HEAT OF BATTLE

"Cut me free," Nicholas said to the Islander behind him.

The Fey woman bent down and picked up Nicholas's sword. She held it in her left hand, the knife in her right, the balance perfect, her legs apart, ready to fight. Other Fey had formed a half-circle around her, fighting to keep the Islanders away. Nicholas glanced to his side. The Islanders had done the same for him.

The pressure on Nicholas's wrists suddenly eased. A man shoved a sword into Nicholas's hand. The grip was slippery with sweat and blood. Nicholas held his free hand out, the sword before him like a shield. "You should have killed me," he said to the woman, "for I have no qualms about killing you."

He swung as he spoke, seeing too late the threat from the side. An angry Fey's knife grazed his rib cage.

"No!" the woman cried. "He is mine!"

"Then kill him," said the Fey. "Before he kills you."

"He won't kill me," she said.

And as Nicholas glanced at her, standing tall and proud, her face glistening with sweat and her eyes sparkling with power, he knew it was true. He couldn't kill her any more than she could kill him.

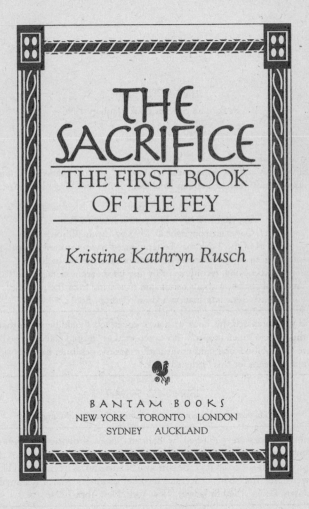

THE SACRIFICE

THE FIRST BOOK OF THE FEY

Kristine Kathryn Rusch

BANTAM BOOKS
NEW YORK TORONTO LONDON
SYDNEY AUCKLAND

The Fey: The Sacrifice
A Bantam Spectra Book / January 1996

ISBN 0-553-56894-9

Published simultaneously in the United States and Canada

Bantam Books are published by Bantam Books, a division of Bantam
Doubleday Dell Publishing Group, Inc. Its trademark, consisting of the
words "Bantam Books" and the portrayal of a rooster, is Registered in U.S.
Patent and Trademark Office and in other countries. Marca Registrada.
Bantam Books, 1540 Broadway, New York, New York 10036.

PRINTED IN THE UNITED STATES OF AMERICA

RAD   0 9 8 7 6 5 4 3 2 1

For my mother, Marian M. Rusch

ACKNOWLEDGMENTS

Thanks on this one go to Deborah Beale for pushing me in the right direction; to Abner Stein, Rich Henshaw, and Richard Curtis, the three fates who backed this project from the beginning; to Harlan Ellison for forcing me to think clearly about fiction; to Renee Dodds for keeping me organized; to Caroline Oakley for her patience; to Tom Dupree for his insight; to Nina Kiriki Hoffman and Jerry Oltion for reading above and beyond the call of duty; and to Dean Wesley Smith for holding my hand during the dark times.

THE VISION

ONE

THE little girl slammed into Jewel at full run, then slid and fell on the wet cobblestone. The girl sat for a moment, her skirts wrapped around her thighs, revealing the pantslike undergarments the Nyeians insisted on trussing their children in. Jewel hadn't moved. Her hip ached from the impact of the girl's body, but Jewel didn't let the pain show.

She hadn't expected to see a child on the narrow, dark streets of the merchant center of Nye's largest city. The stone buildings towered around the cobblestone road. Even though the sun had appeared after a furious thunderstorm, the streets were just as dark as they had been during the sudden downpour.

"Esmerelda!" A woman's voice, sharp and piercing, echoed on the street. The bypassers didn't seem to notice. They continued about their business, clutching their strange round timepieces as they hurried to their destinations.

The little girl tugged on her ripped skirts and tried to stand. Jewel recognized the look of panic on the child's face. She had felt that herself in the face of her grandfather's wrath. Jewel took two steps toward the girl and crouched, thankful that she was wearing breeches and boots that allowed such freedom of movement. "Why were you running?" Jewel asked in Nye.

"Felt like it," the girl said.

Good answer. Nyeian children didn't play enough. Their parents didn't allow it. The girl had courage.

Jewel extended her hand. The girl stared at it. Jewel's slender fingers and dark skin marked her as Fey, even more than her upswept eyebrows, black hair, and slightly pointed ears.

"Esmerelda!" The woman's voice had an edge of panic.

"She won't like your being dirty," Jewel said.

The little girl's lower lip trembled. She reached for Jewel's hand when a screech resounded behind them. Jewel turned in time to see a woman wearing a dress so tightly corseted it made her appear flat, swing an umbrella as if it were a sword. Jewel stood and grabbed the umbrella by its tip, pulling it from the woman's hand.

"You were about to hit me?" Jewel asked, keeping her tone level but filled with menace.

The woman was a few years older than Jewel, but already her pasty skin had frown lines marring her eyes and mouth. Her pale-brown eyes took in the thin vest that Jewel wore in deference to the heat. "What were you doing to my child?"

"Helping her up. Have you an objection to that?"

The woman glanced at her child. Jewel stood between them. Then the woman bowed her head. Her brown hair had touches of gray. "Forgive me," she said, not at all contrite. "I forgot myself."

"Indeed." Jewel put the tip of the umbrella on the cobblestone and leaned her weight on it. Sturdy thing. It would have made a good weapon, and she had no doubt the woman had used it as such during the recent conflict. "Forget yourself again, and your daughter may lose her mother."

"Is that a threat, mistress?" The woman brought her head up, eyes flashing.

"Mistress." Nye term of respect. The Fey did not believe in such linguistic tricks. There were other ways of keeping inferiors in line. "You're not important enough to threaten, my dear," Jewel said, using the linguistic trick to her own benefit. "I was merely warning you. As a kindness."

She knelt beside the little girl again. The girl's eyes were tearstained. "Don't hurt my mommy," she whispered. "I didn't mean to bump you."

"I know," Jewel said. She adjusted the girl's heavy skirts and helped her to her feet. Then she handed her the umbrella. It was almost as tall as the child. "You just remind your mother that we are no longer your enemies. You have to learn to live with us now."

The mother watched Jewel's every movement. Jewel brushed the dirt off the child's skirts, marveling at the thickness of the fabric. Jewel would suffocate in clothing like that.

"You might also want to let your mother know that pants are more practical for children, male or female."

"I thought you weren't going to change our customs." The woman spoke again, her tone full of bitterness, even though she bowed her head again in the submissive gesture the Fey had commanded. Jewel thought of challenging her on her rudeness but decided the battle wasn't worth her time. She was already late for the meeting with her father.

"We change only the customs that interfere with healthy, productive living. Children are born to move, not mince like some expensive fop at a Nye banquet." Jewel smiled and reached a hand under the woman's chin, bringing her head up so that their gazes met. "She wouldn't have run into me if she had been dressed properly."

"You have no right to change how we live," the woman said.

"We have every right," Jewel said. "We choose to allow you your customs because they keep you productive. You are the one without rights. You lost them six months ago when my grandfather became the leader of Nye."

Finally the panic that had been missing from the woman's face appeared. Her round eyes narrowed and her mouth opened just a bit. "You're the Black King's granddaughter?"

Jewel let her hand fall and resisted the urge to wipe her fingertips on her breeches. "Aren't you lucky I was in a good mood this morning? Threatening me is like threatening all of the Fey at once."

The woman's face flushed with terror. She grabbed the little girl and pulled her close. Jewel ignored the gesture. She took a loose strand of the little girl's brown hair and tucked it behind the girl's ear. "Take good care of your mother, Esmerelda," she said, and continued down the street.

At the corner she glanced back, saw the woman still standing in place, the little girl clutched against her side. Jewel shook her head. The bitterness would get the Nyeians nowhere. They were part of the Fey Empire now. The sooner they all realized it, the better off they would be.

Jewel clasped her hands behind her back. The air was warm and muggy after the storm, except in the shadows of the great buildings. Her grandfather had taken the greatest, the Bank of Nye, and made it his own. Four stories of stone standing like a palace in the merchant section, the building was the closest thing to a palace that the Nyeians had ever made.

The streets were nearly empty for midday. The half-dozen Nyeians gave Jewel a wide berth as they passed her on the street. The Fey guards standing in front of each Fey-occupied building nodded to her as she passed. She nodded in return.

Six months since the Nyeians surrendered, and still her grandfather felt the need for guards. Six months without fighting, and she was growing restless.

Like her father.

He had a plan for the next battle. She was ready, even though her grandfather wasn't sure if the entire force was ready to move again. Her brothers didn't think so, but they were young. The last year of the Nye campaign had been the first time any of the boys had seen battle.

Jewel had fought since she'd been eleven—nearly seven years—and she had never progressed beyond the Infantry, much to her father's and grandfather's dismay. Her brothers were delighted. They all assumed that her lack of Vision would mean that she would be passed over as heir to her grandfather's throne.

She hadn't told any of them about her strange dreams. She hadn't even visited the Shaman about them.

Finally she arrived at the Bank of Nye. It stood in the center of a cobblestone interchange. Sunlight touched a small corner of the stone, causing it to heat, and steam to rise from the wet. Through an open window she could hear her father's voice mingling with her grandfather's.

They were fighting, just as she knew they would be.

Every time her father mentioned moving beyond Nye, leaving the Galinas continent and heading out to sea, her grandfather objected. The next place to conquer was an island in the middle of the Infrin Sea. Blue Isle had been a major trading partner with Nye. It had also done some business with countries on Leut, the continent to the south. Blue Isle was a gateway that Nye could never be. But it was a gateway that the Black King believed the Fey were not ready to use.

Jewel knew better than to interrupt an argument between her father and her grandfather. Her father had asked her to wait for him, and wait she would. Outside.

Jewel sat on the flagstone steps and propped one booted foot against the wall across from her. She leaned against the cool stone walls, not caring that the roughness of the stone pulled strands of hair from her braid. This was as close as she could get to the open window, but even if she closed her eyes and concentrated, she could not make out the words.

No one else realized the importance of the battle within. Nyeians scurried by, moving as quickly as people could in six layers of clothing, their round faces red and covered with sweat. Jewel had often joked that the Nyeians had lost the war because they didn't know when to take their clothes off.

Not that the wars had hurt business in Nye. The shops were open, and the street vendors hawked wares as if nothing had happened. Fortunately, the bank was on a street filled with other austere stone buildings, a street where no vendors were allowed. She wouldn't have been able to hear anything at all if the vendors had been camped on the cobblestone.

The Nyeians ducked in and out of shops without once glancing at the open, gaily colored flags outside. The flags indicated the type of merchandise—blue for items made in Nye, yellow, green, red, and purple for items made in other countries. The Bank of Nye had transferred its business to the brick building directly across the street, and more than one trader had entered, a money pouch clutched tightly to his hip.

Jewel closed her eyes and a wave of dizziness hit her. The world tilted, and she suddenly felt great searing pain burning into her forehead. Her father shouted, "You've killed her!" and a voice answered in a tongue she did not recognize. Then he shouted, "Someone help her! Please help her!"

Her breath came in ragged gasps. She opened her eyes. A man leaned over her, his eyebrows straight, his hair long and blond. His features were square. He was neither Fey nor Nyeian. His skin was pale without being pasty. He had a rugged, healthy look she had seen only in the Fey, but his features were stronger, as if drawn with a heavy hand. He spoke to her in that strange tongue. *Orma lii*, he said, then repeated a different word over and over.

He cradled her in his arms, holding her with a tenderness she had never felt before. Then the scene shifted. The strange man still held her, but she wore her father's healing cloak.

A Healer slapped a poultice on her forehead. It smelled of redwort and garlic, and stopped the burning from spreading. "She'll live," the Healer said, "but I can promise no more."

"What did she say?" the strange man asked. His Fey had an odd accent.

"That she'll live," her father replied. He was speaking Nye. "And maybe little more."

The strange man pressed her closer. "Jewel." He kissed her softly. *"Ne sneto. Ne sneto."*

She reached up and touched him with a shaking hand. This night was not how she'd dreamed it would be.

Then the world shifted back. She had moved down two steps, and her forehead tingled with remembered pain. Her throat was dry. A Vision. A real Vision, powerful enough to make her lose her place in the present.

Her heart was pounding rapidly against her chest. She had never heard her father sound so terrified. Nor had she ever seen anyone like that man. His pale skin, straight eyebrows, and blue eyes marked him as not Fey, and his square features and appearance of health meant he wasn't Nyeian. Yet he knew her well enough to cradle her with love.

The bank door slammed open and her father stormed out, his black cloak swirling around his legs. He was among the tallest Fey, and he usually used that height to great effect. Now, though, he seemed even taller than usual.

Jewel had never seen him this angry outside of battle.

She made herself swallow, wishing she had something to ease her sudden thirst. Then she got up slowly, afraid the dizziness from the Vision would return.

"So he said no, huh?" she asked. She had to look up to see his face.

"He said yes." Her father bit out the words as if he resented them.

She frowned. "Then why are you angry? You want to conquer Blue Isle."

Her father looked at her. His eyebrows swept up to his hairline, his eyes fierce. "Because he said I am making a mistake. That I am fighting because I am addicted to slaughter, not because I want to add to the Empire. He said it would be good for me to die on the battlefield so that I don't bring that taste for death to the chair of the Black King."

Harsh words. Too harsh. The fight between the men must have been deep. "He was speaking in anger," she said.

"He believed it was truth." Her father stomped down four stairs, then stopped. At this vantage she was as tall as he was. "No matter what he says, I am taking you with me."

"What about my brothers?" Jewel asked. The last time her father had taken her on a campaign, he had done so that she might care for the boys.

"They're too young for this trip. Meet me in my quarters tonight and bring the Warders. We have a campaign to plan."

He turned his back on her and continued down the stairs. When he reached the street, the Nyeians backed away from him. He hurried across the cobblestone, his cloak fluttering behind him.

Jewel braced one hand against the wall. The dizziness was gone, but a disquiet had settled into the pit of her stomach. She had had her Vision after her father had decided to go to Blue Isle. Were the two connected?

She shook her head. She knew better than to make such speculation about Visions. They existed to guide leaders. She should be happy she had a Vision of such strength. It settled a fear that she would never have the power to be Black Queen.

In spite of herself she felt an odd joy. Her father would take her on her first real campaign—not as a soldier and caretaker for children, but as a leader. One who would help plan.

No matter what her grandfather said about settling, he was wrong about one thing: the fight was in their blood. The restlessness she had felt for the last six months would be put to good use.

She pushed herself away from the clammy stone wall. The face from her Vision rose in her memory.

"Orma lii," she whispered, even though she didn't know what it meant. She was going to face her destiny as a Fey should, in full battle gear, weapons drawn.

THE BATTLE

(NINE MONTHS LATER)

TWO

THE thick, heavy clouds made the afternoon as dark as night. The rain fell in sheets, the huge drops thudding as they pummeled the muddy ground. Nicholas's hair was plastered to his face. A moment outside and he was soaked. No one had seen him step into the courtyard. Lord knew what kind of trouble he would get into for going out into the rain.

The servants had to protect the young Prince from himself, at all costs. Even if he didn't want the protection. He was eighteen, more than old enough to make his own decisions.

His hand brushed the hilt of his sword. The sheath was tied to his leg, the leather thongs chafing against his skin. The jeweled hilt was slick. Fighting in such conditions would be dangerous, but he welcomed the challenge.

The courtyard was empty except for a thin cat running for shelter. The stable doors were closed, and lights burned inside. The grooms were working with the horses. The servants' quarters were mostly dark, except for Stephen's cabin up front.

Stephen was an old man who had served as swordmaster for the royal family. He had taught Nicholas's father to use the sword decades ago and then had had no duties until

Nicholas had turned fifteen. During those years Stephen had become a scholar, studying the history of Blue Isle. He had also become an expert in Nye culture, then had turned his attention to what he called the next threat: the Fey.

Nicholas didn't care what kind of threats he faced as long as he learned to fight. Stephen had been teaching Nicholas for three years now, and though Nicholas had become proficient, he still couldn't beat his swordmaster.

The shutters were closed, but a light burned within. Nicholas knocked. He heard a chair scrape against wood, and the bolt go back before the door swung open.

The flickering candlelight added depth to Stephen's wrinkles. His short gray hair was tousled. He was wearing his winter sweater and a pair of heavy pants, even though it was the middle of summer. "By the Sword," he said. "You're drenched. Get inside before you catch your death."

Nicholas pushed the hair off his face. His hands were red with cold. "No," he said. "Come out. We have practice."

"Not in this weather, we don't," Stephen said.

"I have to learn to fight in all conditions," Nicholas said.

"But I don't have to teach you unless the sun is shining. Now, come in and dry off."

Nicholas stepped inside. Stephen was the only servant who could speak to him with such disrespect, probably because Stephen was the only one whom Nicholas actually trusted.

The air inside was warm. A fire burned in the fireplace, and a book was open on the table. Stephen kept his quarters spare but comfortable. "What were you thinking?" Stephen asked. "You know we never fight in such weather."

"It's been three days," Nicholas said. "I'm tired of being inside."

"You'll be inside until the storm breaks."

"But we don't know how long that will be. It never rains like this in summer."

"I know." Somehow Stephen made the two words sound ominous.

Even though Nicholas longed to warm up near the fire, he wouldn't let himself go any farther without Stephen's invitation. Stephen had only so much space in his single room. He filled it with the table, three chairs, an end table, and a pallet on the floor. A wardrobe stood against one wall. The others were decorated with swords and knives, all different shapes and sizes. Stephen claimed they had once been used in battle, but Nicholas doubted that. Blue Isle had never seen much fighting—even the Peasant Uprising wasn't a real war, according to the Nyeians who visited the palace. Nicholas liked to think that Stephen made up the stories of battles to give himself a purpose. After all, the King really didn't need a swordmaster. Nicholas was learning the art because anything was better than spending his days in a room with Auds.

"Come on in," Stephen said. "I'll give you some mead."

Warm mead sounded good. Nicholas removed his dripping coat and hung it on the peg behind the door. He shook the water from his long hair like one of the kitchen dogs. Stephen sputtered as he was sprayed, and wiped his face.

"They should have an etiquette master for young Princes," Stephen mumbled.

"Sorry." Nicholas grinned. He could never have done anything like that in the palace. Someone would see and report back to his father. Nicholas never quite measured up to his father's wishes. His father wanted Nicholas to be a scholar, to know all he needed to know about the realm. Nicholas wanted to ride horses and win sword fights, and impress women—if only he knew any women to impress.

Stephen went to the fireplace, grabbed a stone mug from the rack on the side, and dipped it into the pot of mead warming at the edge of the fire. He used a cloth to wipe off the end.

Nicholas took the mug, then took a sip. The burning-hot liquid coursed through him, warming him as it went. He liked Stephen's mead. It was sweet, as mead should be, but Stephen always added butter, which he stole from the buttery. It made his mead so much richer than the King's.

Stephen closed his book, then sat at the table. He kicked out a chair, which Nicholas caught with his free hand. Nicholas sighed. "I guess this means we aren't going out."

"I am an old man," Stephen said. "I believe in guarding my health."

"Then maybe we could do some close maneuvers inside. I'm still not as good with a dagger as I would like."

Stephen grinned and glanced around the room. "I value my possessions," he said.

Nicholas did not grin back. He wasn't sure if Stephen had insulted his progress or not.

"And you are doing just fine with a dagger." Stephen rested his arm on the closed book, his hand clutching his own mug. "I think now you are a match for any swordsman who would challenge you."

"Even someone from Nye?"

"Anyone," Stephen said with the same solemnity he had used before.

Cold water dripped off the tips of Nicholas's hair onto his wrists. He adjusted his position so the drops ran down his back. "You really think I'm that good?"

"I think so. Now it's only a matter of practice."

"Great," Nicholas said. He took another sip of mead. He had never expected to receive Stephen's full approval. But Stephen was acting oddly today. "Something's bothering you, isn't it?"

"The weather," Stephen said. "I have lived in Jahn most of my life. I have never seen summer rains like this."

Nicholas shrugged. "Things change."

"That's what I'm afraid of," Stephen murmured.

"What do you mean?"

Stephen shook his head. "An old man's wanderings on dismal summer days. When the sun returns, I will be myself again."

"I hope it comes back soon," Nicholas said. "I am getting restless."

Stephen smiled. He set his mug down, the muscles rippling in his thick arm. "You wouldn't be if you studied as you were supposed to."

Nicholas grimaced. He glanced at the single, shuttered window, then at the glow of the fire. The heat was pleasant, although he was shivering from his wet clothes. He hated the lights in the middle of the day, and he hated to be restricted. Sometimes he worried that all of his practice, all of his work, would fade away. He would lose his skill because the rain forced him indoors for days.

"I am too young to spend the rest of my life in a room," Nicholas said. "Besides, my father isn't that old. He'll live a long time. I won't become King until I'm older than you."

Stephen raised a grizzled eyebrow. "Older than me." His tone was flat, as if the choice of phrasing had bothered him. He leaned back, tilting his chair on two legs, and frowned at Nicholas. "Have you ever thought that your father might need an adviser?"

"My father has a hundred advisers."

"All with their own agendas and concerns. You would be the only one who would share his concerns."

"Me?" Nicholas took another sip of mead. The liquid had cooled and was thick and sugary. "He would never listen to me."

"On the contrary," Stephen said. "I think he would welcome your advice."

Nicholas stood and paced around the small room, leaving boot prints on the wooden floor. He couldn't sit with the thought. His father, listening to him. How very strange. "Has he told you this?"

"Not directly," Stephen said. "Mostly he wishes aloud that you were able to converse with him on several subjects."

Nicholas had heard that, too, and had taken it as nagging. Since Nicholas's mother had died, his father had worked as hard as he could to raise the boy well. Even though servants, and later his stepmother, had done the actual work, Nicholas spent some time every day with his father. The affection between them was genuine, but Nicholas had never thought that he could be his father's equal.

"You're just trying to get me to study harder."

Stephen shook his head. "I am just trying to get you to think. Three quarters of swordplay is mental, you know. The more you use that brain of yours, the better horseman and swordsman you'll be."

"I do better when I'm not thinking about what I'm doing," Nicholas said. He stopped beside the fire and let the heat radiate through his wet clothing.

"You do better when you are so practiced, so used to thinking about it, that you put no effort into the thought. Imagine if you were that way on affairs of state. You are already a better swordsman than your father. You could be a better statesman, too."

Nicholas grinned at Stephen. "You know how competitive I am, and you're using it."

"Yes," Stephen said. He glanced at the shuttered window. The drum of the rain on the roof almost drowned his words. "I think it's time we all do the very best we can."

THREE

RUGAR stood on the prow of the ship, his hood down, water pouring down his face. The rain felt cool and good. He had forgotten the feeling of power it gave him to control the weather. The Weather Sprites had done his bidding to perfection.

By morning the rain would break, and the Fey would be scattered throughout Blue Isle.

If the maps, the Navigators, and the captive Nyeian were right.

Rugar pulled his cloak closer. They should have spotted land by now. The year-old charts suggested that the Stone Guardians were near, yet the view was the same: choppy gray water in all directions. The downpour ruined Rugar's visibility, but he had Beast Riders circling—three Gulls, stolen from his father's private force.

Rugar pushed his wet hair off his forehead. His cloak had been spelled to repel moisture, but sometimes he liked the feel of the water on his skin. His bootmaker's magick hadn't been quite so skillful. Rugar's feet were soggy blocks of ice, chafing against the leather. The wind was slight—just enough to push the ships forward without the crew's resorting to oars or spells.

The ship groaned beneath him, the wood creaking as the prow cut through the waves. The steady drum of the rain drowned out the sound of water splashing against the sides. Rugar clasped his hands behind his back. Normally, he liked travel, but sailing was different. Riding from country to country allowed him to fantasize about conquest, but he had never seen Blue Isle, had only heard about it through myths, histories, and the Nyeians, who were notoriously untrustworthy. Rugar's father, the Black King, didn't even believe the common knowledge: that the Islanders had not seen war. But Rugar believed it. Who would attack that Isle? The Islanders had been smart. They had traded with nearby nations, given them favored status even though (the Nyeians said) the Islanders did not need the goods in return. The Isle was completely self-sufficient.

It was also between the Galinas continent and the Leutian continent. The best point from which to launch an attack that would bring the rest of the world into the Fey Empire. The Fey had already overrun three continents since they'd left the Eccrasian Mountains centuries before. They should not stop simply because they'd reached the end of Galinas. It was Fey destiny to continue until all five known continents belonged to the Empire.

The fact that Blue Isle was rich made the idea of conquest all that much sweeter. Within a few days the Fey would own Blue Isle. Rugar would own Blue Isle.

The Black King would apologize for doubting his only son.

A gull cried overhead. Its caw-caw echoed over the rain and the splash of the waves. Rugar looked up to see one of his own men on the gull's back, his lower body subsumed into the gull's form. Only the man's torso and head were visible, looking as if he were actually astride the gull. The gull's own head bent forward slightly to accommodate the unusual configuration, but that was the only concession to the difference. The Rider and the gull had been one being since the Rider had been a child.

Beast Riders were kin to Shape-Shifters, but like a Shape-Shifter, once the alternate form was chosen, the Rider could not be anything else. The Riders chose the time and place for each Shift, but their moods were always governed by the creature they chose to share their Shape with.

Rugar did not understand what forced a Riding child to choose a gull instead of, say, a horse. Yet he was grateful that some did; he was getting tired of the complaints of the landed Riders. Those that Shifted into horses had worn their human forms all during the trip. They were pacing belowdecks, threatening that if they didn't return to their equine forms soon, they would lose the ability to do so ever again.

Since Rugar had heard these complaints on every campaign he had ever been on, he ignored them. But in such close quarters, his ability to ignore was growing thin. He now wished he had placed the remaining Riders on one of the other ships, and kept only the gull Riders with him. Even they weren't as useful as he would like. Because of their odd physiology, Beast Riders could travel only short distances in their altered form. Rugar would have loved to have sent the gull Riders all the way to the Isle when the ships had set sail, but that would have killed the Riders if there were no places to land along the way.

Rugar stared straight ahead, as if by concentrating he could make the Stone Guardians appear. No one had spoken to him all day. Since the rains had started, no one had spoken to him at all, except when they needed something from him. He checked on the Warders, as he did every morning, trying to avoid the Nyeian they kept in thrall. So far, everything had gone smoothly.

Just as he had planned.

The gull cried again and dived toward the ship. The Rider held on to the neck feathers with his tiny hands, as if he truly had to balance on the creature. Riders always pretended to Ride, even though they became part of the animal. The gull swooped around Rugar, then landed on the deck, skidding a bit on the wood.

He looked down at the creature. The gull Rider, Muce, let go of the neck feathers, straightened his arms as if they were cramped, and tilted his head until he could see Rugar. Then Muce grinned and slowly grew. As he stretched to his full height, the bird's body slipped inside his own. The gull cried as if in protest. The cry halted as the bird's features flattened against Muce's stomach.

Muce, in fully human form, was taller than Rugar, but had a broadness that seemed almost unformed. Muce's dark hair, including the hair on his chest, had a feathered quality, and his fingernails were long, like claws. His nose was not tiny, as a Fey nose should be, but long and narrow, hooking over his mouth like a beak. The nose, combined with his dark eyes and swooping brows, gave his face a nonhuman cast.

He was naked but didn't seem to notice the rain.

"The Guardians are ahead," he said. His voice had a nasal quality. "Beyond them is the Island."

Rugar grinned. "So our schedule is right. We will be there tomorrow."

Muce shrugged. He glanced over his shoulder at the water before them, a furtive, birdlike movement. "From the air it looks as if there are no passages through the Guardians. The water froths, beats against the rocks, and then dead-ends. I swooped down and saw crevices, but the waves reared at me like live things. I don't think one ship will survive, let alone an entire fleet."

"The Nye had to trade with the Islanders somehow," Rugar said.

"Perhaps there is an easier way. The Nye have no reason to tell us the truth."

"No one lies to the Fey," Rugar said.

Muce shuddered and, Rugar suspected, not from the cold. The Fey had a gift for torture.

"You need to gather the rest of the Gull Riders and see if they can spot a way through those rocks," Rugar said. "The more backup we have, the better off we will be. These ships need to go through intact. The Islanders have never experienced battle. We'll teach them what war really is."

"It sounds like a slaughter," Muce said.

"A morning's worth," Rugar said. "Once they see that they have no way to defeat us, they will capitulate. The Guardians are our only obstacle."

"All right," Muce said, although he sounded doubtful. "I will gather the others and see what we can discover."

Without waiting for a response, he stretched out his arms and slowly shrank to his gull form. The gull, as it appeared from his stomach, finished the cry it had been making when it absorbed. It took a few tiny steps backward before launching itself into the air. Muce grabbed the feathers he had held before and, as he flew away, did not look at Rugar.

The gray skies and thick rain drops obscured the Gull Rider quickly. Rugar watched it go. He clenched his fists. He hoped that what he had said to Muce was the truth. Rugar had had no Visions since the ships had sailed.

He had expected to have a Vision before now. As the ships drew closer to Blue Isle, he had thought the proximity would draw more Visions from him or expand on his last Vision, the one that had brought him there. He had seen Jewel—as a woman fully grown—walking through the palace on Blue Isle as if she belonged there. But that Vision was nearly four months old now, and he had not had another one. For a while he was afraid they were going into this battle Blind. Then he had practiced making tiny Shadowlands, as he used to do as a new Visionary. The Shadowlands would capture the cups he had placed in the room and conceal them in a space he had made, proving that his powers were fine. On this trip, then, the Mysteries had given him only one Vision to plan with.

He had spoken to no one about his lack of Vision, not even the Shaman who had consented to go on this trip. Visions were unpredictable things. Perhaps, once he was inside the Stone Guardians, he would be able to See Blue Isle clearly.

No one has conquered Blue Isle before. His father's voice rose out of the mist. The Black King's arguments had haunted Rugar since the ships had left Nye.

No one has tried, Rugar had replied, even though he knew he was wrong. The Nyeians told stories from the dawn of their history which told of a force of long boats, twenty strong, that had been turned away from Blue Isle. The stories were so old that some thought them myths.

When his father had learned of that attempt, his protests had become even stronger. The last fight, when the Black King had learned that Rugar was taking Jewel, had been blistering.

She is the only hope for the Empire. His father had leaned on the heavy wooden desk in his office at the former Bank of Nye. *You cannot take her from here.*

I can do as I please, Rugar had said. *She is my daughter.*

And if you fail, what then? If she dies, what will we do? Her brothers are too young, and at their births the Shaman did not predict great things. Jewel will be great—the best Black Queen of all. If you allow her the opportunity to become Queen.

Rugar had taken a step toward his father. *I saw a Vision of Jewel happy on Blue Isle. Have you had any Visions about this trip?*

His father had not replied.

Have you?

A man does not need Visions to know you're making a mistake, the Black King had said. *We need a rest. We're no longer ready to fight.*

So you have seen nothing, Rugar had said. *Nothing at all.*

Rugar took a deep breath. Rain dripped off his nose onto his lips. The water was cool and tasted fresh. Rugar had had the Vision; his father had not. Rulers followed Vision, even if it was someone else's. Rugar had reminded his father of that, even though it had done no good.

He still made this trip without his father's permission.

But permission didn't matter. Rugar had seen Jewel walking the halls of the palace. He knew the history of the Isle. He would fight the easiest battle in the history of his people.

The Fey would own Blue Isle within a day. The Islanders wouldn't even know they had been invaded until it was too late.

FOUR

AN unexpected gust of wind blew aside the red-and-gold tapestry of the Peasant Uprising, which his mother the Queen, God rest her soul, had stitched in the second year of her marriage. Rain splattered against the flagstone, and the fire in the hearth flared. The room was small, having once served as a bodyguard's bedchamber, and the dampness added a chill. Alexander shivered in the unnatural cold. He reached over the arm of his chair and gave the faded bell-pull a harsh yank.

The rain was making him cranky. He had overslept that morning, spent the afternoon reading and signing long-winded hand-copied state papers, and eaten his evening meal alone. Now, during his private time, he still had to focus on business. Not even a King turned away an Elder of the Tabernacle. Already Matthias had overstayed his welcome, and he hadn't yet mentioned the reason that he had come to Alexander's suite on this unseasonably gloomy night.

Matthias's blond curls hung in ringlets around his shoulders, and his mustache was damp from steam from his mulled wine. He still wore his vestments for Midnight Sacrament, the long black robe with the bright red sash and the small filigree sword on a chain around his neck. He had removed his biretta and set it on the carved wooden table beside him. The curls on the top of his head had been crushed flat by the weight of the cap.

"Highness," he said with a smile, "you realize you are waking some poor sod from a sound slumber."

"I don't care." Alexander stood and ladled more wine from the small jug hanging over the fire. Near the flames, the flagstones were hot against his leather slippers. "They should have tacked those tapestries well in the first place."

Matthias set his brown mug down and smoothed his robe. "This weather has us all upset, Sire, but that does not mean we must abuse the servants."

Or engage in small talk. But Alexander said nothing. He had long ago learned that if he suffered Matthias in silence, Matthias would figure out that Alexander no longer wanted company.

Alexander hung the ladle in its place beside the hearth. Then he returned to his chair, careful to hold his mug tightly lest it spill. "I do not abuse the servants," Alexander said. "If anything, I treat them too kindly. They run the palace when I should. Unlike the Tabernacle. The Auds go barefoot. Don't accuse me of abusing my servants."

"Auds aren't servants, Sire. By the time they get shoes, they've learned to appreciate them." Matthias stuck out his sandaled feet, still scarred from his years without shoes. "Believe me, they appreciate all the comforts they get."

Alexander sighed. As boys, he and Matthias had been educated together. But Matthias, a second son, was destined to go into the Church. Alexander, an only child, was meant to rule Blue Isle from the moment he was born. Matthias always found a way to remind Alexander of their difference.

"Servants can be disturbed to see to my comfort on a rainy night," Alexander said a bit too harshly.

"Of course they can." Matthias smiled. "But you might want to note that the loose tapestry is the one that depicts the revolt that left your great-grandfather a cripple."

Alexander laughed. Some of the tension flowed from him. The rain was making him melancholy. It reminded him of last winter when his second wife had died, the victim of a spirit that had entered on a chill breeze and had lodged in her lungs.

Alexander missed her more than he cared to admit, even though she had been frail and silent through most of their union. Evenings she sat across from him and allowed him to muse while her needle whispered through cloth. Her tapestries were never as lovely as his mother's, but the subjects were always happier.

Alexander took a sip of the wine. Its spices were heavy, and its warmth muted the alcoholic bite. He preferred mead, its honeyed flavor more to his taste. This night, though, he bowed to his guest's wishes. Matthias couldn't get mulled wine in the Tabernacle.

"Much more of this rain and the crops will rot at the root," Matthias said.

Alexander sighed deeply into his mug. Matthias was neither taking the hint nor getting to the point. Alexander didn't want to run this visit like a meeting of the Council of Lords, but he would if Matthias looked as if he was staying much longer. "It has been raining for only two days," Alexander said.

"But there is water standing in the fields." Matthias leaned back in the chair, his slender form almost buried in the cushions. "I spoke with an Aud this morning who is riding across the Isle on a pilgrimage, and he says every field he passed since Killeny's Bridge looks like a lake."

"Do Auds know what lakes look like?"

"My, you are in a mood." Matthias sipped his wine loudly, and the sound echoed in the room.

Alexander shook his head. "No. I would merely like to relax."

. Matthias peered at him over his mug of wine, his blue eyes glinting with humor. "You are being polite this evening? You could have told me that you didn't want visitors. I would have ridden back to the Tabernacle."

"All that way in the rain. I figured I owed you at least one warm drink."

"I am almost through with it." Matthias took another loud sip. He still wasn't getting to the point. The topic, then, had to be one he was reluctant to discuss.

"So," Alexander said, deciding to force Matthias to leave. "You did not abandon your warm room on a night like this to discuss crops with me. Tell me about Nicholas. That's why you're here, isn't it?"

Matthias nodded and cupped his mug between his hands. "Your son, Sire, has the heart of a warrior. He arrives to class each day with cuts and scars on his fingers. He relishes every wound and would waste the Danites' time describing each if I didn't stop by each morning and cut the conversation short."

Another gust of wind blew in, rattling the tapestry. Where was the damned servant anyway? Alexander would have to make sure the downstairs staff was reprimanded in the morning. "I know that Nicholas enjoys the new physical program. But I want to know if allowing him to fight has improved his study habits."

Matthias sighed. "He does study, Sire, but he argues too much. He claims that religion has no bearing on his future as King."

Faith had no bearing on his future as King. Alexander grabbed his mug, feeling the warmth of the clay against his fingers. He didn't quite know how to explain the study of religion to his son. Without the Rocaanists, Alexander's rule would be twice as hard. Often Alexander and the Council of Lords decided an issue, but the Rocaanists spread the word and enforced the King's bidding through prayer and suggestion of the Church. Nicholas would be an ineffective King if he did not learn the subtleties of the relationship between Church and State.

"I will speak to him," Alexander said.

The door to the chamber opened, and a servant, his gray hair sleep tousled and a tattered brown robe hastily drawn over his breeches, stepped inside and bowed. His feet were bare and red with cold. " 'Tis sorry I am, Highness, for me tardiness. The rain has started a flood in the kitchen, and it threatens the hearth fire."

The hearth fire never went out. It was used all night for baking and cooking delicate sauces. It also fed the other fires in the palace.

Alexander nodded. "We have a potential flood of our own. The tapestries need to be nailed more tightly to the windows. The Peasant Uprising is loose and has been dousing us for most of the evening."

"Forgive me, Sire," the servant said, bowing again. "I'll tend to it right away, I will."

He stepped back out the door. Matthias grabbed his biretta and positioned it over the crown of his head. "I think I'd better go, Sire."

Alexander felt a slight, perverse twinge. Much as he wanted to be alone, the fact that he would finally get his wish made him feel lonely. "I'll speak to Nicholas tomorrow."

"Good," Matthias said. He stood, and his slenderness unfolded into uncommon height. Matthias's family had always leaned toward tallness, but Matthias himself would have been considered demon-spawned if he had not shown faith so early. "And I'll let you know if there is a change in his behavior."

The servant entered, carrying a hammer and some wooden nails. Matthias caught the door before it closed and nodded his head slightly, the closest thing he did to a bow. Then he disappeared down the hall. Alexander watched him go. In a way, Nicholas was lucky that Matthias supervised his study. None of the other Elders would have approached Alexander about his son's laxness. A few of the others would have deemed it unimportant, and a few would have used the opportunity, once Nicholas became King, to seize the extra power for themselves. Matthias cared less about power than about preserving the status quo.

The servant pulled aside the loose tapestry, sending more chill air into the room. Alexander stood and wandered next to the fire. He didn't want to catch a chill as his wife had, and if he was going to catch one, it would be now. These rains were unnatural. The summer was usually dotted with rainstorms, but not the constant downpour that the entire Isle was suffering.

" 'Tis rotted the wood is, Sire. Whole hunks are breaking away in the wet."

"Then repair it," Alexander said. He didn't care that the silly wood frames his mother had installed to hold the tapestries were rotting any more than he cared that the hearth fire was threatened by a small flood. Something nagged him about this weather. Something more important than small domestic disasters. Something he didn't dare name aloud for fear of inviting the suspicion of the entire Kingdom.

The weather felt unnatural. In all of his thirty-five years, he had never seen the summer sun blotted for days by rain. He wished he could send a man off to Nye to consult with the Seers there, but the Fey had captured Nye in their last campaign across the Galinas continent over a year ago.

The Rocaanists did not believe in second sight, unless it was prophetic vision sanctioned by their God. And there had not been any Rocaanist prophets for nearly five hundred years. Once he had complained of this to Matthias, and Matthias had told him to listen to the still, small voice within.

But the still, small voice within had told Alexander that Kings were not meant to rule alone. He wished he had had enough sense two years earlier to smuggle a Seer back from Nye, so that now he could speak with someone about this fear in his belly, this feeling that the rains were only the beginning of something deeper, something darker, than anything he had ever faced before.

FIVE

THE cabin was close and smelled of damp. The tick mattress felt clammy, and the indentation Jewel's body had left when she'd risen in the darkness was still there. She hadn't slept well. She never slept well before a battle. She always imagined herself in the middle of a melee, the smell of blood and fear around her, the ring of swords nearly deafening.

Her father had been right. The Fey lived for battle. Jewel could not keep still from all the excitement running through her.

She had lit her lantern and hung it from the ceiling, where it swayed back and forth with the rhythm of the ship. The light's constant movement made it seem as if the walls themselves were moving. Sometimes she could have sworn they had. In the month since the ship had set sail from Nye, she had grown, and now as she sat on the edge of the bed, her knees brushed the rough-hewn wall. She had to bend as she walked into the cabin, and part of her wished to be sleeping below, with the rest of the Infantry, for she could stand upright in the middle of the hold.

But she wouldn't have to wish much longer. By daybreak she would be walking on land again, and she didn't know if she would be sleeping on the cold ground or in her bunk come nightfall. This time she would camp with the Infantry. Her little brothers remained in Nye under her grandfather's care, so she did not have to return to her father's quarters each evening. For the first time she would be a full member of the troop she had been assigned to.

The first time and the last time. When her father learned of her Visions, he would pull her out of the Infantry and he would keep her by his side. She was almost disappointed that she could See. She had been hoping for more battle-worthy skills. Visionaries were leaders, and too valuable to be in the thick of fighting. She had always known that her talents lay in the direction of leadership, but she had hoped she would get fighting skills, like those of a Foot Soldier or even a Spy.

She grabbed her long black hair and swung it over her right shoulder. Then she braided it, quickly and nimbly, wrapped it around her skull, and covered it with an oversize beret. She slipped into breeches, boots, and a leather jerkin. Over that she placed a woolen cape, knitted by one of the Fey's most renowned weavers. The magic woven into the strands repelled liquids, including blood.

She could stay on her bed and wait until the ship made its way through the Stone Guardians. She knew they had been sighted that afternoon. But she would go crazy if she didn't move. Besides, she wanted to be awake to get her first glimpse of Blue Isle, the site of her last campaign.

Then she took the lantern down, opened the glass, and blew out the flame. The darkness was soothing. She set the lantern in its customary position beside the door and let herself out of the cabin.

The deck was slick with rain and sea foam from the unruly waters. She grabbed the wet wooden railing and used it to help her keep her footing. The air was cold and her chill deepened. As she passed the Spell Warder's cabin, she noted light and peered through the portals. They held a Nyeian navigator in thrall. Five of the Warders had circled the Nyeian and were chanting in front of him. They had deepened his trance. His knowledge was critical for this part of their journey. They would not get through the Stone Guardians without the Nyeian's knowledge.

She took the stairs leading up to the prow, where she had last seen her father. He would be planning now and would have no time for her. Still, she wanted to be beside him. She wanted to watch him on his way to his first triumph.

On Nye she had seen the point of the Black King's arguments against fighting. But since the fleet had left, she had come to believe her father more, even though she had not discussed the attack with him. She was a young soldier, having fought only through the last years of the Nye campaign, and she still missed the fighting. She could only imagine how the career soldiers felt. Most of the Fey fought the wars. The Domestics, while necessary, were never valued. Anyone who lacked fighting skills lacked the heart of a true Fey.

Her grandfather was proposing years, maybe even a generation, without a true battle. The Fey would lose their identities, become as soft and cowardly as the Nye. Her father was right; such a thing should never happen.

When she reached the prow of the ship, she found her father surrounded by some of his lieutenants. The rain was still falling steadily, and she could make out only a few faces in the gloom. Oswel, head of the Foot Soldiers, stood hatless near the railing, his long, slender features bent in a grimace. Caseo, leader of the Spell Warders, was speaking, his cowl down and his hands raised toward the heavens. Her father had his back to her, his head shaking slowly from side to side as he listened.

Jewel approached, walking carefully on the wet deck. She slipped beside her father and put her arm around him. She wasn't supposed to hear the highest-level negotiations: she was a soldier of the lowest rank, a member of the magickless Infantry, often used as advance troops to shock the unwary. But since she was the Black King's granddaughter, no one dared order her away.

Her father's woolen coat was dry, but his hair was plastered against his face. On this trip she had reached his height and had only to look across to him. His lips were chapped, his nose red with cold. Only his eyes were unchanged—black and shiny, their almond shape more appropriate to his hawklike features than to the softer Fey faces. He was of medium height for a Fey—Caseo was taller—but her father seemed to tower over all of them.

He acknowledged her by placing his arm around her waist.

Caseo frowned at her, then glanced at Rugar as if telling him to make her leave. Rugar pulled her closer, his gesture clear. Warders might think they were the most important Fey, but they would get nowhere without the Visionaries. Even Warders were subject to the Black King's family.

The Weather Sprite, Hanouk, was speaking. "We cannot time things exactly, Rugar." The only protection she wore against the rain was a thin chemise. Her ribs and collarbone were visible through her skin, her neck and face so tortured by the elements that she appeared four times older than she was. "You must choose to end the rain early or wait for it to end after we land."

Caseo sighed, the sound barely audible above the thud of the rain. "We can barely see to navigate as it is. Our Nyeian thrall is terrified. Before we placed him under, he swore he could not get us through the Guardians without a current map."

"I was there when he was interrogated. The Nyeian sailed to Blue Isle all his life. He will know the way," her father said.

"His knowledge is over a year old—"

"Besides, he's Nyeian. He could be lying to us," Oswel said.

"No." Caseo's tone was flat. "He will not lie to us. But he may not know if the current has altered or if there have been traps set among the rocks in response to our capture of Nye. This is the most delicate protected harbor in the world, Rugar. One false direction and we will sink."

"We will not sink," her father snapped. His grip around Jewel's waist tightened. "The Islanders are isolated. They believe themselves protected here, and they believe the harbor unnegotiable without their petty maps. They know nothing of us or our powers except rumors they may have heard trading with the Nye."

"And we know nothing of them," Oswel said.

"Except that they have not known war for at least ten generations." Jewel adopted her father's tone. "We are a military people. We should be preparing our victory feast instead of speaking of these Islanders with fear."

"The unknown," her father said gently, "is always more dangerous than the known. But Jewel does have a point. We cannot fight with fear." He turned to Hanouk. "We shall arrive under cover of rain and darkness as was the original plan. By the time the ships are in the Shadowlands, the weather shall have cleared."

"I do not like navigating blind," Caseo said. "At least allow the Sailors to do their jobs."

Jewel felt her father stiffen, although the movement was not visible. "You assume that I would place the entire fleet in jeopardy by not placing Sailors at strategic points? Is that what you're saying, Caseo?"

Caseo shoved his hands into the pockets of his robe. Water dripped off the edge of his nose. "I had assumed that you were trusting the Nyeian and the Warders to communicate knowledge to the Navigators. You have said nothing about Sailors."

Jewel bit her lower lip so that she would not respond. She had never heard anyone question her father, but she had never been in a meeting with a Warder before.

"I do not have to approve my plans with any of you," Jewel's father said. "I tell you all what you need to know."

"Then you will be using Sailors—?"

"We have been using Sailors all through the trip, Caseo. Their skills have worked for us for a thousand years. I see no reason to pull them from their posts now." Jewel's father brought his head back, the water beading on his face, making him look fierce. "You may rest assured, Caseo, that I would never rely on the Warders alone."

"You do need the Warders' loyalty for this campaign to work," Caseo said.

"Are you saying that the Warders are not going to be loyal to the Black King?" Jewel's father asked.

"The Black King did not want this mission."

"The Black King funded the fleet."

Hanouk took Caseo's arm. "Arguing with the Black King's son is foolish, Caseo. You have a job as well as the rest of us. Trust Rugar. He is right. The Islanders know nothing of war. We will be feasting in their palace by nightfall."

Caseo kept his gaze on Jewel's father. "Your father always kept me informed on past campaigns."

"I am sure he did," Jewel's father said. "You know everything you need to now, as well."

The rain thrummed on the wood and water. The riggings

groaned, and the ship creaked as it crested a swell. Across from Jewel a rock loomed, going from a shape in the darkness to a menacing presence, its surface shiny with wetness.

"I hope you have asked the Powers to provide a creature of the deep for you," Caseo said, "because if none live in these waters, we shall live and die by our wits alone."

"Our wits," Oswel said softly, "and a Nyeian's memory."

"The Nyeian will help us only once," Caseo said. "We have invaded too deep. He will not have a mind left by morning."

Water leaked behind Jewel's ear and under her cloak. She shuddered. A wave of dizziness hit her. The heavens cleared, and she saw a face looming over her. His eyebrows straight, his hair long and blond. His features were square. *Orma lii*, he said, then repeated a different word over and over. He cradled her in his arms. She smiled at him. His odd look had become familiar.

Her forehead burned. "Are you all right?" her father asked. The pain was greater than any she had felt before. "Jewel?"

A hand tightened around her waist. The darkness returned. The slanting rain was colder, and her father held her against him with such strength, she knew he had been keeping her from falling. The others were staring at her.

"Jewel?" her father asked. "Are you all right?"

She had had another Vision. Or the same Vision. But she deserved her last battle. She wanted it. One more battle, and then she would let him know. Then she would sit at his side as the second heir to the Black Throne.

"I will be glad when this rain ends," she said.

They all laughed, including her father, but the laughter did not reach his eyes. He knew something had happened to her. He would question her about it later. She only hoped he would wait until they had captured Blue Isle.

He turned his attention to the others. "When the rain ends," he said, "Blue Isle will know that the Fey have arrived."

SIX

EVERY morning the Rocaan would wake before dawn, put on his threadbare Danite robe, and light a single candle. In the thin flickering light, his cluttered chambers would look as spare as the cell he had shared when he was a young Danite awaiting his first assignment, five decades before. He would leave his feet bare despite the swollen joints and aches that had the Elders begging him to see a physician. Then he would cross the thick rug, the pain in his feet easing by the time he reached the stone stairs.

On this morning, rising had been particularly difficult. The rain still pounded the side of the building. His joints hurt him more than usual, and the only way he managed to get himself out of bed was to promise himself an extra pastry at breakfast. It wasn't until he had the candle lit and he was following its tiny light up the stairs that he realized the devotions were no longer enough. The thought pained him. It was a matter he would have to take up with the Holy One.

He opened the door to find the hallway brightly lit. The flames in the covered lamps burned fiercely: someone had just changed the wicks and replenished the oils. These small amenities were growing as his age advanced. It was as if the Elders would protect him from aging through comfort.

The large stones that made up the wall were covered with a whitewash that got repainted each week. The carpet was a thin runner of red woven by the Auds in the Kenniland Marshes. They had used wool specially imported from Nye, wool known for its thickness and softness and complete luxury. Even the lamps spoke of elegance, with their carved gold bases to hold the oil, and their precious glass.

He hurried out of the light toward the back stairs, which he had kept purposely undecorated. The rock was worn smooth from the passage of many feet over the centuries. Its icy coldness was reassuring. He used his left hand to steady himself as he followed the narrow staircase, keeping his right extended before him so that the candle would light his way.

By the time he reached the bottom, the chill had returned the ache to his joints and the blood to his face. Only there did he ever feel alive anymore. It was as if the luxury had bred the yearning soul out of him. He needed the poverty, the hardship, to remember what it was like to believe.

The stairs led to a cramped hallway that was part of the original kirk. This palatial cathedral, the Tabernacle as it was now known, had once been a small saint's cottage holding only an incense burner, an altar, and a kneeling cushion so that the itinerant worshiper could feel closer to his God. The original stone room remained, although three centuries earlier the Thirty-fifth Rocaan had added a window, covered by tapestries, which he used to attack assailants who were trying to eject him from the Tabernacle.

This Rocaan had found the room early in his reign. It had been sealed for generations. He had opened it, cleaned it, and restored it to its former simplicity. Now when he opened the thick wooden door, he found his kneeling cushion, an incense burner, and the small hand-carved altar. He'd had the Elders commission tapestries from the life of the Roca, and then he'd hung a simple silver sword, point down, from the wall, to commemorate Roca's death and subsequent Absorption into the Hand of God.

The room was ice cold and smelled of mildew and seawater. The tapestries were soaking wet and dripping onto the stone floor. A wide puddle ran to his kneeling cushion, and a thin trickle ran from the kneeling cushion to the door.

He sighed. He had designed this room to keep him in touch with the simple faith he'd had as a Danite, and as long as the rain continued, the discomforts of his youth would continue too. When he went up for breakfast, he would ask the Elders to commission new tapestries. The rain would certainly have ended by the time the tapestries were woven.

He stepped around the trickle and placed his candle in its small stand. Then he gritted his teeth and stepped into the puddle.

The water was colder than he'd remembered, and he nearly cried out as the shock ran from his aching feet into his legs. He had to hold up his robe to keep the hem from getting damp. He crossed over to the window and brushed the tapestry aside. The tapestry was so wet that it felt three times thicker than normal. The mildew smell was coming from the fabric.

The rain fell at a slant that coated the side of the building and hit him directly in the face. The darkness was so thick, he couldn't even see the river below. If there was going to be a dawn, it would be rendered invisible by the unnatural clouds. The day before, he had searched the records for any mention of a summer like this one, and never, in all the centuries of documentation, had Blue Isle been subjected to this constant dark, winterlike rain.

Some of the Auds whispered that the Holy One was visiting the rain on Blue Isle as a punishment for the corruption of the Rocaan and the leaders of the Church. But if the Holy One was displeased, He would have been even more displeased by the Rocaan's predecessor, who, the Rocaan believed, was more interested in the wealth of the office than in the people's spiritual well-being.

The traditionalists believed that the rain was the beginning of the final reckoning, that the world would slip further and further into darkness until the Holy One, in His compassion, brought the believers to Him in a final Absorption.

In a meeting the day before, the Rocaan had called together his Elders and asked for their opinion of the matter. Fedo used his knowledge of the Words Written and Unwritten as the basis for his opinion that the rains were merely one of the plagues brought to the Isle to test the believers. Porciluna used his knowledge of the Words Written and Unwritten to determine that the rains were a miracle long promised by God. And Matthias, bless his heretical heart, suggested, with no scholarship at all, that the rains might simply be rains, however unseasonable, inclement, and annoying.

Privately the Rocaan agreed with Matthias. He hated attributing motives to the Deities when common sense dictated something simpler, something rational.

Water ran down his face and stained the front of his robe. He let the soggy tapestry fall back into place. His feet were numb. He slogged through the puddle and stopped at the altar long enough to light his incense; then he knelt on the cushion, wincing as the wet fabric squished beneath his weight.

He bowed his head in meditation, allowing the events of the previous day to flow through him. Once he had believed what all children were taught: that the Holy One heard each still, small voice and carried it with the speed of wind to God's ear. As he grew older, such simple belief was hard to maintain. He had spoken to the Holy One with a still, small voice and with a loud, angry one, and none of his prayers seemed to be answered. Sometimes he thought that the Deities sat in front of the Eternal Flame, Roca cupped in God's Hand, and the Holy One at God's Ear, laughing as they listened to the requests of the poor humans below.

Not a charitable thought for a Rocaan to be sending on the wings of the Holy One to the Heavens above. The Rocaan bent his head and tried again. All these trappings of early faith did not wipe away the years of disillusionment. Even the spicy-sweet smell of raw, cheap incense could not bring back the feeling of joy he had experienced as a Danite preaching the Words Written and Unwritten to the congregations along the Cardidas River.

He wished he could go back and speak to that old woman who had approached him in his first year of ministering. She had come to him after a sunrise service, her face wizened with age, her mouth caved in because of her missing teeth. *You ask us to give our lives to the Holy One,* she'd said, her voice quivering, *and in return He will give us peace and joy. I have devoted my life to the Holy One since I was a little girl, and*

I have known no peace and no joy. You must help me, Religious Sir, before I turn my back on the Sword forever.

His words for her then had sounded lame, even to his own ears: *You must believe, and the peace and joy will come to you, sister.*

Only now he understood her despair. Perhaps no one received peace and joy in this lifetime. Most died before they achieved it, and the very old seemed discontented and angry with life. Or perhaps the Auds and the Elders had misunderstood the Words from the beginning. Perhaps peace and joy came after death. Or perhaps, as he feared in the pit of his soul, peace and joy came only to those Absorbed.

There had not been an Absorption since the Roca.

The chill in his knees had spread through his thighs into his groin. Little shivers ran through him, but he would stay until he felt he had somehow touched the Holy One.

His neck was cramping. Outside, the rain beat harder on the tapestries. Maybe the Officiate who had blessed him as a Danite had been right: *We must offer ourselves, failings and all, to the Holy One. The Holy One brings both joy and sorrow to the Ear of God. But you must remember that sorrow is our burden, and God has made no promises to alleviate the pains of the flesh.*

The smoke from the incense had grown thick and cloying. The Rocaan coughed, then wiped his hands against his robe. The kneeling cushion was so wet, the dampness was creeping into the fibers of his own garment.

At what point would God allow suffering to end and piety to be achieved? The Rocaan was an old man by any standard. Someday the chill would become permanent, and he would die frail and ill. All men died, and no requests to the Holy One changed that. Even Roca had died in a way, when he'd been Absorbed, all those centuries ago.

He thought he heard voices in the wind, and the creaks and groans of large ships. The Rocaan sighed. Daylight was coming too quickly. He had not yet made peace with his God. The groanings continued, combined with the slap-slap-slap of waves against a hull. Soon he would hear the longshoremen arguing about the best place to pull cargo ashore, and he would no longer be able to concentrate on the still, small voice within.

Longshoremen. The Rocaan paused, thoughts of the Holy One forgotten. He had been speaking with the Elders about the problems with the sea-going community, how half of them were out of work now that the trading with the Nye had ceased. The longshoremen, in particular, were affected.

He stood, his legs shaking beneath the thin, damp robe. The voices were soft, not the usual shouts and curses that interrupted his moments of worship. He gripped the altar to maintain his balance, then waded back to the window and pulled the tapestry aside.

The rain still fell heavily, and within an instant his face was drenched, water dripping down the inside of his robe. The darkness seemed heavier than it had been before. He placed his hands on the wet stone sill and leaned out, gazing upward. He saw nothing more than the individual drops illuminated by his small candle. The clouds were thick. No light could pierce them. The wind was blowing from the west, guiding any ship in the Cardidas to Jahn with great ease. The creaks of the wood were louder now. He looked, but no matter how much he squinted, he could not see any ships or their lanterns.

His hands were growing numb, and he could no longer feel his feet. If there was a ship below, and its captain glanced up, he would see the Rocaan peering out the window like a common schoolboy. Somehow that thought filled the Rocaan with alarm.

He let the tapestry fall, and as he did, he heard a sound he had not heard since he'd been a boy, fishing with his father. The ululating cry of a man signaling to his mates without words. A cry designed to be a call of the wild, although it sounded like no creature the Rocaan had ever heard. Some kind of prearranged signal that required a pre-arranged action. A cargo ship's captain would not do that.

The Rocaan grabbed his candle and placed it outside the door, careful to set it away from the trickle that had invaded the hall. Then he went back into the room and closed the door after himself, waiting until his eyes adjusted to the blackness before making his way to the window again.

This time he tied the tapestry back and stared at the river below. He heard splashes, and more soft voices, although no matter how hard he concentrated, he could not understand their words. He squinted until finally he could see the outlines of the masts, dozens of them, disappearing into the distance like a ghostly invasion force.

He would have heard had there been a fleet coming to Blue Isle. He would have assigned Auds to minister to their needs, Danites to see to their faith, Officiates to give them contact with the organized Church—and, if they were important enough, an Elder or two to begin political relations. This was different. How different he did not know. He needed the advice of someone else. Someone he could trust. Someone who would look with a clear eye.

He left the tapestry open and went from the room. It felt odd to walk on dead feet. As he bent over to pick up the candle, he noted that his skin was blue. He could not spend any more time in that room this morning. Surely God did not require a man to lose his feet in pursuit of a Blessing. He climbed the stairs, using the wall for support now more than ever, finding that numb feet could not properly judge stair height. When he reached the hallway, he handed his candle to one of the guards.

"Get Elder Matthias for me, and quickly," he said. Then he let himself into his chambers.

As per his instructions, someone had lit his daily fire and placed a tray beside the hearth. He glanced at the warm milk, freshly squeezed from one of the goats housed in the yard, and instead took a small bite of the roll the servants baked every morning. The bread was still hot and doughy in the middle, just the way he liked it. Then he pulled off his robe, leaving it in the middle of the floor, and slipped on the plush red velvet robe of his office, basking in its softness and warmth. He sat on the flagstones and extended his feet toward the fire. A slight needles-and-pins feeling changed almost instantly to deep, agonizing pain as his feet thawed. He grabbed them, startled by the cold flesh on top and the hot flesh on the bottom, and squeezed, as if the pressure would make the pain go away.

At that moment someone knocked on his door.

He sighed; then he backed away from the fire, eased himself into his chair, and put his feet on the ground. He wiped his eyes, swallowed, and, ignoring the pain, called, "Welcome!"

The door opened and Matthias entered, already natty in his pressed black. The robe whispered as he walked. The only concession he had made to the earliness was that he was not wearing his sash or biretta. But his hair was combed and his face already clean shaven.

"I hope, Holy Sir, that nothing amiss has happened," Matthias said, his tone matter-of-fact instead of questioning.

"I certainly hope so as well," the Rocaan said, gritting his teeth. The pain was coming in a steady ache, marred by sharp stabs. "I would like you to go down to my worship room, look out the window, and tell me what you see."

Matthias cocked his head. He was young, the youngest of all the Elders, his skin still unlined and taut. "And what, exactly, am I looking for?"

"I will tell you when you return, since I do not want to influence you. And perhaps, by the time you get down there, what I want you to see will be gone, so do not worry if you fail to see anything at all."

Matthias frowned and clasped his hands in front of his robe. The black robe of an Elder was also made of velvet. The higher authorities in the Church seemed to believe that ranking members should live in comfort. Whenever the Rocaan thought of changing that, he remembered that he would have to give up his soft bed, his morning fire, and his sweets.

Matthias did not look as if he were going to move.

"And one more thing," the Rocaan said, mostly to spur Matthias on, "do not bring a light into the room. I'm afraid you'll have to stumble around in the dark."

"All right." Matthias bowed his head. He backed out of the room slowly.

The Rocaan waited until the door closed before allowing a moan to leave his lips. The pain was easing, but it had been excruciating during his conversation with Matthias. Only the toes continued to hurt. He eased one foot up and massaged it, then the other, noting with pleasure that the blue had left the skin, replaced with healthy red. No toe had an unnatural whiteness, which he had feared. He had seen too many Danites lose flesh to that wintry color.

He took another bite of his roll, then drank some of the milk. Even as the pain left, he felt unsettled. He had not completed his morning ritual. But, if the truth be told, he had not achieved the sense of peace he sought for a long,

long time. This intrusion had simply been a little more startling.

He leaned his head back, then heard footsteps in the corridor. They had more urgency than they had had before. The knock, even though he expected it, was sharp and frightening. No vision, then. He had seen ships.

"Come," he said.

Matthias was already halfway into the room. He closed the door tightly, then hurried down the small flight of stairs. "Ships," he said. "I saw ships. Dozens of them. Should I send for the head of the Port Guild?"

The Rocaan rubbed the bridge of his nose with his thumb and forefinger. The pain in his feet was gone, but a headache had started above his eyes. "Before you go, tell me what you saw."

"It took a moment, in the darkness," Matthias said. "That floor is damned wet in there."

"It's the rain," the Rocaan said tiredly.

"Then I saw masts, and if I looked carefully, I saw the ships themselves. They're not Nyeian. I've never seen them before. And it was quiet except for low voices."

"What were they saying?"

"I couldn't make it out."

"Neither could I." The Rocaan let his hand drop. He opened his eyes. Matthias's face was flushed, his eyes sparkling with the excitement. The Rocaan sighed. "I think you must go to the King."

"Holy Sir?"

A thread of irritation ran through the Rocaan. Did he have to explain everything? Matthias was sharp. He should have figured the problem out already. "The ships are unknown, Matthias," the Rocaan said. "They are not planned for. I suspect our visitors are uninvited."

Matthias shook his head. "That's impossible. No one can get to Blue Isle's shores without guidance."

"Someone had to once," the Rocaan said, "or we would not be here."

Matthias took a step backward, then sat in the armchair near the bed as if he needed something to support his weight. "What would anyone want with Blue Isle?"

The question was soft, almost rhetorical, but the Rocaan

chose to answer it. "We are one of the richest countries in the world. To ignore us would be foolish."

Matthias looked at the Rocaan, his gaze piercing. "You know who this is."

"I have a suspicion," the Rocaan said. "Nye has shared our waters for centuries and still needed help to arrive at Blue Isle's shores. Occasionally other seafaring folk have tried to come to Blue Isle, only to wreck on the Stone Guardians or be savaged by the current. But there is a group that has never tried to attack us before, and now they hold Nye."

"The Fey," Matthias breathed.

"Just so," the Rocaan said. He sounded calmer than he felt. "And if the tales we have heard are true, they are vicious. You must go to the King, and quickly."

Matthias nodded and stood. He hurried toward the stairs and then stopped. "Even if it is the Fey, we'll be able to defeat them, won't we?"

"With God's help," the Rocaan said. He folded his hands across his bulging stomach. Matthias scurried from the room, apparently satisfied with the Rocaan's answer.

But the Rocaan wasn't. He looked at the closed door. "No, Matthias," he said softly, as if he hadn't answered the question before. "They are soldiers and we are farmers, and we shall be slaughtered before we have a chance to learn how to defend ourselves."

SEVEN

THE Cardidas River was over a mile wide at the site of its natural harbor inside the Blue Isle city of Jahn. Although Rugar had known this before he'd arrived, nothing had prepared him for the immensity of the river itself. It had strong currents and dark, brownish waters that spoke of copper in the mud. And the bridge that spanned the harbor was an engineering marvel. It had towers every few feet and stone arches large enough to let ships through. Even in the dark and the rain, the bridge was an impressive landmark.

He didn't need it. The city of Jahn rose around him, filled with impressive landmarks. If the map hadn't shown that the palace lay on the north side of the river, and the religious building on the south, he would have thought that Jahn had two palaces. The Tabernacle was the more impressive of the two, with five towers and white walls that flared like torches in the darkness. It also stood closer to the water. He could barely make out the palace's towers through the rain.

The air on Blue Isle lacked the salty tinge he had grown used to on the open sea. The freshness invaded his lungs, made him feel stronger. He was ready to take this place. Already his troops were scattered through the city. He had watched Jewel's unit leave, his daughter tall and proud in the center of the troop, looking more like a soldier than any of the others.

This would be her last battle. They both knew it. Even though she hadn't admitted what had happened outside the Stone Guardians, Rugar knew. She had had the beginnings of a Vision. She was coming into her Sight.

Rugar remained near the prow where he had stood since the ships had arrived. From there he had overseen the troops, watched as his people slipped away under cover of darkness to take positions that would enable quick capture of the city once the sun came up. Not long now. Not long at all.

Beside him the Navigators had come to free the Sailors. The Sailors had got them all through the Stone Guardians. The rocks were huge, three times taller than the ships. He felt as if he were floating on a cloud surrounding a mountaintop instead of on the ocean. At times the rock walls were close enough to touch. He concentrated all his power on making sure things went smoothly—not his magick power, for his abilities did not enable him to work as a Sailor, but his intellectual power, straining for any movement, any sudden change that would put the ship in great danger.

The Nyeian's mind had disintegrated under the strain, and the Warders had tried to rely on the old maps. But one of the Sailors had discovered a frightened but communicative creature, which called itself a Ze, and it seemed to understand the currents. The Navigators had spread the word of the Ze to the other Sailors, and as a group—with the help of the Ze, the Sailors, and the old maps—the ships had come through with no scratches at all.

The Sailors were still sprawled over the railings, their bodies present, but their minds inhabiting the bodies of the Ze. The Navigators were standing beside them, coaxing the Sailors back to the surface. Rugar rubbed his chapped red hands together. He did need a bit more information.

He walked to the nearest Navigator, Kapad. Kapad had been part of the sea before Rugar had become a member of the Infantry. His eyes were hollow, his own mind still linked with those of two Sailors, and his skin was leathery. His winged brows were silver, but his hair was still black. With his scarred right hand, he held the Sailor's sleeve.

"Don't bring him up yet," Rugar said. "I have a question."

Kapad blinked once, then nodded. The slowness of the response always unnerved Rugar, even though he knew that a Navigator also passed the information to the Sailors he worked with.

"I need to know the kind of magicks they have protecting the harbor." With the back of his hand, Rugar wiped the water off his face. "In fact, I would like to know all the magicks the fish have observed."

Kapad blinked and nodded again. He stood very still for a moment, then said, "He is asking."

"Thank you." Rugar waited, hands clasped behind his back. Even though the Nyeians made no report of magick among the Islanders, the Nyeians might not have known where to look. Rugar did not want any surprises. The Warders believed there was no magick. Magick was extremely rare outside of the Fey—the Fey had encountered only a handful of peoples with even the slightest talents—but Rugar thought it prudent to check.

The Sailor beside Kapad remained motionless. Across the deck another Sailor stood, then staggered backward, his hand to his face. He collapsed on the puddle-covered deck, water splashing around him. His dark skin had an unhealthy pallor and his features looked sunken. The Navigator who had helped him to the surface took his hands, speaking in a low voice. Rarely did Sailors work such long hours. They had been leaning over the rails since the middle of the night. Usually they worked in tandem teams, often leaving one creature and moving into another through the duration of a voyage.

But the Navigators had never encountered Ze before and had asked the Sailors to stay with the creatures until the ships reached Jahn.

The Navigator frowned and leaned against the rail. "Sir?" he said slowly, forming each word as if he were trying to speak while he was listening to someone else. "The Ze claim to have seen no magick here, sir."

That was the response Rugar had wanted to hear, but he didn't believe it. "None?"

"They didn't understand the pictures we were sending them. They asked the others, a sea lion and her young son, some sea otters, a few passing fish, and none of them had seen any magick either. If I hadn't been speaking with them, they would have thought the whole thing impossible."

Rugar smiled. The Nyeians hadn't lied to him, then. He glanced at the palace, looking pale and insubstantial in the distance. He would eat his evening meal in the highest tower, overlooking the sea. "Thank you," he said. He still had much work to do before he got to that meal.

He leaned over the railing and looked at the north side of the harbor. The docks, filled with every ship from a smallest fishing vessel to the largest barge, stood in uniform rows along the harbor's edges. The fish hatcheries, the warehouses, and the grain silos were gray shapes on the city's outskirts. Through those streets his people were scattering in a force one third the size of Jahn's population.

Rugar gripped the rope ladder on the side of the ship and worked his way down. There the wetness felt natural, and the slide of his boots against the wooden rungs the norm. He leaped from the bottom of the ladder onto the dock, wincing as the sound echoed over the rain.

Then he turned and scanned the gray buildings, hoping to see movement. He saw nothing and heard only the rain on the water. He shoved his hands under the wool of his cape and permitted himself one shudder.

The only Fey he could see were two Red Caps talking outside one of the warehouses. The Warders were setting up inside a warehouse, and Rugar suspected that was the one. The Red Caps had little to do before a battle started, but afterward they became invaluable. He was glad he never had to work with them. They made him uneasy. Small and magickless, they were like square, truncated Fey, with the same upswept features and none of the graces. Most Red Caps didn't even bother to bathe. Their very ugliness kept them separate from the other Fey; their lack of magick ensured that they would never attack their betters.

The world rolled beneath his feet. Rugar hated these first moments on land, when the sea still controlled his movements. He wished he had the skill of a Shape-Shifter, able to adapt to any environment.

Rugar walked cautiously along the dock toward the

shore. The rain seemed to be lessening. The Sprites had warned him that they couldn't time it perfectly. He wiped the water off his face with his dry sleeve. Time. He had to do it now.

He had to hide the ships before the Islanders awoke.

Rugar stepped off the dock onto the shore, his boots miring in the muck. Then he raised his arms and closed his eyes, picturing as the generals had taught him long ago, a world with the substance of fog. Around that world he built a box so large that a hundred giants could not hold it. He carefully slipped that box over all the ships. He built a small circular doorway the size of a fist on the east side and marked it with Fey lights, then pushed the whole thing out to sea.

The sound of the rain changed its timbre. Gone was the hollow pounding of water on wood, and added was the slap of drops on water. He opened his eyes.

The ships were gone.

Safe in the Shadowlands.

He had opened the door once again.

Slowly he let his arms drop; then he sank to his knees in the mud. The effort of making the Shadowlands had cost him what energy he had left. But he could not quit now. The cold against his legs would keep him awake. And once the battle started, he would get a second wind.

The ships were gone, and the troops were dispersed. Soon the rain would end and the sun would rise for the first time in days. The people would awake to an empty harbor and a city full of strangers.

A tingle of excitement ran through him, banishing the exhaustion. The Fey would strike quickly and effortlessly.

They would own the city by dinner, the Isle by nightfall. Once the Fey's hold was secure, Rugar would take a ship back to his father to let him know the good news—and to hear his father's apology—in person.

EIGHT

NICHOLAS awoke with a start. Something was different. He sat up on the feather bed, the clammy blankets sticking to his bare flesh, and listened.

The rain had stopped.

He smiled and pushed the blankets aside, then slid off the high bed. The rug, handwoven by his mother, felt damp. It was as if the rain had touched everything. He pushed aside a tapestry and peered out.

The sun was rising, red and fierce, in the east. Raindrops glistened on every surface, catching and reflecting the sun's rays. The brightness made him shield his eyes for a moment until they adjusted. He had forgotten how much he enjoyed the sun.

The courtyard was empty, except for the birds singing in the brown garden. The gardener would be pleased the rains had ceased. He might have a chance to save the vegetables. He had been worried that the palace would eat only apples all winter long.

No breakfast yet, and the fire had gone out in his grate. He was up before the servants. Nicholas grinned. He let out a whoop sure to wake the palace. It had been a while since he'd sneaked into the kitchens to get his own food. He put on a pair of tattered pants, a heavy shirt, and a pair of boots. Then he grabbed his scabbard and attached it to his waist. No sense letting a beautiful morning like this pass. As soon as he finished eating, he would go to the courtyard, rouse the swordmaster, and fight.

Nicholas chuckled, then ran his fingers through his long blond hair to get some of the knots out of it. He tied it all back with a leather thong and opened his door.

The corridor was empty except for an elderly servant carrying firewood up to his father's floor. Nicholas nodded and scampered for the stairs. His boots slapped against the stone as he hurried down.

Other servants were beginning their rounds. A young boy, carrying firewood destined for Nicholas's room, gaped in surprise as Nicholas bounded past him. The round matron who kept the wing was already directing a group of girls toward the gallery at the base of the family tower. A breeze carried the scent of damp ground, and he paused for a moment at the double windows to soak in the sunshine once again.

This time he saw servants crossing the courtyard. The dairymen were coming back from the milking, large buckets hanging from their hands. Some children were playing on the cobblestones while their mothers chatted. A man whisked them all away. No one seemed cross; no one seemed angry. Their spirits all seemed as high as Nicholas's.

He took a deep breath and bounded down the remaining twelve stairs, appearing in front of the great stone arches like a man ready for battle. Then he hurried through the Great Chamber, startling maids already at work cleaning the furniture and scrubbing the ornate stone inlays. His stepmother, in her short reign, had decreed that everything in the palace remain clean—too many servants were idle— and the decree had lasted beyond her.

Once he got to the Hall, he slowed down. This was one of his favorite rooms, and not only because the great state dinners were held there. It was long and wide and had arched ceilings because it connected two towers and had no floor above it. The arched windows matched the ceiling in design, some of the few windows in the palace to have precious glass. His grandfather had installed them to impress visitors, even though the greatest visitors Nicholas had ever seen were mayors from Nye when he was a boy.

He liked the majesty of the room, but more than that, he liked its history. Swords hung from the inner wall, so many he couldn't count them, in styles as old as recorded history. None were ceremonial. Most had nicks and cuts from prolonged use. Some were almost as short as the dirk the swordmaster sometimes carried, and Nicholas's grandfather had once explained that those swords had been for dueling almost four hundred years before.

Nicholas's favorite sword, though, had been his great-great-grandfather's in the Peasant Uprising. Blood still blackened the tip. Legend had it that his great-great-grandfather had stabbed the man who'd crippled him before passing out on the field. Sometimes Nicholas thought he carried the soul of his grandfather's grandfather. No one in his immediate family enjoyed the idea of fighting quite so much. In fact, Nicholas's father had been opposed to his work with the sword until he'd realized that Nicholas would learn nothing if he could not pursue his own interest.

The sun was thin through the mottled glass. The Hall wasn't as enjoyable as usual because beauty awaited outdoors.

Nicholas scurried past the buttery, where he heard men swearing over the churns, and the pantry, where he heard servants laughing as they broke their own fasts. He stopped at the kitchen, and the heat from the great fireplaces and huge stoves made sweat instantly run down his face. Shortly after Nicholas had been born, his father had remodeled the kitchen at the chef's request, adding a high ceiling and ventilation in the roof, but even that did not stop the heat from being overwhelming.

The bakers were making bread in the brick-lined ovens, and the room smelled of smoke and yeast. The chef was scolding an assistant about the quality of the eggs picked for the King's breakfast, while the butler inspected the milk brought by the dairymen. With the roar of the flames, the thump of the bread on the top of the ovens, and the shouted conversations, no one noticed Nicholas when he arrived.

He smiled as he stood. He had missed this, the constant daily drama. It was the servants' duty to make sure none of it reached the upper regions of the palace, but that meant his life was led in too much tranquillity. He was too young to be tranquil, too young to recite the verses of the Words Written and Unwritten foisted on him by overweight Auds, too young to sit, as his father did, and listen to the complaints from region after region about this year's harvest or last year's wool.

Nicholas sneaked inside, slipped past the butler, and stopped by the ovens, reaching for the steaming bread on top. The senior baker slapped his hand so hard that Nicholas pulled it away.

"Is it fingers ye be wanting to lose, boy?" the baker snapped before realizing whom he was speaking to. He stepped back, bit his lower lip, and bowed his head. Sweat dripped off his nose. " 'Tis sorry I am, Highness. I dinna think 'twould be you."

Nicholas laughed. "This morning I am just a yeoman seeking out a simple breakfast."

"Nay," the baker said. "If ye were a yeoman, I'd be tossing ye out on yer behind. Now, get yerself into the pantry with the others, and I'll be bringing yer bread."

"All right," Nicholas said. The conversations around him had stopped. The chef had crossed his arms over his chest, as if he didn't approve of Nicholas's presence either. "But I don't want much. I would hate to overeat on a morning like this."

He hurried out of the kitchen and back into the pantry. The room smelled like bread and was cool compared with the kitchen. Fresh-baked bread loaves already graced the shelves, and the King's cutlery stood in its holders on the wall. A dozen servants remained, sitting on stools around a makeshift wooden table littered with crumbs and cracked cups filled with water. They were laughing, a sound that cut off when Nicholas entered. His chamberlain was inside, and he stepped forward, face red and eyes filled with fear.

"I dinna know ye'd be up, milord," he said. "Ye usually sleep another hour or more."

"How can anyone sleep with the sun back?" Nicholas said. He ruffled his chamberlain's short-cut brown hair. "I would've thought you'd have been outside, enjoying the first light we've had in days."

The chamberlain shrugged, clearly relieved that he wouldn't be chastised for not knowing his master's wishes.

" 'Twas certain I was that I'd be there with ye not long after ye rose," he said.

Nicholas laughed. His chamberlain knew him well. The man was supposed to serve Nicholas in his chamber only, but Nicholas would never have countenanced a man spending such a beautiful day indoors.

"Well, make room," he said, grabbing a stool and shoving it close to the table, "and pretend I'm one of you. I'm going to break fast, then spend the rest of the day in the sun. And if I were King instead of my father, I'd let all of you do the same."

The servants cheered and raised their water mugs high over his head in a toast. He wished, just once, they'd clap him on the back as they would each other, but that degree of familiarity would be nearly impossible for them. He was lucky to gain this much.

The baker came up behind him and put several fresh-cut pieces of bread before him. The butler had added some precious cheese, and the chef had cut one of last year's apples on the side. The food was much more than Nicholas wanted, but he waited until the baker left to pass the extra pieces around.

Then he ate quickly. The bread was hot and doughy, steam rising from the center. The cheese was so perfectly aged that it crumbled beneath his fingers. Its sharpness contrasted with the sweetness of the apple, which was still hard and firm from spending the winter in the cellar.

The others ate their portions greedily. They usually got the leftovers, not the freshly made bread. He wondered how it would feel to eat his breakfast in the room where the fresh bread was stored and not be allowed to taste any. He loved the little luxuries of his life.

While he ate, the conversation flowed around him, mostly full of kitchen gossip—which yeoman was courting what maid. He listened eagerly, even though he didn't know half the names, feeling on the very fringe of a society that he barely understood. No one spoke directly to him, and if he asked a question, the silence afterward lasted a moment too long, as if they were trying to decide who would answer him. Finally the chamberlain would, probably because it was his place to deal with Nicholas. After a while Nicholas stopped asking questions.

When he finished, he got up and excused himself, thanking them all for their hospitality. They laughed with him and thanked him for sharing, but he could see the relief in their eyes that he was leaving. For the rest of the day he would be the topic of conversation in the servants' quarters, while they wondered as to the purpose of his visit and speculated as to the nature of his character.

He went back through the kitchen, waving at the chef and the butler as he passed. With the back of his hand he wiped the sweat off his face and smiled to himself. He left through the open back door, kicking aside the bones the kind-hearted chef had left for the dogs.

Outside, the air was still cool with a touch of damp. But he could feel the heat of the morning was not long away. The sun felt good on his bare arms. There were lots of voices in the breeze, odd cries and shouts he hadn't heard before. But, then, he had never been in the yard this early before.

The cats were sitting outside the dairy barns, grooming themselves after their morning treat of fresh milk. One of the grooms had a mare by the leg, and he was examining her hoof in the brightness of the sun. The cobblestones were still wet, and mud from too many boots had been squelched on top of them. The surface would be slick for his workout, but he could handle slick. He relished a challenge that would allow him to push his own limits.

He went to the swordmaster's rooms at the very edge of the servants' quarters. Nicholas knocked on the door, a sharp report over the palace's early-morning sounds. The door opened, and Stephen stood in front of him, looking sleepy and old in the early-morning light.

"The sun is out," Nicholas said. "I thought we shouldn't wait another moment."

"Boys," Stephen said. He scratched his tousled graying hair and then rubbed the silver bristles on his chin. "I'll be out in a moment."

He closed the door without letting Nicholas inside.

Nicholas paced outside the door, staring up at the sky as if he were afraid the sun would go away. But the sky was a perfect blue without any clouds at all. If it weren't for the standing water, the mud and the wet stones, he would not have believed that the rains had drenched Blue Isle in the dry season.

The shouts in the streets grew louder, and he thought he heard a woman cry in pain. Nicholas frowned. He glanced at the high stone wall as though he could see through it. Sometimes the sounds were too close, as if the peasants could get inside with no effort at all. He was raised with stories of the Peasant Uprising, of the day they had stormed the wall, and only his great-great-grandfather's quick thinking and a chef's vat of oil had saved the palace from being overrun. As a little boy, Nicholas used to enact that battle all by himself, standing on the flat part of the kitchen roof and pouring cups of water down the side of the wall. A manservant had finally stopped him when he'd seen how perilously close Nicholas was to falling into the newly built open ceiling.

Then he heard the pounding of horse's hooves, and he moved away from Stephen's door so that he could see the wooden side gate. The guards signaled down from the towers, and the men double-teamed to pull the ropes so that the gate would go up. Two horses, ridden by Danites with red trim on their hems, marking them as having come from the Tabernacle, came inside. The men let the gate drop behind them as if they were infected by the wild expressions on the Danites' faces.

"We need to see the King!" the rotund Danite said. His voice carried all over the yard.

Nicholas ran forward, his date with Stephen forgotten. One of the guards was speaking to the Danites in a lower tone. The horses were covered with sweat, and one of them reared when Nicholas approached. The Danite struggled to keep hold, but it was a guard who grabbed the reins and calmed the horse.

"On what business do you need to see the King?" Nicholas demanded.

The Danite looked at him, then bowed as best he could on the horse. "We come from the Tabernacle, Highness. The Rocaan saw ships in the harbor this morning, strange ships that arrived in the rain. There are strangers all over the city, and as we rode here, we heard screams in the streets. A woman ran from the alley not far from this place, her clothing in tatters, shouting that she had seen the devil." The Danite's words were clipped. His face was red, and he looked as exhausted as his horse. The Tabernacle was on the other side of the river from the palace.

"We shall go to my father at once," Nicholas said. He stood as tall as he could, adopting the tone his father used for business. "Guard, send someone ahead. Tell my father we will meet him in his audience chamber, and tell him the matter is urgent. You," he said to the groom standing to the side, "take the horses. See that they're well taken care of."

His heart was pounding in his chest, and he was trembling with excitement, but he tried not to show it. Something was happening in Jahn this morning, something that had scared the Rocaan and put terror in the hearts of these Danites.

The guard ran ahead. The Danites dismounted, and Nicholas led them through the door that took them to the inner court instead of through the kitchen. "Why didn't the Rocaan come himself?" Nicholas asked.

"He wanted to," the tall Danite said, "but the Elders thought it would be too dangerous."

Nicholas frowned. How long had the Tabernacle known about this crisis before bringing it to the King?

They went through a narrow corridor, then into the Great Hall, before Nicholas led them through the door which led to the audience chamber.

Four guards stood in front of the oak door. Two of them moved in unison to pull it open as Nicholas and his party approached.

The formal audience chamber smelled musty. His father hadn't used it in weeks. Ancient spears lined the walls, and behind the dais stood the family coat of arms: two swords crossed over a heart.

His father was already inside, seated on the throne, wearing the blue velvet robe he usually wore to a family breakfast. Two of his advisers, Lords Stowe and Powell, stood beside him like silent sentries. They still had morning beards, and Lord Powell's ponytail was askew. Nicholas's father, at least, looked clean shaven.

"What is this disturbance that breaks my routine?" Nicholas's father asked.

Nicholas stepped forward, leaving the bowing Danites behind. "These men rode in moments ago from the Tabernacle. They claim strange ships are in the harbor and strange men are in the streets."

"How many ships?" his father asked.

The rotund Danite stepped forward. "The Rocaan could not tell, Sire. He saw them in the rainy darkness before dawn. By the time the sun rose, the ships were gone."

"Then why didn't he come to tell me himself?" Nicholas's father asked. He was leaning forward, his brow creased and his elbows resting on his knees.

"Because there is more, Sire. There are strange people in the streets, lots of screams and cries. We saw a woman who claimed to be pursued by a devil. We saw blood running like a river from the ports." The tall Danite cast a quick glance at Nicholas as he spoke, as if he didn't want to say that last in front of a boy. Nicholas stood taller. He was no longer a boy. And hadn't his response been the same as his father's?

"The Elders did not think it wise to send anyone important into the streets, which is why we were chosen." The rotund Danite spoke without anger, as if he knew he was of no consequence. "The Rocaan believes we have been invaded. He believes we must act quickly, or perish."

Nicholas felt as if all the wind had been knocked out of him. Lord Stowe gripped the top of the throne tightly. Nicholas's father had turned pale. "Invaded?" he asked, as if he didn't quite understand the word. "But no one can get into Blue Isle. The Stone Guardians protect us, and we have authorized no maps since Nye was overrun."

Then a look of horror crossed his face before disappearing behind the mask he usually wore. The look made Nicholas cold.

"Does the Rocaan know who brought the ships?" his father asked.

"No, Sire," the tall Danite said. "Not for certain. But he has a suspicion."

"The Fey," Nicholas's father said, answering his own question. "They are more skilled than we thought."

NINE

THE sunlight felt warm on his skin. Silence had been cold ever since the fleet had left Nye. He openly attributed his chill to the wind off the ocean, but actually he knew that it was because he wore Fey form again. For too long he had worn the shape of a Nyeian general, shedding that body only days before the fleet had left for Blue Isle.

Steam rose off the mud as the sun hit it. He stood beside the large central building where the guards had their morning meeting. The barracks were twenty-five small, hutlike buildings that formed a perfect half circle. The central building was in front of them. He hid between one of the huts and the building's entrance, leaning on the wet wood wall. The buildings in this part of Jahn were long and two-storied, except for the palace itself. Most of the buildings were made of wood, although some of the older ones had stone facades. The road before him was cobblestone, but the path leading to the central building was dirt.

Silence had spent his morning searching for the closest thing the Islanders had to an army. Before the fleet had left Nye, he had scanned his Nyeian general's memory for evidence of an army on Blue Isle and had come up empty. Apparently the Islanders had no army, only guards who theoretically protected the King. No Nyeian had ever seen the guards fight or do more than hold ceremonial weapons.

It had taken Silence a good hour to find anything that passed for a guard. Finally he had followed to this place three men wearing black tunics and tight pants, thinking the men's clothes were a uniform. When he'd seen that the barracks pressed against the palace like a barnacle on a ship, he'd known he was right.

He hadn't wanted this assignment. He hadn't even wanted to come to Blue Isle. But Rugar was short of Doppelgängers, and Silence hated civilian life. Spying on other Fey for the Black King was not the best use of Silence's talents. Besides, he had been getting tired of the Nyeians. He had lived inside their skins for nearly a decade, and he had nothing new to learn about the culture. The fact that no one understood the Islanders intrigued him. The idea of an easy and prestigious kill also lured him away from Nye.

Rugar had sent all ten Doppelgängers on this trip to get as close to the Islander King as possible. Silence planned to be the one who killed the ruler.

Silence had not yet found the man he wanted, and he had little time. His height and slenderness, his sun-browned skin, his upraised eyebrows and slightly pointed ears, marked him an outsider. How much these people feared strangers was unknown to him. Too many passersby had already noted his presence. He couldn't continue observing for long.

He slid along the wall and approached the main building. Its white wood walls appeared to have swollen with the rain. The building had no windows at all. In order to observe, he would have to slip inside, something he did not want to do, as he was unprepared to make a sudden change.

With his left hand he patted his hip, his fingers touching the hilt of his stiletto. It was still there. Good. He couldn't act without it.

He looked at the barracks around him. For the moment the yard was empty. He climbed the two stone steps to the door and slowly turned the knob. He moved with the stealth for which he had been named, keeping to the shadows, hoping no one would notice his strange presence.

The building smelled of greasy meat, and sweat. He stepped into a narrow hallway, the floor made of rough planks, the walls of unpainted wood. The hall was dark. The only light came from the room beyond, where half a dozen lamps hung from holders built into the wall. He peered around the door. A group of men talked and laughed, empty plates of food still scattered on the tables.

These men were older than the ones he had followed. They had all thickened with age, and their skin lacked the elasticity of youth. On Nye they would be leaders. Probably here as well. He was in luck.

He peered around the door, barely breathing. The men all deferred to a large man with thinning blond hair and large jowls. His eyes were nearly lost in his florid face, and his mouth puckered out of his rounded cheeks.

Perfect. Except that he couldn't prepare there. A Doppelgänger had only a moment before the blood he needed to change dried on his skin. He would have to find a victim somewhere close.

He slunk back to the door and let himself out. The sunlight was blinding. In the distance he could hear shouts, cries, and screams: a sign that his comrades were already at work. He had to hurry. Soon the tableau inside would break up and he would lose his opportunity.

An elderly man ran from a door on the side of the palace toward the barracks. Silence slipped into the shadows. When the man reached the main building's stairs, Silence grabbed him and pulled him between buildings.

The man was thin and bony with age, his skin hanging in wrinkled folds around his features, his pale eyes wide with shock.

"I need your help, friend," Silence said in his most soothing voice. The man shook his head. Silence grabbed the man's shoulder with his right hand, and with his left he pulled the stiletto from its sheath against his hip. In a quick, practiced movement, he jabbed the blade into the man's neck, severing the carotid artery and sending blood spurting like a geyser.

The man's eyes grew wider as his skin grew paler. He gestured wildly, then sank to his knees, all the time gurgling as he tried to call for help. Silence stripped the clothes from his own body, then stood in the spray as if it were a shower, massaging himself quickly so that the blood coated all of his skin. He rubbed what he could into his hair, then, as the stream tapered off and the old man fell face forward in the dust, Silence took his clothes and squeezed what little blood he could get from them.

Then he ran up the stairs and inside the open door. The men were already splitting up. Someone apparently had come to them with news of the fighting near the docks. Silence's quarry still sat at the table, barking orders like a small dog.

Silence's heart was pounding against his rib cage. He had never done this in broad daylight, always preferring the protection of night. Fortunately, all the men except his victim were disappearing through a side door, and no one else had come past the front.

Silence waited until the orders stopped before peering around the door. The blood was growing sticky. He had only a moment left.

His prey sat alone, face red, sweat dripping down his forehead even though the room was not hot. He appeared to be alone.

Good.

Silence stepped into the doorway, knowing that the shock of his naked, blood-covered body would gain him time to cross the room.

"By the Sword," the man said, standing, his chair clattering to the floor behind him. "What in the name of Roca are you?"

"I am your Döppelganger," Silence said as he lunged across the room. He still clung to the stiletto with his right hand, but as he mounted the table, he dropped the blade onto the plates with a resounding clang.

The man was backing up, but he tripped against his chair and would have fallen if he hadn't used his hand to steady himself. Silence leaped on him like a spider, wrapping his legs around the man's torso to hold his position, his elbows in the man's neck to brace his arms. Silence stuck his fingers into the man's eyes and his thumbs into the man's mouth, prying the teeth open and pushing hard against the back of the throat.

Then he pulled and pulled and pulled until the man's essence broke free and fluttered between them for a moment like a frightened child. Silence bit into the mist and sucked it inside, feeling rather than hearing the man's screams.

Then he felt his body mold and twist and expand until it too had a wide girth, small eyes, and a puckish mouth.

The body between his legs and arms vanished, and he nearly lost his balance before remembering to put his own feet on the ground. The bones clattered to the ground. He grabbed a chair and pulled it close to him, sinking in it.

Images mixed in his mind, memories not his own. His stomach churned with the grease of the ancient duck the cook had made, and his head ached from a hangover even though he had had nothing to drink for weeks. The culture wasn't clear yet, and neither was the language, but it would be in a moment. He would just have to wait.

He wiped his hand over the back of his mouth. Clothing. He was sitting there completely nude. Quartermaster Grundy had never been nude in his life. Fortunately, the quartermaster's quarters were in the building. With luck he could get to them and take out the uniform the quartermaster had discarded the night before.

Then both personalities melded, and he clenched his fists. A quartermaster. He had fallen short of captain of the guards. He might have to go through this painful process all over again. This was what came of too little cultural study, too little preparation, and too much arrogance.

Silence shook off his annoyance. He was there. He had invaded an Islander. He had a culture to learn and people to manipulate. He wasn't yet close to the King, but he would be.

Of that he was certain.

TEN

HER hands were gnarled and they ached with the cold. Eleanora winced as she gripped the stale bread crust and snapped it in half. She put the smaller half aside for her midday meal, scraped the crumbs into her dry palm, and took a bite from the larger half. The bread crunched beneath her remaining teeth. She shuffled to the door, opened it, and spread the crumbs on the walk.

She was never so hungry that she couldn't share with the birds.

The sun was out for the first time in days. Its light shone like diamonds through the leaves of the trees. Although the land around her small home was still a mucky swamp, she had faith that it would all dry soon. Maybe then she could walk to Coulter's cabin and see if she could get him to cut her some wood. Someday she might even be able to pay him for his help.

Then she closed the door and went back inside. The single room was dark and colder than the outdoors. She hadn't made a fire since two nights before, when she'd cooked the last of her stew and then slept in the fire's warmth. She was saving her remaining stack of wood, although for what she wasn't sure. Part of her thought she was saving it to keep herself warm on the night she died.

She had no delusions that she would live much longer. A body as old as hers could not take the starvation and the chill. Her clothing hung about her like blankets now, and she could see all the bones in her arms. She was glad she did not have a silver glass so that she could see what suffering had done to her face.

Drew had always thought she had a beautiful face.

But Drew was six months dead, and she would not be far behind him. She had never before realized how much easier life was when there were two to share the misery. He would have found some dry wood while she would have dug roots to feed them.

She missed him more than she had ever thought possible. They had fought from the day they'd met, but they had loved with equal passion. And he had never once blamed her for the lack of children just as she had never blamed him for his inability to farm or to keep sheep. He had been good with his hands, and in the end the neighbors had bargained for his services: a dozen eggs in trade for a repaired wheel; a month's worth of bread for a well-built chimney. She had been living off the last of that charity since he'd died. But when the rains came, the charity ended.

She ate her piece of stale bread, washing it down with a glass of the rainwater she had collected during the night. The water was cool and fresh and sweet. Even the rain brought good things.

Perhaps she wouldn't wait for the mud to dry. Perhaps she would slog her way over to Coulter's. It didn't matter if her skirts got muddy. They were old anyway, and she no longer had anyone to impress.

She swallowed the last of the bread, then pulled open the door again, expecting to scare the birds. Instead she was the one surprised. The crumbs remained, littering the walk. No four-pronged footprints marred the surface of the mud. In the rain the birds had swooped down as soon as she'd tossed the crumbs to them. They had flown overhead as if they'd expected the early-morning ritual.

But they hadn't swooped this morning, and she had been too preoccupied with the sun to notice. She glanced at the trees, the raindrops glistening on their wet branches. The birds should have been singing in the sunlight. Now that she thought about it, she realized she hadn't heard a bird since she'd woken up.

How odd. How very odd.

You must listen when nature whispers in your ear, Drew said. She turned to thank him before realizing that he spoke with the voice of memory. A thousand times each day her mind caught her like this: she would look with a sudden warmth filling the cold places in her heart, only to discover that what she had seen or heard had not been Drew.

Until he died, she had never realized how much a part of her he had become.

The trees, slender birches and mighty oaks, suddenly seemed menacing as they towered above her. If she went a few feet inside the forest, the darkness would overwhelm her. The darkness and whatever had spooked the birds.

No wind, no rustlings of small animals, no sound except the Cardidas half a mile behind the cabin, burbling its way to Jahn. The river never quieted for anyone.

The river. She turned toward it. Sunlight reflected off the brown water, sending ripple lights like stars into the sky. During the night she had awakened, cold and damp on her side of the pallet, arms reaching toward Drew, who was no longer there. The rain had been falling steadily. Through its persistent patter she had thought she'd heard voices on the wind. She had sat up, straining to hear if one of the voices was Drew's, hoping that perhaps he was coming back for her. But they had sounded far away and unfamiliar, and after a while she'd convinced herself that they were simply a trick of the rain.

Perhaps they hadn't been.

She shuddered. No sense in making anything up. She needed to see for herself.

She grabbed her shawl off the peg, then left the cabin and closed the door behind her. The mud sucked at her shoes, seeping into the holes in the soles. She walked around the crumbs—the birds might want them if they came back—and headed deep into the forest.

No one had walked the path in days, and the mud flowed like a river. After a few yards she tried walking on the grass, but discovered that it was mostly marsh. Her luck was better with the mud. At least its depth was consistent.

The trees towered over her, blocking the sun, dripping water as if the rain had never stopped. The sound of drops hitting the ground and of her own feet squishing through the muck were the only sign of life. It was as if she had awakened to an empty world.

She passed the lean-to Drew had built as a blind. All the neighbors used it in the fall and winter when game was scarce, even though hunting in those woods was strictly forbidden by the King. The King never traveled out this far. He didn't suspect that his own people were poaching his deer, or if he did suspect, he didn't seem to care.

She had never walked this far into the woods before without startling some animal.

Her legs were tired, even though she had walked only half the distance to Coulter's cabin. She was in poorer health than she had thought, being unable to walk even a short way without losing her wind.

She suspected her discomfort came from more than old age. The chill she had awakened with that morning had settled in her bones, and she rubbed her hands over her brittle arms as she walked.

When she reached the fork in the trail, her skirts were wet and heavy. She stopped and leaned on the damp bark of a birch tree, bumping it just enough to send a spray of water down on her head. In the distance she heard voices. She frowned. They were as faint as the voices she had heard during the night, the words unintelligible. Then she heard a man shouting. Coulter, telling someone to go away. His words ended in half a cry.

She picked up her skirts to run back to her own cabin when she heard the woman's scream. She recognized it. The same scream had come from her own throat when she'd seen Drew's lifeless body, white and bloated from the river.

By the Sword, she couldn't abandon that. She had no reason to save herself. She had nothing left. But Coulter and his wife, Mehan, had a baby. They had a vegetable garden and weaving and a small flock of sheep. They were young. They had everything Eleanora did not.

She made herself turn and run toward the sound instead of away from it. Her legs wobbled, and she had to go slower than she wanted. Her bones were fragile; all she needed to do was trip and break something. She would be able to help no one then.

As if she could help now. Perhaps it wasn't as bad as she thought. Perhaps Coulter had merely injured himself and his wife was too young to understand the difference.

Mehan's wails were growing. So were the voices. A male voice, speaking Nye, dominated.

She reached the edge of the clearing and stopped. Her face was flushed and she was shaking. She had to grab a tree to keep from falling over.

The Coulter cabin was before her. In the yard stood over a dozen men, slender, tall, almost willowy, wearing pants and a thick leather shirt of a style she had never seen before. They were all dark and had faces that were beautiful and terrible at the same time. They were standing over the body of Coulter, his skin stripped as if it were a dress being torn up for rags, his blood seeping into the muddy earth.

His wife, Mehan, was on her knees beside him, holding his head, which was yet untouched, and wailing at the top of her lungs. Eleanora clung to the tree, her gorge rising. She made herself take small breaths to settle her stomach. She would deal with her distress later when she had a moment alone. When she had time to think.

One of the men stepped forward and grabbed Mehan by the hair. He spoke in a soft voice, and Eleanora caught her lower lip. That was not a man, but a woman. A tall woman who dressed like a man. Eleanora glanced at the remaining strangers with new eyes and realized over half of them were women.

Her stomach turned, and the meager breakfast she had eaten came back up. She tried to retch quietly, using the tree to block herself from the group, hoping that they hadn't heard. Women. Women never participated in war. In the uprisings and revolts of her childhood—even in the Peasant Uprising in which her father had fought—the women had tended the homes, suffered with the wounded, but had never, ever turned weapons upon another being. She had not thought it within a woman's nature.

She ripped a leaf off a nearby bush and used it to wipe her mouth. She was light-headed; the image of Coulter's destroyed body appeared before her each time she closed her eyes. If she wasn't quiet, she would end up like that. She might, even now.

She peered around the tree again. Some of the strangers were pointing in her direction, but the leader was shaking her head. They were having a serious discussion in a guttural language she did not recognize, and the discussion concerned her.

Eleanora waited until they looked away, then slid sideways into deeper brush. Her years in the forest had taught her silence. She could move without cracking a twig or disturbing a bush. Another skill she owed to Drew. She thanked him under her breath.

Mehan was still sobbing, her hands resting on her husband's body. She was repeating his name over and over as if it would bring him back. The woman holding her hair yanked it, and Mehan's head jerked back. The strangers continued to argue, and finally a small one came forward, his features coarser than the others, flatter somehow and shorter. He was dressed in brown, and his face was smeared with blood.

The woman holding Mehan spoke to him, and he chuckled. Then the woman ran her hands down Mehan's arms, and Mehan screamed as the flesh pulled away. The small man caught it as if it were a special treat and stuffed it into an oversize pouch that hung from his belt.

Eleanora watched in stunned fascination. They had special powers. The woman had no weapon, and yet she pulled the skin from Mehan's bones as if she had used a flaying knife. They hadn't got to the cabin yet, but when they did go inside, they would find the baby and, poor innocent thing, he would die as his parents had, a slow, excruciating death.

She could do nothing for Mehan. She was an old woman with barely enough strength to walk through a forest. But she might be able to hide an infant, even for a short while, even until the bloodlust faded.

Only she had little time. Mehan's screams might save her child. Eleanora hurried through the woods to the back of the cabin. Coulter's cabin was big enough to have three rooms, and two springs ago he had added the luxury of a second door. He had done that so the summer breeze could cool the hot kitchen, never foreseeing that it might save his child's life.

She hoped it would.

She prayed as she had never prayed before, making a compact with the Holy One. She had never much believed in God—she had seen too much in her long life to find the promises of the Words Written and Unwritten to be anything more than hope—but at this moment she needed the hope. She needed all the help she could get.

Mehan's screams were long and bloodcurdling. Coulter's had not been like that. What was the point of such torture when the victim would die anyway? Did these strangers get a perverse sort of pleasure from it? Or did they know Eleanora was listening? Were they using it as a lesson for her?

The yard behind the cabin was dark. The sun's rays didn't touch there until afternoon. It still held the cool damp of early morning. No strangers were there; no footprints touched the muck. She damned the mud. When the strangers finally found the back door, they would find her prints and be able to chase her through the woods.

She would have to find a way around that.

She gave the problem to the back of her mind while she concentrated on the cabin. Mehan's screams had turned into moans, which were somehow more hideous in their passiveness. She was losing, but she wasn't passing out.

Eleanora walked through the muck, and as she did, she had her plan. It was meager, but it was a start.

She pushed open the door and stepped inside. The cabin smelled of fresh bread. She couldn't help herself. She had to take a loaf. If she were to help the child survive, she had to eat. She took the warm loaf from the small table. Then she heard the whimpering.

The baby's cries were lost in his mother's sounds of agony. Perhaps the Holy One had heard Eleanora. Perhaps the Words were right when they claimed that Roca loved children above all else.

But she hadn't saved the boy yet. She still had a lot to do. Being in the cabin was only the first step.

She followed the whimpers into the small side room. Coulter had built the baby a cradle, and Mehan had filled it with woven blankets so soft, the baby was being reared like a tiny King. Eleanora stuffed the loaf into the pocket of her skirt, then picked up the baby, blankets and all. His whimpers turned to wails as she touched him.

"I'm sorry," she whispered. "I wish I were your mama."

Her voice soothed him. She put him on her shoulder, remembering all the nights she had wished for someone like him, someone she and Drew had made, tiny and warm and loving.

Outside, his mother's cries ended abruptly, as Coulter's had. Terror froze Eleanora. If they found her, they would kill her the same way—and then what would happen to the child?

She wrapped him in the blankets carefully so that he wouldn't suffocate but so that any cries would be muffled, then hurried to the door with him. Once she reached it, she stopped. She would have to move slowly there. Caution now would save them later. She turned her back and looked over her shoulder, carefully stepping in the footprints she had made before.

The voices continued to argue out front. The small man cackled again, sending shivers down Eleanora's back. The strangers hadn't found her yet. Clearly their magick wasn't all-seeing.

She reached the woods more quickly than she'd thought she would. The footprints looked as if someone had gone into the cabin and was still there. They would spend precious time searching for her in the nooks and crannies Coulter had built for his wife. Then, and only then, would they come to the woods and try to find her.

The baby made quiet sobs against her, his little body quivering. He could sense her fear. She ran her hand over his warmth. They wouldn't make him bleed. No one would as long as she breathed.

She retraced her steps all the way to the bend in the path. Then she stepped off the trail and walked in the marshy grass, cutting across country. She ran as quickly as her ancient body and sodden skirts would let her. The baby whimpered as he bounced, protesting the violent motion, but doing no more.

For all she knew, these strangers were marauding across the countryside. If they had come from the river, and had gone to Coulter's first, then they had come from Jahn. She could only hope that they hadn't reached her other neighbors yet.

She would go to Helter's cabin. They were on Daisy Stream, as far from the Cardidas and from Jahn as she could get by foot.

Helter was a good man. He would know what to do.

ELEVEN

JEWEL wiped the sweat from her brow. Her sword felt heavy and useless against her hips. She was standing in the middle of the road, surveying the scene. The troop, a hundred strong, under the command of Shima, were scouting the parameters of the wall surrounding the palace as well as harassing the peasants who dared interfere with them. Three Islanders were dead, their bodies trampled on the streets for the others to see. Already the murders had made some courageous souls lose their willingness to stand up to the Fey.

The problem had become obvious the minute they'd arrived. The Islanders did not follow traditional wall design. This palace had four gates—one on each expanse of wall.

Jewel was half-afraid that Shima would order them to find three more rams. Each moment they took would allow the Islanders to organize. So far, the Fey had met with no real resistance at all.

Shima was standing near the first gate. She was too thin, her body almost curled in on itself, her long hair white, and her face marked with scars from all the battles in which she had fought. She was a minor Visionary but had no other skills, and had long preferred to lead the Infantry, claiming that an army's strength was in its youth.

She was discussing the problem with one of her lieutenants rather heatedly, her voice occasionally carrying over the dust and haze. Jewel rubbed her arms. She had always thought idleness the scourge of war-making.

Burden brushed against her, his hand cupping her elbow protectively. He was a year younger than she was, but they had always been close. He had joined the Infantry when his family had turned him out at the age of twelve for not yet developing any magick. No matter how much talk the Shamans did, his family would not take him back. Jewel had watched over him from that point, little thinking that he would grow taller and stronger than she. His face still bore a deep tan from the Nye campaigns, and in the last few months his smile had gained a confidence it had never had before.

He was not smiling now. "She's pissing away our advantage." His voice was low, conspiratorial.

"I know." Jewel answered him in the same tone. She glanced around. The other members of the troop were restless as well. If Shima didn't take action soon, the Infantry would take it on their own, and that would be disaster. Most of the Infantry were in their teens—too young to have magick or sense.

"You should talk to her."

"And say what?"

His grip on her elbow tightened and he pulled her closer, as if they were lovers, embracing. The tactic wouldn't fool Shima, but Shima was still arguing with her lieutenant. "You already have a plan. I can tell."

Jewel glanced up at him sideways. He had trimmed down since the Nye campaigns. The thinness accented his high cheekbones and made his eyes more prominent. "What makes you think that?"

"Your impatience. You chafe when someone else misses the obvious."

Well, Burden hadn't missed the obvious. He saw how annoyed she was. And she had Seen what to do as clearly as if the battle had already been fought. They didn't need four rams. They needed reinforcements to guard the other gates while they broke into one.

"If I speak to her, she'll think I'm pulling rank."

Burden shrugged. "What she thinks won't matter."

"She's my commander."

"You are the Black King's granddaughter. In the end we will all answer to you."

Jewel sighed. Part of the point of serving in the lower divisions was to learn humility. And humility didn't come naturally to her. She wiped the sweat from her forehead. It was gritty. Even after a rain the air there had a level of dirt she had never felt before.

A group of soldiers stood in front of one of the shop doors, playing with the people within as cats played with mice. The soldiers' laughter filtered over the road. Shima didn't seem to hear. She was gesturing at the gate, then at the ram. The troops were splitting off, wandering down the road to see what kind of loot they could find.

Jewel pushed past her other comrades, touching an arm here, a shoulder there, noting their relative calmness. Even though they were about to go into battle, they didn't seem worried. Fighting there was different from fighting in Nye. The Nyeians had an army that had defended their northeastern border countless times against raiders—and had not lost, until the arrival of the Fey.

These people, on the other hand, seemed to have no idea what defense was about.

Sunlight fell on the wall, making the damp gray stone almost bright. If she squinted just right, she thought she saw lookouts hidden in tiny towers behind the gate. Another thing to plan for.

As she approached Shima, the words of the argument grew clearer. ". . . say we rip apart one of the buildings and use the lumber as rams," the lieutenant was saying.

Shima shook her head. "The wood won't hold against these gates. No. It's better to return to the ships. We still have supplies there."

"But the ships are in Shadowlands," Jewel said. She stopped in front of them, her back to the other troops. "And I can assure you my father will not get them out."

"Your father's carelessness got us into this mess in the first place!" Shima snapped. "Year-old maps. No schematics of the buildings. No knowledge of the Islanders themselves.

Lucky for him they're sheep. What was he thinking, bringing us here unprepared?"

"He prepared as best he could. If we had sent Fey here with Nyeians, we would have lost any element of surprise."

Shima started to answer her, but Jewel held up her hand.

"We are losing that element of surprise now," Jewel said. "As you so aptly pointed out, we do not know what these people are capable of."

"You forget yourself," Shima said, straightening to her full height. She had nearly half a head on Jewel.

Jewel took a step back so that she did not have to look up. "I believe you forget yourself," she said. "And if I have to, I will take over this troop so that my father's mission will be carried out."

The lieutenant was standing to the side, his eyes wide, his face flushed with the heat. A silence was growing around them as other members of the troop realized that a power struggle was going on. Only the laughter of the taunters in front of the store provided a distraction from the tension. Jewel could hear nothing on the other side of the gate. It worried her. She knew they could hear the argument, but she wasn't sure if they understood it.

Shima's gaze moved away from Jewel and surveyed the people behind her. Something in their posture must have convinced her, for when she looked back, her angular features had tightened even more. "I take it you have a solution."

Jewel nodded. "Send a small band for reinforcements. We need a double team. Then divide us in half. One half remains here to batter down this gate. The other half divides into thirds. Each third will guard a gate. That way if anyone in the palace tries to bolt, we have the advantage. We will also be able to enter that second way."

Shima nodded at the lieutenant. "Grab four and head for the docks. We need another hundred as quickly as possible."

The lieutenant bowed once, then scurried away. Jewel did not watch to see whom he chose as his companions. Her gaze was still on Shima.

Shima's entire frame had acquired a rigidity it had never had before. She barked orders at the remaining troop, dividing it now along the lines Jewel had suggested, and ordering the battery to begin as soon as the soldiers were in place. Then she looked at Jewel.

"The plan is a good one. Did you pull it from some military history lesson that I forgot?"

Jewel understood the nature of the question. Shima was still a good commander, although she was not as flexible as she should be. "No," Jewel said. "I Saw it."

Shima took a step back. A Fey with Vision was always powerful; a member of the Black King's family even more so. "I cannot risk you now."

"You have no choice." Jewel let her hand drop against her scabbard. "I have come here to fight."

"At my side, helping me envision the battle."

"No," Jewel said. "You don't need me. You are simply letting your anger at my father's tactics interfere with your good sense. Think for a minute. He can envision a battle better than any of us. His mind is so expansive, it can make a Shadowlands large enough to hold all of our ships. Do you believe that he would have brought us here if his Vision had failed? Or do you believe he would willingly lead us into a defeat?"

Shima looked away. About thirty soldiers were disappearing around the wall. The remaining soldiers had rolled the ram into place. "I believe," she said slowly, "that your father's thirst for conquest has tainted his Vision."

Jewel drew in her breath in shock. No one had dared speak out against her father before.

Shima grabbed her hand. The woman's grip was tight, her skin hard and callused. She leaned forward so that only Jewel could hear her words. "Every night since we left Nye, I have seen my own body, broken and bloody on the banks of that damned river. And I am not alone. There are hundreds of dead Fey. These people may not look menacing, but my Vision tells me they will kill us."

Jewel shuddered. She remembered the Vision she had had, the deep pain, the man whose features were not Fey, and the concern he was expressing over her. Was she dying in that Vision? She couldn't tell.

"My father would not have brought us here if that was true," Jewel said. "Fey die in battle. It happens in every campaign."

"But not to the extent I saw. Not in such a hideous way. It was as if they had partial Foot Soldiers' skill."

Jewel made herself swallow. Of all the Fey, the Foot Soldiers disgusted her the most with their love of torture, their willingness to use their bare hands—to use touch—as a method for killing. Each victim of a Foot Soldier died of mutilation and blood loss rather than direct assault. "There's no point in telling me this now," Jewel said. "We're here. We're committed."

"I'm telling you this because I don't think I can lead with that Vision clogging my sight."

Jewel nodded, understanding finally reaching her. Shima was not making mistakes because she was angry. She was making mistakes because she was afraid.

"I'll stand beside you," Jewel said.

Shima looked at her for a moment, and Jewel thought she saw fear in her commander's face. Then, as suddenly as it appeared, it was gone. That glimpse, more than the verbal confirmation, made a shiver run through Jewel. Commanders weren't supposed to be afraid. They were supposed to be confident and strong.

Not inexperienced, like Jewel.

"We should use this gate," Shima said. Her tone had a question in it, as if she were asking if this gate fit into Jewel's Vision.

"It's beside the stables," Jewel said. "We can free the horses and prevent any escape or notification."

They both knew total prevention wasn't possible. Any commander inside would understand what was happening the minute the battering ram hit the gate and would prepare his people to come out the other sides, fighting.

But they didn't know if there were commanders inside. For the first time Jewel began to understand Shima's frustration.

Jewel glanced around. The taunters had left the building. The door was closed. The dust had settled on the street, and only a small fighting force remained. Several of them stood around the battering ram, ready to pick it up and move into position. Picking it up was the most difficult task of all. It had once been an ancient oak tree, its thick trunk shorn of leaves and branches. The Spell Warders had warned her father to build a ram once they arrived on Blue Isle, but he insisted on bringing it with them, although its weight required them to bring an extra ship.

"Let's go in!" Shima said.

The small troop cheered. The twenty soldiers stationed beside the ram hefted it together. They looked small next to the bark sides, their faces red with strain. They stood for a moment, catching their breath, then jogged forward until the end of the ram slammed into the gate door.

The sound boomed through the street. Jewel felt the ground vibrate beneath her feet. Her entire body was tense. There were chips in the gate where the ram had hit. The troop stepped back in precision, then jogged in again. Another boom and vibration. Jewel listened, but could hear no response from behind the gate.

Across the street the door opened a little way. The sunlight reflected off white skin. Jewel could almost smell their fear. No one had ever tried to break into their palace before. One of the few things anyone knew about Blue Isle was that it had never been invaded.

Another boom. This time tiny pieces of wood flew in all directions. Jewel glanced at the gate, afraid the wood had come from the ram instead of the gate itself. But the gates were splitting down the middle, dry pale sticks pointing toward the bright-blue sky.

The troop was silent as it watched. The only sounds were the soldiers' boots scuffling against the dirt in a rhythmic pattern, followed by the boom and vibration as the ram hit the gates. Shima watched, arms crossed, features smooth. Jewel wondered if she had spent the entire trip from Nye with this kind of taut fear in her system, and if she had, how many others had as well.

Voices echoed from down the street. The heavy sound of booted feet moving in unison eclipsed the sound of scuffle. Both Jewel and Shima glanced up. They couldn't see the reinforcements, but they could hear them.

The ram slammed into the gate again, and this time the sticks fell, leaving a small hole. Goose bumps rose on Jewel's arm. She could see more cobblestone and the gray stone of a building, legs scurrying by. Horses whinnied in panic, and voices speaking in a language not Fey carried across the morning air.

Only a few more hits and they would be inside. Jewel

glanced up to see Burden staring at her. The sun caressed his face, shining on his high cheekbones and beautiful dark eyes. When he saw her, he smiled. She smiled back. A kind of curious joy filled her. She loved battle. She shouldn't have let Shima's fear infect her.

Shima walked behind the ram to wait on the other side for the reinforcements. The ram pounded the gate again, splitting all the way through the hole. The rammers pulled it out and backed up. The hole was large enough to put soldiers through, but no one had attacked from above. They still felt as if they had time to enlarge it, to open the gates forever.

The reinforcements arrived, a fighting force as large as the troop Jewel was a part of. They spanned the road—trim, slender soldiers in identical leather, family swords hanging from their hips.

The group carrying the ram ran forward and slammed it against the gate, a little lower this time. With a crack and clatter, the remaining wood gave way. Someone screamed inside, and it took Jewel a minute to realize that the scream had come from a horse. The soldiers set the ram down, grabbed their swords, and ran inside.

Half the reinforcements did the same, sounding their battle cry. The rest of the reinforcements ran to their positions at the other gates. Jewel unsheathed her sword and followed the troops inside. She assumed Shima was behind her.

The first soldiers had already set the horses free, and the frightened animals were stampeding through the melee, trying to find a way out. Grooms struggled to close the stable doors. The troop was squeezed into a narrow corridor between the stable and another building. Some of the soldiers on the periphery were fighting guards, the clang of metal upon metal resounding over the din. Babies were crying, women screaming, and horses rearing up, trying to kick anything in their way. Still the troops pushed forward, and ahead Jewel could see the stone walls of the palace's first tower rising above her. This palace had windows, and from above she watched someone push a tapestry aside and overturn a bucket onto the troops, the falling liquid so hot that it steamed in the warm air.

Jewel screamed a warning, but it was too late. The liquid

coated the troops beneath the window, and their screams mingled with those of the horses. Jewel turned away, still trying to push forward through the teeming mass of moving bodies. The bitter stench of sweat and fear filled the area and mingled with the dust, making her want to sneeze.

More guards spilled out of the palace, and the clash of steel against steel became almost deafening. Other Islanders joined the fight, carrying whatever they could find—axes, knives, sticks. Jewel could see it all but couldn't participate in any of it. She was still trying to pull out of the mass in the center. Finally she broke free near a pair of double doors on the lower part of the palace itself. The heat from this corner was immense, and she fancied she was near the kitchen. She glanced up—no windows above her.

Then the doors opened, and a small group of men emerged, most of them older, brandishing makeshift weapons. The man in the lead held a long serrated knife, his white clothes coated with dirt and grease. Jewel noticed the details even as she lunged for him, swinging her sword at his belly. He bent over to dodge the blow. She slammed her sword into the leader's knife, the shiver of impact running down her arm. His knife slipped through his fingers, cutting his hand, and she rammed him through.

He stumbled backward, almost taking her with him, but she tugged on the sword, and it pulled free from his body. Blood seeped onto the white cloth, and he stared down at it as if shocked that he could bleed. Then he tumbled over, still alive, but harmless.

His other companions had scattered. She would leave them to the fighters behind her. She wanted to see what was inside.

She pushed in through the door and found herself in the kitchen. The walls blocked the noise of the battle, making the large, hot room almost unbearably quiet. Bread burned in the brick-lined ovens. A hearth fire was unattended. At the edge of the kitchen, near the pantry, servants were running pots of hot lard and boiling water up the back stairs, making a kind of chain so that they could continue scalding the invaders.

Jewel backed out slowly. This was not a place to go alone. She needed help, others to help her destroy that chain.

She went back outside into the noise and the dust and the blood. The screams were fainter now, overcome by the grunts and clangs of battle. She peered out over the melee, and suddenly her vision blurred.

She was standing beside the river with her father, his voice rising in panic. Bodies were strewn across the shore, Fey bodies, their features hideously changed, as if they had melted in the hot sun. She was coated in blood. Her father was shouting orders, but no one seemed to be listening to him. They were all staring in disbelief at the bodies before them.

An arm tugged her into the hollow of a wall as a knife whistled past her face. Burden stood beside her, his skin coated in sweat. "What in the name of the Powers were you thinking?" he shouted. "You nearly let that man kill you!"

She didn't know which man he meant. She hadn't seen anything but the knife. For a moment her mind had been somewhere else entirely.

"We need to get you out of here," he said.

She shook her head. "Grab some more soldiers. We have to go inside. I know how to stop them from pouring garbage on top of our people."

He glared at her for a moment, then let her arm go. They didn't have time for discussion, and he obviously knew it. He went to the edge of the crowd, grabbing arms and pulling soldiers out of the fray.

She clutched her throbbing elbow, breathing deeply. Shima had infected her somehow. Jewel hadn't felt fear until she'd learned of Shima's Vision. When this was over, Jewel would have to talk with the Shaman to see if a Vision could crawl from mind to mind like a snake.

Until then she refused to let the fear overtake her. For if it conquered her in battle, she would die.

TWELVE

OUTSIDE the window a man screamed. The sound was hoarse, loud, and long, more like that of an animal in agony than anything human. Matthias froze on the steps, his right hand on the damp stone wall to brace himself. There, on the staircase between the first and second floors, the battle felt closer.

He swallowed the lump of fear in his throat and, with shaking fingers, pulled the cord holding the tapestry. The thick fabric unrolled and slammed against the wooden window frame, blocking some of the sound. The scream continued, growing higher and more pain filled with each instant. Matthias hurried past the window, hating the sudden darkness that made the steps treacherous, but feeling it necessary.

He had seen too many people die that day.

In hideous ways. The stripping of the flesh inch by inch made his stomach turn; the blood darkening the mud outside; the bodies strewn around the Tabernacle, abandoned and without hope. So far the Tabernacle itself had been spared, although he didn't understand why. It was clear, from the sumptuous towers, tapestried windows, and jeweled doors that the Tabernacle contained more wealth than any other building in Blue Isle except, perhaps, the palace itself.

Bile rose in his throat and he swallowed again. If the Fey weren't there to plunder the Isle, then why were they there? The only answer he could come up with after seeing their horrifying performance on the streets below was simply that they enjoyed killing.

He hurried down the remaining stairs to the first floor. The Danites crowded against the doors and windows, holding anything they could find as weapons. Some even clutched their tiny symbolic swords, a fact that would appall any other Elder. Matthias believed that God would understand a man who would save his own skin any way he could.

Understand and maybe even forgive.

A few of the Auds and some of the servants ran back and forth through the red-carpeted rooms. The men's faces showed their confusion. Some of them even tried to peer over the Danites to see what was causing the noise outside.

The scream finally ended in a bloodcurdling howl. The silence that followed was even more frightening.

Matthias clutched his robe around his chest and hurried past the closed and locked offices, past the ivory busts of previous Rocaans, past the gilt-framed portraits that hung from the corridor walls. One of the Auds, a small, balding man he didn't recognize, grabbed him by the arm, oblivious to the breach of etiquette.

"Please, Respected Sir, we need palace guards here. Only they can save us."

The man's grip was strong. It rooted Matthias into place. He glanced down at the hands on his arm. They were bare, in accordance with an Aud's disdain for ornamentation, the fingers thick and blunt, the nails bitten through. Matthias slowly brought his gaze to the Aud's face.

"The only one who can save us," Matthias said slowly, "is the Holy One carrying our prayers to God."

Matthias shook free and continued down the corridor, not waiting for the Aud's response. More servants ran past him, carrying sticks and bits for firewood. One large man in chef's white lugged a large sacred sword ripped from the Servants' Chapel door. Matthias bit back a reprimand. The man could wait for discipline if he survived the day.

Which, Matthias was fairly certain, none of them would.

He took a deep breath to calm himself. He had never seen such fighting. It had begun shortly after he'd sent the Danites to the King. People were slaughtered all over the streets by Fey with swords. Then this latest group of Fey arrived, and with a simple touch, they could flay a man alive. Matthias had watched three such killings from the Rocaan's windows before he'd realized deep in his soul that the pain and suffering were real—that neither the Holy One nor Roca himself would swoop down from the heavens to protect the true believers.

Although, so far, they had protected the Tabernacle.

But that wouldn't last long.

Finally he reached the bend in the corridor that attached the newest wing of the Tabernacle to the earlier kirk. There the stone was older and flaking, the carpets threadbare, the lighting simple candles placed in tiny gold holders. He grabbed one of the candles, then shoved a key into the lock of a small wooden door.

The key turned slowly and the lock itself groaned at the use. For a moment he was afraid it wouldn't open at all. Then he felt the mechanism give. He pushed the door open and coughed at the dust that floated out to greet him.

He glanced over his shoulder. No one was in the corridor. He stuck the candle in first, then followed it, closing the door behind himself.

The candlelight was meager. It illuminated only his hand and arm and small patches of the surrounding wall. He couldn't see the stairs, didn't know if they had rotted away from disuse. The air was stale and dust filled. He took a step, using the toe of his leather shoe as a guide to find the edge of the stair. He found it and stepped down gingerly.

Something caught in his hair, and he muffled a cry, flailing with his left hand until his fingers tangled in the sticky strands of a spider's web. He grimaced but made himself move forward, hand extended outward in front of his face to prevent any of that gooey stuff from touching him again.

By the Blessed Sword, he had never envisioned himself doing this when he had awakened that morning. He had expected to go through his routine, to finish negotiating with the Rocaan over the land south of Killeny's Bridge for the Auds, to speak with the King's son Nicholas about his lack of faith, to sup with the Rocaan. Matthias had never imagined that by evening the world as they knew it might be gone.

But no one had envisioned this, and even if they had, they hadn't known how to prepare for it. They had no soldiers, only guards who had trained on stories of peasant battles generations old. The sea and the rocks had guarded Blue Isle. Until now.

The deeper beneath the Tabernacle he went, the colder the air grew. The chill had a dampness to it. Water dripped somewhere ahead of him. There was a rank smell down there of swamplike decay, and he didn't want to think what manner of creatures he might find as he went forward.

The stairs twisted into the darkness. Matthias leaned on the rotted railing, counting the landings, two, three, four. On the fifth he stopped, holding his candle forward in the vain hope that he would be able to see the bottom.

And he froze. The edge of the landing had fallen away. The stairs were gone. These passages were not the answer. He had hoped to hide the Rocaan down here. But not even a young man would survive the jump to the bottom.

He swallowed. His throat was dry. He had never realized how much being alone terrified him. He clutched at the sword around his neck more from habit than any desire to call upon the Holy One. He had to get back upstairs and find another solution.

But he didn't want to go back to the chaos. He wanted to wake up and discover this was all a nightmare, that he would be warm in his bed, and the rain would still be beating outside, marking the continuation of the unnatural summer. He wanted to start the day all over again, not visit the Rocaan's hellhole, not see those ghostly masts on the Cardidas, not feel that frisson of terror rising in his stomach.

The drip-drip-drip of the water was fading behind him. His meager candle was burning low, the wax warm as it melted across his fingers. He didn't move very quickly, afraid of being alone in the darkness, but the force of his imaginings kept him moving. He knew, in the rational part of his mind, that he would go upstairs to find things still the same: the Auds and servants panicked, the Danites prepared, the Officiates blocking the door to the Rocaan's suite, but the part of his mind that held dreams and terrors had locked on to the images of death it had seen that morning.

He didn't want to die that way.

He didn't want to know that nothing lived beyond the grave, that Rocaanism was the vision of a crazed, charismatic man who had managed to collect believers all over the Isle centuries ago. Matthias paused and rubbed his free hand over his face. In times of trouble the true believers were turning to their God, and he—scholar, leader, rational thinker—had nothing to turn to at all.

Even though he had tried to believe. He had tried to believe, since he was born the second son in a land-owning family, the son who would live in his brother's shadow or make a shadow so large in the Tabernacle that no one—not even his brother—could ignore it. The moral part of him had thought it wrong that he was using the Church for personal gain, and that part was crying the loudest now, telling him that this fix he was in was his fault for denying the power of the Words Written and Unwritten.

He climbed the stairs two at a time, clinging to the rotting railing for support. The candle's flame guttered; in a moment it would go out entirely. His fear of the darkness won over his fear of the real world—he pushed the door open with a strength he didn't know he had—

—Only to feel the door open a few inches and then jam. Light poured in as his candle flickered out. Voices, shouting in a language he didn't recognize, echoed through the corridor, followed by screams and thuds. For one crazy moment he thought of running back down the stairs, but knew he couldn't. He had a duty to the Rocaan—a duty he valued as much as his life. He couldn't forsake the old man now.

Matthias shoved on the door again, this time opening it far enough to stick his head through. To his great relief the corridor was empty except for the prone body of an Aud blocking the door.

God. They were inside now.

The terror he had felt below rose like bile in his throat. He shoved again, a strength born of panic coursing through him. The Aud's body slid to the side and he got out, slamming the door behind him. Blood was spattered all over the stone walls and was running down the door.

He had to get upstairs. He had to *see*.

The screams and clangs were coming from the direction he had originally come from. He would have to go through the servants' wing.

Matthias stepped over the body of the Aud and ran down the corridor. The shouts grew fainter as he moved. There were signs of turmoil everywhere: candles knocked on the floor, tables overturned. Someone had slashed a portrait of the Tenth Rocaan, the canvas curling forward, chips of paint scattered on the floor.

Matthias had rounded the final corner past the Servants' Chapel when he saw them. A band of twenty Fey, tall, slender, and frightening in their dark leather. They were standing over the body of another Aud and arguing in that guttural language. A deep laugh interrupted them, and a shorter Fey, wearing a red cap, his features gnarled, reached down to the Aud, took long, dripping strips from the body, and stuck them into a bag around his waist.

It took a moment before Matthias realized the strips were the man's skin.

He couldn't repress the groan of shocked horror that left his throat. The Fey turned in unison, and Matthias's gaze met all of theirs, their eyes equally dark, bleak, and empty.

The little man took a step forward, and that broke Matthias's paralysis. He screamed as he turned, unwilling to die as the Aud had but knowing that he probably would. If he ran down the corridor from which he'd come, they would catch him, and flay him, leaving his blood to drip down the walls. He had nothing to defend himself. He would be helpless before them.

Instead he turned toward the Servants' Chapel, thinking he would grab one of the ceremonial swords. They were the right size, and Roca would not mind if his symbol was used to save one of his faithful's life.

If Roca existed.

If Matthias was considered faithful.

Still, at this moment, his soul was less precious than his life.

He pushed open the double doors into the chapel, placing his palms on the empty spot where the sacred sword had been. His feet slipped on the slick stone. Someone had kicked the carpet aside and spilled liquid on the floor. It took a moment before he realized that the wetness was blood.

The pews were overturned and bodies were everywhere, most of the feet bare and intact. Danites, Auds, servants, all dead. But he couldn't stop to absorb the destruction. He had to keep moving, to find a weapon that would save his own life.

He scurried up to the altar. The podium was on its side and shattered. A dead servant lay across the sacrificial table, the skin on his face half-gone as if someone had been trying to carve him up there, on the holy place. The entire chapel smelled of blood. And all ceremonial swords were gone.

Matthias whirled on his feet, trapped. If he left by the back way, he would be in the front of the building, and if he left the way he'd come, he would encounter the Fey.

As if they heard his thought, they charged in both doors. The group had split in half and they were running at him, hands chillingly empty of any weapons at all.

He would not die like this. He would not let them kill him there. He pushed the body of the servant, looking for his weapon, but finding nothing. Then he saw the glittering vials of holy water the Rocaan had blessed the night before for Midnight Sacrament. The vials were made of heavy, thick glass. Perhaps they would stop the Fey while Matthias thought of something else.

Matthias grabbed vial after vial and flung them at the Fey, at the group before him, then at the group to his right. The first glass hit the stone and shattered, and the Fey screamed in pain. Then the next glass shattered. Matthias kept throwing until he realized that the Fey were no longer advancing.

The stench in the room had grown. It smelled as if something was burning. It took a moment for him to realize that all of the Fey were clutching their legs and screaming. They had fallen to the ground and were rolling in the blood. He glanced behind him. He had thrown maybe ten bottles, certainly not enough glass to cut that many men.

Then he realized that they weren't bleeding, but their clothes were peeling from them as if trying to get away. He stood for a moment, his hand over his mouth. They were lying in the water, and every time it touched part of their bodies, they screamed. The little man was already dead, his eyes rolled back in his crushed face.

Matthias's hands were shaking—the entire thing had left him terrified—but he had to know. He had to know. The glass couldn't have killed them, so the water must have.

The holy water.

Matthias took a vial and walked down the steps, his heart pounding so fiercely he felt as if he couldn't breathe. He uncorked the bottle and waited until he saw the Fey who had looked at him first. The creature was still alive, his legs and hands a mass of burns, his clothing ripped and tattered.

His gaze met Matthias's, his skin pale and his dark almond-shaped eyes wide with shock. "What have you done?" the Fey asked in accented Nye.

The words startled Matthias, made him wonder if they were faking, if that was how they had caught all the others. He tossed the water forward, and it landed on the Fey's perfect features. The creature screamed until his lips melted over his mouth. Matthias stood, riveted, tears in his own eyes, watching the creature—the man—flail as the flesh melted over his nostrils and his body could no longer get air.

The other Fey were still moaning, oblivious to their leader's death. But Matthias watched for what seemed like forever as the leader clawed at his featureless face with his misshapen hands. At long last the body stopped moving.

Matthias staggered back up the stairs. The screams in the chapel were drowning the screams from elsewhere in the Tabernacle. But here and in the other chapels scattered through the building, he had the power to stop it all.

Quickly he tied the hem of his robe around his waist, making a giant pouch, which he filled with holy-water vials. Then he took as many as he could carry.

He carefully skirted the wounded and dying Fey and made his way to the double doors of the chapel. He had to move slowly, but it was a small price to pay for his own survival.

THIRTEEN

HE had blood on his lips. Scavenger wiped the back of his hand over his mouth, but that only made the problem worse. The sticky substance smeared across his skin. He hated this part of his job. He smelled of iron and death, and would for the next few days.

Scavenger staggered down the road between the buildings, bodies spread around him. When he had followed the Foot Soldiers up this road toward the palace, he had thought the area reeked of fish. Now he could smell only himself.

Ahead of him, the warehouses and docks covered the rocky shoreline. The dark-brown water of the Cardidas glittered beyond them, empty of ships. Only a small, odd Circle of Light indicated that ships were in Shadowlands. In the bright sunlight the Circle was nearly invisible. Still, he glanced at it, reassured by the closeness of everything familiar.

The area near the docks was as empty as the river. The bridge, which had been filled with panicked horses and screaming Islanders a few hours before, was bare except for a few bodies hanging off the sides. He couldn't see any Red Caps working up there, but Red Caps were short and probably weren't easily visible over the stone wall. Good pickings, and so close to the Shadowlands. If only he were so lucky.

He had walked for what felt like miles to return to the warehouse. The sun was growing warm, and the mud was slick. He felt twice as heavy as usual with his cargo hanging from the pouches secured to his belt. Made from sheep bladders and spelled by the finest Domestics, these pouches kept even the slimiest material safely wrapped inside. He had seen a Red Cap with bad pouches once; the poor man had dribbled blood all the way to the camp, only to be slapped by one of the Warders for leaving a trail.

Scavenger was cautious not to leave a trail. All his life he had been careful not to make any mistakes. Still, it had got him nowhere. Red Caps were victims of their birth: short, squat, magickless, they had no function at all outside of war. In peacetime the Caps had settlements outside the Fey areas so that "real" Fey wouldn't need to be reminded that not all of their race grew tall and slender and beautiful.

Still, he missed the peace. During the last year his hands had been clean, and he hadn't been covered with filth. He didn't have to take orders from Foot Soldiers and hold strips of some poor person's skin in his hands.

Scavenger swallowed and licked his lips, wincing at the blood taste. Then he took a step down the incline leading to the warehouses, lost his footing, and slipped along the side of the path, holding himself up with one hand so the pouches around his waist wouldn't burst. By the time he reached the bottom, the blood on his palm was his own. He wiped it against his pants and hurried into the Warders' new den.

They had chosen the largest warehouse near the river as the place to set up their quarters. The doors were made of gray, weathered wood, splintered in some places. A few Islander bodies were scattered outside, and more lay on the shoreline, most killed by Infantry instead of Foot Soldiers. The bloodletting would occur later, if at all.

Scavenger hurried up the wooden ramp and pulled the doors open. The building smelled of rotted fish and stale water. He sneezed, glad for a different stink to wash the blood from his nostrils. Already someone had made Fey Lamps and left them along the wooden floor, the trapped souls inside beating against the glass, the light fresh and strong and lovely. Scavenger stopped and stared into one of the lamps. A slender man hovered inside, his tiny face wrinkled with confusion. The Islanders had probably never seen Fey Lamps before, and that poor man probably had no idea that he was trapped inside one, destined to remain until his soul gave up. He probably didn't even remember his capture. The Wisps usually worked very quickly, aided by the Domestics.

"Are you a Cap, or someone I should worry about?" Caseo's deep voice rumbled from deep within the warehouse.

Scavenger stood, heart pounding. Caseo was the most powerful of the Warders, and the most willing to use that power. "Number Fifteen," Scavenger said, his own voice rising on the last syllable.

"Well, then, come forward, boy. The day has only begun."

Boy. Scavenger's mouth set in a hard line. He had not been a boy in over thirty years. Just because he had no magick and because his body had never grown willowy and straight didn't mean he was a boy. He was as much Fey—adult Fey—as the rest of them.

He took a deep breath, unwilling to face a Warder while angry. He had done that once and found himself working with the five-day-old corpses in the battlefields outside Uehe. He had been almost twenty then, and had never seen—or smelled—that kind of putrefaction before. He hadn't allowed himself to see it since.

"I am coming, sir," Scavenger said. He followed the trail of lights. They illuminated bare walls, made of unpainted wood. From hooks hung a handful of torn nets. Most of the hooks were empty.

He rounded a corner and found himself in a room that held more light than a meadow in the noonday sun. Fey Lamps hung from the walls and the ceilings as well as stood on the floor. Most of the furniture had been pushed against the walls except for an oversize table and ten stools for the older Warders. All twenty of the Warders were inside, bent over small pieces of paper, their robes pulled tight. Solanda, the Shape-Shifter, was with them and was pacing like a trapped animal.

Scavenger stared at her for a moment, her tawny hair,

golden skin, and unconscious grace marking her as the most perfect of all the Fey. Even the dark-brown birthmark on her chin—the mark all Shape-Shifters were born with—added to her beauty.

Caseo was leaning forward, his hands spread on the table's surface. He was studying some paper as well, a map perhaps, although Scavenger couldn't get close enough to look. Caseo's hood was back, revealing his gaunt features. He turned toward Scavenger, eyes dark holes in his narrow face.

"Well, boy," Caseo said. "Bring it here. I'm sure there is much more waiting for you."

Scavenger swallowed the insult and came forward. The Warders at the foot of the table stepped aside. Solanda reached around Caseo and picked up the paper, tucking it under her arm and turning her back on Scavenger as if his ugliness offended her.

He stopped at the table's edge. The edge brushed against his chest. The table was long and made of a thick wood. Ancient bloodstains marred the wood's surface, and he knew that the Islanders had used it for cleaning fish. The fishy smell was particularly strong in this room.

Scavenger pulled his pouches off his belt and reached up to set them on the table. No one helped him, although the movement was clearly difficult for him. The pouches slid into large, wobbly, bladder-shaped things, disgusting packets of disgusting material. Now he understood why Solanda had turned away.

Caseo grabbed one, hefted it in his right hand, and grinned at Scavenger. "Where'd you get it?"

"The palace," he said. "They're inside already."

Caseo's grin grew. "Maybe this won't take as long as we thought. The waterfront is taken, as are most of the shops. We need to keep some of these pitiful creatures alive to help us tend the land."

Caseo bent over the pouch and, holding it carefully with his left hand, untied it with his right. He put the leather thong on the table, then reached inside the bladder and pulled out a long, slim strip of skin, curling with length and black with blood. He held it gingerly between his thumb and forefinger.

"Are they all cut so fine?" Caseo asked.

Scavenger nodded. "The Infantry pushed in quickly, left a lot of them alive, and the Foot Soldiers didn't have to do much work."

"Completely untouched," Caseo said, addressing the other Warders. "Look at this. Curling, thin, pristine. Rugar was right. This will be a haven for us."

Scavenger bit the skin off his lower lip. He had heard the dissension, of course. The worry that Rugar's Vision was going. But Caseo's words had a calming effect. Pristine. Generations of Islander lives untouched by any harmful magick. No wonder the souls in the Fey Lamps burned so brightly. All the Islanders on Galinas had met the Fey before. It made the fighting that much harder, for the nourishment the Blood Users took was thinner in those places.

"Excuse me, sir," Scavenger said, knowing he was not needed anymore. "Can I go?"

"In a minute, boy," Caseo said. He set the skin back in the pouch and handed it to another Warder to seal. Then he took a tiny rag offered from yet another Warder and cleaned off his fingers. He turned toward Scavenger, leaned his hip against the table, and crossed his arms. "You say you found these pickings at the palace."

Scavenger nodded. "I'm sure there'll be more."

"I'm sure," Caseo said. "That's why I want you to round up the Caps working the harbor area and bring them to the palace with you. We've done all we're going to do down here, and the Foot Soldiers are long gone. Knowing the Caps, they're probably skipping stones across the water rather than searching for more work."

Scavenger pursed his lips and straightened his back. Now he knew that Caseo was baiting him on purpose. The Warders—everyone, for that matter—knew how much a good Cap hated his work. The Cap who liked the work was slipping into madness and was therefore unreliable.

"May I go?" Scavenger repeated, this time not making the necessary bow to Caseo's power.

"And see how he doesn't deny it? Were you skipping stones before you found us, boy?"

Scavenger pulled more pouches from the inside of his shirt and threaded them through his belt. When he was done, he said again in a level tone, "May I go, sir?"

Caseo waved his hand. "You have already wasted enough time. Go now."

Scavenger spun and stalked out. Red and green colors flashed in front of his eyes from the brightness of the Warders' room. As the darkness swallowed him up, he heard Solanda's voice, as warm and rich and musical as he had imagined. He had to strain to hear what she said.

"If you keep baiting the little troll, he will come after you."

Scavenger felt his face heat. "Little troll" was worse than boy. He bowed his head and scuffled out. It was his fate to be hated, something he deserved for being ugly and short and having no magick. But sometimes he wished a day could go by without anyone reminding him of his hideousness. That would be a day to remember.

He pushed open the double doors and stepped into the sunlight. Screams, clangs, and the sounds of battle echoed from all sides. The noise was louder than it had been before, probably because he was near the water, where the battles all along the riverfront carried on the waves. He hurried down the ramp, not even glancing at the bodies, looking for other small, blood-drenched Fey like himself.

It took a moment before he realized something odd was happening across the river.

Instead of the wild joy of a successful Fey battle cry, he heard sobs of pain. He shielded his eyes and hurried down the dock, staring at the huge building on the other side of the water.

The building was constructed like a fortress, with four towers flanking one central tower. The towers all had windows, and each were painted with a giant white sword pointing downward. The building did not have walls like a fortress, only passageways connecting one tower to the other. Its stonework looked uneven, as if parts of the building had been built at different times.

As Scavenger squinted, he could see people being pushed out of the windows. Tall, lanky people, dressed in brown leathers, wearing no armor, only the casual battle dress of the Fey. Most of them were not screaming. Islanders in black robes were leaning out the upper portions of the towers, pouring liquid from tiny bottles onto the fighters below. A huge cloud rose over the battle area, and as its tendrils reached across the river toward Scavenger, he backed away. Still, he caught its scent—putrid and rotting, like the bodies he had had to tend when he'd been but a boy.

Over there, in the fortress, the place he remembered from the attack plans as the seat of the Islanders' religion, Fey were dying. They had some kind of magick there—that's why the building had no walls. They didn't need the protection. They could kill as the Fey could.

He bit his lower lip and squinted. Black-clad figures were mingling among the Fey. Sunlight glinted off heavy bottles, and more liquid fell. Each time it touched a Fey, a bit of steam arose. He glanced at the warehouse. If he warned Caseo, they might be able to get word to Rugar, and he could bring the ships out of Shadowlands and they could leave.

But Scavenger could find Rugar on his own. Then Caseo would have to fend for himself.

Scavenger ran down the dock, the half-formed plan sounding good in his mind, until he realized he had no idea where Rugar was. Besides, the Fey needed the Warders. They came up with new spells, new fighting methods. If something different was happening, the Warders had to know first so that they could save everyone.

He damned the Mysteries that had led him to this place, that didn't allow him the personal revenge he wanted. Then he ran up the ramp, slammed his hands on the double doors, and hoped that Caseo would believe him.

FOURTEEN

ALEXANDER had been in the War Room once; his grandfather had proudly shown it to him when he'd been a boy. He had learned how the room had been used to stop the Peasant Uprising, and how it was designed to keep the lessers in check.

Alexander was inside now, a boy no longer, but a King suddenly thrust into war. He had changed into a peasant shirt and long pants—an irony not lost on him—but one his son had insisted on, and one that made sense. He needed the freedom of movement that robes did not give him. He had his sleeves rolled up, and he, his advisers, and Stephen, his son's swordmaster, were poring over plans of the castle: twelve men in a room the size of his bedroom suite.

It felt as if they were hiding.

The room smelled damp and musty. Ancient maps, tattered and chewed by mice, covered one wall. Lord Stowe had ripped one down and used it as a cloth to dust off the long, filthy table that stood in the middle of the room. The advisers had insisted on coming there—the uppermost tower, protected by one long flight of stairs and a secret exit behind the throne. It had been designed by someone wilier than Alexander. The design made it impossible to trap anyone inside—unless, of course, the attackers knew the building's plans.

And no one knew the plans of this room. Each King learned it from his predecessors. Nothing was written down. Not even the advisers knew of the escape route that wound its way through a false wall all the way to the dungeons below.

Alexander had first come into the room alone to see if his memory was as clear as he had hoped. He tested the secret door and, except for a spiderweb the size of his head, the hidden passageway looked like a viable way of saving his own skin.

If only he could find Nicholas. He wanted to be able to save them both.

Nicholas had vanished after the meeting with the Danites, ostensibly to find Stephen. But Stephen had found Alexander, and neither of them had seen Nicholas.

They had said nothing after that. They knew where Nicholas was. Somewhere in the midst of the fighting, loving the moment, not thinking of the future.

Or dead. Or dying. All alone below.

Alexander had dispatched four guards to search for Nicholas but had given up when one of the guards had come crawling back, his right arm hanging from his side, the blood stanched with a piece of tapestry from one of the lower windows, with news of what they had all feared.

The Fey had broken through the gate and were now inside, attacking the castle.

Lords Oast and Stowe had climbed to the roof and watched from above. When they came back in, their faces were ashen and their hands shook. They repeated what the guard had implied.

It would take a miracle for anyone to survive the slaughter going on below.

So Alexander was trying to put it out of his mind. No one would let him go, and he knew little about sword fighting. At least Nicholas had practiced at it. Alexander stayed in the War Room and tried to plan a defense they had never thought they would need.

"When the peasants stormed the palace," Monte, the head of the guards, was saying, "they were turned back with swords and flaming torches. All it took was a concentrated effort." He was a large man, all muscle and no fat, with arms the size of Alexander's thighs. His face was lean, and his hair more brown than blond. He kept it short against fashion.

"But they were an angry, uncoordinated force." Stephen stood, one foot on a shaky stool, the other on the ground. Even though he had twenty years on all of them, he stood straight, his body unbent by age. He had a power that none of the others seemed to have. "The Fey are fighting machines. They originated in the Eccrasian Mountains and brought all the magick of that place with them. They managed to overrun two continents before Galinas. When they took Nye, we should have prepared for this. They will not stop until they control the entire world."

Alexander ran his hand through his long blond hair. He had to think of something besides his son. "Are you saying we have no hope against them?"

"Those Danites had no idea how many ships they'd brought," Lord Powell said. His hair was falling around his puffy face, his ponytail almost totally undone. He looked as if he had been in the thick of the fighting, even though he hadn't left Alexander's side. "Enough to fill the Cardidas at port. Even if they had sailed over here on a whim, they had a month to make plans."

Alexander glanced around the room at the men, their eyes wide with fear, their faces pale, their hands shaking. They had already decided the fate of this battle. They were ready to roll over and let the Fey take Blue Isle from him. Him, Alexander, whose family descended from the Roca. Nicholas was fighting below and would die at the age of eighteen if Alexander allowed the situation to continue.

And he would not. If the Isle was lost to the Fey, it would be lost in a fair fight.

"Are you suggesting," he said as calmly as he could, "that we allow this superior force to take the Isle?"

"N-n-no, of course not," Powell said. He backed away a little. "But I—honestly, Sire—I don't see how we can prevent it."

"You don't, do you?" Alexander felt a rage surge through him. He stalked Powell, backing his adviser toward the table. "I have never led a battle, but I know this. We will not roll over and play dead because we are frightened of some magicians who have crossed the Infrin Sea. We will not give up Blue Isle because we believe the Fey to be unbeatable. We will fight them with every breath in our bodies, and if it looks as if our land will not survive, we will destroy it ourselves before they steal Blue Isle's riches. We will make it worthless to them. We will find a solution, or every man, woman, and child in this country will die trying. Do I make myself clear?"

No one answered. If anything, their eyes had grown wider, their faces paler.

"Do I?" His voice echoed in the room. In the silence he could hear faint screams and cries coming from below.

"Very." Stephen left his stool and stood beside Alexander. "I have made it my life's work to study the history of warfare, the methods of the fight, and that includes the Fey. I welcome the opportunity to put my knowledge to use."

"Good," Alexander said. "And the rest of you?"

The silence continued. No one met his gaze. Finally Powell shrugged. "Sire, we have never been in this situation before. We—"

"As if I have." He couldn't keep the sarcasm from his voice. What was the point of advisers if they didn't advise? Still, he couldn't spend all day discussing. He had to make decisions now. People were dying below.

"Sire—" Powell started again, but Alexander cut him off with the wave of a hand.

"We are under attack and our people are fighting as best they can below, with no planning, no guidance, and no help from us. The Fey have broken through our walls, and they never should have done that. Your people should have stopped them." He pointed at Monte. "But they're inside now, and we have to get them back out. They had the element of surprise, but we have strength. We have this fortress that my family built during the Peasant Uprising. We have to solidify it. Monte, put your men together. I want a coordinated attack near the gates, and I want those gates blocked. No more Fey can come into this area. Do you have that?"

Monte nodded—then waited, hands behind his back.

"Well, get to it, man," Alexander said. "I am your King, your commander, and you will do what I say. *You will all do what I say.*"

"Yes, Sire." Monte started toward the door and then stopped. "But we're sworn to protect you."

"Leave a contingent on the stairs," Stephen said. "That should be sufficient if our other plans fail."

Alexander glared at Stephen for a moment before realizing that the elderly swordmaster wasn't rebuking him, but actually helping him. Monte was staring at both of them, and Alexander suppressed a small sigh. "Do as Stephen says."

"And use your swords," Stephen said. "Do not let any of those vermin touch you. Some of them can kill with simple touch."

"Yes, Sire." Monte backed out of the door, then pulled it closed. Alexander turned to the others. They were still scattered about the room. Some were watching the empty door as if Monte would come back and save them from Alexander's scrutiny. Others were staring at the floor.

A sorrier bunch he had never seen. Why did it take a crisis for him to realize that his help was insufficient? "Stephen, you will stay with me. Lord Holte, you will coordinate attacks on the third floor. Do not let those creatures get beyond that level into the towers. Lord Stowe, you have the second floor. If the Fey have already entrenched there, work with Holte in preventing them from getting any higher. Lord Powell, you will concentrate on the first floor. Lord Oast, you will work on the yards and grounds. The rest of you shall serve as runners and messengers between those commands and our post up here. The goal is to drive the Fey from this castle. Once they are back in the streets, then we will worry about getting them off Blue Isle."

"Sire," Powell said, extending his hands, "we have no military training. We don't know what we're doing."

"Then you'll learn in the thick of battle. And, Powell, that's the third complaint. You will help Lord Oast on the ground, and Lord Enford will take the first floor. If there are any detail problems, deal with them yourselves. The key is to be leaders here. Give our people something to rally around. I will not let those marauders take over Blue Isle, and anyone who helps their cause even inadvertently will die by my hand. Is that clear?"

The men were staring at him now. Powell's face was red, but he did not make another protest. Alexander's throat was raw, his muscles tense. If someone touched him wrong, he would spring. This was a long shot. He knew it and they knew it. But he couldn't hide in the tower room and allow the Fey to overrun his country without putting up a fight.

"When we have this palace back, we will reconvene up here and make plans to drive them out of the city. Until then I do not want to see any of you again. I expect to be victorious." He took a deep breath. No one else attempted to speak. The sounds from below had grown louder. "Now, I want this room cleared except for Stephen."

"Before we leave, Sire," Powell said, "I would like the swordmaster to tell us what we should know about the Fey."

More stalling. Alexander was about to start into them again when Stephen put a hand on his arm. "I can tell you nothing about the Fey that you can't learn below," he said.

Powell nodded and turned, hands clasped behind his back, walking slowly as if he expected Alexander to rescind his orders. But Alexander wouldn't. He didn't need to be questioned, especially now.

It took only a moment for the men to leave. The last one closed the door behind him. The latch clicked in the silence. Alexander waited a moment, then sank into one of the chairs.

A faint cry he had never heard before echoed from below. It had a victorious sound. He closed his eyes and for one moment allowed himself to be a person instead of a King.

"We will need more of a plan than that," Stephen said. His voice was soft. He had moved closer; Alexander could feel the heat of the man's body, smell the faint odor of sweat that surrounded him.

Alexander sighed, then opened his eyes.

"They're too powerful for us to drive them from the palace." Stephen was leaning on the table. "Once they're in, they're in."

"What can they do?" Alexander asked.

"That we can't?"

Alexander nodded.

"They can kill with a single touch. They can enchant. Some even say they can take over a man's body and make him do their bidding."

"They can't be all-powerful," Alexander said. "If they were, they would have been here sooner."

"Oh, they can die." Stephen rested his hands on his knee. Even though his voice was calm, his hair was mussed, and half a day's growth of white beard covered his cheeks. "In fact, they can die as easily as we can. Pierced properly with a sword, too much blood loss. They're not superhuman, Sire. They simply have more talents than we do. It's as if they are conquering us with bows and arrows and we haven't even learned how to use a stick yet."

Alexander leaned back in his chair. He had been a fool to think that Blue Isle's natural defenses would be enough to keep creatures like the Fey away. He had had warning from the day they'd captured Nye. The Fey had gone as far east as they could. The next stop on their campaign had to be Blue Isle.

"What do we do now?" he asked, not sure he really wanted to hear the answer.

"We make it until nightfall," Stephen said, "and hope we live to see another day."

FIFTEEN

RUGAR had created a garrison not too far from the Cardidas. Early in the fighting he had commandeered an inn, allowing owners and guests to flee on the theory that the fear they spread would be more valuable than the blood they shed. Terror won campaigns more quickly than death did. Killing sometimes made the defenders angry, made them rebel. But a bit of mercy now and then, heavily laced with fear and supposition, gave a troop strength.

The inn was a two-story wooden structure, with a large common room that hadn't been cleaned in this century, and a kitchen so filthy he didn't want to touch the cooking tables or the dishes. The straw-filled mattresses in the five rooms upstairs had lice: if his people were to stay the night there, he would make certain the mattresses were burned, and the place cleaned.

He had wiped off a large wooden table when he had arrived, moved it closer to the door, and used it as his base. He sat cross-legged on the top and dispensed orders as if they were food rations, allowing his officers to consult before they made a move or altered his original plans. The realities of Jahn pleased him. The invasion was even easier than he had thought it would be. The Islanders gave in to their surprise and ran in terror instead of fighting back. Only at the palace had he heard of any coordinated efforts to stop the Fey—efforts that showed just how inexperienced the Islanders were.

Outside, the shouts and screams of various battles floated across the air. An hour or so earlier he had heard the ringing thuds of the battering ram against the palace gate, and the cries of triumph once his people had broken through. It would be only a matter of time now before the Fey held Jahn. Once the palace was taken, these spineless people would capitulate to their new rulers.

Dust had risen in various parts of the city from the scuffling and the fighting. The air had a raw smell to it—blood and fear and sweat overlaid the city scents of baked bread and sewage. The activity all around him made him restless. He had been planning this attack too long to stay cooped up in a makeshift garrison on the edge of the city.

He climbed down off the table, feeling the air cool his legs. He ran his hand through his black hair. No one had come to see him for some time now. His duty as coordinator was done, unless there was some crisis, which he did not expect. His troops were spreading all over the countryside, seeding terror everywhere they went. They were to capture each house, each village, each town they went through until they reached the Isle's edge or until the Islanders surrendered. His orders were to keep the actual destruction to a minimum: the Fey had come to Blue Isle because it was rich, and that prosperity had to be maintained, or the Isle would be worthless to them.

His guards flanked him as he stepped outside: Rusty and Strongfist had been with him since he'd been a boy. They had always protected him, and he had always watched over them. They were getting older, but their bodies were still lean and trim, their actions quick and full of strength. They would go with him wherever he went.

He took a step forward when suddenly the scene in front of him disappeared. His mouth clamped shut, although he had to scream. Something was burning his face, seeping into his nostrils, filling his eyes. He couldn't breathe. He clutched at his face and fell forward, and then the scene shifted again. He was in a wooden room with benches overturned, thirty Fey on their backs with their faces melted away, their bodies already turning stiff with death. A black-robed Islander male was running from the room, small glass bottles cradled in his arms.

Water, falling from the sky, made him feel weak. The more that landed on him, the weaker he grew until he was little better than an Islander himself. That extra muscle, the one in his mind that created something out of nothing, had burned away to an ash, and the cinders scattered to the winds.

He was lying facedown on the muddy ground, his face half-buried in muck. He had to turn so that he could breathe. Rusty was kneeling beside him, his sun-wrinkled face creased with worry. Rugar eased himself to his elbows and wiped off his nose and mouth. "I'm all right," he said, his voice harsh, as if he hadn't used it for a long time.

He looked up and into the blinding rays of the sun, he saw hundreds of Fey, scattered on roads and around buildings, their faces gone, their bodies twisted. Nearby, Islanders were digging a large hole and filling it with limestone. Horror filled him as he realized that the hole was a mass grave. No Fey were left to retrieve the dead.

His chin was wet and his mouth dry. His back ached. He was lying half-in, half-out of the mud hole, his mouth open and drool running down his face. He must look like an idiot. Fortunately, Rusty and Strongfist had seen the Visions overtake him before.

Only never like this.

"Tell me I blacked out," he said, pushing himself into a sitting position. "Tell me that the exhaustion finally got me and you let me dream."

"Your eyes were open," Rusty said. His normally dark skin was ashen. "You had the Look."

"I have never seen you do this before, though," Strongfist said. His voice was shaking. "It was as if an unseen force assaulted you and laid you flat."

Rugar's eyes had been open. His mouth had been open. He had felt, tasted, and smelled the Vision. He closed his eyes and reviewed the scenes in his mind. Jewel had not been among the dead. Neither had he. Except, perhaps, at first. But he didn't know if that moment of great pain was his own death or simply part of the Vision, being able to feel what that black-robed Islander had been doing to the Fey.

Chills ran through him. Some of that had to do with the mud. He was encased in it.

"Are you all right?" Strongfist asked.

"I'm fine," Rugar said.

"Let's clean you off," Rusty said, taking one of Rugar's arms.

Rugar shook free. "No," he said. "I need to think. Leave me here and let me think."

"We can't leave you alone," Strongfist said.

Rugar glared at him. They would do what they were ordered. Strongfist backed away. Rusty glanced at Strongfist. They had been with Rugar long enough that they didn't need the words.

"We will be near the inn's entrance," Rusty said. "We'll be able to see you from there."

"Fine," Rugar said. He didn't care what they did as long as they left him alone. He bowed his head, letting his brow rest on his mud-coated knees. His body was shivering with emotion. He had to separate the emotions raised by the Vision and the emotions he was feeling.

The Visions had been filled with terror: fear of dying, panic at being unable to breathe, horror at all the bodies strewn about the grass. The smell of limestone brought with it the rot of death. Normally he would have had days to sort this. But now he had to loosen the terror himself.

Sitting would do him no good. He needed to move. He put a hand in the soft earth, feeling the warm, viscous liquid close around his skin. He stood and the mud dripped off him. What a wonderful commander he made, the son of the Black King, looking tall and proud in the land of his enemies.

That thought made him smile. He shook the mud off as a dog would, then leaned his head back. The sun was shining on ground made muddy by his own Weather Sprites. His troops were scattered throughout Blue Isle, wreaking havoc, putting fear into the people, killing the leadership. Everything about the campaign had gone well. The terror he was feeling came strictly from the Vision.

And this Vision conflicted with the other he had had. He made himself step out of the mud hole and pace on the squishy grass beside the path. His father had told him, all those decades ago, that Visions came in random order. He might see the evening of his death at the age of eighty mingled with the birth of his child at the age of twenty. The Vision he'd had of the dead Fey could take place years from now. None of the faces were clear. If they had been, he might be able to pinpoint the events in time.

But his Visions of Jewel had been clear. She was only a few years older as she walked through the Islander palace with a babe in her arms. He could place that Vision in time, and that time was soon.

These Visions had come because he was on the Isle. He had not had Visions on the sea. Perhaps he was Blind on the sea. He had heard of such things before. Visions also came easier when he was exhausted, as he was now. His mind was more susceptible to them.

He should be thankful that the Visions had returned.

"Rugar!" The voice was breathless. Rugar closed his eyes and kept pacing, hoping the voice's owner would get the hint not to disturb him now or that his bodyguards would come and take the voice away.

"Rugar! By all the Powers, Rugar, you need to listen to me now!"

Finally he recognized the voice. It belonged to Caseo. Caseo, who was supposed to be in the warehouse with the other Spell Warders, taking the Red Cap spoils and devising specialized spells for the Blue Isle campaign. Rugar suppressed a sigh. He knew how ridiculous he looked, but he didn't care. He crossed his arms and whirled. "You're away from your post."

"With good reason." Caseo's eyes were wild. "Rugar, they are slaughtering us."

"Who?" Rugar didn't know if this was another of Caseo's exaggerations.

"The Islanders. Across the river. Upon my soul, I have never seen anything so gruesome." Caseo's gaunt features looked even more hollowed by the bright daylight. Caseo valued his position as leader of the Warders. He would not leave at a time like this to spread a rumor.

Rugar felt the chill return. "What's happening?"

"I don't know exactly. The smell comes in clouds, a great putrefying stink, and then it clears, and we can see black-robed Islanders pouring some liquid on our people. They are screaming, Rugar, screaming as they die."

Rusty and Strongfist approached. They kept a respectable distance, but they got close enough, as if Caseo's very wildness made them nervous.

Rugar's mouth had gone dry. "Where is this exactly, Caseo?"

"In that huge building across the river. The one with all the towers and without the gates. The one the Nye said belonged to the religion."

The words barely registered. Instead, in his mind's eye, Rugar was seeing a black-robed man running from a room, carrying glass bottles in his arms. *Water, falling from the sky, made him feel weak.* Water. "Liquid," he said.

"What?" Caseo asked.

"No wonder," Rugar murmured. His people were dying. In droves, as they never had before. No wonder he had been knocked flat by the Vision. The first and second parts were no Casting at all. They were Present. But if he didn't stop this now, the third part of the Vision would be Future.

He grabbed Caseo by the shoulder. "You must take me there," Rugar said. "Take me there now."

"I can't," Caseo said. "They'll kill you."

Rugar shook his head. "I saw it all in a Vision. We will stop them. We have to."

SIXTEEN

THE Rocaan's chambers had never been so mussed. Mud covered the floor. The couches were pushed against a wall, the tables moved into the middle. Someone had kindly closed the door to his bedchamber. At least forty people filled the room, some bending over vials, others carrying trays of filled vials into the corridor. The conversation was deafening, but occasionally it would still when a particularly loud scream would echo from the courtyard.

Despite the growing heat, the Rocaan sat by the fire, wearing his heavy robe, his feet still bare. His discarded breakfast sat on the table beside him. Someone had pulled the tapestries back from the window, letting in the blessed sunlight, and the cries of agony from the courtyards below.

Holy water. His holy water was killing them. The sacred water used by Roca himself to clean the sword before the Soldiers of the Enemy used it to run him through. The secret passed from Rocaan to Rocaan in an unbroken line, from generation to generation. Passed in small vials to the congregation during Midnight Sacrament so that they could clean their own swords in a ritual purification.

And here he sat, the Fiftieth Rocaan, knowing how few

vials there were in the building, that the water killed, and that without it, every human on Blue Isle would die.

If he ever needed to reach the Ear of God, now was the time. Only he couldn't feel the presence of the Holy One. He was on his own.

He felt that way too—the only person in the chamber not moving or planning or discussing. He wanted them all to leave so that he could think. His very being felt that it wasn't right to use holy water to kill, no matter how well and fast it worked.

The Elders were running the operation in the Rocaan's chamber. They had the Auds searching the sanctuaries, chapels, and back rooms for more holy water. The Elders had said nothing to him, had not consulted him beyond Matthias's quick announcement of the effect of holy water. To that, the members of the Rocaan's staff, the clergy, and the highest authorities in the Tabernacle had cheered.

Cheered.

The Rocaan put his head in his hands. His palms were hot and clammy. His body ached with the strain of the morning. Even his chair felt uncomfortable. He drew up his knees so that his bare feet disappeared under his robe, a trick he hadn't used since he'd been an Aud.

Earlier, the ululating cries had scared him, brought him to his knees in honest prayer for his own people. He had clutched the tiny silver sword he wore around his neck, wondering if he could accept it into his body with the same ease and grace that Roca had all those centuries before.

The martyred hero who, in death, had captured the love of God.

The Rocaan wanted nothing more for his people than to capture that same love. Instead they were fighting back with a force he didn't recognize or understand. Rocaanism did not condone murder, yet what were they doing but murdering with the very substance that he had blessed?

Warm fingers brushed his arm and he jumped. He looked up to find Matthias bending over him. Beside him the wood snapped, and two Auds fought over who would take the next group of vials to the Danites on the floor below. Matthias's blond curls were mussed, and his mustache looked ragged, as if he had been chewing on it. There were hollows under his eyes that had not been there earlier.

"Holy Sir," Matthias said, "we must speak."

The Rocaan glanced around his chamber. Danites stood in groups of three, arguing. Vials covered all the tables, and Auds brought even more. The screams of the dead and dying rose from below, adding an odd counterpoint to the dull roar of conversation.

"Holy Sir?" Matthias repeated.

In the space of one morning it had all changed to this.

"Yes," the Rocaan said. "We do need to speak. Alone."

He did not understand how his chambers had become the central command for a war he did not want. It was almost too much to bear. "Get them out," he said to Matthias. "Get them out and we will talk."

"But they feel safe here."

The Rocaan glanced bitterly at the vials. "They have another safety now."

Matthias followed the Rocaan's glance and frowned. He squeezed the Rocaan's wrist and then got up. One by one, he spoke to the other Elders, all of whom looked at the Rocaan before nodding. The Elders spoke with the Officiates, and within minutes the vials and the people had left the room.

The screams from outdoors had grown louder. Only the crackle and snap of the burning wood sounded familiar. A trickle of sweat ran down the Rocaan's brow, past his eye, and onto his cheek. It felt like a tear, but his eyes were dry.

"They're gone, Holy Sir." Matthias stood in front of him, hands clasped and head bowed. His curls were thinning around his crown.

The chamber seemed bigger with all the sofas pushed aside. Vials were scattered on the tables, and some trays sat on the floor. The Rocaan pushed himself out of his chair. Suddenly the heat was too much for him. "You do not believe in Roca, do you, Matthias?"

Matthias brought his head up quickly. Standing at full height, he was nearly a foot taller than the Rocaan. "I am an Elder."

The Rocaan nodded. "A second son. A family decision. You have an apt mind, a quick wit, and a penchant for reality. Very valuable, and rare in an Elder."

"We do not have time for philosophical discussion," Matthias said. "People are dying."

"And we are killing them." The Rocaan took Matthias's hand and led him to the window across from the bed. He pulled back the tapestry depicting the first Rocaan touching the Ear of God, and looked out.

The sun gave everything a white, pure light. Water still clung to the moss growing near the window. Bodies were scattered on the courtyard, faces gone, arms and legs wrapped around torsos as if trying to block pain. The Rocaan had never seen anything like it.

He stepped back and pushed Matthias forward, standing behind him so that Matthias could see nothing except the death below.

"The Words Written and Unwritten forbid murder," the Rocaan said.

"These creatures are evil," Matthias said, his voice shaking. "They have a power that slays men with the touch of a finger."

" 'The evil that men do corrupts entire nations,' " the Rocaan quoted. " 'We must fight such evil by being good.' "

" 'We must be strong in the face of our enemies.' " Matthias turned so that he faced the Rocaan. He stood so close that the Rocaan could feel the heat of his body.

"Strong, yes," the Rocaan said. "But not even Roca fought back with physical force."

"We don't have time for this," Matthias said. "Even as we speak, our people are dying all over the city. Only here have we found the answer."

"The answer lies in the holy water," the Rocaan said. "And it is not a simple question of blessing the Cardidas. The secret of holy water was passed from Roca to the first Rocaan and has been passed to each Rocaan like a closely guarded key. Only I can create this weapon, and so you must listen to me."

Matthias bit his upper lip. His lower teeth were yellow and crooked.

"Roca did not give us holy water so that we could kill," the Rocaan said.

"No, Roca gave it to us that we might live," Matthias said. "And we did not understand its secret until now. When it touches a holy man, it purifies him, and when it touches an evil man, it kills him."

The Rocaan shuddered. "You are not thinking. If holy

water killed evil men, then murderers, thieves, anyone with sin in the heart would die at Midnight Sacrament. This goes beyond that. It is almost as if the Fey's presence has caused a new magick to blossom. A magick I cannot condone."

Another scream rose from below, long and loud and male. At the same time, someone pounded on the door. "Holy Sir!" the voice cried. "We are running out of holy water!"

Matthias licked his lips. His eyes glittered with a panic the Rocaan had not seen before. Matthias swallowed as if he were nervous about speaking and then bowed his head. He did not look at the Rocaan as he spoke. "If you do not bless more water, Holy Sir, then you shall be breaking the highest law in the Words Written and Unwritten. For you are right, they say that a man may not murder, but there are wars written in the Words and in our history. The King's defense against the Peasant Uprising was called a jihad by that Rocaan. Are you saying that defense is not viable?"

Matthias had the mind of a scholar. The Rocaan had used it in the past but could not follow it now. He wouldn't defend himself until he understood the argument. "What law am I breaking?"

Matthias looked up, his pale skin flushed. "You would be committing murder, Holy Sir. Mass murder. You would be— you are—condemning us all to death."

The Rocaan took a step backward. This he had not considered. The pounding on the door made his head throb.

Matthias followed, using his tall body as a weapon, a weapon that intimidated. "We cannot survive against magickal touch. If we do not defend ourselves against these creatures, we will be slaughtered like the lambs kept outside the city. Even as we argue, the King could be dying. The King, the direct descendant of Roca on earth. It is our duty under the Law of the Sword to protect all believers. The Fey are not believers. They are Something Other. A test, perhaps, sent to slaughter us all. Perhaps we of this generation were meant to discover new properties in the holy water. Perhaps all of this is a sign that the prayers the Holy One has taken to God's Ear were heard. And you would have us forsake all that. You would try to be as great a martyr as Roca. He died to save us, Holy Sir. Your action would not save us. It would slaughter us all."

The pounding on the door continued. Neither man acknowledged it.

The Rocaan sank back in his chair. He was not used to making quick decisions. Never in his years as Rocaan had he had to make a decision without lots of prayer, lots of consideration. Yet he, in a matter of moments, had to make a decision that would change the faithful's relationship with God and Roca forever.

"Holy Sir! Please!" the man outside called.

"Please," Matthias whispered.

"Forgive me," the Rocaan murmured under his breath. He spoke to the Holy One, asking for forgiveness for not one, but two sins. He would break two laws this day. He sighed. "Tell them that their water will come."

Matthias nodded and went to the door. The Rocaan stared at the fire, at the red embers glowing at the base of the flame. He waited for the still, small voice to speak from within. But no voice spoke. No voice indicated which path was right and which path was wrong. *A man is cursed who must make decisions based only upon his own knowledge.*

When Matthias finished speaking to the man outside, he closed the door. "And where will we get this water?" Matthias asked.

The Rocaan stood slowly, feeling every one of his years. "We shall make it," he said.

Matthias gasped. "Are you dying, Holy Sir?"

The Rocaan shook his head. "No. But I refuse to let the blood of the invaders stain my hands alone."

SEVENTEEN

SOLANDA paced the warehouse. Its rectangular shape, which had seemed large that morning, now felt tiny. She had sat in each chair, rubbed her hands on the scarred tabletop. The smell of fish made her stomach growl. The uneven boards rocked under her bare feet. She avoided the bags of blood and skin; they disgusted her. The creatures that used them were not true Fey. There were only a handful of true Fey, and she was lucky enough to be one. And unfortunate enough to be the one traveling with Rugar.

She owed him, but not this much.

No windows. She hated the darkness. She stopped for a moment by a Fey Lamp and crouched in front of it. The little soul inside batted against the glass like a butterfly caught in a jar. Solanda reached out with her long finger and traced the cool surface. The creature batted harder. If she opened the glass, the soul would get away. As a child, she used to open Fey Lamps and try to catch the fleeing souls. She had succeeded only once, and the soul had burned her mouth.

She stood and paced again. They had no right to leave her alone. Caseo swore he was going for Rugar, that the crisis across the river would have ramifications for them all.

She had never felt so useless. Rugar had forbidden her to look outside or to get involved at all. He had no job for her yet—might not have a job for her at all.

If the invasion didn't go as planned, she would become key to the takeover of Blue Isle. As things stood, she was a reserve weapon. They hadn't needed her in the Nye campaign, and now she had traveled across an ocean—water, damn them all—to hide in this filthy warehouse guarding packets of blood used by her inferiors.

She would take this no longer.

The next time she circled around to the main hallway, she left the room and its wonderful lights. She rounded the corner and crossed the boards. The wood felt slimy beneath her bare feet, and the fish smell had grown. Her stomach growled again. Rugar left her with orders to stay in that awful warehouse with no windows and no food and did not tell her when anyone would get back. If someone returned before she did, let them worry. She wasn't the type to stay in one place.

The restlessness came from her cat self. She had learned, over the years, not to fight some of the feline impulses. They served her well. Others merely annoyed her. The only problem with being a Shape-Shifter was choosing the permanent altered form. She had done so as a child of three when her constantly shifting form threatened her health. Every Shifter reached that point. Solanda's had come earlier than most, and she resented it. To this day Solanda had told no one that she had made her choice to Shift into the form of a cat because her baby self thought cats were the prettiest creatures she had ever seen.

She walked down the long hall. The wood got drier, and the smell receded. When she reached the outside doors, she placed both hands on them and pushed. Sunlight cascaded in, blinding her for a moment, bringing sound. Screaming cries, thuds, and running feet. She stood in the open doorway blinking against the light, hoping that no one saw her.

Gradually the glare faded. The ramp leading from the warehouse was empty. She stepped onto it. The wood was warm from the sun. She turned her face toward the light, letting a chill she hadn't even realized she felt slip from her body. The Cardidas River slapped against the docks in the harbor. She paused. People had been screaming a moment before. There. If she listened hard enough, she could barely hear them. The sounds of battle had been closer a moment before.

The hair prickled on the back of her neck. She was no longer alone. She turned her gaze toward the road. A man stood behind her. He was barefoot, as she was, but he wore a black robe that hung on his body like a bag. He was holding a bottle in his hands and looked confused, as if searching for something. She slipped into the shadow of the building but did not go inside. He was one of the humans. He had to be looking for Fey.

A great smell was rising off the river. Fetid and thick, it hung in the air like a fog. She glanced across the water. There, at the large building, she could see Fey, and more Black Robes. Only the Fey were screaming. That was what was missing: the victory cry.

No wonder Caseo was frightened. Fey never lost battles.

She had to get back inside. She slid along the side of the building when the man in black saw her. He let out a small squeal of surprise, then ran toward her, shaking the open bottle like a weapon.

Like a weapon.

He seemed to think he could kill Fey.

Across the river Fey were screaming, dying, surrounded by Black Robes.

Fear coursed through her, quick and sudden. If she ran back inside, he would find her. He would find the blood. He would find the lamps. He would hurt their stash, and Caseo would never forgive her. Her panic made her freeze.

The Black Robe had such a silly face, chubby and pink, his eyes a pale blue that she had never seen before, his lips chapped where he bit them, his head balding. His eyebrows were straight and pale on his light skin. His fat hid his cheekbones, and his eyes were round. Even the Nyeians had more color to their skin. She couldn't die at the hands of a man as ugly this one. And she wouldn't.

She felt her body slide into itself, felt her mass compact into the smaller form. The man had stopped running, as if he couldn't believe his eyes, and then he started again, making little frightened eeps as he ran. Finally her change completed. She glanced down at her hands, pleased to see the familiar golden paws, the soft fur, the whiskers sticking out of the side of her nose. She twitched her tail and jumped off the ramp, running away from the stupid Islander as fast as she could.

Under the side of the warehouse, past the fish stink, her movements lightning quick and silent. His feet squished on the marshy ground, the sound a heavy counterpoint to her fear. She kept to the side of the warehouse until she saw a hidden place behind the stairs in the back. She crawled beneath the stairs, deep in the shadows, remembering to keep her eyes covered. A real cat would never have thought of that, but she had learned young that the eyes reflected, giving everything away.

She was panting, her heart pounding. Those bottles. They held death in those bottles. And he had seen her change. Silly fool. She would have to remember his face now and kill him when she had the chance.

The squishing sounds grew closer. She peered over her paws, careful to keep her eyes half-covered. He stopped beside the stairs. His toenails were long and yellow, curling upward, dirt spattering them. Hair grew on the top of his feet, blond and curly. She was glad she was too far away to smell them. The heightened sense of smell was both an advantage and a disadvantage.

The fish stink made the emptiness in her stomach grow. She wanted him gone so she could eat. Then she would find someone who could help her. She would find this annoying Islander and kill him.

He squished past and she remained motionless until she could no longer hear him. His footprints were wide and filling with water from the saturated ground. Her paws were cold, and she hated the dampness on her fur.

The screams and cries were growing again. Then she heard voices, speaking a language she didn't understand. She peered through the slats in the stairs, saw more Black Robes standing together, holding bottles as if they were swords. Her Black Robe wasn't with them. They talked for a moment, then sneaked off in different directions.

She leaned back on her haunches, a feeling she had learned to trust rising in her gut. Caseo had thought the problem was across the river: the stink, the dying. He made the decision to find Rugar and warn him not to cross the river. Perhaps Caseo would warn Rugar away from the Black Robes.

But the problem was here now. Here. On the warehouse side. Caseo would not be able to come back. And the Black Robes were hiding, ready to launch a secret attack.

Solanda licked her right leg nervously, her sandpaper tongue catching on the soft fur. The grooming soothed her, a soothing she missed in her human form.

She would wait there until the Black Robes went away. Then she would hurry into the city and see if she could find someone—Caseo, Rugar—anyone to warn, anyone to send the message that the Black Robes were coming, the Black Robes were hiding, all ready to kill.

She finished working her way down the leg, stopping at the paw to clean the mud from her pads. A purr she couldn't repress started in the back of her throat.

The trip had a purpose after all. She would not be useless, as she had been in the Nye campaign. Those hours getting splashed, feeling her coat get soaked, waking up with rats the size of her cat form staring at her face, were not in vain. She would prove once again that Shape-Shifters were the most superior Fey.

She was pleased to have the chance.

EIGHTEEN

HIS arm was getting tired. Nicholas stood halfway up the steps in the kitchen, hacking and slashing at the tall, slender creatures who threatened to overwhelm him. Fighters were packed along the stairs and into the kitchen itself, spilling into the pantry and beyond. The last time he had had a chance to look, kitchen staff clubbed at the Fey with any weapon they could find. Women were sticking wood into the hearth fire and making torches. Still the Fey poured in from the door beside the ovens. The room was stifling and smelled of fear.

Nicholas had forsaken grace and finesse and all the fine points of sword fighting that Stephen had taught him. Nicholas's entire sword had become a weapon. He had slapped a man in the face with the flat of the blade, chopped a woman's thumb off with the sharp edge, and knocked another man unconscious with a rap of the hilt against the crown of his head.

Weapons clanged, and people were shouting. All through the pantry, the kitchen, and into the courtyard he could hear that eerie call that marked a Fey victory.

He and the other Islanders wounded the Fey, caused them to stop, step back, and disappear. But still the Fey were gaining. Most of the kitchen crew had no weapons. The servants had gone into the hall and taken weapons off the walls. Nicholas had ordered the steaming bucket brigade that had worked for nearly an hour before the Fey surged into the kitchen.

They had caught him between floors and probably would have killed him if he hadn't been working with Stephen. But Nicholas's expertise with the sword had caught his attackers by surprise, and he had managed to hold two steps and the space around them for longer than he had imagined possible.

The stairs were slick with blood.

Nicholas's hair was plastered to his head. His body was drenched in sweat. Only his grip on his sword was firm. He had been standing in the same position—his right foot two steps up, the other braced against a wall—long enough for the muscles in his right leg to cramp. He heard the clang of swords behind him, and he could see the chef fighting at the base of the stairs. The butler guarded the door to the pantry, using carving knives. Other servants fought with the weapons they found, but they had no experience. The Fey were relentless. For each one Nicholas wounded, another appeared, and for each one killed, another slipped past him and disappeared up the stairs.

He had no idea what was happening anywhere else. He was afraid that no one was defending the front stairs as well as he was, and that the Fey were already swarming the entire palace, and his father was dead.

Nicholas's arm moved on its own. He was fighting a Fey who appeared to be younger than he was. The details blurred: all the Fey had black hair, dark skin, and startling upswept eyebrows. But they had differences in fighting, in the degree of fear they brought to Nicholas and his sword.

Bodies were scattered on the steps and on the floor of the kitchen. The brick-lined ovens were open, and someone had shoved the wounded inside, adding to the stench. One young servant lay on his back, his chest split open, his head smashed against the stone floor. Nicholas would look away and bodies would disappear, or they would get stepped on, trampled beyond recognition, but every time he looked back, that young servant remained, sprawled on the steps in that awkward position, his eyes open and staring at the ceiling as if in silent supplication to the God Matthias served.

The Fey in front of Nicholas was fighting with an unusual style. She—Nicholas was finally getting used to the females in battle garb—was stabbing frenetically, her movements so quick, he sometimes couldn't see her arm. She had nicked him more than once, drawn first blood on him where no one else had been able to touch him all day. He parried her thrusts more with logic than through any visual acumen. Finally he shoved the sword toward her belly, and she failed to defend. She toppled backward, and it took all the strength of his tired arm to keep his sword in his hand. As she rolled down the steps, she took two more Fey with her, temporarily blocking the tide of Fey swarming at the stairs. Nicholas used the moment to glance over his shoulder.

"I need help here," he said. "Please get someone down here."

" 'Tis none," a voice answered from above.

Swords clanged around him. The Fey were recovering below. Nicholas peered around the corner and saw the baker and three other Islanders fighting more Fey. He didn't recognize any of the three, but they recognized him. "Please," he repeated.

"Lor," said someone higher above. " 'Tis Good Nicholas."

People shoved around him, and more came down, pushing the Fey away. He moved off his steps and was about to climb up the rest of the stairs when something hit him from behind.

He toppled forward, clinging to his sword and keeping it away from his body as he fell. He skidded down the blood. His free hand landed on the sprawled servant's chest, and Nicholas cried out in disgust. He snatched his hand away and started to get up when someone grabbed him by the hair and tilted his head back.

A woman stood over him, with the same upswept eyebrows, the same black hair tied in a long braid. Her eyes were sparkling, her cheeks flushed with exertion, her free arm extended as she prepared to stick her knife into his throat.

He had never thought the angel of death would be so beautiful.

"Lor!" came the voice from above. "Unhand him! 'Tis Nicholas! They got Nicholas!"

The cry caught her attention for a crucial moment. He couldn't swing and hit her, but he grabbed her ankle and pulled. Her grip on his hair loosened, and he yanked his head away. She thrust her knife and he brought up his sword. They clanged together, but he wasn't braced properly and he fell.

Voices rose, calling his name. She reached around him, and her knife scratched his Adam's apple.

"Drop the sword," she said in Nye. He froze. He couldn't pull on her ankle without jeopardizing his neck, but he didn't have the leverage to stab her himself. Her action stopped the Islanders beside him from saving him. The sounds of the battle continued, uninterrupted. Voices shouted near the hearth fire, and he heard his chamberlain yell for help from the direction of the pantry.

The Islanders on the stairs had gathered around as if the other Fey presented no danger at all. His people, the servants in the castle, the people who recognized him, encircled him, but held their weapons helplessly as if they didn't know what to do.

The nearby Fey had stopped fighting as well. They were watching the woman with the same intensity that the servants were watching Nicholas.

The woman smiled. She wasn't much older than he was. "You're important to them," she said. "I think maybe you should come with me."

He would be damned if he went with any of them. But he had no choice. He was not Roca. He would not be a martyr for any cause, particularly one he didn't yet understand. She pressed the point of her knife in harder and pushed on his chin, indicating that he should stand.

"Drop the sword," she repeated.

He could do nothing with it, so he let it go. But his grip on her ankle tightened. She wore leather boots so soft he could feel her ankle bones through them.

"And let go of me." Her eyes sparkled as she spoke. She seemed to like the challenge he was presenting her.

The cool blade of the knife still pushed on his chin. He could feel the metal slowly warm beneath his skin. "I do not believe you will kill me," he said. The words had a choked sound thanks to the pressure of the knife tip. His Nye wasn't as fluent as hers.

Her lips parted and her face paled. The sparkle left her eyes. "What does *orma lii* mean?"

He started. *Orma lii* was Islander. She spoke the words with the accent on the second syllable instead of the first, her pronunciation slow with incomprehension. He almost didn't understand her. The clash of swords and screams of pain continued. Only in their small circle near the base of the stairs had the fighting stopped.

A Fey beside her, a tall, excessively thin boy with large eyes, hissed, "Jewel!" as if he were shocked that she had lost the focus of her attack. But Nicholas was curious. She had seen him before. Her eyes held recognition.

"It hurts to speak with a knife scratching my throat," he said.

"If you think I will remove it to ease your discomfort, then you think me a fool," she said. "Answer my question."

"I do not believe you slashed your way into my home to ask me the meaning of a simple phrase. You could have asked anyone once you docked, and saved lives."

"I don't find your wit amusing," she said, but the sparkle had returned to her eyes. She was enjoying the verbal battle—and enjoyment was out of place.

Murmurs ran through the group around them as translations flew in two languages. More people had joined the crowd. The fighting had stopped in the pantry. Voices carried over the din: *They've got Nicholas!*

"It was not wit," he said. "I have no knowledge of why you are here."

"I believe it's obvious." She pressed the flat of the blade harder against his chin. She hadn't altered her stance, but she had become a conqueror once again. "Stand up."

He tightened his grip on her ankle. She winced, more in exasperation, it appeared, than in pain.

"So you really want me to cut off your pretty head?" Her tone was casual, as if they were discussing a second helping of pheasant.

A slight gasp echoed behind them. Then the baker pushed his way down the steps. "Me, take, ma'am," he said in broken Nye. "Please."

She ignored the baker. Instead she looked at Nicholas,

and a full smile spread across her face. Her beauty took his breath away. He had never seen the combination of ethereal features and sheer power.

"You appear to be worth more to me alive than dead," she said. She moved her head, command style. "Burden, Rielle, get him to his feet."

The fighting had stopped all the way to the hearth fire, although Nicholas could still see movement near the door. The Fey were holding their weapons against their sides, all staring at the woman.

The skinny Fey who had spoken before and another male Fey came to Nicholas's side and pulled him to his feet. The woman moved her knife away. They trussed his hands behind his back, yanking so hard, his shoulders cracked. The leather thongs they used cut into the skin on his wrists.

She shoved the knife into her belt, obviously trusting the Fey around her to protect her back. She took a step forward until he could feel the heat of her body. She was as tall as he was. He had never met a woman of his height. It felt odd to look into her eyes as if she were a man.

The hair around her forehead was damp with sweat. "What is it about you that they so admire?" she asked. "Are you someone important?"

His heart was pounding hard, and he had to work at keeping his breathing even. They were so unprepared. He had no idea who or what this woman was, only that she could kill him if she wanted. He didn't know if surrendering was best, or if dying was. All he knew was that he didn't want to die.

" 'Are you all right?' " he said.

Her eyebrows straightened as she frowned. "What?"

He had thrown her off again. He felt an odd power in that. She was used to being in control. "It means 'Are you all right?' "

Her lips parted, and that haunted look returned to her eyes. "Say it for me in your language," she said softly, as if they were alone and she were asking for words of love.

He replied with equal softness in Islander. Tears rose in her eyes, but she didn't look away.

The skinny Fey holding Nicholas spoke in a language he didn't understand. She waved her hand at him with a downward, dismissing motion, and then replied in the same language. She never took her gaze off Nicholas.

"Who are you?" she finally asked in Nye.

"Does it matter?" he said. The disagreement between the two Fey added a level of panic he had not felt before. "You are going to kill me anyway."

She shook her head once, then wiped the blood off his throat with her thumb. Her skin was warm and calloused. "No," she said. "I will not."

The sudden tenderness confused him. He glanced at the skinny Fey holding him and saw anger in the boy's eyes. Nicholas's own people were watching, standing very still. The crowd had grown huge. All movement in the kitchen had stopped except near the door. The battle cries were now coming from the courtyard.

The baker was sliding through the crowd. He was weaving his way toward the pantry door. Nicholas understood the plan. The baker was going to get help if he could.

She, too, glanced at the crowd around them, then back to him. "I could torture any one of them until they told me your name."

"No," Nicholas said, mimicking her tone. "You will not."

"Such courage for a man in such a desperate position. If I were to kill you"—and as she spoke the words, she whipped the knife out of her belt and returned it to his throat, the movement so quick that he would not have been able to stop it even if his hands had been untied—"they would lose something precious."

The servants, blood covered and already battle weary, had looks of utter horror on their faces.

She was standing so close to him, he could feel her breasts pressing on his chest. "If I threaten you, I control them." She smiled, but it didn't reach her eyes. "You give me such power that I think I'll keep you."

She turned to the Fey behind her. "Modify something in here for a makeshift prison, and disarm those poor people." They moved to do as she asked. Then she faced Nicholas. "Tell your people that if they continue to fight, I will kill you."

He said nothing.

She grabbed his bloodstained shirt and pulled him even closer. "Tell them."

The collar dug into his neck. He nodded. She stepped back so that he had a clear view of everyone in the kitchen. The servants, from the young boys who cleaned out the hearth to the women who directed the work in the dining hall, watched him with wide eyes.

"My friends," he said in Islander. "It doesn't matter what they do to me. What matters is Blue Isle. Kill these creatures. Kill them all."

For a moment the Islanders just stood; then they surged forward, almost as one body, catching the other Fey unaware. Knives went into Fey backs, grunts of pain echoed as Fey were bashed on the head, screams sounded from the far side of the room as an elderly woman pushed a Fey soldier into the hearth fire.

The Fey woman grabbed Nicholas, her knife again at his throat. "What did you tell them?"

"I think that is obvious," he said.

NINETEEN

RUGAR ran a stained hand through his caked hair and took a deep breath. He hurried down the dry patches of the muddy street toward the main street. Caseo, Rusty, and Strongfist followed. Even before Rugar arrived at the road, he saw things which made his internal chill grow.

Fey running, their long forms without grace. They weren't waving their weapons or moving in an order. They were fleeing. Rugar had seen that action often enough in battle to recognize it. Behind them waddled overweight Islanders in black robes, shaking small vials of clear liquid. Some Fey clutched their arms. Others fell screaming to the cobblestone, writhing in an agony Rugar didn't want to comprehend. A stink rose—burning flesh and something even more acrid, something he didn't quite recognize.

The beating of his heart increased at the sound of terrified footsteps. He stopped in the shadow of a deserted storefront and watched as his mighty warriors collapsed in the face of armorless creatures brandishing what appeared to be water. His throat was dry, and he finally understood—from a victim's point of view—how terror spread from person to person like fire in a wind.

Caseo came up behind him, his breath ragged, not from exertion but from fear. "They're killing us," he said.

"We're letting them," Rugar replied. His words were stronger than his confidence. He, too, wanted to turn and run.

But he couldn't. He was their strength.

The mud had dried on his face, making talking difficult. He brushed the flakes away and shook them out of his hair. He needed to rally his people.

"Caseo," he said, "send word to the troops near the palace. We need to inform them of this threat. If they know, they won't be as frightened. When that task is done, I want you to gather the Spell Warders and see if you can counteract this poison. Try to find out what kind of powers these religious Islanders have."

Caseo nodded. Having an assignment seemed to calm him. He hurried down one of the back alleys, his reedy form moving with a purpose he had seemed to lack only a moment before.

"Rusty," Rugar said to his guards, knowing they were there without having to look for them. "Get word to the remaining troops inside and outside the city. They, too, need to know about this turn of events."

"What about you?" Rusty's gravel voice came from the area in the back and to the left of Rugar.

"Strongfist and I are going to see if the danger is as bad as Caseo says." The shard of fear dug deeper into Rugar's heart. His father had warned him. But none of them had realized that the conquerors' terror seemed more powerful than any victims' terror Rugar had seen. Perhaps because he shared it.

Before him the Fey were still running like frightened deer, oblivious to anything but escape. A young infantry boy tripped and fell on the cobblestone. The black-robed Islander, hurrying past, dumped the remains of his vial onto the boy's back. The boy screamed, his features locked in a look of pain and surprise. His back steamed, and he was rolling, rolling, rolling as if to put out flames. Then, suddenly, he stopped moving. Even from Rugar's distance he could see that the boy was dead.

Rugar turned away. His people were dying, and he had to find a solution. Quickly, before the terror spread and ruined the morale. All they needed was a way to kill the Black

Robes. The Warders needed to know where to focus their spell designs. Since he had sent Caseo to the palace, he would have to go to the warehouse himself. Rugar slipped between two buildings and followed the narrow alley, heading in the direction of the wharf.

The smell grew stronger as he walked, but the screams had faded, replaced by low murmurs and the cries of beings in pain. At one intersection Strongfist moved as if to go to someone, but Rugar caught his arm. He didn't dare lose his guard now. And, besides, until they knew what caused this odd wounding, they were better off not touching their comrades.

By the time they reached the edge of the wharf, the smell was a ghost in his nostrils. The eye-stinging smoke had lifted, leaving only the white buildings of a thriving seafaring people, the sunlight reflecting off the wide waters of the Cardidas, and bodies strewn across the muddy ground like abandoned children's toys.

He let out a small cry and went to stand in the carnage. He had stood among the dead before on countless battlefields, but they had never been his dead. Oh, he had lost a few here and there, but never so many and so hideously. A Spell Warder, recognizable only by his robe, lay at the base of a ramp coming out of the warehouse. Three Foot Soldiers, side by side, their faces gone, their hands fused to their chests, still twitched near his feet. They were suffocating— he knew that—only he had never realized that it was such a long, horrible way to die. They had no nostrils and no mouth and no indication of where those features had been. He was not a Healer; he had no idea how to save them.

No Black Robes lurked among the carnage, only a golden cat mincing around the bodies, stopping on occasion to paw at the remains. The reflection of light off the water was nearly blinding, and the rare moan breaking the silence was more horrifying than the screams.

Strongfist had left his side and was walking among the dying. He stood beside a shaking woman, his hands hovering over the remains of her face as if he were afraid to touch her. Finally she stopped, and he hunkered down beside her, his shoulders rounded in defeat.

"These Islanders have a great magick." His voice shook

with disbelief. They had never encountered any other beings with the same or stronger abilities.

"Perhaps they're Fey."

Rugar whirled toward the new speaker. Solanda stood where the cat had been, the skin around her eyes loosening in the last throes of change. She was naked. Her hands and feet were stained with mud.

"What did you see?" he asked, grasping for anything. If they were Fey, there might be an ancient magick, a way of revenge.

"I saw them kill with their magick liquid," she said, her voice as smooth as a purr. "But we kill with many devices, from our hands to our minds to our knives. Perhaps they have the same powers as well."

"The Nye said nothing of this."

"You believe the conquered?" Her words hung in the air. She placed her hand on one slender hip, and her eyes were as unfathomable as a cat's. "They had many reasons to lie to us."

He hadn't relied entirely on the Nye. His people had looked up the histories, listened to the legends. No one had thought that the Islanders would have magickal powers.

Only those with the evil Visions had even suspected Rugar had made a mistake.

The moans around him made the hair prickle on the back of his neck. "What did you see?" he repeated.

"At first I saw only a few of those smelly little men," she said. "Then I changed and hid. And from my hiding place I saw even more. This poison kills." She looked down at the Infantry soldier beside her. Two slender, perfectly formed hands grasped weakly at smooth skin where the face had been. "They have no Shape-Shifters, though, for I terrified one of their number when I changed before him. They also appear to have no women."

Those facts seemed irrelevant to Rugar. Finding an immediate solution to this nightmare was the only thing that would satisfy him.

"I do have something that might interest you, though," she said. "If you will follow me."

She grabbed his hand and pulled him away from the dying boy. Rugar stumbled over bodies, over twisting Fey reaching for him. The stench was overpowering: burned flesh and fear and the beginnings of fetid decay, all overlain with the muddy scent of the river and the sharp odor of fish. Hands brushed his ankles. And the cries of the dying sounded discordant, like a choir out of sync and out of tune, yet filled with devastating emotion.

Solanda's hand felt curiously cold in his, as if she, too, were part of the dead. She held him tightly, squeezing his fingers together, her nails digging into his flesh. She was as frightened, as bewildered, as he was.

He glanced toward Strongfist, who was still hunched over the dead woman. For a moment a fear touched Rugar: a fear that this horrible death was catching, like an illness that sweeps from person to person with no discrimination. But Strongfist's features had not changed. He still leaned forward, shaking back and forth, as if the carnage were too much for him.

Rugar looked away from Strongfist, back in the direction they had come. No black-clad Islanders lurked. They must have felt they had done their piece there and were moving to other venues. How terrifying for his Fey: to be attacked by creatures they knew nothing of and then to die in ways they never had before.

When Solanda reached the warehouse, she did not go up the ramp. Instead she crept along the building's side, keeping to the shadow. Her grip remained tight on Rugar's hand. It was cold in the shadows—the sun had given the day its only warmth. A chill ran down his back. At least there were no dying there to grab for him, no one reaching for his unguarded flesh.

"Hurry," Solanda said, and it wasn't until that moment that he realized he had slowed in the safety of the shade. Everything had reduced itself to small points and images: the chill; Solanda's dry hand in his own; a single voice, rising above the rest in a wail that mimicked the Fey victory cry; Strongfist huddled like a child against the destruction before him; the sunlight on the river reflecting joyfully into the fetid air. Taken as a whole, it was too much. Taken as a single image, it merely overwhelmed.

Solanda stopped at the other end of the warehouse. The ground was muddy there, but the only prints belonged to a woman and a small cat. This was where she hid, then, and where she chose to protect her find.

She released his hand and bent over. He rubbed his fingers. Her nails had left tiny indentations in his skin. She moved gingerly, with a delicacy and grace only the Fey Shape-Shifters possessed. She braced one hand on the side of the wooden building and, balancing precariously, reached with her other hand into the darkness under the stairs.

The wail had stopped abruptly, making the underlying layer of moans suddenly audible. Rugar leaned against the warehouse, then pulled away when he realized that the wooden slats were swollen with water.

Solanda stood. She held a pouch between two fingers of her left hand. With her other hand she carefully pried the top open, holding the fabric apart so that Rugar could peer inside.

A vial sat in the center. It had an ornamental shape, with a narrow neck and a wide bottom. The glass had been carefully cut into fake diamonds that looked like the reflections off the lake. Even through the odd triangular shapes, he could see liquid sloshing within. The bottle was stopped with a cork that looked no different from any other cork Rugar had seen.

"How did you get this?" he asked. His skin crawled at being so close to a foreign agent of death, and yet he gazed at it with fascination.

She closed the pouch, pulling the leather thong tight, then slipped the thong around her wrist. "I watched them hide a small stash. When they appeared to be gone, I checked it. There are still a dozen or more bottles there, but I slipped the pouch over this one, careful not to touch it. I believe the Warders can use it to see what kind of magick we're fighting."

He let out a small breath of air. He would not have thought of risking his life for a single vial of poison. Yet she had done so. He was sorry he had ever thought her dispassionate or cold. She might have found the source of their salvation.

Only he didn't know how to reach the Warders. He had sent Caseo to the palace. If Caseo had come to find him, then Caseo had sent the other Warders away. Rugar glanced at the warehouse, a shiver running through him. Was there more death waiting inside?

"Do you know where the rest of the Warders are?" he asked Solanda.

She clutched the leather thong as if it could protect her from all the horrors around them. She wouldn't meet his gaze. "Caseo sent them to the Shadowlands."

Rugar straightened. Only he had the authority to send Fey to Shadowlands. Yet the order made sense. "Did they make it?"

Slowly she lifted her head. She had the deliberate, unshakable calm of a cat. "I don't know. He asked me to wait in the warehouse while he went for you."

Rugar frowned. The order made no sense. Shape-Shifters were rare enough, and Solanda was the only one they had brought with them across the Infrin. But Shape-Shifters could hide in plain sight, as Solanda had done. Which meant there was something in the warehouse to protect.

"The Red Cap pouches," he asked, "are they—?"

"In the warehouse? Yes." She took a deep breath, as if she was expecting his censure. "But none of the Islanders have gone inside."

Rugar nodded. No excuse for her to leave her post in a normal situation, but this was not a normal situation. The moaning and the shifting, dying bodies were evidence of that.

But the Shadowlands. That was an idea. It would give him time, give them time, to determine what kind of weapon the Islanders were using against them.

"Take that into the Shadowlands. Tell the Warders to begin work at once and warn them how deadly this stuff is. If you see a Red Cap on the way in, make him start hauling pouches. We'll keep everything in Shadowlands until we have this problem solved."

She glanced at the vial, and something like fear crossed her face. She would not be able to change while carrying it. She would have to find a way in without using her feline form.

"Go quickly," he said, letting her know he understood her dilemma.

She started around the building, then froze. He came up

behind her, feeling the rigid spring in her stance. The sound hadn't been evident behind the warehouse: the building itself must have blocked it. But on the side, the clop-clop of horses' hooves rose above the moans and whimpers of the sufferers. He glanced around the building. The riders wore black robes. Dozens of horses and riders, all, he presumed, carrying more vials to the Islander fighters.

Solanda let out her breath in a hiss. She could return to her hiding place under the stairs, but Rugar and Strongfist were trapped. They couldn't hide in the warehouse: eventually the warehouse would be searched.

"Put that back in its hiding place," Rugar said to her, "and hide with it."

"Where will you go?" she asked.

"I'm going to get Strongfist. Don't worry about us. We'll be all right." He turned his back on her without watching her change, a process that had always made him nervous. Instead, he launched into the field of the dead, stepping over bodies, wincing as hands brushed him, as voices pleaded for mercy, as Fey writhed in final agony. The pounding of the hooves grew stronger, and he wondered if the Islander soldiers could see him from the bridge.

Strongfist sat in the center of the bodies, his knees up to his chest, his arms wrapped around them as if he could isolate his heart from the sight of all his dead comrades. He looked up when he saw Rugar, but Strongfist's eyes were glazed.

The hooves were closer, echoing on the wooden bridge. Rugar crouched beside his bodyguard, feeling the man's terror. They had nowhere to hide.

Except right there.

"Play dead," Rugar said.

Strongfist looked at him as if he were crazy. Rugar put his arm around Strongfist's shoulder and pushed him onto his side. Rugar flopped beside him, facedown in the mud. The mud was thick and goopy there. He shoved his hands in it to the wrist, making it look, he hoped, as if they had dissolved.

The stench this close to the bodies made his eyes water. He prayed he was right, that the disfiguring was not catching, for if it was, both he and Strongfist were now infected.

He felt the pounding hooves more than he heard them.

The horses had to be almost on top of them. He hoped that Solanda was well hidden.

His heart beat in time to the horses' hooves. He closed his eyes and waited for the death in his Vision to come to pass.

TWENTY

ELEANORA stopped at the fork in the path. She was deep in the forest, where the trees grew tall and thick. No sunlight filtered through the branches, but even there the leaves dripped with the remains of the rain. A large and twisted oak had grown into the intersection. She used the oak's gnarled roots as a chair, not caring about the damp wood pressing against the only dry portion of her skirt. Her stomach was growling, and she was dizzy from too much exertion. The baby was heavy. She made a cocoon of his blankets and cradled him on her lap.

His little forehead was wrinkled, his pale-blue eyes staring up at her as if he had a thousand questions but didn't know how to frame them. Since they left the house, he had made almost no noise, and she had been frightened that she had hurt him. Yet he seemed fine.

He was only a few months old. She had nothing to give him, no way of keeping him fed. Helter's house was farther away than she had thought, or perhaps her exhaustion combined with her panic made it seem farther. The fork was the halfway mark. She was so tired that she wondered if she could go on.

She leaned her head against the trunk, feeling the dampness against her scalp. Maybe a moment to catch her breath. She had heard nothing behind her on the road, no sign that those evil creatures were following her. If she hadn't been carrying the baby, she would have thought she'd made it all up.

A little food might revive her. She took the bread out of her pocket and ripped off a large hunk, eating it so quickly she barely tasted the doughy freshness. Her mouth watered at the unexpected treat, and she had to stop herself from eating the entire loaf. If she did, she would waste it. Her stomach wouldn't be able to hold that much food that quickly.

She shoved the rest of the loaf into her pocket, then set about tending the baby. She couldn't change him, although he needed it, and she had no milk. He wasn't ready for hard food, and she didn't want to risk choking him. Finally she settled on giving him drops of water from nearby leaves. He balked at the lack of a nipple, but when she put the water on her fingertips, he sucked greedily.

"Poor little one," she whispered. How quickly his life had changed. She ran a hand over his soft head, feeling the silky strands of hair against her palm. His lower lip trembled, but he didn't cry.

Her hands shook as she wrapped the baby in his blankets. Then she placed him against her right shoulder, cradling his head with her right hand and supporting his bottom with her left. She had tried carrying him a variety of ways, and each made her arms ache. Odd to have lived as long as she had and to have gained no experience with babies.

Ah, Drew, she thought. I never believed I'd need it.

She slowly got to her feet and walked around the tree so that she left no footprints on the trail. She took the right fork, which led to Daisy Stream, but she didn't use the path. Instead she walked parallel, behind the first row of trees. Branches hit her in the sides, and water ran down her face. She was able to protect the child from the worst of it, but when his little back got whacked with a twig, he began to whimper. By the time she could no longer see the gnarled oak, the baby's whimpers had turned into sobs.

"Please," she whispered. "Please shush."

His crying grew louder. He was responding not to her words, but to the fear that was rising within her. She was merely an old woman. She had no special strengths. She didn't know why she had gained this burden when this morning all she had to look forward to was a slow death.

When she had gone around several corners, she crossed through the trees to the path. No matter how magickal those creatures were, they wouldn't be able to see her prints from the fork. She adjusted the baby so that his face rested against her chest, muffling his cries as best she could without smothering him. The trees were thinning, and she could hear the gurgle of a stream. Perhaps the fork was not halfway. Perhaps she had misremembered it. Perhaps she was closer than she thought.

She stumbled against a root, pain shooting up her leg. Her grip on the baby loosened, and for a moment she thought she was going to drop him, then land on him, killing him. But she caught him, then regained her balance, stopping as the pain waved through her.

The baby's cries had become shrill screams. She put him back in his position against her shoulder, then patted gently between his shoulder blades, trying to soothe him. But he would have none of it. It was as if he suddenly knew that he was orphaned and that he might not live through the day. But he couldn't know that. He was probably tired and cold and hungry and wet.

Gingerly she leaned her weight on her sore leg. The pain was fierce, shooting from the arch of her foot into her thigh, but she could walk. She limped the next few steps, then regained her earlier pace, deciding that a little pain was worth her life.

The trees were thinning into shrubs, and the darkness of the forest was fading. Sunlight streamed through holes in the branch canopy above her. But aside from the baby's cries, she heard nothing.

Her throat was suddenly dry. What if she was wrong? What if those creatures had come from the coast instead of from Jahn? Perhaps all the people between Daisy Stream and the Infrin Sea were dead. More bodies, more blood. If she closed her eyes, she could see the stripped skeletons lying in their yards, the tall, thin creatures watching from doorways and laughing at her.

If everyone was dead between Coulter's home and the Infrin Sea, then she had no reason to hide in the forest. She and the child would have to die too. Or perhaps she could bargain for his life. They could raise him anyway they wanted to. They would get rid of her; she was just a meddlesome old woman. But a child. A child was precious to any race.

The baby shuddered, gulped, and then stopped crying. Little shivers ran through him, though, as if he was too tired to make a sound.

She rounded another corner and saw the clearing ahead. The sunlight fell across the grass, and she saw people moving, children playing near the edge of the forest.

They were alive, then. The creatures hadn't come there first.

Relief gave her the extra energy she needed. She couldn't run, but she tried, hobbling as quickly as she could across the mud and the wet.

As she burst out of the trees, the children screamed and ran away in terror: only then did she realize what an awful sight she must make.

"Help!" she cried. "Please! Someone!"

Her legs would take her no farther. She managed to stay upright for the sake of the baby. The sun felt warm on her skin, but her clothes were heavy with water. The baby started to wail again.

Three men and two women ran toward her. She recognized them: Helter and his wife, Lowe; Pier and his wife, Vy; and Arl, who was unmarried. Lowe took the baby, and Eleanora felt as if a great weight had been lifted from her. She pitched forward. The men caught her and eased her to the ground.

"Eleanora?" Helter asked as if he were uncertain.

"Yes," she said. She closed her eyes, feeling the world spin. It was all right. She was with friends and safe now. But not for long.

She sat up. "The baby needs care," she said. "He's Coulter's. His parents are dead."

"Dead?" Lowe asked. The baby whimpered in her arms.

"Murdered," Eleanora said. Then, in gasps and bursts, she told them the story of her morning. Vy glanced from her to the baby as if only the child made Eleanora's tale real. Pier supported her with his thick arm. Arl watched the forest as if he expected the creatures to burst through it at any moment.

When she finished, there was a long silence. The children had crept back up and were listening, their eyes wide. She wished she hadn't spoken in front of them, but she had had no choice.

She had black spots in her vision. She wouldn't be able to continue much longer. The fear and exertion had finally caught up with her. "I haven't eaten," she said into the silence.

Her voice seemed to snap Lowe out of her shock. "Yes," she said. "And this baby needs to be changed." She cradled him close.

Helter nodded. "Let's go inside. We need to make plans."

Plans. Eleanora closed her eyes for just a moment. They would rely on her for the plans, and she didn't even know if the creatures were human. She had no idea if knives wounded them or if they could even die.

"Come on, Eleanora." Pier's voice was soft against her ear. "We'll take care of you."

She hoped so. As Pier helped her to her feet, she opened her eyes.

Arl hadn't moved. He still stared at the forest, a look of quiet horror etched on his features. "They're going to come for us, aren't they?" he whispered.

"I'm afraid so," Eleanora said. Of that she had no doubt.

TWENTY-ONE

THE Black Robes scurried by him. Scavenger blended into the shadows along the wall of the empty storefront. He was across the dusty street from the palace, but it seemed as if he were miles away. Since he had run to Caseo to report the evil across the river, he had seen over fifty Fey die. No blood, but that hideous stink, the shrill cries of pain. The Black Robes had not seen him yet, but he knew they would want to kill him, since he had Islander blood on his clothes.

Caseo had ordered him to the palace to continue his work, but Scavenger couldn't. His pouch was empty. He couldn't bear to cross into the walls, to be trapped in a world even more Islander than this one. Besides, the blood magick no longer worked. He had seen Foot Soldiers attempt to touch the Black Robes. The Black Robes would toss liquid onto the Foot Soldiers before the incantations were complete.

The Islanders were winning.

When he had arrived, he had peered through the hole in the battered gates and seen Islanders in hand-to-hand combat with Infantry. The Foot Soldiers had just arrived, and they had begun their deaths by touch. They looked for Red Caps—three were already working inside—and when he saw that his comrades were so busy, he slunk back into the shadows. Scavenger needed to concentrate on his own life. They had enough blood pouches in the warehouse to last half a year.

If they lived that long.

The wood of the building was still damp from the rains. He could feel it through his shirt, clammy against his skin. His entire body was shaking. There was nowhere to hide. It was only a matter of time before they found him and covered him with that awful poison.

The Black Robes had paused at the gates of the palace, peering inside with what seemed to be trepidation. Fey guards littered the street, moaning and crying as they died. Scavenger tried to turn his gaze away, but he could not. The horror of melted hands, of missing faces, held him rapt. He could almost picture himself there, dying in hideous agony.

Strange that it should bother him now. He bathed in the blood of others, gathered it for use in magic poisons. He had seen more people die than he cared to think about. But he had seen only a handful of Fey die. Not dozens, like this.

The Black Robes hadn't gone in yet. The melee inside seemed to frighten them. They held out the remaining bottles and counted among them. Scavenger crept to the side of the building, making certain that he did not step into the open. Some of the Fey near the side of the road saw him and yelled for him to help them. He put a finger to his lips. He couldn't help them if he died too. Didn't they know that?

The Black Robes didn't seem to hear. They seemed less fearsome now that they weren't moving. There were only about twenty of them, and each seemed to be down to a bottle or two. Certainly not enough to attack the force that had spread itself through the palace.

Scavenger licked his dry lips. Perhaps the Fey inside didn't even know of this new danger. Someone would have to warn them.

He put a hand on the side of the damp building. To warn them meant that he would have to find a way across the road so that the Black Robes didn't see him. He had already warned Caseo. He was not heroic enough to warn the people twice.

"See how they skulk and hide as if their little lives are worth something."

The voice was unfamiliar and nasal. Scavenger whirled, his heart pounding. A heavyset man with puckered lips, large jowls, and beady eyes stood in front of him. The man was Islander and wore the uniform of the King's guards.

The man smiled at Scavenger's fear. "Your pouches are empty, boy."

Scavenger bit his lower lip, unable to speak. His hands went to the dry, empty pouches hanging flaccidly at his side. Then he realized what the man had said. How did Islanders know about pouches?

"Wh-who are you?" he asked, turning slightly so that his back was against the wall instead of facing the street.

The man's smile grew, making his eyes nearly disappear in the folds of his face. "Quartermaster Grundy," he said lightly as if he found the name amusing.

"Y-you have no bottle," Scavenger said.

"Of course not," the man said. "It would kill me."

Scavenger let his mouth drop open; then he closed it quickly. Kill—? He frowned, then collapsed against the building as the strength left his legs. Fey. The man was speaking Fey. There was no way for an Islander to know that language. He peered up at the man's piggish eyes. He was too far away to see if they were flecked with gold.

"Who are you?" he repeated.

The man laughed. His cackle rose over the moans of the dying. "Ah, Scavenger, I am your friend Silence. Don't you recognize me?"

The Doppelgänger. Scavenger slid all the way to the ground, his butt landing in the drying mud. The relief flowing through his veins made him weak. "I thought you were going to kill me."

"I would like to." The smile had left Silence's face. "You have no blood for me. I am in the wrong body. I need a change."

Scavenger leaned his head against his knees for just a moment. He took deep breaths, trying to calm himself. Silence. Somewhere Silence had learned tolerance of Red Caps. He was the only Doppelgänger who spoke to Scavenger as if Scavenger was worth something.

When he felt as if he could breathe comfortably, he glanced at the Black Robes. They were still huddled by the door of the gate. "A quartermaster?" he said as if the word had just occurred to him. "Someone who manages the barracks?"

"I had little time for preparation," Silence snapped.

"What are those Islanders over there with the bottles?" Scavenger still hadn't looked at Silence. The Fey on the street closest to the storefront had stopped moaning. They looked dead.

"They're Danites. Religious Islanders." Silence's tone was flat. Scavenger finally looked at him. His skin was red with the heat, sweat trickling down his hairline. The body was a poor choice all around for its lack of exercise and mobility. "I don't pretend to understand this. Grundy has no knowledge of Danites having magickal powers. Nor does he think of them as warriors. Either I picked an exceedingly stupid host or something is odd here."

"Everything is odd," Scavenger said. "It is as if we are cursed."

Silence nodded. He was staring over Scavenger's head at the street beyond.

"Are you going to absorb one of them?"

Silence shook his head. "Grundy has his uses right now. I am not sure if a Danite is the proper place for me either. They usually don't have access to the King, which is my assignment, and they aren't supposed to be powerful. I am wondering if a Fey has turned on us."

"No one would do that," Scavenger said, but the conviction had left his voice long before he'd finished the sentence. He remembered the conversations on the ship, the Visions that contradicted Rugar's calm. No Fey would go against a Vision. But no Fey had ever helped the enemy either.

"Shima's troop led in?" Silence asked. The question seemed less for information and more for confirmation.

Scavenger nodded. The Black Robes were talking among themselves. They didn't seem to notice the Fey writhing at their feet.

"Then Jewel is inside," Silence said.

Scavenger froze. The Black King's granddaughter. Women of that lineage were supposed to have special powers, but Jewel's hadn't manifested yet. She was still young and serving with the Infantry as part of her experience.

"There's no way we can stop the Black Robes," Scavenger said.

"We don't have to stop them," Silence said. He gazed over Scavenger's head at the fighting beyond. "We have to save the future Black Queen."

Scavenger swallowed. That meant crossing the road, going into the fray. He wouldn't do that. "We'll die in there."

Silence shook his head. "I won't. They won't kill a quartermaster."

"But if you get splashed—"

"I'll be careful."

"Or one of our own could attack you."

"They won't," he said with a confidence that Scavenger didn't believe. He had seen Doppelgängers killed by Fey before.

The pounding hooves were growing closer. Scavenger's mouth was dry. "I can't let you go alone."

"As if you'll make it, all bloody, your little face smeared with death?"

Scavenger wiped his mouth with the back of his hand, but it did no good. The blood was caked on. "They'll get me anyway."

Silence shook his head. Grundy's head. Sweat dripped off the chin. "Oh, no. You're going to hug the back alleys and the side streets. You're going to avoid any and all Islanders, like a good Red Cap, and you're going back to the ships."

"The ships?" Scavenger said, feeling a brief second of hope. The ships were safe. No Islander could get to the ships. "But they're in Shadowlands."

Silence nodded. He crouched so that he was face-to-face with Scavenger. Now Scavenger could see the gold flecks in the eyes; the slightly imperfect formation of the lids. "Look," he said, his voice thrumming with accents that were Silence's even though the pitch was not. "You have to go to the Weather Sprites and ask for rain."

"That's Rugar's job."

"Rugar might be dead by now."

A chill ran down Scavenger's back. They could all die. The horses were close; he could feel the vibration of the hooves beneath his feet. The Fey had never lost like this. Never, in all his experience, in all history. Rugar dead? On this afternoon anything was possible.

"Why rain?" he asked, just in case the Sprites asked him. He was the lowliest of the low. He had no right to demand anything, even if Rugar was dead.

"Because," Silence said, "it will at least give us a chance to escape."

It would dilute the poison and give them cover. Scavenger nodded.

"You're going for Jewel?"

Silence patted Scavenger on the shoulder. "Someone has to." He stood. "Good luck."

"To you too," Scavenger said.

But Silence didn't appear to hear him. He walked past Scavenger, his gait rolling and slow, not at all like the lithe and agile Silence. He stepped into the street as the horses, bearing more Black Robes, were stopped by the other Black Robes. Scavenger held his breath. The Robes waved Silence over. He swaggered toward them. Scavenger bit his lower lip. They would kill Silence. But instead they laughed and patted him on the back.

Silence shot one quick glance over his shoulder at the alley. Scavenger ducked in and away. Back alleys and side streets. He had to make it to the river.

If he made it to the river, he might survive.

TWENTY-TWO

THEY were going to die. All of them. He knew it.

Lord Powell huddled near the broken gate, his hair hanging over his face in a tangled mass, his shirt ripped and his arms covered with blood. He had barely got out of the palace alive. Then he had peered into the street and seen more of them, those evil creatures that were torturing everyone he knew. The screams and cries, the scent of blood and piss and fear, were enough to drive him insane.

He had found a safe corner behind shattered wood, held a sword tightly in his right hand, and waited. If any of them came toward him, he would kill them. He would kill at least one of them before they killed him.

But no matter what the King had said, they were all going to die. The King had known it; they all could see it on his face. He wanted them to die fighting for Blue Isle when they knew nothing about the conquerors. Perhaps living under the new rule was better than dying. There was only one way to find out.

He would surrender—that was what he would do. Nicholas was already in their clutches. Powell had seen that as he'd sneaked through the kitchen. Caught by a woman. The servants had made it clear who Nicholas was. Powell had got out of the kitchen before they could identify him. He didn't want to be a pawn. He wanted to live and not be tortured, not die. He had seen too many people go down.

The wood of the wall dug into his back. A man screamed and fell in front of him, landing faceup. A Fey put a booted foot on the man's chest and shoved a sword through the man's throat. Powell suppressed a gasp as the man's blood spattered his leg. But he didn't move. He would die if he moved.

The Fey didn't notice him. He pulled the sword free and returned to the fray.

Outside the gate, horses neighed. Powell peered through a hole in the wood. Danites. What were they doing there? Was the Tabernacle gone already? His grip tightened on his sword. Damn, he wished he'd learned to use the thing.

The Danites were holding bottles and talking excitedly to one of the quartermasters. A Danite held out a bottle and the quartermaster shook his head, laughing. "I'm a guard," the quartermaster said, his voice rising above the din. "Not a priest."

The quartermaster crossed the yard, his sword out but at his side. Powell turned away from the gate. Around him people were screaming, crying. He wiped his face with the back of his arm, wincing as the drying blood stuck to the damp skin of his forehead.

They had been laughing.

The Danites had been *laughing*.

He frowned, peered through the gate again. The Danites were gone. Only the quartermaster remained, an odd expression on his fleshy face. Powell bit his lower lip. How could they laugh at a time like this? Had they planned this? They were, after all, the ones who had notified the King. They were the ones who weren't following procedure, who acted as if there had been no warning at all. What if they had done this in some misguided attempt at a coup?

No. He shook his head slightly as a bloodcurdling scream was cut off behind him. The quartermaster caught Powell's movement and turned. Their gazes met. There was something cold in the guard's smile. Powell nodded to him. Ingrate. He had no concept of how to behave toward his betters. The quartermaster probably thought it funny that one of the lords was hiding near the gate, ready to make his getaway.

Powell would stop him. He would find out what made that self-important soldier laugh. Powell gripped his sword tighter, turned away from the opening, and held the sword in front of himself like a shield. There were no Fey close to him. They were crowded near the doors to the palace.

Powell took a step forward, then another, reluctant to leave the small safety afforded by the shattered wood. Then the quartermaster appeared in front of him, huge body more muscle than fat, a block against the destruction before them. The quartermaster's grin was warm. Powell wondered how he ever thought it cold.

"Waiting for me?" the quartermaster's voice boomed across the courtyard. Powell glanced around in panic, then placed his left forefinger over his lip to indicate silence.

"Right." The quartermaster crouched in front of the newly dead man. Powell glanced down at the body. The head was nearly severed from the neck, and blood collected in a small puddle near his feet. "A present?" the quartermaster asked.

Powell frowned. The heat, the noise, the sunlight, something was getting to him. He wasn't hearing correctly. "What?"

The quartermaster laughed and stuck his hands into the blood. Then he smeared it all over his body. A shiver ran through Powell. Something was wrong; something was very, very wrong. He eased himself away from the quartermaster, but the quartermaster grabbed his arm.

"Not so fast," the man said, and that cold look was back in his eyes. "I need you, *Lord* Powell."

The quartermaster's grip was strong. Powell tried to shake himself free, but couldn't. The quartermaster stared at him while using his remaining hand to pull off his clothes and cover the rest of his body in blood.

Powell glanced around. Everyone he saw was fighting a Fey, except the Fey still ringing the door. No one to help him. No one even noticing. He had no choice.

He brought up his sword and slammed it onto the quartermaster's wrist. The sword cut into the flesh and shuddered when it hit bone. The quartermaster screamed, his grip loosening. Powell yanked himself free and ran, his legs betraying him as he stumbled his way across the yard, back toward the palace. Anything to free himself from that crazy, crazy man.

A body slammed into his back and knocked him into the mud. The wind left him. Powell tried to roll, but the thing on him was too heavy. He peered over his shoulder and saw the quartermaster's face, chin digging into Powell's back. The quartermaster's hands and feet slid around front, and Powell was pinned.

He struggled, but something was pulling at him, yanking him away from his own skin. There was no pain. He couldn't grab on to anything. For a moment he broke free and hovered over his own body.

The quartermaster wasn't on him. Instead, a long, skinny Fey held him, its naked body covered with muck and blood. Its face had a rapt, almost feral expression. Then it looked up, saw Powell, and took a deep breath.

Powell tried to grab something, anything, but he was being sucked toward that feral being. He was surrounded by air—he was nothing but air himself—and then—

—he was Quartermaster Grundy, nothing more than sensuous appetites and pomp, eating breakfast and talking to his men when this thing, this—

—Silence, Fey, a Doppelgänger, nothing more than half a being himself, wounded in Nye, nearly died, taking a ship to a new island for an easy fight—

I'm drowning in them, Powell thought, and then he did.

TWENTY-THREE

THE pounding hooves faded. Rugar kept his eyes closed for another long few minutes for good measure. His right cheek was stuck in the mud, and he was breathing shallowly. The stench of the bodies caught in his throat.

A disaster. It was all a disaster. They had greater magicks than he ever thought possible. He had a real war on his hands now.

The mud was cold against his skin. The chill had worked its way through his body. He needed to think, and there was no time. He had called off the troops, but he would have to do something with them while he decided how to meet this new threat.

He opened his eyes. The body beside him was huddled in a mock fetal position, arms above the melted head. The face was completely featureless. Rugar shuddered. He knew what it was like to die like that, to feel his entire body change, his nostrils close, his mouth seal. He swallowed, but the stench of death remained in his throat like a piece of bread that had gone down the wrong pipe.

Far away the screams and slap of metal against metal rose and fell like a counterpoint to his own breathing. His heart pounded against his rib cage. He was alive. Many of his own people weren't.

He swallowed again and sat up, slowly pulling his hands out of the muck. He wiped the goo on his clothes. His fingernails had turned blue, his fingers white with cold. Around him bodies stretched for what seemed like miles. The sun glinted off the river, the light adding a clarity to the scene.

Dead. He had not seen a massacre like this in all his years as a soldier, although stories of early battles told of such fights, days when the Fey realized that their magicks did not always protect them.

The Fey had ridden down the Eccrasian Mountains, leaving death in their wake. But when they encountered the swords of the Ghitlus, the Fey learned how to die at someone else's hand. They retreated up the mountains, fashioned their own swords, and thus the Infantry was born. The Infantry, and the Fey's ability to absorb its enemies' power and use it for good.

Rugar had brought a full contingent. It would take little to see how the liquid would work. All he had to do was find the time.

The Fey had retreated before. They could again.

The mud was drying on his hands. He scouted for Solanda, but couldn't see her. He needed that bottle she had stolen. That bottle and time. Caseo had sent the Warders to the Shadowlands. It would take little to send the entire force there. Rugar had already made the Shadowlands big enough to hold the ships, and the ships had enough supplies to help them return. The Islanders would be confused about where the Fey had gone, and the Fey, when they learned the secret of the bottles, would once again have the element of surprise.

Anything. Anything to get them out of this mess.

He took a deep, shuddering breath to get control of himself. Then he reached across the destroyed body to Strongfist. Strongfist had burrowed his left side into the mud, his nose and right eye visible only to the most careful viewer. Rugar's filthy hand hovered over Strongfist's shoulder, but didn't touch.

"They're gone," he said quietly.

Strongfist didn't move.

"Strongfist," Rugar said. "They're gone."

Then he did lower his hand and touch Strongfist, relieved to feel the warmth of a living man beneath the cloth
of his jerkin. Strongfist opened his eye, his gaze as cold as
the ground.

Rugar flinched. They would blame him, just as his father
would blame him. But he had to be strong to turn this defeat
into a victory. And the best way to do that was to keep the
troops on his side.

"I have a plan," he said. "But first we need to assemble
our people in the Shadowlands."

Strongfist sat up. Mud dripped off his hair onto his side.
He made no attempt to wipe himself clean. "Retreat?"

"Until we learn the secret of their magick," Rugar said.
"And then we will kill them all."

Strongfist snorted and looked away.

Rugar grabbed Strongfist's chin and held it tightly,
squeezing the jawbone. "You can die here if you want,"
Rugar said. "But I shall note that you gave in after one
battle and died a coward. And your name shall be evoked
whenever Fey speak of dishonor."

"None of us will live that long," Strongfist said.

Rugar stared at Strongfist. The man's mud-covered face
was empty. He had served Rugar for years, faithful in all but
this. And who could blame him? They sat in a field of death.
If Rugar killed all who had lost faith on this day, he would
destroy most of his remaining troop.

"We will live. And we will win." He let go of Strongfist's
chin. "We need to call a retreat into the Shadowlands. I
need your help spreading the word."

"Fey do not retreat," Strongfist said.

"Fey do not die meaningless deaths." Rugar stood. The
bodies spread before him in all directions. "We shall go to
the Shadowlands and perfect our revenge."

TWENTY-FOUR

ANOTHER knife poked his back. The Fey woman's knife was against his throat. She held him, hard, her hand clutching the back of his head as a lover's hand would. Nicholas stood at the base of the stairs. Around him swords flashed, people yelled, and blood spurted. Sweat ran down the side of his face like tears.

Nicholas waited to die.

The woman's dark eyes held an odd kind of hurt. The fight went on around them, as if they were encased in glass.

Something smashed in the pantry, and a handful of Fey ran up the stairs. More Fey surged through the open door. A maid was passing torches made from sticks of wood and pieces of her skirt to any Islanders that passed her.

The unseen knife poked harder at the small of his back. Another hand gripped his shoulder—not her hand, one less friendly, one with more power. A male voice shouted above the melee, and Nicholas recognized the voice of the angry Fey male who held him.

The woman shook her head once.

The knife dug in deeper. The woman shouted, clearly an order, although Nicholas didn't recognize the tongue. The knife's point moved away from his back, although the pain remained, changing from a sharp, immediate threat to a dull ache.

His hands were tied, but if he got away, someone could cut him free. She hadn't moved, her knife point still a heartbeat away from killing him.

"Get it over with," he said in Nye.

Blades flashed. Someone screamed. The servants behind her were fighting with pots and knives. Most of the Fey were using swords.

Still she didn't move. The male Fey's grip on Nicholas's shoulder grew tighter. He too spoke, and as he did, Nicholas felt his body shift. He was going to stick his knife through Nicholas's back.

Nicholas brought his arms up as high as he could, catching the man behind him in the stomach. The blow wasn't hard, just surprising, and the man let out a grunt of pain. Nicholas took one step back, ducked and twisted away, then tripped over a body lying on the floor. He stumbled, caught his balance, and backed into the chef.

"Cut me free," Nicholas said in Islander.

The woman bent down and picked up Nicholas's sword. She held it in her left hand, the knife in her right, the balance perfect, her legs apart, ready to fight. Other Fey had formed a half circle around her, fighting to keep the Islanders away. Nicholas glanced to his side. The Islanders beside him had done the same for him.

The pressure on Nicholas's wrists suddenly eased. A man shoved a sword into Nicholas's hand. The grip was slippery with sweat and blood. Nicholas held out his free hand, the sword before him like a shield. His shoulders ached, his arms tingled, and his hands hurt with the effort of movement.

"You should have killed me," he said in Nye to the woman, "for I have no qualms about killing you."

He swung as he spoke, seeing too late the threat from the side. The angry Fey shoved his knife in the opening left by Nicholas's movement. The knife grazed his rib cage. Nicholas brought the sword back and slapped the Fey with the flat side of the blade.

"No, Burden!" she cried in Nye. "He is mine."

"Then kill him," Burden, the Fey, said in the same language, his breath coming in huge gasps. "Before he kills you."

"He won't kill me," she said.

And as Nicholas glanced at her, standing tall and proud, her face glistening with sweat and her eyes sparkling with power, he knew it was true. He couldn't kill her any more than she could kill him.

But she didn't have to know she was right. And he didn't have to kill her. It was clear that she was in charge of this group. She was as valuable to them as he was to his own people.

He thrust, and as he did, the Fey beside him screamed. The chef had shoved a knife into the Fey's side. The woman parried Nicholas's thrust, her gaze not on him, but on the boy.

The Fey sliced at the chef, cutting through the skin on his lower arm. Blood spurted on Nicholas, hot and searing, coating him. He stepped away, his feet slipping on the wet. The Fey man staggered, swinging wildly.

The woman swung again, and Nicholas caught her sword in a clang, keeping out of the range of her knife. The chef fell to his knees, ripping at his shirt and struggling to bandage his arm with one shaking hand.

A man screamed. Nicholas held the woman away from him, his muscles aching with strain. He had been fighting most of the day, using his body in ways he never had before, fear filling him. Exhaustion was clear in the trembling of his muscles.

She, however, didn't seem to weaken at all. Her body was thin but strong. Her arms had visible biceps, unlike any woman he had ever seen. Through sheer endurance, she would defeat him. He had to outthink her.

Something crashed above them, and a body tumbled down the stairs, rolling too quickly for Nicholas to see if it was Fey or Islander. The distraction gave her a second's advantage. She dived in with her knife, and he backed away only to feel the slap of a blade against his back. He held his sword out to deflect her, but turned to find Burden using a blade bloody from the wounded chef to try to stab Nicholas in the back.

Nicholas used his forearm as a shield, wincing as the bone deflected the blade. Then he grabbed Burden's face and shoved him backward. Other Islanders turned on him, and Nicholas faced the woman, her knife inches from his belly.

"You won't," he said in Nye.

Before she had a chance to answer, he knocked the knife from her hand, then shoved his sword against her belly. She gasped, her own sword useless at that angle. He pushed her backward, through the crowd, her own people too involved in their own fights to see her predicament.

Finally her back hit the wall beside the pantry door, and she stopped. She glanced down at his blade, then back up at him. "You won't either," she said.

In one quick movement he dropped his sword and cupped his damaged hand around her small neck. "I don't have to," he said as he pressed his body against hers to hold her in place. "I have you and I can tell, from our very short acquaintance, that your people won't like that."

Her gaze met his, and again he was struck by her height, her strength. She didn't flinch. Her body was warm beneath his.

His arm ached with pain. He longed to switch, but couldn't. He called for help from some of the servants around him, but it took a moment for anyone to respond.

As he waited, he studied her. The upswept eyebrows, the nut-brown skin, the small bones that gave her face a delicate air, marked her as different. She was breathing as hard as he was. They were inhaling and exhaling in unison.

"Your back is unprotected," she said.

"It's a risk I'm willing to take to hold you," he said, and meant it.

TWENTY-FIVE

SHE was covered in so much dirt and blood that she felt like a Red Cap. Shima fought by rote, maiming and killing and struggling as if she were alone on the field. The fight had moved into the organized chaos that was the middle of all battles, and even if she wanted to give instructions, no one would be able to hear them.

The sun felt warm on her back. She was still in the courtyard. Most of her troops had gone inside, but she remained out, waiting for the reinforcements. Dozens of Fey remained in the yard, fighting the Islanders that could still stand. The Islanders were inept fighters, their technique poor. Most didn't even use swords, preferring wooden clubs or makeshift weapons that broke when Shima hit them with force.

Perhaps she had been wrong. Perhaps Jewel was right. Perhaps the Vision had been false. The attack certainly seemed easy enough. A day's worth of effort and these Islanders would be subdued.

At least the Islanders had stopped pouring boiling water from the windows above. The mud was deep there, the scalded skin of injured Fey gleaming redly around her. People were moaning. Bodies lay where they had fallen, eyes open and reproachful toward the sunny sky.

She stabbed the Islander across from her, then ducked behind a column to catch her breath. She had been fighting steadily since they'd entered the wall, allowing her troops to move inside without her, relinquishing their command to Jewel without telling a soul. Shima had known that would happen on one of the campaigns. She had simply had no idea it would be this one.

The clang of metal against metal mingled with the cries of pain. She used the back of her hand to wipe the sweat off her forehead. Her skin came away dark with grit and dried blood.

As she was about to step back into the melee, she saw an Islander soldier near the gate coat himself with the blood of a fallen colleague. The action made her pause. She had seen no evidence that the Islanders used the same weapons the Fey did—indeed, she had no idea that they had the same kinds of powers.

A Doppelgänger, then? It would be useful to know which one.

She eased around her column, protecting her back, and peered over the fighters. The soldier grabbed a slender man of medium height, and then they both disappeared.

A bleeding Islander slammed into her, then fell to the ground. The Fey who had injured the Islander was already engaged in a battle with a man wielding a club. Shima stood for an extra second, long enough for the slender man to stand—alone, naked, and uninjured.

As she had suspected. A Doppelgänger. She gripped her sword tightly and pulled her knife from its hilt. Then she fought her way through the crowd, adding the final blow in more than one battle, stopping once herself to stab a man in the stomach.

The Doppelgänger bent down. She could see only his naked back. Then he stood, slipping a shirt over his head, and bracing himself as he pulled on a pair of breeches. It seemed as if it took forever, but she finally reached his side.

"Which one are you?" she asked as softly as she could.

He gazed down his long, slender nose at her, and for a moment she thought she had made a mistake. Then he smiled.

"Silence," he said in Nye, and held a finger to his lips.

Not a command, but an acknowledgment. He glanced around and apparently saw no one watching them. He leaned toward her and whispered in Fey, "Outside are Danites. They carry holy water—a potion—that can kill us. I have seen too many of our people die today. You must retreat and do so through the other gate. Go to the river. Convene in the Shadowlands."

A potion that killed? Fey didn't die in campaigns. Not in great numbers. Not in numbers huge enough to panic a Doppelgänger. The fear that had been building all day made Shima suddenly dizzy.

"Jewel," he said. "Where is she?"

"Inside."

"I'll get her out. The only way she can be safe is as one of my prisoners."

Shima took a deep breath. Something was giving her a way out. She would make it if she acted now. She had to believe that.

She peered through a hole in the gate. Islanders wearing black robes and no shoes stood in the street. They all held bottles and did not look as frightened as she felt.

"Those are Danites?" she asked.

"Yes," he said.

"They do not look dangerous."

"That potion can kill on contact. Call retreat."

Retreat. Never in her fifteen years as a leader had she called retreat. Never had she heard anyone do the same. If she hadn't seen Silence change, she would have thought him some kind of knowledgeable Islander spy, out to infiltrate their ranks.

She swallowed. "You will handle the inside?"

"Just Jewel," he said. "The rest is up to you."

She nodded. "Get away from me now," she said, "before they wonder why I don't kill you."

He pushed past her without looking back. The Islanders crowded around him as if he were someone to protect. He must have picked a powerful Islander to overtake.

Then she looked away from him. Call retreat.

She climbed onto some broken wood and shouted with all her strength, but her voice didn't carry above the sounds of fighting. She tried again, projecting with all her power:

"Troops! Through the west gate and down to the river. Immediately! Avoid the Islanders! They have a powerful magick!"

The Fey near her looked up, startled, some losing their advantages and getting clubbed or stabbed. The word rippled through the crowd like a wave. She was about to yell again when something wet hit her back. She turned.

A black-robed Islander scurried past her, a vial clutched in his wet hand. The Visions had been right.

"Retreat now!" she screamed as pain seared through her. She convulsed and fell, her body changing like an untutored Shape-Shifter's. Her last coherent thought was that they had all been fools to risk everything for this wretched Island. Then she began her last, fruitless fight for survival.

TWENTY-SIX

ALEXANDER paced. His steps raised decades-old dust. It coated his hands and face and made him sneeze. If the room had a window, he would open it. Then the noises from below would be even louder, and he would be a visible target.

He hated this forced inactivity. His people were doing his bidding; he could expect no more. Sometimes he wished he had the spontaneity and naïveté of Nicholas. If Alexander hadn't felt the weight of obligation, he would have been below, fighting until he could no longer move.

Not that it did any good from up here. The closest they had to a war leader was Stephen, who had studied war as Matthias studied his religion. Even the guards knew little about actual fighting. They had to protect the royal family against angry peasants at times, or from fights within, but nothing like the Fey. The Fey had defeated the greatest armies in the world.

Stephen sat on a stool in front of the table. He was tracing plans on sheets of paper, then crumpling them and tossing them into a corner. Soon all of the old maps and documents that filled the room would be piles of discarded paper. Alexander's father would have been appalled at the destruction. Alexander figured: let Stephen crumple everything in the room. History didn't matter if Blue Isle had no future.

They should be discussing, thinking, planning, but the task was too great. Alexander wasn't sure how to begin.

"How long are we going to remain up here?" he asked.

"Until the sounds of battle die out below?"

Stephen looked up from his doodles. "Or until someone brings us word."

"Seems foolish to me," Alexander said. "To keep me alive when I might rule over nothing."

"There is always a Kingdom as long as the King is alive," Stephen said. "They can't—and won't—kill everyone on the Isle. It's not their way. They conquer, and then they make their territories work for the Empire. They're very efficient. They'll install Fey governors here who will make the survivors work harder than they have ever worked. Blue Isle has resources to offer, resources the Fey can't tap alone. They will keep some of our people alive. People who will rally around you."

"Even you seem to be planning for our initial destruction." Alexander sat on the bench across from Stephen. Dust rose and Alexander sneezed. Then he brushed his hair away from his forehead.

"We're fools to think we can survive this kind of initial attack. We will be among the defeated, Sire. We need to accept that. But we must not accept that defeat." Stephen rubbed his stubble covered chin. "And that is why you must remain here."

Alexander sighed and placed his head on his arms. Dju had warned him of this. On the representative's last visit before the fall of Nye, Dju had asked for a private audience with Alexander. *They will overrun us*, Dju had said. *They will come for you next.*

But no one can penetrate Blue Isle without our help, Alexander had said.

The Fey can. They have strengths beyond our ken. Already they have breached our eastern borders, and we have been preparing for this for decades. Our soldiers are trained and ready. You have no real soldiers, Sire. The Fey will destroy you in an afternoon.

Why are you telling me this? Alexander had asked.

Because your lack of vision concerns me, and your ideas that you are not part of this world concern me even more. It may be too late for Nye, but it is not for Blue Isle.

He hadn't listened. He had been warned several times, and by people he trusted, and he still hadn't listened. He had preferred to believe that the Isle would protect them, as it had always done. And in his lack of foresight, he had condemned his people to death.

His son to death.

"I wish Nicholas were here," he said.

"As do I," Stephen said. "We need him as well as you."

Alexander brought his head up. Stephen was looking away, his cheeks flushed. His businesslike words had hidden his own concern for Alexander's son. Stephen had given Nicholas as much care—maybe more care—than Alexander had done.

And if Nicholas survived the day, it would be because of Stephen, not Alexander.

He needed to think. They came in by the river. They not only planned to invade, but to conquer and settle. Stephen had said they were vulnerable to the same things Islanders were, but had more power at their command. If the Islanders could find a way to reduce the size of the Fey's force while avoiding the Fey's power, they might have a chance.

And Stephen was right: it would take surviving the day.

Alexander drummed his hands on the table, then stood. "We need a specific plan," he said. "Something more than hoping that we will survive and using me as a rallying point."

Stephen threaded his fingers together and placed his hands behind his head, leaning back. "What are you envisioning?"

Voices rose outside the door. Alexander froze. Stephen stood slowly, pulling his sword and moving beside the door frame. Then someone pounded on the door itself. Alexander put his hand on the hilt of his dagger.

"Come," he said as the door burst open. Monte, head of the palace guards, staggered in, his clothing covered with blood, his forearm slashed and dripping from a handful of small cuts. Dirt streaked his face. He had a Danite in tow, a round barefoot man whose black robe was in tatters. In his hand he held a bottle usually used in Midnight Sacrament.

"Well?" Alexander's hand remained on his dagger. Stephen hadn't moved from his crouch beside the door. The guards crowded against the opening, their backs to the room.

"We . . . have . . . them, Sire," Monte said. His words came in large gasps, as if he couldn't get enough air.

" 'Them'?" Alexander asked, not willing to hope.

"The . . . Fey, Sire. . . . They're . . . dying."

"All of them?"

"Not yet," the Danite said, his head bowed. His voice rumbled from a place deep inside him. "But soon. Holy water kills them, Sire."

Stephen stood and let his sword down. "It what?" he asked.

"Kills them." The Danite glanced at the swordmaster. "It's like they melt."

Alexander felt something let go in his chest, a holding, a panic. He didn't even acknowledge the Danite, but addressed his remarks to Monte. "Is this true?"

Monte nodded. "I've seen . . . it myself, on the . . . way up here. . . . He used that bottle, and . . . they started to flail and . . . scream and die. It was hideous. . . . It was . . . wonderful."

"So they're out of the palace?"

"Not yet," Monte said. He seemed to be catching his breath. "When I saw the Danites, I figured . . . I should bring them to you first. They're coordinating an . . . attack on the Fey inside now."

"Is there enough holy water?" Stephen asked the Danite.

"I don't know," the Danite said. "But we have got more from the Rocaan. Hundreds of Fey are dead between here and the Tabernacle."

"Hundreds," Stephen breathed.

"It's a miracle," the Danite said.

"A miracle we need to use," Monte said. "Quickly. . . . If we didn't have this weapon, we would all be dying."

"Then make sure it is distributed to all who need it. I want to know when the Fey have left the palace."

"Yes, Sire." Monte let go of the Danite. "Give the King your holy water."

"No," Stephen said a bit too quickly. "Give it to me."

The Danite glanced between them, confusion evident on his face.

"Give it to Stephen," Alexander said.

Monte bowed, then turned as he headed for the door.

"Wait," Alexander said. "Monte, as you came up here, did you—" He paused, not wanting to seem vulnerable, but finding no way around it. "Did you see my son?"

Monte did not turn around, but his shoulders stiffened. "No, Sire."

Alexander wished he could see Monte's face. It seemed to him as if the head of the palace guards was lying. Alexander swallowed. He could make Monte turn around, but now was not the time. The guards were sworn to protect the King and the Prince. If Monte knew where Nicholas was, he would make sure someone was there to help.

"All right, then," he said. "Get this counterattack started, and make sure someone else comes up here with more holy water for the guards outside."

"Yes, Sire." Monte nodded once, to acknowledge the King, then let himself out the door.

Stephen pushed the Danite. "You go with him."

"But—"

"King's orders," Stephen said.

The Danite frowned in confusion, but left as well. Stephen closed the door behind him. "Odd," he said, leaning against it. He brought the bottle to his face. The water inside glistened.

"I would have liked to question that Danite more," Alexander said.

"Not yet, Sire," Stephen said. "Let's see how this counterattack goes first."

"You are supposed to follow my wishes," Alexander said, noting that Stephen did not use a term of respect in his address.

"I am supposed to protect you." Stephen put the bottle of holy water on the conference table. "How were we to know that Danite was one of us?"

"He was with Monte," Alexander said. Stephen watched him. Alexander frowned and peered at the bottle. "You think this is a ruse to get at me?"

"It could be, Sire."

"Then why would Monte—?" Alexander stopped, remembering the conversation earlier after the advisers had left the room. "You think Monte might be under the Fey's magick?"

"We can take no chances," Stephen said. "At the moment the only two people we can be certain of are me and you."

"By the Sword." Alexander sat heavily on the bench. "And we can trust each other only if we remain together." This level of caution was beyond him. Not to trust people he had known all his life? How could his world have turned itself upside down so quickly? "We can't live like this."

"If this holy water works," Stephen said, "we will devise a test for those who are near you. It might all be moot, anyway."

"If the holy water works," Alexander repeated, putting his face in his hands, not willing to let himself feel. "If it works, we have hope."

TWENTY-SEVEN

THIS body's slenderness belied its lack of strength. Silence cursed as he scurried across the courtyard. He hated the part of his magick that forced him to duplicate his hosts exactly. The first Islander host had been too fat, and this one was no better, remaining slim by relative youth and excellent heredity, not through exercise or a good diet. He was getting winded already.

The battle continued around him. Fey and Islanders fought outside the back entrance leading to the palace kitchen. Shouts and screams echoed in the air. Swords flashed. Near him an elderly servant used an iron barrel rim to slash at passing Fey. Silence kept swiveling his head, afraid that the Danites were nearly upon him. They wouldn't try to kill him, thinking he was their precious Lord Powell, but if some of that holy water splashed on him . . . He shuddered. No one deserved to die like that.

He was still disoriented from the change. Islander personalities did not mesh well with his own. In Nye he would change and be that person immediately. Here even his knowledge of the culture came slowly.

This second change made everything slow. The changes depleted him more than he cared to admit.

Behind him, Shima called a retreat. Her voice trembled as she yelled.

The clothes he had stolen were too tight. He hoped no one would notice that he dressed differently than Powell had been a moment before. At least he had remembered to grab his stiletto in all the confusion.

He slipped behind a column, cowering as he had seen Powell do. He hoped no one saw him speaking Fey with Shima. That would make him suspect from the start. But he couldn't worry about that now. He had to find Jewel, and quickly.

Shima's commanding voice broke off in midcry. He turned, saw the Danites clearing their way through the crowd. The stench was rising—and the tone of Fey voices was changing from victory to terror. He took a deep breath, then pushed into the melee that blocked the door to the kitchen.

Islanders slashed at Fey with clubs of burning wood, with knives, and with swords stolen from the dead or dying. The Fey—the Infantry—were fighting back with their own swords, youthful faces covered with sweat. The stench of the dying hadn't made it to this area yet. It smelled of smoke and fear.

Both of his personalities recognized faces. Most of the fighting Islanders were kitchen staff, although a few of the guards had made it this far down. The butler was staving off two Fey with the handle from the butter churn, screaming as he did so.

All of the Fey in this area were from Shima's troop: Infantry members too young to have discovered their magicks, or the unfortunates who had no magicks to speak off. He weaved his way around the fighters, glad for Powell's relative height, each step another step between him and the Danites.

He kept to the walls. The screams and cries and shouts were a blur to him. He couldn't tell which were in his native tongue and which were in Powell's. He squinted through the smoke and near darkness, hoping to see Jewel.

It wasn't until he got near the stairs that he realized something had changed.

Islander and Fey stood side by side, forming a semicircle. Their expressions seemed identical: a mixture of confusion and hope. All held their weapons at their sides, as if they were afraid to use them.

Burden stood near Silence, his sword bloodied. He was breathing heavily. Silence followed Burden's gaze.

There, in the center of the circle, Nicholas held Jewel while his men tied her hands. She wasn't struggling.

Silence swallowed, a cold terror running through him. She wasn't wounded by the Danites, for she would be dying. Could the Islander boy have bested her in a fight? Jewel, granddaughter of the Black King, one of the strongest of all the Fey?

He pushed his way through the standing crowd, his heart pounding wildly at the risk he was taking. Fey or Islander could strike at him at any moment. He took advantage of the oddness of the situation to protect him.

"Well done, Highness," he said in a voice that carried. "Our first prisoner. Is she yours?"

Nicholas glanced up, and a wariness crossed his features. "Lord Powell. Shouldn't you be helping my father?"

Jewel was watching him, a slight frown on her forehead. Some Fey claimed to be able to recognize a Doppelgänger no matter who he was wearing, but she had never been one of them. Still, Silence felt as if she could look through his disguise.

"Your father sent me here," Silence said, and with that statement an image jumped through his brain. He knew where the King was, and he knew how to get there. Perhaps if he could stay ahead of those Danites, he might be able to demoralize these Islanders after all.

But Jewel came first. Rugar could not lose his oldest child.

"I am supposed to monitor the ground." He held out his hand as he came forward. "But you seem to have it well under control. Let me take this prisoner to your father."

"I don't know if she is a prisoner yet," Nicholas said. Then Silence noticed the dagger in the boy's left hand. The fear that was dogging him grew.

"Oh?" If Silence was going to rescue her, he had to sound diffident. And Powell thought he knew the boy: all reckless curiosity and flamboyance, with little real strength. Silence hoped his host was right. "Well, then, if she's not important, kill her."

The words came more easily than he expected. Nicholas's grip on his dagger tightened, but he shook his head. "She's important," he said softly.

Silence took a step closer. Jewel didn't move, her gaze trained on his face. "Then let me take her for you. You can finish up here. The Danites are coming with a potion that kills these creatures quickly, leaving no time for even a death cry. We have the situation well in hand now."

The Islanders had finished tying Jewel, but Nicholas still clutched her against him. "Where would you take her?"

"To the barracks. We need to be able to question these creatures, and since you think she's important—"

"I'm taking her to my father."

"What?" Silence couldn't hide his surprise.

"They all listen to her, they all follow her. She's someone important. My father can question her, maybe even bargain with her."

The boy's stubbornness made Silence's chill grow. Silence forced himself to smile. "She is probably just a division commander. She probably knows nothing more. We won't need to bargain, since we have our holy water. We are going to win, Highness."

"Are we, milord?" The boy smiled in return. "Then indulge me." He took Jewel's arm and pulled her to the stairs. "You know where my father is. Take me there."

Silence swallowed. Behind him he heard the cries of dying Fey. He glanced over his shoulder. The Danites were at the door, making their way into the room. The stench preceded them. All the Fey would die. All of them. Even Jewel.

He tried not to let his fear show and scanned his mind for Powell's knowledge of the castle. Not all the pieces were there yet, but some of them were. Even if Silence got Jewel, he would have to take her through the Great Hall, the lodgings, and finally into the streets: the streets from which the Danites had come.

To the Islanders, though, he was one of their rulers, one of their lords. He would be able to free her and take her to the Shadowlands later, when the path was safer.

The screams were growing behind him. He wished for one moment without Islander presence. He would scream a warning to his people. But that was the price of his profession. He had known it since he'd been a boy at the battle of Issan.

"All right," he said, striding closer and taking Jewel's free arm. "I'll take you."

Color filled Nicholas's face as Silence touched Jewel. Jewel didn't move. Silence looked down and saw that her face had gone vacant, her eyes glazed.

A Vision.

He bit back an oath. The Black King's granddaughter, fighting in the Infantry, when her entire body could be paralyzed by a Vision. She had kept it secret from all of them. She had to. Rugar wouldn't have let her fight with this kind of magick.

"What's wrong with her?" Nicholas asked, his voice rising, a boy again and not the man he was pretending to be.

"I don't know," Silence said. "Perhaps it's some kind of trick. Let me take her from here—"

"No!" Nicholas said. "She's coming with me."

The tension in her body relaxed, and she crumpled in their grasp. Silence put a hand on her back, but Nicholas used his body to brace her. Powell's knowledge of the boy did not extend to kindness toward women. If anything, he showed an atypical lack of interest in them.

Perhaps he was one of the cruel—the kind who took Fey women and tried to destroy the magick in them by force.

Jewel's eyes fluttered. Her gaze focused slowly on Silence's face, and she smiled. "Silence," she whispered in Fey.

He couldn't respond. He couldn't make a movement that would give himself away, although he wanted to say something, anything. Instead he squeezed her arm, the terror in him deepening. His responsibility was no longer to Rugar and the Black King. It was to the Fey themselves. For the loss of Jewel meant the loss of their future.

TWENTY-EIGHT

SHE came out of a sound sleep gradually, hearing the cry of a baby, and wondering why Roca tortured her so. She wished Drew were beside her to cradle her as he used to. *It's only a bird, beloved,* he would murmur. *Only a bird.*

But as she stirred, the sound continued. A baby's cry, deep and heartbroken. And a woman's voice, quiet and soothing. Eleanora frowned. Her body ached. As she opened her eyes, the room spun. The ceiling was thatch, and she was lying on something soft.

The room was small with rough, unsanded walls. A table stood beside the bed, with a single candle on it. The window, at the bed's foot, had no tapestry covering it. The room smelled of drying mud and fresh milk.

She blinked; then the memories came back. They had had to help her to the half circle of cottages that formed the village of Daisy Stream. When they'd got to Helter's cabin, she had passed out. Her frail body had not been able to take any more. They must have put her on their bed.

But those creatures hadn't come.

"I think we should go to Coulter's and see what she was talking about." A male voice filtered through the window.

"They might have gone in a different direction." A

woman—Vy?—said. "She wouldn't have taken the baby otherwise."

"Really?" Helter asked, his voice soft. "We all know how she covets children."

A lump rose in her throat. She pushed herself up, willing the dizziness to go away. *Covets children.* And she had thought Helter was her friend. He was Drew's friend and nothing more. Maybe not even that.

"She doesn't covet children," Vy said. "She cares for them, just like many women do. She never took anyone's child before. In fact, she brought Gitwen's son home when he ran to the river that time. She could have kept him at the house. It was right after Drew died."

Eleanora ran a shaking hand over her face. The baby had stopped crying, but the woman was still crooning in a nearby room. Helter's cottage was big, even compared to Coulter's. Helter's family had lived there for generations, and Helter's father had always believed that separate people needed separate rooms.

She used the wall to brace herself and sat up slowly. Splinters dug into her fingers. This room had to be a more recent addition. She pulled the blanket off her legs. The dizziness was strong for a moment; then it faded. Too much effort for an old and starving woman.

"Why don't we send a group to Coulter's? If there's a problem, we need to know, and if she took the child, Coulter needs to know." Helter spoke forcefully. It sounded as if he had moved closer to the window.

She took a deep breath and eased herself to her feet. Then she smoothed the blankets on the bed—a feather mattress suspended on a wood platform—how much more comfortable than her pallet on the floor—and walked to the door.

The bedroom opened into the kitchen. Like Coulter's, this room had a hearth stove, very small, that heated everything. The table was old enough to have scratches. Lowe had the baby on her shoulder, her hand patting his tiny back. His little face was red from crying, his eyes squeezed shut, his breathing even. When Lowe saw Eleanora, she smiled.

"He'll be all right," she said. "He misses his parents, but he will be fine."

"Did he eat?" Eleanora asked. She kept one hand on the door frame to brace herself.

"We warmed some goat's milk for him. He drank it all." Lowe's gaze ran the length of Eleanora. "How are you?"

Eleanora smoothed her hair. "Shaky. But fine. How long was I asleep?"

"Not very long," Lowe said. "You need more rest than that."

"There's been nothing on the path? No one following me?"

Lowe shook her head.

Eleanora pushed off from the door frame and crossed the room, letting herself outside. The sun was out, but the air had the coolness of twilight. The cabins were dark. All of the villagers sat around the meeting stump just past Helter's front garden. Helter stood near the edge of the garden, beside the blooming berry plants. He had sounded closer inside.

The conversation stopped when people saw her. Helter turned.

Eleanora hadn't seen this many people in years, maybe not this many at once in her entire life. She cleared her throat. "If you send people to Coulter's," she said, "make sure they can defend themselves. And make sure they can hide."

Helter had the grace to look away from her. "No one has come up the path."

She shrugged. "Maybe they don't know there are settlements this far out. I was afraid they were going to follow me. Maybe they didn't even know I was there."

"You've got to admit," Helter said, "that your story is fantastic."

"Just because it's strange doesn't mean I lied." She kept her hands loose at her sides, trying to look relaxed. Any bit of nervousness would make her even more suspicious to him. "If I was going to steal a child, do you actually think I would be foolish enough to bring him here—a place where you knew his parents—and then tell you where he came from? I'm old, Helter, not stupid."

"I think we need to take her seriously," Vy said. She was sitting at the edge of the semicircle, leaning against the stump. "These creatures sound frightening. If they can kill Coulter, they can kill anyone."

Helter turned back toward the group. "I sent Arl down the path to see if there's anything to report."

"Arl?" Eleanora stepped gingerly near the garden. She stopped beside Helter. "He's little more than a boy."

"He can hide as well as an old woman," Helter snapped.

She flushed. "I'm not ashamed for what I did, Helter. I saved a child's life. Now it's up to you to save your lives. These creatures are heartless things—"

She stopped. A rustling from the wood made her start. She whirled, making herself dizzy again, but this time she managed to stay upright.

Arl was crossing the clearing with a Danite beside him. The Danite was not one Eleanora recognized. The Danite who supposedly managed the kirk near Daisy Stream hadn't made rounds to this area in over a year.

"They're horrible things." Arl stopped at the edge of the meeting circle. His young face was pale, but his eyes had a faraway look Eleanora had seen only in the aging. He leaned on the Danite.

The Danite was thin and almost as young as Arl, his hair cut close around his skull, his black robes dripping wet and his feet covered with mud. He clutched a small bottle.

"Coulter's dead," Arl said, "just like Eleanora said. The bodies—" His voice broke and he shook his head. "I've never seen anything like that."

"Where is the woman?" the Danite asked.

"Here," Eleanora said. Her dizziness had receded a bit, but she didn't want to take a step forward. She bowed her head and waited, fearing that he, too, would censure her.

He came close and touched her forehead with wet fingers. "You are Blessed," he said. "Not many see the Fey and live."

"You know what they are?" she asked.

He nodded. "I rode in from Jahn to see if they had attacked the countryside. The city is under siege, but we have been driving them back. They're demons. Holy water destroys them."

"He killed those remaining at Coulter's with a splash of water," Arl said. He glanced at Helter. "Good thing, too. They were going to come for me."

"I told you to hide," Helter said.

Arl wiped a shaking hand across his brow. "They knew that Eleanora had been there. They knew she took the baby. They thought she would be back, so they had scouts in the woods. The Religious Sir arrived just in time."

"What are these creatures?" Vy asked.

"Demons," the Danite said in a patient tone, as if she hadn't understood him the first time. "They came in boats from across the sea, but they have magick, and the boats have since disappeared."

"Why would the Roca allow this?" Eleanora asked.

"The Roca has provided for His people, for those who believe." The Danite held up the vial of holy water. "This is all I can spare for you now, but let the boy come with me, and I will have him return with more blessed water on the morrow. We have placed some outside the city, for country use. And there will be more. One of the Elders promised that when the Fey menace is gone from Jahn, we will send Danites and Auds through the countryside with vials of holy water in case the demons come again."

Helter turned to Arl. "Are you willing to go with him?"

Arl nodded. His eyes were shadowed, his face drawn and worn. He looked twice as old as he had when Eleanora had arrived that morning. "No one else should have to see those horrors. I—I know what to avoid now."

His gaze met Eleanora's. They shared ghosts now. Ghosts and terror.

"Is the baby all right?" he asked so softly that Eleanora could barely hear him.

"He's fine," she said, knowing how important it was to touch life after that kind of carnage. "Lowe has just got him to sleep."

Arl smiled. Then he touched the Danite's arm. "Come, let's go see him and get a bite to eat."

"And then we'll have to go," the Danite said. "Those demons won't wait for us. They'll come here as soon as they can."

They headed to Helter's cabin, already a team, a force against the creatures that invaded their land.

Eleanora watched them go. Helter sighed, then looked at her. "I owe you an apology," he said. "I should have listened."

"I know," she said, finding a bit of strength in his words. "But should haves don't matter anymore. We have to find a way to protect ourselves." And soon. She didn't have the heart to ask if the boy and the Danite had made sure they hadn't left a trail. She didn't want to know if the Fey would find them easily.

TWENTY-NINE

HER Vision made her dizzy. Jewel shook her head and took a breath. Silence held her. She recognized him after the Vision. She had seen him change; the clothes he wore now were the ones he'd put on after killing the man in the courtyard.

But she didn't have time to think about her own situation. The Black Robes coming through the door, the stench of rot that had been part of her earlier Vision, and the miasma that rose with the glistening water the Black Robes spread decided her. Jewel's body went slack. The men who held her could do with her what they wanted, but she had to save her people. Shima had been right. This was a place of death.

"Run!" she cried in Fey. "Run for your lives!" The Fey around her looked shocked. Burden raised his head, his mouth open.

"Run!" she said again. "Those Islanders behind you bring death. I saw it! As the daughter of Rugar, I command you! Run!"

The man from her Vision shook her a little. Silence tightened his grip on her arm. Suddenly she knew what she was feeling from him. Fear. He was terrified. She couldn't recognize it on his strange face.

Burden came toward her, but she shook her head. "I am lost," she said to him directly. "This time you must listen to me. Get these people out of here. They will die otherwise."

He had to hear the command in her voice. He had to understand that she wasn't speaking as his friend or as a frightened Infantry soldier but as his future commander. He nodded, then raised his sword above his head.

"The Black King's granddaughter says to flee!"

The Black Robes were coming closer. Silence pulled on her arm. He said something in Islander to the man beside her, the man from her first Vision, and together they pulled her toward the stairs.

She slid in blood, stumbled over bodies. She wasn't used to moving without her arms, moving without power. Silence did not look at her. His Islander face was slender, with a hooked nose and longish blond hair. Perhaps she had been wrong. Perhaps she had taken an Islander for one of her people in the confusion following her vision.

"Silence," she said quickly, not looking at him but looking at Burden's back. "Silence, if that is you, squeeze my arm three times. Otherwise, I will fight this with my people now."

The squeezes were quick and light: one, two, three. The man from her Vision looked at her with puzzlement. He said something to Silence, who snapped a response.

Four dead Islanders lay at the base of the stairs. Another was sprawled along the stone steps. The stench was following them, combined with thumps and screams of agony. Fey screams.

The hair on the back of her neck rose.

She stumbled, and the man from her Vision held her up. He seemed to know her, too, and was as protective of her as she had felt of him. Silence glanced over his shoulder, biting his lower lip. The man put a gentle arm around her back, and she recognized his touch.

"We are taking you to the King," he said in Nye.

"My people are dying down there."

"Be glad it's not you."

More bodies had fallen on the stairs. Most of the Islanders were below and had seen the fight. The cries went on, many cutting off abruptly. One Fey Infantryman crumpled in a doorway, dead from sword wounds. She opened her mouth, preparing to warn the Fey up there, but there were none. Either they had heard her, or they had already retreated.

Retreat. It was not a Fey word. She closed her eyes and let the men drag her up yet another flight of stairs. The Fey did not retreat. She wondered if her father was alive to know of it. She wasn't sure if she wanted him to be alive or not: to preside over such a defeat would destroy him, and yet she could not imagine life without him.

And here she was allowing herself to be taken to their King. With Silence beside her. He was one of the best. She had to trust him to save her. She couldn't trust the man from her Vision, no matter how much she was drawn to him.

The men were talking in Islander again. She wished she had a Doppelgänger's skill to absorb the language immediately. She wanted to know what they were saying, and she couldn't ask either of them.

The man's voice rose a bit and Silence shrugged. They rounded yet another corner and went up another flight of stairs. The tapestries had been torn off the windows there, and there were no bodies. The steps grew narrower and sharper. They were no longer in a public place.

They passed a handful of Islanders coming down the stairs. All of them bowed—to the man? to Silence?—she wasn't sure.

"Who is this man you allow to touch me?" she asked in Nye to the man from her Vision.

He smiled. She had never seen him smile before. His beauty made her gasp. The heavy bones and the odd shape to his features gave him a strength she found appealing. "What?" he replied in the same language. "Are you no longer curious who I am?"

She was curious about all of this, about why she had even allowed herself to be taken when her people were dying below. Burden would have told her that the Black King's granddaughter had to survive. Silence had shown her that without saying a word. But she had always been a fighter. Perhaps, after seeing their King, she would have some wisdom to take back to her father, if he lived.

"How far away is this King?" she asked. "Doesn't he monitor his own battles?"

"He has never fought one before," the man said softly. "We are not a warlike people, as you are."

The condemnation in his tone stopped her from asking further questions. Silence said nothing. The stairs continued to wind round and round. Her limbs were tired. She hadn't realized until that moment how much effort she had put into the fighting.

When they reached the top of the flight of stairs, the man beside her stopped. Five guards stood in front of a large wooden door. The man from her Vision spoke to them, and they bowed their heads. The Islanders had shown respect to him, not to Silence. She resisted the urge to look over her shoulder.

She didn't have to. One of the guards opened the door, and the men led her inside.

The room was large and dust filled. Papers were crumpled on the floor, and footprints traced the dirt. There were no windows, but if she strained, she could hear the cries from below. The walls, then, weren't all stone. A long table filled the center of the room, surrounded by chairs and benches.

There were three men in the room that she didn't recognize. One was a Black Robe clutching a bottle. She caught her breath but didn't allow herself to move away from him. *Show no fear*—one of the first rules of capture. *Fear is weakness.* The second was an old man with stubble on his chin. His watery blue eyes peered at her as if she were a great curiosity.

The third was a slender man with dark-blond hair and blue eyes. He was younger than she'd expected. The man wasn't tall, but his grace made him seem taller than he was. He wore pants and a loose shirt as if they were uncomfortable. His gaze kept shifting to the man from her Vision, and she could feel his barely contained joy.

She glanced at the man from her Vision and felt a start deep within her. He was a younger version of the man across from her.

"I suppose you had a reason for bringing me here," she snapped in Nye, looking at the man who held her.

"Have manners," he said in return. "I am presenting you to the King."

"Well, then, present me. Which of these cowards is your King?"

At the word "coward" the grizzled man and the Black Robe took a step backward. If she had ever needed confirmation of her suspicions, she had it now. The third man was the King.

"I am King," he said in Nye. "My name is Alexander, and I would take your hand as is our custom, but Stephen here says you people can kill with a single touch."

"If that was true," she said, not willing to give away any secrets about Fey magick, "your son would be dead."

A brief look of horror crossed the King's face as he glanced at the man who held her. Anger swept through her —anger at herself. She had held the Prince of Blue Isle and had failed to use him. She should have known whom she held when the peasants were willing to die for him.

The King questioned his son in their own language, and his son shook his head.

"And you," the King said to her in Nye. "Who are you?"

"My name is Jewel." They knew nothing about her people. They would not know who she was just from her name.

"Jewel. As in something precious? Or is that a translation?"

"*Jewel*," she said in Fey, and then translated it into Nye. "Jewel is my name in Fey. For a period our people named their children with real words in the L'Nacin custom."

"The conquered live on in the conquerors," the man the King had called Stephen said.

She did not answer. She didn't even look at him, but out of the corner of her eye she kept watch on the Black Robe. His grip on the bottle was so tight that his knuckles had turned white. She could feel behind her the tension in Silence's body.

"What are you going to do with me?" she asked.

"My son thought you were important enough to bring to me," the King said. He leaned against the table and put a foot on the bench. "Who are you, Jewel?"

The Prince hadn't taken his hands from her. She glanced at him sideways and found him watching her. Her heart thumped. Linked by Vision to a Prince she had never met. How strange to be in this place.

"I am merely a member of the Infantry."

"He says the others have placed some importance on you."

The Black Robe brought his bottle to his chest as if his movements depended on her answers.

She shrugged. "Our group leader was outside. I am second in command after her."

"No," the Prince said. "They treated you with more respect than that."

She snorted. "You are isolated here. You are judging my people's actions by your people's standards. You know nothing of our customs. Leaders of all stripes, even those born of the moment, receive respect."

"You could have killed me," the Prince said. "You did not."

"I was a fool," she said.

The Black Robe uncapped the bottle. He spoke to the King. Stephen bit his lower lip and stared at her. The King looked from the bottle to her.

"I think," Silence said in Nye—the first words he had spoken since they had entered the secret room, "that we should discover who she is before we use her as an experiment."

She stiffened. She couldn't help the response. She hadn't Seen her own death. Weren't Visionaries supposed to be able to do that? But she had Seen the Prince leaning over her, asking her if she was all right.

The Prince tightened his grip and pulled her closer. "What does that stuff do?" he asked the Black Robe.

The Black Robe answered in their language, and the Prince's face paled.

"We know nothing about these people," he said in Nye. He wanted her to understand, although she didn't know why. Perhaps so that she would know he was sparing her life again? "Killing her would accomplish nothing. But learning their customs from her would prepare us for the future."

The Black Robe spoke to the King. The King shook his head. Then he put an elbow on his knee and leaned toward her. "The Danite says that he isn't sure what a single drop would do. He suspects it won't kill you. He says a splash will most certainly kill you. He suggests that we torture you if you don't talk of your own free will."

"And he calls himself a man of God," Silence said.

Jewel took a step backward into Silence, warning him to protect himself. Fool. Couldn't he see that taunting them would get him nowhere, would only make them suspicious of him? They already knew the wrong things about Fey power. They might guess he was not the right man.

The Prince steadied her, then frowned.

The Black Robe spoke sharply to Silence. Silence responded in the same language. The Black Robe's face flushed.

She ignored them as best she could. She kept her gaze on the King. "You haven't discovered if I will speak of my own free will yet. Why do you talk of torture so early?"

The King studied her. He had lines on his face and gray streaked in his hair. Sadness. His entire bearing had an edge of sadness.

"You seem amazingly fearless for one who could die in an instant," the King said.

She stood straighter and shook herself free of the Prince's grasp. "I am a soldier," she said. "I have been trained to die all my life."

The King's face remained impassive, but Stephen's mouth opened slightly, as did the Black Robe's. A thrill ran down her back. They truly did know nothing of her people. She could speak to them of her own free will—lie to them—and help the Fey by placing the wrong kinds of fear in them. She would have to think on the proper way of doing it. She only hoped she would have enough time.

The King stared at her for a long moment; then he stood as if he couldn't contain his energy. He paced around the large room, passing the other men as if they weren't there, and then stopping in front of her.

He was shorter than his son by an inch or two. She found that she had to look down to meet his eyes. And in them, she saw the restlessness he had just displayed reflected, and then she understood why her taunt had reached him: he hated being trapped in this room while his people were dying below.

"What are you doing here?" His words were low and full of anger. He didn't mean her, but all of them, the Fey her father had brought.

She saw nothing wrong in telling him the truth. "The

Fey own half the world," she said. "Blue Isle happens to be one of its richest corners, and we want it for ourselves."

"We have done no harm to anyone. We trade freely with those who would trade with us. You had no reason to take us by force." He spit a bit as he spoke the sibilants. She felt the spray on her chin and neck but did not turn away.

"We do not trade with anyone," she said.

"But we would not have refused you!"

She stuck out her chin, made her posture firm so that he would understand she was speaking with authority as she restated, "We do not trade with anyone."

He tilted his head back and looked up at her. There were shadows beneath his eyes that could not have come from the day's battle. "All that death," he said slowly, "for something we would have given you."

"You would not have given it all to us."

The Prince let go of her. She felt the loss of his warmth. She relied on him, even though she didn't know him. He took a step to the side, closer to his father, where he could watch her face. Silence remained behind her, looking to them, perhaps, as if he were protecting the exit, when in fact he was guarding her back.

"Is there any way we can stop this bloodshed? Can we negotiate with you?"

"The Fey do not negotiate," she said, but she did not know if that was true. The Fey had never been in a situation like this one before.

"You are asking the wrong person," the Prince said, "if she is only an Infantry leader, as she claims."

"Who leads your force?" the King asked.

"Rugar," she said.

"Rugar? He is—"

"The leader." She was not willing to explain how military hierarchies were related to political hierarchies. It was clearly different here—something the Islanders would have to figure out on their own.

"How do I find him?" The King stayed close to her, as if his presence would force her into speaking the truth.

"For all I know," she said, keeping her tone level, "he could be dead. Our leaders fight."

Again, the insult. The King's face flushed, and the Black

Robe took a step closer. The King held out his hand, stopping the progression.

"It seems an odd battle plan," Stephen said from behind her. "How would there be direction if a leader died?"

He wanted to trap her into revealing the very thing she had decided to keep to herself. "We have our ways of knowing what needs to be done," she said. Let them take that implication as they would.

The Black Robe burst out in a torrent of words. The King replied with a firm tone, then added a comment to Stephen, who nodded.

"I thought you were going to cooperate with us," the King said.

"I am answering your questions."

"You are not saying anything of import."

"Then ask better questions."

The Prince said softly, as if he was trying to help her, "Have a caution. He is our King."

"He is not my King."

"Your insolence doesn't make things easier," Stephen said.

She shrugged. The movement was painful. Her arms had fallen asleep. "Then you will learn nothing at all."

The Black Robe took a step toward her, flinging water from the vial. Time slowed. Even though she backed out of the way, she didn't seem to be moving fast enough. The Prince pushed her, and she stumbled. She looked up to see that he had stopped the water with his own body.

Her heart was pounding furiously. Silence still held her arms as if he were trying to save her, when, in fact, she had become his shield.

"What was that?" she said to the Black Robe. "Are you so anxious to use your magick that you can't wait for orders from your King?"

The Prince peeled off his shirt, revealing a slender, muscular chest. He wiped the water from his face and flung the shirt into the corner. "I wouldn't provoke him any further."

"This man behind me said that man is a religious being. Is it your religious people that specialize in murder?" Jewel's terror made it impossible for her to be quiet. Silence's grip tightened on her shoulders. The Black Robe held up the vial of poison as if brandishing a sword.

"Get out," the Prince said to him.

The Black Robe looked at the King. The King spoke sharply in his native tongue. Black Robe responded, gesturing at Jewel. The King repeated a phrase twice before the Black Robe bowed once and left.

As the door opened, the guards outside peered in. The Black Robe pushed past them. Then the door slammed shut.

"Your customs are very strange," she said in Nye. Silence's grip on her was still tight. "Is such disobedience common?"

"This entire day has been uncommon," the King said. "And I would not be seeing you now if the Danite hadn't come to let me know that over most of the city your people are dying. Your invasion is failing."

Silence's fingers dug into her shoulders. She wanted to pull away but couldn't. She couldn't take their word for it, but since the arrival nothing had gone as planned. Still, they didn't know about Silence.

"If we are failing," she said, "then why do you need me?"

"Because," the King said, "I do not believe defeating the Fey could be so easy." He ran a hand through his thick hair. "Milord, take her to the dungeons and put a guard on her that you can trust. I don't want to come down there to discover another zealot has been there before me."

"I will go with her," the Prince said.

"No," the King said. "You will stay with me."

Jewel swallowed hard, unable to believe her luck. Would she and Silence get a chance to be alone? It would be almost too easy.

"Lord Powell doesn't know the guards," Stephen said. "I will accompany them and return within a few minutes. Besides, I want to see this defeat for myself."

"I can handle her," Silence said.

Stephen smiled. "You would probably abandon her at the first sign of trouble. Do I have your permission, Sire?"

The King nodded. He spoke to them briefly in their own language. Jewel wished her arms had not gone dead. Silence could knock the old man unconscious and free her; then she could rejoin the others. It would be simple.

She hoped.

THIRTY

THE sun was setting. The sky over the Cardidas was blood-red. Long shadows hid the Rocaan on his balcony. He felt empty, hollow. Below, bodies littered the courtyard like discarded waste. The stench was so thick, he could almost touch it. Rot and burned flesh. From forever forward he would recognize it as the smell of anguish.

Matthias was inside, supervising the last of the holy water they would make that day. Vials and vials of the water went out the doors on trays, as if every person on Blue Isle had come to Midnight Sacrament and needed a Blessing at the same time.

As far as the Rocaan could see, the fighting had stilled. Lights flickered in the harbor, but the ships were gone. He had been staring into the twilight so long, he thought he saw an occasional Fey disappear over the waters of the Cardidas. Perhaps he was watching souls take flight.

Ah, Holy One. The Rocaan leaned his head back. He could not believe that God would sanction such destruction.

The stench touched him, seeped into his own body. He would never wash it clean. If only the confusion hadn't been so great, if only he had been able to consult with

Elders other than Matthias. Matthias had never believed. Matthias used his brain to justify everything.

Matthias was terrified of the Fey.

The Rocaan's entire being ached—the joints in his hands and wrists and elbows, his shoulders and his back—all from the work he had engaged in during the afternoon.

He couldn't blame Matthias for all the destruction. Matthias, even though he had helped with the holy water, had not made the decision. The Rocaan had.

He had no idea how many were dead. He had counted almost a hundred bodies on the ground below him.

The lights flickered again over the harbor. Five Fey stood on the pier and then disappeared. The sounds of fighting were gone. Now the city was filled with the moans of the survivors. Oh, if he could only go back to the day before, when his greatest concerns had been his aging body and the unceasing rain. He had never believed that an entire world could disappear within the space of a day, but it had, and it had taken his life with it.

What crime would it be to take his body as well?

A man must live with his own actions. For it is on how he learns from his mistakes that he will be judged.

A man should not be allowed to make such dire mistakes in the twilight of his existence. Nothing in the Rocaan's life had prepared him for this. Nothing. It was a choice no sane God would allow: choose between killing hundreds of Fey and hundreds of Islanders. Of course the Rocaan would choose his own people.

But what if this was a test, a test like the one the Roca had faced just before his death? The story was as familiar as the pain the Rocaan felt when he woke every morning. The Roca, when asked to choose between leading his people into a battle they could not win, or slaughtering the Soldiers of the Enemy, decided instead to offer himself as a sacrifice.

The Words Written and Unwritten were clear on the sacrifice itself, on how the Roca died and was Absorbed into the Hand of God. But the Words were silent on the fate of the Roca's people, and on what became of the Soldiers of the Enemy.

Until this moment the Rocaan had always been caught in the ritual and ceremony surrounding the miracle. He had never thought of the human consequences. The canonical law did not say if the Roca was successful in finding a third alternative to the crisis facing his people. Instead, it focused on the fact that the Roca, holy being, had found a place before the Eternal Flame, cupped in God's hand, able to do God's bidding from that moment forward.

But what was God's bidding? And how was a Rocaan, the Roca's emissary to the world, able to know?

"You need a lamp."

Matthias's voice made the Rocaan start.

"I prefer the darkness," the Rocaan said. "It hides the truth of the day."

Matthias stepped onto the balcony, the open door leaving a triangle of light on the floor. His blond hair was mussed, his face drawn. "At least we survived," he said.

"But at what cost?" the Rocaan asked. He stretched out his legs in front of him, feeling the strain of the overworked muscles.

Matthias sank into the chair beside the Rocaan. For a moment the odor of Matthias's nervous sweat overpowered the stench of death. "We had no choice, Holy Sir."

"We did not think of other choices," the Rocaan said. "We followed blindly the path laid before us. Perhaps I should have given myself to them, as the Roca did so many generations ago."

"And then what?" Matthias said. "They would have slaughtered you, and no one would have been able to save us."

"I am not a savior," the Rocaan said. "I am a purveyor of destruction." He stood, ignoring the shooting pains in his back and feet, walked to the edge of the balcony, and leaned on the railing. The lights continued to flicker in the harbor.

"The Roca knew he was Beloved of God," Matthias said.

"The Rocaan is also supposed to be Beloved," the Rocaan said. The wood was still damp beneath his arms. "And you forget that there were people involved in that story, too, and Soldiers of the Enemy. You are a great scholar, Matthias. What became of the people the Roca swore to defend? What became of the enemy?"

" 'The enemy is always with us, within ourselves.' "

"I can quote the Words Written and Unwritten. They say nothing on these points. What of the history?"

"The history?" Matthias sounded confused.

The lights continued, nearly a dozen of them, circling the same point. "Yes. We study the Roca. We believe he was a man. We use the Words as a guide, but we know nothing of the human truth." The Rocaan gripped the wet wood. "It did not matter until now. I had never even thought of it until this moment."

"There is historical precedent for what we did today," Matthias said. "The Forty-fifth Rocaan, the Twenty-third—"

"May all have missed what the Holy One was trying to tell them. Perhaps it is the duty of a Rocaan to sacrifice himself for his people every few generations. Perhaps it is a test of faith, of the religion itself. Perhaps, in failing to do our duty, we have destroyed the very foundation of our belief."

The chair creaked behind him as Matthias stood. He came to the railing and stood beside the Rocaan. Matthias's height prevented him from leaning on the railing. He put his hands behind his back and stared over the carnage to the river. "You speak of things we cannot know," he said softly. "The Fey would have killed you. That much is certain."

"And perhaps I was to be Absorbed into the Hand of God. Perhaps that is the duty of the Rocaan. Not leadership in this world, but in the next."

"There is nothing about that in the Words Written and Unwritten."

"The Words are full of such admonitions," the Rocaan said, "about the Roca himself. Tell me, Matthias. Who are the Soldiers of the Enemy? We do not know. Such a general name. Perhaps they were Cemeni and the other leaders of the Peasant Uprising. Perhaps the Forty-fifth Rocaan failed to follow the model set by the Roca. Perhaps we have new Soldiers of the Enemy here now, and perhaps I have failed."

"I think God never makes easy choices," Matthias said.

"And I think that is an easy answer for a complex problem." The Rocaan let exhaustion fill him. "I cannot stand more of this day. I am going to my chambers."

"Wait." Matthias put a hand on the Rocaan's shoulder. "What are those lights?"

"They have been flickering all evening."

"I thought I just saw someone disappear into them."

The Rocaan patted Matthias's hand. "I think they are Fey souls meeting their own version of God."

"Or a new style of Fey magick that we are unfamiliar with. What happened to the ships, Holy Sir? Ships like that do not disappear from our harbors, and yet our people couldn't trace them."

The Rocaan felt an odd chill mixed with an even odder hope. If the Fey weren't dead, then he had another chance to serve his own God. He looked at the dark courtyard below, as if he could see the bodies rising whole and strong. "What do you think it is?" he whispered.

Matthias shook his head. "I do not know," he said. "But I promise you an answer by morning."

THIRTY-ONE

THE Shadowlands leached the ships of color. Rugar stood on the deck of the *Feire,* watching as more and more of his people staggered into the Shadowlands, bloody, beaten, and terrified. In all of their history the Fey had never encountered someone with more power than they had.

His clothes smelled of mud and the odd rot that had set in on the bodies near the port. Since he'd entered, he had made the entrance circle near the dock wider and ringed it with newly made Fey Lamps. He had one Foot Soldier outside, changing the lamps as their powers faded. Already a hundred Fey had entered the Shadowlands. He wanted to make sure all the other survivors did too.

He had not seen Jewel, even though he searched for her. He hoped she had gone to her quarters on the *Eccrasia,* but he had not yet had a chance to search.

"Sir, another!" a Weather Sprite called to him from her position near the prow of the ship. He stiffened. This Shadowlands had been a creation of haste and confidence, meant to house ships and perhaps fifty of the invading force. The strain on his creation was showing. Corners were breaking, sending bits of light and glimpses of the ships to anyone who was observing. He was glad for the dark. Otherwise, the Islanders would find them.

He tugged at his caked clothing, wishing for a moment— just one moment—to search out his missing daughter and to bathe himself. But he was the only one who could repair the Shadowlands. He crossed the deck, his footsteps echoing in the hollow nothingness that made up the Shadowlands. Soldiers, unwilling to go into the darkness belowdecks, crouched against the railings, leaning against each other for comfort. He nodded to them, trying to reassure them, faking a confidence he didn't feel.

This failure had caught him off guard. He had prepared himself for a quick battle, and a quick victory. Another mistake. If he had known that the invasion would become a long, drawn-out series of attacks, he would have slept more. He would have prepared himself for the strain on his own resources.

As it were, he would have to work with the Spell Warders on finding a counterspell to the Islanders' magick poison. He would also have to keep repairing the Shadowlands while his scouts looked for a new opening. Then he would have to create another Shadowlands, a firmer one that would withstand the presence of his entire fighting force. No one had built a Shadowlands like that since the Black Queen at the battle of Ycyno two centuries before. He only hoped he had the strength.

The Weather Sprite stood near the railing at the edge of the prow. He pointed to the hole in the Shadowlands, but he didn't need to. The sound of water lapping against the dock was clear, as was the cool breeze, filled with the scent of death. He peered at it and saw that it faced the far side of the river, near the ghastly palacelike religious building where the destruction had started.

"Thank you," he said. "I can tend to it now."

But he stood for a moment, gazing through the hole at the crispness and clarity of the real world. He didn't relish living in a Shadowlands, not even for a few days. Its grayness was depressing; it dampened the spirits instead of raising them.

Then he reached up and gripped the soft edges of the Shadow with his fingers. He closed his eyes and, with his Vision, closed the hole, made a seam, and willed the seam away. When he opened his eyes again, the hole was gone. Only grayness faced him. A never-ending grayness.

And silence. That disturbed him the most. None of the soldiers talked as they returned. They found a place to collapse and remained there, nearly motionless.

The Fey had lost battles before, but this was different. In the past the enemy had had greater numbers—as this one did—but those numbers had been trained. The enemy had also had more advanced weapons. The advantages had always been in the physical world, not in the magickal one. The Fey had been seduced into thinking they were the only ones who had conquered that realm. The shock of discovering the truth, and the horridness of the deaths visited on them, affected him profoundly—yet he was the one who had to revive their spirits.

He hurried along the deck until he reached the connecting bridge built especially to link ships hidden in Shadowlands. Nothing natural occurred in the Shadowlands—no water, no ground, nothing except air that a Visionary poured into the hiding place. The walls of the Shadowlands were porous, an invention of an early Black King, and allowed the air to filter through. Nothing else did filter through, not even sound, which made the Shadowlands dangerous to leave.

Since this was a simple Shadowlands, the walls were tight and spare. As he crossed the bridge, Rugar could feel the damp coldness brushing against him. The next Shadowlands he built—the one built for a longer fight—would not have this design flaw.

He crossed quickly and stepped onto the bridge of the flagship, the *Eccrasia*. Here the soldiers conversed in low voices. He heard only snatches:

". . . black robes . . ."

". . . never would have believed that something so ungainly . . ."

". . . on horses . . ."

". . . entire room full of bodies . . ."

". . . no faces . . ."

". . . most still alive . . ."

He had seen the destruction himself. The thought of identifying the dead filled him with a different anguish. And he couldn't get his father's words out of his head.

No one has conquered Blue Isle before.

And his own cocky response: *No one has tried.*

But he had checked only Fey and Nye records. Perhaps Blue Isle had been attacked from Leut, even though it was farther away. He had thought Leut had no real history of trade or warfare this far north from its land mass, but he had not checked. Perhaps all that he had known about Blue Isle was wrong. It certainly seemed that way after this morning.

On the way to his own cabin, he stopped at Jewel's and knocked. The portal was dim, and he heard nothing inside. "Jewel," he said softly.

No one answered.

When he came back from his cabin, he would open the door and see if she was resting inside. But he doubted it. She was always at his side during a crisis.

He put his hand against the door and leaned his forehead against his knuckles. If she was dead, he would never forgive himself. Jewel, the brightest of all his children. But he had seen her, walking through the Islander palace as if she owned it.

She couldn't die.

He would have known.

He tried the door. It opened easily, and he stepped into the darkness. He lit the lantern she had stored in the traditional place beside the door, finding it odd that the thing did not sway as it would have if the ship had been resting in water.

The cabin was small—and empty. The cot still bore the indentation of Jewel's body, and a nightdress lay across the mattress as if she had expected to use it later.

He sat on the edge of the cot. She could be a hundred places—with the wounded in the hold of the *Feire* or working with the Warders herself. She might even still be outside, helping the rest of the stragglers to Shadowlands.

Next time—next time after a campaign—he would ask her to come to him first so that he wouldn't worry about her, so that he could fight with a clear mind. This was the reason the Black King's advisers had suggested that family members not fight in the same unit. But no one had listened because Fey tradition called for family to remain together.

It was not like him to worry like this.

Perhaps this rout was just a test, and a reminder of his

own arrogance. The Black King's son, the best commander in the entire Fey military, suffering a defeat at the hands of nonwarriors. Far enough away, though, that the majority of the Fey people, and his own children (except for Jewel), would not need to know of it if he turned this victory around.

He picked up the nightdress and clutched it in his hands. The cotton fabric came from the base of the Eccrasian Mountains. It was rare and expensive. It was also warm, not from the fabric itself, but from the dream spell woven into it. Jewel loved the nightdress and had worn it for a year. She had had it made, she said, especially because she had no special magick.

"Rugar?" The voice was soft, and male.

Rugar looked up slowly, unwilling to be caught in this moment of vulnerability. A young Fey stood in front of him. He was slender and tall, and wearing the tunic of the Infantry. His left sleeve was ripped, and his arm hung free and useless. A stained bandage was tied just above his elbow.

He took a step into the light. His face was smeared with blood, not like a Red Cap's, but like a man who had been spattered in battle.

"I'm sorry," Rugar said. "I can't place you."

"Burden." The boy's name seemed to weigh him with even more sadness.

A friend of Jewel's. One who had served with her and had cast an interested male eye at her. The one Rugar had hoped she would pursue first, before she decided on her mate, thinking an Infantryman would be good training for the life ahead. A chill ran down Rugar's spine. He twisted the nightdress around his fingers.

"Were you looking for Jewel?"

Burden shook his head. "I was looking for you."

The fabric wound around Rugar's thumb and forefinger, trapping them. He clenched his fists around the material and pulled it to his chest, as if it could protect him from anything Burden might say.

"You were serving with Jewel." It was not a question. He remembered that much of Jewel's unit.

"Under Shima." The boy clutched his bad arm with his good. "Shima is dead."

"I pray she died as a warrior."

"She died telling us to retreat." Burden's words were clipped. There was anger behind them. "Then the poison hit her. I saw her after. It took her a long time to die."

Rugar untangled his fingers from the nightdress. He should stand and take control of this conversation from a lowly boy who had no powers at all, but he could not. He heard the blame and felt it was deserved. Shima had warned him she would die on this mission. She had said he was making a mistake.

"And Jewel?"

"Jewel led us into the palace." The boy leaned against the door frame. He was pale from blood loss.

"Is she dead?" Rugar asked.

"I don't know," the boy said.

"You didn't stay with her?" Rugar stood, finding a direction for his anger, a direction away from himself.

"I nearly died defending her." The boy pushed away from the door frame, rising to his full height. He was standing up to the next ruler of the Fey and knew it, but that did not deter him. His anger was that great.

Rugar recognized the emotion. He had seen it on hundreds of battlefields. "Then what happened?"

"They captured her."

"Captured?" Rugar stumbled over the word. "They took prisoners?" He had heard nothing about it. It seemed a sophisticated thing for nonwarriors to do.

"They took a prisoner. Only one."

The most precious one. Jewel. Rugar sat back down. The cot was hard against his buttocks. All the aches rose to the surface, along with a panic he had never felt before. "How did they know who she was?"

"She seemed to know the man who captured her. She spoke to him in Nye and spared his life."

"She spared his life?" None of this was making any sense. Jewel, acting contrary to orders. Jewel, who understood better than most the necessity for rules on the battlefield. "And she allowed him to take her? *You* allowed him to take her?"

"The Black Robes came into the place, and she told us to retreat. I tried to get to her, but the man hustled her away." Burden was swaying ever so slightly. If he did not get care, he would collapse there from the lack.

"You need to tend to yourself, son," Rugar said, his voice

tender. This boy, this Burden, had tried to save Jewel. That in itself should count for something. "I am grateful that you came to me."

"We need to get her back."

"Yes," Rugar said. "We do."

Burden stared at him for a moment, then touched his good hand to his forehead and backed out of the light. His footsteps, uneven but firm, echoed as he made his way along the deck.

Rugar gripped the edge of the bed. They had Jewel. And their poison. They could torture her. They could kill her and lie to him about her death. Somehow they had known the quickest way to defeating Rugar's spirit.

They had captured his heart.

THIRTY-TWO

ALEXANDER leaned against the closed door. He was shaking. The girl had had an odd beauty, with those upswept brows, high cheekbones, and dark eyes. Her height had been imposing, and she had known how to use it.

I am a soldier. I have been trained to die all my life.

But Alexander hadn't, and her closeness had unnerved him. The War Room seemed empty without her.

"She's stunning, isn't she?" Nicholas said.

Alexander brought his head up. His son was standing in front of the table. He was covered with blood, and his hair had fallen out of its ponytail. Yet he stood with his right foot on the bench and his right arm resting on his thigh. So casual, so comfortable, for one who had come so close to death.

"She is our enemy."

Nicholas shrugged. "Better to have a magnificent enemy than one we are ashamed of."

Like the bunch of peasants King Constantine had defeated. The words fell unspoken between them.

Alexander pushed away from the door. He had thought the blood and terror of the day would have cured Nicholas's romanticism. Instead the girl seemed to add fire to it.

He walked over to his son and put his hand on Nicholas's shoulder. Flecks of blood dotted his cheek and neck. Nicholas looked up at him, and finally Alexander saw the boy hidden inside the man's frame.

"You could have died," Alexander said.

Nicholas shook his head. "I was fine."

"I would not have been able to bear it if you had died."

Nicholas smiled awkwardly at his father. "You mean the Kingdom could not bear it if I died."

Alexander shook his head. His hand was now covered with blood. "No," he said softly. "I could not bear it."

Almost two decades ago Alexander had held Nicholas the night the boy was born. Only then Nicholas had been so tiny that Alexander's hand covered the boy's back and bottom. The baby had been fragile against Alexander's shoulder, his tiny head soft and wobbly. For those first few years Alexander had gone into the boy's room and watched him sleep, marveling at the tiny miracle he had helped create. His wife had never known of Alexander's nocturnal roamings—she had asked him to leave her bed when she was swollen with Nicholas, and she had made it clear that he did not need to return unless something happened to the boy. His second wife had never given him children, and this overgrown child, still fragile in his flesh-and-blood shell, was all the future Alexander had.

Alexander sighed and wiped his hand on his pants. More than anything he wanted out of that room. But not yet, not until his advisers told him all was safe. "You should have stayed here with me," he said.

"But, Father, they were fighting below."

Alexander nodded. "And dying."

"My place was with them."

"No," Alexander said. The girl's words still echoed in his head. *Our leaders fight.* "We don't fight. I don't know what their system is, but ours relies on you and me as thinkers, as leaders, and as figureheads. If you died, it would demoralize Blue Isle. And that would be the last thing we need."

Nicholas snorted. "You don't think they would fight for their homes?"

"We are part of their home." Alexander patted a spot beside him. "Sit, Nicky."

The childhood name. Nicholas looked at the place Alexander indicated, but did not move.

"Nicholas," Alexander said, "you are tired. Don't let pride get in the way of allowing your body to rest."

Nicholas smiled—a small, fleeting grin of acknowledgment—and then sat beside his father.

The blood had stained Nicholas's skin. The boy was slender and more muscled than Alexander had ever been. The sword practice with Stephen had given him strength.

Alexander sighed. He had to get through to Nicholas, because if he did not, he might lose the only thing he truly valued. "I know," he said, "that you need to be different from me. I am more of a scholar. I prefer talks with Matthias to exercise. I prefer examining Kingdom reports over riding a horse. What you don't see yet, Nicky, is that you *are* different. You are stronger and smarter, and you have your own concerns. If you would just finish the last bit of your education, I would be able to use you as an adviser."

"I don't see why books are important—" Nicholas started, but Alexander raised his hand for silence.

"I need you now, Nicky," Alexander said. "I need you to understand what it means to be King and to stand by my side. We know little about these creatures that have invaded us, and what we do know could be wrong. Even touching that girl could have got you killed. Just breathing the same air—"

"She wouldn't hurt me."

This time Nicholas's words stopped Alexander. He ran a hand through his hair. He, too, had seen the girl's odd attractiveness but knew it for what it was—a temptation. Nicholas was young and at the age when anything female attracted his attention. Alexander almost said so, then didn't. He had to keep his son on his side.

"What makes you say that?" he asked.

Nicholas flushed. He looked down at his hands. Alexander looked too. They were nicked and bloodstained. A long cut still oozed on the back of his left palm.

"I say that because she had me," Nicholas said.

Alexander grabbed Nicholas's hand and pulled it away from the scab. "What do you mean, 'had you'?"

Nicholas stared at their joined hands until Alexander let go. "I was fighting on the steps leading out of the kitchen.

"I had found a place on the first landing that protected my back and gave me a good brace, as Stephen had told me to do, but I must have moved, because the next thing I knew, someone hit me, and I toppled down the stairs."

Alexander resisted the urge to close his eyes. He kept his breathing even. Nicholas's story was not reassuring him. The more he heard, the more he wanted his son out of the fighting.

"I landed next to this dead body"—Nicholas shuddered—"and when I looked up, she was there, with a sword at my throat."

One quick movement this afternoon and his son would have been dead.

"She didn't kill me, Dad. She didn't even try. It was almost as if she knew me."

Alexander's body was covered with a fine layer of sweat that hadn't been there a moment before. He gripped his knees to keep his hands from shaking. "She probably knew who you were."

"No," Nicholas said. "She was surprised when the staff volunteered to protect me."

By the Holy One. Alexander felt the sweat roll down his back. The boy tossed off details as if he were talking about a riding trip outside the city.

"She even asked me who I was. I wouldn't tell her. But she knew me, Dad. And even though her people wanted to kill me, she wouldn't let them."

"Then you got the upper hand?"

"There was an opening," Nicholas said. "I took advantage of it."

His son must have felt Alexander's nervousness, because he was no longer elaborating. Alexander didn't want him to. Nicholas was safe. That was all that mattered. That, and the fact that Nicholas would never get into the same situation again.

"You have no idea," Alexander said slowly, "what she might have done to you. She might have been enchanting you. Maybe they wanted someone to infiltrate us. Maybe this is part of a plan."

Nicholas shook his head. "She seemed surprised when she realized she was captured."

Alexander sighed. They would argue about this forever.

"No matter what you think of the girl, you need to be at my side from now on. Think, son. What would have happened if you had died at her feet? How would those servants have felt? Would they have kept fighting?"

Nicholas's flush grew deeper. He knew the answer as well as Alexander did.

"I know you have wanted something to test you your entire life." Alexander put his hand on the boy's naked back, surprised at the clamminess of Nicholas's skin. Nicholas, despite his bravado, had been under a great strain. Alexander softened his tone. "Well, you had that test, and you met it with courage that hasn't been seen since your great-great-grandfather. Our people will discuss your exploits for years. That's all we needed. They know now that we will sacrifice everything for Blue Isle."

Alexander took off his own shirt and put it around Nicholas. "But we can't sacrifice everything, because if we do, we lose the only strengths we have. Do you think it was easy for me to hear that girl's taunts? I would like to be fighting out there too." He stood, unable to sit still with what he was saying. "Even through these walls I can hear the sounds of the dying. And I would like to be out there, saving just one life—"

"Yes, Dad, that's it," Nicholas said, clutching the shirt around him.

"—but I forget that by the correct actions in here, I can save more than one life. I can save hundreds of lives. I can save Blue Isle." Alexander put his hands behind his back, considering his words before saying them. "Nicky, we are lucky to have the holy water. Lucky to be able to drive the Fey away. Lucky that girl was so frightened of the Danites that she came with you. Nye fought for years and lost an entire generation of young men against the Fey. Did you know that? And now the Fey own the country. You heard her. She said, 'You would not have given it all to us,' and she is right. We would not have. We are still a people, still a country. We still make our own choices. You heard her, Nicky. She speaks fluent Nye, but Nye is a dead language because the country it represents is now part of the Fey's Empire. We are small, but we are sovereign, and I mean to stay that way."

Nicholas slipped his arms through the shirt. He was

cringing just a little, as if the strain of the day was finally getting to him. "How do you plan to do that, Father?"

Alexander shook his head. "I don't know. The Fey have practiced warfare since the Roca was Absorbed. We have never fought. We have only traded. It is as if the Roca had given us the holy water all those generations ago to protect us from this very threat."

"Faith, Father?" Nicholas said. "You were never religious before."

"Then how do you explain it?" Alexander said. "The Fey came here with a strong fighting force, enough warriors to take over the city before night fell. We have no experience, no real knowledge of what to do, and yet we have held them off. Call it luck, call it fate, or call it God's will, but we have survived. And I mean to continue."

Nicholas leaned back. His face was drawn with exhaustion, the shadows under his eyes so deep that his eyes looked sunken.

"I need your help, Nicky," Alexander said. "We need to make these decisions together. We need to learn together. Because they will come after us. The Fey are smart. They know the value of leadership, and they will destroy what they can."

"But you said we won this time."

"The battle," Alexander said. "We won't have won the war until the invasion force is dead."

"Or sent packing back to Nye."

"No," Alexander said. "If they go to Nye, they will try again. We have to prevent them from leaving here if it is the last thing we do."

THIRTY-THREE

JEWEL held a torch in her left hand. Her wrists still burned from the pressure of the ropes. She leaned against the exit, the stairs behind her, her breath coming in quick gasps.

For the moment she was safe. The enclosed landing provided a measure of security that would disappear in a matter of seconds. The King's people had to have heard the screaming. It still echoed in her ears. She had glanced over her shoulder only once, hoping Silence was behind her, but he wasn't. It was a vain hope anyway. According to his training, her life was the important one.

She had to get out of the palace alive. Then she had to make it back to the Shadowlands. Silence had managed to tell her while Stephen was getting a torch that the Fey should meet in Shadowlands.

Those were the last words the two of them had spoken to each other.

She pushed the door open and peered through the crack. The hallway was littered with bodies. Fey bodies, hideously deformed. She looked away. She had come so close to dying this day. Only the Prince had saved her with his quick movement. Otherwise she, too, would be lying disfigured on an Islander floor.

If they saw her, they would kill her.

The hallway was dark except for the thin light of a single torch stuck into the wall. She could see no one except the bodies. Broken furniture was scattered around them, and the floor was wet. She hoped the magic woven into her boots to protect them from rain would protect them from this false water as well.

She pushed the door open the rest of the way. The stench of rotting flesh made her want to gag. She bit her lower lip and stepped out, into the wetness. The water beaded on her boots, and she let out a small sigh. Then she crouched beside the bodies, avoiding their twisted faces, looking for their weapons.

The weapons had been taken.

The Islanders weren't completely ignorant about war.

She didn't recognize this hallway. Silence and Stephen had been taking her to the dungeons when Silence had slit her ropes, shoved the torch into her hand, and told her to run.

And she had, the Powers forgive her. She hadn't even waited to see if Silence got his advantage. She knew the drill: a Doppelgänger was supposed to defend the Black King's family with his life. But that didn't make it easy the first time. She had never needed a real defense before.

Footsteps echoed down the hallway. She stood and ran across the floor for the stairs. More bodies were sprawled along it, most of them Fey. A few were slaughtered Islanders. They were blood covered, but their bodies were still intact. No Foot Soldiers had made it into the palace, no Red Caps had followed. At least, not obviously.

All the carnage. She hoped her father had returned to Shadowlands. She would have no way of telling if he was among the dead.

She hurried down the steps, rounded the corner, and found herself in a Great Hall. More bodies littered the passageway, most of these Islanders. The Fey had made it far before the poison carriers had found them. Her father had been right: if the Islanders hadn't produced this secret potion, the Fey would have owned Blue Isle by now.

Whoever had been coming down the hall had not followed her. She stopped next to one of the Islander bodies. This one was slender and male. It also wore a pale-tan robe which, if she could remove it, might give her just enough cover to make it back to the docks.

Silence had kept his stiletto, and she saw no other weapons on the ground. At least this floor was dry. She wouldn't have attempted touching anything on the floor above with her bare hands.

The man's throat had been cut. The neck and shoulders of the robe were crusty with blood. She untied the string around the collar, then discovered that the string was merely ornamental. She would have to lift the robe off the man. A dirty job, fit for a Red Cap. But she had no choice.

She stood and placed the torch in a holder on the wall. Then she went back to the body. She pushed the edges of the robe until it gathered around the body's waist; then she lifted the legs and pushed the back as well. Her breath was coming hard, so hard she was afraid anyone passing would hear her.

The thought made her move quickly. She set the legs down as quietly as she could; then she pulled the torso up by its arms. Its skin was barely warm and clammy. It felt dead. The thought sent a shudder through her. She put one hand behind the back, and with the other yanked the robe upward. This Islander wore nothing under his robe, and she averted her eyes from its pale, withered flesh. The robe caught on the back of the skull, and she had to work it free before pulling it all the way off.

Then she slipped the robe over her own head, wincing at the strong, fetid odor of blood. The robe had a hood, also blood encrusted, but which might prove useful as she made her way through the streets.

She was taller than the dead man. The robe came only to the middle of her calves, revealing her delicate boots. The Islanders did not have boots like hers—at least, not any she had observed. For a moment she paused, looking at the man's feet, but his shoes were made of a thin leather, obviously untreated. She would risk being seen before she would risk placing her feet in that unreal water.

Voices echoed from the floor above. They were speaking Islander, its odd, flowing tones almost familiar to her now. She grabbed her torch out of its peg and, stepping over bodies, followed the trail down the Great Hall.

The windows were filled with glass—an expensive thing,

but then, Blue Isle was known for its riches. In the courtyard she saw movement: Islanders collecting weapons off the dead Fey. She followed the hall into the pantry, wincing at the stench of rotted bodies. These comrades she knew. She refused to look at them. The hearth fire still burned, and some of the smell came from there. Part of a corpse lay on the flagstones, partially burned. Someone had pulled it from the hearth fire.

She stepped around it, past the brick ovens, which were now cool, and through the open door. Moaning came from one corner of the courtyard. With her free hand she pulled up the robe's hood. A young Islander boy sat near the closed stable doors, his arms wrapped around the body of a dead man. The boy was sobbing.

A woman saw Jewel and called out in Islander. Jewel shook her head, hoping the movement was universal and kept walking. The woman followed. Jewel ducked her head deeper into her hood and resisted the urge to run. If the woman stopped her, she would see that Jewel was Fey. If the woman had that poison, then Jewel was doomed.

She stepped over more bodies and pushed through the destroyed gate. The woman called out one more time, but Jewel shook her head again, wishing for only a few phrases of Islander besides the one her Vision and the Prince had taught her. *Are you all right?* would start a conversation, not prevent one.

Jewel hurried down the street. That morning the street had been so full of promise. Now it was littered with the disfigured bodies of her friends. She gave the palace one last glance. Silence was still in there, fighting for his life, or perhaps even dead.

Because of her.

And Burden, and Shima, and the others. She didn't know how many of her friends lay at her feet. How many could she have helped if she hadn't allowed that Islander boy to take her away?

The streets were eerily quiet. She seemed to be one of the few people moving about. The Islanders were probably hiding, holding their silly water weapons and figuring a way to destroy the Fey. The only Fey she saw were dead.

Dead.

She picked her way over body after body, the stench a

live thing in her nostrils. Now that she was away from the palace, she knew she would make it to Shadowlands. No one was out to stop her. And once inside Shadowlands, she would find her father. If she couldn't find him, she would take over.

She would make certain the Warders found a counter-spell against the poison.

Then she would make these Islanders pay.

THIRTY-FOUR

THE torch was warm in Matthias's hand. He held it out in front of him, using the other hand for balance. He kept close to the wall as he made his way down the stairs. No one had lit the torches on the lower levels of the Tabernacle, and the darkness unnerved him. The bodies were gray lumps; the overturned tables and chairs provided a maze that he had to step gingerly through. A faint odor of burned flesh lingered in the stairwell. The floors were sticky, and he didn't want to think about what he was walking in—or on.

His throat was dry. As the stairs leveled out onto the first floor, he repressed the urge to run to the door. So many dead in this holy place. It offended sensibilities he didn't think he had. The bodies, contorted and gray, also brought superstitions he thought he was clear of to the surface. He had never believed the dead could walk until now: until he saw motionless limbs seem to move under the torch's shadows, sightless eyes reflecting firelight, mouths open as if to speak. Perhaps, if he pinched himself hard enough, the nightmare would end and morning would come.

He put his hand down to his side as he left the protection of the stairs. Only a few more feet and he would be outside. The closeness of the bodies there made the hair on the back of his neck rise. He tripped on a chair leg and nearly dropped the torch. For a moment he wrestled with holding the torch or catching himself. An image of his body falling with all the others made him gasp in panic. Finally he reached out and grabbed a hunk of clothing, catching his balance. When he realized what he had done, he bit back a scream.

The smell of the dead was almost more than he could bear. When he got back, he would have to order some of the remaining Auds to begin cleanup. But before that he would have to figure out what to do with the bodies. They couldn't just go into the Cardidas.

He stood slowly, his grip on the torch so tight that his hand ached. When he had volunteered to go to the docks, he hadn't thought it through. All the dead. All the reminders of the horrors of the day.

Finally he reached the doors. They were propped open by fallen bodies, but someone had cleared a pathway between them. As he stepped into the moonlit grounds, he let out a breath of relief. He felt safer without the walls of the Tabernacle around him.

The bodies were scattered there, not bunched together as they had been inside. The light from the moon augmented the light from his torch, and stars twinkled in the sky. If he looked up, the world was the same world he had grown up in. He could almost hear the sounds of the city at night: the street women calling, the occasional drunken fight. But those sounds were absent now. An odd quiet had fallen on Jahn. Except for splashes near the river, and the lapping of the water against the shore, the city was silent.

The breeze off the river had a slight, damp chill. Matthias brushed a strand of hair off his forehead. The exhaustion he had felt earlier had left him. It surprised him to note that his body, so bitterly overused this day, had reserves of strength within it.

He brought his torch down to his side, wondering if it made him obvious. Probably, and he didn't know who or what was marauding this night. He turned and pulled the unlit torch from beside the door, letting the stick fall to the ground, and stuck his own torch into the slot. The flame reflected off the open doors. As the breeze moved it, the light occasionally revealed the interior of the Tabernacle.

Matthias shuddered. He didn't want to go inside again.

He wiped his hands on his already filthy robe and picked his way across the inlay tiles, keeping to the small paths left between the fallen bodies. This tile had been one of his favorites, depicting the Second Rocaan carrying the Words Written to worshipers outside of Jahn. The joy on the Rocaan's face as he gazed at the Words reflected Matthias's own joy when he studied. Now he wondered if he would ever be able to look at the tiles in the same way again.

Small losses. He could focus on the small losses without thinking of the larger ones. The larger ones would make him crazy.

The walls surrounding the Tabernacle grounds prevented him from seeing the Cardidas. For a second he thought he heard voices carrying over the water. He held his breath and listened as intently as he could, but he couldn't tell if he was hearing actual words.

Little shivers ran up his back. The whisper of the river sounded like the whisper of the dead. He gripped the tiny sword around his neck and ran his fingers over its dull edge. If he ever needed to believe in God, in Roca, it was this day. *The belief of cowards*, the Words Written and Unwritten said, *is assured*.

He did not like to think of himself that way. But before now he had never known the truth behind that aphorism.

He should have sent an Aud to do this. Someone expendable. But he didn't know the Auds well enough to choose one who wouldn't embellish his tale, and he didn't know how many were still alive. The Rocaan wanted the lights investigated, and Matthias had promised he would do so. He couldn't go back on his word now.

Young trees stood near the gate, their leaves rustling in the breeze. Matthias let go of the tiny sword and pushed the gate open, thanking the Holy One that someone had had the presence of mind to close it, at least. Except for the occasional body, the road was clear. The mud was rutted from wagon wheels and horses' hooves, and hundreds of footprints. It seeped under the wood of his sandals, soiling the bottom of his feet. The cold ooze squished between his toes, and he closed his eyes, willing impressions from the day—the melting faces of the Fey, the blood spilling across pristine floors—away from the sensation.

He had a clear view of the river from there. The lights continued to flicker at irregular intervals, almost like a door opening and closing. Voices rose again from the river, speaking in a language he did not understand.

He crept as silently as he could along the edge of the road, wincing whenever his feet squished in the muck. If only he had more information about the Fey. Could they become invisible? Were they around him now? He resisted the urge to put his hands out in front of him like a blind man, to push away unseen forces.

The only voices he heard came from the river. And the ships were gone. Perhaps they made the ships invisible. But if they had done that, then he would still be able to hear the water lapping against the wooden hulls, and he did not. Only the voices, low and conspiratorial, and the odd lights.

When he reached the bridge, he paused. He could either go back for holy water and then cross the bridge to see what was going on, or slide down the bank and get as close as he could on this side of the river.

If he needed to risk a life, he could send an Aud. The Rocaan needed Matthias. He clearly did not want Matthias dead. If he had wanted that, he would not have shown Matthias how to make the holy water, a process as startling as any Matthias had seen within the Church.

He clung to the wood railing that led up the footpath side of the bridge. The river was almost a mile across, not counting the harbor's mouth on the other side. In the daylight, things would look far away. At night they had an even eerier cast.

Still, he would follow his plan. He took the muddy footpath down the side of the bridge to the water's edge. He had to keep one hand against the wet ground for balance. Weeds grew tall there, brushing against the sides of his robe, tickling his bare arms. He rustled as he moved, a sound he feared would carry over the water. Finally he crouched beneath a tree that had grown crossways over the river, providing welcome shade in the daylight, and the illusion of cover now.

The voices on the other side had stilled. One light appeared and disappeared over the wide dock that led into the warehouses. The ships had originally been moored there. He sat, breathing quietly, waiting for his eyes to adjust to the moonlight over the river, and the odd darkness that he was in.

After some time—he wasn't sure how much, but long enough for his body to stiffen—he thought he saw tiny lights flickering in a small, perfect circle. Even though he couldn't judge exactly, based on the distance, the circle could have been no bigger than his head. It floated above the pier like a tiny beacon.

Slowly he shifted position, careful not to make any noise. He brought his knees up to his chest and wrapped his arms around them. The larger lights disappeared as he rustled his way to this position. He hoped that the Fey hadn't heard him, that they weren't around him now. Invisible presences had been hard for him to grasp in his religious studies, but there, faced with a magickal enemy, he had no trouble at all. He didn't move again for a while, trying to be another body in the darkness.

When he was about to give up, he heard footsteps and voices carry across the water. He squinted as if that would make his vision penetrate the darkness. Four figures moved on the pier—no, five. One of them had an arm around another, who appeared to be having trouble walking.

They were tall, all of them taller than he was, and rail thin. Not Islanders. Islanders were stocky and short. They had thought him demon-spawn when he was a boy because he shot up so quickly and so high in his fifteenth year. He caught his breath and watched.

The Fey moved into a single-file line. The figure in the front paused and gestured at the ones behind. A voice carried across the water, deep and low, speaking again in that guttural language Matthias did not understand. Then the first put his hand through the small circle of lights.

The light grew until it covered the dock. Now Matthias could see the remaining four more clearly. They were blood covered, and the one being held up by the others appeared to be unconscious. Wounded.

The light appeared to be coming from nowhere. It was as if an edge of the night sky had ripped, letting out trapped daylight. He could see the effect of the light shining on the pier, but not the source of the light itself, as if a building blocked his view inside an open door. But there was no building, and no sound of water against a ship's hull. The

fear that had haunted him all night returned, raising goose
bumps on his skin.

They pushed the wounded Fey into the light, and he
disappeared. Then, one by one, the others followed. Once
they were gone, the light remained for only a moment before disappearing too. He blinked against the darkness. The
world was as it should have been again.

Except for the tiny circle of light remaining above the
pier.

If he were a courageous man, he would return to the
Tabernacle, grab all the holy water he could, and toss it
inside that circle of light. But he was not. He was not a true
child of Roca. He did not believe in self-sacrifice for the
good of others.

"Forgive me," he whispered to the Holy One.

He rested his forehead on his knees. The breeze ruffled
his hair and caressed the back of his scalp. He sat there until
the implications of what he had seen became clear to him.

The Fey had not evacuated. They were regrouping. They
would try again. The battle fought today in Jahn was not a
definitive defeat. Instead it was the beginning of something
long and terrible.

THE SIEGE

(ONE YEAR LATER)

THIRTY-FIVE

EMAQUE crouched on the deck of the ship. The *Uehe* was one of the smaller ships, chosen for its ability to navigate difficult passages. The Weather Sprites had ordered a heavy rain. The icy drops coated him, seeping into his skin. He had not had the wealth to order protected garments, and since he had lived in the Shadowlands, he had not had the need. Still, the rain with its bluster and chill was better than that gray, empty place. Rugar had done what he could to get the Fey to make it home, but home was not a fog-drenched place with opaque walls and no sky. No one was made to live in the Shadowlands this long. Emaque was amazed that they all had.

Some of the water dribbled into his mouth, and he licked the cold wetness off his lips. He leaned against the wooden railing and waited for the call. When he'd first got aboard, he had needed the railing to keep his balance. It had been a year since he had been on a ship—since that awful day when they had lost the First Battle for Jahn. He had not been chosen for the later excursions to the Infrin Sea, for which he was thankful. Too many Fey had died in the skirmishes and battles during the past year. No one had cited any figures, but he guessed their force had gone down by half. After the First and Second Battles for Jahn, Rugar had stopped attempting complete attacks. Still, the guerrilla fights and surprise tactics weren't working that well either. And the Warders had yet to find any way to counteract the Islander poison.

Emaque had not been called to fight upon land, and he had avoided the escape attempts on the river as well. The first two ships were sunk, and most of the crew on the third and fourth missions did not make it back alive. He wasn't sure he wanted to be on this trip, but he saw no choice. As a Sailor, his obligation was to the Fey and to the sea.

Imatar, the other Sailor on the voyage, crouched against the rail directly across from him. Together they were to guide the Navigator through the treacherous mouth of the Cardidas River, past the Stone Guardians and into the sea. Once free, they were to bring Rugar's message to the Black King.

The rain thrummed on the deck, and the Cardidas raged against the sides of the ship. The ship was rolling just enough to make balance difficult. Most of the crew were at their stations or belowdecks. Emaque could barely see anything through the rain.

The rain was making him reflective. If he had known that he would live on Blue Isle for over a year, he never would have volunteered for this duty. But he had seen the chance for extra bounty, and he had had his eye on one of the Domestics. She wouldn't have him unless he could buy his own ship. She hadn't wanted to live the mobile life of a military wife. She had liked Nye and wanted to settle there.

She probably had. She certainly wouldn't have waited this long.

He sighed and shifted position. They were almost to the mouth. He could smell the salt on the air, as if the rain itself were diluted with it. Excitement built in his chest. It had been too long since he had used his real skills. He was tired of building houses and furniture and working with his hands. It was time to be as the Powers demanded: time to speak to the deep.

He stood, unable to wait any longer. Imatar motioned him down, but Emaque couldn't crouch anymore. The green trees on the side of the river, the brown mud, the murky grayness of the river itself, were a balm to his eye. Since he had moved to Shadowlands, he'd missed color more than anything.

The river was widening as they reached the mouth. Emaque remembered this from the trip in, the Ze warning him about the sandbars and sudden drop-offs in this part of the river. He had been the first to speak to a Ze that night. Now all the Sailors used Zes when they could.

The Ze were long, eellike fish, with a passion for the slimy weeds that grew on the side of rocks. For all their willingness to help, the Ze were little more than gossip fish who chose to go from rock to rock and to live their lives through the misfortune of others. On the way in to Blue Isle, Emaque had had to suffer through a steady stream of personal history about each creature that swam by in order to get the bits and pieces he needed about the passageways themselves.

He leaned on the railing and looked at the hull cutting through the water. The spray bit his cheeks, mixing with the soothing touch of the cold rain. The sensation, coming from something other than Fey creations, warmed him and took his mind off the treachery ahead.

"You shouldn't be standing." The voice made him start. Emaque turned. Kapad stood behind him, wearing water-protected rain gear. The droplets beaded on the wool, making him shimmer.

"It doesn't matter," Emaque said. "We're almost to the mouth."

"I know," Kapad said. "I'm going to set up the link early. I don't want any mistakes this time."

Some of the crew of the fourth ship had blamed their failed mission on the Navigator and the Sailors. The crew claimed the Navigator didn't link with the Sailors early enough, and hence missed the warnings of the Ze.

"Me first?" Emaque asked, hating to link with the Navigator before finding an intelligent creature below the waters that would lead. The Fey-to-Fey link always made him uncomfortable, invaded, a feeling he could avoid only by diving deep into a sea creature's brain.

"You're standing," Kapad said. He held out a hand, wizened and crisscrossed with tiny scars. More than his name, the hand showed him part of the Black King's generation. When Kapad had started, Navigators could link through any blood vessel on the hand. Now the regulations required that they link through the fingers only.

Emaque sighed and took one more quick glance at the trees, the water, and the rain. In a moment it would no longer be a private joy. He held out his right hand, extending the forefinger, and winced as Kapad pricked it with the small picker each Navigator received at the end of training. Emaque's blood eased from his body then, dark and red as it mixed with the rain, dripping onto the deck below.

Kapad pricked his own finger, then held the fingers together. For a moment Emaque felt nothing, and then the link, like a small voice inside his head. The link from Fey to Fey was a Navigator skill that Emaque couldn't replicate if he tried. It had evolved so that the Navigator could listen and respond to the information the Sailor pulled from the deep.

It felt as if part of Kapad settled right behind Emaque's eyes. "Imatar next," Kapad said, and the words created an odd echo effect, resounding first in Emaque's head, and then repeated in his ears. "Why don't you start delving for the Ze? The sooner we get help, the better. I'll send over a crew member."

Crew members always guarded Sailors, just in case, in their excitement, they tried to plunge overboard themselves. Emaque had never had the urge, but he had never met some of the creatures the older Sailors had.

Kapad crossed the deck, stopping to speak to one of the officers. No matter what Kapad's orders, Emaque refused to start without a crew member present. During his training he had seen a Sailor dive over to be with a dolphin who had enticed him. The man hadn't known how to swim and had died before the rescue crew and the dolphin could get him out of the water.

Emaque took a deep breath to calm himself. Almost free. Just through the Stone Guardians, where the mouth of the river dumped into the sea, and he would be away from Blue Isle for the rest of his life.

A young woman came up to him and identified herself as his watch. He looked her over: her body was long and wiry, with muscles corded on her arms. She had enough strength to hold him, if she had to.

"You ever done this before?" he asked. Across the deck Imatar and Kapad touched fingers.

She was staring at him solemnly, her brown eyes wide. "On Nye a few times, and on the way here," she said. Her voice was soft, barely audible above the pounding of the rain.

"All right," he said, relieved he didn't have to go into a full explanation. "The important thing is to hold me no matter what. The last time a ship tried this channel, Islanders shot arrows at it. What you have to remember in a situation like that is that it might seem right for you to let me go and take care of yourself, but if I go, then the Navigator loses his way, and we all die."

"What about the other one?" she asked, pointing to Imatar. He was standing alone now on the other side of the deck, watching Emaque. "What if you die and he lives?"

"Then we're half-blind." Emaque had heard the question before. Crew members often had no magick at all or small magicks like weak Domestic talents: the abilities to make ropes hold, ways to clean the deck and keep the wood from rotting, methods of keeping the food from spoiling. They did not like to be relied on, and hated the job of watching a Sailor. Sometimes Emaque thought that crew members did have magick, but their fear of responsibility kept their talents hidden.

We are only a few miles from the mouth. Kapad's voice sounded tinny in Emaque's head. *I am at my station. The watch reports ships ahead.*

Emaque sent a nonverbal acknowledgment; then he looked over the edge of the ship at the swirling water, his greatest fear clutching at his stomach. He always worried that below there would be no sentient creatures to lead them.

Imatar is gone. Go now, Emaque.

Emaque didn't have to be told twice. "Now," he said to the woman, and then leaned over the edge. She placed her hands on his back so that she could feel any shift in his body if he planned to jump.

The spray was sharp and biting there, and the river water had more than its share of debris on the surface. He cursed under his breath. No matter what happened on this trip, he would get bruised.

He plunged his mind into the deep, searching for a spark of intelligence. He felt nothing, as if he weren't in his body or any body, as if flesh no longer mattered. All he could see in this state was the spark of intelligence. Different kinds of creatures had different sparks. He searched, seeing tiny pinpricks and faint glows. It took a moment before he saw the kind of fire he was looking for. He slipped in.

Pardon the invasion, cousin, he said, as he always did, the words covering the physical jolt of having his consciousness land in a strange place. Then he felt the automatic cold—no surprise there—and the soft, soothing bulk of the water around his new frame. Buoyancy was a joy, and being able to breathe there, in the depths, made that joy even firmer.

NOT INVITED. NO. NO.

It was a Ze. He could tell by the pattern of speech, and then by the feel of the body.

Peace, cousin. I mean you no harm. I am merely looking for my way.

NOT INVITED. GO, OTHER. GO.

I will leave if you guide me through the mouth, through the channel, past the Stone Guardians.

NOT INVITED. GO NOW. GO.

The water was murky at this level. The light that filtered through was dim. He got a sense of rocks at the bottom, which probably interested the Ze, and other fish swimming by. Two bottom feeders were nibbling at the refuse along the sand between the rocks. Ahead he saw a bigger shape, probably a creature he didn't know.

The last time I spoke with one of you, he told me all about the fish around him, as well as guiding me through the Stone Guardians.

ZE DIE. GO, OTHER. GO NOW.

Ze have died? Because of what? Because of us?

Emaque! Kapad's voice sent an urgency. *We haven't time. Find something else.*

ZE TAKE OTHER THROUGH FLOW. THEN DARK FALLS. BODIES BREAK SURFACE. LEAK DARK. BRING EER. ZE DIE.

Eer. He cast back in his memory to the conversation he had had with the first Ze. He had seen one Eer. It was four times the size of the Ze, with a wide mouth filled with jagged teeth, puny eyes, and razor-sharp scales. Drawn, according to that Ze, to any destruction of life, the Eer would continue that destruction, killing and eating everything in its path.

He could say nothing. The Ze's fear was legitimate.

Find something else, then! Kapad commanded, voice as firm as before.

What about Imatar?

Imatar is not your concern.

Emaque felt the urgency then. He didn't know how he felt it: before, he had always been separate from the creature, his consciousness, and himself. But if Kapad wasn't answering questions about Imatar, then Imatar had found nothing either.

He knew the Ze couldn't hear Kapad, and he wasn't sure the Ze felt the same urgency he did.

Go now. Now.

Wait. Emaque directed his thoughts to the Ze. *Even if I leave you, we will be in these waters. Without your help we will be in them longer. Chances are there will be more bodies to attract the Eer without your help.*

Before no Eer. Too many. Now. Go.

That's not true, Emaque said. *There were Eer before. Your people knew what Eer were. There just weren't as many chances for an Eer to go crazy. Whether you help me or not, the Eer will go crazy in this area soon. You're better in the sea. Take me with you. Escape the Eer and help me at the same time.*

The Ze swam in small confused circles for a moment, then stopped and nibbled some weed off a rock. Then it pointed itself toward the mouth of the river.

Quick, then. Before Eer.

The Ze jutted forward, its tail flapping, its small body straining. It kept to the bottom, maneuvering around the rocks as if searching for food. It took Emaque a minute to realize the Ze was keeping close to find a hiding place.

How are the currents up top? he asked, knowing that while the Ze was giving them a path, it wasn't completely helping the ship.

Sea strong. This Ze wasn't as talkative as the first Ze had been, and if other Sailors hadn't had the same experiences with Zes, Emaque would have thought his first experience odd.

This Ze was terrified. The carnage in the area must have been horrible.

And when do we get to the Stone Guardians?

CIRCLES. MUCH DANGER. EVEN ZE DIE IN CIRCLE WATERS.

Great, Kapad sent to him. *We pick a day with currents so strong, they kill fish.*

Emaque ignored him. *Is there any way around the Stone Guardians that is safe?*

SOMETIMES. DURING SPAWNING.

When do Ze spawn? Kapad asked.

How the hell should I know? Emaque sent back to him. He watched out of the fish's eyes and saw other Ze flanking them like a protective force. They knew so little about Zes. Did they have their own version of telepathic powers? He worked so hard at discovering routes, he didn't know the rest. The lack of knowledge made him uneasy. He occupied the mind of the creature without welcome and didn't even know what the creature was.

The rocks grew darker. Smaller fish darted among them. The weeds waved in the current as if pointing the way for them. Emaque wished that the Ze would look up; he wanted to see the position of the ship's hull above them. The bottom curved downward, and the water took on a life of its own, tumbling in an underwater fall. Even though Emaque could not see the Stone Guardians, he figured the Ze had taken him to the mouth of the river.

Ships, Kapad warned. Emaque thought he could hear fear in Kapad's mental voice.

We need to go as quickly as we can. There will be fighting on the surface, and maybe dark waters and more bodies.

HIDE. GO NOW, NOT INVITED. HIDE.

The Ze started to head for the rocks. Emaque wished for more than mental power. *No! They'll find you here. Get us out of the Stone Guardians while there's still time.*

HIDE, the Ze said again.

No! We'll all die!

That stopped the Ze. Emaque was afraid that it would swim in circles again, but it didn't. It started swimming toward the surface. Above them, and a bit to the back, Emaque saw the hull of the *Uehe*. Other things blocked the opaque surface light all around, but the Ze's eyes weren't that good.

The water had cold pockets as it fed into the Infrin. The current pulled at the Ze's body, and the little fish swam higher as if to get away from them. The *Uehe* was following them: did that mean Imatar had not found a spark? or that his spark was even more reluctant than Emaque's?

Do these circle currents reach the surface?

SOME. FAST. MOVE FAST. ONLY SAFETY.

It took him a moment to understand that. The only safety was in moving fast. He hoped the *Uehe* was moving as fast as it could.

The other shapes blocking the darkness seemed closer. Below, an Eer played in the swirling waters. The Ze swam even faster, its companions fanning out like a decoy force. Had he hit an important Ze? Or did they all know something was happening? He had never seen fish act this way. If he survived, he promised himself he would learn more about the creatures he invaded.

Muck floated in the water: bits of seaweed and fish dung, plus garbage from the surface, leaves and grass and dead bugs. They were very close to the surface now. Through the fish's eyes he could see the other shapes more clearly.

Hulls. But not Fey. Small boats.

Islander.

They're around you! he sent to Kapad.

Keep going, Kapad sent back. *Let us handle the surface.*

But the boats are small. He knew that small boats sometimes got lost in a crew's zeal for finding larger ships.

The Stone Guardians are ahead.

Emaque couldn't see them. The debris in the water continued to churn. The Ze kept looking down, apparently watching for the Eer.

It swam over several small whirlpools. They felt like tugs against its body.

Are we going through the Guardians near the surface? Emaque asked.

BOTTOM SHARP ROCKS. NO SAFETY. ONLY SAFETY NEAR AIR.

No wonder the Zes had been good choices in the past. They had a fear of the current dashing them against the rocks.

Powers! Kapad's thought was sharp and sudden.

What happened? Emaque asked, but he got no answering response. *Kapad! Kapad!*

Finally, faintly, *Keep swimming. We're almost free—*

And then nothing. But he couldn't be dead. If one man

died while linked, the other died too. Kapad was still alive, but not communicating. Maybe he needed all his effort to filter both Imatar's and Emaque's perceptions.

The Stone Guardians loomed, craggy and ominous in the water. They were really one stone with a lot of jagged edges, as well as caves and carvings through the center. One Ze had tried to lead the ships through a cave on the way in: the Sailor had to pull out at the last minute and find another host to prevent disaster.

Weed grew along the rock's porous surface. Some tendrils were long as hair and just as fine. The Ze barely looked at them in its panic.

DARK! it cried. DARK!

At first Emaque thought it meant the Guardians, and then he understood. The water was turning dark around them, as if the rain on the surface had turned to blood.

Emaque fought the urge to pull up, back into himself. No. They had reached the Guardians. They were almost free of this horrid place. Almost.

The Ze swam even more quickly toward the rocks. It went so near the surface, the spines on its back cleared the water. The air felt as heavy and suffocating as water did when Emaque was in his own body. The Ze headed toward an opening between the Guardians that the Ze on Emaque's previous trip had warned him against.

EER! EER!

Emaque didn't see the Eer but knew it had to be wallowing in the blood.

No, Kapad cried. *The channel is too narrow. It will sheer the ship.*

Is there another way?

NO TIME! EER!

I don't see the Eer. Please, can we find another way?

OTHER SAFE FAR AWAY. ONLY ESCAPE FROM EER.

Please—Emaque thought.

NO! And the Ze plunged into the space between the Guardians. For a moment Emaque hung on and then realized the futility. He would be too far to return to his own shell.

You'll have to trust Imatar, he sent, and pulled out of the Ze.

The sudden blindness shocked him. He scanned the area

around him and saw no sparks at all. Then he remembered to look outside the water.

His consciousness zoomed back into his own body, and immediately he became aware of two things: his left side had fallen asleep all the way to his arm, and sharp pains shot through his back. He was drenched, his hair plastered to his face, his clothing stuck to his skin. The ship had stopped moving, though, and so the spray did not catch him in the front.

He opened his eyes. The water below him was laced with blood, and already bodies floated on the surface. He stood slowly, not sure what the pains in his back were, and found that he was alone.

The girl had left him. He didn't see her or her body on the rain- and blood-slicked deck. He squinted and scanned the horizon. The small ships were returning to Blue Isle. The *Uehe* was still heading for the Stone Guardians, being drawn by the current.

Kapad! Turn us around!

I am. Kapad's voice was faint in his head. Too faint when they were this close.

The blood was flowing back into Emaque's left side. The pain as the nerve endings came alive was exquisite. He put a hand on his back to cover the pain there and felt the ripped tatters of his shirt, and long, deep scratch marks—so deep, the skin had been tattered around them. The girl had hung on so tightly that something had had to drag her away. He looked again at the bodies in the water and this time recognized her uniform and build. She had tried. Somehow she had saved him—at the cost of her own life.

He hadn't even asked her name.

The ship finally turned. He felt it groan as it moved in the water. Kapad had said nothing, unusual for him. Emaque squared his shoulders. No time for sentimentality. He gazed across the deck. It was broken up as if things had been shot through it, like the cannon fire the L'Nacin had used and then their underground had later sold to the Nye. He wondered if the vessel was even seaworthy. But the crew was supposed to take care of that. Only he didn't know how many of them were still alive, if any.

Imatar was not on the other side of the deck, in his place. Maybe he, too, had come to himself. Or maybe his guardian had moved him—a dangerous and tricky thing, but one sometimes made necessary by battle.

The rain had turned to a light mist: the Weather Sprites had decided to seed only through the Stone Guardians. As the ship continued to turn, Emaque saw even more bodies in the water, and wood from a destroyed Islander ship.

Emaque? Kapad's essence seemed even fainter this time. *I need help—*

Emaque hurried across the deck, avoiding the holes and the broken equipment. A body, badly twisted and melted, crouched under a chair. He shuddered. They had met the Islanders, and the Islanders had used their poison. He wasn't sure he wanted to see what had happened to Kapad.

Still, Emaque grabbed the railing and mounted the steps that led to the pilothouse. They were slick, and they shouldn't have been. He clung as he moved, and when he reached the top, he first looked to the Guardians. They were behind the ship now. Emaque silently thanked the Powers. He would never have been able to navigate a ship through those mountainous rocks.

Then Emaque looked at the wreckage that was the pilothouse. The glass had been broken on all sides, and most of the crew were hideously dead, the stench from the potion and melted flesh rising over the stench of blood.

Kapad's body was undamaged, but he huddled at the base of the great wheel. Emaque went to him.

"Imatar's dead," Kapad whispered, the words having that curious echo effect in his ears and head.

A chill ran down Emaque's back. He had to sever the link with Kapad, and quickly.

"Ship first," Kapad said. "There's still crew alive. You have to get us to Shadowlands. Can you pilot?"

"If I have to," Emaque said. "With your help."

"I don't know how much help I can be," Kapad whispered.

I'll die if you do, Emaque sent.

I won't die. As if that were a promise any man could keep. Kapad couldn't keep his eyes open. He stretched a shaky hand to Emaque.

Where's Imatar? Emaque sent.

The tainted arrows got him when we saw the ships. Someone said the girl took yours. They're getting wise to our ways,

Emaque. Kapad's eyes fluttered open. *We have to sever the link.*

Emaque nodded. He took the tiny gold scissors from Kapad's breast pocket and snipped the air in front of Kapad's nose, and then in front of his own. No one was certain how that magick worked, except perhaps the symbolism severed the link in the minds.

Kapad looked up at him. "We'll never get off this damn island," he said, and died.

THIRTY-SIX

THE rain had stopped, but the air still felt damp. The Rocaan stood at the edge of the pit, his tiny filigree sword in one hand and a pouch filled with burial herbs in the other. The Danites usually Blessed the dead, but lately, when it came to mass anonymous burials, the Rocaan had been doing the work himself.

This burial pit was on a small hill overlooking the Cardidas, just outside of Jahn. Other pits were hastily covered, and someone had posted a sign warning the curious away. The grave diggers waited at the edge of the hill, their backs to the Rocaan. Diggers were unclean, and unable to take part in any religious ceremonies.

Two Elders, Porciluna and Andre, stood a respectful distance away. None of the Elders believed the Rocaan should be there. They believed him too old and frail to stand in the wind.

The rotting smell from the mass grave was mixed with the odd perfumy scent of lime. The Rocaan stared at the bodies below, wrapped in cheap linen and tied head and toe. He hoped the Holy One had guided their way to God's side. No one deserved to end up like this, one slab of meat among many, resting on a thin layer of dirt between them and other dead.

This group of twenty—mostly men—had died defending six hovels to the south of Jahn. Apparently Fey had raided the meager store of goods the families had stored, and they had come out brandishing weapons. None had had holy water, having used it to fight off a previous raid.

The Fey had killed them all and escaped, just as they had done on a hundred other raids up and down the Cardidas. Of the families, only four women remained alive, and ten children. The orphans' quarters were already overrun. If the children stayed at their homes, they would starve, and if they went to the orphans' quarters, they wouldn't be any better off.

The Rocaan had condemned them all. Listening to Matthias on that wretched day of the invasion, over a year before, had been a mistake. He had known that Matthias reacted from his own scholarship and his own mind, not from any still, small voice, and yet the Rocaan had listened. If he hadn't, if he had sacrificed himself, perhaps all of these unfortunates would be alive.

The paupers' graves bothered him the most. He did not do burial work for those who could actually afford him. He left that to the Danites. But these people, whose families still mourned, and who had fought for their homes, didn't have enough money for an individual resting place. Instead they were given an anonymous home in a worthless plot of ground as a reward for all their sacrifice.

He couldn't ask them for forgiveness. Such forgiveness had to come from his God, and within his own self. But he could use all his powers as a Rocaan to make sure that the Holy One saw and rewarded even these poor souls.

Porciluna was watching him, arms behind his black robe, concern on his round face. Andre stood beside him, hands in the pockets of his robe and head down. Of all the Elders, Andre was the only one who understood the guilt that the Rocaan was feeling, who even accepted the thinking that had brought the Rocaan to this place. During the invasion Andre had saved a small cadre of children who had been in the Tabernacle for a faith class, and he had not killed a single Fey. Instead he had threatened them with the holy water, and splashed some on the floor before him, and the Fey, already familiar with its powers, had run.

The Rocaan held the sword out before him, his hand extending over the pit. "Holy One," he said, letting his voice reverberate as if he were doing Midnight Sacrament, "I am your increasingly unworthy servant. But I beg you to overlook the messenger and hear the message."

Out of the corner of his eye he could see Porciluna's feet shift. The words were not the correct ones for the ceremony. But they were right for the prayer the Rocaan had to offer.

"These souls have given everything because it was asked of them. In return they have nothing, and their families even less. Please, Holy One, find their Beings and transport them to the side of God. Bless them with Your presence, and reward them for their love."

Then he slipped into the words of the ceremony. "Bless the Honored Dead. Treasure their Beings, and we will treasure their memories upon this land."

He bent and planted the edge of the filigreed sword in the soil, his hand scraping against the lime. Then he reached into his pouch as he stood and scattered the herbs across the bodies.

"As the Roca honored God, so have you. As the Holy One has spoken to God, so have you. As God has loved us all, so have you. You return to the cycle of life, that in dying we might all live. It is with the Roca's highest Blessing that I leave you so that the Holy One may Absorb your soul."

Then he touched his scented fingers to his forehead, whispered one word of personal blessing, and backed away from the pit. The wet ground was particularly soft over the other pits, but he had no choice but to walk on them. Since the Fey had arrived, countless lives had been lost. The day of the invasion had been particularly devastating, but there were skirmishes inside and outside of Jahn. He let the Danites take care of the communities outside the city because he wasn't up to such travel. He could do only so much.

As he reached the Elders, he paused and glanced at the pit one final time. The grave diggers were shoveling the pile of dirt beside the pit onto the bodies to make an even layer. They had to leave dirt, though, so that there would be some for the next group. Sometimes these pits held bodies eight layers deep.

"You are exhausting yourself," Porciluna said. His voice was raspy from too much wine and fine food. Since he had become an Elder, he had grown to double his size. "You cannot continue coming here. The Danites can bless the dead."

The Rocaan shook his head. "These people have died because of my sin. The Danites cannot acknowledge that."

"How could you have sinned?" There was no respect in Porciluna's tone. "You did not ask the Fey to Blue Isle."

"Let him be," Andre said. He took the Rocaan's arm and helped him across the marshy ground. The air smelled of loam and the tang of the Cardidas. "The Holy Sir has more knowledge of the Mind of God than the rest of us. If he believes he has somehow done something to bring this scourge upon us, I will believe him and help him find a way to banish it."

"You're saying that the Holy Sir is a sinner? That is blasphemy in the Ears of God." Porciluna punctuated his words with pants, his breath short as he tried to keep up.

"It is blasphemy," the Rocaan said, "to argue at the site of death. And Elder Andre was merely saying that unlike the rest of you, he believes me."

"Thank you, Holy Sir," Andre said. He helped the Rocaan down the steps leading to the road. Their carriage waited, a large black conveyance with tiny swords embroidered in the corners on all three sides. The driver, sitting up front, picked up the reins when he saw the Rocaan. The team, two matching black horses, pawed the rutted road as if anxious to be off.

Porciluna opened the door, and the Rocaan climbed in. He sat behind the driver, his legs outstretched before him, his body almost collapsed with exhaustion. Porciluna and Andre sat across from him.

"Holy Sir," Porciluna said with some surprise. "You left your sword at the grave site."

"It belongs there," the Rocaan said. To mark the place of Absorption. To mark the site of a crime. To mark his guilt.

"We should send the driver for it. The grave diggers will merely take it."

The Rocaan leaned forward. "Porciluna, you have no faith in the human spirit."

"Indeed, I have too much," Porciluna said.

"We are to believe the best of others, not the worst."

Porciluna's cheeks flamed. "In this last year I have seen the worst of everything the world has to offer."

"And the best," the Rocaan said. "For as many tales of horror, there are tales of giving. Have faith. Not just in Roca, but in Blue Isle itself."

"It is hard, Holy Sir," Porciluna said. "Blue Isle is no longer a place I know."

"It is no longer a place any of us know," the Rocaan said. "But hardship should bring us closer to each other, not pull us apart. And it is the duty of the Church to maintain unity."

Even as he said the words, he winced inwardly. By making the holy water a weapon, a tool of destruction, he had ruined the Church's chance to play a benevolent role in this crisis.

Even the Elders had forgotten the mission of Rocaanism. It was time he put things right.

THIRTY-SEVEN

RUGAR sat on the Meeting Block in the center of Shadowlands. The sound of pounding wood echoed hollowly from all directions. It had taken three weeks for his people to find the best location for the larger Shadowlands, and a week for him to build it properly before he could allow anyone to move in. The Battle for Jahn had left him exhausted—more by the failure than anything—and the following skirmishes did nothing to rest him.

At least this Shadowlands was the proper kind for a military base. He didn't spend most of his time repairing the walls or making sure the ships were linked. The ships remained in the first Shadowlands, in Jahn Harbor. This new Shadowlands was outside of Jahn near some abandoned cabins in a deserted section of woods. The loneliness of this place made foraging difficult, but it also ensured that the Islanders did not attack.

The Shadowlands was like a great box with nothing inside, but it did have a top, a bottom, and walls. They were barriers to the touch and felt solid but had no visible form. Somehow the air came through those barriers. Shadowlands made by poor Visionaries or inexperienced leaders sometimes did not have that quality, and the air disappeared quickly. More than one campaign had lost soldiers because a poorly equipped leader had tried—and failed—to build a proper Shadowlands.

This one now looked like no Shadowlands he had ever seen before. Most he had lived in had been for a week or two during a campaign in a specific location. Some Shadowlands had been for leaders only and were like a personal tent. Others had tents inside for the troops. But none had individual buildings like this one.

Getting the wood had been most difficult. He had sent parties out in groups of five to chop trees and bring them into the Shadowlands, where Domestics molded them to the proper shape. There still weren't enough homes for everyone. Many crowded into cabins much too small. The Shadowlands had space enough, but getting materials had been the problem.

As were other supplies. He had nightmares about water, dreaming that the Islanders had switched the water supply with their poison, and all the Fey in the Shadowlands were dying of thirst. The Domestics had said that they could purify waste water and had convinced him to keep a store of it, but he couldn't bring himself to do that unless there was an actual emergency. Instead, he sent parties to the Cardidas every day to bring back the needed buckets.

Jewel was presently overseeing the rationing of the day's water. He was so thankful to have her beside him, and even more thankful for Silence, who had saved her. She had stumbled back late the evening of the First Battle for Jahn, wearing a bloody Islander robe, her wrists bruised, telling the horrific tale of being held by these Islanders. Rugar had forbidden her to leave the Shadowlands since.

He couldn't wait for her to join him. News was long in coming from the *Uehe*. It had him half-worried and half-excited. The scouts he had sent to the mouth of the Cardidas weren't back, and they knew he wanted word immediately. The longer they waited, the better the chance that the ship had made it through the treacherous channel.

He hoped it would. He prayed it would. He used all his powers, limited as they were on effecting the future, to ensure it would. Unless a ship got out, the Fey had no chance of leaving this place.

The pounding made his head throb. He had had to live

with that pounding since they had moved to this Shadowlands. New houses, new construction all the time. He had his people prepare for a long siege, and he wanted them to be comfortable. He wished he could make it so that they would have nothing to worry about, but that seemed beyond his power. Even food had become an issue.

They could grow nothing in there. The formlessness of the Shadowlands did not allow anything to be planted in the ground. Many of the Domestics brought soil in from the outside and built large soil boxes so that they could grow gardens. So far they weren't working. Jewel had suggested tending gardens outside the abandoned hovels—and if the Domestics couldn't make a go of the interior gardens, he would give it some thought. Instead he sent his people out in raids. Usually for meat, but sometimes to steal vegetables from unsuspecting Islanders.

So much balancing. He had never worked so hard or worried so much in his life. Campaigns had always been difficult, but not like this, where he had to take into account everything, from housing his troops to feeding and clothing them.

Someone laughed behind him. He turned. Jewel was threading her way through the stacked wood that the Domestics were molding for the house to be built in the back of the Meeting Block. He still couldn't get used to the lack of color in the Shadowlands. The odd opaqueness made her look sickly: her dark skin mottled, her black hair colorless. She waved when she saw him. He waved back.

She was speaking to Burden, who laughed again. He touched her arm—an easy gesture that turned into a caress. Rugar straightened. Burden was overstepping himself. He had ever since the night of the First Battle for Jahn, as if he had some moral superiority over Rugar. As if his actions in the battle had given him a right to Jewel. She wasn't dissuading him, and Rugar like that even less. Too many children were conceived out of boredom. He didn't want his daughter to be tied to a child in a place like the Shadowlands.

Jewel slipped out of Burden's grasp and ran to her father. Her hair flew behind her, and he smiled in spite of himself. She was beautiful. Even in this gray place his daughter had a joy that made everything lighter.

She sat beside him, crossing her legs as he had done, knees meeting. "Water rationed," she said. "It's getting easier all the time. Everyone is bringing the right-sized containers now, and no one is fighting anymore. Pretty soon we might be able to let them collect water on their own."

He shook his head. "Someone would always take too much."

"We almost have too much in storage right now," she said. "Gia says we'll have to build another storage tank soon."

"Good," he said. "Right now we can't have enough."

She leaned back and placed her hands flat on the Meeting Block, gazing up at the opaqueness that anywhere else would have been sky. "You think the scouts are dead?"

"I don't know," he said. "I'm not willing to speculate."

"The last time, the scouts made it back after the survivors," she said reflectively.

"The last time, the Islanders fought from the land. If they had fought from the sea, then the scouts would have come back first."

"You know," she said, still not looking at him, "I've often wondered why no one has come for us. Grandfather should have sent reinforcements by now. The Black King never lets a force stand on its own for longer than a month or two. Do you think he's all right?"

"He's fine," Rugar said.

She sat up. "You've heard from him?"

"No," Rugar said. "I just know he's not coming."

The words hung between them. She ran a hand over her long hair, smoothing it, then grabbed a strand and twisted it around her forefinger. Finally she said, "That's what you were fighting about that day in Nye, that day I was waiting for you. He said he wouldn't back you up."

Rugar looked at his hands. That conversation lived in his head, moment by moment, day by day. He had thought that when he became an adult, he would make good choices, strong choices. He had thought that his father was too out of touch with his people to know the future. He had forgotten that the Black King was a great Visionary, greater perhaps than Rugar, because the Black King had had decades to perfect his magic. What had his father Seen? And why hadn't he said anything?

"I'm right, aren't I?" she asked. "He didn't want us to come here."

Rugar swallowed. He couldn't keep this inside anymore. "He said that our people were tired of fighting, that they needed a few years to rest and to enjoy the fruits of their triumphs. Some soldiers, like me, had fought their entire life, and now it was time to reward them. He said that to push on with the battle was to force our people to a place where they could lose for the first time in our memories."

"He was right," Jewel said, drawing her knees to her chest.

"We know that now," Rugar said. "But he could have been wrong."

"Why'd he let you go?"

"Wisdom." Rugar had thought that through too. "It allowed him to get on with the business of ruling his Empire without the distractions. But he was angry that I took you."

"I wanted to go," Jewel said.

Rugar nodded. "And you were in my Vision of this place. Jewel, I swear to you, I saw you walking through that Islander palace as if you owned it. An older you. I thought it meant we had won."

"We're not done yet." She rested her chin on her knees. "I want to know why Grandfather thought us a distraction."

Rugar glanced around. The pounding continued, but Burden had left, and he didn't see any others around him. "It was brilliant when I finally realized what he had done." Rugar sighed. "You're too young to remember, but when I was a boy, we stopped the fighting for a year. We had a truce with L'Nacin, and we might have stopped our westward march at that point, but a lot of our soldiers didn't adapt to civilian life. Many couldn't even tolerate guard duty—no action. So they formed outlaw bands, marauders, and they pillaged L'Nacin, raping and murdering, and then selling what they stole, even if the booty was slight. There are always people who cannot let go of the excitement of war. So your grandfather remembered this and ordered me to take only volunteers, thinking that the people who volunteered for this mission would be the ones who would have gone outlaw otherwise."

"Some didn't come willingly."

"That's true," Rugar said. "Some came because I'm their

commander, not the Black King. And some came because they don't believe the Fey should stop with Galinas. Still others came because they love fighting."

She dug her chin into her knees. She wouldn't look at him, and that unnerved him. He wanted some response from her other than this cold contemplation.

"I can't believe he would abandon his own son to the whims of fate."

Rugar sighed. She was young yet, unused to making difficult choices. Someday she would understand that to follow the heart wasn't always the best thing for a ruler. "He tried to convince me against it. We argued for a month. You just remember the day he gave in."

Rugar did too: the look on the Black King's face when he said *See if you can put a force together* was a look of farewell. He had not seen the troops off, as was his custom. In fact, he had left the province the day before.

"But to abandon you—"

"I'm an adult, Jewel. I make my own choices for good or ill." Rugar smiled, wondering if he would have the same strength his father had.

"But you're next in line."

Rugar nodded. "And I am twenty years younger than he is. If he serves as most Black Kings have, he will die as an old man. I'll have a reign of ten years at the most. Losing me isn't the great crime of this trip. Losing you is. The fact that he let you come along shows how much he wanted to believe in me. You were his inheritance, not I."

Her face sank lower against her knees until only her eyes and nose were visible. Rugar put out his hand, and it hovered over her back for a moment; then he pulled it away.

The pounding continued, a monotonous sound. They had an odd mix of Domestics with them. Those who could shape the wood could not force it to hold together. They had to use the old-fashioned method with a hammer and wooden nails.

"If I don't come back," she said, the words muffled against her skin, "what then?"

The question didn't surprise him. He had been expecting it most of her fighting life. What did surprise him was that it had taken her so long to ask.

"Your brother Bridge will become Black King."

"Bridge," she breathed. They both knew she was the better choice. She had bested Bridge in everything, from sword fighting to military strategy. "Why didn't you tell me this before we left?"

"Because," he said, "I thought we'd win."

She closed her eyes and hid her face behind her knees. This time he did put a hand on her back, feeling the rigid posture, the stiff muscles. She didn't acknowledge his touch. He had betrayed her by treating her as a child, and now he could have cost her the future she had trained for.

He had never intended that.

"Shima had Seen her own death. Others came to you, saying that this mission would be a failure. Your own father told you not to go, and still you came." Although her words were angry, her muffled tone was soft and full of disbelief. "Didn't you at least question yourself?"

"No," he said.

She brought her head up, her dark eyes shining. "Why not?"

This time he looked away, unable to face that loss and earnestness mixed in her features. "When I was a thirteen-year-old boy, I had my first Vision. I saw a black horse, running through a field, a Beast Rider hiding beneath the blanket across its back. Two armies flanked the horse, and they watched as it reached the Oudoun leader. The Beast Rider stood, the horse reared, and its hooves tore the leader apart. I told my field commander about it, and he laughed at me. So I told my father, and when a Beast Rider came to him with that exact plan, my father approved it, and that was the decisive end for the Oudoun War. My father said he had never heard of a Vision so clear in its detail in one so young. It indicated great power. I saw the Shaman. I talked with other Visionaries. They made me create tiny Shadowlands. They dissected my Visions. The verdicts were all the same. I was a powerful Visionary. And my powers seemed to grow as I got older. I saw no reason to doubt this Vision of you. Even though it was shorter than many I've had, it was still strong, and detailed."

"But when they speak of Vision," Jewel said, "they say that it is the duty of a Visionary to compare his Vision with the Vision of others."

"It is," Rugar said.

"Then why didn't you?"

"I did," he said. "Think about it, Jewel. We are not immortals. Fey die in campaigns. Just because Shima Saw her death, and others Saw failure, didn't mean that we would all fail. It simply meant that there would be a cost. I expected a cost. And if I had thought that cost would have been you or the family or the people themselves, I would not have done this." He looked back at her after that. Her mouth was parted slightly, her eyes wide. They had not had a conversation like this one for a long, long time. If ever. Jewel had never really been an adult to him before. Now, with his father across the sea, and his advisers unwilling to listen, he had no one but this black-eyed girl.

"What did you hope to gain?" she said.

"Have you forgotten already?" He stared at her until she looked away.

"No," she said. "I haven't forgotten. But we aren't on our way to Leut, and Blue Isle doesn't seem particularly wealthy to me. Not now."

"Oh, but it is," he said. "I wasn't wrong about that. Look how they've sustained this campaign they were unprepared for. They have no food shortages, and the people are well fed."

"Not all of them."

He shrugged. "Even the wealthiest nations have poverty. You look to see how many people suffer, not whether people suffer at all." He glanced around, realizing for the first time himself how lucky they were to be trapped there—if they had to be trapped anywhere. Otherwise they themselves might have starved. "The Isle is supporting us now, too, Jewel, and there is almost no effect from it. We're raiding their gardens and killing their livestock, and still they eat."

Jewel stood, put her hands on the small of her back, and stretched. Then she glanced at him, and her face had lines he had never seen before. "So we won't be rescued. Not even if a ship gets out?"

"If I believed that, I wouldn't have sent a ship. No, your grandfather will send help if he has word that we're alive—and alive in large numbers. But he also needs to know about their poison, and he needs to have Warders working on a way to combat it. Then, and only then, will he send an invasion force large enough to take the Isle and rescue us."

She nodded and sat. "So that's why you've been sending the ships."

He frowned. "What did you think I should be doing?"

"Fighting." The word sounded so simple, especially when she said it. "We're here to conquer. I thought you should have mounted another battle, and another, and another."

"Jewel," he said, "we've already lost over a third of our force. The Second Battle for Jahn showed me that we can't do that as long as they have their poison. The Warders' first spell didn't work, and they can't seem to come up with anything else. As long as we have no way to fight that poison, we have no way to fight. Better to hold on until we solve the problem and send for reinforcements."

She drew herself back into the protected position. "I just hate it here," she said. "I even dream in gray now. Sometimes I want to go out onto the Isle just to remember what green looks like."

"I know," he said. If he had known another way to build a Shadowlands, he would have. But he didn't. And the only thing he could think of was to let the others use their skills to improve the box he had trapped them in.

He and Jewel sat in silence for quite a while. He felt half-ashamed for telling her, as if his failure were compounded. The decision had seemed right at the time. He had never made a real mistake before. And Blue Isle would have been a step closer to Leut. Even if the Fey never went past Blue Isle, they would have the Isle's wealth. And if they decided to move on, they would have the Isle as a base. Without Blue Isle they could not have Leut. The wars would be done then.

And what would he have done? He, the Black King's son, the Prince destined to fight forever and rule not at all. He fathered children, training them in the art of war, and let the Black King train them in the art of leadership. Rugar would never be other than a military leader; the Visionary whose Vision had led them to this disaster.

Lights flickered near the Circle Door. Rugar looked up. The Circle Door opened, revealing a bit of green from the forest outside, mixed with the scent of pine. One of the scouts tumbled in. His long hair was matted and covered with brambles, his clothing torn, and his arms lined with scratches. Jewel got up and went to him, bending over him as if she were a Healer who knew what she was doing. Others came running: a real Healer, a Domestic, and Burden crowded around him. Rugar waited on the Meeting Block.

"Get him some water," Jewel said.

Dello, the Domestic, nodded and ran to the nearest cabin, her waist-length hair flying behind her. Neri, the Healer, crouched beside Jewel. Neri's frown of concentration deepened her wrinkles. She was tiny, but talented. She ran her hand over the scout's head, smoothing his hair and comforting him with that simple touch.

"He'll be all right." Neri's voice was soft.

"What news is there?" Burden asked.

Rugar stiffened. That boy would have to be dealt with. He knew better than to pull information from a scout before the leader had it.

"He needs to talk with my father," Jewel said.

Dello returned with the water. She brought the scout's head up and helped him drink.

Rugar stood. "Bring him to my cabin. Now."

He waited until Dello, Neri, and Burden helped the scout to his feet. The scout staggered a few steps, then walked on his own. Jewel flanked him. When he stood, Rugar recognized him as Hiere, the scout he had assigned to the river's north face.

Rugar's cabin was farther into the Shadowlands. It was one of the first built. Originally, it had been used as a meeting place, then he and Jewel had taken it over as living space. He needed privacy, especially for meetings like this one.

He went in. The furnishings were still sparse: a few chairs and a table. Both he and Jewel had torn apart their ship cabins to form their own bedrooms down a narrow hall. He lit the lamps and turned. All five waited for him.

"Jewel may stay," Rugar said, "and Hiere. The rest of you can go."

Burden paused for a moment, as if he were going to say something, and then went out the door with the others. Rugar waited until they had disappeared into the opaqueness before asking the door to close.

He offered Hiere a chair. Hiere sat and couldn't quite hide his sigh of relief.

"Well?" Rugar asked, even though he was afraid he already knew the answer.

Hiere shook his head. "They almost made it," he said. "They reached a passage in the Stone Guardians and then stopped. The attack was quick and bloody. I thought"—his voice broke—"I thought for a moment that they would make it. I really thought—"

"Are they all dead?" Jewel asked.

"No," Hiere said. "Someone turned the ship around. But it's badly damaged. I'm not sure if they'll make it back."

"They have usually let our injured come home," Rugar said. "The Islanders don't seem as bloodthirsty as—" He didn't finish the thought. Of course they weren't as bloodthirsty as the Fey. The Islanders hadn't learned the necessity of slaughter yet.

Hiere nodded. "They almost caught me. I had to outrun a group of them near the cabins."

"Did they see you come in here?"

He shrugged. "If they did, they didn't follow. I'm sorry, Rugar. Sorry to bring such news."

Rugar patted the scout on the shoulder. "The news is not your fault," he said.

"Why did you run?" Jewel asked. "What about the invisibility?"

Hiere looked at her for a long moment, his dark eyes sunken in his face. He clearly hadn't eaten in a long time. The water had only temporarily revived him. "I used all my reserves when I was hiding at the mouth. They attacked the ship in small boats, but they had archers hiding throughout the woods. I had to stay invisible or they would have found me." He picked at a scab on his arm. "They know we're going to keep trying until we get out. Respectfully, sir, they don't need to come in here. They will eventually get all of us at the mouth of the Cardidas."

Jewel's gaze met Rugar's over Hiere's head. The truth of that statement caught her as well. Rugar nodded.

"Jewel, help him to the Healers. Hiere, you're the first to report. Thank you for your bravery in returning to us quickly. I'll send a band out to see if they can help bring the *Uehe* in."

Hiere staggered to his feet. Jewel supported him by placing a hand on his back and ducking under his arm. She led him to the door and helped him outside. Rugar walked to the door and stood beside it. His daughter was a tall, strong woman, and the weight of Hiere bent her. He was more exhausted than he let on.

Or more discouraged.

Rugar closed the door and sank into the chair Hiere had just vacated. The wood was hard against his body. He had hoped this ship would have made it to Nye, and the Black King would have sent reinforcements. But it wasn't going to happen now. Not until they found a way to fight that poison themselves, and they were getting nowhere with it.

He had never been in a position like this. He had nothing to draw on, no reserve army, no help from his father, no unlimited ground. Not even Old Stories or history to give him a grounding. He would have to find a solution on his own.

Rugar put his head in his hands. He needed a new strategy, and he had no ideas at all.

THIRTY-EIGHT

NICHOLAS never thought he would outgrow sword practice, but in the last few months he had felt that the time had been wasted. He sat in the courtyard, the sun beating down on the cracked dirt, the unnatural rains of the past year a distant memory. There had been reports of rain near the Stone Guardians, but the storm had never come into Jahn. Rain made him nervous now; it always made him think of Fey attacks, even though he had fought that first battle in sunshine.

First and only battle. Despite the other fighting—some of it in Jahn, his father had not let Nicholas out of the palace. His father said Nicholas's life was too precious to waste. He was also convinced that the Fey now knew who Nicholas was—and would try to kill him if they could.

Nicholas's sword rested across his legs. He had been polishing the blade, waiting until the practice began. He suspected he was early; Dunbar had never kept him waiting in the past. Unlike Stephen. Stephen had always kept Nicholas waiting, believing the experience good for the Prince.

Only now Stephen no longer taught sword fighting. He no longer had time for Nicholas, always running to keep up with Nicholas's father, always sitting in on the advisory meetings. The war had changed Stephen. It had changed all of them. Nicholas felt as if he were disobeying his father each time he took a horse outside the palace walls.

A shadow fell across the dirt. Nicholas looked up. Stephen smiled down at him. "Are you ready to practice?"

Nicholas's heart leaped, but he kept the joy off his face. "What about Dunbar?"

Stephen shrugged. "He says you were contemplating quitting sword lessons. I think now would be the wrong time to stop, don't you?" His words were a bit slurred these days. The red scar that ran across his right cheek pulled his lips slightly off center and made the right side of his mouth almost immobile. He had received the wound on the day the Fey woman had disappeared. The day of the invasion. The day Lord Powell had died.

Nicholas stood and sheathed his blade. "Father won't let me go with the soldiers. If I can't fight, there is no point to practice, is there?"

"And what of defense?" Stephen asked. "Should the Fey ever get into the palace again, you will need your skills."

Nicholas grinned at him. "Honestly, Stephen, fighting just hasn't been the same with Dunbar. He's good, but he's not you."

Stephen smiled back. He patted the hilt of his own sword. "Should we begin, then?"

"Here?" Nicholas glanced around the courtyard. It was empty, but Stephen had always taught him that blades belonged in a site away from passersby.

A bit of surprise passed through Stephen's eyes so quickly Nicholas thought he imagined it. Then Stephen said, "No, no, of course not. In our old place."

Their old place was an alley between the servants' quarters and the guard barracks. The alley was rarely used and was wide enough for both men to parry and fight.

"All right," Nicholas said. He led the way. A groom nodded as he passed, leading one of the King's stallions. The horses rarely got good exercise anymore. Since the Fey had arrived, Nicholas's father did not take the horses on their rides, and he forbade Nicholas to as well. He truncated the grooms' routine, preventing them from going far from the palace. It was as if, with the walls and gates repaired, Nicholas's father believed that the thin wood would keep the Fey out.

Stephen did not keep up and chat as he used to. Once Nicholas turned to find Stephen frowning at him. When Stephen noticed Nicholas looking at him, Stephen smiled, but the smile did not reach his eyes. Perhaps Nicholas's father had ordered Stephen to fight with Nicholas. Perhaps the King had finally become convinced of the importance of fighting altogether.

Finally they reached the alley. Sunlight didn't touch the ground there, but the dirt was still hard. The alley was closed on the guard-quarters end but open to the courtyard. As they went in, another groom passed, leading a mare, and nodded as he headed toward the stables.

"I remembered this as being more private," Stephen said.

"It's even more private now that the guards don't come through here." Nicholas frowned as he took his usual place. It wasn't like Stephen to complain about passersby. Sometimes a handful of servants stopped and watched the fight, picking sides and cheering as if they were watching a real battle.

"Well," Stephen said, unsheathing his sword with a flourish, "it has been a long time."

"It has." Nicholas unsheathed his. He stood, knees bent, sword ready. But at that moment Stephen stepped forward and his blade clashed against Nicholas's, sending a shuddering jolt through Nicholas's arm.

"Hey!" Nicholas said. Stephen had never started early before.

"New tactics," Stephen said as he withdrew and danced back, amazingly light for a man his size and age. "The Fey do not wait for an invitation to fight."

That they didn't. Nicholas remembered the battle all too clearly. He stepped into the spot vacated by Stephen and lunged. Stephen parried, and the clang of blades echoed in the open air. Nicholas led the attack, each movement he made blocked by Stephen. Then, suddenly, Stephen held a dirk in his left hand, and he sliced at Nicholas when he came close.

Nicholas had to twist away from the new blade and, in doing so, left his right side undefended. Stephen's sword point grazed the skin of Nicholas's belly. The pain was sharp and instant. Nicholas looked down at the blood staining his blouse.

"First blood!" Stephen cried with an exhilaration that Nicholas had never heard.

"But we never—"

"Stop complaining, boy," Stephen said, lunging again and again. Nicholas had to parry each movement, his arm already growing tired from the odd, rapid fighting. "It's a new world."

"I guess," Nicholas said. His left hand felt empty. He hadn't fought much with a knife or a shield, but he had never had to defend himself against two blades before—except in that first battle. So that was what Stephen was doing—mimicking actual fighting conditions. If Stephen wasn't going to fight fair, neither would Nicholas.

He backed away from the sword, then slammed the flat of his blade against Stephen's knife hand. Stephen lunged with his sword, but Nicholas dodged and hit Stephen's knife hand again, then turned the sword and cut Stephen's thumb just below the knuckle. The injury was enough to loosen Stephen's grip on the knife, and Nicholas flicked it away.

The knife clattered against the servants' quarters.

"Second blood to me," Nicholas said.

Stephen's jaw set, his scar dark against his pale skin. He was no longer smiling. He lunged, stabbed, lunged, swung, and fought like a madman. Nicholas had to block each thrust or get wounded himself. Stephen was hitting with such force that Nicholas was afraid to stop fighting, afraid that Stephen would really hurt him.

It was odd, too odd. Stephen had never fought this way, not in all the years Nicholas had trained with him. His eyes were too bright, and his movements stronger than those of a man who hadn't fought in nearly a year.

Nicholas kept defending himself, anticipating, blocking, holding the swords together as long as he could. And each time the blades separated, and Stephen moved away for another swing, Nicholas took a step backward. The alley no longer seemed friendly. The darkness felt like an enemy, and Stephen had the feral expression of a man Nicholas didn't know.

Sweat ran down Nicholas's face. He hadn't practiced either, and although he was strong, his body felt the lack.

He bit his lower lip almost through, his gaze never leaving Stephen. Nicholas kept moving backward until he felt a warmth on his skin. The sun. He was in the courtyard.

People were gathered on all sides, watching with a seriousness they had never shown before. No one cheered. They all had the same uneasy expression. When he reached the center of their semicircle, Nicholas stopped defending and stepped forward, attacking with the remains of his strength. He kept lunging toward Stephen's weakened left, forcing Stephen's blade to cross his own belly. Finally, in one quick movement, Nicholas nicked Stephen's left arm again.

"Third," Nicholas said. His breath was coming in gasps. "Enough blood, Stephen. We quit."

"We're not done," Stephen said. He was still in the alley, his sword held ready before him. "You need to know how to fight in difficult situations."

"I'm done," Nicholas said. He threw his sword onto the ground between them. It landed in the dirt, and dust rose around it, dirtying the blade. Stephen looked down at it, then up at Nicholas. Stephen took a step forward, his sword poised for attack.

Fear rose like bile in Nicholas's throat, but he held his position. "We're done, swordmaster."

Stephen froze and then glanced at the crowd around them. He held the position a moment longer than he should have. When he stood, he was not smiling. "A man never throws his sword in the middle of a duel."

"It was not a duel," Nicholas said. "We were practicing."

"Times have changed, Highness," Stephen said. "You need to learn to fight in war."

"I have fought in war." Nicholas was shaking. He clenched his teeth, willing the shaking to stop. "I no longer need sword practice. And you shall never draw blood again in training. Is that clear?"

"Highness—"

"Is that clear?"

Again the look. Stephen's eyes held something—defiance—before he smiled and bowed his head. "It's clear, Highness."

"Good," Nicholas said. He crouched to pick up his

sword, not willing to take his gaze off Stephen. "I'm going to get cleaned up. You need to have that thumb attended."

"Yes, Highness."

Nicholas pushed his way through the crowd and took the entrance into the Great Hall. There, in the anteroom's coolness, he leaned against the stone wall. His body dripped with sweat and he was exhausted. He pushed up his shirt and examined the wound on his stomach. It was small, more of a cut than anything serious. The blood had already slowed to a trickle. His shirt was ruined, and he would need a poultice on the wound itself. He sighed. He hated the way things had changed. He should have known that Stephen would have changed too.

Stephen hadn't had a sword in his hand since he'd fought the Fey woman. She had attacked them and left Stephen for dead. When he'd come to, he hadn't known that Lord Powell was dead. At first he had thought Lord Powell captured until someone pointed out that the bones near his feet were those from a human skeleton and were covered with fresh blood.

Of course all of that anger and fear would come back the next time Stephen held a sword. Nicholas hadn't lost the feeling of fighting in battle; no reason Stephen should forget the moment of his worst defeat.

Nicholas took the stairs to his room two at a time. He didn't relish the idea of telling his father that sword-fighting practice was a thing of the past. An odd irony considering how hard Nicholas had struggled to be allowed to fight in the first place.

He opened the door to his chambers and went in, kicking the door closed behind him. He winced as he pulled off his ruined shirt. The action opened the cut again, and he grabbed a cloth off the dressing table, pressing it against his stomach. Nothing serious, but annoying just the same.

Nicholas stuck his head into the bucket of ice-cold wash water, letting the chill travel down his sweaty body. Then he yanked his head out and shook the water off. The droplets landed on his naked back and chest. He grabbed a towel and scrubbed the wet off his face, then dipped it into the water and washed off the rest of the sweat.

He dried off, then sprawled backward on the softness of his bed, letting the feathered mattress enfold him. His body tingled from the exercise, and his stamina was good. But he had worked too hard on that fight. If he'd wanted that kind of battle, he could have gone into the woods and waited for a Fey to appear.

A knock at the door startled him.

"Yes?" Nicholas said.

"Yer Highness, yer father requests yer presence." The voice belonged to his chamberlain. "Says there's news."

How often had he heard those words in the last few months? News was rarely good anymore. It was more dead, or sunken ships, or a food crisis near the marshes. His father had placed a food tax on the outlying provinces that hadn't been invaded by the Fey, and the landowners weren't happy with it. But with the Fey so close, Jahn would have suffered a food shortage if his father hadn't taken action.

"Come in, then," Nicholas said. "I'll need your help."

The door opened. His chamberlain entered. He was a gaunt man. His son had been Nicholas's chamberlain for three years, but the boy had died in the battle. His father never spoke unless he had something he felt was important to say. He apparently stepped into his son's job because the family relied more on the palace income than it did on the subsistence farm he had tried to maintain.

The chamberlain bowed his head. "Highness."

"Clothes," Nicholas said, as if it weren't obvious. "I was going to dress myself, but there isn't time."

The chamberlain peered at him. "You're bleeding, Highness."

"It's not serious," Nicholas said. "It'll be all right if I give it a chance to scab. But I don't have time to wait for clothing. Find me a cloth to keep against this cut, and a shirt that won't show blood."

The chamberlain disappeared into the wardrobe. Nicholas slipped out of his pants and threw them beside the bed. The chamberlain returned with a strip of cloth, which he wound around Nicholas's waist. Then he went back and got a dark shirt and fawn pants, which he helped Nicholas put on.

"Did my father say what the news is?" Nicholas asked as he adjusted the wide lace cuffs on his sleeves.

"No, Highness. But it seems important. 'Tis men on horseback."

Nicholas nodded. "Thank you," he said by way of dismissal. Then he ran his fingers through his damp hair and pulled it into a ponytail. The chamberlain picked up Nicholas's discarded clothes. Nicholas strapped his knife around his waist—he no longer went anywhere without a weapon —and headed to his father's audience chamber.

He took the winding staircase down two steps at a time and wondered what had happened now. The last time he had been called down the stairs, only a day ago, was for the news that the fifth Fey ship had been defeated at the mouth of the Cardidas. He couldn't hope for good news two days in a row.

He hurried through the passageway, entering the audience chamber alone and unannounced.

In the last year the audience chamber had lost its musty smell. The spears still lined the walls, but guards now stood between them. Real swords rested in a stand behind the dais, as did vials of holy water.

His father was seated on the throne, Stephen and Lord Stowe beside him. Stephen raised his eyebrows and half smiled as Nicholas came in. Nicholas did not acknowledge him.

Two men wearing stained clothing and days' old growth of beard stood at the base of the stairs, looking a bit confused by the sudden delay.

"Nicholas," his father said. "We started without you."

"I'm sorry, Father." Nicholas walked to the stairs, nodding as he passed the men. They smelled of sweat and horses. They had been riding for some time. "I only just heard that you'd be here."

His father nodded as if the matter was really of no consequence. Nicholas took his place behind the throne, between Lord Stowe and Stephen.

"All right," Nicholas's father said to the men below. "Continue."

" 'Twas one of their scouts we was following, Sire," said the man on the right. He was stocky with broad lips and a red nose. "He was watchin' the whole battle at the mouth of the Cardidas."

"Why didn't you capture him there?" Lord Stowe asked.

"Dinna see him, milord," the other man said. He was

stocky as well, but his stockiness looked more like muscles. "He showed up outta nowhere right in front of us."

"Showed up out of nowhere?" Nicholas asked.

"Ye see, Highness, 'twas like we seen an outline, and then it become this man," the first said.

"But you let him go," Lord Stowe said again.

"Yes, milord," the second man said. "We thought if he was scoutin', he would have ta report somewheres, and since they left the river, we knew that ye been lookin' for them."

"We have," Nicholas's father said.

"And we know where they are."

Nicholas leaned forward, his arms on the back of the throne. His posture was not quite disrespectful, but only because he was Alexander's son and would occupy the throne one day. "We already know about where they are. We've heard tales of their disappearing in the woods to the west of Jahn, near a bunch of old hovels."

"Not disappearin', beg pardon, Highness," the first man said. He took a step forward. He seemed to be the one with the courage. "They got a door."

"If they have a door, why can't we see it?" Lord Stowe asked.

"Ye can," said the second man, who then bowed his head and added, "milord."

Nicholas didn't move. If these men were correct, they had found the Fey's hiding spot. The lords had been hoping for this. They hoped they could find a way to trap the Fey inside.

The first man glanced at his companion, clearly exasperated, and continued for him. "Ye canna see the door in the day. They got tiny lights around it, like fireflies. The lights blink at different times, so ye gotta be lookin' for it. But it makes a circle that a man can put his head and shoulders through."

"What did you do after you found the door?" Nicholas's father asked.

"We waited until we dinna see nobody, then we walked around it. 'Tis like they say about the one in the river. Ye canna feel nothing except if ye close yer eyes and pretend. Although them lights at the door are hot if ye touch one."

"How do you know this is the proper door?" Stephen asked, his voice full of disdain. Nicholas shot a sidelong glance at him. Stephen was standing at attention, not looking at all tired from their exertion earlier.

"Beg pardon, sir, but we seen the creature go through it."

"You what?" Stephen asked. Color flooded his face. That news shouldn't upset him. Unless he knew something that Nicholas didn't.

"We seen him go through. He was runnin' from us fast as he could—him not knowin' that we was gonna let him go—and he dived through that door like he was headin' into a lake. Then he vanished," the second man said. He didn't add the niceties for Stephen.

"A man that was half-visible when you first saw him," Stephen said, his tone implying that the man's story seemed too tall to be true.

"Aye, sir," the first man said, ignoring Stephen's tone. "But this was different. 'Twas like that circle ate him. He went through a door."

"It is in the right location," Nicholas said.

"Lord Stowe," his father said, "I want you to take these men to a room where they can clean up and rest, as well as eat whatever they want. Then I want you to get a scribe and have them tell everything they remember, every nuance and every detail. We will need that to go over."

Nicholas stood up, astonished. The meeting was just getting interesting. His father never broke up a meeting so quickly, especially when they were getting such valuable information. Perhaps he had caught Stephen's tone and was going to reprimand him for it.

"I'll take care of it, Sire," Lord Stowe said.

"When you're done, report back to me."

"I will, Sire."

Lord Stowe led the men out of the room. The guards continued to stare straight ahead, as if they had heard nothing. Nicholas waited for his father, unwilling to challenge him in public.

"Stephen, Nicholas, come with me," his father said. He also pointed to one of the guards and indicated that he should accompany them. Then his father left the dais by the small door in the back. It led to a tiny chamber that had once been a listening booth. The last time Nicholas had been in there had been when he was a boy. He saw his first spider there, crawling across the floor, and screamed so loud he had interrupted his father's audience.

All four men barely fit inside. The chamber had four scarred chairs that looked as if they belonged in the servants' quarters. Alexander pushed one against the door, and the guard sat on it, facing them. Nicholas and Stephen took two other chairs. Nicholas's father remained standing.

"What happened?" Nicholas asked. "Why did you end that? They weren't done."

"We have enough information to begin plans," his father said. "We need to get to those Fey as quickly as we can. We have the advantage of surprise."

"If those men are right," Stephen said, "we would need hundreds of fighters."

"Not with enough holy water," Nicholas said. "We send in some fast-moving people. Maybe even that whole secret construct they have would disappear if touched. We don't know."

"What if those men are wrong?" Stephen asked. "Then what?"

"Then nothing," Nicholas's father said. "We have lost nothing."

"I think we should go with a small force, observe, and see if the men are right," Nicholas said. "Then if they are, we get enough holy water to drown the place and do a two-pronged attack, one with arrows and the other with men carrying the vials. We could rout them in no time."

"Stephen?" his father asked.

"I still think we should gather as many men as we can and send them in. We are safer in larger numbers."

His father templed his fingers and put them against his lips. "We don't know what kind of powers this secret place gives them," he said. "We shouldn't risk a lot of our own people until we have knowledge. If we can defeat them in one attack, fine. If not—"

"We have tipped our hand. They will know that we can get them, that we know where their secret place is," Stephen said.

"I suspect they already know that," Nicholas said. "The men said their scout knew he was being followed."

"But he wouldn't have gone in if he thought they saw him," his father said. "We'll have to act quickly. Stephen, I want you to fetch Monte. We'll have a meeting after dinner tonight and finalize plans. Then we'll send out a force after dark."

"At night?" Nicholas asked.

"They said lights surround the door. It makes sense, doesn't it?"

"I guess," Nicholas said. Something was odd about this conversation. It left him unsettled.

"All right, Sire," Stephen said. He stood and bowed. The guard got up and moved the chair away from the door. Nicholas's father stood and watched Stephen walk through the audience chamber. Then he dismissed the guard and eased the door closed.

"What was that?" Nicholas asked. "I have never seen you make plans on such little information."

His father grinned. "War councils are supposed to act quickly."

"But not that quickly. We don't know everything."

His father shrugged. "We know enough."

Nicholas tilted his head back and watched his father. He leaned against the door as if he didn't want anyone to come in.

Nicholas took a deep breath before asking, "What's really going on? What are you trying to do?"

His father stared at him for the longest time. His blue eyes seemed to look right through Nicholas. Nicholas remembered the look from his boyhood—that steel-eyed gaze that commanded Nicholas to confess anything he had done wrong. His father opened his mouth once, then closed it.

"Father?" Nicholas said.

His father ran a hand over his face and sighed. "This is an important opportunity for us, Nicholas," he said. "We have to make the most of it."

"But why Stephen and me? Why not wait for the other lords, have a council?"

"There isn't time, son," his father said. His voice was sad. "We're all out of time."

THIRTY-NINE

THE Fey Lamps glowed from the ceiling and the walls, lighting the small cabin like the sun. Caseo stood on the wooden floor, hands behind his back, staring at the lamps. The souls inside were still bright after a week of use. That fact had disturbed him for a year. These people were untouched by magick, indeed, seemed to have no magick of their own, and yet they had defeated the Fey with a poison more potent than anything Caseo had seen before.

He walked to the cold fireplace and leaned against it. He had insisted, when Rugar had given permission for Warders to have a building for their work, that the fireplace be made of stone. Caseo picked the stones himself—at some risk—late at night on the banks of the Cardidas. He wanted stones no bigger than a man's head and no smaller than a man's fist. Their shape had to be almost square, and he permitted no carving to make them fit. He had supervised the Domestic who had made the mortar, adding different protective spells into each batch.

Aside from the Fey lights and the stools scattered about, the room was sparsely furnished. A Domestic had made a rug for the floor that they kept rolled up against the wall.

This place was not made for comfort, but for work. Critical work.

The table in the center of the room was made from wood, again with Caseo's supervision. He had followed the team of tree cutters into the forest and picked out the tree himself. He had chosen one that was strong and vibrant, hoping those qualities would transfer into the table itself. They seemed to.

Finally he let himself look at the vial on the tabletop. Its cut-glass sides sparkled in the bright light. One of the other Warders had called it beautiful, but he saw no beauty in it. In the last year that vial had become a personal enemy. The only spell with a secret that he couldn't break.

The sharp edges of the stone cut into his back. The Fey lights gave off no scent, so the room smelled of his own sweat. He had been there for a day with no fire because he still wasn't sure what temperature extremes might do to the water inside the vial. That could be the next experiment. He wasn't sure of that either.

Also, the room's chill helped keep him awake. With the defeat of the fifth ship, the only hope the Fey had was to conquer this poison. Or to find a way around it. He and the other Warders were the only ones qualified to find that solution.

They had used half the bottle this year, working drop by drop. One Warder had died and—the Powers forgive them —the rest had watched with fascination. They had even studied his twisted body to see what they could learn from it. It had been grisly work, and they had all noted that the liquid had somehow changed the very fabric of his being. Not just his skin molded and changed, but his bones, his internal organs, everything that made him into a living, breathing being had been altered.

The slowness frustrated him more than anything. He had been in the cabin since he'd heard the news about the last ship, mostly staring at that bottle as if it held the answer— though he knew it didn't. Fey had died from water held in other containers as well. No, something about this water was different from any other water he had encountered. Different from any other water on Blue Isle, so far as he could tell. The Fey drank from the Cardidas to no ill effect.

They had found another stream not far from the Shadowlands, and its water was fine as well.

Somehow the Islanders had altered this water. Whatever they had done, he would find because in it was the secret he was looking for.

He wished he had a way of examining each drop of water as he would look at a clump of dirt. A man could see the elements in dirt. He could get it wet and test various aspects of it. But water, unless it had something floating in it, was not as easily read. This water had nothing floating. That had been the first thing he looked for.

What they had done was to experiment on tissue from Fey cadavers, and a few samples taken from living Fey. That, at least, had yielded some results. He found that the solution, if diluted, had slower effects and sometimes not quite as dangerous effects. He wasn't sure how to use that information in battle, unless some enterprising Fey could get to the supply of poison and dilute it. But if they could do that, then they could just as easily get rid of it or substitute real water.

Their most significant finding was that if the solution was washed off with real water quickly, the damage to the tissue was minimal. That, at least, had a practical application, one he had presented to Rugar. If someone was injured in battle with a weapon dipped into the poison, or injured by the poison itself, cleaning the wound very, very quickly would ensure minimal damage.

Rugar had not applied that finding to the ship heading to the Stone Guardians. *Warriors do not have time to wash themselves in the middle of battle,* he had said. *We need a better solution than that.*

Caseo planned to speak to him again. The solution they had found was better than none.

He touched the edge of the table. The wood was warm and firm against his fingertips. Although he had been alone with the vial a hundred times since they had come to the Shadowlands, he had never touched it. He was afraid that somehow even the bottle itself would contaminate him.

Perhaps it already had. The bottle was all he thought about. He even dreamed of the poison. He hadn't worked on new spells since they had come to the Shadowlands, and even his interest in reviewing innovations made by others had lessened.

He felt that until they had solved this problem, there was no point in working toward a future. Until they conquered the poison in this bottle, the Fey had no future at all.

FORTY

HIS rooms were cold. Matthias sighed, looked up from the book he had been studying, and noted that the sun had set. He reached for the velvet bellpull and gave it a firm yank. The Aud should have been there before dark to light the fire and close the tapestries. Lately, though, the service in the Tabernacle had got particularly bad. He blamed some of it on the turnover. Auds were leaving the city to join country villages. They figured they would be safer there. They were probably right.

He lit his lamp and continued his study. The book he was poring over had particularly bad hand-lettering, but he felt it worthwhile. He had been studying all the old texts, looking for clues to the questions the Rocaan had asked him on the night of the invasion. So far he had found few references to the physical representatives of the Soldiers of the Enemy. Most references were to their symbolic meaning.

This particular text, though, was a history of the Tabernacle itself, written a century before. What fascinated Matthias were all the hidden areas of the Tabernacle, built for various monastic and special purposes. He had not had a chance to ask the Rocaan if he knew of these areas, and he wasn't sure he was going to. But he was taking notes. He planned to investigate all the secret areas himself.

When he heard the expected knock on the door, he gathered his papers and marked his place before he bade the Aud to enter. He swiveled in his chair and was startled to see Porciluna.

"You should stand when a colleague enters the room, you know," Porciluna said.

On Porciluna the Elder's black robe looked expensive. His filigree sword rested on the top of the mound that was his stomach. His sash was not tied so much as wrapped around him, a slash of red on the black. Despite the hardships of the last year, Porciluna still looked like a creature of leisure, and Matthias hated him for that. Matthias had lost a considerable amount of weight, which he couldn't afford, and noted each morning when he did his toilet that a new worry line appeared in his face.

He did not stand but set his pen down carefully so that he didn't get ink on his hand. "Did we have business, Porciluna?"

Porciluna pursed his lips and shook his head. "But I thought that you might want to know what happened today."

Matthias indicated a chair next to his. He turned his chair outward so that he could see Porciluna. Porciluna took the chair offered, sighing as he took the weight off his feet. Matthias clasped his hands in his lap. Usually when someone came to him, it meant a village hadn't had enough holy water, or there had been yet another series of Fey-related deaths. Sometimes he thought this war would end only when there were no people left to kill.

"What?" he asked, his hands clasped so tightly, he could feel the strain in his fingers.

"The Rocaan insisted on doing another ceremony for the honored dead."

Matthias let out breath he hadn't realized he was holding.

"He left his own sword at the grave sites, even though I warned him it would be stolen and sold, and he is not talking sense." Porciluna smoothed the strands of hair on his balding head. A touch of color rose in his cheeks.

"What's he saying now?" Matthias asked softly.

"That his actions caused the Fey to come. His sinning caused all of this."

Matthias picked up his pen and put it in its holder. He would get no more work done this day.

Porciluna grabbed his arm. "How can you be so calm? Don't you see what's happening here?"

"I see a lot of things happening," Matthias said. "None of them good."

Porciluna's palm was damp. His grip tightened on Matthias. Matthias looked down at the hand, and Porciluna let go. He smoothed his hand on his own robe. "I am worried, Matthias. The Rocaan doesn't seem to be in his right mind. He is letting affairs of the Church slip. He spends too much time in that cell of his. He presides over funeral ceremonies best left to others, and now this."

"He's been talking like this since the invasion," Matthias said.

Porciluna shook his head. "No. Not like this. He has asked theological questions and had us digging through texts for answers. But something in the way he acted this time. I feel as if he plans to make a change. He plans to do something that he believes will make the Fey leave. Something . . . crazy." He spoke the last word so softly, Matthias almost didn't hear it.

Bile rose in Matthias's throat, and he swallowed to keep it down. One more stress. One stress too many. The one he wanted to ignore. "You think the Rocaan has lost his mind?"

"I see little of the man I used to know," Porciluna said.

A knock on the door made them both jump. They glanced at each other—who could have heard them?—and then Matthias remembered the Aud he had called.

"Come in," he said.

The door opened, and the Aud shuffled in, carrying a candle. Its tiny flame made Matthias realize how dark the room had become. He could see only Porciluna in the light given off by the lamp on his desk. The rest of the room was in shadows.

"I thought I had orders to light the Elders' rooms when darkness fell," Matthias said sharply.

"My apologies, Respected Sir. I am not usually in charge of the rooms. Your man seems to have disappeared."

Another one. This was disturbing him as well. "All right, then. I want the tapestries done, here and in the other Elders' quarters, as well as the lights, and lighting the night fires. Make sure that someone has taken care of the Rocaan as well."

"As you wish, Respected Sir." The Aud went to the first lamp and lit it.

The brightness in the room increased, revealing the velvet sofa, the ornate chairs flanking a table decorated with tiny swords. The Aud went from light to light until a softness filled the room. Then he pulled and fastened the tapestries in front of the windows, blocking out the darkness and replacing it with scenes from the Roca's life.

Matthias and Porciluna watched the Aud move from place to place, saying nothing. Once the Aud glanced over his shoulder at them, and then continued, as if he found their behavior strange. Finally he crouched in front of the fireplace and pulled pieces of wood together to build a fire. The small thumps and shufflings he made were the only sounds in the room.

Matthias looked away, grateful for the respite from the conversation. He had been ignoring the Rocaan, and the problems there, worrying more about the Fey and the future. It had been easy to stay away from the old man; he didn't seem to be comfortable around Matthias these days, as if he blamed Matthias for all the decisions he had made during the invasion. Matthias should have realized that someday the problem would come back to him, since he was the one the Rocaan had trusted with the secret of holy water. On the day of the invasion Matthias had been the Rocaan's choice to succeed him. Matthias doubted if the Rocaan felt that way now.

Wood snapped behind him, and the faintest scent of smoke filled the air. He turned. The Aud was replacing the grate. Then he stood, wiped his hands on his robe, and bowed his head. "Anything else, Respected Sir?" he asked.

"Not in here," Matthias said, hoping that the Aud heard his pointed reminder to remember the other chambers.

The Aud nodded again, then let himself out.

Once the door had clicked shut, Porciluna said, "All the little things seem to be coming apart."

"They do, don't they?" Matthias said. "Just another sign,

I guess. Although"—he chose his words carefully—"these do not mean that the Rocaan is crazy."

"He's not thinking clearly," Porciluna said. "He is tending to the wrong things."

"The Rocaan is a man of faith." Matthias stretched his legs and leaned back in his chair. The wood creaked from his weight. "There are times when he will not follow logic but that still, small voice within."

"We are all men of faith," Porciluna said.

"Are we?" Matthias raised his gaze to Porciluna's face. Porciluna's features looked soft, as if the candlelight had wiped any edges off it.

Porciluna straightened, placing his hands on his knees. "If we weren't, we wouldn't be Elders."

Matthias smiled. "Come now, Porciluna. Save that talk for the faithful. You know as well as I that many men are here because they have nowhere else to go, and that others are here because if they are sufficiently ambitious, they can live a life of luxury."

"If you're implying that I am here for such base reasons—"

"I'm not implying anything," Matthias said. "But if we are going to have a true discussion about the future of the Tabernacle, we need to do so honestly. I have watched you, Porciluna, and I can predict your actions. If you were listening to a still, small voice, I would not be able to. You are an ambitious man who enjoys this life. I do not know if you believe in the Roca or in God."

"All the men here are good," Porciluna said.

Matthias studied him, knowing he would get no more out of Porciluna than that. "Yes," he said after a moment. "They are. And there is a lot of wisdom in the Words Written and Unwritten."

"But they say nothing about what to do with a Rocaan who is unfit," Porciluna said. "I think we should call a meeting of the Elders. Take a vote, maybe remove him."

Matthias folded his hands over his stomach. It was growling. He hadn't eaten all day. "It's unprecedented," he said. "It might cause a schism in the Church that we don't need."

"It might save us."

The words hung in the silence. The wood snapped again,

an explosion in the quiet room. Then logs tumbled as the fire burned itself down.

Matthias pushed himself out of his chair, clasped his hands behind his back, and walked over to the fireplace. The Aud had built a lovely fire. The red and gold sparks flew up the chimney, and the fire itself burned tall and hot. "What bothers me," he said, letting the warmth caress the front of his body, "is how do we judge? If you study the words, the Roca often seemed irrational. Perhaps true faith is a form of insanity."

"It seems to me," Porciluna said, "that he cannot reconcile what he knows of Rocaanism with the powers of holy water."

"You mean, he cannot countenance the fact that it causes death?"

"Death in unbelievers."

Matthias laughed. "If that was the case, then half the leaders of the Church would be dead. I have trouble with that property of holy water myself, and I have not the purity of spirit the Rocaan does."

"So you do believe that the events have hurt his mind."

"I think the events of the past year have changed all of us." Matthias put one hand on the mantel. "But if they've hurt his mind, I don't know. I do know that he has questioned his actions since that day. And I also know that, more than any of us, he listens for the still, small voice. Perhaps he is hearing it. How are we to tell?"

Porciluna stood. "I plan to call the meeting of the Elders."

Matthias pushed away from the fireplace. His skin was hot in the front, but the rest of the room still felt cool. "If you say one word about removing him, I will fight you every step of the way."

Porciluna frowned. "Why? You're the logical choice to be the next Rocaan."

"Inherit an office that your actions would rob of all its powers? I think not, Porciluna. The Rocaan shall remain until he dies in office. And when he does, the next Rocaan will be his choice for a successor, as it always has been."

"But he has already made the choice," Porciluna said.

"Oh, no." Matthias turned back to the fire. The flames had died down but were still burning more blue than red.

He could not see anything reflected in them. "He taught me the secrets of holy water so that he would not have to bear the responsibilities of its use alone. Never once did he say anything about my succeeding him. I think the lesson was more my punishment for forcing him into taking action."

"We could hold the meeting without you," Porciluna said.

"But you won't," Matthias said. "You can't get rid of the Rocaan without my help. You'll have no one to take his place. And I will not replace him without his blessing." He turned and faced Porciluna. "Do I make myself clear?"

"Clear enough," Porciluna said. His tone made Matthias cringe.

"Don't make a mockery of this," Matthias said. "Right now we need to be unified."

Porciluna pursed his lips. "All right. We'll be unified. For now. But I warn you, Matthias, if the Rocaan gets worse, we'll have to take action."

"I'll let you know when he's worse," Matthias said. "I'll let you know when to take action."

"Always in charge, eh, Matthias?" Porciluna bowed slightly, just as the Aud had done, but unlike the Aud, Porciluna's expression was mocking. "I'll let myself out. Good night."

Matthias didn't answer him. Once Porciluna disappeared through the door, Matthias locked the door after him. Then he leaned on it.

A revolution in the Church couldn't come at a worse time. He hoped he had staved it off. For if he hadn't, more than the fate of Rocaanism was at stake. The fate of the entire Isle was.

FORTY-ONE

HE was cold, and he hadn't had a decent night's sleep since they had left the ships. Scavenger curled up behind a pile of wood, near the back of Shadowlands. He no longer kept night or day hours. He paid attention to the niceties of time only when his services were needed. Until then he slept when he felt like sleeping, and ate when he felt like eating.

As if he had that kind of choice.

He pulled his coat over his short legs and patted a pile of empty pouches together as his pillow. The gray mist that formed the base of Shadowlands had a chill to it, even though Rugar denied it. And the ground beneath the mist, the invisible ground that no one could see, felt like the flat end of a sword blade. Cool and smooth and completely lacking in warmth.

A year they had been in Shadowlands, and no one had seen fit to give the Red Caps somewhere to sleep. He had spoken to Tazy, the head of the Foot Soldiers, several times about this, and Tazy promised each time to do something.

He had done nothing.

Scavenger even thought of speaking to the Warders, but he lacked the courage. And he certainly didn't have the courage to speak to Rugar. Rugar would probably ignore him anyway.

Scavenger curled against the wood. It felt damp. He shivered, wishing for something more comfortable to lie on, and closed his eyes. Everything looked gray. He was so tired of gray. He had even sneaked out one day and wandered through the forest, and when he had returned—in full view of Rugar's daughter and her Infantry companions—no one had said a word. It was as if he didn't exist.

He had never existed for them. He was a tool, as their swords were tools, to be used only during warfare, only at the right time. It galled him that he had no recourse. As a young man he used to dream of growing into his magickal powers late—very late—and becoming a Shaman or an Enchanter, who could twist them all. At the very least he hoped he would become a Dream Rider, so that he could control their subconsciouses while they slept.

But he had grown no magick, just as he had failed to grow tall, and so those dreams had become nothing more than fantasies of revenge, fantasies he could never complete.

Now that Silence was gone, doing his duty somewhere in the city, no one spoke to Scavenger, no one except the other Red Caps. They discussed the best places to sleep or the places to steal food outside Shadowlands. Nothing terribly illuminating.

"Boy!" A foot prodded his back.

Scavenger kept his eyes closed. He didn't move. He had learned long ago that if he ignored people who sought him out, they often went away.

"Boy!" The prodding became almost a kick. A sharp pain ran up Scavenger's spine.

The idiot would kick him to death if he didn't respond. Scavenger opened his eyes. One of the tall Infantry boys stood over him. He spent most of his time with Rugar's daughter. Scavenger remembered thinking the boy's name was appropriate.

"Boy!" the boy said as he kicked him.

Scavenger rolled away. Burden. That was what the child was called. Burden, because his parents thought he would come to nothing. They suspected he would be a Red Cap, but he grew too tall, too graceful, too beautiful. A Fey as tall as that would come to his magick eventually.

"What?" Scavenger said, careful not to let resentment into his tone. If he complained about each time he was called "boy" by someone younger than he was, he would have been killed by now.

"We need this wood. You'll have to move."

Scavenger sighed, grabbed his cloak and pouches, and sat up. His back would be bruised where the boy had kicked it. The spot had been a good one for a few days. Now maybe he could steal Vulture's place under the Domicile stairs.

"Oh, and boy?"

Scavenger looked up at this Burden. The boy's mouth was set in a thin line.

"Don't sleep in public places anymore. It's not seemly."

Scavenger clenched his teeth, but he couldn't hold back the words. "Do you have a better idea?"

The boy raised his chin as if Scavenger had slapped him. "Excuse me?"

"I was wondering if you knew somewhere else I could sleep. No one seems to want Red Caps in their cabins."

Burden shook his head slightly, as if he couldn't believe what Scavenger had said. "We all build our homes, Cap. I suggest you do the same."

"You have the help of Domestics. They won't even talk to me."

Burden shrugged. "Haven't you a leader? Go talk to him."

Scavenger stared at the boy for a moment, unable to believe what he had heard. Of course Red Caps did not have a leader. Foot Soldiers ordered Red Caps about, as did Warders, but no one organized them. Red Caps were forbidden by the Black King to organize. If more than two were seen together in a public place, they could be arrested, even killed.

"There's no one," Scavenger said. "If you don't want me sleeping near your precious wood, I would suggest you talk to someone."

"Has anyone ever told you that you should be more cautious about how you talk to your betters?"

Scavenger swallowed his first response. "I am in a dilemma, sir. You tell me not to sleep in public, but no one has helped me make a private place. You tell me to talk to the leader of my unit, but I have no unit and no leader. I simply want to do what you tell me."

Burden shook his head. "I didn't mean for this to be such a production," he said. "Look, boy. Just sleep somewhere out of the way. Figure we need the wood and water." He pointed to an empty gray patch near the very edge of the Shadowlands. "Sleep somewhere like that, a space no one will ever use."

For a moment Scavenger pictured his hands wrapped around Burden's neck, his little fingers choking the air from Burden's lungs. But Burden was Infantry. He was trained to be strong, even if he had no magick. He would be able to overpower Scavenger in a moment, and then Scavenger would have to face the Warders or Rugar for punishment.

Scavenger tucked his pouches under his arm, grabbed his cloak, and stood. "Sorry, sir. I'm glad you told me what to do. I will move out of your way now. Thank you for the help."

"Certainly," Burden said. He turned his back on Scavenger and began lifting pieces of wood to carry them somewhere else.

Scavenger stood for a moment and watched the boy's easy strength. Such grace, such confidence even though he was still Infantry. It was as if he knew he would get his magick someday.

And he would. Fey who grew tall and willowy grew into their magick. A Fey who stopped growing at child height, as Scavenger had, would never get magick at all.

But they all treated him as if his brain had stopped growing as well. And it hadn't. The boy didn't even recognize the sarcasm Scavenger had used in speaking to him. The boy probably thought Scavenger wasn't capable of such an advanced way of speaking, just as the boy didn't realize that Red Caps needed comfort too.

Scavenger sighed. He would go to the Domicile and see if he could beg some food from the Domestics. Then he would scout the Shadowlands for a new place to sleep.

FORTY-TWO

A full moon gave the woods a silvery glow. Theron led his party quietly down the path. Twenty fighters, even armed as heavily as they were with holy water, seemed hardly enough to take on the entire Fey army. Still, the plan made a lot of sense. If the Fey could be destroyed with a touch of the liquid, perhaps their secret hiding place could be destroyed as well.

He just hated being the leader of the team that launched the attack.

The group following him moved more silently than he'd expected they would. He had grown up in the woods—one of the reasons Monte had chosen him for the job—but except for his friends, the rest were city boys who had shown a particular aptitude for fighting. Theron hadn't expected them to be so calm nor so quiet.

The full moon helped. The woods weren't as dark as he had seen them. It was almost like daylight out there, a thin, silver daylight, but daylight just the same. The air smelled of pine and the Cardidas, which followed a mile away. The rustling of animals had spooked the troop a few times, but he recognized the sounds. A deer rooting, a hawk hunting, a tsia baying for its mate.

It had rained just a bit as the force was setting out, and that, too, had been in their favor. Theron saw the prints of another person on the path, just ahead of them, and he knew that someone had been there before. The prints probably had no relation to the attack, but he couldn't be too sure. He had warned the others to be prepared, that the Fey might have advance warning.

The goal, as Monte had explained it to him, was to get as much holy water through the Circle of Light as possible. If the attack force could get through that Circle as well, so much the better. What Monte hadn't said—and hadn't needed to say—was that the force probably would not come back.

The Fey were smart, Theron had to give them that. When Monte had described the location of the hiding place, it had not surprised Theron. In fact, it made him realize again just how smart they were. He knew the area. Most of the hovels had been abandoned years ago. One was owned by a childless couple who were probably elderly or dead by now. The only true cabin had been the site of a spectacular murder on the day of the invasion—the Fey obviously making plans that early for a base in the region.

The woods there were tamed, but empty of Islander life. Too close to Jahn for some, too far for others. No stream that fed off the Cardidas, and the Cardidas itself a bit wild at that point. No one had thought to start a village there. That part of the forest was too hard for conventional living.

Finally he reached the double oaks mentioned in Monte's description. The sight of the two trees, their roots almost blocking the path, soothed him. When he had seen Monte read the instructions off a sheet, he had wondered how many hands the instructions had gone through. Theron was terrified they would find themselves in the woods completely lost, advantage lost, and the Fey finally warned of their arrival.

The slaughter would be horrible.

The slaughter was always horrible when the Fey had the element of surprise. They killed quickly, ruthlessly, and viciously. A party of twenty would be dead even before the leader had realized the Fey were nearby.

Theron stopped at the double oaks and put a finger to his lips. The others stopped too. He could barely make out the faces in the weird silver light: Kondros, Matio, and Adrian, Theron's friends since they were boys; Bendre, Cyta, and Lysis, the only volunteers for this campaign; Ure, Surl, and Ort, members of the King's guard; and the others, stretching back into the dark. They all watched him silently. He couldn't even hear their breathing.

He pointed toward the Cardidas. They had all known that they would leave the path eventually. He waited until they were together before showing them the way they would have to go. Theron put a finger to his lips and slipped off the path.

The ground was damp from the rain, and the air had an earthy smell. The landmarks were as Monte had told him: a large rock to the left, a slender deer trail through the weeds, a dead tree pale and thin in the moonlight. When Theron reached the spot where the Circle of Light should be, he stopped again. Monte had not mentioned the most obvious landmark of all.

A circle in the ground large enough to fit several people inside comfortably. There was no fire hole inside the circle, nor did there appear to be any trampled grass. The circle itself was made of dirt. Grass poked through, as did tiny flowers. This circle stood in the middle of the clearing where Monte had said they would find a Circle of Light in the air.

The hair stood up on the back of Theron's neck. He hated changes and misinformation. It made him nervous. If Monte hadn't made it clear that this plan was the King's, Theron would have stopped right there and turned the troop around.

The moonlight in the Ground Circle seemed brighter than anywhere else in the forest. It was almost as if someone had taken a lamp and hung it from a tree so that the light would spill into that one patch of ground. But there were no tree branches above it.

Theron swallowed. He scanned for the Circle of Light, wondering how he would see it in the bright moonlight. The sky was an odd blue-gray there, also tainted by the moon.

No animals rustled. The troop was alone in the woods.

A hand grabbed his shoulder, and it took all of Theron's discipline to keep from crying out. He glanced over. Kondros, his round face clearly visible in the light, then nodded toward the clearing. Theron shook his head. Kondros pointed. Theron followed the direction indicated by Kondros's finger.

There, just above the circle on the ground, was a matching circle in the air. Only this circle was composed of flickering lights. He stared at the lights, thinking they were somehow familiar. Then he realized they mimicked the will-o'-the-wisps he had seen near the Daisy Stream at night when he'd been a boy. But they weren't will-o'-the-wisps. They had a regular pulse and a different shape. He almost believed that if he touched one, it would speak to him.

Kondros's grip remained tight on Theron's shoulder. Theron had taken a step into the clearing without realizing it. He glanced at his friend.

The Circle was bigger than he expected. They would have no trouble going through it.

Theron put his hand on Kondros's. Kondros nodded and let go. Theron turned to the group and help up three fingers. The gesture was repeated by the men in the front so that the men in the back could see.

He was thankful he had described four different plans with them. The third was the most cautious method of attack.

The group fanned out around the clearing, staying away from the Circle itself. The first squad of four—Cyta, Adrian, Ort, and a young recruit named Luke, whom Theron suspected to be too young even to serve with the guards—opened the pouches on their hips and pulled out the holy water. Someone in the guard unit a few months back had modified the containers. Instead of the religious vials, the men now carried goat bladders with spouts on the top: a quick squeeze, and water streamed from the spouts. In this new form the water had twice the distance of a splash tossed from a bottle. A fighter could actually aim the spout, squeeze the bladder, and shoot an arc of liquid two body lengths with accuracy. The containers created a new weapon, one that kept the fighters away from the Fey and their strange powers.

The remaining group placed their already tainted arrows into bows, waiting for Fey to appear. They stood in firing position around the edge of the clearing, knowing that they would have to be vigilant.

Theron tensed. He was the only one who had not drawn his bow. Instead, he clutched a knife and his own container of holy water. The others could shoot. If he saw a Fey, he would kill it with his own two hands.

The four leads crouched as they crossed the clearing. Cyta was the small unit's leader. He paused with a movement of his hand when they reached the outside of the drawn circle. Then he shot a bit of holy water inside. Nothing screamed, and nothing disappeared. The light remained bright, the clearing empty.

Cyta stepped over the dirt line. His skin turned silver in the light. Adrian followed, as did Ort. Luke hesitated before stepping across. He was the only one who looked back to see if someone—or something—was behind him.

Theron's grip on his water container tightened. His entire being was on alert. Kondros's breathing suddenly seemed very loud. The faint shuffling of feet, the slight movements the other men made, put Theron's nerves on edge.

Cyta walked toward the Circle of Light. His expression was rapt. He held his container before him like a shield. His three companions followed. Cyta stopped in front of the flickering Circle. Slowly he put his free hand forward. It went past the lights and looked as if it were eaten by blackness. Then his entire body shook, and he flew backward, landing outside the circle on the ground, and near the trees.

The others shot their holy water at the center of the Circle of Light. The stream of water hit something solid in the middle and doused them instead. They turned and tried to run, but slammed against the edge of the drawn circle as if they were encased in glass.

The light in the clearing grew brighter, as if someone had added extra candles to the moon. The men remained frozen, as if they couldn't believe what they were seeing.

Suddenly Fey appeared behind the men, across the clearing. Theron opened his mouth to shout a warning when hands gripped him around the waist, spinning him around. By instinct he squeezed the container and shoved his knife forward at the same time. The knife went into the Fey's stomach and, as he started to scream, water hit him in the face. But the others were not prepared. Bows went flying, and men screamed as Fey swords ran them through.

Theron stepped away from the melting Fey and sprayed his water at the Fey around him. They screamed and fell back, clawing at their faces, their chests, their arms. Kondros, bleeding from the side, pulled out his own holy water and sent great jutting arcs of it in all directions. Theron ran after the Fey still stabbing at his men, spraying and missing.

The Fey ran for the Circle. Theron, Kondros, and several others followed, the holy water like streams in the air. The water sparkled as it flew, still falling short of the moving Fey. They jumped over the dirt circle and disappeared into the Circle of Light.

The three Islanders were still inside, struggling to get out. Six of the Fey women grabbed them and dragged them through the light circle.

Theron ran after them, Kondros at his heels. The silent clearing was now full of screaming and the stench of burning flesh. As he reached the Circle, Theron shot the holy water. It arced toward the odd light but splashed against the air as if it were hitting glass. It ran down the sides, creating a visible barrier that seemed to have grown from the dirt line itself.

Kondros passed him and pounded on the barrier where the water had made it visible. Cyta joined him, then Theron. Their fists hit a substance as smooth as ice, as strong as metal. The door into the Circle of Light was open, and inside they saw a white light, and no floor. The three Islanders inside were floating with the Fey toward houses built in the light. Then darkness shrouded it all again.

Theron fell forward into the circle, landing face first in the damp grass. A grunt beside him told him that Kondros had fallen as well. Cyta crouched above them.

"They controlled this," he said. "They knew."

They knew. And they had planned it for prisoners. Prisoners with holy water. Perhaps the three could escape. But if Theron had been taking prisoners, he would have separated the weapons from the warriors immediately.

"They wanted to capture some holy water," he said. "And we let them."

"We didn't know," Kondros said.

"I knew." Theron's voice was soft. "The plan had no

strength. That was why I took such odd precautions. It was almost as if the King planned to sacrifice us. If he was going to attack their stronghold, why so few men? Isn't that relying too much on a weapon?"

"It should have worked," Cyta said. "You saw how it affects their bodies."

"Yes," Theron said. "And fire destroys wood. It destroys our bodies. But it forges iron."

"We have to get out of here," Kondros said.

Theron pushed himself off the ground. He wiped the dirt from his face. How many dead? How many wounded? He had always vowed to die with his men if they were attacked. How could he live?

"There's no great hurry," Cyta said. "If they wanted us all to die, they would have killed us." He took Kondros's hand and pulled him to his feet. "No. They want us to go back and report on this."

"They know that capturing the holy water will scare everyone," Theron said.

"They want us to know who is in charge," Kondros said.

Theron ignored Cyta's offer of a hand. He got to his feet on his own. "They're not in charge. They have a fortress that we can't get into, but the fortress is on our land. They're trapped here. We can kill them all if we like. We're not going to scare that easily."

He hoped. He sighed and left the other two standing outside the Circle. He went back into the woods to see if anyone else had survived.

FORTY-THREE

SOLANDA hurried down the darkened street, the cobblestone cold and hard against her paws. Even this far from the docks, the smell of fish was almost overpowering. She swallowed the excess saliva in her mouth, promising herself that she would indulge in an entire salmon when this mission was over.

The houses were still dark and quiet. Most of the people slept. A few had got up to man the boats, but she had avoided them. Islanders had a fondness for cats, calling her and offering her food whenever they saw her. She could resist the calls, but not the food. One woman had offered her chicken livers, petted her, and then taken her into the house and wouldn't let her out. Solanda had had to wait until night, change to her human form, and then open the door herself to get away. She didn't want that to happen again.

Especially tonight. Rugar had sent her from the Shadowlands when the moon had been at its highest. She had gone quietly through the woods, glad she had changed inside Shadowlands when she'd seen the party of Islanders approach. A battle just outside the Circle. These Islanders didn't know what they were getting into.

She was sorry that she had to miss it. She missed victory. At night she lay on the mattress she had stolen from one of the hovels—stolen and repaired, on her own, since the Domestics were overworked—and recounted the successful campaigns she had been in. Sometimes she remembered how it felt to be a victor, to take over entire cultures, to keep what one liked about them, and to change everything else. Once they conquered an area, the Fey set up governors whose job was to keep the area producing, to keep the populace under control, and to change as little as possible. Certainly the laws were different: the Fey brought their own legal system, their own government, but art, language, custom remained the same.

Here things were still in flux. Here she felt out of control. She hated living in the Shadowlands, hated having to do as Rugar told her. He feared for her and would not let her loose in the city as was her wont, because she was the only Shape-Shifter on this trip, and he was afraid to lose her.

This fear would make him lose his advantage. A Shape-Shifter was no good if she was used only for petty errands. A Shape-Shifter worked best as a spy, deep under cover in the new land, learning secrets from the natives. Shape-Shifters had won some of the longer campaigns for the Fey.

She raised her head, followed the faint scent of unfamiliar urine along the curb. She stopped, sniffed, noted that two male cats were debating the territory. The street was empty except for her, and for the dark buildings on the side. She ran down the cobblestone, not wanting to get involved in a petty turf war. It had happened to her before, and she had gone back to the Shadowlands scratched and bleeding because she hadn't acted like a normal female cat.

The wall around the palace had been poorly repaired. The Islanders had done a hasty job: nailing wood over the holes, using broken boards to cover destroyed areas, trying to use the same gate with new boards placed haphazardly over the shattered center. She slipped through the bottom of the gate, under a broken board, careful to avoid the shards of wood—she hated getting slivers in her coat—and she pranced along the path, carefully avoiding the puddles of horse urine and the big patch of horse dung. The smells inside the palace always assaulted her—too many people in too close an area; animals loose in the back part of the yard;

an oversize vegetable and herb garden tended the old-fashioned way with old-fashioned fertilizer.

Once the Fey took over, they would change some of the unsanitary practices of this little backward community.

If they took over.

She leaped onto a rock outside the kitchen and made herself catch her breath. Almost unbidden, one paw came up. She licked it, then wiped it over her face, washing off the residue of the odors and the night's march. She hated these doubts that crept into her mind. Rugar had inspired them. He wasn't taking the kind of leadership role that he should. He should come out of hiding in the Shadowlands. He should take advantage of the special talents of his people, and he should assassinate these Islanders as they slept.

But he was afraid they slept with poison beside their beds. He was afraid that he would lose his entire force and be left with nothing.

And he did have a point. Of the six Doppelgängers they had brought, they had lost two, both in the Tabernacle. The first had died during the First Battle for Jahn, and the second had mistakenly touched something he had thought filled with regular water and discovered their poison instead. She never would have found out what had happened to him if she hadn't been on the prowl a few days later and overheard two of the Black Robes discussing how one of the brazen Fey had tried to sneak into the Tabernacle, and died by his own hand.

Now she was supposed to send two more into that evil place. The Spell Warders were having no luck deciphering the secret to the potion. Doppelgängers in the right position should be able to learn it on their own.

The kitchen door opened and the cook looked out. His face was already red from the heat of the fireplace. Beads of sweat stood on his forehead, and the back of his white uniform was pasted to his back. The sweat stench was almost as overpowering as the smell of food coming from inside. Her stomach rumbled. She put her paw down, looked up at him, and meowed.

When he saw her, he smiled. "Yer early this day, little miss. Trying to sneak ahead of the others, are ye?"

She meowed again, then jumped off the rock and rubbed against his leg. He ran a large hand over her fur. His skin smelled of freshly dead chicken, spices, and wood. She licked the fat of his palm and tasted salt.

"Wait, little miss. I got a treat for ye from the butcher. I'll get it before yer little friends come, and ye'll have it all to yerself."

She sank back on her haunches and watched as he closed the door. Voices echoed through the courtyard as the servants began their day. A horse neighed. The sky was turning pink. It would be a beautiful day.

He opened the door and set a plate of chopped chicken liver before her. One liver, but more than enough to sate her small appetite. She wound through his legs, contemplating a run through the kitchen, but the liver won. She went to the dish, eating so fast she could barely taste the food. When she was a cat, she ate like a cat—quickly, sometimes so quickly that the food came back up—all taste and sensation and desire. The liver was gone in a moment.

She sat back and licked her whiskers. He was still watching, a fond smile on his face. The door to the kitchen was open, and the heat from the fireplace was palpable.

He saw where she was looking and stepped outside, closing the door behind him. He crouched and held out his hand. She sniffed it to see if he held any more food.

"Ye canna go through there, little miss. They'd have me head for sure. But ye come back in the mornings, and I'll make sure ye get something special."

She let him pet her, both as a reward for the information about the kitchen, and as thanks for the chicken. The liver left her thirsty, and she would need to get a drink of something. She took one more wistful glance at the empty bowl, then stalked into the yard, licking her whiskers as she walked.

Rugar had told her not to bother Silence. The information he brought from the King himself was perfect. Tel, on the other hand, had spent the last year in the stables, and the information he had heard wasn't as valuable as Rugar had expected. In Nye, and in L'Nacin, the stable masters were privy to most knowledge because the leaders used the horses so much. But on Blue Isle apparently only the young Prince used the horses and then rarely talked about affairs of state.

She hated the stables. More than once she had spooked a

horse and nearly been trampled. She sat, finished washing her face, then searched for a puddle of rainwater, putting off the mission as long as she could. The only untainted puddle she found was in a mud hole near the stables. She took a quick drink, then winced at the grittiness of the water. It would do. For now.

The stables housed only fifteen horses. They were separated by large stalls, and the clean floor was covered with fresh hay. She sneezed as she entered, more from the pungent smell of the horses than from anything else. The front of the stables was empty except for the tack and several bales of hay. She jumped on top of one of the bales, waiting until she saw Tel.

She had seen him twice since his change, both times in a designated meeting spot. He wouldn't be expecting her now. She wasn't sure how she would contact him. Both times she had seen him, she had been in her Fey form.

A stable boy came from the back, leading a black stallion. The horse was prancing. Solanda slipped even farther back on the bale, hoping the horse wouldn't see her. It didn't. The boy led the horse outside.

Someone else was whistling by the stalls. She craned her neck and tried to see past the beams and bales into the back. But she couldn't. She wouldn't go down that hall and risk getting trampled.

Two more stable boys passed with horses before she saw the man she wanted. Tel was dressed as a groom now, and ordering the others about. She waited until the two were gone before she walked on the wooden railing of an empty stall.

His human form was broad-shouldered and muscular. None of the Blue Islanders seemed very tall, however, and Tel's host was no exception. His hair was brown, and nothing in his face revealed Tel's presence.

When he saw her, he swore. He opened his mouth and looked away from her, probably to call one of the stable boys for help, when she meowed at him and raised one paw. He looked back at her, his brow furrowing in puzzlement.

She sat next to the support beam and said in Fey, "I'm thirsty. Bring me some fresh water outside this smelly building."

"But—"

"A Doppelgänger should never question his betters," she said, and jumped off the wall. Straw dug into her pads, and she silently cursed him for his job. She shook the strands off her feet, then went outside to wait.

The sun had peeked over the gate. The day would be hot and steamy after the night's rain. She found a patch of sunlight, letting the warmth soak into her bones.

Presently Tel came out, carrying a ceramic dish filled with water. He set the water in front of her, then sat down cross-legged beside her.

"Who are you?" he asked in Fey.

"First," she said, looking around to make sure no one else was in earshot. She didn't see anyone. "Talk to me in Islander. I've picked up enough of it this last year to be conversant. Second, treat me like a cat you've been trying to tame for some time. Use that stupid baby talk Islanders use when talking to us. Third, I will still use Fey. Maybe no one will realize what I'm doing. And fourth, idiot, I am the only Shape-Shifter Rugar brought with him."

"Solanda?"

"One and the same. Now, if you don't mind, I'm going to have a drink." She stood and bent to the water, scooping it into her mouth with her tongue. Spoiled horses didn't have to drink out of mud holes for their nourishment. She drank half the bowl—she hadn't realized just how thirsty she was —before sitting again and looking at Tel.

"You have water on your whiskers," he said in Islander.

"Brilliant observation," she said. She shook her head, splattering him. He wiped off his arm, lips pursed. She hated Doppelgängers. Thought they were as important as Shape-Shifters, but they lacked so much natural talent. "I'm here from Rugar. He says the quality of your information is poor. He wants you in the Tabernacle."

"What?"

A stable boy brought another horse outside. Solanda moved closer to Tel, rubbing her head against his leg. She purred. Tel put a tentative hand on her back. She wrinkled her nose at the stink of horses.

She waited until the stable boy was gone before continuing. "He wants you to discover how they make that poison. The Spell Warders are having no luck with it."

"By the Sword," he said, an expression she had never heard, but she assumed it was a human oath. "I could die."

"You could be kicked to death by a horse too. Wouldn't it be better to die knowing that you had got information that could save us all?"

He looked around, scratching behind her ear as he did so. She couldn't help herself. The scratching felt good and she leaned into him.

"Listen," he said in Fey. "I have heard that we can die just from going into that place."

"Not true," she said. "I have known Fey who've been inside."

"Have they lived?"

No. They had all died. Even the Doppelgängers. "They were careless," she said. She pulled away from his hand, even though the touch felt good. "If you refuse this assignment, I will bring a Red Cap here to douse you and turn you to your old form. You'll have to make it back to Shadowlands alone and unprotected."

He wiped his hand on his pants legs and stared down at her. "You play mean," he said in Islander.

"The poison terrifies me. I want off this wretched place. The last ship didn't make it, and I'm beginning to be afraid that Rugar is going to settle. I don't want to settle. I want to move on. Nye wasn't heaven, but it was better than living in the Shadowlands."

Tel stared at her for a long moment. His eyes narrowed, and she finally saw the Fey in him. He, too, lived in terror of the poison.

He took a deep breath, rubbed a hand over his forehead, and sighed. "How long do I have before I'm supposed to go?" he asked in Islander.

"Right away," she said. "I don't think I'm the only one who is impatient."

He frowned at her, then picked up the bowl of water and tossed the water onto the ground. She almost commented on his rudeness—he could have asked her if she wanted more—but then realized that was what he wanted.

"Rugar expects a message as soon as you're in the Tabernacle," she said. "A courier will be waiting for you down at the warehouse near the old Shadowlands at midnight tomorrow."

He didn't respond, even though she knew he had heard her. He turned his back and went inside the stable. She watched for a moment, fighting the urge to follow him. He was too comfortable. She recognized the signs. She had seen it twice in Nye—Doppelgängers who had turned, whose hosts had proved stronger than the Fey self. She would warn Rugar. He could decide if Tel formed a threat to the rest of the community. She hoped not. Too many in their small force had died in the past year.

But she didn't have long to reflect on it. She still had one more Doppelgänger to talk with, and she wanted to do so before the nobility woke.

Now she wished she had sneaked into the kitchen. She trotted across the courtyard, glad she had had the water. As the sun struck the damp dirt and stone, steam rose. She wanted to finish her duties so that she could find a nice, cool piece of shade and sleep.

She rounded a corner, went past the kitchen and along the archway, dodging the feet of busy servants, most of whom took no notice of her. The sounds in the yard had increased—the chickens squawking as they got fed, horses neighing and people shouting greetings to each other. A ragged black cat with half an ear hissed at her from a hole a fallen stone had left in the wall. She hissed back for good form, then scurried away. Other cats lived in the yard, and the last thing she needed was a fight.

Finally she found the door she was looking for, the one that opened into the corridor outside the Great Hall. She bumped against it, thinking it would open from her weight, but it didn't. She scanned the yard, hoping to see someone coming toward her. When no one did, she lay as near to the door as she could, her muscles tense so that she could spring through at a moment's notice.

She had catnapped for about an hour when the door finally opened. She slipped between the booted feet that made their way out, ignoring the shouted "Hey!" and scampering down the hall. She had no idea where to find Quest, but her best chance was there.

The inside of the palace was cool after the growing heat outside. She hurried down the corridor, enjoying the cold stone against her pads. The air smelled of dust and freshly baked bread, an odd combination. She headed toward the kitchen because she wasn't sure where else to go.

Finally she heard voices: a woman speaking softly to a man at the base of the stairs. She stopped and peered around the corner. The woman was one of the servants. She was slender and very blond, her hair paler than her skin. Her serving dress was cut low across the bodice, but it appeared as if she had tried to pull the bodice higher. She held a feather duster before her like a weapon. The man was Quest in his human role as master of the hall. He was giving the woman instructions, and she was arguing with him. Suddenly he took the duster from her and tossed it across the floor. It skidded to a stop near Solanda. Solanda didn't back away quickly enough.

"Oh, lordsy," the woman said. "I dinna let this one in, sir."

"But make sure you get it out," Quest said.

The woman hurried toward Solanda. Solanda ran past her and careened into Quest's leg. He cried out as she dug her claws into his pants leg and climbed up his side. He was brushing her away, but she bit his hand.

"Get this thing off me!" he yelled.

The woman came over, apologizing as she walked.

"Stupid," Solanda hissed in Fey. "I have to talk to you."

The woman grabbed her and Solanda yowled, digging her claws in harder. " 'Tis sorry I am, sir. I dunno how she got in here."

"Go about your dusting," he said. "I'll take care of the damn cat."

"Sure is a strange one, that," the woman said. "I dinna ever hear nothing meow like that before."

"Go," Quest said, "or I will discipline you immediately."

The woman hurried to her place in the hall and picked up her feather duster; then she disappeared down the corridor.

"I hope to hell this is you, Solanda," he whispered in Fey as he pulled her off, "because if it isn't, I'll make sure you don't live through the day."

"Testy," she said. "Get me out of this corridor and we'll talk."

He cradled her with one hand, pushing her body against his shoulder as if she were a child. He went up the stairs, past the first landing and the tapestry-strewn window, and onto the first floor. As one of the ranking officers of the house, he had special privileges, such as a room in the palace proper.

His room was small, though, with an ancient feather bed that needed airing. It had one uncovered window that gave the place a larger feel. He set her down on the mildewed rug—obviously a discard from the nobility—and immediately went to his washbasin. He pulled off his shirt, revealing long scratches on his side and arms.

"Couldn't you have done something else?" he asked.

She jumped onto the bed and sneezed as dust rose around her, the motes floating in the window's light. She sat, then wiped her nose and mouth with the side of her paw and sneezed again as more dust got into her nostrils. "Don't you ever clean this room?" she asked.

"I barely have time to sleep." He grabbed a ripped cloth and dipped it into the water. "Master of the hall has its benefits—and I do hear a lot—but I work harder than I have ever worked before."

She sighed. Complaints. She hated complaints. As if she didn't work for the cause. Still, she didn't have to *pretend* to be the enemy every day.

He wiped the blood of the scratches, wincing as he did so. "By the Powers, these things hurt."

"Cat scratches," she said without apology. "If I were you, I'd get a Healer to look at them so they don't get infected."

"They don't have Healers here."

"They must."

"Butchers is more like it," he said. "They have no knowledge of the Mysteries."

"Well, the wounds don't really matter," she said.

He stopped wiping. "They want me back?"

"No." She sat with her front paws pushing on the feather bed, her back paws braced behind her. She couldn't relax in this room. The smells, the dust, were driving her crazy. "Just a moment."

She closed her eyes, willed and imagined her human form. Her body grew and stretched, the power surrounding her. At some point the tickle of the dust was gone, replaced by the faint odor of mildew and sunshine. The bed's softness eased the jolt of her change. When she finished, she was sitting in the same position, only her knees pushed into her breasts, and her hands were flanked by her legs.

The avid and shocked expression on Quest's face made her stay that way. She had forgotten about the heightened sexuality of Doppelgängers.

"Sorry," she said, wishing she had something to cover her nakedness. "I've been a cat too long today."

His smile held understanding and irony, neither of which she wanted to see. He set the cloth down on the stand and sat beside her. She didn't move away. No sense in antagonizing him.

"They don't want you back," she said, continuing the conversation, hoping it would distract him.

It did. He leaned away from her so that he could see her face. "My information's been good," he said.

She nodded, liking his defensiveness. "But it's not the information we need. The power here is diffuse, it seems."

"The Rocaanists make no state decisions."

So he had already thought of this. "No," she said. "But they know the secret to the potion."

He paled. She did admire a Doppelgänger's ability to absorb everything about its host.

"You've already thought of this," she said.

"I've heard rumors," he said. He ran a hand through his thinning hair, then winced when the movement pulled at the scratches. "They found bones over there. And then one of the Auds melted. Only they think that a Fey was hiding in an Aud's clothing."

"We lost two in the Tabernacle," she said. "Rugar was hoping not to send anymore, but we can't find the secret to their poison."

"How do you expect me to do that?" His voice rose just a little. "The holy ones have to touch that stuff every day."

"Not all of them," she said. "Even I know that."

He didn't even have the grace to smile at trying to fool her.

For a moment she wished she were back being a cat. It was hard to hide the anger. Both of these cowards were fighting her. "You should know better than to let your fear overcome you," she said. "We need the answer to this. We need it or we will all die. Do you think you can avoid this poison forever? What happens when they start testing loyal-

ties with it? You know they will. They just haven't thought
of it yet."

"Oh, they've thought of it," he said. "All of the King's
advisers have been touched."

All? She wondered at that. "Well, then," she said. "You'd
best discover the secret."

"You have no sympathy," he said, the smile finally crossing his face. She wondered why her coldness amused him.

"None." She let the word hang between them.

He touched her arm. "I'd forgotten how beautiful Fey
women are."

She looked down at his hand. "I find Islanders repulsive."

He flushed and pulled his hand away. "I'm not an Islander," he said despite his movements, but with a resigna-
tion that meant he understood.

She brought her legs down and stretched, deliberately
taunting him now. The movements felt good. In the space
of a single night, she had forgotten how wonderful long
limbs felt. When she finished the stretch, she turned to face
him and sat cross-legged. He let his gaze roam her body, but
he did not touch her.

"Rugar did not send me to entice you or to reward you,"
she said. "He isn't pleased with the information he's received from you. He was hoping that the Doppelgängers
would give him the knowledge he needed to defeat these
people. Instead, you have all grown comfortable in your
imitation Islander lives."

"All?" Quest asked.

"We've spent too long here, and they've discovered
Shadowlands. If they can find a way in, they can defeat us.
We will never see our families again. We will never leave
this place."

"That's not my fault," Quest said.

"No," she said. "It's not. Completely. But I'm appalled to
know you have thought of going to their religion and have
not done so for fear of your own life. You are our sacrifice.
That is what your powers make you. And instead, you hide
here and then talk as if you are doing us all a favor by
cleaning their King's palace."

"It's not like that—" he said.

"Really? It certainly seems that way."

"I thought I was getting enough information here."

This time she was the one who smiled. Coldly. "If you were getting enough information here, then you would have known that they had found their way to Shadowlands." She put up a hand. "Don't deny it. I saw the surprise on your face. You shouldn't have to hear it from me."

He leaned his head back against the stone wall and closed his eyes. She stood and splashed some of the water onto her face, then wiped it off with another of his ripped cloths. Some of her feline habits never went away. Whenever she was nervous, her face felt dirty.

This fear disturbed her. How many others did it paralyze? Perhaps that was why the Spell Warders couldn't find the secret to the poison. They were too afraid of it. She would have to talk with Rugar when she got back. The Fey, in the shock of their defeat, had lost their ability to take risks.

"You're right," he said, his voice soft. "I hate to admit it, but you're right. How soon does Rugar want me to leave?"

"Now," she said. "Only give me time to get out of this hellhole. That woman heard me talking to you."

She set the damp cloth down and faced him. The color in his cheeks remained high.

"You understand what you need to do?" she asked.

"I need to find the riddle of that poison."

"As quickly as possible," she said.

He nodded. "I have some ideas. I have choices as to who to take on. I will get it for you. For Rugar. Tell him, Solanda."

She smiled—a real smile this time. "I will tell him," she said. "Now, if you'll excuse me." She settled on the rug, then let her body slip into itself, her mass compacting and somehow lessening, although the Warders had never figured out how that happened either. The feline form felt like an old friend—she hadn't been out of it long enough—and she sneezed at the dust and mildew.

"I wished we could do that as simply," Quest said.

Her tail twitched. His magick would never come as easily. Her kind were the only true Fey. The rest were imperfect, unable to achieve even half the magick she could.

He stood and grabbed his shirt. The wounds had dried on his skin.

"One other thing," she said.

He slipped the shirt on and adjusted it, then looked down at her.

"Rugar expects to hear as soon as you are settled in your new form. A messenger will meet you tomorrow night at the base of the bridge just crossing the Cardidas after dark. Make sure you are there. If not, we will assume that you did not survive the transition."

He swallowed visibly, his Adam's apple moving up and down. "I'll survive," he said.

FORTY-FOUR

ALEXANDER entered the War Room alone. He shut the door on his guards and leaned against it, still winded from the climb up the stairs. He was not as young as he used to be, and his body reminded him of that fact daily. When he crouched, he needed to brace himself to rise, and when he climbed stairs, he had to pause on every other landing to rest.

The room smelled of candle wax. Someone had thought ahead and lit the lamps inside. It was not bright enough, but it would do. Such a waste to spend a sunny morning in a room with no windows.

He sighed and brushed the hair from his face. His hand was shaking. He hadn't slept more than an hour or two—and that was in snatches. He kept coming awake at every noise, waiting for the messenger to tell him what had happened on the raid against the Fey. When the news came, over a light breakfast of freshly baked bread and milk, it left him stunned. He had been expecting the worst, but somehow, when the worst had happened, he found himself ill and shaken. He had been unable to finish eating. So he faced this meeting tired and hungry, his mind full of images of the men he had sent to their deaths for nothing more than to satisfy his own suspicions.

The War Room had changed in the last year. It had the polished shine of a room well used. The table glowed. He had replaced the odd assortment of stools and benches with padded chairs. The washbasin he had asked for sat on the other occasional table, along with a matching pitcher. An assortment of knives and swords stood in a specially built case. A sleeping mattress was rolled against the wall, and a plush carpet with a blue, gold, and brown—patterned weave covered the floor. Some dried meat, pickled vegetables, and kippers were stored on the shelves, along with regular water. Vials of holy water covered a lower shelf. He wanted supplies up there in case something trapped them inside.

New maps had been copied and hung on the wall. On one of them, the artist had marked the sites of all the battles and skirmishes since the Fey had arrived. On another the artist had noted all the battles of the Peasant Uprising, in the vain hope that it would show the King where to stage current battles. But so far, the Fey had chosen the sites.

He pushed off the door and walked around the room. Soon the others would arrive and he would have to take action. But for the moment he was alone and able to think. So much of this was new: the constant vigilance, thinking in terms of war instead of commerce. No ships had left the Isle since the Fey had arrived because Alexander feared giving the Fey a map of the correct route. The Islanders were complaining of shortages, but mostly in exotic goods. The only area that concerned him was that of cloth, since the Island woolens were coarse and uncomfortable. But for centuries Blue Isle had been self-sufficient. With a little time and patience it would be again.

All of that planning he could handle. The loss of life, on the other hand, kept him awake. The nightmares were getting worse instead of better.

Alexander stopped pacing in front of the vials of holy water. Unlike his son and all of his advisers, Alexander had killed no one in this war. On this night that would change.

Yet what he was about to do was different. He wasn't killing in the heat of the moment. He had planned this, and already his stomach was churning. He didn't want to think about all the possibilities. But he had to.

For the sake of the Kingdom.

He took a deep breath, grabbed one of the vials, and pulled off the stopper. The slight pop made him wince. He set the stopper down, fighting the urge to sneeze when the faintly dusty aroma of the water reached his nose. He gripped the vial by the neck, took it to the basin, and poured it in. That way the water was easily available. He also half hoped that he wouldn't have to use it at all, that he could think of a way to get them to dip their hands into the basin voluntarily. But he knew that would never happen.

A rap on the door startled him. He capped the empty vial and replaced it on the shelf, heart pounding. He wasn't ready for this meeting. He would never be ready.

The guards weren't to knock unless at least two of his advisers had shown. The knock echoed again.

" 'Tis Lord Stowe, Sire, and Lord Fesler." The guard's voice sounded muffled through the door.

"Come," he said, tugging on his shirt. Since the invasion he had changed from robes to the pants and shirts his son preferred. They gave him more mobility and made him less visible among his staff. No one had advised him to make the change, but he felt it prudent. He walked over to the chair at the head of the table as if he had been there all along.

Lord Fesler came in first, a slender man with hollowed cheeks who looked as if he had never slept. He had not been one of the King's trusted advisers until after the war had started, but during the past year his soft comments and his wry observations had had more truth in them than most. Alexander didn't like him but had learned now more than ever that liking meant little in a world at war.

Lord Stowe followed, his brown curls pulled back behind his head. He had deep circles beneath his eyes. He pushed the door closed and took his customary seat beside Alexander.

"You've heard," Alexander said.

Stowe nodded. "They came to me after they spoke to you."

"The raid?" Fesler asked.

Alexander shook his head, unable to say more.

"We'll discuss it when the others get here," Stowe said. The knock sounded again. Alexander's hands were shaking. He gripped the back of the chair, the wooden edges biting into his palms, to hide his nerves.

"Captain of the guards, Sir Monte, Lord Egan, and Sir Stephen of His Majesty's Swords." A different guard this time, his voice ringing through the door clearer than the others had.

At the mention of Stephen's name, Alexander's mouth went dry. "Come," he said again, hoping that his voice sounded the same.

The door opened, and Stephen came in first. His face had no expression at all, but his eyes seemed to take in everything. He stopped at a chair on the other side of the table, in full view of Alexander.

Lord Egan followed. His back was hunched, hiding his bulk, and his round face still showed signs of his famous joviality. But he hadn't smiled much since he had found a place among the King's council. His advice, like Fesler's, had been sound and necessary.

Monte stopped in front of the door to give additional instructions to the guards. The War Room was no longer a secret among the staff. Most knew that it existed, although only an elite cadre of guards knew exactly where it was.

Alexander pulled his chair back and sat in it. He looked at all of his advisers. It felt as if his own gaze were jumping like Stephen's was. He wasn't sure if he should look at the swordmaster or ignore him.

After a moment the chair was too confining. He wanted to pace. Nicholas was late, and it bothered him. Nicholas was always late. Alexander frowned at the thought. His son would be the only adviser who would be announced alone.

He had waited to test his son last. His son and his most trusted adviser. Of all the advisers, only Nicholas had been alone with his father since the war had started. Nicholas had other chances to betray, but none like this.

None like this.

But Nicholas was infatuated with the Fey girl. Nicholas had touched her. Nicholas thought her "magnificent."

Alexander stroked the arm of his chair, his fingers still shaking. The invasion had brought him to this. A distrust of his own son. The future of his people. He hadn't wanted to face this thought, but he might have to, in just a few moments.

The sense of urgency didn't leave him, although he knew that at present his people were fine. Still, this was the moment his father had warned him about. The moment when being King took more resolve than desire. The moment when he lost his humanity for the sake of his country.

"Something has disturbed you," Stephen said, looking at Alexander's hand.

This man missed nothing. Alexander bit back the rage that filled him. He met Stephen's gaze. The man's eyes were cold. "Yes," Alexander said calmly. "Something has."

A knock on the door was followed by, "His Highness, Prince Nicholas."

Without waiting for Alexander's invitation, the door opened. Nicholas entered. His hair was tousled and he was still rubbing sleep from his eyes. He did not apologize for being late.

He looked normal. The boy Alexander had raised. The child he had held.

If Nicholas was enchanted, Alexander would have known.

Alexander let out breath he didn't know he had been holding. "We need to get under way. Have a seat, my son."

Nicholas nodded. He pulled out the chair next to Stephen and sat. Alexander watched, lips pursed. Nicholas took too many risks. It would cost the boy someday. Alexander would have to talk with him. Warn him. Again.

Alexander stood, unable to sit any longer. He paced around his chair and glanced at the water in the bowl, glad to see it was still there. Then he took a deep breath. "We received news of the raid on the Fey's hiding place this morning. Five of our people survived. Two were badly wounded. Three weren't injured at all. Three others were captured. Theron, the leader, came back here to get help for the dying and the dead."

"Captured?" Monte asked, his tone implying all sorts of horrors none of them wanted to think about.

"Along with holy water," Alexander said.

Lord Egan slumped in his chair. Beads of sweat appeared on his brow. "Now they'll know how to defeat us."

Lord Stowe shook his head. Unlike the others, he had had hours to think about this. He knew, just as Alexander did, that nothing was absolute. "None of us knows the secret to holy water. None of us knows how it works. And taking our people will not change that. The Fey can't handle the water, so if they were to study it, they would need human hands to conduct the test."

"Throwing the water at the Fey hideout did not dissolve it?" Stephen asked.

Alexander stopped behind his chair. He leaned his elbows on top of it and considered the question. A reasonable man would ask it—that had, after all, been the plan. But a spy would want to know what had happened to his camp. All of Stephen's questions in the past few months had been like this. Maybe even in the past year. "No," Alexander said. "The mysterious hiding place still stands."

"I don't understand this," Lord Fesler said. "This was supposed to be a secret raid. How did they best us in a secret raid?"

"There were things we did not know," Alexander said. "They apparently have a circle in the ground with some magick properties. They seem to have the ability to erect a barrier that holy water cannot penetrate. Theron has developed a theory. He believes that water to them is like fire to us. It will consume our skin, our lives, and most of the things we use. But it will not destroy stone, and it will temper iron. We have only one element to use against them. They have many to use against us. Fortunately, our one weapon is more powerful than anything else they have."

"It sounds as if they are going after the secret," Nicholas said.

"I would be too," said Alexander. "We are trying, in fact, to learn as much about them as we can and are thwarted on every path. Perhaps we can find a way."

"We have been unable to capture them," Lord Egan said.

"We haven't really tried," said Monte.

"Do you think we have a chance against people like that?" Stephen asked.

Alexander stood and crossed his arms. "What do you think, Stephen? You're the expert on the Fey."

He frowned just a little. "I am no expert."

"On the day of the invasion, it was you who gave us all instructions about the Fey. On that day, before the girl arrived, you told us many things about the Fey."

"The girl," Stephen said softly. "We had a prisoner."

"Yes," Nicholas said. "And if it weren't for you and Lord Powell, we would have kept her."

Alexander wasn't going to allow his focus to shift away from Stephen. "You told us that the Fey were fighting machines, that they would not stop until they control the entire world."

Stephen shrugged. "It was obvious. And true."

"You said you have studied the history of warfare, yet it is Lord Stowe who has contributed the most history. What happened to all your knowledge, Stephen?"

"It was merely reading and oral history, most of it worthless, Sire."

"You didn't think so during the invasion."

Lord Stowe was watching both men as if they were sword fighting. Nicholas had pushed his chair away from Stephen, so that he had room to stand quickly. Lord Egan leaned back, his face a mask.

Stephen glanced at them all before looking at Alexander. "You seem to have an agenda, Sire."

"I am simply curious at your lack of willingness to put your knowledge to use. On the day of the invasion, you said to me that you wanted to be useful. It was one of the reasons I included you in the meetings in this room."

"Haven't I been useful, Sire?"

The words echoed in the silence. Lord Fesler rubbed his thumb against his forefinger over and over again. Stephen's eyes glittered as he awaited Alexander's response.

"Not in the way you promised, Stephen."

"Perhaps I could not be."

"No, perhaps not." Alexander leaned against the end table. The water in the bowl sloshed beside him. "You also told us that the Fey could kill with a single touch."

"And we saw that later. Reports of men being killed by touch."

"Yes, we did." Alexander wanted to look at the holy water but couldn't give himself away. "And then the others left, and you said something interesting to me."

"I told you they could enchant," Stephen said.

The response surprised Alexander. Somehow he had thought Stephen would not remember that conversation. "And you told me that they could take over a man's body to make him do their bidding."

The room was so silent that he could hear Egan's labored breathing. Everyone was watching Alexander, except Nicholas, whose gaze remained on Stephen.

"What happened in that corridor, Stephen, with that female Fey?"

Stephen touched the scar on his cheek. "I told you," he said. "She broke her bonds and attacked me. When I came to, she was gone, there were bones at my feet, and the guards were standing over me, concerned that I was dying."

"Why didn't she kill you?" Alexander asked.

"I don't know. Maybe she didn't have to. Maybe Lord Powell fought harder."

"I thought the Fey could kill with a single touch."

"Not all of them. I *told* you that. I said some of them could."

"Do you think she could?"

"Obviously she could," Stephen said. "How do you think Lord Powell died?"

"Then why didn't she kill you? She touched you, didn't she?"

Stephen paused, his mouth open slightly, as if shocked by this line of questioning. "Her knife touched me," he said.

"Her knife touched you," Alexander said. "Then how did she knock you unconscious? Did she touch you, Stephen?"

"What are you trying to say, Sire? That she took me over?"

"Someone cut her bonds, Stephen. Someone set her free. Lord Powell is dead."

Color ran into Stephen's face. "It could have been anyone," he said. "Someone else could have helped her. Your son was taken with her. Why didn't she attack him? Have you asked yourself that?"

Alexander clenched his fist. "Are you saying Nicholas is enchanted?"

Nicholas's eyes were wide. He was staring at his father in disbelief. "Father—"

Alexander waved a hand to silence him. Nicholas needed to wait. Alexander couldn't afford that distraction. Not yet. "Don't change the focus of the conversation, Stephen. We are talking about you."

Stephen gripped the edge of the table. "Why are you accusing me of this now? You've trusted me all year."

"Someone let the Fey know that we were going to attack them last night. Only you and Nicholas knew the plan."

All of the lords looked shocked. Monte reached for the knife at his belt. Nicholas stood.

"And you wouldn't think of accusing your son?" Stephen asked with a snarl that Alexander had never heard before. In all the years he had known Stephen, Alexander had never heard such contempt in Stephen's tone.

Alexander didn't think. He whirled, grabbed the basin, and flung the contents toward Stephen. Stephen screamed and launched out of his chair, grabbing Nicholas and using him as a shield. The water splattered the table and chair and sloshed near Stephen's shoes, but did not touch him.

Lord Fesler grabbed another vial off the shelf. Monte rose, knife extended. Stephen pulled a knife himself and placed it at Nicholas's throat.

"Use that," Stephen said to Fesler, "and I will kill this sorry excuse for a boy."

"Do it," Nicholas said, his voice strained against the knife. "He won't have time to kill me."

Alexander gripped the dripping basin, breathing hard, terror pounding in his chest. Either way he was risking Nicholas. "What did they do to you, Stephen?" Alexander asked. "I thought of all of us you were the most incorruptible."

"Did you?" Stephen said. "There are ways to get to everyone."

"He's not Stephen," Nicholas said. A drop of blood ran down his skin and disappeared under the collar of his shirt. "If he was Stephen, he would not need to be frightened of the holy water."

"The boy thinks he is so clever," Stephen said. "But what do you know of the Fey and their magicks? Nothing. Nothing at all. Perhaps the water will merely break the enchantment."

Fesler took the stopper off the vial.

Stephen smiled. "It will cost a Prince's life to find out."

"Do it," Nicholas said again.

"And lose what pitiful advantage I have? I don't think

so." Stephen backed toward the door, his grip on Nicholas tight.

Alexander set the basin on the table and held up his hands. "Let my son go, and you can go free."

"Really, Sire, I am not that stupid. Your son will get me out of here."

"You can't get out of here when you're pulling him," Lord Stowe said. "If the King gave his word, then he means it."

"But he didn't give his word, did he?" Stephen smiled. The smile looked odd on his face. "He merely made an unsubstantiated promise."

Alexander opened his mouth to give his word, and in that moment Nicholas stomped on Stephen's foot. The older man grimaced and Nicholas grabbed his arm, pulling the knife away from his throat. Alexander reached behind himself and grabbed the water pitcher, flinging the contents at Stephen. Lord Fesler needed only the suggestion: he tossed the holy water at Stephen. Alexander's water hit Nicholas and splashed on Stephen, but Fesler's holy water hit Stephen on his left side.

Nicholas pushed away from Stephen and scrambled across the room, hand at his throat. Stephen's clothes peeled off his skin. A haze filled the room, followed by the stench of burning flesh. Stephen screamed. The lords looked on in horror. Nicholas stood beside his father and grabbed his arm. Alexander leaned into him, relieved at his son's strength. Relieved that his son was still his son.

Stephen slipped onto the floor, his legs jelling into a single mass. He tried to push the water off his skin, but his hands were melting, the skin dripping off like blood. He cried out again before collapsing on the floor.

Alexander could no longer see him, but he heard thuds that stopped after a few short moments. The haze and stench grew. Alexander had to swallow hard to keep the meager contents of his stomach from rising.

Finally all sounds stopped. He patted Nicholas's hand, then took it off his arm and made his way around the room. The body was unrecognizable. Only the eyes remained, open and staring at nothing. The stench was so strong that Alexander felt as if it had got inside him.

Alexander stood over the body. His trembling had increased. One mistake and he would have died. If he had been a bit less cautious, if he had ever allowed himself to be alone with Stephen, Stephen would have murdered him. Alexander's eyes were watering from the smell. He wished now that he had approached it all differently. He wished he had tested his advisers from the beginning.

"By the Bloody Sword," Lord Stowe said. He was now standing behind Alexander. Nicholas approached too but said nothing. Lord Fesler was pale, and Lord Egan still sat at the table, his hand over his mouth. Monte had moved closer to the body, still holding his knife.

"You hit him with the holy water," Nicholas said to Lord Fesler.

Fesler nodded.

"We'll need to test anyone who comes near the King with holy water from now on," Nicholas said.

"We tried that already," Lord Stowe said.

"How did we miss Stephen?" Monte asked. "He's with the King all the time."

"At first," Alexander said, not looking at any of them but still staring at the body, "he avoided the tests. Always some excuse. I never really noticed. But one afternoon he took a vial and poured it onto his hand."

"He couldn't have."

"Not unless he planted it himself," Nicholas said.

"He probably replaced the water with regular water," Monte said.

"Then why didn't he do that up here?" Fesler asked.

"No one gets into this room without me," said Alexander. He was shaking so hard, he had to sit down. He took the closest chair, the one Nicholas had been using.

"I don't understand," Lord Stowe said. "He looked like Stephen, but he disintegrated like a Fey. Is this what happens when you're possessed?"

"If it was that easy," Nicholas said, "then why haven't we seen others like this?"

"Maybe we have," Lord Fesler said, "and didn't know it."

"He looked like Stephen," Alexander said. "He acted like Stephen. He remembered things only Stephen would know. He had to be Stephen, changed somehow. That woman transformed him in the corridor."

"Or before," Nicholas said.

Alexander shook his head. "Before, he was speaking against the Fey. After, the things he said could have been taken for concern if we had only paid attention."

"But you knew," Lord Egan said. "How did you know?"

"I knew there was a leak," Alexander said. "I tested all of you. It wasn't until Stephen that I had a direct link. Stephen gave himself away. But I never expected this. Ever. I had thought, when I threw that water, to startle him. To test him. I had never expected to scare him."

"They could be everywhere," Lord Fesler said, his voice soft. "We would never know. They could be in this room, and we would never know."

Alexander put a hand to his forehead. The thought had occurred to him. The Rocaan's task would be doubly difficult. Not just holy water for war, but for tests as well. Daily tests—and how far would they go? Each servant? Each person who came near the nobility? What about the people on the streets? What about the children? Where did the distrust end?

"How many of them are there?" Egan asked.

Alexander sighed. "I don't know," he said softly. "But they just won this battle." He backed away from the body and turned to the curious faces around him. "Not only do they have our people and our holy water, now they have our confidence as well. We will never completely trust each other again."

FORTY-FIVE

JEWEL pressed her hand against her forehead, as if she could push the headache out the back of her skull. She had been awake almost thirty hours, and she could feel the tension in her back with each movement of her shoulders. The buckets of water were heavy. She wished the Domestics had assigned her another task.

She pushed open the double doors that led into the Domicile with her backside, letting the rust-iron stench of blood overwhelm her. The Domicile was the largest building in Shadowlands. Rugar had decreed it the most important, since he figured it would have to act as hospital as well as the foundation for most of the interior work done on the Shadowlands. The building was long and narrow, divided into sections. Rooms for chefs, rooms for weavers, and a private room for the Shaman. Some of the rooms were small. The main room, the one she had walked into, was the size of three rooms, and currently the hospital.

Seven Infantry filled the beds with sword wounds to the gut. Another had a slash along his arm, and one body rested on the cot near the door, waiting for someone to take it for ritual cleansing and disbursal. Jewel set the water down near the cot and stretched. Her back cracked and popped as she straightened it. She had never sat out a battle before, and the smells, leaching through the walls of Shadowlands, had terrified her more than the glimpse of darkness when the first Fey had come through the Circle Door.

The prisoners, though. The prisoners intrigued her. And she was not allowed to see them until her father and Caseo had spent time with them.

Neri approached Jewel, face drawn and white with exhaustion. Since the move to Shadowlands, the Domestics hadn't had much rest. The strains of a battle so nearby had drained them even further. Neri bent and picked up one of the buckets.

"Thanks, Jewel," she said. Her smile was as tired as her eyes. "We've done all we can for the moment, I think."

Jewel nodded toward the beds. "Will they be all right?"

Neri shrugged. "With Infantry it's hard to tell. We do what we can, but most of them lack the magick necessary to heal themselves." Then her eyes widened just a little. "No insult intended," she said.

"None taken." Most of the Fey did not know, even yet, of Jewel's Visions. In fact, many believed that her capture during the First Battle for Jahn had been because she had no magick power of her own.

Seven more wounded, perhaps seven more dead. And no reinforcements. The Fey would become servants of the Islanders through attrition if this continued. Just by the sheer numbers. Eventually, there would be no Fey left to go to battle.

Her father's revelation that the Black King would not help them had shaken her to the core. It made the entire situation different. They were as helpless as the Hevish when the Fey had surrounded them on all sides, cut off access to the roads and rivers, and interrupted their trade. The Hevish were a small but determined people, and they had fought a pitched battle from their fortified country for five years. But time worked against them. Slaughter of the young, then of the older generation, as well as starvation, had defeated them.

A trapped people could not withstand a siege. Especially when the enemy had all its resources at its command.

Unless the Warders found the secret to the poison, the Fey had to find another way out of the situation. If only they had brought more Doppelgängers. One could be assigned to take on the person of a sailor the Islanders had hidden, and navigate a ship out of the treacherous bay. But Rugar had used the Doppelgängers traditionally, in battle and out, to gain information about the enemy. Now three were dead, and the two he had sent into the Tabernacle would probably die as well.

She stepped off the porch into the swirling mist. Over the past year she had grown accustomed to losing her feet in the murky edges of Shadowlands. She no longer blinked to clear the misty grayness from her eyes. The world looked right with blurred edges. She was afraid that if she stepped back into the real world, its brightness would blind her.

Her father was probably back in the cabin by now. She walked quickly past the buildings still under construction, past the arguing craftsmen. The pounding was something else she had got used to. She paused in front of the Warders' cabin. Smoke plumed out of the chimney. In the early days of Shadowlands, the Fey had not allowed fires. This was before they had learned that the walls were somehow porous, and that the air in Shadowlands remained as clear as the air outside it.

Still, the fire intrigued her because the temperature was comfortable. Her father had seen to that. They were doing something. A shiver ran down her back. Something with the prisoners? She hoped not. She wanted to see them before the Warders began their experiments.

But she was supposed to see her father first. She walked past the Warders' cabin to her own. The cabin her father had built for them had been the meeting place at first, and that was his excuse for its size. But he had made it the meeting place so that he wouldn't have to justify a larger cabin to the others. He had said that people would envy them if they thought the cabin had been built for privilege, but would understand if it existed for utility.

Sometimes she felt his justifications were silly ways to avoid confrontation over rank that should have been inevitable in their position.

If she didn't return to Nye, her grandfather would make one of her brothers Black King. He had already thought of that possibility. It was the reason he never let more than two members of the same family fight in the same battle. He protected his heirs. And he had precedent. His own father had picked a second son to succeed him when it appeared that the first son had died in a raid. Fortunately for Rugad, his brother had returned almost a decade after the father's death. The claim did not hold.

She wished she had known more about her grandfather's opposition before she'd left. She wished she had listened more closely to the arguments she had overheard, instead of concentrating on the oddity of her first Vision.

But she had had a Vision about Nicholas, the King's son. She had been meant to come to Blue Isle.

Or had it been a warning?

She would never know.

Finally she reached her own cabin. Just outside, she stopped. Two guards stood at the door. Burden was one, a scowl across his slender face. He must have tangled with her father again. The other, Amar, stood with his legs apart and arms crossed. His muscles bulged. She had always liked Amar, even though he was of her father's generation and had never shown any sign of magickal ability. He had been a solid Infantryman and a loyal guard to her entire family.

She nodded at them as she approached. "Is my father all right?"

"He is taking matters into his own hands again," Burden said.

Burden's attitude grated on her father. It was beginning to bother her as well. "How unusual," she said, "for the leader of this party, and the Black King's son."

Burden flushed. Amar tried to hide a smile. Jewel noted it, feeling her own eyes sparkle, but she didn't let the mirth move to the rest of her face. She passed them both and went inside.

The room seemed small and dark without a fire. Her father sat on the table, one foot on a chair, the other dangling. Only his eyes moved when she came in, tracking her progress from the door to his side.

"You were supposed to be here," he said.

"I couldn't just sit."

"You were supposed to sit and think."

She shrugged, unwilling to fight. "Sitting and thinking doesn't work for me, although I did come up with a few things."

"Save them." He pushed the chair away and jumped off the table. "I have some prisoners for you to meet."

Her heartbeat accelerated, and she caught her breath. He hadn't wanted her to see them until the Warders were done. "Why did you bring them here?"

"Because Caseo explained his experiments, and I decided he could waste the poison before he destroyed possibly valuable lives." Her father's tone was flat, but Jewel heard the anger underneath.

"You said the prisoners were his."

"And they will be," Rugar said. "When I am done with them."

"Have you already questioned them?"

"I have, and so have a few others. They're not answering anything."

"And so you want me to try? I have no experience with this."

"You have more experience with Islanders than most of us here. You're one of the few who has had a prolonged discussion with them."

Jewel's mouth had gone dry. She had, but the context had been different. "What about Solanda?"

"She's not back yet. And we have no Doppelgängers here."

"I haven't been among the Islanders in a year. Surely Burden or some of the others—"

"They know how to kill the Islanders. If I need help with that, I have an entire campful who will have creative suggestions." Her father's flat tone was gone. His frustration was clear. She was finally understanding what he faced.

The military crew sometimes forgot that the enemy was more than a fighting force, more than creatures to be bested or killed. Since Rugar had isolated the Fey, he had never bothered to get to know the enemy. So Rugar was going to have to rely on Jewel's very meager experience.

"Where are they?" she asked.

"The extra room," he said. "I wanted to talk with you alone first."

She nodded. The prisoners couldn't really escape anyway. The guards were more for show. They would be trapped in the Shadowlands, unable to get out. But if they got their hands on the poison, they would be able to do a lot of damage.

She went down the hall, tucking the loose strands of hair into her braid and tugging on her leather vest. Her exhaustion had lifted at the thought of seeing the prisoners. She half hoped Nicholas would be among them. She had wanted to see him again, to talk with him, so that she could better understand what had happened between them that day. By all rights they should have slaughtered each other. Instead they had toyed with each other as if they were childhood sweethearts.

Her cheeks flushed at the memory. No man, not even her dear friend Burden, had brought such an instant response. She knew what her grandfather would say if she was to tell him of the event. *Go with the magick, girl.* It was his phrase and, he said, the secret to his long life as Black King.

Go with the magick.

She flung open the door. All three prisoners were sitting. Their wrists and ankles were bound, and another rope bound them to chairs. The ropes looked loose, so the Warders must have placed an additional binding on the three. They were looking down, but none of them had that magnificent blond hair she remembered of Nicholas.

"It is rude to snub someone who has just entered a room," she said in Nye. Her Islander was still poor, even though she now had some of the basics.

The man farthest to her left raised his head. He wasn't as old as her father, but he wasn't young either. His long face had crow's-feet near the eyes, and a sensitive mouth. The squareness of his features startled her. Islanders were like Fey made without whimsy. "It is also rude to tie your guests to their chairs."

She smiled. Perhaps all Islander men were verbally aggressive. "Point taken," she said. "But you are not a guest."

The center man bit his lower lip and stared at her. He was little more than a boy, with a boy's leanness and lack of grace. His pale skin had acne scars, and his eyes, deep and blue, were wide with fear.

"I couldn't have got here on my own," the first man said. "Your friends brought me. Where I come from, that makes me a guest."

Jewel nodded. "Where I come from, that makes you a prisoner."

"Wh-what plan you to do us?" the boy asked. The boy's Nye was poor. He had clearly never been off the Isle.

The third man shushed him. As he turned to the boy, the third man's profile revealed a hawkish nose and thin lips.

"I'll give the orders here," Jewel said.

The third man glanced at her as if seeing her for the first time. He was older than the others, his eyes as narrow as the rest of him. He didn't like her. She could feel the hatred come off him in waves.

"That's because you ain't tied up, bitch," he said. His Nye seemed as poor as the boy's, but it was clearly an affectation. He had a stronger mastery of the colloquialisms than any other Islander she had heard of.

"Oh," she said, keeping her tone light, "I suspect I would give the orders whether I was tied up or not. In Shadowlands the Fey dominate."

"But not on the Isle," the third man said.

"Not yet," she said agreeably, and closed the door.

The third man said something to the others in Islander. She caught the words "alone" and "us" combined with what she believed was another curse specifically designed for women.

"You will speak Nye or you will never speak again," she said.

The color fled from the boy's face. "Sorry, missus," he said, "but Nye—a—no is—for me."

"You do just fine." She smiled at him and kept her voice gentle. He would be easy to break.

The third man spoke to the boy in Islander. She heard him use the word "play." He understood, then, that she was toying with them. She pulled her knife off her belt, walked over to him, and grabbed him by his hair. It was coarse and greasy and smelled of sweat and dirt. It hadn't been washed in days. She pulled his head back and placed the knife against his grime-encrusted cheek.

"I told you that you will speak in Nye or never speak again," she said. "Would you like me to cut out your tongue from the inside of your mouth or through your throat?"

"Lady! Please!" the boy cried.

The first man snapped something at the boy. The curtness and the directness in his tone made it sound like a name.

"I am speaking to you, old man," she said.

"You expect me to apologize to you, bitch?" he asked, his voice hoarse from the pressure of her knife.

"What I said was that you are to speak Nye. I don't care if you apologize to me or not. My ego isn't fragile, but I prefer you to speak in a language I understand. If you can't follow that direction, you won't speak at all. Is that clear?"

"When you make threats," the man said, "you should follow through on them."

"You're right," she said. She took the knife away from his neck. It left a small cut. She wiped the blood off on his shirt and shoved the knife back into the hilt. "Excuse me for a moment."

She opened the door, called her father in Fey, and asked him to send Burden into the room. She heard him yell for Burden, then heard Burden's affirmative response. She left the door open, then turned to face the prisoners. The third man watched her, chin up, blood dribbling down his neck. The first man looked more relaxed, and the boy's eyes were wet.

When Burden came in, he closed the door.

"Take him out of here," she said in Fey, pointing to the third man. She walked over to his chair. In Nye she said, "The Warders want to use you to find out what makes Islanders work. They need you alive for that and wouldn't be too happy if I killed you—even accidentally. So they will remove your tongue—you won't need it, anyway—and then they can start work on you."

"It's a bluff," the man said.

"She never bluffs," Burden said. He came up behind and untied the rope that held the man to the chair, lifting him easily by one armpit. "Say good-bye to your friends, because you won't be able to speak to them after this."

"Ort, say you will. Please!" the boy said in his poor Nye.

"Sorry," Jewel said softly. "But he was right. A woman should always make good on her threats. That way she is taken seriously."

The first man was watching her without fear, as if he was studying her. He had a different kind of intelligence from his friend. The older man—Ort?—had more bravado than courage. But this man had strength.

She returned her attention to Ort. "Get him out of here," she said to Burden in Nye. Then she added in Fey, "Have the Healers put a silence spell on him—and keep him away from Caseo."

"My pleasure," Burden said in the same language. He pushed Ort ahead of him and ordered him forward in Nye. When they left the room, Jewel closed the door behind them.

"Now," she said. "We'll begin again. I prefer to speak in Nye. While you are here, you will speak only Fey or Nye, even between yourselves. And you will answer our questions."

"No know Fey," the boy said, his voice breathless.

"And you barely know Nye," Jewel responded with a smile. "That's all right. You'll learn."

"So you don't speak Islander," the first man said.

"I don't care for the language. It is too harsh," she said. She ran a hand on this man's cheek, getting her fingers—still stained with Ort's blood—close enough to his nostrils that he could smell the rusty-iron odor. "And what is your name?"

The muscles in his face stiffened. She could feel the movement under her fingertips. "Does it matter?" he asked. "You're going to kill me anyway."

She smiled, slid her hand down, and chucked his chin before moving away. He had stubble there, like the men of Nye. "If we were going to kill you," she said, "we would have done it before bringing you in here."

"You would—a—have die Ort," the boy said.

"No," she said, keeping her tone reasonable. "If he doesn't cooperate with me, I will simply make him wish he had died. And, unfortunately, now he won't even be able to say so."

She took Ort's chair, shook the ropes off it, and swung it around so that she could sit, facing them. "I would like to know your name," she said again to the first man.

"It's not important."

She leaned her head back, just a little. "Well, then, you'll need to explain this to me. In Oudoun they believe that true names should be hidden, that someone who knows a true name has power over the person whose name it is. Yet the Nyeians never said the Islanders believed that. Is this because they felt we didn't need to know? Or do you think they wanted to give us an advantage?"

The boy looked confused. Either she was speaking too quickly for him, or this wasn't a custom. He looked at the man, then back at her.

"Are you afraid of me?" she asked him.

His Adam's apple bobbed as he swallowed. "Yes, ma'am."

Something like anger flickered over the man's face, but it disappeared so quickly she wasn't able to identify it. "Let the boy be," he said. "He shouldn't have come with us."

"Then why did he?" she asked, willing to let them take her where they would.

"Asked," the boy said. "And—"

"He has never fought before. He was a last-minute choice. He should be home with his family." Two spots of color appeared on the man's cheek. She liked his courage.

"You should have thought of that before you allowed him along," Jewel said.

The boy glanced back and forth between them. "Can hurt it? To tell names?" he said to the man.

The man sighed. "No, I suppose not. Everyone knows anyway."

By that she assumed he meant everyone outside. When the three weren't among the dead, or part of the returning wounded, the others would guess that they were among the prisoners. Rugar had been very firm with the Fey force. Allow some Islanders to return. Let them know that the Fey had captured both poison and prisoners. That might turn the tide a bit.

"The more you help us, the kinder we will be," Jewel said.

"We heard—" the boy said, deliberately avoiding the man's eyes "—the *Fey*—" and he used the Fey name for themselves, an odd choice, she thought "—not kind."

"That's true," she said. "We aren't in battle. No one should be. But we're not in battle now. You are prisoners, and you need to figure out a way to keep yourselves alive."

"What do you plan for us?" the man asked.

She saw no harm in telling him that. He would never escape, and if he was allowed to go free, any stories she told would make the Fey even more frightening—one of Rugar's goals. "We plan to discover what makes you different from the Nye. We can do that verbally, or we can let some of our experts figure that out their own way."

"Cultural differences?" the man asked.

"And physical," she said.

The boy didn't understand the exchange. He probably didn't know the words. But the man knew the words and the subtext. All the color had left his face.

"He's a boy," the man said.

She nodded. "Useful. Too bad we didn't capture any of your women."

"Women?" He seemed stunned at the idea.

"If you're different, they have to be different too," she said.

"Different?" he asked.

"From us." Her words were soft, and for a moment he looked perplexed. Only at that time did she notice the similarity between their races: when he frowned, his eyebrows rose like wings. And she nearly gasped from the wonder of it. What if they were all related on some level, as fish were related, as cats were related? That the Fey were not a different kind of creature, but a superior version of the same creature, something that all Islanders could aspire to. It would explain their poison water: somehow they had reached a Fey-like plateau without realizing it, and the effect on the real Fey was devastating.

"We're different," he said. "We're not aggressive."

"You do quite well," she said, thinking of all the dead and wounded she had seen that morning.

"No," he said. "That's not what I mean. You people have this odd desire to take over everything. We're content to live on our Isle without interference. Why don't you just leave us alone?"

And in his words she heard another voice: *All that death for something we would have given you.* She shook off the memory as something to save until later. "We are not a commercial people. It's better to own something than to pay for it, don't you think?"

"You can't own everything," the man said. "You can't own me no matter what you do to me. Even if you control my body, my thoughts will remain mine."

She stared at him, wondering if his naïveté was genuine. Then she remembered that they had had no contact with the Fey before this year, and knew nothing of Doppelgängers. "Then you should have no problem in giving me your name," she said.

He leaned back in his chair, a smile touching his face. The ropes were cutting into his clothes, making an oily crease on the filthy fabric. He didn't seem to notice. "Adrian," he said. "And my son, Luke."

So in trade he gave her three pieces of information, the connection being the most useful. The boy was staring at him, confusion even more evident. Adrian was right: the boy should have stayed home.

"Your son isn't fluent in Nye," she said.

"We didn't think he would need it." The "we" surprised her. A woman back home, perhaps, who helped him with decisions? Solanda had said that women did not do such things in Islander society. Another man, then? The older one?

"So he is not your only son."

Adrian started. The question had caught him by surprise. Her smile grew. "The oldest son learns the trade. The younger sons till the fields. Is that how it goes?"

"No," he said. "The oldest son inherits."

"And what becomes of the younger sons?" The favored son, she guessed, from the warmth evident between them.

"Whatever they choose."

"You send them into the world with nothing and hope they will survive?"

Adrian shrugged. "I did."

She crossed her legs, letting her right ankle rest on her left knee. "So you do have ownership," she said. "And you struggle to maintain the size of the land. We do not. We all inherit, so the land must increase, or we would have an ever-diminishing holding."

"Also—girls?" the boy asked.

She nodded. "And younger sons."

He flushed. Adrian glanced at him, and she saw tenderness in the look. She wondered how she had missed it before. "What are you going to do with us?" he asked.

"My people need information from you," she said. "We

will get it anyway we can. I am sorry to torture your father, but we have no choice."

At that he smiled. "Ort is not my father. He is an old man with more passion than sense."

"He's not as dumb as all that," she said. "His knowledge of colloquial Nye is better than any I have heard here. He should be at home as well, helping to negotiate a peace."

"No one has negotiated a peace," Adrian said.

"No one has offered." Jewel put her hands on her calf.

"Is that what you wanted us here for? So that we could go back with word that you want peace?"

She shook her head. "You're not going back. We can't let you out of here."

"What—place this is?" the boy asked. "No sky."

"Or sun or rain or weather." She leaned forward just a bit, feeling closer to the boy than she wanted to. "This is where we live until we win."

Adrian laughed. "The Fey have never been in retreat before. What makes you so sure you will win?"

"You," she said, and believed the calmness in her own voice.

"Me?" The smile on his lips didn't meet his eyes. "I am no one. Just a man who joined a fighting force last summer to defend his homeland."

"And has some degree of expertise because he came on this important raid," she said.

He shook his head. "We're not a fighting people. I am the first man in the history of my family to face battle. I was in the raid because I was convenient, not because of my skill."

Probably true, but not really relevant. What was important was the fact that the three of them had used the poison and probably understood how it was derived. The added side benefit, as Caseo had pointed out, was that the Warders could learn the effects of the poison on the Islanders themselves.

She sighed and leaned back. "You could save yourself some anguish," she said. "You could tell us how your poison works."

"I think you've seen how it works," he said dryly.

Vividly. And it frightened her. But she wouldn't let him know that. "I want to know what makes it work."

He laughed. "Then don't ask me. I throw the stuff. I don't make it."

"It's made?" she asked. One of Caseo's theories had been that the poison was from a stream or a lake somewhere.

"I believe so," he said. "But I don't know. I am not in the upper echelons of Rocaanism."

She frowned. "What was the poison used for before?"

"The water? It is used in our religious ceremonies. The holy water is passed through the congregation, and they dip their fingers into it and use it to clean off the tiny ritual swords that members always carry."

"Did you have a sword?" she asked.

He shot a quick glance at his son. The boy was looking at his hands. "I am not a believer," Adrian said.

"Your religion, then, it is not political or required? It is a choice?" That was new to her. She had never encountered that before.

He shrugged. "No one says anything if that's what you mean. I feel it's not right to mouth platitudes if I do not believe them."

But his son believed. She could tell from his attitude. The boy couldn't speak Nye, but he did understand it—when he wasn't feeling a pressure to respond. She spoke half a dozen languages like that. If she didn't concentrate on them, she understood them. But the moment she was required to perform, she couldn't. She would have to remember that about him and warn the others.

"Did you have a ritual sword, Luke?"

At the sound of his name, the boy's head jerked up. His eyes were shiny with fear. "They—it—not anymore," he said.

"Someone took it."

He nodded.

She swallowed, wanting to run from the room, to warn her people not to touch the sword's blade. But they had probably figured that out. Fortunately, the ritual symbol for the religion was easily recognizable as a weapon. "What's the purpose of cleaning the little sword?" she asked.

"The Elders say the Roca did that to his own sword before he died," Adrian said.

Jewel smiled. "For a nonbeliever, you are very knowledgeable."

"We are all raised in the Church," Adrian said.

"So what do they do to make your water holy?" she asked.

Adrian shook his head. "I don't know."

Jewel sat up. "You don't know? Or you won't tell me?"

"I don't know," he said. His tone was sullen.

She turned to the boy. "Do you?"

He glanced at her, and then at his father. Adrian nodded, as if in encouragement. "I—I—" the boy stammered. "Ah, no."

"But you were all raised in the Church."

"That doesn't mean we understand everything about it. Religion needs to be somewhat mysterious to work," Adrian said.

The hair rose on the back of her forehead. The Mysteries. Perhaps they disguised them in different ways. "Yet you know how to use this poison."

"As a religious item? Of course. We didn't learn about its other properties until you folks came on the scene—at least, none of us outside the upper echelons of Rocaanism knew."

She didn't move, didn't allow her expression to change. If they didn't know about that particular property, how had they discovered it? She had to talk with her father. They needed more knowledgeable Islanders. "What does this poison do to you?" she asked.

"Nothing," Adrian said.

"It—" The boy said a word in Islander, then flushed. His eyes were bright with fear.

"What did he say?" she asked Adrian, her tone harsh.

"It purifies." Adrian's voice was soft. He didn't look at his son, but Jewel could feel his concern. She had frightened both of them with her treatment of Ort. They were afraid she would do something to Luke as well.

"Purifies," she said softly. "And how does purification make you different?"

"It makes us acceptable to God," Adrian said.

The words sent a shiver through her. "And the Fey, then, can't be purified?" she asked. "We are unacceptable to your gods?"

"That—*Danites*—they say." The boy spoke almost eagerly, as if in giving her that information, she would forgive him for slipping into his native tongue.

She suppressed a sigh. So. Not only were they fighting a powerful poison, they were also fighting a superstition. It was a good thing her father had sent Doppelgängers to the Tabernacle. Perhaps they would find an entrance into the Islanders' Mysteries. She couldn't understand it all, not in this conversation. So she switched the subject. "Who is your commander?"

"On this mission?" Adrian asked.

She nodded.

"Theron. He was picked by the King."

"So the King directs the battles?" She had trouble believing that. The man she had met was inexperienced and frightened. He didn't seem capable of leading a force like this. But, then, Islanders had not seemed capable of defeating the Fey.

"Some," Adrian said. "But we have no formal system. We are not military people."

"So I gathered," she muttered. "Tell me about your military, or what exists of it."

He shook his head. "We have no military. We have the guards who protect the King. The rest of us fight to save our homes, our children, and our lives." He jutted out his chin as he spoke, as if she were going to rebuke him for his defiance. Instead, she had to suppress a smile. She liked their aggression, their passionate belief in their own rightness. Perhaps that, more than anything, gave them strength.

"You make yourselves sound so noble," she said.

"We are," he said.

"We value our own principles as much as you value yours," she said. "Just because you do not believe in them does not make them wrong."

She regretted the words as soon as she spoke them. He had got to her. And she hadn't wanted him to.

"Your principles are wrong," he said, "if they cost me my life."

She stared at him for a moment, suddenly finding his defiance unappealing. She didn't want to think in his terms, even though he had a point. "You're safe enough," she said blandly.

"Like Ort?" he asked.

"Ort will live."

"How well?"

She let the words hang in the silence. Then she stood and looked down at him. "What other plans does your King have for fighting the Fey?"

He didn't tilt his head to look up at her. Instead he leaned back in the chair as best as his ropes would allow and gazed up without moving much, so that they still seemed to be on the same level. "Even if I knew, I wouldn't tell you that. I am not a fool."

"No," she said, "I suppose you aren't." She had already got enough from this conversation. She started to walk away when an idea hit her.

She paused, then gazed at Adrian over her shoulder. He had turned to his son, whose lower lip was trembling like a babe's. When they noticed she hadn't left, their faces returned to neutral masks. But in that moment she had seen despair, and great love.

"What kind of help would you give me if I let your son go free?" she asked.

Adrian opened his mouth, but she waved a hand to silence him.

"Don't answer me now. Think about it." She smiled, knowing she had him hooked. "The exchange would have to be an equal one. You would have to give me something worth a life that hasn't even reached its halfway point."

With that she let herself out of the room. As soon as the door closed, her knees buckled beneath her. She braced a hand against the rough wood wall, ignoring the splinters that dug beneath her palm, and took a deep breath. She hadn't realized how much energy she had put into that meeting. Another sign of the low level of panic she carried with her always. Part of her believed they would never leave this place. Such a belief had never bothered her before. She had no real home. Her family had been moving since the day she'd been born. But she had a community that included her grandfather and her brothers, as well as most of the Fey. This world here, in the Shadowlands, was a small, pale replica of the world she had left behind.

When the moment of weakness passed, she went down the hall. Her father was standing beside the fireplace, staring at the piles of ash, his hands clasped behind his back.

"Well?" he asked without looking at her.

"They claim they know nothing about how to make the

poison, but it figures into their religion. The older one—Adrian—says that it is part of the 'mystery' of religion." She walked up beside him and stared down as well. A charred log was half-buried in the ash. Grayness everywhere. How she longed for real color.

"The mystery?" He straightened and finally sought her face as he was speaking to her. "Do they know?"

"About our Mysteries? I don't think so. But I don't know. They could all be lying. They may know more about us than we could ever learn about them."

"Then why haven't the Doppelgängers reported it?" he asked.

She shook her head. "The coincidence feels odd to me. First the poison, now the fact that it is connected to a mystery."

"You are looking for signs where there are none, child," he said.

"You shouldn't rule things out this early in an interrogation," she snapped. She had just spent her time discovering information only to have him dismiss it and call her "child" as if she were little more than a tiny girl with hopes and dreams instead of knowledge and experience.

He sighed and returned his attention to the empty hearth. She wondered if he looked there because the cottage had no windows. It had no need for them. Everything looked the same outside, and the temperature remained the same as well.

"What else did you learn?" he asked.

"That our remaining two are father and son. And that the father might be willing to bargain for his son's life."

Rugar smiled. "You are very effective, Jewel."

"Yes," she said more sharply than she intended. "I am."

She left his side and pulled out a chair, sinking into it, letting the exhaustion creep over her. When he said nothing else, she felt as if she had to fill the silence. "I think they should be put somewhere together and given some freedom from those bonds. When the Warders are done with their companion, he should be placed with them as an example for the father of what might happen to the son. I think we will learn more from them that way."

"I'd like you to continue to interrogate them," Rugar said.

"In due time." She would pick the time, although she did not tell him that. The exhaustion she was carrying created little black spots around the edges of her vision.

"Have you ever thought," she asked, "of negotiating a peace?"

"What?" He barked the word out, as if shocked that a child of his would suggest such heresy.

"A peace. Until we figure out a way around all of this."

He looked at her as if she had lost her mind. "The Fey never negotiate from a position of weakness."

She shrugged. "We don't have to keep the peace. Once we learn what we need, we might be able to conquer them after all. No one said we had to do it fairly."

"Whatever made you think of this?" His voice had a gruffness she hadn't heard before.

"The situation," she said. "If Grandfather doesn't come, and we keep losing people, we will die here. But if we stall and discover what gives them their power, we might have a chance to survive."

"It sounds like a coward's solution," he said.

"It's sensible," she said. "We've already lost more on this campaign than any other in my memory."

"Things will change."

"Right." She stood, and for the second time that day her knees buckled. She pitched forward, feeling the blackness overwhelm her, but helpless to stop it. Her father caught her, his arms warm and strong around her. His scent mingled with the leather of his clothing, and his chest was firm. Pain slashed her forehead.

Her father was shouting, "Someone help her! Please help her!" but his voice sounded too far away. She opened her eyes. A sword hung over her head. They were in the Tabernacle, with all the lords and all the Fey leaders gathered around. The ceremony. She had ruined the ceremony. A man leaned over her, his eyebrows straight, his hair long and blond. His features were square. Nicholas. Tears floated in his eyes. He cradled her in his arms with a tenderness she had never felt before and said, *Orma lii.* Islander that sounded as familiar as Nye. *Are you all right?* Then he said her name over and over.

Someone poured water over her face, and she cringed. Nicholas raised a hand to stop it.

"Let them!" her father said, pulling Nicholas's arms away. The burning in her forehead eased.

Then the scene shifted. Nicholas still held her. She was wrapped in her father's healing cloak, but she was in a room made of stone, lying on a mattress that made her sink as if she were in water. A Healer—Neri—was bent over her, chanting. She slapped a poultice on Jewel's forehead. It smelled of redwort and garlic. "She'll live," Neri said, "but I can promise no more."

"What did she say?" Nicholas's Fey was heavily accented, barely understandable.

"That she'll live," her father said in Nye, "and maybe little more."

Nicholas made a keening sound in his throat and pressed her closer. "Jewel." He kissed her softly, then brushed her hair away from her cheeks. *"Ne sneto. Ne sneto."* I'm sorry. I'm sorry.

She touched him back. This night was not how she had dreamed it would be.

His arms tightened, and then he grabbed her shoulders, shaking her. "Jewel! Jewel!"

Not Nicholas. Her father. She felt a vague disappointment, as if the pain was worth Nicholas's touch. The darkness receded. She opened her eyes and found herself staring at the ceiling of their cabin. Her mouth was open, and drool ran down her chin. She brought her head up slowly, half expecting the burning in her forehead to stop the movement, but there was none.

"Are you all right?" her father asked.

She nodded, feeling a dislocation, as if she had been in two places at once. "I haven't had enough sleep," she said.

He eased her toward the chair. "You had a Vision."

She had to squint to see him. He looked older than she remembered. Maybe she hadn't looked at him, really looked at him, in a long time.

"Didn't you?"

The tone was off as well. He had never spoken to her with that mixture of awe and anger. Only to his father. What had gone wrong?

She put a hand to her head, unable to think, wondering why she felt like lying to him, why she had been lying to him about her Visions all along. "I suppose I did," she said.

"Tell me what you Saw." Not a request, a demand. And he didn't seem to care how she felt, even though she had nearly passed out. Was this how it was supposed to be between them? Was this how *his* father had acted toward him when the Visions had started?

"I think it was personal," she said, wishing her brain would clear, knowing that it wouldn't, that she needed to sleep before she could think clearly.

"In our family Visions are never personal," Rugar said.

She took a deep breath and then pulled her hand away from her head. The echo of the burning pain remained there, and for a moment she thought she felt scarred skin under her palm. Then she touched her forehead again. Smooth, as it should be.

"Does it matter what I Saw?" she asked.

"Of course it matters!" he said. "We have to do this together now."

"Then why don't you tell me what you See?" she asked.

He blanched. His face went from its normal dark to a grayness as deep as the Shadowlands within a matter of seconds. His eyes glittered. "You don't need to hear about my Visions."

"I think I do," she said, "if I am going to tell you mine."

"When did we find ourselves on opposite sides?" he asked.

"When you got so intense."

He laughed then and sank into a chair beside her. He took her hand. His palm was clammy. "I was worried, Jewel. That's all. I had never seen you do that before. It's startling when it happens to me. I never realized what it looked like."

"You never saw your father have a Vision?"

He shook his head. "You're the first."

The oddness again, but she decided to trust him. Perhaps he was right; perhaps her faint had startled him. It had certainly startled her.

She closed her eyes and recited the Vision as closely as she could. She didn't tell him she had seen the same thing twice before, nor did she tell him that this Vision had altered slightly. She understood it better, knew the language, knew the people involved. The Vision's evolution startled her more than the Vision itself.

When she finished, he was staring at her. "What do you think it means?" he asked.

Finally she had had enough. "You're the expert," she said. "You tell me."

For a moment his gaze seemed empty. Then he shook his head. "I don't know," he said. "I honestly don't know."

FORTY-SIX

THE air smelled odd in the sanctuary. Goose bumps ran up Matthias's arms as he quietly closed the oak doors behind him. The carvings dug into his palms, and he knew without looking that he had just placed his hands over the scenes of the Roca's birth. Normally he loved those: the water funnel surrounding and protecting the baby; the frightened faces of his parents; the face of the Holy One etched in the clouds. But on this day he didn't stop to look. On this day he pulled his hands away from the door and stood in the silence.

A faint scent, one he had learned to recognize in the last year. Blood. In this, the holiest of places.

His mouth had gone dry. He wanted to swallow, but couldn't. He clenched his fists so that he wouldn't touch the tops of the pews as was his custom to make sure no one had altered the carvings there. Instead he pulled off his sandals and set them by the door so that his feet would make no sound on the polished floor.

When the Rocaan walked down this aisle, the Auds walked before him, rolling a red carpet. Other Auds followed, rolling up the red carpet where he walked, so that no other feet touched it besides his. Matthias had often thought that the ritual made the Rocaan look as if he were walking on an island of red.

Blood-red.

Matthias's feet were sticking to the polish. Ahead he saw no one. He seemed to be alone, a fact that unnerved him even more than the odor.

The sanctuary was usually his favorite place. It made him feel refreshed. And sometimes, when the choir sang, he almost felt as if he could touch the Ear of God.

Nothing appeared to be disturbed. Rows of pews glistened in the light flowing down from the stained-glass panels inserted into the ceiling. The panels also depicted various events in the Roca's life, and as the sun revolved in the heavens, the sanctuary's interior light reflected different colors on the floor below. At night the lights were invisible, and the place had a dark, mysterious air not disturbed by the candlelight.

The pews had red cushions that so far appeared unstained. Ahead, the red rug covering the altar also appeared clean. No one had touched the silver bowl containing the holy water, and the vials in their shelves under the Sacrificial Table appeared undisturbed. If an attack was to happen here, someone would go for the water immediately.

He was being foolish.

He was being cautious. The smell was faint but ever present.

The air was cold. He shivered once, then continued his measured pace. Finally he reached the center of the sanctuary, where the pews were truncated to form a small circle on the floor. Above him, the largest replica of the Rocaan's sword hung, pointing downward. He had often wondered what would happen if the sword fell in the middle of a service. But it never had. It was held with ropes that the Auds constantly replaced—a different rope done on a different day by a different Aud, always overseen by a different Officiate. The sword was four times larger than a human being, and encrusted with jewels. Its point gleamed menacingly in the multicolored light.

Matthias had half expected to find something unusual in the circle, but the floor was polished there too. The smell seemed to have grown stronger, though. He ran a hand through his hair, his fingers tangling in the curls, glad he hadn't worn his biretta. He had planned to come there to plead with Roca to give him faith—the attack on the Fey hiding place had shaken him somehow—but this distraction had taken all resolve from him. A man couldn't speak to his God when the sanctuary smelled of blood.

Past the circle, the pews jutted back into the aisle and continued until they reached the stairs leading to the altar. The carved wooden chairs on the altar lacked the shine they normally had. Someone had been sitting in them since the morning cleaning.

It could have been one of the Elders. Matthias wasn't the only one who used this sanctuary, instead of the tiny chapel on the third floor, to pray. But that thought didn't stop his heart from racing even faster than it had a moment before.

He made himself walk slowly so that he looked at each pew as he passed, making certain they were empty. He wished he had a small vial of holy water in the pocket of his robe, as he used to when this war first started. He had become lax of late: he had seen no Fey in so long, only the dead reminded him that the country was under attack.

His breath was coming in short gasps as he walked up the steps. The hair on the back of his neck prickled. The square Sacrificial Table, nicked with the cuts of a hundred consecrated swords, was empty, but the rug beneath it had a dark blotch, as if someone had spilled water and forgotten to mop it up.

He knelt and touched the spot. It was damp. He brought his fingers to his nose and winced. Blood. Just as he suspected.

He glanced around quickly to see if he was still alone. He was. He saw no one else, but he couldn't be sure he was alone. Stupid, stupid of him not to have got help the moment he noticed the smell.

Matthias swallowed and rocked back on his heels. Now he had reason to get someone. He started to stand when his gaze caught something near the leg of one of the chairs. With a shaking hand he reached over and grabbed it—

—and nearly dropped it. It was smooth and white, but still damp, as if someone had wiped it clean. He kept it in his hand and brought it closer to his face. A bone. A tiny one. Like the bones of a person's fingers.

His trembling had increased. He sat down on the carpet,

away from the blood spot, and looked closely at the weave. No more blood, no more bones. Whoever had caused the blood had missed this particular piece of evidence just by chance.

"Matthias?"

Matthias started and almost stood but forced himself to remain sitting. He recognized the voice. It belonged to Andre, one of the Elders. "Come here," Matthias said, slipping the bone into his pocket. He would save that surprise for later, once he determined what was going on.

Andre came down the aisle that Matthias had walked on. Matthias's throat was dry. He hadn't heard the door open. He hadn't realized he was concentrating that hard. But it made sense.

"Smell something odd?" he asked as Andre walked.

Andre stopped, sniffed, and shook his head. "Candle wax, a bit too much polish. Nothing else."

Matthias frowned. Were his senses that much more finely tuned than Andre's? It seemed strange to him. "What are you doing here, anyway?"

"I could ask you that," Andre said. "I have never seen anyone worship here by sitting on the floor."

Matthias again resisted the urge to stand. Andre made him nervous. His piety seemed so pure compared to Matthias's scholarly approach to religion. His ignorance was equally irritating, and his recent friendship with the Rocaan even more so.

"Come here," Matthias said again.

Andre came closer. His shoes squeaked on the polished floor. Matthias's feet were cold. His entire body was cold. Andre crouched beside him.

"What did you do?" he asked.

Matthias bit back an angry retort. "Nothing. I found this. Touch it."

Andre extended one finger and pushed on the carpet. It made a slight squishy sound. He glanced at Matthias as if confused, then brought the finger to his own nose and sniffed. "Blood," he whispered. "In the sanctuary?"

Matthias nodded. "We need to find out what has happened. I want you to assemble the staff as well as all the Auds and Danites who are assigned to this place. I will speak to the Rocaan and gather the Elders. Between us we should find out who saw anything, if anyone did, and who is missing, if anyone is."

Andre wiped his finger on a dry spot on the carpet, as if he couldn't stand the feel of blood against his skin. Matthias watched him, then asked, "Did you see anything?"

Andre started as if he hadn't expected Matthias to speak again. "No," he said. "Except you. I just got here."

Matthias nodded. Someone had to have seen something. Someone had to know what caused the blood. Perhaps an Aud was injured. Perhaps someone had driven an enemy from the building.

"Do you think the Fey did this?" Andre asked.

Matthias looked at him, not willing to hear that thought, but now that it was out, it chilled him. "I hope not," he said.

"It could be a miracle," Andre said hopefully.

Matthias smiled. "There have been no miracles for hundreds of years."

"Life is a miracle," Andre said primly.

"Perhaps," Matthias said, "but I prefer to think of it as business as usual."

Andre shot him a look that Matthias had never seen before. Something cool and calculating lurked behind the man's eyes. "It is a miracle," he repeated, but for the first time since he had known Andre, Matthias didn't believe him.

Matthias stood up. His perceptions were probably off, thanks to the desecration of the sanctuary. The Rocaan would be heartbroken, and Matthias wasn't sure the old man could handle more upset. He seemed not only distant, but a bit crazy these days, as if he heard the word of God when no one else did. The Rocaan's actions worried Matthias. Porciluna hadn't mentioned a meeting of the Elders recently, but Matthias kept expecting him to. With this new crisis it became even more important for the Elders to be unified.

"Get an Aud in here," Matthias said. "Don't let anyone touch that spot."

Andre nodded. He stood too, and for a moment Matthias considered telling him about the bone. But then he decided that the detail could wait. The Rocaan would need to know first.

Matthias retraced his steps down the aisle. Andre went out the Danite door toward the back, the one the Rocaan always used when he conducted the ceremony himself. Matthias took one more glance at the sanctuary. The blood smell was stronger than it had been before. He didn't know what had happened there, but he wasn't sure he wanted to guess.

He didn't like the idea of anything going wrong in the Tabernacle itself.

When he reached the doors, he stopped to grab his sandals. His feet were icy cold, his toenails blue. He suspected the reaction was as much from fear as from the chill in the room. He had lied to Andre: the incident was probably Fey related. He had spent some time studying the incident in the dungeon tunnels with Lord Powell and Stephen. There had been blood there, too, and bones.

Just like the invasion. In the barracks, the morning of the attack, a guard had discovered bones littering the floor, and another body beside them. A few other sites had found bones, some very close to the palace. Monte, head of the guards, had guessed that they were somehow connected to the Fey, but whether the bones belonged to dead Fey who had been completely destroyed by the holy water, or whether the bones were human, no one could say.

Bones and blood. Bones and a body. His grip tightened on the prize in his pocket. Something had happened there, and someone had cleaned it up. He was determined to discover who.

He ran a finger along the carvings on the door, touching the sword held aloft by the doomed Roca. The Roca was in profile, his features grim. His eyes, though, did not look human because the wood did not have real expression. What did the Roca know that they had forgotten? What gave Him all the power, the ability to be remembered, to be Beloved by God?

Matthias leaned his head on the door. For the first time in his adult life, he wished that he had real faith, not knowledge. Because, for the first time in his life, he was beginning to understand that only faith would get him through.

FORTY-SEVEN

SOLANDA cocked her head. The voice mewed again. She sat on the side of the road and washed her face with her right paw. The sound didn't come from the forest; she heard the voice inside her head. She sighed. Shape-Shifters often had spillover magick from the other disciplines, but she had never experienced it before.

The trees seemed impossibly tall. The sunlight filtering through them had a sparkly quality. Birds chirped behind her, but the birds near her were silent. She didn't mind. She hadn't been hunting. She had been heading to the Shadow-lands.

The voice had been bothering her since she'd left Jahn. At first she thought she was being followed. Then she realized that the voice was saying nothing, just making small whimpering sounds. Panicked sounds. It called to her, warning her that she was missing something important.

She dug her paw into the corner of her eye and rubbed hard, getting the dirt out. She didn't have to return to Shadowlands right away. Rugar always let her follow her own whims. He already knew about the Doppelgänger appointments; he didn't need her for more than errands anyway. And this latest errand was done. If this voice turned out to be a simple trick on the part of the Mysteries, she would come back as quickly as she could.

Better to get this voice out of her head.

She stood up and looked both ways before she continued down the path.

The way to the Shadowlands was along the river. But the voice urged her to go north, away from the river into the forest. The path had originally been an Islander travel route, rarely used now because of the Fey's stronghold there. Few Islanders had lived in these parts in the first place, and most were gone by the time the Fey had arrived.

The farther north she went, the more the path narrowed with disuse, although footprints were carved into the dirt—probably formed with the mud that had been so thick from the rains. She passed a small wooden building—not a cabin, but something that she would have thought a lookout station if the Islanders had been military people. The wood was worn and weathered, and the roof was falling off. Obviously it hadn't been used since the Fey had arrived. She wondered what it was originally for. The path forked there, and she was about to follow the better-traveled portion when she glanced at the other fork. No. She needed to see what had been abandoned first.

The unused part of the path slanted downhill, and its smoothness eased her aching pads. She had walked too far without resting or eating. The quiet of this place almost made her turn Fey, but then she remembered the story of Aio, the Shape-Shifter who had got too comfortable and was slaughtered shortly after returning to two-legged form. It was a cautionary tale Domestics told Shape-Shifter children, but it had saved Solanda many times.

She would heed that memory now.

She moved into a patch of birch trees, their white bark welcome contrast to the green of the forest around them. The path had grown even narrower, and blades of grass pushed up through the dirt. No one had come that way in a long time.

The path descended another small hill, and she found herself in a clearing. The grass had grown tall, and brambles thick as weeds threaded through the trees. A cabin stood in the center of the clearing, its door open, its furniture broken and scattered on the lawn. Other Fey had been there before her and had probably taken all useful items into the Shadowlands.

She found a path under the brambles, glad for her feline shape, and a cat's ability to make itself twice as small as it should be. She winced as her stomach brushed against thorns on the ground. She pushed with her hind feet and dug her claws into the dirt ahead of her until she made it into the clearing. Then she stopped, picked the thorns out of her belly with her teeth, and washed her face again before surveying the ground around her.

Scattered pieces of wood and broken pottery hid in the tall grass. Wooden nails were embedded into the ground, many point up, and she had to avoid them to keep from injuring her paws. She sniffed the destruction, looking for the voice that had led her there.

Then she saw the skeletons.

They were in the middle of the clearing, and the grass had grown around them. The woman's was sprawled a few feet from the man's. Her clothing was tattered and hung on the bones, rotted and chewed by bugs. A few strands of hair still remained underneath her skull, which was forced back as if she had been screaming when she died.

The man was crumpled, his bones scattered as if an animal had got to them. But she knew no animal had. The marks on the bones came from Foot Soldiers indelicately lifting skin, muscle and blood from a dying being. Sloppy work. She would have to report it to Rugar.

Islander skeletons: she could tell from the inelasticity of the rib cages, the firmness of the bones.

And they had been dead a long time. Not a fresh kill. Probably dating from the First Battle for Jahn. Some of the units had not fought in Jahn—which would explain how they knew about such an empty place to put the Shadowlands at all.

The voice in her head was silent: she was supposed to be there. But the skeletons told her little more than the obvious, that an Islander couple had lived there and the Fey had killed them. She left them to disintegrate in the tall grass and made her way to the cabin itself.

The steps remained, but they were covered with dirt and animal tracks. She stopped to investigate. Beneath the dirt was a black stain. The blood had been so heavy at one time that it had seeped into the wood. No amount of rain would wash that stain away.

She climbed to the top, slowly, uncertain of what she would find. The inside of the cabin was dark and smelled of dust. Mice had left tracks in the dirt on the porch, and the tracks mingled with those of various birds. A much larger catlike animal had left pad prints twice the size of hers along the porch's edge—it had disdained the steps and leaped to the porch from the ground. All the tracks led inside and then out again. Apparently nothing left to steal.

But she sniffed the air again for good measure. With all that activity, the last thing she wanted to do was startle some huge animal that ate cats. The cautionary Shape-Shifter tales also warned of Shifters who had got themselves in a bad situation, without time to change to a more conducive form.

She smelled nothing different, so she went inside.

Most of the furniture was gone, leaving only bare floor with more tracks. Some of the tracks were human and Fey— she recognized the print of Fey boots and felt her suspicions confirmed. Much of the interior had found its way into Shadowlands.

The cabin had a large front room, and two branching rooms. There was an economy of design she had not seen in many buildings there, and an attention to comfort that was rare in Jahn. The fireplace was centrally located between the front room and the kitchen, and the windows made the room feel lighter than it had from the outside. It must have been a pleasant place to live, in better times.

In the back the kitchen had a door leading to what must have been a healthy garden. Some plants still grew untended, their leaves intertwining with the weeds. The pantry door stood open, and a small hearth stove stood off to one side—a luxury in a cabin this size, and one she was surprised that her people hadn't stolen. Perhaps they hadn't had a means to get it to Shadowlands.

She felt odd there, as if she were missing something. She went back into the front room and then into the first side room. It had been a bedroom. The furnishings were gone, but the headboard was still nailed to the wall. She stared at it for a moment, wondering what sort of life the people who had lived there had. Had they been happy so far from others? Had they liked their comfortable house? They had certainly died in prolonged pain, a price she would not like to pay for anything. She had seen the Foot Soldiers work, and it disgusted her. She couldn't imagine what it would feel like to actually suffer their touch.

A slight breeze rustled through the uncovered window, carrying with it the scents of grass and dry air. She looked up, sniffed, but smelled nothing unusual.

The voice in her head was still silent. If she hadn't felt its presence so strongly, she wouldn't believe now that it existed. But it did. And it wanted her to know—something.

She left the bedroom and crossed the small hallway to the other room. It too was empty. Sunlight reflected off the dust-covered floor, a large yellow patch that made her want to lie down, rest, and warm herself. But she didn't. The anticipatory feeling was stronger there, as if she was close to something.

In this room nothing remained on the walls except a small stain on one side. On closer inspection she noted that the wood was darker there, as if the sun had never faded it. The stain was about a foot high and a yard wide, as if someone had kept a long board against the wall. But she could tell no more from it. If this was what she was supposed to seek out, she had no understanding of its meaning.

She stood for a moment in the warm sunlight, letting it caress her fur. This was a side trip, one that she didn't entirely understand.

She sighed. She would go back to the path and follow it in the direction she initially headed, to see where it led. Then, if she found nothing of consequence, she would return to the Shadowlands.

Her tail twitched at the thought, sending dust motes through the air. She watched them glisten in the rays of sunlight—and then she saw something in the corner. Reluctantly she got to her feet and padded over.

She had to blink in the sudden darkness, hating the contrast between the sunlight and the rest of the room. The chill air against her fur made her shudder. She approached the corner slowly, almost on her belly, jumping each time she saw a dust mote move. The cat part of her had control, and the Fey part of her felt a slight embarrassment, as if her behavior were completely unseemly.

Finally she reached the spot and peered ahead, half-tempted to switch to her Fey form so that she could see more clearly. The object was round and half-hidden in shadow. She couldn't tell if it was the rolled-up body of a dead mouse, or something more sinister.

With a tentative paw, she reached out and batted it.

The thing rocked and she jumped away, her feline reflexes taking over. She sat and stared at it for a moment before realizing that her paw had not touched fur. It had touched wood.

A thread of relief ran through her. She had suspected, since the Fey had arrived on Blue Isle, that the Islanders had more powers than they let on, and that someday a Fey would touch something—a dead body, a bit of food—and die as hideously as they did when touched by the water poison. That was one thing she liked about traveling in her feline body: her aversion to water was considered natural.

She got up and approached the thing again, this time batting it harder with her paw. The thing rolled toward her and hit her front legs. She sniffed it, getting the scents of dust, dried wood, and something else, something that might not have been noticeable to anyone else.

Baby sweat.

She batted the ball away from her and noted an entrance hole and an exit hole marring the ball's perfection. Someone had made this. She could imagine a stick going through it or a string, something to make this a plaything for a very young child.

A baby.

The voice in her head was beginning to make sense now. But she didn't inspect the ground that closely. The child might already be dead. The skeleton of an infant would be harder to find than one of an adult.

She batted the ball around the room for a moment, enjoying the rolling sound of wood on wood. Then she let it roll back into its corner—the house must not be completely level—before she went outside.

A baby. This changed things. The Foot Soldiers knew to capture babies instead of killing them, but if they hadn't found the child, it would have starved to death on its own. If it could crawl, it might be in the yard. If something else had killed those people, the child would be dead as well.

But she suspected it wasn't dead. If the child lived, she would find it.

FORTY-EIGHT

THE Rocaan held it in his palm—a tiny, thin bone about the size of the tip of his thumb. A stringy bit of matter—flesh, muscle, he wasn't sure—still clung to its end, as if that would indicate who it came from. Or what. He leaned back in his chair and shivered despite the heat of the fire roaring in his fireplace. He had been cold for almost a year now, and he suspected that the cold did not come from the outside.

The tapestries were fastened over the windows. He hadn't allowed the tapestries away from the windows since the invasion. His memories of the bodies in the courtyard had spoiled the view. An Aud now came in every morning to light all the lamps, illuminating the etchings on the walls.

Matthias, his blond curls mussed, sat across from the Rocaan. Matthias looked odd without his biretta, like a man who had recently awakened and not yet got his bearings. His sash was twisted, and there was dirt on the shoulder of his robe. Matthias—even in the height of the battles around Jahn—had never looked this disoriented.

"You're sure it's human?" the Rocaan asked. He had never seen a bone before, at least not a skeletal bone. He had seen only the bones the cooks threw to the dogs that guarded the river's edge.

Matthias nodded. "I have been around bodies," he said. "It's human."

And then the Rocaan remembered: when Matthias was an Aud, he had been part of the group that had reclaimed the bodies from the Kenniland Marshes. A few had risen to the surface during a particularly bad storm, and someone had guessed—probably Matthias, based on his scholarship— that more would be beneath the marshes' surface. All of the bodies had been dead a long time. The Rocaan had over- seen the burial, but the bodies were already in their coffins. It had taken Auds and townspeople almost a month to reconstruct the skeletons they had found in the marsh. The dead, they had assumed, were part of the Peasant Uprising and had been buried in a mass grave.

"What would it be doing in the sanctuary?" the Rocaan asked, not sure he wanted the answer.

Matthias shook his head. "I've been wondering the same thing. The blood has me the most bothered. There were blood and bones discovered in and near the palace during the invasion, as well as in the guard barracks. This has something to do with the Fey."

The Rocaan clenched his fist. "They leave us nothing. Don't they understand the concept of holiness?" He closed his eyes and leaned back, wishing this would all end. They had taken so much from him. Now the only place he would be able to worship would be the tiny room from which he had first seen the Fey.

"I don't think it matters to them," Matthias said.

The Rocaan opened his eyes. He didn't like sitting across from Matthias. Matthias was tall and thin like the Fey, and he was the one who had suggested the use of holy water as a weapon. He had never believed in God or the Roca, and he twisted the Words Written and Unwritten into something that could do his bidding.

Matthias should never have learned the secret to holy water. Now the Rocaan would have to choose—forcefully, decidedly—his successor before he died. Andre was a possi- bility; he had faith. But Andre had no knowledge of the world. That was the problem with the faithful: they refused to examine the present.

He swallowed. He set the bone in a silver bowl on the table beside him. It clinked as it fell, and Matthias winced. The man had never shown this much sensitivity before.

The Rocaan didn't like it.

He nodded to Matthias as a form of dismissal. Matthias didn't seem to understand the gesture.

"I will take this all under advisement," the Rocaan said.

"Take what under advisement?" Matthias asked. "All we know is that there could be a problem in the sanctuary. We don't even know what it could be."

"If I hear of anything out of the ordinary—"

"You're saying that pools of blood are ordinary now? I already sent Andre to call a meeting of all the inhabitants of the Tabernacle. If someone is missing, then we will know what happened."

The Rocaan didn't like Matthias's tone. The sarcasm didn't belong in their relationship—whatever it had become. "You shouldn't have acted without me," the Rocaan said.

"Why not?" Matthias asked. "All the Elders are authorized to act in your stead. We run the Tabernacle."

"Yes, but I lead it." The Rocaan said the words softly. He wanted Matthias to hear the undertone, to understand that things do not always go according to plan.

Matthias leaned back and pursed his lips together. He apparently heard. "Well then, Holy Sir," he said after a moment, "I will cancel the order."

"Do that," the Rocaan said. He closed his eyes. He didn't want to see anymore, to think anymore. He wanted the fire to warm him, and he wanted these days of worry to end.

The chair creaked as Matthias's weight shifted. Then someone rapped on the door. The Rocaan sighed and opened his eyes. Matthias was standing, his hands clasped over his belly. He was looking at the door with a wistful expression as though he were a little boy gazing at something forbidden.

"Get that," the Rocaan said, not bothering with the niceties. "I'm not available except in an emergency."

Matthias nodded without really looking at the Rocaan. The Rocaan squinted. His assessment was wrong. Matthias wasn't wistful. He appeared frightened. A shiver of fear ran down the Rocaan's back. He had seen Matthias alarmed, but never terrified. What would frighten him so?

Matthias made his way to the door. He opened it and slid out, so that the person behind it wouldn't see the Rocaan in his high-backed chair. The Rocaan brought his thumb and forefinger to the bridge of his nose and pinched. The pain felt good. It woke him up, made him remember that he was alive. He picked up the silver bowl and stared at the bone. Someone had died in the Tabernacle. Or someone had poured blood and planted a bone in the most sacred spot on Blue Isle. A Fey ritual? Did they hope to gain power that way?

Perhaps he should ignore the King's order and send a small ship off the Isle. Nye had a tiny band of Rocaanists who might be willing to leave the country now that it was under Fey domination. They had lived with the Fey for over three years. They would know if this was some kind of Fey trick—and they would know what to do about it.

An ache was building behind his eyes. But they would also want holy water to take with them to Nye when they returned. The Rocaanists on Nye had no real leaders. The Aud who had formed the band had died years ago, and they had worshiped without instruction for nearly a decade. It had been the Rocaan's decision to let them continue on their own, thinking it best to keep Rocaanism confined to Blue Isle. The risk he would take sending that ship out would be greater than the information he received. With some thought he would be able to learn what he needed right here.

The problem was that neither side was talking to the other. He had never even met a Fey. He had seen them only from a distance, during the invasion, when they had fought his people on the courtyard below. The Words Written and Unwritten said that any man who did not know his enemy was a fool. The Words preached knowledge at all costs. And the Rocaan had allowed them to ignore the knowledge in the face of terror.

The door opened, and Matthias slipped back inside the room. If anything, he looked even paler than before. He was winding a curl around his forefinger, a gesture the Rocaan had never seen before. Matthias nodded once, as if in acknowledgment that he was interrupting the Rocaan.

"They found more," Matthias said.

The Rocaan shivered with chill. "Blood?" he asked.

Matthias nodded. "And an entire skeleton. In pieces."

The Rocaan turned away, his gaze catching the fire. The flames crackled and spit on the wood, rising in strange shapes, as if they held the answers. "What do you think it is?" he asked. "Do you think they're trying to enchant us?"

"I don't know," Matthias said. "But it hasn't worked on the palace, if that is the case. I'd like to see if anyone is missing, and I would like to send word to the King so that they know we have found the same phenomenon here."

The Rocaan sighed. Even when he didn't want to, he was doing Matthias's bidding. How strange that it should work out this way. Matthias should do his bidding instead.

"Who brought the news?"

"Porciluna." To his credit Matthias said no more. But the Rocaan could tell that he wanted to push forward, to act.

The Rocaan waved a hand. "Have your meeting. Send someone to the palace. Tell the King that I wish to see him. Tell him—" that the Rocaan was tired. That he wanted this war over. "—that he can pick the time and place."

Matthias stopped twisting his strand of hair. "As you wish," he said, and backed out of the room. His fear had more power than his arguments.

The Rocaan watched him go and somehow could not shake a feeling of doom.

FORTY-NINE

SCAVENGER tied the last full bag against his hip, put a hand on his back, and stood up. The air smelled of rotting flesh and bloating bodies, a smell he was beginning to detest. Sweat ran down the side of his face even though it was cool in the shade of the trees. A bird chirped overhead and quit when he looked up, as though his very expression silenced it.

He had been working since dawn of the day before, with five other Red Caps whom Rugar claimed could be spared. Spared from what, he didn't know. It wasn't as if they were fighting other battles somewhere and needed Red Caps to collect the blood and tissue. But he knew better than to ask. No one answered a Red Cap's questions.

Still, they were shorthanded. This kind of work required at least ten Red Caps, working as quickly as they could. He placed the most recent flesh strips in bags on his left side, so that he knew which ones weren't as good as the first. Caseo would be angry at the waste. Scavenger would tell him to blame Rugar.

As if that would do any good.

His hands smelled as bad as the clearing. He wiped the sweat off his brow with his wrist. No one acknowledged the work he did. No one really knew how dangerous it was, except for other Red Caps. To do this kind of stripping in the heat of battle was deadly—not all Red Caps took the strips from Foot Soldiers—but not nearly as deadly as doing it here, in the silence of this clearing. Each time he touched a body, he was afraid he would brush some of the Islander poison, that his own body would melt and betray him and he would suffocate because he had no way to breathe any-more. He had dreams about that. He would wake up gasping for air. If he knew any way out of this godforsaken place, he would take it. But he knew none.

It was his own fault that he was out there. He made the mistake of telling Tazy, the head of the Foot Soldiers, that he would go anywhere to get out of the grayness of Shadow-lands. It too leached into his dreams. He used to dream in color on Nye. Now everything was gray, sometimes dark and sometimes light, but always gray.

He needed to escape. He would go crazy there if they made him stay much longer.

"Nearly done?" A voice sounded just behind his ear. He looked up to see Vulture standing beside him. Vulture was even shorter than he was and weighed twice as much. They had gone to school together, and Scavenger still remem-bered the day when they'd been the only postpubescent males in the class, the day the teacher pulled them aside and told them that they might as well quit because the magick would never come to them.

Scavenger shook his head. His body ached. "There's too much work for all of us."

"It's almost wasted now," Vulture said. "Can't get much useful off decayed flesh."

"Maybe the Domestics can."

Vulture wrinkled his nose. "They won't come near this kind of body. And the Shaman didn't bring any Tenders."

"That's right. I forgot." The forgetting had been a means of self-defense. The Red Caps would have to dispose of the remains themselves now. He stretched. The blood bags hung heavy from his belt. "You know what bothers me?"

Vulture tied a bag to his own belt. "What?"

"No Islanders. Remember at the Second Battle for Jahn, when they were dragging the dead away from us? And at the

Skirmish for Cardidas Port, how they tried to kill us when we bent over a body?"

Vulture looked up, a frown on his round bloodstained face. "They've had two days."

"Exactly."

Vulture shuddered. "What if they had poison on these bodies? What if it is a different kind? We'll die slow—"

"Maybe," Scavenger said. "But I don't think it's that. If they wanted us to die, they wouldn't have wasted lives. Something else is happening."

"It makes no sense," Vulture said.

Scavenger glanced at the Circle, knowing where the lights would flicker but not seeing them. He took a deep breath. "Maybe they don't want to come back here. We won here. We took some of their people, killed most of their people, and captured their weapon. Maybe they're finally afraid of us."

"I think they've been afraid of us all along," Vulture said.

"Yes, but maybe they think we can get them now."

"I don't think they ever doubted that," Vulture said. "We knocked their cozy world into pieces a year ago—"

"And they've managed to hold us off." Scavenger sighed. He hated it here. He hadn't liked Nye either. It was the work. Maybe he should have run away as he had planned after they'd captured Nye. He could have got a farm, or a small house, and lived there, unbothered. But he knew that wouldn't work. No one wanted Red Caps around. Nyeians would have shunned him, and if the farm failed, he wouldn't have been able to eat. At least being in the military kept him fed. More or less.

He patted the pouches hanging from his belt. "I don't think we can do much more here," he said.

Vulture nodded. "Why don't you see if Tazy will come out here and make that judgment? I think we can all use a rest."

Scavenger didn't have to be told twice. He crossed the clearing, stepped across the dirt line into the Ground Circle, said the chant, and then stepped through the Circle of Light. The lights burned his skin, and then he was inside, in the cool gray that was the Shadowlands.

A group of Domestics were standing near the meeting square. They saw him and turned their backs, continuing the discussion as if he weren't there. With a sigh he kicked away the cool grayness, revealing an opaque layer of nothingness at his feet. He didn't even have his own place to wash up—and if he had, someone would want to know why he was cleaning himself instead of working.

He walked carefully, head down, so that he wouldn't see the others stare at him. When he reached the Spell Warders' cabin, he knocked.

There was no answer, and he was going to let himself in and stack the pouches in the back room as he had been told when the door flung open. Caseo stood there, looking as tired as Scavenger felt.

"You're a mess," he said.

Scavenger shrugged. He wouldn't let Caseo anger him today. "I have pouches."

"Are you sure they're any good? You stink of decay."

Scavenger looked down. He hated the Warders. They had refused to listen to him during the First Battle for Jahn. He had begged them to let him see the Sprites, to ask for rain. But the Warders wouldn't listen to him. They almost hadn't let him into Shadowlands.

"The bodies have been out there for two days," Scavenger said. "We can't preserve them because you say it taints the magick. No one has told us to quit yet. So I bring you pouches."

"By the Mysteries, do I have to do the thinking for all of you?" Caseo snapped. He turned to someone in the cabin whom Scavenger didn't see and said, "Get Tazy or one of the other soldiers to stop these imbeciles from tainting our supplies."

"We're not imbeciles," Scavenger said.

Caseo turned, his face tilted, his eyes shining as if Scavenger had said something amusing. "What?"

Scavenger jutted out his chin. "I said that we're not imbeciles."

A smile played on Caseo's lips. "What would you call it, then, when only one quarter of your brain works properly?"

"We're just as smart as you are," Scavenger said. "We're just not as lucky."

"Ah," Caseo's smile grew. "You call it luck. How strange. As if a gift from the Powers will come from the skies and rain luck on you, and then you will be as fortunate as I am. Such small, unworthy dreams, boy."

"I am not a boy. I am a man full grown."

"You are a boy," Caseo said. "You have not yet come into your powers. Isn't that what you believe?"

"I have powers," Scavenger said. "I am just as Fey as you are."

Caseo grinned. "And just what are your powers, boy?"

"I am stronger than you. I have more stamina than you. I have *physical* abilities where your abilities are magickal. I am just as worthy as you are."

Caseo's grin became a deep chuckle. "If you were strong or worthy, you would at least be a part of the Infantry. You are nothing, boy. Nothing at all. You are well named—a creature that steals from the dead. We have conquered a dozen societies, boy, and none of them value the people who work with the dead. Only the outcasts and worthless ones put their hands on bodies."

With shaking hands Scavenger untied pouches from his belt. They dropped to the ground with squishy thuds, but none of them broke. "I make your work possible," he said. "Without me and the rest of the Red Caps, you wouldn't be able to perform your vile spells. You would be nothing."

Caseo's grin faded, and for a moment Scavenger thought he had got to him. Then Caseo nodded. He extended a hand. "How would you like to test the theory that you are as much Fey as I am?"

Scavenger stared at Caseo's palm, untouched by calluses, the nails polished and buffed. The man had never done physical labor in his life. Scavenger put his own hands behind his back. "What do you want me to do?"

"Come with me," Caseo said. "And bring the pouches with you."

"No," Scavenger said. "Let someone else carry the pouches."

"You are a Red Cap," Caseo said. "Whatever else happens, we all must do our jobs."

The remark made Scavenger flush. He leaned over and picked up the pouches by their tied ends, holding them together in his fists. The weight was hard on his arms—he was used to carrying them around his waist, which made them feel like part of him. But he said nothing as he followed Caseo up the stairs and into the Warders' cabin.

Scavenger had been inside many times, but he had never been allowed to linger. The other Warders sat around a table, and except for the closest, who wrinkled his nose as Scavenger passed, they did not seem to notice him. Caseo pointed to the back wall where other blood pouches had been stacked. Scavenger placed his pouches on top.

The main room was stiflingly hot. A fire blazed in the fireplace—covered with too much wood—a waste and a crime when a number of Fey still had to sleep on the ground or in crowded buildings with no heat. The Warders were all balding, bony creatures—even the women—with eyes that saw beyond the simple, everyday pleasures. A shudder ran down Scavenger's back. It was one thing to spar with a single Warder, quite another to face the entire troop.

They sat with their hands under the table, and they all wore heavy robes despite the heat. Scavenger appeared to be the only one sweating. He licked his lips, longing for a glass of water, and knowing they wouldn't offer it to him.

A bowl of water sat in the very center of the table, and to one side, an open pouch of blood. A strand of skin lay in another bowl, in pinkish water. The skin had a freshness that the skin he pulled today did not have.

"What are we doing?" Scavenger asked.

The Warders all looked to Caseo at the same time. It was as if they had no volition of their own, even though Scavenger knew they had. He had met each of them individually on the ships, had dealt with them more than once when he'd brought in pouches or helped with the blood supply. They seemed shocked that he dare speak aloud in a room with people so much his betters.

"This Red Cap," Caseo said, putting his hand on Scavenger's shoulder, "has said he is as much Fey as the rest of us. And I suddenly realized that he can help us all in determining that. We assume that it is our magickal powers that make us Fey. He has none and yet considers himself one of us. I think a bit of a test is in order, don't you, Warders?"

They did not respond. Scavenger shook Caseo's hand off his shoulder. Even when the man was trying to be civil, he still patronized Scavenger. Even when they were trying to work together.

"I've never heard anyone say that magick powers make a Fey," Scavenger said.

Caseo's smile was back. "Of course not," he said. "But what makes us different from, say, the Nye? Our powers."

"We look different," Scavenger said.

Caseo shook his head. "People from different parts of the world look different from each other. All the peoples around the Eccrrasian Mountains share our dark coloring, just as the peoples on Blue Isle all have round features and pale hair."

"Our military might makes us different," Scavenger said. "Our determination to be the strongest people in the world."

Caseo laughed. The other Warders watched, their faces expressionless. It was as if their bodies were in the room, but their minds weren't. "How could we conquer so many people on strength alone? You are a naive child, Red Cap."

"I am not a child," Scavenger said. "I am only ten years younger than you are. I remember you in school. I remember when you got your powers."

"We will have this discussion until you prove you are as worthy to be called a Fey as I am," Caseo said.

"So," Scavenger said. "I'll prove it."

Caseo's smile was slow and reached his eyes for the first time since Scavenger had known him. "All I want you to do," he said, "is to take a bit of skin you brought with you and place it in the bowl of water."

"What will that prove?" Scavenger said. "Is it a spell I'm supposed to know? I have no training there. And don't lie to me. I know you all were trained once your powers appeared."

"It is a spell," Caseo said, "but I'll give you the words when you put the skin in the water."

Scavenger shook his head. "The test is unfair. I have no magick. That we all know. I have been tested by two Shamans. I have worked with some of the greatest Shamans of our time, and they have shown that I have no magick." He glanced at the bowl, then at the other bowl with the skin already in it. He had seen no spell that required skin in water. But he did know that the Warders were testing the Islander poison. By placing Islander skin in Islander poison, they were seeing if its effect on Islanders was the same as its effect on the Fey.

A shiver ran down his back. He went to the corner and picked the last pouch he had made off the stack. He opened it, and the stink of rotted flesh almost made him gag. The Warder closest to him turned green. He brought the pouch back to the table, letting the stink affect them all. He grabbed the edge of one skin and held it tightly between his finger and his thumb.

"I am a Fey," he said through clenched teeth, holding his anger back so that he didn't grab the bowl and spray everyone in the room with its contents. "That poison will kill me."

Caseo shrugged. "That remains to be seen. No Red Cap has yet died from it."

"Such a test," Scavenger said. "If I die, I prove that Red Caps are worthy of your respect. And if I don't, I prove that we are not true Fey."

"You said you are strong," Caseo said. "Prove it. Touch the water. Help us solve this problem. If you live, then we will know that it affects only those of us who are magick."

"I may not have magick," Scavenger said, "but I have brains, and what you are proposing is a kind of murder."

Caseo shook his head. "I am convinced that you will live. I am convinced that magick alone will cause the poison to work."

"Then why don't you test it on one of the Infantry?" Scavenger said.

"No," Caseo said, raising his arms, "I think we shall test it on you."

Scavenger had been afraid of that. He tossed the skin at the bowl. Warders screamed and backed away as drops splashed around the table. He didn't wait to see if any of them would die. He ran for the door, yanked it open, and dashed outside.

Damn them. Damn them all. They believed that he was so worthless, he could die for their experiments. He had heard the drill before, on Galinas. One might die that all might live. It was how the generals totaled the winning. If more of the enemy died than Fey, the battle was a success. Lives meant nothing. Especially lives that had no magick.

He was through with that. He was through with them all.

FIFTY

NICHOLAS stood in the Great Chamber in the private wing of the Tabernacle. The oriel cast a thin light on the room itself, but he was impressed by the real glass panels. They depicted the Roca's Absorption. The Roca himself was in the center panel, calmly cleaning his sword. The Soldiers of the Enemy stood around him, tall and faceless in their black armor. The Roca's own people crowded the pews and balconies, and their mouths were agape with fear and awe.

The rest of the Great Chamber was just as ornate. Gold leaf covered the walls. On the supporting beams the leaf was shaped into small swords. The chairs were stiff-backed and uncomfortable. He preferred to stand on the red-and-black woven carpet while he waited.

The tables were made of wood with the sword pattern woven into their legs. Each detail added to the whole and made him feel stifled. He had never really believed anything in the Words Written and Unwritten. Studying them with Elder Matthias had been a burden he had been happy to relinquish when the Fey had come. He understood his father's protests: a King should know about his subjects, and Rocaanism was the single greatest force in Island society, but that didn't mean Nicholas had to believe it. He just had to know how to manipulate it.

The grate had wood stacked in it, but there was no fire. The simple stone fireplace almost seemed out of place. The stones were roughly cut, without carving or ornamentation. As he inspected them, he guessed that they predated most of the room—that the trappings of the religion had come much later, when such things grew important.

The door opened and the Rocaan entered, followed by Elders Matthias and Porciluna. Nicholas's own guards were outside the room waiting, as they had been instructed.

The Rocaan's face had more lines in it than Nicholas had remembered. The man looked small in his velvet robe. Its color exactly matched that of the carpet, and the black sash he wore (with filigreed swords hanging off it like tassels) brought out the accents. He did not wear his ceremonial hat, and his balding head looked naked without it. When he saw Nicholas, his eyes widened.

Protocol required Nicholas to bow to the Rocaan. When Nicholas became King, the Rocaan would bow to him.

Nicholas made sure his bow was sweeping and respectful. As he rose, he said, "Beg pardon, Holy Sir, but my father believes that the two leaders of Blue Isle should not share a room until the Fey menace has passed."

He had expected a gracious comment in response, but the Rocaan said nothing. Matthias glanced at Porciluna as if he, too, found the behavior odd.

"My father says I am to report to him all that you say, Holy Sir."

"Your father set the time and place for this meeting," the Rocaan said. His voice was weak and tremulous, not the powerful speaking voice that Nicholas had heard over a year before. "He could have informed me that he was not coming."

"Yes, Holy Sir," Nicholas said. The muscles in his shoulder were tightening. "But he was afraid that you then would come to him. He believes that it is best—"

"That we not meet." The Rocaan nodded. "I believe he is wrong. That we need to be in contact. But he is frightened. A fear I understand."

Nicholas was about to deny the statement, and then he realized that the Rocaan was using it as a door to open his own side of the conversation. "You, Holy Sir? But you have God and the Holy One on your side."

"We all have God on our side, young man," the Rocaan said. As he spoke, he turned to Matthias as if he couldn't believe that Nicholas did not know that. Matthias shot the Rocaan a sheepish smile that turned glittery and hard when the Rocaan returned his attention to Nicholas.

"My father says you have urgent business—" Nicholas began, but the Rocaan held up one hand.

"I know," he said. "I am thinking about whether I want to discuss it with you."

Nicholas straightened. That was enough. The King ruled the nation, and he determined that his son would meet with the religious leaders. If the Rocaan pushed him around now, he would try to do so when Nicholas became King. "I am heir to the throne," Nicholas said. "I am the one you will be dealing with in the future. You may as well get used to it now."

He left off the respectful title. The Rocaan didn't even seem to notice. "I am not certain whether we will deal, young man," the Rocaan said. "But we are faced with a dilemma now that I had hoped I could discuss with someone who has done more living than you."

Nicholas opened his mouth and then closed it again. He didn't want to defend himself. It would be the worst thing, but he also knew that this old man could ruin Nicholas's reputation among the Rocaanists. The last thing Nicholas wanted was to be saddled with a reputation for weakness this early in his life.

"You are a prejudiced old man," Nicholas finally said.

Both Matthias and Porciluna straightened. Not even they, apparently, insulted the Rocaan. The Rocaan tilted his head, as if Nicholas's comment fascinated him.

"Prejudiced, young man?"

Nicholas nodded. "You have decided, without evidence, that I am not worthy of your confidence, even when my father sends me in his stead. Now, I may assume you are showing disrespect to my father—which I am sure you would never do—or I can take you for your word that you would rather speak to someone older on the assumption that someone older would be wiser. That is, of course, the accepted opinion. But you forget, Holy Sir"—and he made sure the title had a spin of sarcasm—"that my father would not send me in his stead if he did not have a full belief in my abilities to handle any situation."

Nicholas's words echoed against the gold walls. His own faith in his father had been shaken when he'd realized that his father had been testing Nicholas's loyalties. But despite those fears, his father had been alone with Nicholas numerous times. The test of Nicholas had come with Stephen because, as his father explained, chances were Nicholas was loyal. Still, Nicholas caught the threads of fear and relief in his father's tones, and understood what the tests had cost him.

The Rocaan put his hands behind his back and studied Nicholas. Matthias started to say something, and the Rocaan shot him a look that obviously demanded silence. Nicholas didn't appreciate the scrutiny. He crossed his arms in front of his chest and stared back at the Rocaan.

Finally the Rocaan nodded. "You are quite right, Highness. I let my expectations get the better of me. I am not as flexible as I used to be, especially in situations of crisis."

Nicholas smiled. "I understand, Holy Sir. These are trying times for us all. Now, you mentioned a matter of some urgency. Would it be possible to sit and discuss this?"

Matthias was staring at Nicholas as if he had never seen him before. Good. In the past Matthias had thought of Nicholas only as a wayward student. It was time that Matthias, too, learned that Nicholas was a man, capable of ruling Blue Isle if he had to.

"Yes," the Rocaan said. "We should be comfortable, even though I find this room quite cold. Porciluna, if you would be so kind as to light a fire for us. I think we should sit near the oriel. I am finding more and more comfort in the Roca's Absorption these days."

Matthias hurried around the Rocaan and pulled out chairs so that they would fit in front of the oriel. The Rocaan sat in front of the panel with the Roca on it. Light streamed from the window onto his chair, making him glow. He appeared younger than he had a few minutes earlier.

He patted the chair beside him for Nicholas. Matthias took the chair to the left, leaving Porciluna a chair farther away. Porciluna was still bent over the grate, struggling with the fire as if he hadn't made one in years. With each step he wiped his hands on a cloth he had taken from his robe. The cloth was growing black with ash.

Nicholas sat. Up close, the smell of mothballs and aging flesh was much stronger. The Rocaan's eyelashes had sleep on them, and his robe, though well pressed, had a slight stain on the corner. His hands were covered with as many wrinkles as his face, and liver spots dotted the skin like freckles.

Nicholas hadn't realized until this moment how old and frail the man was.

The Rocaan reached out and patted the back of Nicholas's hand, as if to reassure himself that the boy was real. Nicholas had never had to establish a relationship under crisis before. He finally understood how difficult such trust was.

"I do not mean to offend, Highness," the Rocaan said, "but would you mind if I Blessed you before we began our talk?"

A Blessing was an honor usually reserved for special occasions—weddings, coronations, or funerals. But it also involved touching the forehead with a ritual sword covered in holy water. A good precaution for them both.

"I would be honored to receive your Blessing, Holy Sir," Nicholas said. "How would you like to proceed?"

The Rocaan took the chain holding the silver sword off his head. Then he pulled a small vial of water from the pocket of his robe, and from another pocket he pulled a tiny cloth. He must have planned this when he'd heard that Nicholas was coming. He certainly wouldn't have asked as much of the King.

The Rocaan poured half the water from the vial onto the cloth, then polished the tiny sword with it. "We do not need kneeling here," he said to Nicholas. "The Holy One knows that you are submissive in your heart."

Behind the Rocaan, Matthias rolled his eyes. He knew better than all of them that Nicholas was not submissive in areas of religion.

"Bow your head and extend your left hand," the Rocaan said.

Nicholas did as he was bid. His heart was beating triple time. He had not been Blessed since he'd been a child—and he had believed then, in a young, unfocused way. He did not believe now, thinking that Rocaanism was mostly stories told to the less intelligent to keep them in line. For a moment, though, the childhood belief came back to him—not strong enough to qualify as faith, but enough to give him fear. What if his lack of faith caused the Blessing to fail? Would he melt like the Fey?

He closed his eyes. The point of the tiny sword scratched his palm, encircled the third finger of his left hand, and drew blood from his fingertip. The sharp stab was momentarily painful, nothing more. The Rocaan placed his other hand on Nicholas's head. The Rocaan's hand was bigger than he expected, and warm, sending heat through him.

" 'Blessed be this man before Us,' " the Rocaan said. " 'May the Holy One hear his Words. May the Roca guard his Deeds. May God open his Heart.' "

Nicholas swallowed, wishing the moment would pass. He felt no different, except for the tiny pinprick of pain in his fingertip. At least he was not dead. He had had an odd fear of holy water ever since he had seen the Fey die from it.

"Blessed be," the Rocaan said.

"Blessed be," Matthias repeated.

"Blessed be," Porciluna said from across the room.

Then the Rocaan took his hand off Nicholas's head. Nicholas felt as if a great weight had been lifted. He raised his head, and the Rocaan was smiling at him, revealing teeth broken and yellowed with age. "Welcome to the Tabernacle, son of my friend, grandson of my oldest friend."

"Thank you for the Welcoming, Holy Sir," Nicholas said, "and for the Blessing." He could breathe now. They had both touched the holy water and were sure of each other's influences. But the Elders hadn't. He wondered if he should ask them to leave and then decided against it. Whatever the Rocaan planned to discuss, the Elders probably knew.

A whiff of smoke filled the room, and then wood popped and snapped behind them. Porciluna had got the fire started. He walked quietly across the floor and sank into the remaining chair.

"Forgive the precautions," the Rocaan said. "I am not used to this world filled with enemies. Before we had only to watch for the overly ambitious and evil among us. Now we must watch everything, for without caution we will die."

"The Fey have destroyed life in Blue Isle," Nicholas said, agreeing.

"Not destroyed," the Rocaan said. "Damaged. Perhaps, with work, we can repair it."

"Perhaps," Nicholas said, although he did not believe it. A change like this would leave a permanent stamp upon the community.

The Rocaan apparently didn't notice the subtle disagreement in Nicholas's tone. "We asked for this meeting," he said, "because we have had some alarming events here in the Tabernacle. We have found bones."

Nicholas frowned. "Bones, Holy Sir?"

"Bones," the Rocaan said. "One bone in the sanctuary itself, accompanied by a bloodstain as large as this chair, and a full skeleton, disassembled, in the Servants' Chapel near a spray of blood."

Nicholas felt a chill, even though the fire sent heat through the room. "Do we know what they belong to?"

"They're human," the Rocaan said. "Matthias and several others have assured me of that. And, it appears, they are from two different bodies. The bone found in the sanctuary is not missing from the skeleton found in the Servants' Chapel."

"No reports of fighting," Porciluna said. His voice was thin and grating, just as Nicholas remembered it.

"And no one missing from the Tabernacle," Matthias added.

"Have you checked servants?" Nicholas asked, knowing that most of the nobility would have missed that. The servants were often unseen.

"Matthias assembled the entire staff, as well as the Auds assigned here, the Officiates, and the Danites," the Rocaan said. "No one was missing."

"What about visitors?" Nicholas asked.

"We have not had any unannounced visitors since the invasion. We believe it is safer that way. Even Midnight Sacrament is held in the smaller chapel on the grounds, with Danites at the doors as a protection." The Rocaan's tone implied that he did not like the arrangement. "We thought the palace might be able to help, since Matthias says you found bones and blood on the day Lord Powell died."

Nicholas nodded. His father had told him to be completely honest with them. Nicholas was glad for the Blessing now. Even knowing that he was talking with the real Rocaan made him nervous. Sharing information seemed both dangerous and necessary.

"I captured a Fey woman on the day of the invasion and brought her to my father for interrogation at Lord Powell's suggestion. After speaking with her for a few moments, my father decided to put her in the dungeon for later interrogation. He assigned Stephen, my swordmaster and a self-proclaimed expert in the Fey, to accompany Lord Powell and the woman to the dungeons." Nicholas ran a hand through his hair—his father's gesture, a thought that made him stop immediately. "They took the passages so that they wouldn't get caught in the corridors. When Lord Stowe went to the dungeons later, the woman wasn't there. So we sent guards into the passages. I went with them. We found Stephen unconscious and wounded against the wall. The woman was gone. All that remained of Lord Powell was a pile of bones and a large pool of blood."

"Are you sure that was Lord Powell?" the Rocaan asked.

"Who would it have been?" Nicholas asked. "The woman escaped. Her ropes were cut."

"The bones could have belonged to anyone," the Rocaan said. "They could have added a guard to their retinue. Lord Powell might be in their custody even as we speak."

Nicholas's throat was suddenly dry. In all the times he had thought of that incident, he had never come up with that particular twist. To be a prisoner of the Fey for an entire year was a thought he wasn't sure he wanted to contemplate. "There's more," he said, pushing the thought away. "Stephen began to act strangely after he healed. He made suggestions that were unlike him and refused to work with me on the sword. After a few skirmishes where it became clear that the Fey had inside information, my father believed that someone in the palace was spying for them. He tested all of us. Two nights ago, in the raid on the Fey hiding place, we learned that Stephen had been providing the information. My father confronted him in front of all of us and—" Nicholas's dry throat seized up on him for a moment. He had to clear it before he could continue. "—and

Stephen got hit with some holy water. He—melted—just like a Fey."

Matthias whistled. Porciluna ran a hand over his sweating face. The Rocaan frowned as if he didn't understand the implications of what Nicholas had said.

"Before he took the prisoner to the dungeons," Nicholas said, "Stephen had apparently told my father that the Fey could enchant a man and make him do their bidding."

The Rocaan pushed himself out of the chair and walked over to the fire, holding his hands over the flame as if he had suddenly become cold. The room was too hot. Nicholas found it was difficult to take a deep breath.

"So you're saying an enchantment can make a man die like a Fey?" Porciluna asked.

Nicholas shook his head. "I don't know. But we do know that Stephen was working for them, and he died like them. And he was the only one who survived the attack in the passages."

"Left there," Matthias said. "Left there as a spy."

"They stole blood and skin from the poor people they killed," the Rocaan said. His voice sounded very far away. He was hunched over the fire as if he couldn't quite stand upright. "Perhaps their magick requires blood in order to function."

"What did Stephen say about the attack?" Porciluna asked.

"He said he couldn't remember much," Nicholas said. "It seemed believable. He was clearly hit on the head. I even attributed his personality change to the invasion, and to his injury. I never suspected that he would work for them."

"Why not?" The Rocaan turned.

"Because he was too honorable," Nicholas said. "He taught me that a sword is more than a weapon. It is a symbol of hope for our religion, and it has powers that should not be lightly used. He taught me to honor the sword, to thank it, and to use it with reverence. He also taught me to honor my enemies, to understand them, and to realize that in understanding them, I might gain more than I would ever gain in fighting them."

"Perhaps this understanding led him to join their side," Porciluna said.

Nicholas shook his head. "He knew more about the Fey

than all of us combined. He had studied them. He had talked with people who fought them. When the Fey took over Nye, he thought it terrible. He believed they were voracious, that they absorbed cultures instead of letting them be. He would never have gone to them—not willingly."

"The bones and the blood." The Rocaan leaned against the fireplace, careful that his robes were nowhere near the fire itself. "They must be part of a magick ritual to take over a person—to 'enchant,' as the Prince said. And leaving them at the site must be part of the ritual."

"If that's the case," Matthias said, "then the ritual in the sanctuary failed, and the one in the chapel was successful."

"Because most of the bones were gone," Porciluna said.

Nicholas shook his head. "This doesn't seem right. Then what happened to Lord Powell? And why haven't we found any more unconscious people?"

"Perhaps it happened too long before," the Rocaan said.

"The blood was still wet in both cases," Matthias said.

"A big stain like that would take time to dry," Porciluna said.

"Yes, but we had Midnight Sacrament for the Elders the night before. Someone would have noticed it then, and the sanctuary was cleaned before that," Matthias said.

"Andre conducted Morning Sacrament in the chapel for the staff," Porciluna said. "He noticed nothing unusual."

"Did you see if anyone saw anything odd?"

Matthias shook his head. "Both areas were empty for several hours before the blood was found. How long was Stephen unconscious?"

Nicholas shrugged. "We don't know. It was well after dark when Lord Stowe began the search."

The Rocaan stuck his hands into his pockets and walked toward them. "We are getting nowhere here. We have no knowledge, only speculation. But we have a solution."

"Holy water," Nicholas said.

The Rocaan smiled at him. "Yes. We test everyone to make certain they do not—melt, as the Prince so delicately put it—and we trust no one who refuses to touch the water."

"I think we might need this at the palace as well," Nicholas said. "We will need more than we have, I'm afraid."

The Rocaan nodded. "I will see to it that you get some. Matthias, you will need to help me."

"Pardon me, Holy Sir," Nicholas said. "But if someone in the Tabernacle is working with the Fey, then the vials of holy water you already have might be tainted. It would take little to replace them with real water. You will need to keep the holy water in hands you can trust, and you will need to make certain that it is holy water you have in the vials. Is there a way to do that?"

The edges of the Rocaan's eyes crinkled as if he was about to smile and was suppressing it. "We can do that," he said. "I have already thought of it. The holy water I used with you I made myself just before we met."

The two Elders did not seem startled by this news. "So far," Matthias said, "we have been fortunate that the Roca provided us with a weapon against the Fey—"

The Rocaan winced at the word "weapon." Nicholas filed the reaction away to think on later.

"—but that weapon will not serve us forever. They have not conquered half the world by being stupid. We have been lucky; they thought us easy to take. But we can't lose that advantage now. We need to outthink them and anticipate them. The water is one way. There have to be others."

"Why hasn't anyone just told them to get off this damn Island?" Porciluna asked Nicholas.

The oath startled Nicholas. He glanced at the Rocaan and saw nothing in the man's face that led him to believe Porciluna's attitude was a problem. Apparently they all had wondered that.

"If they leave with a bottle of holy water, they put all their people at work on it. Once they find a way to neutralize it, they return with more ships, more power, and destroy us all." Nicholas looked at Porciluna as he spoke. "It is a risk we do not want to take."

"Yes," the Rocaan said, "but this presupposes that we will not learn how to defend ourselves in their absence."

Nicholas bit his lower lip. "I think the chances of that are less than the chances they will learn how to deal with us. Whom would we go to for information? And what would we do when we had it? Nye had years of warning before the Fey arrived, and did nothing. All of Galinas has struggled to defeat them. They have powers that we do not. And they use them. We cannot learn as quickly or as well."

"Perhaps," Matthias said, "we have other weapons at our disposal that we are not aware of."

"The Roca's sword?" the Rocaan asked. "The gold with which we decorate our Tabernacle? The food we eat? How would you test these theories, Matthias?"

The amount of anger in the Rocaan's words made Nicholas want to back away. He held himself rigid, though, and pretended as if he had heard nothing unusual. He would have to report this, as well, to his father. The last thing they needed was divisiveness among the Rocaanists.

"I am merely suggesting," Matthias said slowly, as if he were speaking to a child, "that Blue Isle might have advantages Galinas never had."

The Rocaan stood. "We are wasting our time discussing things to which we have no answers. Matthias, you are to come with me. I will send a delivery of holy water to the palace, Highness, and I will test the messenger before it leaves here. You should test again on the other end." He nodded at Nicholas. Porciluna and Matthias stood reluctantly. Nicholas remained seated, the unease he had felt since he had arrived growing.

The Rocaan made his way to the door, the red velvet in his robe sweeping behind him. He placed his hand on the knob and then turned to Nicholas. "I think we forget, Highness, that the Roca, in all his wisdom, swore to protect us. We merely have to understand how those protections work." He smiled. His features looked gentle in the fading light. "We will be safe. I know it."

FIFTY-ONE

SOLANDA was tired and thirsty by the time she reached the end of the path. She had followed the voice, a small command in the back of her head, for miles until the path began to trail the side of a stream. Daisies grew alongside it, big white flowers that had no scent. She had never seen so many in one place. They hid the grass, making the banks of the stream look white. She walked around them, past a large tree that split the path, and onto a clearing.

Her tongue protruded from her lips, and she was panting. But she wasn't certain if the water was safe to drink, and so she pressed on. When she reached the bushes that separated the forest from the clearing, she stuck her head through them and stared.

Several cabins stood in a small semicircle. Only a few were as fine as the abandoned one she had seen. Children played around an oak stump so large that the Fey would have used it for a meeting place. Five boys and three girls of varying ages danced in a circle, singing, their hands clasped.

Solanda sat down. The words of the song sounded like nonsense, although she wasn't sure of that. The dance was a familiar one—she had seen older Fey use it to create a Ground Circle before opening a door into Shadowlands.

How strange that small children this far from Jahn had learned the same thing.

Or perhaps not so strange. Any beings that stood upright might think to join hands and dance in a circle. The difference was that here she didn't understand the song. And the song was probably what created the magick.

A woman stood near one of the houses, a basket of wash on her hip. Her breasts were enlarged from a recent pregnancy, and she smelled of milk. But the baby scent was not the one Solanda was following. The woman watched the children with a parent's intensity. In the distance men's voices were shouting rhythmically, as if they were working. The breeze carried the odors of sweat, children, and fresh fish.

Instantly Solanda's mouth watered. It had been a long time since she had eaten. The voice in her head was still, as it had been in the house. She had found the place she was meant to be.

Approaching the woman seemed best. Women on this Island seemed to have a special fondness for cats, as if the animal's grace and freedom appealed to them. Solanda had seen little grace or freedom among Island women.

Solanda walked out of the clearing, careful to brush in some dead leaves as she did so. The grass was soft beneath her paws: this part of the Island had no troubles with drought. If anything, it was a bit swampy. She would bet that the river overflowed at least once a year.

The children continued to dance. Up close, their words were no clearer and the melody was unfamiliar. The woman sighed and smiled, placing a hand on her other hip. She looked as if she wanted to call one of the children away but was unwilling to break up the group.

Solanda was afraid the woman would leave before she had a chance to catch her attention.

Another woman came out of the second house. This woman was older, with the loose, wrinkled skin brought on by malnutrition and age. Her clothing was clean, though, and well tended, even though it had a lot of mended rips. And, oddly, she smelled of baby.

A familiar baby.

Solanda's ears pricked forward.

". . . doesn't like them playing this kind of game now

that the Fey have arrived on the Isle," the first woman was saying. "He believes that any mention of magick is enough to bring them too close."

"Superstition isn't going to get us anywhere," the older woman said. Her voice was deep and tired. "The Fey are too ruthless to be popping in and out of a scene every time someone speaks of magick."

She spoke with authority. She must have been in Jahn during some of the battles. Only skirmishes occurred this far out. Solanda crossed the small dirt path, away from the children, and staggered the last step toward the women. She wound around the first woman's legs, meowing plaintively.

The woman stepped away. "Look at that filthy thing, Eleanora. Where did it come from?"

Solanda bristled. She was not filthy. She had made sure of that. Besides, she thought Island women liked cats.

"Oh, I think she's beautiful," the older woman—Eleanora—said, and crouched, holding out her hands. "Come here, gorgeous."

Solanda stopped winding around the first woman's legs and peered suspiciously at Eleanora. At least she didn't use that awful baby speak so many people used with cats. And she waited until Solanda was willing to come to her.

"Don't go near it," the first woman said. "They carry disease. You'll bring it to Coulter."

"Nonsense," Eleanora said. "I have lived near cats all my life. They're obsessed with cleanliness." She hadn't broken her eye contact with Solanda. "Come here, beautiful. I promise not to hurt you."

The first woman took another step back. "What will you do with it when you get it?"

Solanda was now free of the woman's legs. She didn't move, preferring to watch Eleanora from a distance.

"I'll feed her and give her some water. She looks like she hasn't had any for a long time." Eleanora hadn't moved her hands. She was used to cats. "Hey, gorgeous, I have a rug in front of the fire, a little extra fish, and lots of water."

With a soft meow Solanda went over to Eleanora and sniffed her fingers. They smelled of fish and baby sweat.

"That's it, gorgeous. I won't hurt you." Eleanora used a soothing tone, a gentling tone, but one that held respect, not contempt. In spite of herself, Solanda was growing to like this woman.

Solanda rubbed her mouth against the woman's hand, dripping a bit of saliva onto the woman's skin. Now her own scent mixed with that of the baby. So far, the voice hadn't returned to her head. She was apparently on the right track.

Eleanora cupped Solanda's chin. The gesture was friendly, not confining. "Would you like to come in and have some dinner?"

Solanda purred. Eleanora let go of Solanda's chin and then went to the next cabin. The children were still singing behind them. Solanda followed Eleanora.

"You're a fool, Eleanora," the other woman said.

Eleanora ignored her.

The steps up to the cabin were coarse, the wood poorly sanded. The small porch had been made later, out of logs, and was uneven. As Solanda stepped across the threshold, she was assaulted by smells: fresh bread, fresh fish, and dirty diapers. The main room had toys on the floor, and an expensive iron mesh in front of the fireplace, probably to keep the baby away from the flames. There was no real kitchen to speak of, only a pantry that lacked a separate fireplace. The bread must have come from someone else.

Eleanora poured milk from a pitcher into a bowl, then put the bowl on the ground. Solanda drank it, even though she knew too much would give her the trots. She didn't care. If it got too bad, she could go into the woods and be Fey for a few hours. That would take care of any discomfort.

"I don't have a lot of fish. It spoils fast unless I pickle it. Better to let you finish these last few bites." The woman spoke as she worked, pulling bones from the flesh before setting pieces on a small plate. Solanda appreciated the effort. Here was a woman who cared about beings smaller than herself.

When she put the plate in front of Solanda, Solanda's feline side took over. She inhaled the food so quickly, she barely had a chance to taste it. Then she sat on her haunches and cleaned her face, slowly and delicately, making certain no pieces of fish fell off her whiskers onto the floor.

Eleanora took the plate away. "Liked that, did you? Well, then. We always have a bit extra if you want to stay."

For the moment she did. Solanda finished cleaning and then spread out on the small rug before the hearth. She closed her eyes, meaning to doze, but all the travel of the last few days finally got to her, and she slept.

A shriek woke her. She opened her eyes to see a small boy wearing only a diaper walking toward her, his pudgy legs spread wide and thumping in the ungainly fashion of a being that has just learned to walk. She feigned sleep, figuring she could sprint away if she had to, as the toddler got to her. His fat fingers were clutching the air in anticipation of reaching her. He was bending over when Eleanora appeared and scooped him in her arms.

"No, Coulter. Be nice to the kitty."

Exactly, Solanda thought, and then she stretched herself awake. And as she awoke, she studied the child. He was the one whom she was there for. She knew it with a depth that matched her ability to Shape-Shift. Something about this child had drawn her miles away from her home.

He looked no different from other boys of his age. He had big curious eyes—blue—a color she had never seen in Fey children—and hair too brown to be called blond. His legs were still pudgy enough to have dimples for knees, and his toddler's stomach protruded over his diapers. He was jabbering at the woman who held him. Baby speak: half real words, half a garble of sounds. Solanda didn't even try to follow the train of thought.

Instead she rolled onto her back and revealed her belly to him, more as a sign to Eleanora that Solanda was worthy of trust. She needed some time there, to see what made the child special, and she could use the fresh food. Besides, a bit of diversion from life in the Shadowlands would be nice.

"Ah, Coulter," Eleanora said. "The kitty is being nice to you. Here is how you pet it."

She bent down, keeping one arm wrapped protectively around the child, and rubbed Solanda's stomach. Solanda purred and squirmed. Touch felt so much better in her feline form.

The boy, Coulter, reached out a pudgy hand and patted Solanda's tummy gently. Instantly a burst of power ran through her, and she almost Shifted.

"By the Sword," Eleanora said, and pulled back.

Coulter protested and reached for Solanda. Solanda

stood. Had she started to Shift? She cleaned her face as a pretense for examining her body. Nothing was different. Each hair was in place. But Eleanora must have seen the momentary waiver. Solanda had to make that look like a trick, but she didn't want the boy to touch her again. So she went and rubbed on the woman's legs.

"You spooked me, gorgeous," the woman said.

"Me!" the little boy said. "Me!" He was reaching for Solanda. If she concentrated on her form, she might be able to hold it while he touched her. Then she would be able to see what kind of power he really had.

"Be careful," Eleanora said again.

The boy cooed as he reached for Solanda. His touch hit her fur like a bolt of lightning. She had to bite on her back teeth—hard—to hold herself in the cat form. He had a power, and he was too old to have Fey blood. An Islander with power. Rugar would love to know of this.

But how to tell him? Solanda would need to think a bit before she made a choice on how to act.

She moved away from the baby's hand and bumped against Eleanora's leg, showing a preference as best she could. Better that the child did not try to touch her. Better that she kept her shape constant. It had been too close, a moment before.

Eleanora crouched and put the baby down. "Leave her for now, Coulter. We will teach you how to be with the kitty while she's here. We'll have you feed her. That will help."

He continued to reach for Solanda, and she dodged, using Eleanora's legs as protection. The boy had determination. His blue eyes glinted as he chased her.

"Coulter!" Eleanora said, and scooped him up again.

Solanda dived under a chair and huddled there. Here was the key they had all been looking for. Somehow this baby had survived the attack on the other cabin. Somehow he had drawn Solanda to him. He had power. She had been touched by children before, and that had never forced a change. No. There was something about him. Something important.

She lay down under the chair and placed her chin on her paws. The elderly woman was explaining to the child in words he probably couldn't understand why he shouldn't grab for a cat. Solanda tried to ignore the love there.

The old woman had been kind to her. Kindness was rare in any country, and Solanda would repay it by breaking the old woman's heart.

FIFTY-TWO

THERON'S hands were shaking as he approached the site. He felt older than he had the last time he'd walked down this road. Cyta and Kondros were both silent as they walked beside him. They weren't exactly disobeying orders, but they weren't obeying any either. No one had said that they could return to the battlefield. No one had said they could collect the dead.

This was the first time the King had allowed the dead to rot. Before, he had always sent teams to bury them and Danites to bless them. It was almost as if he was ashamed of the defeat. Theron was. He was even more ashamed of returning from the battle alive and whole. He should have been wounded. He should have lost a limb or blood or anything, something to show that he had suffered as much as his men.

But he could never suffer that much. He had not died.

Or been captured.

Cyta had mentioned trying to launch a rescue squad, someone to go after Adrian, Ort, and Luke. But Theron wasn't ready for that yet. The King might have something planned for that rescue. Perhaps that was why he didn't want anyone near the battle site. But that didn't seem right.

If he had wanted a rescue, he should have mounted one by now.

Kondros said he believed that the King counted the prisoners as lost. Bodies that belonged on the pile with the rest of them.

Theron couldn't bear that. Adrian had been a friend. A good man. Someone you could trust in any situation. Ort was a great fighter, and Luke was just a boy. Their lives couldn't end because a ruler saw them only as bodies to be launched against an enemy.

Theron stopped at the edge of the path before it opened into the clearing. His throat was dry and his heart was pounding in his throat. "You two don't have to go on," he said quietly.

"And let you go back there alone? You must be kidding," Cyta said.

"We've come this far," Kondros said. "We can go all the way."

"But I don't think we can bury all the dead—and do we dare do it without a Danite?"

"Better than letting them rot," Cyta said.

"If they're still there," Kondros added.

"I guess there's only one way to find out." Theron rubbed his damp palms on his pants, then took a deep breath and stepped off the path. He remembered walking this way in the darkness, remembered his misgivings, and wondered why he hadn't listened to them. Because he had trusted his King. He wasn't sure he would do that again.

They had barely gone ten paces when the smell hit them: rich and fecund and sour, it invaded their nostrils and tried to sink into their bodies. The stench brought tears to Theron's eyes. The King should be there. He should know what his plan had led them into.

Cyta had turned green. Kondros, his lips puckered in distaste, ripped the hem off his shirt and tied the material around his nose. Cyta, hands shaking, did the same. Theron brushed the pouches filled with holy water that he had hung from his belt. He was glad for them. He would never have come this far without them. Quickly, he ripped his shirt and brought the rag up to his nose. The cloth blocked the invasive nature of the smell, but didn't make it go away.

Two days. They should have returned sooner.

As Theron reached the edge of the clearing, he heard voices. They spoke in a guttural language that he recognized as Fey. The hair stood up on the back of his neck. He glanced at his companions. Cyta's green color had stayed, and a sweat had broken out on his forehead. Kondros bit his lower lip.

Quietly, Theron parted the tree branches and peered into the clearing. The bodies were stacked like cordwood near the dirt circle. There were no lights flickering in the air, no Fey visible. Then a short, squat man came out of the woods behind. He was covered with dirt (or blood?) and carried in his hands long dripping strips of something (cloth?). Another short man came from the same area, his hands stained and empty, pouches hanging from his belt like the pouches hung from Theron's.

They spoke, and he realized these were the voices he had heard. Sounds traveled in this clearing. Instinctively he tamed his breathing. Cyta and Kondros did the same.

A third Fey—a woman—dragged a body by its heels from the woods on the other side. The face looked odd, as if someone had carved holes in it. Then Theron realized that it was missing skin.

Instantly he felt nauseous. They were mutilating the dead. He had heard that the Fey did that, but he had never seen it. He glanced at his companions. Three against three. Good odds, unless more Fey came from the Circle.

Theron grabbed a pouch and opened it. With the other hand he took the knife from his boot and dipped it into the water. Cyta and Kondros did the same. Then Theron retied his pouch and attached it to his belt again. He held his knife out before him and was about to go into the clearing when someone grabbed him from behind.

A hand that smelled of rot covered his mouth and pulled him backward. The sharp edge of a knife bit into his throat.

Cyta and Kondros both turned, one hand on their pouches, the other holding a knife. Their eyes were wide.

The stench of the man holding Theron made him gag. "Now," the man said in badly accented Nye. He was whispering. "If you throw that stuff on me, it will bring the others, and that will bring still others. And we, none of us, want that."

Cyta and Kondros didn't move. Theron's eyes were watering. He held his breath, wishing he could speak. The pain in his throat was sharp, and he thought he felt the coolness of blood trickling down his neck.

"Now," the man said, his voice close to Theron's ear. "I need your help, and I believe you need mine. So how about we have a little chat, away from this clearing?"

Theron kept gesturing with his eyes, wishing he had the power to communicate with his mind. *Throw the water on him. Throw it!* But his friends didn't seem to get the message. They were watching the man, not Theron.

The man pulled Theron backward, keeping the pressure on his neck steady. His hand clamped even harder on Theron's mouth, fingers digging into his cheek, forcing him to bite the flesh inside. He let out a breath, then took another as he stumbled backward, his gaze on his friends, his free hand opening a pouch. He gripped the knife tightly with the other hand. All he had to do was shove it into the man's leg, and the man would die. But he might kill Theron in the process.

They crunched through dead leaves and branches. Theron watched the clearing, expecting the other Fey to follow, but they did not. When they were what he believed to be a safe distance from the clearing, he turned his knife hand and shoved the blade at the man's leg. Immediately the hand over his mouth moved and knocked Theron's knife away.

"Kill him!" Theron shouted.

The man's knife dug deeper into his throat. "Do it," he said to the others, "and I'll kill him. You"—he moved his head as if he were nodding at someone—"slash those pouches off his belt, yours, and your companion's, then drop your knife. You drop yours now."

Cyta dropped his knife. Theron shook his head just a little, trying not to jar the blade at his throat. Kondros shrugged, then reached over and cut Theron's belt off before cutting away Cyta's and his own.

"Now," the man said, "we're going to talk for a minute."

He pulled Theron against him, keeping the pressure on his throat. He took his other hand off Theron's mouth and encircled his waist. The man's grip was strong. Theron couldn't have broken it if he'd tried.

"You are too close to the Circle," the man said. "Islanders this close to the Circle will die, didn't you know that?"

"We came to get our comrades," Theron said. The blade pushed against his Adam's apple, making speaking painful.

"The dead?" the man asked. "The dead do not care how they end up. Be thankful they can be useful."

"Useful? To you? They don't want to be useful. They want to be Blessed," Theron said.

"Shh, Theron." Kondros held up a hand and faced the man. "You said you needed our help."

A little shudder ran through the man's body. Theron felt it in his back. He frowned, thinking that, for a moment, Kondros might be taking the right tack.

"You know nothing of us," the man said. "I can tell you."

"You would tell us about the Fey?" Kondros said. "Why should we trust you?"

"Because," the man said, his voice soft. "They just tried to kill me. I want to get out of here."

"One of their own?" Cyta's voice rose with incredulity.

It sounded like a lie to Theron too. "No," he said. "We can't trust you."

"Let Theron go," Kondros said, "and you will prove your trustworthiness."

The man's body shivered again. Theron watched his friends' faces. They betrayed nothing. He waited, holding his breath—that stink was overwhelming—and then the man let go. The knife dropped and the arm released Theron.

He stumbled forward, and Cyta caught him. Theron turned to see who their attacker was. Another short Fey—he hadn't realized that they were short—stood behind him, his face and arms smeared with blood and dirt. His clothing, originally red, was covered with brown stains as well. Only his dark coloring, telltale eyebrows, and high cheekbones made him look any different from the Islanders.

"What do you want from us?" Theron asked.

The man wiped the back of his hand against his forehead, as if he was unwilling to smear his face. "Take me somewhere safe."

"There is nowhere safe for you among our people," Kondros said.

The man shook his head and glanced over their shoulders at the clearing. "I can't go back there."

"What happened?" Cyta asked.

"They tried to kill me," he said.

"How?" Kondros appeared to have infinite patience. Theron was ready to snap at the man.

"They had some of your poison. They were going to pour it on me as an experiment."

Theron let his breath out slowly. So they were trying to figure out holy water. Already this man had given them some information they could use. But was this a plant? He didn't understand why the man would come to them instead of to his own kind.

"And you ran away?" Kondros asked.

The man nodded.

"We'll take you somewhere safe," Theron said, "if you get our people buried."

The man frowned, then shook his head. "It doesn't matter what happens to them. They're already gone."

"It matters to us," Theron said.

"No." The man's word was soft. "All that is there is the useless parts. We have taken the rest. They're gone."

"Taken the rest?" Cyta asked. Theron's stomach turned again. "For what?"

"Magick," the man whispered, as if he had said a holy word.

"Oh, God," Theron said, and the statement was half a prayer. No matter what, the King or one of his advisers had to speak with this creature.

"If you come with us," Kondros said, "you need to get rid of your knife, and you need to let us have our protection back."

"Don't pour the poison on me," the man said. "I ran from that."

Theron could feel the man's terror. If all the Fey felt that way, holy water was a better weapon than he had thought. "How do we know that they're not going to come after you?"

The man smiled. The smile was not a happy one. "I'm a Red Cap," he said. "They won't even notice that I'm gone."

"I think we should just leave him here," Cyta said in Islander.

Kondros shook his head. "What if he's telling the truth?"

"Then we missed an opportunity," Cyta said. "But if he's not, we'll die."

"I won't hurt you," the man said in Nye. "I promise. You may tie me up if you like. Just get me away from here."

Theron touched his neck. Blood smeared against his skin. The cut wasn't scabbing yet. "We could just kill you."

The man nodded. "You could. But I will tell you all you need to know about the Fey. I will tell you everything."

Theron looked at Kondros over the man's head. They couldn't make that kind of decision. A lord would have to, or the King himself. Maybe they could bargain this man's existence for a burial of their friends. Or a rescue of Adrian and the others.

"All right," Theron said, giving a small nod. "We'll take you somewhere safe."

FIFTY-THREE

JUST being in the Tabernacle terrified him. Tel clasped his hands together and sat in one of the wooden chairs, trying to keep himself calm. So far, he had managed well enough. Seeing Matthias just after the change had been awkward and frustrating. If Tel had had a bit more strength, he would have attacked Matthias then. But Tel might not have come through the experience sane. He hadn't had a chance to get near Matthias in the meeting later in the day.

The Elder's—Andre's—private rooms were austere, although they looked as if they had been built for opulence. The main room was wide, with a fireplace that extended to the ceiling, and a balcony that overlooked the entire city. The bedroom was also big and had another huge fireplace. Neither fireplace looked as if it had been used much, and Andre had chosen to sleep on a cot. He had furnished the main room with wooden furniture—no cushions—and had removed all the rugs, leaving only the tile floor. Still, it was better than the stables, where Tel had been before.

But not much better.

Not enough to make up for the danger he was putting himself in. If only he could stay in the private chambers.

When he ventured out, the Tabernacle was his worst nightmare.

He saw holy water everywhere. One of the Auds had brought him a flask of wine with his luncheon, and he had poured it into a mug, staring at it for the longest time, his tongue dry with thirst, wondering if the wine was made with the poison. But he knew it wasn't—or at least the Andre part of himself knew. Still, his hand shook as he brought it to his mouth to drink.

Even as Tel walked the halls, leaving the meeting and coming back to his rooms, he saw the water. Auds cleaning the walls, buckets of brownish liquid filled with damp cloths beside them, filled him with terror.

And to his surprise, none of the terror was worth it. He had thought that if he took over one of the Rocaan's assistants, an Elder, he would learn the secret to the poison, only to discover that no one but the Rocaan himself knew how to make the stuff.

No wonder the old man had looked haggard and ill since the Fey had arrived.

Tel wasn't quite sure how to get the information either. Did he become the old man? What if the holy water was part of the old man's makeup? What if, in becoming Rocaan, some part of the body changed? Tel could imagine himself, covered with blood, trying to absorb the old man, only to feel himself melting as so many other victims had. The image left him in the uncomfortable wooden chair, feet pressed together and hands wringing. He knew this place was safe, except for the cabinet near the door, where Andre kept his own supply of holy water, for both worship and protection.

The Rocaanists all imbued the water with mystical qualities. Andre had believed that the Roca gave them the water as a protection. Its use in Midnight Sacrament had taken on a special meaning to him after the Fey had arrived. Andre believed that the Roca had known about the Fey and had given the water to the Islanders as protection.

Not a bad idea, when one thought about it, although Tel didn't know how a man at the dawn of time had known that invaders would arrive at Blue Isle now. Perhaps the Roca really had had the Ear of God.

Tel shook himself and stood up. Andre had a loose body

that Tel had tied into knots. He moved his shoulders, hearing the cracks and pops. If only he could return to the stables, where he could work with the horses and ignore the crisis around him. He had snapped at Solanda because he had known she was right: he had gone to that place all Doppelgängers were warned about, the place where it became more comfortable to be someone else than to be himself.

He wouldn't make that mistake here.

He was running the risk of making a different mistake. He had been told in his training all those long years ago that Doppelgängers risked their lives for the troops. No Doppelgänger was more at risk than Tel was right now. And he was so frightened, he wanted nothing more than to be in his room.

Still, he had other problems to contend with. He was supposed to conduct Midnight Sacrament that night—actually handle vials with the holy water in it—and he was supposed to meet his contact at the same time. He wasn't sure how he was going to accomplish both tasks.

No one ever got out of Midnight Sacrament. It was one of the most important duties an Elder could perform. He paced on the bare stone floor, his hands clasped behind his back. He had to find a way out of this, and he had to do it soon. Because if he didn't show up at the meeting place, the messenger would assume he was dead, and he would have no help from Rugar.

Assume he was dead. Tel sat down. If they assumed he was dead, he could go back to being a groom. Life as a stable boy wasn't glamorous, but it was safe. And the Fey weren't going to get off this island for a long, long time.

A shudder ran through him. He knew what he was contemplating. If he got caught, the Shaman would speak his punishment. Tel had seen a Doppelgänger punished for abandoning his duties just once. The Doppelgänger was forced to go through a dozen Nye prisoners, changing into one after another in rapid succession until his own being broke under the strain. Then he was whisked away by the Spell Warders to be used in their strange and secretive experiments.

No one ever heard from him again.

Tel gazed out the window. In the courtyard below, children played a game under the supervision of an Aud. Normally, Andre would be down there, but Tel couldn't stomach playing with Islander children. Not at this juncture. He believed the meeting covered him: all of the Elders had been stressed by it. Matthias had a look of trapped terror, and Porciluna's face remained red during the entire thing. Tel had spent most of the meeting wondering about the additional bloodstain. Had Rugar sent another Doppelgänger there?

If so, then Tel might be less important than he thought. He could leave, and no one would be the wiser.

Except the other Doppelgänger, who, if he too were present at the meeting, would know that Tel was around. What if they both left? Then the Fey were doomed never to learn the secret.

Happy screams, mixed with laughter, floated up from below. The children came there every afternoon at Andre's instigation, although he wasn't always part of the playtime. Andre had believed that indoctrinating the children young —and making such indoctrination fun—would help the religion. It had worked so far, and it had made Andre the Rocaan's favorite.

Tel turned away from the window and leaned on the cold stone wall. He wiped a hand over his face. If he merely stayed where he was, and was cautious, he might learn the secret of the holy water from the Rocaan. Or he could transfer to Matthias's body after a few days. Andre's memory said that Matthias had also learned the secret on the day of the First Battle for Jahn.

The key was to do both the Midnight Sacrament and to meet his contact. The contact would wait. It would be part of his instruction to give a Doppelgänger as much time to arrive as possible. If Tel made it through the Midnight Sacrament, no one would know who he was. He would be trusted completely.

The shaking returned. He rubbed his hands together. He couldn't wear gloves—he wasn't even sure that would work. Even if it did, gloves were not an option. The Elder had to pour the holy water onto cloths he touched with his bare hands.

But the Rocaan had given him a solution earlier. Tel just hadn't seen it until now.

He hadn't been willing to see it until now.

They were going to switch all the holy water with holy water the Rocaan especially prepared. Tel was an Elder. The Auds would trust him. Excitement built in his stomach, making the trembling worse. Now all he had to do was find a source of vials and clean water.

The Cardidas had clean water. And he could get the children to help him haul it up as one of Andre's games. No one questioned Andre's games.

A relief filled him that was so strong, he felt his face flush. He was ready to be a Doppelgänger again. He would discover the riddle of the poison, and then he would leave Blue Isle. Forever.

FIFTY-FOUR

THE Rocaan paused and rubbed his eyes, wincing as the dirt from his fingers made the stinging worse. He hadn't spent a long time at study in years. He leaned back in the wooden chair he had placed in front of his scrolled desk, listening to the wood creak beneath his weight. His eyes were tearing. He needed better light.

He stood slowly—he had been sitting in the same position since Alexander's boy had left him hours before—and gripped the back of the chair. The others thought the Rocaan was working on the holy water, but that was Matthias's task for the day. The Rocaan would do his in the morning when he was feeling fresh and alert.

Tonight he would continue his search for answers and draw his own conclusions without the benefit of Matthias's twisted scholarly mind. Today the Rocaan had reread the Words Written, trying to see if he had forgotten anything, misinterpreted anything, failed to understand anything. He found himself skimming the familiar text, and after a while, he had to force himself to read aloud. Even that hadn't helped completely, because he started adding the Words Unwritten, like a descant floating high above a melody. Belief did not seem to allow for thought. The Words had taken the position of ritual so long ago for him that he couldn't even remember when they had been fresh.

If they had ever been fresh.

His father used to recite the Words before each meal, and the Rocaan had grown up chanting the text of his religion as if it were the lyrics to a song. Perhaps he had never sought meaning before. Perhaps what he most resented about Matthias was not his lack of belief, but his ability to set the recitation aside and see the Words for what they really were.

Try as he might, the Rocaan could not see the Words Written for what they were, but what the religion had intended them to be, a small part of the ritual, a part of the teaching, a part of the healing. For hidden between the lines of the text were the Words Unwritten, and behind those were the stories that provided the backbone of the faith. Stories illustrated by the ancient paintings in the Tabernacle, by the oral histories, not considered part of the Words, memorized by one particular Elder—in this case Eirman—to chant at Absorption Day Services.

A rap on the door startled the Rocaan out of his reverie. Instead of bidding the knocker—he knew it had to be an Aud—to come in, he went to the door himself and looked through the view slit. The Aud who stood in the corridor was impossibly young, perhaps no more than fifteen, a boy who barely had enough age to make a lifelong decision, and who probably hadn't. The Rocaan was half tempted to open the door and demand if the boy's parents had forced him there as they had Matthias, or if the boy had come of his own free will.

Instead he pulled the bar back and opened the door, blocking the boy's entrance with one hand placed on the door frame, his arm against the opening. "I would like dinner brought to my room," he said, not allowing the boy a chance to speak. "I will light my own fire and lamps tonight."

The boy nodded, his face flushing red as he moved. Then he bowed his head and disappeared down the corridor, his bare feet slapping against the carpet. The Rocaan waited until the boy was gone before closing the door. He had always thought it ridiculous that the leaders of the Church were waited on like nobility. If anything, they should be the servants, working to help the others. But somewhere someone had decided that the Elders and the Rocaan needed care if they were to continue the spiritual quest, and their material needs were provided for them.

But perhaps it was the physical needs that provided the spiritual insights. Lord knew how distant he had become from his God, his fellows, and himself since he had become Rocaan. And he should have become closer.

When he'd been a boy, watching the Rocaan at an outdoor service near Kenniland Marshes, he had thought it would be such a magickal thing to be Beloved of God, and all that it implied. The Holy One would sit on the Rocaan's shoulder, and the Roca himself would act as guide. The Rocaan had never coveted the position for himself—to do so would be to violate all the tenets of his faith—but when he found he had it, he had thought that something, someone, would swoop down from above and bless him, that he would truly feel Beloved of God.

Instead, he was an old, tired man with no hopes, no dreams, and no understandings.

He pushed away from the door, grabbed flint and a candle, and lit it. Then he lifted the cones off lamps and touched the candle to the wicks. The Auds were usually more frugal, lighting only the lamps near the Rocaan's bed and near his favorite chair. But he lit every lamp in the room. Finally he eased his elderly body into a crouch and built a fire, as he used to do when he was an Aud, serving the Danite in charge of his parish almost sixty years before. His hands still remembered the routine.

He opened the grate, then piled the wood on the stone, added kindling and tinder, and lit the fire. The Danite he had served had never had fires of this size. He had always saved the wood for his Auds, so that they would have enough for their common room where they said their daily prayers. But wood wasn't plentiful in the Kenniland Marshes, although it was near Jahn. The forests here were thick and strong, replanted each season like any other crop.

His legs were wobbling from the strain of the position. He braced one hand on the stone side of the fireplace, another on the floor, and stood. Not much strength left in his old body. What little of it he had once had was leached by sitting all day, eating and sleeping in comfort. His father had not lived this long. He had died when the Rocaan was still an Aud, digging in the marshes for mushrooms. They had not found his body for nearly a week.

The Rocaan leaned against the fireplace after he stood, feeling the warmth of the flame through his velvet robe. Then he turned, staring at the room, ablaze in light. As he had hoped, the faint paintings and etchings became visible.

On the ceiling above him, the Roca receiving the blessing of a child. This etching, like the others, was done in gold, and showed only in the right light. The wall behind his desk showed the first Rocaan receiving the approval of the Holy One in a blaze of white light. He didn't know much about the First Rocaan. No one kept the oral histories then, except of the Roca himself. He wasn't even sure how long the First Rocaan had served. He supposed he could figure it out, roughly, using generations and averages of the ages of the Rocaans, but even that would not be right. What of the Thirtieth Rocaan, who put on his ceremonial sword and fainted, never to wake again? He was God's Beloved for a matter of weeks only, as was the Twenty-fifth Rocaan, who was stabbed by an insane Aud just after the ceremony. Nor did it account for his predecessor, the Forty-ninth Rocaan, who'd been touched by the Hand of God as a boy and who had become an Elder by the age of thirty, Rocaan by the age of thirty-one, and who was God's Beloved for over sixty years.

The oral histories were imperfect gatherings of fact, put together by men who had no concept of the things that would be important to faith. Who were the Soldiers of the Enemy? Not even Matthias could find that. Nor could the Rocaan find any other reference to them in the Words Written and Unwritten. He knew of no other paintings of them, except those that showed the Roca's Absorption to the Hand of God. And in those they were small men in armor, their backs to the viewer or their faces obscured by the Roca's light.

The Rocaan's legs were giving out on him. He stumbled to a chair and sank into it, covering his face with his hands. Blue Isle had not needed a history before. Islanders were a group, unified by their homeland, separated by rivers and marshes and mountains. While they spoke of history, they did not use it for much besides storytelling, not like the Nye, who believed that the past, not the future, held the secret to their existence. Islanders believed that God held that secret, and belief in God was sufficient for all their needs.

Until last year it had been.

Now he wondered if the Nye weren't right. And if the Islanders hadn't lost more than stories when they'd let go of their past. The Rocaan was an old man, and he remembered little of his childhood. The King could recite his lineage, a long string of names that went back to the Roca himself. The Rocaan leaned his head on the back of the chair and whispered, " 'And when the Roca Ascended, his two sons stepped forward. The eldest said he would stand in the Roca's place as Leader of Men, and then a voice came from the Sky—in a peal of thunder—and commanded that the second son take the Roca's place as Beloved of God. And from that moment to this, only second sons could become Elders and then Beloved of God.' "

The Rocaan himself was a second son, as had been the Rocaan before him, and the Rocaan before him. The King was always the eldest son. How odd, though, with the commandment in the story buried in the Words Unwritten, that "second sons could become Elders and then Beloved of God." Not second sons of the King, nor second sons of the current Rocaan, but second sons only. It was as if an admonition had been dropped. Why make the Kingship hereditary and the Rocaan not? Had Rocaanism lost its power because the Rocaan did not have the King's blood?

Despite the warmth of the fire, the Rocaan shivered. A chill had risen in the back of his neck and traveled down his spine. Alexander had had only one child, a son. Alexander's father had had only one child as well. There was no way to test the theory, no way to see if the second son of the King would ascend if touched by holy water and a ceremonial sword. Had a King failed to have two sons? Had a Rocaan failed to reproduce? Or was the stricture against women in Rocaanism a constant from the beginning? Even that the Rocaan did not know.

When the Forty-ninth Rocaan had summoned this Rocaan to his deathbed, the dying man had touched the younger man's forehead with a finger dipped in holy water, drawing a sword on the Rocaan's forehead. *You shall be Blessed of God*, the dying Rocaan had said. Then he had closed his eyes and whispered, *May God forgive me*. For decades the Rocaan had wondered what his predecessor meant. He had been filled with such sorrow and such joy at the moment: sorrow at the loss of a mentor, and joy at being chosen to succeed him. In the next few days the dying Rocaan had shared what little energy he had, making the new Rocaan Keeper of the Secrets.

The Secrets. He reviewed them each night like a ritual prayer, but he did not understand most of them. Like the Ritual of Absorption, which no Rocaan had ever performed, but which had traveled down from the beginning of the religion. Perhaps that ritual was as garbled as the Words Unwritten. Perhaps parts were missing, parts forgotten by elderly, dying men trying to carry on a tradition.

A knock sounded at the door, followed by a soft voice identifying the Aud who had left earlier. The Rocaan moved his hands from his face and sighed.

"Come," he said, and the boy entered, carrying a tray of food. The scent of fresh mutton stew with gravy, potatoes, and onions filled the room, and the Rocaan's stomach growled. The chef had also put fresh bread beside the plate, knowing the Rocaan's penchant for doughy food. The Rocaan's nightly cup of mead reflected the light.

The boy set the tray on the table. The stew was still steaming.

"Holy Sir," he said, keeping his tone respectful, "would you like me to douse some lights?"

"No, boy," the Rocaan said. "I need them tonight."

The Aud nodded and clasped his hands over the front of his coarse black robe. He turned, revealing the black bottoms of his very dirty bare feet as he moved.

"Boy?" the Rocaan said. "Where are you from?"

The Aud stopped, faced the Rocaan again, but kept his head bowed. "The base of the Snow Mountains," he said.

The Rocaan nodded. He had been to the Snow Mountains just once, as a Danite. The villages there were small because the winters were harsh, and it took a certain type of person to brave the deep snows. Some said that the peasants who survived the Uprising fled to the Snow Mountains, but no one had wanted to pursue them.

"What stories do your people tell of the Roca that you have not heard since you became an Aud?"

To the Rocaan's surprise the boy flushed. " 'Tis blasphemy, Holy Sir."

"Blasphemy?" the Rocaan asked. "How do you know this?"

" 'Tis a self-centered focus that feeds lies." The boy was paraphrasing the caution that all novitiates receive.

"But no one told you it was blasphemy, then?"

"No, Holy Sir."

"Then please, boy, share it with me."

The boy shook his head.

"I have the Ear of God," the Rocaan said. "If I determine it blasphemy, we shall Bless you again, wipe your lips with holy water, and pray for forgetfulness."

The boy swallowed so hard, his Adam's apple bobbed. "Yes, Holy Sir."

"Come," the Rocaan said. "Sit beside me. The chef gave me too much bread for an old man to eat." He was conscious of the dietary restrictions that limited Auds to one meal of meat per week. He did not want to violate that for the boy, but he also didn't want the boy to watch him eat.

The boy brushed off the back of his robe before sitting in the chair beside the Rocaan. The boy took the bread with an eagerness the Rocaan remembered. Auds were never fed enough, nor did they get enough sleep. It was part of the ritual indoctrination. Any boy who was strong enough to survive the routine of work and deprivation was strong enough to serve God.

But the boy did not eat until the Rocaan took a bite. The stew was rich and heavily herbed. The tastes exploded across his tongue. Like so many who had lived through the starvation of early religious life, he had grown fat and accustomed to luxuries—so much so that in an unconscious fashion he never wanted to be deprived again. Perhaps that, too, was wrong. Perhaps much in Rocaanism needed rethinking.

"Tell me, boy," he said softly.

The boy chewed and swallowed. The Rocaan handed him the mead and the boy took a sip. Then he sighed, as if he knew he could not get out of telling the Rocaan what he needed to know.

"It is said by the people of the Snow Mountains that the Roca was born there during a blizzard to a very poor family. Green lightning mixed with the snow to show the power that was unleashed that evening." The boy did not look at the Rocaan as he spoke. He tore the bread he held into small pieces and placed them on his robe. "People did not go near the family for fear of that power. They did not believe in God then, did not know of wisdom or of anything beyond this life of pain."

The Rocaan set his spoon down. This story was old. He could tell from the cadence in the boy's voice, and the rhythm of the story itself. The boy spoke it as the Rocaan spoke the Words Unwritten, as something he had learned so young, it was a part of him.

"As the Roca grew older, it was said he had the winds under his command. He could bring a storm or turn it away, and often did, to protect his family's land. When he learned that other boys did not have this talent, he ran into the mountains to find out why he had been chosen." The boy put a piece of bread in his mouth and chewed. He glanced at the Rocaan out of the corner of his eye, then looked away.

"A great storm rose that night, but when it cleared, people in the valley saw that there was no snow on the mountaintop. Shepherds claimed that the storm had stopped at the tree line, and that the sun had shown even though it was dark. After that night the Roca came down and told the people of the valley about God. He also told them that, without his leadership, they would die in a great war, and they all bowed down and worshiped him. The Roca stayed in the valley until the Soldiers of the Enemy arrived, and then he took his wife and sons and came to Jahn."

The Rocaan picked up his cup of mead and took a long, hard sip. This story did not exist in the official oral histories, nor was it in any of the scholarly works. Yet it covered a period the Rocaan had never heard covered.

"Why do you think this blasphemy, boy?" he asked.

The boy was about to eat another piece of bread. He set the bread back in his lap after the Rocaan asked the question. "Because it is about the Snow Mountains. They make it sound as if the Roca is theirs only, as if he comes from them."

"But the story also makes it clear that they treated him as an outsider, and that they were afraid of him."

The boy nodded. "I told Elder Eirman about this, and he

said that I should stop listening to such tales and to get about my own studies."

"I shall speak to Elder Eirman. As the historian, he should investigate these stories, not deny them."

"Then you don't believe it's blasphemy?" The boy spoke quickly, his question revealing his youth and the depth of his fear.

"If it is blasphemy, it is not yours. And who is to say at this early date? We do not know where the Roca was born or how he came to be before he fought the Soldiers of the Enemy. Perhaps your story is true."

"If it is true," the boy whispered, "then why don't they speak it in church? Why is it told late at night, during great storms, in hushed voices as if the people are afraid that God might hear?"

"I don't know," the Rocaan said. He handed the boy another piece of bread. "Thank you for telling me. Your soul is safe, child. You are innocent of any wrongdoing."

Tears filled the boy's eyes, but he kept them downcast. He took the extra piece of bread and picked up the crumbs of the first with his free hand.

"Do you know other boys with these kinds of stories?" the Rocaan asked.

"We do not talk, Holy Sir," the boy said, and the Rocaan smiled at his own foolishness. Of course the boys didn't talk. Auds were forbidden to speak to each other because it was believed that they could learn nothing from each other. They were innocents, and innocents in equal ways. They could only learn things of value from their betters. While the rule made certain that the Auds did not band together and protest their living conditions, it also made certain that stories like this one were buried.

How many of the Auds the Rocaan had served with had known this tale? And how many other tales had Elders suppressed all these years?

"Thank you for indulging an old man, boy," the Rocaan said. "When you leave, I would like you to find Elder Eirman for me and bring him here."

"You will not tell him about me, will you?" the boy asked, then clapped his hands over his mouth. Slowly he brought them down, his face bright red. "I am sorry, Holy Sir. You have God's wisdom."

And sometimes even God's wisdom was not enough. The Rocaan smiled at him. "I will keep your secret, boy."

The Aud bowed his head. "Thank you, Holy Sir," he said; then he took his bread and left the room.

The Rocaan leaned against his chair, exhausted from the encounter. Stories of the Roca that existed outside the religion. He would never have thought it if he hadn't been studying so intently. Perhaps if he asked all the Auds who served him, they would each have a different story of the Roca's origins. Perhaps the Danites would as well, although he doubted if they would say anything. If this boy, after being an Aud only a few years or even months of his short life, was afraid to speak, imagine how Danites, who had lived with the secret for at least a decade, felt.

It was time to lift the strictures from this religion. The arrival of the Fey had caused him to question holy water. Perhaps the Fey would cause him to question other things. Perhaps the Fey were not evil at all, but merely a testing, to keep the faith pure.

FIFTY-FIVE

THE little filth had deprived him of his chance to work with the water. Caseo rubbed his hands together. The Warders were gone, except for two, Touched, the youngest, and Rotin, the second-oldest. They seemed as frustrated as Caseo at the lack of progress. And then to have that filthy Red Cap betray him. A Red Cap's life was worthless. The creature could have done something useful, and it had not. Instead, it acted frightened when it alone might have held an answer to the way the Islander magic worked.

Touched was hanging Fey Lamps. Rotin had her bald head cradled on her arms, as if the day's work had exhausted her. Caseo knew better. He had worked with Rotin since they'd been children. She did her best thinking when she was tired, frustrated, and hiding.

He put on the gloves the Domestics had made him especially for the poison work. Even though he trusted the magick, he still was cautious and had yet to spill on them. His hands didn't shake until late at night, after everyone had left, and he was alone. Then his entire body trembled with the risks he took daily. He went around the table and picked up two bowls, one with water alone, and one with a strip of Islander skin in it. He placed them with the other bowls filled with an inch of poison, all showing failed experiments, in the corner, on a table protected by Caseo's most powerful spell so that no one would stumble against them accidentally.

"It seems to me," Touched said as he stepped down from the chair he had been using to hang the Fey Lamps, "that we are going about this wrong."

The use of the word "wrong" almost made Caseo spill the second bowl. He set it down quickly, breathing heavily at the nearness of his miss.

"You're suggesting that I don't know what I'm doing?" The fear that had risen in him made his question harsher than he had intended it to be.

"No!" Touched's eyebrows rose in protest. Of all of them, only he looked odd with the baldness all Warders acquired after initiation, as if he were not meant to be a Warder at all. Caseo could still see the missing hair floating like a nimbus around Touched's head. "I'm saying that—"

"We're doing this wrong." Rotin sat up. Her voice was raspy from the herbs she used. Her eyes were red-rimmed, and her entire body moved as if she were exhausted. "I know you don't like criticism, Caseo, but really, that is a childish, egotistical way to lead anything."

Caseo stiffened, unwilling to look at them. He backed out of his magick corner and examined his gloves for droplets before removing them. "We're not discussing me," he said.

"No, we're not. We're discussing our solutions to this poison." Rotin rubbed her eyes. "Let Touched speak. Your jealousy of him can be so counterproductive."

Caseo bit back anger. He was not jealous of Touched. He merely did not like children. And Touched was not yet twenty, too young to be a Spell Warder. Too young to be considered one of the great powers of the race.

"What are we doing wrong?" Caseo asked, unable to keep the sarcasm from his tone.

Touched shoved his hands into the pocket of his robe. The gray material blended with the colors of the Shadowlands, making him look almost invisible. Only the brightness of the Fey lights, shining on his bald scalp, gave him any warmth at all.

"We don't dissect magicks," Touched said. His voice

squeaked on the word "dissect." He cleared his throat. "We create them. We might never find out how this works by reversing our process."

Despite himself, Caseo felt a leap in his heart. He knew what the boy was saying. "You want us to create this kind of poison? With the same properties?"

Touched nodded, his eyes sparkling in a way that showed how he deserved his name. "We can test it on Fey dead. Some folks died of other than poison causes in the last battle, right?"

Rotin shrugged. "No one has checked."

"And even if they have, the magic is gone from them," Caseo said.

"There is no proof that it is magick caused," Touched said. "Even Infantry died in Jahn on the day of the First Battle. That suggests that magick is not an issue."

Caseo frowned. The magick had been his theory; he was not so willing to part with it. "We never know if the Infantry has magick. Some just don't have magick in enough quantity. The Red Caps have no magick at all, and none of them died."

"None of them were in the thick of the fighting," Rotin said. "Let the theory go, Caseo. The fact that the little Red Cap defies you shows that he has enough sense to save his own life. Would you volunteer for an experiment that might kill you horribly?"

"Of course not," Caseo said. "But my life is worth something."

Touched sat in his chair, appearing to melt into the wall with that peculiar talent he had for disappearing when controversy started.

Rotin had never been threatened by Caseo. She wrinkled her nose at him. "A Red Cap's life is worth something too. Someone has to be willing to work in the heat and stink to give us materials. We all need to be divided up when we die. Who would do that if the Red Caps didn't?"

"Domestics?" Caseo said, although he knew they would shrink from the job. "Perhaps we could design a spell that would enable them to do a Red Cap's job without touching a body."

"There's no need when the present system works so well. And on a battlefield, a Domestic is always overworked."

Rotin reached into the pocket of her robe and removed a packet of herbs. Then she reached into the other pocket and took out a tiny mortar and pestle. She ground the herbs together and licked her finger, placing it in the mixture.

"Doing it straight now, Rotin?" Caseo asked.

She licked the herbs off her finger and shuddered with an almost orgasmic pleasure. The problems of being a Spell Warder, denied sexual experience in return for a touch of all magicks. Her eyes were shiny as she looked up at him. "You don't allow us much time to ourselves these days. I take my enjoyment as I can."

"The others have left," he said. "You could have left too."

Touched was watching from the corner, his eyes bright under the Fey Lamps. He was too young to have any vices or to understand the losses he had volunteered for.

"I knew you were reaching a dangerous level of frustration," she said. "The next thing you will do is kidnap babies and pour poison on them."

"Children have magic," Touched whispered.

"*Dormant* magic," Caseo said. Rotin knew him too well. He had thought of that, but the children in camp were all too close to puberty to be of use to him.

"If you're going to take anyone," Rotin said, "it should be Infantry, who are by far the largest force we have here, and who are interchangeable."

Caseo licked his own lips, wishing for the first time that he had a taste for her herbs. He had tried them once, but the resulting sensation overwhelmed and frightened him. He preferred to be overwhelmed by his own magical power rather than to be overwhelmed by an outside force he could not control.

"So you have been thinking along the same lines I have," he said.

She smiled. "I know how your mind works, Caseo. I may not share some of your abilities, but I know where frustration takes you."

Touched had backed himself so far against the wall that, if he forgot himself, he would slip through it. "You're talking about taking Fey lives to test magic," he said.

Rotin nodded. "It wouldn't be the first time."

"The first time was when?" Caseo said, delighting in her

game with the boy. "When the Fey came down the Eccrasian plain?"

"Against the swords of Ghitlus," Rotin said, her grin growing, her back to the boy so that he couldn't see her. "The Warders believed that the swords had magical properties, having never seen metal weapons before."

"And so they tested swords against all kinds of spells and finally determined that the swords themselves had special powers. Then, with the Black King's permission, they tried the swords on Infantry," Caseo said.

"And the Infantry died. But so did Ghitlans who faced the sword," said Rotin.

"The Spell Warders thought, 'What an odd magick that kills its own,'" Caseo said.

"So the Warders did more experiments," Rotin said, "and discovered that they could hex swords and they could put magick properties on swords that changed swords. And eventually they concluded that swords had no magical properties of their own, but that they were made of a specific material that allowed them a kind of strength we had never seen before."

Touched's eyes were wide. No one had briefed him on the difficulties Spell Warders sometimes faced. He was probably like so many others, figuring that Warding was one of the most powerful positions among the Fey, not realizing that with power came difficult choices.

"Now, be fair," Caseo said, baiting Touched even further. "You know that they didn't come to this conclusion intellectually."

Rotin nodded. She scooped out the last of the herbs with her little finger, then slipped the mortar and pestle back into her pocket. "Oh, I had forgotten," she said. She turned, grinned at Touched, then rubbed the herbs across her teeth. "It was with the Ghitlans that we learned the art of torture."

He sucked in his breath. She licked the herbs off her teeth and put the bag away, shuddering as their effect hit. Touched's eyes filled with tears.

"You're making this up," he whispered. "You're making this up to justify your own cruelty."

"I wish I were, boy," Caseo said. "Warding is not an easy position. They told you that when you took the oath. And I told you that you were too young to do it, too young to understand the choices, remember?"

"You were jealous of me," Touched said. "Until me, you were the most talented Warder ever."

Caseo shot a look at Rotin. How many minds had she influenced with her drivel? "No, child," he said. "I simply understand choice. You don't. I know that one little Red Cap's life is worth a lot less than a hundred other Fey lives. I know that a bit of torture, judiciously applied, will teach us more about the properties of this water than any of the 'experiments' we do. And I am not above ruining one life to save a thousand."

"You're mad," the boy said.

"Am I?" Caseo asked. "Your family lived through the Nye campaign, did it not?"

Touched swallowed. His father had been in the thick of the fighting. The Warders had come up with a new spell to be used by Beast Riders, which probably saved all the lives on the front. The Fey all knew it.

"We discovered the Beast Rider spell through judicious experimentation. One hundred fifty Nye prisoners died in various ways before we discovered the quickest and most effective way—the most painless, you might say."

"Why didn't you tell me this before I joined?" Touched asked.

Rotin shrugged. "A discipline does not reveal its secrets to outsiders. Besides, you never balked at hanging Fey Lamps, or working on spells to aid the Weather Sprites. How many creatures do you think died or drowned because of those rains last year?"

"I didn't," Touched said.

"You have the abilities to be a Warder. Therefore you are a Warder. Or you become nothing. You know the choices," Caseo said.

"I thought being a Warder was an intellectual skill," Touched said.

"It is," Rotin said.

"I didn't think it involved torture and killing."

"It does," Caseo said. "And now you must live with it. We all had to." He glanced at Rotin, her eyes still glazed. "And we all do it in our own individual ways."

Touched glanced at both of them. Then he opened the door and ran from the building.

Rotin leaned back, stretching her arms over her head. "I think you were a bit harsh on the boy."

Caseo shook his head. "We need him. He is talented and he is right. We were going about this wrong. But we have limited resources. And if his revulsion saves us time and resources, then we are better off."

"Time and lives," Rotin said. "You mean time and lives."

"That's what I said, isn't it?" Caseo asked.

"You are a cold one," Rotin said.

"If the boy can help us neutralize the poison, so much the better. But I am hoping for more. He gave me an idea. We create spells. We need to make that water a more effective poison."

"It's already quite effective," Rotin said.

Caseo braced his fingertips on the table. "Not against Islanders," he said. "And it needs to be. We need it to be. Imagine them pulling out their little water pouches and dying by their own hands." He laughed, delighted at his own idea. "And that's the beauty of Warding, Rotin. The ability to twist something harmful into something useful."

FIFTY-SIX

NICHOLAS swung off his horse. He was tired and covered with sweat, his long blond hair plastered to his forehead and the back of his neck. The stallion was lathered. He had run it too hard after his meeting with the Rocaan.

The courtyard was busy in the early evening. The twilight cast everything in pinks, golds, and shadows. Two stable boys were leading his father's favorite mare and the new gelding into the stables. A dairymaid was struggling over a butter churn, and the cook was outside, calling the dogs.

Nicholas wiped a hand over his face, wincing at the scents of leather and horseflesh. The events at the Tabernacle had disturbed him. The bones, the blood, the reminders of Lord Powell's death and of Stephen's. Sometimes Stephen's face came to him in dreams, melting, drowning in his own tears. *They're killing me,* he would say. *You can see it, Nicky. You can stop it.* But Nicholas hadn't seen it until too late.

The second groom came out of the stable and took the reins of Nicholas's horse. "I'll take him, Highness," the groom said, bobbing his head. He was young, with hair cropped short and a face darkened by the sun.

"Where's Miruts?" Nicholas asked, removing the saddle. The stallion was breathing as hard as he was.

The groom came alongside him and helped, using his body to push Nicholas away, as if reminding Nicholas that tending the horses was not his job.

Nicholas glanced over at the groom. He was perhaps the same age as Nicholas, but held himself as if he were much older. His cheeks were flushed, and he kept his eyes turned away.

" 'Tis sorry I am, Sire, but I dinna know," the groom said. He patted the horse's side, then snapped his fingers. "Take Ebony inside," he said to one of the stable boys, "and give him a proper rubdown."

The stable boy nodded and led the horse inside. Nicholas felt a pang watching it go. He had felt linked during that long ride along the Cardidas, as if the horse's effort purged him of the tension from the Tabernacle.

The tension had returned.

"Well?" he said.

" 'Twas yesterday mornin' when I last saw Miruts," the groom said. "And he was actin' strange afore that. He spooked the horses sometimes, and he done odd things. Like yesterday, he spent a long time talkin' to a cat."

"A cat?" Nicholas asked.

The groom nodded. The red in his cheeks grew. "He give it some water and then petted it."

Whatever Nicholas had expected, it was not this. "It doesn't sound that odd," he said.

"Oh, but 'tis," the groom said. " 'Twas Miruts who told me that I should not touch another animal except the horses. Such highbred creatures, he said, easily spooked and we wouldna wanna spook the King's stable."

"So you think he's been going against his own orders for some time."

The groom shrugged. "He'd been skittish since the Fey come, Highness."

Suddenly Nicholas came alert. "His behavior changed when the Fey arrived?"

" 'Twas the invasion." The groom looked up. He was biting his lower lip. "He was never the same after that. I ask him once what was happening for him, and he said the world couldna be as it was. Not ever again."

They all had felt that way. Nicholas's own behavior had changed. But not enough. Not the way Stephen's had. "How much did he change?"

"He was the same, I guess," the groom said, although his tone sounded uncertain. "But he got sloppy, and he liked things he never liked afore."

"Such as?"

"The palace, Sire." Now the groom was biting his upper lip. His lower lip was bleeding. "Beg pardon, but he dinna really care who he was helping. Then the Fey come, and suddenly he wants to know everything. Like who's where and who's doin' what and why. 'Twas like he woke up and liked people bettern horses."

And suddenly Stephen forgot his expertise on the Fey and rarely left the King's side. Nicholas swayed a little. He would have to go into the kitchens and see what he could find to eat. He had missed luncheon and probably supper.

"What else?" Nicholas asked.

The groom smiled a little, then wiped the back of his hand over his mouth. " 'Twas Miruts lived only for horses. Now 'tis like horses is his job and nothing else. He never used ta be with the fellows at night and just chat. But he started last fall. Sometimes he would forget his extra work or to check the others"—the groom looked down—" 'Twas me that took up the slack, Highness."

The groom obviously wasn't saying that to make an impression. He sounded annoyed.

"Where do you think he went?" Nicholas asked.

The groom shook his head. "He never left afore. I dinna think it of him. He—well, he used ta—care about his work."

"Did you see him talking with anyone you didn't know?"

"No." The groom frowned. "But sometimes he would leave at dusk, which was bad, doncha know, because so many bring their rides back about then, and he would go to his cabin and leave a light burning, like he went in there ta just sit. Used ta be he would stay here with the horses till near bed. I used ta wish I had his place because he never used it 'cept to sleep, and sometimes not even then."

As big a change as Stephen, if not bigger. Nicholas's mouth was dry. He cleared his throat, then said, "Did you ever find any bones in the stables? Unidentified bones?"

"Bones, Highness?" The groom frowned at him as if Nicholas were crazy. "Only when the dogs try to bring the bones the cook gives 'em. Big smelly things, those bones are, sometimes with the meat still hangin off 'em. But real bones, no, Sire."

Nicholas nodded, feeling a deep relief. The head groomsman must simply have been unnerved by the Fey. Everyone's behavior had changed. Nicholas himself felt as if he had grown up in the last year and become an older version of the self who had woken up on that bright sunny morning.

But he wasn't quite willing to let the subject go yet. "You're sure?" he asked. "Not even last year, just after the invasion?"

"Oh, then." The groom attempted a small smile, but it failed, leaving his eyes sad. "We cleaned up lots of bones last year, Highness. And bodies. The whole courtyard was littered with them. A lot of us in the yard had to handle them Fey, Highness, and most of us was afraid that even dead they could hurt us. But we found lots of bones."

"Lots of bones?" Nicholas asked, forcing the words out.

The groom nodded. "Mostly we thought them Fey just melted, Highness. You know, until nothing was left on them."

"In piles?" Nicholas asked.

"Bones in piles, you mean, Highness?" The groom frowned. "Twice. Once near the gate, right near the body of a guard. 'Twas his throat they had cut. One of the stable boys was helpin' me, Highness, and he thought maybe the guard dumped his whole bottle of water on the Fey while it was tryin' to kill him. Lot of good that did the poor bastard, eh, Highness?"

Nicholas was shaking. The skin melted. That's what Lord Stowe said. That was what had happened to Stephen. But it didn't melt away. It didn't completely disappear. This was a tactic the Fey used that no one yet understood.

"You said twice, that you'd found them twice," Nicholas said.

"Ah, that's right," the groom said. "Miruts found the second pile in the stable. He was cleanin' it out when I come in the next day." The boy looked up at Nicholas. "Lor, in the stable, like you asked. What does it mean, Highness?"

"I don't know yet," Nicholas said. "But Miruts touched them, right? What was he doing with them?"

"He was takin them outside in piles. He"—the boy looked down—"he, ah, had given some of the longer ones to the dogs."

"And you didn't like that."

The groom shook his head. He kept his eyes downcast. "Sorry, Highness. I mean, I didn't think it Rocaanist, if ye follow. They had been living creatures once with brains, more like us than animals. And I wouldn't give none of them horse's bones to the dogs. I sure wouldna do it to no being that thought and spoke and fought like them Fey do."

Neither would Nicholas nor, he doubted, his father, nor anyone in the guards. It was a particularly cold thing to do. Bodies were buried and Blessed. Even the Fey bodies left in the courtyard were buried in an unmarked area of unconsecrated ground near the river. Protectively covered with limestone and holy water so that they wouldn't rise again, but buried nonetheless.

Not fed to the dogs.

Nicholas licked his lips, not liking what he was thinking. "Was there blood near the bones?"

The groom nodded, his eyes widening. "A large stain. Both times, Highness."

"But you said a man's throat had been cut near the gate. Wouldn't that create a lot of blood?"

"Sure, Highness."

More sweat ran down Nicholas's face, even though he felt chilled. "And was there blood?"

" 'Twas a lot."

"Near the man?"

"And the bones," the groom said.

Nicholas swallowed, the movement hard on his dry throat. He hadn't forgotten the discussions after the Fey had arrived: how they could kill with a single touch; how some of the guards had disturbed the Fey peeling skin off bodies; how some Danites believed the Fey collected blood.

"Highness? Are ye all right?"

"Yes." Nicholas ran a hand over his face, wiping the sweat off his brow again. He was hungry. He was tired. He had been disturbed by the conversation with the Rocaan. The mood was just carrying to this moment, that was all.

"Are we done, Highness? I want ta make sure they're takin' good care of Ebony."

Normally, Nicholas would have waved the groom away, but he did not. He still had questions, questions he wasn't sure he wanted the answers to. "Do you remember fighting in the stables that day?"

"During the invasion, Highness? 'Twas no fighting here. Me and the boys, we held them off and kept the doors closed. We dinna want them anywhere near the good horse-flesh, if ye know what I mean. We was afraid of what they might do."

"You kept the doors closed?" Nicholas asked.

"Aye, Highness." The groom was looking at him again, a small furrow between his brows.

"Then where did the bones and blood come from? Did Miruts say?"

The groom nodded. "He said he found them in the morning when he come in."

"And the horses were fine?"

"Yes, Highness. 'Twas the first thing I asked."

"And was there any sign of a struggle?"

The groom shrugged. "Hard to tell, Highness. The bodies was still all over the yard, and the whole place was a mess, if ye remember."

"I remember," Nicholas said. And he remembered the stench, the terror, the way that he couldn't sleep for days afterward—and when he did, he dreamed of the woman, the one who got away. "So it looked as if there had been a battle inside after all."

"Only near the blood, Highness. Some of the hay bales was messed, and the horses was skittish, but that seemed right ta me. Lots of fear and stink around here, so they shouldna been actin' too normal."

"Did he go to Midnight Sacrament?" Nicholas asked.

"Miruts?" The groom looked at Nicholas as if he were crazy.

"You go, don't you?" Nicholas pointed to the tiny sword around the groom's neck. "Did he go with you?"

"We dinna see each other outside the stables, Highness. I dinna think he had nothin' to do outside the stables."

"So he never went to Midnight Sacrament?"

"I never seen him," the groom said. "But I always go to the chapel in the palace."

"It would seem likely that he would go here too, wouldn't it, with his preoccupation with the horses?"

The groom shrugged. It seemed that the implication that Miruts didn't go to Midnight Sacrament disturbed him more than the talk of blood and bones had. "We dinna talk about his beliefs, Highness. He did go to Absorption Day with me once, though."

"This year?"

The groom shook his head—one quick, frightened movement. "The year afore last. At the Tabernacle. We took Missy and the gelding because they hadn't got their ride yet that day."

An unusual occurrence, then. Going to the Tabernacle was always an honor for the lower classes, particularly for Absorption Day. It spoke of some belief. "Was it his idea or yours?"

" 'Twas mine, Highness." The groom licked his bleeding lips, then met Nicholas's gaze. "They important, Highness? His beliefs?"

Nicholas had heard that the lower classes believed that they could be punished for not following Rocaanism. Perhaps some of the Danites fostered that belief. When he became King, he would make it clear that believers could do whatever they wanted, think however they wanted. "Normally his beliefs aren't important at all. But they might be, when combined with his disappearance."

The groom rubbed a hand against his thigh, a nervous habit he didn't seem to be aware of. "You think it has somethin' ta do with the invasion, then?"

"I don't know," Nicholas said. "I certainly hope not."

But he remembered Stephen's face as the holy water hit him, the sure, clear knowledge that he was going to die. Nicholas had known Miruts—not well, but he had known him. Miruts loved his horses enough that he would chastise the King's son if he brought a horse back as tired and lathered as Ebony had been. Miruts was not the kind of man who involved himself in politics and intrigue unless it affected his horses.

"At the Absorption Day," Nicholas said, "did Miruts take part in the ritual?"

The groom frowned in memory, his upper teeth digging into his lower lip. Then he took a breath. He had left tiny bite impressions on the skin beneath his lip.

"He bought the holy water, Highness. We shared it."

And Stephen had taught Nicholas that a warrior covered his sword in holy water to protect it before going into battle. Stephen had always had a vial stored near his swords.

Exhaustion made Nicholas's limbs tremble. Stephen had been right on that day so long ago. The Fey could take over men's minds and capture their spirits. How many people in the palace were working for the Fey? And how would the King ever know?

"Thank you," Nicholas said. He patted the groom's arm. "We'll search for Miruts, but until he returns, the horses will be your responsibility. Can you take care of them?"

"Aye, Highness." The groom's face lit up for the first time. Horses, it seemed, were his passion as well.

"I'll talk to the master of the yard, and if Miruts doesn't return, you will inherit his cabin as well as his job." Nicholas smiled at the boy's joy. "See to it that you use it as little as he did."

"Aye, Highness!" He turned, about to run into the stable, before bowing deeply.

"Go on," Nicholas said, suddenly feeling infinitely older than the groom in front of him.

"Thanks, Highness!" the groom said, and ran into the stable. His voice, high and excited, echoed into the night.

"And so old Miruts is forgotten," Nicholas whispered. It saddened him, somehow, that the groom he had relied on had also been co-opted by the Fey.

Then he froze in the middle of the yard as the darkness fell around him. His swordmaster, his favorite groom. What if they weren't trying to get to his father? What if they were trying to get to him? That would explain the woman and her vacillation between ferocious warrior and attracted female.

But Nicholas had nothing to offer.

Unless they assassinated the King.

He swallowed. A breeze had come up, drying the sweat off his forehead, sending a chill even deeper into him. All possibilities, but none of them certainties. He needed to get out of those clothes, then he needed something to eat, and he needed to speak to his father.

Nicholas crossed the courtyard in long strides, seeing tall, slender shapes lurking in the shadows, shapes that proved to be bell pulls or cleaning equipment when he got up close. This day had left him as shaken as the day Stephen had died, only for different reasons. He pulled open the kitchen door and stopped.

Two women he didn't recognize stood in front of the hearth fire, arguing about whose duty it was to keep it burning. It had burned down to embers, and if someone didn't start it soon, it wouldn't be ready for the next day's cooking. The chef was in the back corner, arguing with a serving boy, and the butcher, his smock covered with ancient blood, leaned against the wooden meat counter, arms crossed.

No food sat on the counters, and Nicholas could smell only the remnants of the night's meal. Usually he found something to steal, a bit of mutton left for the servants, a slice of bread not yet put into the pantry. And he had never, ever seen the hearth fire out.

"What's going on?" he asked, his voice booming over the din.

The arguing stopped. All of the parties looked at Nicholas, equal mixtures shock and chagrin on the faces. Then, as a unit, the men bowed and the women curtsied, holding the position. Nicholas wasn't used to royal treatment in the kitchen. He liked it when they pretended he was one of them.

Of course, he had started it by being imperial. A headache pounded behind his eyes. "Stand up!"

They stood. The women clasped their hands in front of their bodices, as if they were waiting for a reprimand. The butcher braced himself against the counter again, and the chef rubbed his shoulder as if it hurt him.

"What is going on?" Nicholas asked, his tone softer this time.

" 'Tis duties, Highness. There's been some problems today," the chef said.

"Then where is the master of the hall? I'll speak with him."

"We dinna know, Highness."

The headache suddenly grew fierce. "He's missing?"

"Yes, Highness."

Nicholas grabbed a stool and pulled it close, then sat down and rested an elbow on the counter. He waved a hand at the women—"Get the hearth fire started so that we'll have breakfast tomorrow"—and rubbed his eyes. Duty demanded that he would no longer be the boy he once was.

"Get me some dinner," he said to the serving boy. "Whatever is left and some mead, and send someone for the assistant housemaster."

"Beg pardon, Highness," the chef said, "but the master dinna have help. He give us each our areas and expected us to work 'em."

"Then what happened in the kitchen today?" Nicholas asked. "It shouldn't matter that the master was gone."

The chef shot a quick glance at the butcher, who made a dismissive motion with his head. The butcher again crossed his arms over his chest.

"His Highness wanted roast pig, smoked over the stone hearth outside. 'Twas most of the day I was gone, Highness. I sent a message to the master of the hall that I wouldna be here and would he look in on the workers. No one said he was gone."

The serving boy came in carrying two plates and balancing a mug of mead, his little finger hooked in the handle, and the body of the mug resting against his stomach. He slid the first plate in front of Nicholas—several slices of bread and newly whipped butter, and a sliced apple, then said, "Beg pardon, Highness, but the pork is still hot. Dinna know if you wanted ta be riskin' it, though."

Nicholas raised a brow. "When did you serve my father?"

"Just afore sundown, Highness."

Nicholas nodded. "Then the meat should be fine." He smiled at the boy as he set down the second plate and the mead. Nicholas took the mug first and guzzled its contents, enjoying the richness, and not caring as to the effect. He wiped his mouth with the back of his hand and gave the mug back to the boy. "Get me more," he said, "and make sure I see the other heads of the household."

The boy nodded, glancing quickly at the chef to make certain that he and not someone else should perform the duties. The chef gave one surreptitious nod, which Nicholas chose to ignore.

The liquid helped his headache a bit. He put a slice of pork on a piece of bread, added a slice of apple, then put another piece of bread on top of it. Then he took a bite of the sandwich. His stomach rumbled. He hadn't been this hungry in a long time.

"The master of the hall is missing," Nicholas said. "Has anyone searched for him?"

"The housekeeper," the chef said. "We have na seen him in the kitchen areas, and we looked in the wine cellar, the buttery, and the pantry."

"Could he have been doing some special work for my father?" Nicholas asked around a second mouthful of food.

"Oh, no, Highness," the chef said. "If he was, we would know."

"What do you think happened to him?" Nicholas asked. He took a sip of the mead. His headache was easing. He had let himself go too long without food.

"I dunno, Highness," the chef said.

"Has he ever done anything like this before?" Nicholas asked.

The chef shook his head.

The hair rose on the back of Nicholas's head. This disappearance seemed as odd as the groom. Nicholas finished his sandwich, then pushed the plates away. The serving boy entered again, followed by three women. Nicholas recognized them—he had seen them every morning—but he didn't know their names. They all looked as if they had been awakened from a sound sleep.

"This is Agnes, Highness," the serving boy said as the stoutest and eldest woman curtsied. "She is the main floor and east wing."

"Agnes," Nicholas said.

"This is Charissa, Highness," the serving boy said as the young blond woman curtsied. Nicholas watched with interest. He had watched her slender form with interest more than once. "She is the public-visitation rooms second floor and above as well as the west wing."

"Charissa," Nicholas said.

"And this is Evadne, Highness," the serving boy said as the third woman curtsied. She was middle-aged with salt-and-pepper curls and muscular arms. "She is the north and south wings."

"Evadne," Nicholas said. "You may all stand. Thank you, boy, for finding them for me."

The boy nodded, then backed away, knowing that he had been dismissed.

"Have any of you seen the master of the hall?" Nicholas asked.

All three women glanced at each other, then shook their heads. "Beg pardon, Highness, but he has na been around all day," said Charissa.

"Nor yesterday afternoon neither," said Evadne.

"When was the last time you saw him?" Nicholas asked.

"Morning duties meeting," Agnes said. "Yesterday. He dinna show for this morning. We made do."

"Not well enough," the butcher mumbled.

"What?" Nicholas asked him, even though he had heard.

"Beg pardon, Highness," the butcher said.

"Has he ever missed your morning-duty meetings before?" Nicholas asked.

"Nay, Highness. The house would fall apart without it, you know, and then we would all be in bad trouble." Evadne. She kept her eyes downcast as she spoke to him.

So they thought they were in trouble. He stared at them for a moment, wondering if he could use that fear, then despising himself for the thought.

"Well, you're not in trouble now," he said. "You're merely helping me solve a mystery." He suppressed a sigh. He would have to interview the entire household staff if he wanted a straight answer, and he didn't have the energy for it that evening. When he finished there, he would have to go to his father. He took another sip of mead.

"Have any of you found anything odd around here recently? A stack of bones, a large spot of blood? Like the time we found the bones next to Stephen in the corridors." He spoke to Evadne on that one because he remembered her standing in the shadows, a mop and bucket beside her, her face tight with fear.

"Not since the invasion, Highness," she said, turning pale with the memory.

"Did you find more than that in the palace during the invasion?" he asked.

"Beg pardon, Highness," Agnes said, "but 'twas a mess. We had ta work for three days just ta get the bodies and blood outta here. Then we could start on the cleanin' and repairs."

"But did you find more?" Nicholas asked.

Charissa tucked a loose strand of hair behind her ear. "I helped the master of the hall clean some out of his chamber," she said softly. "He asked me not ta say nothin', but I guess it dinna hurt."

"He asked you not to say anything?" Nicholas squinted. What an odd request. "Had he ever asked you that before?"

"No," she said too quickly, a flush building on her cheeks, "he never asked me."

Nicholas stared at her, not sure if he wanted to pursue the issue. Finally he said, "When he asked you to keep quiet before, was it about personal matters?"

Her flush grew to a deep, painful red. She nodded once.

"Not anything like this."

She shook her head.

"Was there blood?"

She took a deep, shaky breath. "A lot." Her voice was soft. "Near the door. I wiped it up, and I was thinkin' "—her voice trailed off and she took another deep breath—"I was thinkin' how he couldna slept in there the night before, the smell was so strong."

"Smell of blood?"

Again she nodded.

"But this was the night of the invasion. Do you think anyone slept?"

She shrugged.

Nicholas gripped his mug tightly, feeling the ceramic strain beneath his hands. Bones in the stable the night of the invasion. Bones in the palace. Bones near the gate, and blood, lots of blood. Then two men, reliable men, disappear on the same day. That day bones appear in the Tabernacle, but no one is missing. The details were connected, but he wasn't sure how.

"And you saw nothing strange yesterday. Nothing that made you just the littlest bit nervous?"

"Beg pardon, Highness." Charissa courtesied again, keeping her bright-red face low. "But I'd like ta talk ta ye alone if I could. I seen some things. 'Twould be best if I dinna say here." She glanced at the others, and they all watched her, curiosity on their faces.

He was familiar enough with the camaraderie downstairs to know that it was based, in part, upon gossip. Any fuel to the gossip might damage or build reputations.

"I wouldna talk ta her alone, Highness," the butcher said. "She's known for talking with her skirts around her waist."

Nicholas suppressed a smile. "And what harm would that do to me?"

The butcher leaned his head back as if he just realized what he had said. "None, I guess, Highness. But it wouldna be good for the lady, Highness."

"If she already has a reputation, then maybe a few minutes alone with me will improve it." Nicholas stood and extended his hand. She took it hesitantly. Her fingers were coarse and work roughened. He squeezed them, but glanced at the people standing around him. "You others need to search this place once more, see if you find anything new about the master of the hall. I want you to bring to me first thing tomorrow morning the people who saw him last. If he can't be found, we'll appoint a new master then."

"Aye, Highness," they said in rough unison.

He gripped her hand tightly, then tucked it in his elbow as if she were a great lady. With her beside him, he left the kitchen. He took a torch from the corridor wall and led her into the Great Hall. The weapons looked menacing in the flickering light. He set the torch in the torch holder above the state chairs and bade her to sit. Then he sat beside her.

"You know something else?" he asked.

"Beg pardon, Highness," she said, running her hand through her hair, a nervous gesture that he found very attractive. "I need me job, and what I have to tell ye sounds a wee bit crazy."

"You and the master of the hall were lovers, weren't you?" Nicholas asked, unable to suppress the question.

She shook her head, eyes downcast. The flush was back, deep and painfully red. "Not lovers, Highness, though I— spent some nights in his chamber."

Nicholas frowned. This was beyond his experience. Why would a woman be in a man's chambers if they weren't lovers? "I don't understand."

She waved a hand, as if she couldn't control her emotions. "I just wanted ta keep my position, Highness."

Nicholas sucked in a breath. Never had he imagined anything like this went on in his own home. "And he threatened you?"

"Not since the invasion," she said. Then she looked up, as if she was afraid that Nicholas would punish her for the answer. "He'd been nicer since then."

"Nicer?" Nicholas's head was spinning. Nicer. "He hurt you?"

"Nay, Highness." Her eyes were filled with tears. He took her hand. Her fingers were cold. "He just made it clear that if I dinna—do what he wanted, he would have me dismissed. And I couldna have that. Me ma uses me allowance for the others, she does."

He blinked. He thought he had known the world of the servants. He had been wrong. "You have no father?"

She shook her head. "He died when my sister was a wee one. We got a small farm, and me little brother tries to keep it, but he was only seven when Pa died, and me ma was ill. So I come here. I have ta stay, Highness. Please." Her hand was shaking. He rubbed it with his own.

"You'll stay," he said. "I'll guarantee it. If anyone gives you trouble, you come see me."

She blinked and a tear fell. He wiped it off her cheek. "Thank ye, Highness," she whispered.

He was sitting close enough to feel her breath on his face. The butcher's words came back to him, and for a moment he wondered if this wasn't a way of manipulating him. He squeezed her hand again, and let it go.

"Now," he said. "Tell me what you meant by 'nice.' "

Her smile was shaky. She wiped a second tear off her cheek with her wrist. She swallowed. "After that morning with the bones," she said, "he dinna ask me ta his room again."

"Not ever?"

"Nay, Highness. I—ah—I asked him if I done something wrong, and he said no, he had other things ta think about now, and he dinna need me anymore. I asked if I still had work, and he told me I was a silly one ta worry that."

"So he stopped being intimate with you," Nicholas said, more to himself than to her. The chill from her hands had filled his entire body. "Did he pick another girl to be with?"

She shook her head. "It—beg pardon, Highness—but it

got ta be a joke with the maids. They wondered if maybe the Fey had took his—his—you know."

Nicholas rubbed a hand over his face. A change of pattern. Just like the groom. Just like Stephen. Finally something to warn the Rocaan about. He would send a message in the morning.

"But other than that, he was normal?"

She rubbed her hands on her skirts, then sighed. "Nay, Highness. He wanted ta know what people heard, and when no one had any news, he got angry. He was gettin' real angry at me, because I do the west wing where the chambers are, and he thought I would hear more gossip than I did. I kept tryin' ta tell him that no one was in the chambers when I came, and if he wanted gossip, he should tell the chamberlains, but he dinna like that."

"Gossip," Nicholas said. He nodded. "So what did he do when he was angry at you?"

"He yelled at me, Highness. And the other day he threw my duster clear across the floor—" She brought her eyes up to him as if she were flirting with him. But he recognized the look. She was measuring him.

"This is what you wanted to tell me. What you didn't want the others to hear."

She nodded. "But I'm not crazy. I want ye ta know that. I'm not."

"All right," he said. "I've heard you talk. You seem fine to me."

"When he threw my duster, it landed in front of a cat, and he started yellin' at me for letting a cat in. I dinna let the cat in, and I told him so, and he told me ta get it out anyway."

Nicholas was leaning forward as she spoke. Miruts had seen a cat before he disappeared too.

She was watching Nicholas intently. "When I went ta get the cat, it run ta the Master and up his leg and—here's what's crazy—it started talkin' ta him."

"Talking?" Nicholas asked.

She nodded. "I swear. But it wasn't Islander. 'Twas Fey. I heard enough of them bastards ta know what it sounds like. And I said, that's an awful strange meow, and he said, forget the cat, he would take care of it. So I left and went around the corner and watched him, and he took the cat up to his chamber. And I never did see him again after that."

"The cat spoke Fey?" Nicholas said.

"I know it sounds crazy. That's why I dinna want the others ta hear. But I swear. I swear."

Stephen had said, on the day of the invasion, that the Fey had powers that Islanders didn't. But he never said they could turn into cats. He did say they could take over men's bodies and make them do their bidding. Maybe they could do that with dumb animals as well.

"Do you remember what the cat looked like?" Nicholas asked.

She frowned. " 'Twas orange." Then she shrugged. "It looked like a cat."

He patted her hand, afraid to touch her any more than that. Then he smiled at her, wishing she didn't have a reputation with the staff, wishing that he were like his grandfather, a man willing to roam the lower halls. But his father had told him that bastards threaten a dynasty, and the best way to avoid bastards was not to make them at all. Before the Fey arrived, Nicholas had hoped he would have a wife by now. But the dynastic concerns had disappeared under the weight of the war. Perhaps he should figure a way to revive them.

He stood and offered her his hand to help her up. Then he thanked her and started to follow her as she left the Great Hall. But he stopped himself. Better that he didn't know where her quarters were. Better that he let her disappear back into the bowels of the palace, to deal with her problems, her life, and her livelihood. He had promised her that he would help her if she needed it, and help he would.

But right now he had bigger concerns.

He watched her make her slow way down the corridor. She glanced toward the kitchens once but did not enter them. He leaned against the cold stone wall and took a deep breath as she disappeared into the darkness. Then he closed his eyes, feeling the exhaustion carry him.

The Fey had been in the palace. Somehow they had overtaken the master of the hall and Nicholas's favorite groom. Maybe some of the people he had spoken to this evening were taken by the Fey. He would have to tell his father. And he would need the new holy water immediately.

All of the palace staff would need to be tested. All of them. Even the lovely Charissa.

And he would have to warn the Rocaan even more. Somehow the bones and blood led to the Fey's ability to make a man do their bidding. That meant there were two spies in the Tabernacle. They might try to kill the Rocaan.

Suddenly he opened his eyes, exhaustion forgotten. If he had spies in the Tabernacle, he would assign them to learn the secret of holy water.

No sleep for him tonight. He needed to speak to his father, then get another horse out of the stable and return to the Tabernacle. He didn't trust this message to anyone but himself.

FIFTY-SEVEN

WHEN Jewel emerged from her room early the next morning, she was alone in the cabin. But the fire burned brightly in the hearth, and steam rose from one of the iron pots. At least there would be tea, even though their supply was getting terribly low. She suspected that she and Rugar had the last remaining tins.

She ladled the water into her mug. Her father had left a tea strainer out for her; they had been sharing strainers since it became clear they would be trapped on Blue Isle for a long time.

He also left some fresh bread on the table. She carved a slice. He had probably had some business with the Domestics. Lately he had been leaving early to supervise some of their work. He was becoming worried that the food supply would dwindle, and anything they could do to increase the yield would help them all.

A knock on the door startled her. She swallowed, set the bread back on the plate, and called, "Who is it?"

"Caseo."

She took a deep breath. He was not the man she wanted to see before she had finished her breakfast, but she doubted she had a choice. "Just a moment."

Before she got up, she took another large bite of bread, then wiped off her mouth. She unlatched the door.

Caseo didn't wait for her to ask him in. He ducked under the threshold and stepped inside. "Late breakfast?"

She was in no mood to be civil. "I'd offer you tea, but I would worry that you were going to stay if I did."

"Nothing should stop a Fey from being a good host," he said, eyeing her cup.

"Except an unwanted guest." She returned to her chair, slid her cup closer, and took another bite of bread. She chewed it slowly and swallowed before speaking again. "Did you come for me or my father?"

"You," Caseo said.

"Well," she said, "I can tell you already that the poison will probably kill me, and that no, I will not participate in your experiments. So thank you very much for considering me, and be sure to close the door on your way out."

"When and if you become Black Queen," Caseo said slowly, "I would hope that you have more patience with your subjects than you display with me."

Jewel sighed. "I am not Black Queen yet, and I find you difficult at best, Caseo. Insulting me is not the way to work with me."

He sighed, clearly impatient with the enforced politeness. "The prisoners," he said. "I want to use them. I assume you're done with them."

So he was going to be direct. Perhaps that was best. "I spoke to them only yesterday."

"And had a Healer still one of their tongues. Nice idea, but you can't interrogate a man who can't speak."

"No," she said, standing so that she met his gaze. "But you can scare his companions into talking."

"So you are done," he said.

"I've only begun with them." She leaned against the table. "But tell me what you plan to use them for, and I will consider your request."

"You know what I want them for. I need to figure out this poison."

She crossed her arms. "I've already asked them about it. They know nothing."

"Well, perhaps you didn't ask them properly," he said.

She stared at him. Just because he was older didn't mean

that he could speak to her that way. "I don't have to defend myself to you, Caseo. I asked the prisoners, they said they didn't know, and I was satisfied with their answers. Now, you be satisfied with mine."

He stared at her for a moment, then crossed his arms as well. "I would really have preferred to talk with your father."

Jewel shrugged. "Then find him. It will do you no good. I'm in charge of the prisoners."

Caseo leaned toward her, using his height as a weapon. He placed his face inches from hers. "You are preventing us from discovering the one thing that could save us."

She didn't move. "I am doing nothing of the sort. I am discovering the information in my own way. And if you were so worried about finding the answers, you would be in your own cabin right now, working."

"I have worked!" The words exploded from him with such force that she felt the puffs of air from his breath. "I have worked for months!"

"And you're finding nothing?" she asked the question softly.

"Nothing, nothing, absolutely nothing except what you already know—that it can be diluted, the effects slowed or reduced, with real water. That is all we have learned. All. In months of intensive work." He put his hand on her shoulder. "So you see why we have to do this. You see why we need those prisoners. We have little hope of finding the answer on our own."

She stepped away from his grip. "I doubt that, Caseo. I have full confidence in your abilities. You are tired, that's all."

"Why is it that everyone questions me?" He straightened to his full height.

"I am not questioning you," Jewel said slowly. "I am saying that I believe in you."

"But you will not work with me."

She suppressed a sigh. Her father had been right when he called Caseo temperamental. "All right," she said, using her softest, most reasonable voice. "Tell me what you will use the prisoners for."

"Experiments," he said. "First to see if the water affects them. Then to learn if they know more than they told you.

Finally to discover if we can recreate the effect on Islanders."

She didn't move, but in her mind's eye she saw Adrian's face and the caring look he had shot at Luke. Her promise that if Adrian cooperated, his son would go free. She didn't want to see Adrian mangled and melted beyond recognition. But she also didn't want to spend the rest of her life in the Shadowlands.

"How would you do that?" she asked.

"We create spells. We do not dissect them. We would work on what we do best, creating spells." He spoke with such enthusiasm, she almost thought the idea his until she realized he had not credited it. Apparently one of the other Warders had pushed him in this direction and he believed the Warder to be right.

"So anything could happen to these men."

"Yes," Caseo said.

She nodded and pushed away from the table. He had a point. The Fey had tortured prisoners before. She had helped late in the Nye campaign by bringing the prisoners to the commanders herself. She had seen things at Luke's age that he couldn't even imagine. Still, she didn't feel right throwing the prisoners to Caseo.

"I am not done with them," she said. "When I am, they will be yours. Until then work with the Red Caps on obtaining some fresh skin from the bodies outside. See if that will help you."

"We already have skin," Caseo snapped. "We need those prisoners. You're delaying the inevitable by being stupid—"

"And you are making me angry," Jewel said. "I do what I believe best for this troop, and only my father will overrule me. Do you understand that, Caseo?"

He crossed his arms and leaned back, peering down at her with that frightening hooded gaze.

"Do you understand?" she asked. "Because if you don't, I am sure my father would be all too happy to explain it to you."

"You are an Infantry soldier. You have no jurisdiction over me," Caseo said.

"I am the Black King's granddaughter. I own your very life," Jewel said. "Don't tempt me to take it."

"You wouldn't," Caseo said. "I am the best Spell Warder you have."

"If you were," Jewel said with a smile, "you would have thought of this idea, instead of one of your other Warders. You are no longer the best, Caseo. You let a lucky, magickless people get the best of you. Aren't you ashamed of that?"

"I have nothing to be ashamed of. It was your father that brought us here. It was his failure of Vision that trapped us here, not mine."

She was so tired of hearing that, so tired of thinking it herself. "If you were able to do your job, we would have controlled this Isle long ago. But you can't beat a simple spell that most of the Islanders don't even realize is magick."

Caseo took a step toward her. "Don't shift the blame onto me, girl," he said. "Do you know why we moved Shadowlands? Because your father's Vision is breaking down. He should have been able to expand the first Shadowlands with no trouble at all. Instead, his abilities failed him. Magick always fails first on water."

"If you knew that, then why trust his Visions?" Jewel asked. "You came with us, after all."

"He was once the best Visionary of us all. But sometimes Vision decays, Jewel. Especially when it is used to See the same things over and over." Caseo's face had turned dark. His brows leveled over his eyes, making him seem angrier than he was.

"If what you say is true, then you have still failed," Jewel snapped. She was shaking. No one had quite maligned her father like this. "Warders are supposed to bring these concerns to the Black King, and in his absence or if he is the one with the problem, they are supposed to bring it to the Shaman. Have you talked with her?"

"I have been a bit busy," Caseo said. He stood to his full height.

"So you haven't." Jewel pushed off the table. "Yet you threaten me with my father's inability to do things. You try to fob off your mistakes on someone else, and you demand that I give you prisoners even though you won't say what you'll do with them. I have no reason to help you, Caseo."

"Except to help yourself," he said.

"I see no evidence that helping you will help any of us.

And if I catch you spreading those lies about my father without going through the proper channels, then I will make sure you are on the next small boat heading for the Stone Guardians. Then we will see what kind of stuff you are made of."

"You have no right to threaten me, girl."

Jewel tilted her head back at him. "I have every right," she said. "I am your better and always will be, even if we stay on Blue Isle forever. It would serve you well to remember that."

"And it would serve you well to remember that without Warders, you would have no idea how to use your powers at all." Caseo flung open the door. Gray mist spilled in. The Weather Sprites must have been attempting to experiment with rain again. "You are a naive child, Jewel. Look around you. Fey do not make these kinds of mistakes unless their magick is dying. We are trapped by your father's unwillingness to admit that he is losing his Vision."

"If I hear you attack my father one more time, I will take this to the Shaman myself. And you will run the risk of losing your position as head of the Warders." Jewel backed him toward the door, pointing her finger at his chest.

Caseo stopped in front of the door and glared down at her. "I need those prisoners."

"You will get what is left of them when I am through with them." She put her hand in the middle of his chest and shoved. "Now get out and don't bother me again."

He let himself be forced through the door. When he reached the porch, he tilted his head toward her, his eyes suddenly bright with an idea. "You have come into your own Visions, haven't you? What are they telling you? Do you see the decay of Shadowlands? The rescue of our troop? A life forever on Blue Isle? Or do all of us die hideously because your unwillingness to help me allows the Islanders to poison us all?"

"If I had my Visions," she said, "*if* I have them, I would follow them. And if I saw the poison destroying us all, I would find a way to make certain you Warders were more efficient. Now, get out of here before my father comes back and I am forced to tell him of your lack of faith in him."

"Caseo believes in no one." Her father's voice echoed in the gray mist. "That is something you will have to learn about senior Spell Warders, daughter. They are so corrupted by their power that they forget others have powers too."

"Ah, Rugar," Caseo said without turning around. "You have forgotten to teach your daughter to listen to her betters."

Rugar stepped out of the mist. His hair was damp, and he had circles under his eyes. "She listens to me and to her grandfather," he said. "Now, what are you bothering my daughter about?"

"I want those prisoners. I think they hold the secret to the poison." This time Caseo did turn, but only halfway so that Jewel could still see his face.

"And what did my daughter say?" Rugar asked.

"That he can have what's left of the prisoners when I am done with them," Jewel said, hating to be discussed in the third person.

Rugar shrugged. "Sounds fair enough, Caseo. I will make sure you receive them when she is through with them."

Caseo muttered a curse under his breath. He stalked down the steps without looking back at Jewel and disappeared into the mist. Rugar grabbed the railing and pulled himself up, his movement young and athletic even though he was three times Jewel's age.

"You angered him," Rugar said, taking her arm and helping her inside. He closed the door after them.

"I don't care," Jewel said, pulling her arm from his hand. "He's an insufferable ass, and he thinks he can order me around."

"Technically," Rugar said, "he can order all of us around, at least when it comes to magick. He is in charge of the spells, and he can change them at a moment's notice."

"We don't use spells."

"No," Rugar said, "but it's the Spell Warders who determined that Visionaries have a place in this culture. We used to be considered crazy until the Warders realized our Visions had truth, that we saw one possible future. Once we learned that, we became even stronger than we are."

"Ancient history, Father," Jewel said. "It has nothing to do with Caseo."

"It has everything to do with Caseo," Rugar said. "There is no such thing as ancient history for the Warders. Time is fluid for them. Some of them, it is said, can move backward or forward in time as they are needed. It is also said that a Warder never dies, but merely finds a new body to live in."

"I see no great ancient wisdom in Caseo," Jewel said. "He is a pompous, insufferable man."

"Yes," Rugar said. He cut himself a slice of bread and turned it over in his fingers. "But he is the best we have here, the best your grandfather allowed us, and we must make room for that. And we must cooperate with him as best we can so that we can change our fortunes here."

"I don't believe he will discover the antidote to that poison."

Rugar looked up at her; then set the bread down. "If he doesn't, Jewel, no one will. He is our only hope to solving the riddle of that odd magick."

"He won't do so by bullying me," Jewel said.

"And you won't help by fighting him." Rugar leaned on the table, much as Jewel had earlier. "Sometimes, Jewel, part of ruling is dealing with people we don't like because they are the ones in a position to help us."

"I know that," she snapped. "I'm not a child. But I have not Seen any—I mean, I do not see any evidence of his ability to solve this riddle."

Rugar stepped toward her and took her elbow again, but this time his grip was firm, his fingers digging into her flesh. "You Saw something new, Jewel?"

"No," she said, unwilling to look at him. The change in him when she mentioned her own Visions unnerved her. Part of the problem with Caseo's charges was that they felt too true. Why would her father treat her this way if his own Vision was working properly?

Rugar let go of her arm. "It seems to me, daughter, that you more than anyone have a stake in helping Caseo determine the root of that poison."

Involuntarily she touched her forehead. She could almost remember pain she hadn't felt yet. She hadn't thought of the Vision in terms of something that *would* happen, but in terms of something that *had* happened. Even though she knew that Visions were preventable, she hadn't thought of it with this one. It was her first Vision, her badge of adulthood, and she was clinging to it as that and nothing more.

She sank into a chair. The remembered pain made her forehead tingle. "What should I do?"

Her father smiled and crouched beside her like a supplicant. He took her hand. His was warm and rough from the work he had been doing in Shadowlands. "We don't always know what we can do," he said. "Sometimes we don't discover how to change the Vision until too late. And sometimes we misunderstand the Vision. That's why we usually ask for interpretations. Maybe we should take this Vision of yours to the Shaman."

She shook her head. If she could avoid the Shaman, she would. "It seems straightforward."

"So did my Vision of you in the Isle palace, walking through it as if you own it. But taking that Vision into account along with yours gives it a whole new meaning."

Jewel frowned. She squeezed his fingers. "What do you mean?"

"Are you in the palace because of the young Prince?" Rugar asks. "Or because they injure you and you cannot leave?"

"Was I injured in your Vision?"

He shook his head. "You looked like your mother, regal and lovely."

She shrugged. "Then how can our Visions be related? Or if they are, then we did discover an antidote to the poison."

"Perhaps," Rugar said. "But I am not as trusting as I once was of the simplicity of these things."

Jewel let that sink in. Then she bowed her head. "Did Grandfather ever have a Vision about this place?"

Rugar dropped her hand and stood up. "Your grandfather has reached the end of his Vision."

"He's Blind?" Jewel asked.

Rugar picked up the poker, moved the grate, and rolled a log over so that the fire could get some air. The flames spouted as he put another log on top.

"You left him knowing he was Blind?" Jewel asked. "You left him to rule without Vision?"

"Most Black Kings have no Vision at the end of their reign." Rugar slid the grate back into place.

"Is that why he opposed this mission, because he needed your Eye?"

Rugar laughed. "No, child. He has other Eyes, lesser Visionaries. He knows, like I do, that a man must follow his own Vision or change it. His Vision led him to Nye. Mine led me here."

"But if he can't See—"

"He can still rule. A man does not rule by Vision alone. He leads, he directs with Vision. Once he has achieved that Vision, he maintains. If my father does nothing else in his life, he will be remembered as one of the most successful Black Kings. He conquered the rest of Galinas for us. He gave us control over half the world." Rugar stood and leaned against the stone fireplace.

Jewel looked down at her hands with their short, stubby nails and calluses. "Are you losing your Vision?" she asked softly.

"What makes you ask that?" His voice had a harshness to it she heard him use only with the troops.

She didn't want to tell him about Caseo. She wasn't sure why. She certainly had no reason to protect him. But it felt as if she were protecting all of them by not saying who had planted the idea in her mind. "It stands to reason that if Grandfather has lost his Vision, you might too."

"Not all Visionaries go Blind," Rugar said. "Nor do all of them reach the end of their Vision."

"I have heard that some have false Visions, and that it leads to craziness." She spoke that last softly. She had heard it in the schoolroom from one of her many teachers when she'd been a girl. When another teacher had overheard the exchange, Jewel's teacher had been dismissed. Jewel never saw her again. She couldn't even remember her name.

The color in Rugar's cheeks was high. "I have seen Spell Warders reduced to gibbering fools by a single mistake. I have seen Beast Riders get stuck in their animal and die because of the change. I have seen Shape-Shifter babies die because their caregiver left them alone too long and a Shift came unbidden. I have never seen a Visionary lose his mind. Ever."

Jewel nodded. The force with which her father spoke had some fear behind it. "But have you ever heard of it?"

He picked up the poker and pushed at the grate, closed his eyes and sighed. Then he rubbed his left hand over his eyes, opened them, and put the poker away. "It is said that after the Fey started spreading away from the Eccrasian Mountains, the Black King lost his Vision. He was a young man and had not yet fathered children. He had false Visions and led the Fey in circles. The Shaman tried to depose him, but there was no procedure for that. The Warders refused to develop new spells, and the Fey refused to follow him. They camped at the base of the mountains for almost a generation while he followed his false Vision, then went Blind. With his Blindness came a deep despair, and gradually he lost his mind, memory by memory, until he was little more than a child. The Warders and the Shaman met and tested Visionaries until they found one who could see beyond the next battle. She became the first Black Queen, and her line was long-lived and strong. They ruled well until the entire family was murdered hundreds of years later."

"Have any other Visionaries lost their minds?"

Rugar nodded. "A few. But none were in power like that. They were always removed, or sent away quietly, or made into regents. It is not something we talk about much."

Jewel was breathing heavily, as if she had been involved in quick swordplay. "Why don't we talk about it?"

"Because," he said, his eyes full of the same fear she felt, "if most of our people knew about it, they would doubt all Visionaries. How can we tell a true Vision from a false one? And how do we know when a Vision has been averted? Or when it is one that was never meant to happen at all? How do we tell a mental breakdown from a successful use of foreknowledge? We can't, Jewel. We have only our minds and our reality to rely upon. We must trust in ourselves completely."

Her forehead still tingled. Remembered pain that never happened. Visions and insanity. She hadn't really linked them, not even when she had seen her father get the Look or fall into one of his Visions as he had in the middle of the Nye campaign. That was the way things were. All Fey knew that Visionaries sometimes acted strangely, just as they knew Red Caps stank of offal and blood.

Caseo. Caseo was an evil man who wanted to get his way and would use any method to do so, even by undermining her faith in her own father. "You weren't going to tell me about this, were you?"

Rugar shook his head. "You need complete confidence in your Visions. One way to achieve that is to believe that they will always come true unless your actions change the future."

"Is there history of craziness in our line?" she asked softly.

"No," Rugar said. "But in the last three hundred years, several of our ancestors have reached the end of their Vision. Some died before that end could be achieved, but anyone who has lived to your grandfather's age has become Blind."

She made herself swallow. Her mouth was dry, and it felt as if she were swallowing air. She grabbed her cup of tea and drank it, even though it had got cold. When she was finished, she set the cup down. It rang softly on the wooden tabletop. "That's why you wanted to come here, isn't it?" she asked. "You wanted to get to the end of your Vision."

He set the poker down and wiped his hands on his pants. He looked older than he had when he had emerged from the mist not an hour earlier. "If your grandfather dies when the seers say he will, I will be an old man. I will never be a Visionary Black King. Just a placeholder for you or your brothers. I will be Blind. I owe it to myself, to our people, to follow my Vision as far as it will lead. And if I never become Black King, so be it. I will enable you to be a better Black Queen."

"You're afraid to be King without Vision."

He ran a hand through his hair, a gesture he rarely used because it gave away his discomfort. She had seen it only a few times in his life, always when he was under great stress. "It is one thing to rule with Vision and to have lost the Vision. It is another altogether never to rule with Vision. We hold our power through Vision, strength, and political skill. I have never been much of a politician. I am a wonderful Visionary, but that will go someday. And my strength will go with it. I would bring nothing to the throne and jeopardize my family's place if I was to believe otherwise."

Jewel blinked, feeling disoriented. "Why can't I see beyond the single Vision, Father? Why don't I See myself as Black Queen?"

"Sometimes," he said softly, "a single Vision is so strong that it overpowers all the others until it happens. And sometimes a single Vision is all that we get of our lives."

"How do I know that I will See more than that?"

"Because your mother and I both had Vision. It should be very strong in our children," Rugar said.

"Should be," Jewel said. "But what if it isn't?"

"It will be," Rugar said. "I watched you have a Vision. It commands all of you. Sometimes Visions come to people in dreams or in flashes, but when the Vision is strong, it takes over the entire person, as it did you."

She swallowed, wishing for another cup of tea, but not willing to make it. "My Vision has us with the Islanders, and yours has me in their palace. What if fighting them is wrong, Father? What if our destiny is something else entirely?"

He stared at her as if he didn't recognize her. "We fight, Jewel. That is what we do."

She pulled her braid forward and fiddled with the end. She had been thinking this for some time, but she hadn't known how to approach him. Even now she wasn't sure if this was the correct method. "I know," she said. "But what happens if this place is different? We can't seem to conquer it by force. Perhaps we're here to learn something new. Perhaps that is what our Visions mean."

His expression hadn't changed. He crossed his arms over his chest, much as Caseo had done. "I'm listening," he said.

"We have many powers," she said. "We can enchant and beguile. We seem to use those skills only when we have conquered a people, but what about before? In my Vision the Prince cares for me. It is very, very clear. And if the Prince cares for me as strongly as he seems to, then perhaps we have another way into their world, another way to take control of this place."

"Jewel, you're talking about methods that take years. We don't have years."

"We have already spent a year here, Father, and all we have to show for it is this gray temporary home in the woods outside their city. We have lost half our people, and we are no closer to finding a solution. The Black King won't save us, and we can't find a way out of this place without risking even more lives. It seems that years spent conquering these people subtly are years better spent than hiding in the Shadowlands."

He flinched as if she had hit him. Then he looked into

the fire as if it would provide answers. "I need time to think about this," he said.

"I know," she said softly.

"We may need to see the Shaman."

She nodded. Then she flung her braid back over her shoulder. She wasn't sure if she had won a victory or lost something precious. "There's one more thing, Father," she said.

He didn't look up. "Go ahead."

"I think I'm going to let the prisoner Luke go free. The young boy. I believe if I do that, I can get somewhere with his father."

This time Rugar did look at her. "You're convinced of this?"

She nodded. "It was a deal I made with the father. He's had time to think of it. If I let the boy go free, I will do so only after I have received valuable information."

"If you let the boy go free," Rugar said, "make sure he will still be useful to us."

Jewel grinned. "I'll make sure he'll help us whenever we want him to."

FIFTY-EIGHT

THERON'S hands were shaking so badly that Kondros had to double-check his knots. The little Fey man sat docilely in the chair, his hands tied behind him, and his feet tied to the chair legs. They had come to Kondros's house, as close to the palace as they could get without going into the gate. To call the place a house was to be charitable. A bootmaker had the front of the building, and Kondros a room in the back, off the bootmaker's apartments. The building smelled of hides and tanned leather, appropriate since the little man reeked almost as badly.

The little man hadn't struggled at all. He had gone to the chair willingly and not protested when Theron tied his hands behind his back. Theron wouldn't let the little man out of his sight. His neck still hurt from the knife cut, and he was terrified that the little man was going to use some kind of spell on him, make Theron do his bidding because he had now touched Theron's blood.

Cyta had gone for Monte. The three men had decided on the way back that they wanted to involve someone close to the King, but they didn't want to risk anyone too close. They didn't know if the little man planned a trick on them or not.

The room was small for three people. It would be crowded with five. The little man had one of the four chairs that surrounded a table, and Kondros sat on the mat in the far corner of the room. The fireplace took up one wall. There was no window, and the door opened onto an alley with a lot of traffic. They kept the door closed, even though the room was stuffy.

Theron didn't even have room to pace. His forefinger touched the slash on his neck. The scab was in place now, and he didn't feel any different. Maybe the stories he had heard were lies made up by the Fey so that the Islanders would be frightened of them.

Kondros had placed a bottle of holy water on the table. After checking the knots on the little man's wrists, Kondros sat down beside the bottle and let his fingers play with its sides. The little man's eyes kept darting to Kondros's fingers, and then to Theron's face. Clearly, the little man was frightened of that water. That fear, more than anything, made Theron believe the little man had told them the truth.

Without warning the door opened inward, making Theron scramble backward. Kondros grabbed the holy water, and the little man squeaked his protest. Cyta came in, his face red and sweaty from exertion, followed by the captain of the guards. Monte was a small man, powerfully built, who stood straighter than any other Islander Theron had ever met.

Monte slammed the door behind him and walked over to the little man. He wrinkled his nose as he got close, as if he couldn't believe the stench. "Why didn't you men clean him up?" Monte asked.

"He won't let us bring water near him," Theron said.

"Smart creature, aren't you?" Monte asked.

The little man licked his lips. "Who are you?" he asked in Nye, his voice shaking.

Monte hooked his booted foot around the leg of the chair behind him, pulled it forward, and sat down. "I understand you want to join our side," he said in Nye. "That's an odd request."

"They tried to kill me," the little man said.

"It's their job," Monte replied. He glanced—once—at the holy water near Kondros's hand.

"No," the little man said. "My people. They tried to kill me."

Monte leaned forward and put his elbow on the table so that his face was closer to the little man's. "And why would they do that?"

Theron's shaking had grown worse. The situation bothered him. He pulled a chair and sat on it too, arms crossed tightly over his chest. What if the little man was the beginning of some odd invasion force? What if he was going to take over Monte and the rest of them, and then get to the King?

"I'm not important to them," the little man said.

Monte chuckled softly. "Not important? With as many men as they've been losing, everyone has to be important to them."

The little man shook his head. "I'm a Red Cap. I take care of the dead, and that gives me no value. I have no magick. I am not worth anything to them."

"It seems," Monte said, "that you have a lifelong problem. It would make no sense for you to defect now."

"They tried to kill me." The little man spit out the words with such force that Theron resisted the urge to back away.

"You said that," Monte replied as if the little man had shown no anger at all. "But I don't understand why."

"They're trying to find out how that works," the little man said, nodding toward the vial of holy water. "They wanted to experiment with some of it on me."

"Why would they want to do that?" Monte asked. "They already know it will kill you."

The little man shook his head. "They think it might have no effect on people who lack magick."

Cyta and Kondros glanced at Theron. What an explanation. If it was true, then the Roca had given them a very potent weapon indeed. Only Monte didn't move.

"How do we know you lack magick? We have only your word on that," he said.

"If I had magick, I would not be sitting here trussed like this."

"Unless you were trying to infiltrate us. Unless you were trying to make us believe you are something other than what you are."

The little man bowed his head and shook it once, as if he

couldn't believe the position he was in. Then he licked his lips and tilted his head back. "I have never done anything like this before," he said. "I wouldn't even consider it if I were back in Nye or on the continent. I would just run away, resign, or join some of the Fey who have chosen to stay away from the wars. But I have no choice here. I can't stay in the Shadowlands. If I do, they will experiment on me in my sleep, and I can't live alone outside of the Shadowlands, because if I do, one of you Islanders will kill me. So I thought if I came to you, if I told you things you didn't know about us, maybe you could help me, but you won't trust me."

"We have no reason to," Monte said. "We have only your word. And that is worth nothing to us."

The little man exhaled loudly. Theron sat stiffly, his fingers again creeping to his neck. "He didn't kill me," Theron said, uncertain why he was defending the little man.

"Of course not," Monte said. "Why should he? You were his way to me. Or to the King. What's your real plan? Assassinate the King?"

The little man shook his head. "We've had people closer to your King than I am."

"The girl," Monte said. "We know."

"No," the little man said. "You don't know. The only thing we have in our favor at the moment is your awful ignorance. And that ignorance could get you all killed. I am willing to betray everything I was raised on for safety. I am the key to your winning this war."

Monte glanced at Theron. "Let me see that wound," he said. He tilted Theron's neck back, and Theron winced at the pain as the scar pulled. "I hope you don't mind if I clean it with a bit of holy water."

Theron frowned. "Holy water's not for—oh," he said as he understood. "I don't mind."

Monte grabbed the vial from Kondros. The little man cringed as if he expected the water to come toward him. Monte poured a bit on his handkerchief and dabbed at Theron's neck. The kerchief came away bloody.

"Well," Monte said. "He didn't enchant you."

"I can't," the little man said. "I have no magick. Would I smell like this if I did?"

Monte ignored him. He handed the vial back to Kondros, spilling a drop on Kondros's hand. Kondros grinned at him and wiped the drop away.

"He already tested me at the palace," Cyta said.

"Good test," the little man said, his voice shaking. "None of our people would survive."

"Want me to touch you?" Monte asked.

"No!" The little man screeched the word. "I said I would help you! What more do you want?"

Monte shrugged. "Maybe you won't die, if you lack magick, as they say."

The toe of the little man's boots pushed at the plank floor. He backed the chair up as far as it would go. "No. I don't believe that. There are Red Caps missing. I think they died from the poison like everyone else. Please. Please. I am making you an offer. Please. Don't kill me. Please."

Monte sighed and set the vial down. He put the kerchief down beside it. Theron's heart was pounding. The little man's fear was infectious.

"All right," Monte said. "I'll accept your offer. But you will have to do things on my terms. I will not take you anywhere near the King, and you will answer every question I put to you. I will have a guard on you at all times, with holy water beside him, and if you make so much as one wrong move, we will spray you. Is that clear?"

The little man's mouth worked but nothing came out. Finally he nodded.

"If your information is not useful, we will kill you. If your information is wrong, we will kill you. Is that clear?"

The little man swallowed. "Yes." The word came out as a near whisper. Theron truly believed the little man was terrified. "What happens when you learn that I'm telling you the truth?"

"We'll negotiate then. At the very least, we'll let you live. And if you are telling us the truth, that is more than your people were willing to do."

The little man nodded and looked away. Monte pushed his chair back and stood. "I want you men to take him to the guard barracks. We'll put him in the keep alone, and one of you will guard him tonight. Tomorrow I will have new guards posted. Until you hear from me, though, none of this has happened. I don't want word to get out in this city that we have a Fey prisoner." He glanced at the little man.

"If it does, I may not be able to keep my word about keeping him alive."

"We won't say anything," Theron said. Then he looked at his companions. "Will we?"

They shook their heads. They both crouched without Theron saying another word and started untying the little man's feet.

The little man was watching Theron. When he saw Theron's gaze on him, he mouthed, "Thank you."

Theron nodded, not wanting to have a Fey indebted to him. Once the Fey man was in Monte's prison, Theron hoped he would have nothing more to do with him.

Monte was watching them help the little man to his feet. "Whatever else happens, men," he said, "you did the right thing by bringing him to me."

Theron wasn't so sure. He had wanted something more decisive to come from this meeting—a way to kill all Fey quickly, or even better, a way to rescue his friends.

FIFTY-NINE

TEL paced Andre's chambers, reviewing the Midnight Sacrament. Andre's memory of the ceremony was very detailed, so detailed that Tel found it confusing. He knew if he relaxed and let his mind take over, he would be able to perform it correctly, but he wasn't sure he could relax. One slip, and he would die.

Damn that Solanda. She had sent him here, to this place of death, to discover a secret that he couldn't know unless he became their religious leader, or Elder Matthias. If Tel took over either of those two men, he could send the secret back to Shadowlands, and stay here, substituting real water for the poison and protecting his people that way.

Only he wasn't a real hero, and he was frightened. He might not live through the night.

The sound of horse's hooves and a voice shouting at the gate made him hurry to the window. In the darkness he could barely see the Danites standing guard at the gate. A horseman stood there, talking with them. He heard the voices floating over the air and leaned forward to see if he could make out what was being said.

When he heard the name Nicholas, he froze. The Prince was back on an urgent matter. Had they discovered the bones in the stable? Had something else happened? He didn't know, but his mouth had gone dry. The guards stood away, and Nicholas's horse hurried through the gate into the courtyard.

Tel leaned back inside, his heart racing, the indecision gone. He had to go to Midnight Sacrament now. If the Prince had discovered something, Tel had to be around to know what that something was. The messenger be damned; Tel would get another message to the Shadowlands when he had a chance.

Which meant he had to perform Midnight Sacrament. And he had to protect himself. He gripped the wall for support, the stone digging into his fingers. The fear had left him light-headed. But he had no time. He knew only one way around all of this. At least he was prepared.

He grabbed Andre's service robe and slipped it on. The children had helped him bring buckets into the Tabernacle. He had stolen new, unused vials from the storage room and filled them with river water, and then he had, with the help of an Aud, brought them to his room. He tied the belt around his waist, nervously adjusted the sword, and put on his biretta. Then he pulled the bell pull, hoping that the Aud who was supposed to respond wouldn't be too late.

He glanced out into the courtyard again, but couldn't see the Prince or his horse. Andre hadn't been summoned for a meeting, so chances were that Nicholas had come to see the Rocaan or a specific Elder. If only Tel had picked Matthias when he had been trying to rise in the ranks. But Solanda hadn't left Tel much time, and he had taken the first he could get. Tel had had only Miruts's limited knowledge of Rocaanism to go on, and from that perspective he had done well. It was only when he settled into Andre's body that he realized he had made a mistake.

There was a soft knock at his door. "Come," he said without inquiring who it was. Andre never did. Elders did not think themselves at risk there.

An Aud stood at the open door, head bowed. "Yes, Respected Sir?"

Tel took a deep breath, then swept his hand toward the box of vials he had left on one of the tables. "Please take those down to the sanctuary. We have new holy water from the Rocaan for the service tonight."

"Yes, Respected Sir." The Aud went to the table and picked up the box, groaning under its weight. Tel held the door for the Aud, then followed him into the corridor, knowing that it wasn't customary, but not caring. If anyone asked, he could say he was making certain the new holy water made it to the sanctuary.

In truth, he wanted to know where the vials would be. So he followed the Aud through the corridors, holding his robe close to his sides so that he wouldn't brush anything or knock anything loose. His biggest fear was that there was another poison in this building, a poison the Warders and Rugar did not know about.

As Tel went past the audience rooms, he heard voices. The Aud continued, head down, as if he heard nothing. Tel wanted to stop, to listen, to see if he was missing anything, but he didn't dare. He needed to know where those vials were at all times.

The voices grew louder as he passed the closed door. Two Danites stood outside, their heads bowed, hands clasped in front of them. Tel ignored them as a good Elder should and stared straight ahead, listening with all his power.

He didn't recognize the soft voice, although it sounded familiar to Andre. The louder voice, the one that spoke with energy and feeling, was Nicholas's. The words were muffled, but some of the sentences were clear:

". . . some kind of pattern, and since it is unusual, we must take it as a threat."

The soft voice responded. Tel couldn't make out the words.

"Well, it certainly isn't normal, and anything abnormal we must assume is Fey. Besides, this happened near Stephen . . ."

And then Tel was beyond the door. He could hear no more. He resisted the urge to glance back. Stephen. Stephen. The name was familiar to him, but he wasn't sure through which of his personalities or why.

He followed the Aud down the narrow back stairs to the sanctuary. The Aud kicked at the closed door at the base of the stairs. When it opened, he walked through. Tel put his hand on the door, trying not to cringe as his fingers touched the wood, and then slipped inside also.

The rooms behind the sanctuary were used as storage and

quick-changing rooms for Elders who ran late. Extra robes hung on the walls, covering the various swords, each done in a different style. The floor was covered with handmade tile, depicting a Rocaan crowning a King, and the browns and reds of the tile gave the room some life.

Tel was glad he had followed the Aud, because vials of holy water stood everywhere, some in boxes, some out.

The Aud stood in the middle of the mess, holding the box, his young face red with exertion. "Where would you like me to set this, Respected Sir?"

Tel's hands were shaking. One misstep in this room, one casual bump against those vials, and he was a dead man. "Let's take the vials under the Sacrificial Table," he said, relieved his voice was calm, "and replace them with these."

The Aud pushed open the door to the sanctuary with his back. Tel started to follow, but the Aud grinned at him. "I can do the job, Respected Sir. There is no need to supervise me."

"Still," Tel said, "this is an important task. The Rocaan wants to make sure it is done right."

The Aud who had opened the door initially said, "The Rocaan didn't seem to mind when we brought the rest of these down here. I think he'll trust us to put them under the Sacrificial Table."

Fear was making Tel jumpy. "Yes, but I am in charge of this particular box, and I am going to make certain it is in its place before Sacrament."

The Aud shook his head. "All right," he said. "But I wouldn't want to go against tradition just to supervise a task that would have been done well anyway."

Tel almost asked, *Go against tradition?* and then his Andre memory worked for him. Elders were not supposed to be seen before Midnight Sacrament since sometime before they theoretically became the Representative of God.

But he had already called attention to himself, and it was his life. "I'll watch from the door," he said, and carefully, clutching his robes so tightly to his side that it constricted his walk, he made his way to the door. When he reached it, he pushed it open with his shoulder.

The pews were already filled with the faithful. Many had their heads bowed in meditation, others had arms raised in prayer. Some stared at the Sword hanging from the ceiling.

Andre used to love Midnight Sacrament for its simplicity. Tel appreciated its shortness.

The Aud crouched behind the Sacrificial Table. He took the vials of holy water out of the box and then took the vials off the shelves built under the table itself. Tel watched very carefully as the Aud placed the old bottles back in the box. Then, slowly, Tel let the door ease closed.

The other Auds were watching him as if he had gone crazy. He smiled at them, then shrugged. "No detail is too important," he said.

He backed away from the door and stood near an empty counter, careful not to let his body touch it in any way. He couldn't control his shaking. What if the Warders were wrong? What if the deaths had nothing to do with the water itself but with the rituals that created it? What if he went into that sanctuary and the Isle God struck him down?

Foolish thoughts. He made himself take a deep breath. Very foolish thoughts. If the Isle's God was going to strike him down, it would have done so when he'd killed that parishioner on the street after morning services, and then attacked Andre in the Tabernacle itself. The God would have to have been deaf not to have heard Andre's pleas as he'd struggled with Tel.

He rubbed a hand over his face. He had to remember all that he had learned. How Esx, the ancient Doppelgänger too old to practice his trade, had taught all the young boys to eschew sex and sexuality except in the host bodies, to have the only joinings be with the victims. In those teachings, which began when Tel's magical abilities had appeared at age twelve, Esx had taught them that if gods were as all-powerful as their worshipers claimed, no Fey would exist. They would have been struck down by the all-powerful gods whenever the Fey invaded the gods' lands.

Esx had lived through four major campaigns and the transfer of twenty-five bodies. He had kept the last because he had grown accustomed to it. In all of that experience he had to have faced moments like this one. He would never have made that comment about gods without reason.

The Aud pushed the door open and came back into the room, struggling yet again with the heavy box. His black robe was damp with sweat, and he reeked. Andre would have thanked him for his help, but Tel could not bring himself to do that. Instead, he said, "Remember to place those aside so that they can be refilled with more of the new batch."

"Yes, Respected Sir," the Aud mumbled, and Tel thought he heard surliness in the tone.

Then another Aud came to him, carrying a large silver sword. Tel made himself smile, although his heart was pounding. The sword was ancient and had never been used in combat. Its ornate hilt was the model for all the small swords that the Rocaanists wore around their necks. The Aud extended the sword to him, hilt out.

"Is it prepared?" Tel asked, thankful again that his voice sounded calm.

The Aud flushed. The question must have seemed unusual. "As always, Respected Sir."

Tel reached for the hilt quickly. If he was going to die, it would be better here, in the back, near all the holy water, than in front of the worshipers in the sanctuary. Fewer witnesses, less chance to corroborate the story.

But he touched the hilt of the sword and felt nothing except the cool softness of the metal. His eyes filled with tears of relief. The Aud hadn't lied. He had wiped the sword clean of all water: contaminating it in religious terms so that it could be Blessed in the Midnight Sacrament, recalling the action of the Roca before he was Absorbed.

"Thank you," Tel said, perhaps as much to their nonexistent God as to the young Aud who had handed him the sword. He gripped the hilt tightly, then took a deep breath to brace himself. His biggest test in this body—perhaps his biggest test ever—would come in the next few moments.

He slid the sword through his sash, then retied the sash tightly so that the sword wouldn't slip. Then he opened the door and stepped onto the altar. The door closed behind him with a slight click.

Slowly heads came up and arms came down. The sanctuary, which had seemed cold and large in the morning, was now hot and crowded. He stood, as Andre used to, and waited until the gathered people were done with their meditation and prayers.

Some had been there for hours, he knew. It was custom for the people to cleanse their minds and spirits in communication with the Holy One before attempting Absorption with their God. He also knew that some hoped for true Absorption, but that it had never happened—not in the history of the organized Church.

Finally the entire congregation looked at him. The faces were unfamiliar—not anyone Miruts had known—and oddly familiar. He had the feeling of having stood before them as recently as the previous morning. He knew that the ceremony he performed tonight was, in many ways, linked for them to the ones Andre had performed in the past. All of the Elders knew that the congregations appeared to support a particular Elder, and Andre's liked his soft-spoken style.

Tel's heart was pounding. Time to start. If he did it right, no one would know who he was. No one would be able to guess he wasn't who he appeared to be.

He swung the sword over his head and caught its tip with his left hand. He was surprised at the blade's softness, although his Andre memories had warned him that it would be.

" 'There are enemies without,' " he said, projecting his voice without making it sound loud.

" 'And within,' " the congregation responded.

Despite his fear, he almost smiled. They had no idea. " 'We are surrounded by hatred—' "

" '—greed,' " the congregation said—

" '—lust,' "

" '—cruelty,' "

" '—and loss.' " He took a breath where Andre always did. The body did not know this, the mind knew this. He was shocked at how rote the service was. He brought the sword down with both hands so that the flat of the blade faced the congregation. " 'We chose to fight, not with weapons—' "

" '—or with cunning,' " the congregation said—

" '—but with faith.' " Slowly he brought the sword down and laid it flat on the Sacrificial Table. The light from above reflected off the tiny images etched in the blade. "Tonight the Holy One will take our troubles to the Ear of God."

The last was not a quote from the Words Written and Unwritten, but a part of the ceremony that had been added centuries before by the Twentieth Rocaan. Tel raised his hands again, this time without the sword. The sleeves of his robe fell away, revealing his bare arms. The congregation mimicked his posture.

"When the Roca asked for God's ear, he begged for safety for his people. Yet they were besieged by enemies, and it appeared that God did not listen. The Roca brought the enemies to the holiest of places, and there he asked God to strike them down. When God did not, the Roca thought to strike them down himself, but he thought, 'Would that mean that I believe I am better than God? For if God is not willing to do this thing, He in His wisdom must have a reason. And I am but a lowly creation, not a creator. I do not have the ability to see more than my small corner of the Isle. I cannot even see what is across the water. I cannot see God in his holy place. I cannot see the beasts in the trees. I am lowly, unworthy of making decisions for my God.' "

Tel brought his arms down, as the ritual decreed, and fingered the sword. "So the Roca ordered his men to stand at his side, their blades out but useless. And when he was approached by his enemies in that holy place, he welcomed them and bade them to wait until he cleaned his sword. Then he took the water left him by a fallen comrade and cleaned the blade."

Tel's hands were shaking as he reached to the shelf below the Sacrificial Table. Danites had emerged from the doors behind him and flanked him. He took a vial in each hand and passed them to the Danites without looking at them. When they had a grip on their vials, they processed to the pews, the first Danites to the pews farthest in the back, and there they waited, one hand on the vial's bottom and the other around its neck.

The congregation did not watch them, but instead used that moment of silent progression to offer their remaining prayers to the Ear of God. Slowly arms came down and heads bowed until Tel spoke again.

He waited until the last Danite was in the aisle. Then he took the last vial and set it beside the sword. Fear made his chest ache. He took a small cloth from the second shelf. A lump had risen in his throat, and he cleared it softly before continuing.

"As he cleaned his blade, the Roca told this to his men."
His voice sounded shaky. This next quote from the Words
Written and Unwritten frightened him more than any other
part of the service. "He said, 'Without water, a man dies. A
man's body makes water. His blood is water. A child is born
in a rush of water. Water keeps us clean. It keeps us healthy.
It keeps us alive. It is when we are in water that we are
closest to God.' But his men said—"

" 'Holy Sir, when a man stays too long in water, he
dies.' " The congregation and the Danites stated the rote
response.

"And the Roca looked at them all with great pity in his
eyes. 'A man dies only when he is not pure enough to sit at
the feet of God.' " Then Tel picked up the vial and pulled
out the stopper. A faintly bitter scent reached him, and bile
rose in his throat. He made himself swallow once, twice, to
keep himself from vomiting, the terror so overwhelming, his
entire body was shaking. " 'When you touch water,' the
Roca said to them all, 'you touch the Essence of God.' "

He poured the water from the vial onto the cloth. It took
a moment for the water to seep through, but when it
touched his hand, he made an involuntary groan. No one
else seemed to notice. The Danites took his action as a cue
to pass the vials down the rows, and parishioner after parishioner poured a few drops of water onto their own cloths.

Tel watched for a moment, mesmerized, wondering if the
very smell of the water would contaminate him and corrode
him from the inside. But his hand did not hurt, and no foul
stench rose from him. He let out a breath he hadn't even
realized he was holding, and as the air passed from him, an
elation filled him.

Carefully, he put the cloth on the blade. He had to do
this properly as well. To rub back and forth was considered
bad luck. Early Rocaans believed that it released the demons in the blade, the demons that caused the blade to be
used as an instrument of war. He didn't want that. What if
they were right? What if there was something trapped in the
blade, something as deadly as the water?

He stroked downward from the hilt to the tip until water
glistened on the silver. Then he removed another cloth
from the lower shelf and blotted the water without drying it

off. He turned the sword over and repeated the procedure again.

A low murmur had filled the sanctuary: people asked for verbal blessings from the Holy One. In case they were Absorbed, they wanted to go with religious words on their lips. Tel wanted to laugh at the seriousness with which they all took this folderol, but Andre had believed it utterly, and enough of that belief came through the memories that Tel felt as if he were committing heresy by even having the thought.

The congregation had finished, and the Danites had retired to the back to await the end of the service so that they could collect the empty vials. Tel lifted his sword by the hilt, his movements so practiced that it took no effort to lift it into position. The position brought some of the fear back: the blade's tip pressed against his flat stomach, the pressure just enough to mime the Roca's Absorption.

"We allow no enemies here," he said in accordance with the service. His words sounded hollow, his throat dry. "The Roca has protected us from all that would threaten us. We shall not die by the Sword. Instead, we live by it."

He let go of the sword, and it clattered against the table, knocking the vial over. The remaining water spilled along the surface and dripped onto the carpet. He used all of his control to keep from jumping away.

"Go forth," he said, "and remember what a gift it is that the Roca has given you."

"We go with thanks," the congregation said.

Tel picked up the small sword around his neck and touched it to his forehead. Then he raised his arms and bowed to the sword hanging from the ceiling. The others did the same as they stood. No one spoke as they left the sanctuary.

He turned toward the back door, but found that he couldn't go in. He was trembling so badly that he was afraid he would accidentally knock one of the vials of real holy water upon himself. He stood near the Sacrificial Table, thinking of the words he had just spoken, and wondering if they were true. Their former leader had given them a weapon against their enemies. The holy water—the poison —had truly kept them all safe this past year.

But it did not keep them safe any longer. A viper was in

the nest. The enemy had infiltrated their holiest of places and survived.

He bowed his head and breathed a silent word of thanks to whatever had protected him in this place: the Mysteries, the Powers or the Islander God.

SIXTY

THE Rocaan sat alone in his audience chamber, his head buried in his hands. For the first time in his entire career, he missed Midnight Sacrament. But he didn't care. He was shaking all over. The strain was too much for him. He was an old man. Didn't God care about that? Shouldn't a man have peace in his old age?

Not a Rocaan, and he knew it. He served the place of the Roca on the Isle, and it was his duty to keep his people protected from their enemies, a duty he was somehow failing.

Enemies were never supposed to be allowed within, and yet if young Nicholas was to be believed, they had somehow found a place in the Tabernacle, perhaps even corrupted an Aud.

Or, God forbid, an Elder.

The Rocaan brought his head out of his hands and sighed. The room was bright with torches, and the wood carvings made it feel warm. But he shivered with an internal chill. What if he was the one corrupted and he didn't even know it?

But he would know it. He wouldn't be able to touch holy

water. Young Nicholas had said that his swordmaster had died touching holy water.

The Rocaan stood. His legs ached, and his knees cracked as he moved. Too old. Why hadn't God brought this before a younger Rocaan? But if He had waited, whom would He have had to tap? Matthias? Andre? Or no one at all?

Torches burned from their pegs overhead. No one had bothered to light the chandelier, and its carefully crafted glass baubles hung low. The paneled walls depicted the reign of the first Rocaan as he converted the countryside and subdued his brother, the King. All of the chairs were pushed against the walls, except for the two he and young Nicholas had used.

Two men had disappeared from the palace the day the blood and bones had appeared in the Tabernacle. Those two men had acted strangely since the Fey had invaded. Both men had cleaned blood and bones from their favorite places. Both men had spoken to a cat.

The Rocaan would order, as Nicholas had requested, anyone who saw a cat in the Tabernacle to kill it on sight. The chefs would have to stop feeding their pets around back, and the Rocaan would probably extend the order to dogs as well. No sense in having any dumb animals threaten the safety of this holy place.

Then he would touch all his people with holy water. Before that he would watch Matthias make a mixture, to make certain that he wasn't under Fey influence and simply pouring water into bottles. And the Rocaan would have anyone report strange behavior to him. Anyone reported more than once would have to be tested by water again. And again.

The Rocaan sank into another chair. His body felt twice as heavy as it had when he'd woken that morning. Not exhaustion, per se, but disillusionment. He had thought the Tabernacle a fortress, and then the Fey had invaded it. Enemies within.

" 'There are enemies without and within,' " he whispered, quoting, but condensing the Words. " 'We choose to fight . . . with faith.' "

He picked up his sword and placed it against his forehead. The tiny silver filigree was cool against his skin. "If ever I needed your guidance, Holy One, it is now."

He waited, but no still, small voice came to him. Only a rush of panic and fear. He closed his eyes. The Roca had led his enemies to the holiest of places, but he had not killed them. Instead, he had offered himself as a sacrifice that his own people might live. And by doing so, he had become Beloved of God.

But he had not desired to become Beloved of God. The Rocaan lifted his head. *And that was where all the Rocaans made their mistake. The Roca had desired to protect his people, and nothing more.*

The thoughts didn't feel like his, but like a voice whispering in his ear. He didn't move. Was that the still, small voice? It had a certainty that he had lacked for decades.

And here he was, questioning it.

But he wasn't questioning the certainty. He was questioning the voice. And perhaps it didn't matter where the voice had come from. What it said was right. The Roca never, in all of his teachings, asked to become Beloved of God. Love was something that God bestowed as a reward for the selflessness with which the Roca had acted.

Yet if the Rocaan acted with selflessness now, it would seem that he was trying to curry favor. He had to examine his own heart and see if it was pure. He had to cleanse it of the ambition to become Beloved, and leave only the desire to do the right thing, the proper thing. To protect his people with minimal bloodshed as the Roca had done.

So far he had failed to do that.

But the Words did not tell whether the Roca had failed before the Absorption. No one knew what made him bring the Soldiers of the Enemy to the holy place. Frustration? Failure to do something earlier? Wisdom and prevention? The Rocaan had no way of knowing.

He sighed and let the sword fall against his chest. If only he had known sooner that the Elder in charge of the Oral Tradition was stifling it. What Rocaan had thought that up and believed it good for the people? The answer to that question was lost forever, although the Rocaan thought he knew. Through the Rocaans numbered in the late twenties and early thirties, there was a lot of political intrigue and assassination. The Rocaan in those days held as much power as the King, maybe more, and because the position was not hereditary, more Elders believed they should get the position than did. Perhaps, in those days, the Elder in charge of the Oral Tradition was told to keep it silent, not to give any region or any one extra power.

He gripped his sore knees. He had changed that now. When he met with Elder Eirman, he stressed that the Elder was to take stories about the Roca from the various Auds and Danites and record them. The stories might not be true, but they might shed a light on the history that was missing.

They might help a future—or current—Rocaan.

He closed his eyes. The heaviness was so deep in him that he was afraid he would have to call someone just to help him out of the chair. He started to lever himself out when the door into the audience chamber swung open.

Elder Reece bowed to the Rocaan. The younger man was wearing his Danite's robe, which he always wore at Midnight Sacrament when he was not performing it. Reece was thin to the point of gauntness. He was not wearing a cap on his balding head, and as he faced the Rocaan, he licked his lips nervously.

"Forgive me, Holy Sir," he said, "but I believed I might disturb you in the audience chamber."

The Rocaan sighed. He had wanted to go to his own chamber. But he supposed he could wait a bit longer. Maybe when Reece was done, he would help the Rocaan out of his chair.

"What is on your mind, Reece?" the Rocaan asked.

Reece nodded and swallowed, self-effacing bobbing movements that made the Rocaan want to demand that the man learn self-respect. But Reece had always been timid. Elders were supposed to exhibit different qualities, and none of the others could have taken that one.

"You said, Holy Sir, that we were to report to you when we saw something out of the ordinary," Reece said. "I thought you might like to know about the Sacrament, since you didn't attend."

The Rocaan sighed. Timidity was trying at the best of times. "I know the ritual, and I probably know who was there, since Andre presided. What happened? Did he skip?"

"Oh, no, Holy Sir. His delivery was quite heartfelt." Reece looked up. "Would that all of us were able to achieve that degree of feeling in the ritual itself."

Or in life. The Rocaan's leg aches were growing worse.

He wanted to stand. "You said that something was out of the ordinary."

"Yes, Holy Sir." Reece tugged on his sash; then, for a brief moment, his gaze met the Rocaan's. "I don't know if you remember when I first came to see you, years ago?"

"What does this have to do with anything, Reece?" the Rocaan snapped, unable or unwilling to remember their first meeting.

"Well, Holy Sir, if you do not remember, I need to refresh you. It's important." Reece looked extremely sincere.

The Rocaan sighed again and made himself remember what he could. "I recall something about the ceremonies."

"Yes, Holy Sir. I had a reaction to holy water, if you recall. It makes my skin blister. You said that it should not worry me, that as long as I had faith, I would be welcome in God's service."

The Rocaan sat up straighter, his tiredness forgotten. He did remember now. And he remembered that Reece was not the only one who had had trouble with holy water in the past. An entire kirk near the Cliffs of Blood had had a reaction to the Rocaan's holy water. He had figured that it was because his recipe relied on the old recipes, whereas the more recent Rocaans made holy water without the seze. They believed that the Roca did not know of seze, an herb which grew only in the Kenniland Marshes, so they thought the herb a late modification. The Rocaan was a purist and had no evidence that the Roca knew otherwise, so he went back to the original recipe. Once his recipe started going to the outskirts of the Isle, the towns near the Cliffs of Blood reported rashes after Midnight Sacrament.

"I do remember now," he said. "But I thought we gave you dispensation to wear gloves."

"Yes, Holy Sir. But sometimes I spill a drop or two on bare skin, and the blisters return almost immediately. The last time was so bad that Elder Vaughn sent for a doctor."

The Rocaan had not heard of this. "What was bad?"

"The blisters spread up my arm until I was in such pain, I could barely stand it. The doctor prescribed a salve, and I healed."

The Rocaan nodded. How odd. He had allowed gloves for all the congregations near the Cliffs of Blood. He wondered if any of their symptoms had worsened. Doubtless he would have heard of it if they had.

"And what bearing does this have on tonight?" the Rocaan asked. Poor Reece. The Rocaan would never consider him to become Rocaan. The congregation would grow old and die before Reece made his first decision.

"I spilled half a vial of holy water on my left arm, Holy Sir." Reece pulled up his sleeve and extended his arm. The skin was pale and covered with freckles and short blond hairs. "But I am not injured."

The Rocaan touched Reece's arm. The skin was smooth. "And they will not show up later?"

"They have always appeared before the Sacrament ended, Holy Sir. The last time so fast that I thought my entire arm engulfed in flames."

The Rocaan gripped Reece's elbow. "Help me up." Reece grabbed back and pulled. The Rocaan stood. His heart was pounding. This was precisely the thing that young Nicholas had warned him about. "You are certain that the vial contained holy water."

"A Danite handed it out at the service, Holy Sir. Andre took the vials from beneath the Sacrificial Table. Before service an Aud was replacing bottles. I assume that was your directive. We had discussed this, that all the water would be replaced."

"Yes, we had," the Rocaan said. He let go of Reece's arm. His palms were covered with sweat. He had been making the holy water properly. But that meant Matthias hadn't been. And Matthias had discovered one of the bloodstains. Just as the missing people in the palace had.

"Help me to my room," the Rocaan said.

"Yes, Holy Sir." Reece put an arm around him to brace him. The Rocaan leaned in, his mind already far ahead of his body. He would make a new vial of holy water. Then he would wake up Matthias.

They would settle this thing between them once and for all.

SIXTY-ONE

THE mist that the Weather Sprites had created left a dewy coating all over the Shadowlands. It also gave the air a chill it didn't normally have. The weird ground that was not really visible beneath the grayness was as slick as a newly laid marble floor. Jewel slipped once and caught herself before dropping the torch she carried. After that she walked as carefully as she could. She hoped her father would talk the Sprites out of experimenting again soon.

Odd magick, Shadowlands. The Sprites could normally create rain without much effort at all. But something in the Shadowlands itself prevented it, just as it had prevented the sunshine they had tried for days earlier.

Finally she found the building she was looking for. The Domestics, at Rugar's command, had hastily constructed a shed for the prisoners. The shed was small, and its boards were mismatched. She hoped the prisoners were tied or spelled, because it would take little effort for a man of Adrian's strength to break through the flimsy construction.

She opened the door and was glad that she had remembered the torch. Only Fire Domestics could have seen in this darkness. She placed the torch in the holder built high into the wall—almost too high; she hoped it wouldn't start the makeshift room on fire. The prisoners huddled together on the floor, blinking in the light. The close room smelled of unwashed bodies and excrement. No one was taking care of any of their needs.

"Have you eaten?" she asked in Nye.

The older man, Ort, grunted harshly and turned his face away.

"How—eat?" the boy asked. "When no—mouth, ah, toe? toe?"

"Tongue," she said, impatient with his poor language skills. "And he has a tongue. He just can't use it unless we let him. Of course, we could remove it permanently if he likes." And she smiled sweetly at Ort's back.

Adrian leaned against the wall, just watching her. His hair was plastered against his forehead, and his feet were braced against Ort's body. Apparently he too had noted how flimsy the walls were and had been trying to push them down.

She ran her gaze over him slowly so that he wouldn't miss her scrutiny. "And what did you plan to do when you escaped the shed? Stand where you think the exit is and beg someone to open it for you?"

"I would have thought of something," he said.

She leaned against the door frame, as much to avoid the stink as anything. She couldn't close the door. Four of them wouldn't fit in the shed. "Have you considered my offer?"

"You're treating us like animals," he said as if he hadn't heard her. "No one should be kept like this. We haven't had water since yesterday."

"Well, then you'll piss less, won't you?" she said. She shoved her thumbs in the waist of her pants. "I see our friend Ort is as rude as ever. The head of our Spell Warders has been asking for prisoners to use in his experiments, Ort. I suspect you would like to volunteer."

The man didn't move. He kept his face averted.

"No," the boy said. "Please. He—ah—means it not."

"He's a full adult," Jewel said. "He knows what he's doing. One thing you'll need to learn about life, boy, is that you can't protect others from themselves."

"As if you're so old and wise," Adrian said.

She stared at him a moment. He stared back. Nights of maltreatment and no food seemed to have strengthened him instead of cowed him. "You did not answer my question."

"You must want something from us desperately if you're willing to deal with me," he said.

She sighed, as if the conversation had been a trial, and grabbed the torch. "I am not desperate. You merely touched my heart the other day. I see that I was wrong about you. I will be letting Caseo know that he can have you. And I'm sorry, Luke. Caseo is not known for his kindness."

"*Papa!*" the boy cried in Islander. It was one of the few words she knew.

"I will, however, not tell him that you are all related by blood. It's the least I can do." She made certain that her smile was cold. Then she slipped out of the shed and closed the door.

As the latch snicked shut, she heard the boy cry out again, and then Adrian shouted, "Wait!"

She hesitated just a moment. If she opened the door, would she be playing it right? It probably didn't matter. The man was probably playing her, not allowing himself to bow too far to her whims, but not willing to jeopardize his son.

She pushed the door open and held the torch inside. Adrian had bent his tied legs so that he didn't touch Ort. "I'll talk to you," Adrian said. "But I want to see Luke free first."

"Nice try," she said. "But I am a woman of my word. I will set your son free if you talk with me and give me something worth his life."

Ort grunted again and shook his head. Adrian ignored him. "What would you consider worth that much? I already told you I don't know the secret to holy water."

"I thought perhaps the deal might jog your memory."

"I can't remember something I don't know."

"Then you have nothing to bargain with," she said. "I would hear what you have to say before I let your son go free."

Ort grunted louder and turned toward Jewel. Then he shook his head at her three times. She smiled at him. "You're not part of this," she said. "Attempt to influence this one more time, and I shall give you to Caseo right now."

Adrian was staring at her. His face was thinner than it

had been even the day before, and there were deep lines under his eyes. The decision had been weighing on him heavily. Ort watched him carefully, as did Luke.

"I—ah—may to speak him—ah—in Islander?" Luke said.

"No," Jewel said. "I want to hear anything you have to say."

"Please, lady. I no to speak Nye good."

She almost relented. But she couldn't trust the boy any more than she could trust the men. "No," she said.

The boy blinked away tears. "Papa, please. No. I—ah—I stay. With you."

"You're just a baby," Adrian said. "And there's no future here."

"Papa, please. Please."

Ort watched them both. Then he looked up at Jewel. The fury in his eyes was as palpable as a slap. She stared back at him, unwilling to let a prisoner get the better of her.

"All right," Adrian said. "I'll deal with you. On your terms. But with one change. I would speak to my son in my own language before he leaves. You can get someone fluent to listen in, if you want, I don't care. But I want him to be able to talk with me."

It was a reasonable request, particularly with someone listening in. "Done," she said. "But you must realize that your son may not go free. Your information has to be worth his life."

Adrian swallowed. "I know that."

Ort turned his head away and leaned his forehead against the wall. Jewel crouched in front of Luke. "Luke," she said, "I promise you that I will listen carefully to your father and make a sound decision. I know Ort believes that I will listen and then betray my promise. But I will not do that. And neither will you. I want you to understand this: if your father and I set you free, you must recognize that the Fey can be fair. You must speak to that. Is that clear?"

The boy glanced at his father. Adrian nodded once. Then Luke nodded hesitantly.

"I trust you will explain anything he didn't understand," Jewel said to Adrian.

"If you give me the chance," he said.

"It depends on your information." She leaned toward

him and untied his legs. She wasn't quite certain where she would take him. She didn't want him in her cabin again, not after that meeting with Caseo.

He shook his feet as if to shake the pain away. She put a hand under his elbow and helped him up.

"I'll be back, Luke," he said. "Don't let Ort cause more trouble."

"Yes, Papa." The terror on Luke's face made Jewel's heart twist. She had never seen a people so unused to the ways of war. On Galinas all of the nations had warred with each other. The history of every country from Nye to Alarro was a history of wars.

She helped Adrian out the door, trying not to wince at his odor. Finally she decided to take him to the Domestics. Someone could clean him off while she waited.

She pushed the door closed and secured it. Then she led Adrian to the Domicile. He watched the ground as he walked, as if he couldn't believe what he was walking on. But he said nothing. She led him up the stairs and knocked on the door, unwilling to drag him into the hospital wing when he was this dirty.

Mend, the Domestic who answered the door, looked as haggard as Adrian. She was tiny, her skin unnaturally pale from being so long away from the sun. Her hands were bent and callused from all the work she had had to do. Even though she was a mildly talented Domestic, she was one of Jewel's favorites because she worked so hard.

"I have a prisoner here, and I need him cleaned and placed in an empty room," Jewel said.

"We don't have empty rooms," Mend said.

"Oh, I think you do," Jewel said. "I'll take care of that part, if you get him cleaned without unbinding him."

Mend nodded. She took his arm and led him to the side of the building. Jewel watched for a moment to make certain everything was under control, and then she went inside.

The seven Infantry in the beds were looking better. One was even propped against pillows. The Healers had been working hard. They had sent a group into the forest to pick herbs, hoping that there would be the right ones on the Isle. Apparently there were.

Jewel nodded at them and went down the narrow corridor. When she reached the first room, she pulled it open. It was small, as she had hoped, and filled with weavers. Threads were scattered everywhere and looms clicked and hummed. The weavers looked at her expectantly.

"I need the room," she said. "I'm sorry."

They nodded as a unit, as if they were used to being thrown from the place they were in. But they did not move right away.

"Take things with you if the magick requires that they not be touched by anyone but you," she added. "I'm afraid I will need the room right away."

Then she closed the door and stepped out, allowing them privacy to finish their spells and to collect their work. From the infirmary one of the men moaned, and the sound sent a shiver through her. Maybe she was making a mistake allowing this man's son free. These Islanders, for all their naïveté, were adept at harming Fey, something no other people could claim.

Behind her the door opened and the weavers emerged, most carrying their wheels. They walked down the corridor away from her, as if they had a specific place in mind to reestablish their workroom. She waited until they were gone before entering the room.

Wool bits littered the floor and the air still had the taint of magick. She loved Domestic magick. It felt so normal, so warm. The air sparkled with it because it was always used to make something better instead of to conquer something. If she had it to do all over again, she would have learned Domestic skills instead of fighting skills. Not that either of them would do her any good. She was a Visionary, and Visionaries belonged in the military or in government. Only a select few became Shamans, and she—even as a young child—had not had the compassion for that.

Only two chairs remained in the room, set near each other as if waiting for two occupants to have a conversation. Something about Domestic magick allowed them to know these sorts of things, to put out the right clothes, or make the right meals, or make the rooms they were in feel just right. It was that talent she envied more than anything else. Even the ability to see possible futures did not allow her to be that sensitive to other people's needs.

There was a knock on the door. She turned, but it was

already half-open. Mend stood there, her hand on Adrian's arm. His clothes were cleaned, and he looked refreshed despite himself. And that awful odor was gone.

"Thank you, Mend," Jewel said softly. "I can't tell you how much I appreciate it."

Mend nodded and blushed just a little as she let go of Adrian's arm. His hands were still bound.

"Come in and sit with me," Jewel said.

He walked forward, his back straight, his movements confident. Mend watched him cross the room as if she, too, were fascinated with him. Then she saw Jewel's gaze on her. Mend smiled, backed out of the room, and closed the door quietly behind her.

He reached the chair and sat. She sat across from him. They were so close that their knees almost touched. "All right," she said, not willing to waste any more time. "What do you have to offer me?"

He swallowed hard, his Adam's apple bobbing. She could feel his nervousness, but his gaze never wavered. "Myself," he said.

"I already have you," she said. "I want something worth that boy's life. Worth his future. And I warn you, Adrian. Don't play with me."

"I'm not playing," he said. "You have my body, and at best, you can offer it to your devils for experimentation. But you do not—and will not—have my mind."

She smiled. "You underestimate us. Just because we have been kind to you doesn't mean that we can't take what we need."

"If you could do that," he said, "you would not have taken me at my word about holy water. You would have done what you could to pull that secret from me."

"I thought you said you don't know anything about it."

"I don't." He smiled. "But you didn't even try your techniques to see if I was lying."

"How do you know that?" she asked. "Magick is not flashy. It's something fine and subtle. Something that seems as natural as breathing, at least to us. Can't you feel the magick in this room? The weavers were here, doing their work. There are magick traces here. Can you feel them?"

His mouth opened a little and then closed. He obviously hadn't felt them. Most nonmagickal beings had no real sense of how magick worked. "So," he said finally. "Why aren't you going to get the information from me any other way?"

"Information voluntarily given is often more valuable and more complete," she said. Then she leaned forward and put her elbows on her thighs. "What do you offer me, Adrian?"

"Myself," he said again, his voice calm and steady. "In service to you until the end of the war."

"And what do you offer that we can't get for ourselves?"

"Intimate knowledge of the Isle and its people."

"No battle plans, no magick formulas. Just information about the way the system works?"

He nodded. His Adam's apple bobbed again. He was nervous, although he was trying hard not to show it.

"Until the end of the war," she said, leaning back. Her chair squeaked with her movements, and bits of wool floated in the air. "What if the war doesn't end?"

"Beg pardon?" he asked.

She smiled. "There are border clashes between L'Nacin and Oudoun that have lasted for centuries. This could do the same."

"Centuries," he repeated. "There isn't room on this Isle for a war that lasts centuries."

"You'd be surprised," she said. She placed an arm on the chair back, making her body look as relaxed and comfortable as possible. "You are, what? Twenty years older than your son?"

"Twenty-five," he said.

"That means that he will, in theory, outlive you by twenty-five years." She pretended to consider that. Then she shrugged one shoulder. "I will accept nothing less from you than your life in exchange for his. You advise us on matters Islander. You teach us the secrets of your homeland and keep us apprised of all that we should know, and you do so until you die. Or until your son dies, whichever comes first."

"My life?" This time he let the anguish show on his face. Such a choice. She wasn't sure she would make it. "For my son's." He took a deep breath. "What happens if we win the war?"

"You won't," she said. "The Fey will never allow it. You

may win battles, as you did with the First Battle for Jahn, but you will never defeat us. We will fight you until there are none of us left. And even then the Black King will probably send reinforcements. You will never win."

He looked a bit startled at her vehemence.

"I mean we want you for the duration of your life. Nothing less." She smiled at him. "And if you lie to us, even once, your son dies. And if you lie to us after your son has children, his children die. We are ruthless, Adrian, especially with people who cross us."

"How would you keep track of him?"

"We have our ways," she said. "We will know where he is each moment of the day. This can be of great benefit to you. If there is an attack, one of our people will protect him. And his children, when the time comes. But if you fail us, he will die. We do not give second chances."

"My life."

"For his." She took her arm off the back of the chair. "You get the better part of the bargain. Your life is shorter. We will give him an extra twenty-five years of protection if you live out your normal life span. If you cheat us and kill yourself, of course we will kill him."

"Do you have that great a need for my knowledge?"

Shrewd man. She liked that about him. "No," she said honestly. "We have a need for your interpretation. Ways a culture work are easy to discover. Understanding why it works that way is sometimes very difficult."

He looked away from her, at the point in the wall that would have had a window if the Fey had seen any point in installing windows in Shadowlands. He was not a young man. He understood what he was giving up. She could only hope that his love for his son was strong enough to make this kind of deal possible. An inbred knowledge of the culture would provide more than even a Doppelgänger could.

"What do I have to do?" he said.

"You will live in the Shadowlands, with us," she said. "You will be available whenever any of us wants you."

"And my son?"

"I will make sure he leaves Shadowlands today. You may watch if you like."

He still wasn't looking at her. His jaw worked, and he

blinked several times, hard. Then he swallowed again. "When do I see him again?"

"You won't," she said. "You will be with us now."

His head whipped around, his hair flying, his eyes flashing. Again, she was astonished at the power of Islander expressions, as if their emotions were somehow stronger than hers. "No," he said. "No. I won't work with you under that term. I don't care what you do to me. If I can't see my son, I won't work with you."

"You will not see him," she said. "We cannot let you out of here, nor can we let anyone else in."

"No," he said again. "I will not work for you for twenty years only to discover that you killed my son five minutes after you set him free."

A point she hadn't thought of. Not that it made any difference to her. She had other uses for Adrian's son. "You will see him once a year, then," she said, "in a prearranged time in a prearranged spot. You will always be accompanied by one of us, and you will speak Nye or Fey unless one of your guards is fluent in Islander."

He blinked, apparently startled at her easy concession. She stood before he could recover and think he might be able to get her to concede other points.

"And that is all. Have we a deal, Adrian?"

He looked up at her. Emotions warred across his face. He opened his mouth, closed it, then shut his eyes as well. He bowed his head and sighed. When he looked up again, his lashes were wet. "A deal," he said softly.

"Good." She went to the door. "I will have Mend return to untie you. We will find suitable clothing for you, and a place for you to stay. I will make sure she brings you a meal."

"Wait!" Adrian said. "I would like to spend the last few hours with Luke."

"I understand that," Jewel said. "But I will not have you giving him ideas, and I don't have someone to supervise you yet. You will have a chance to talk to him before we set him free."

She pulled the door open.

"You realize," he said low and deep, "that if anything happens to Luke, I will kill you. Not anyone else. Just you."

She turned back to him. He was staring at her with an intensity she had never seen before. Hatred. Pure, deep, and unabashed, just as Ort's had been. Only unlike Ort's, Adrian's felt personal. Didn't he realize that she had helped him? She could have got what she needed without setting Luke free. She could have coerced Adrian, or more likely, Luke himself. The information would not have been as comprehensive and detailed, but that had never stopped them before.

"I understand the passion," she said, keeping her tone level. "But I would warn you that if you kill me, my people will make certain that no drop of blood in your line remains to pollute the Isle. And once each and every one of your relations die—probably in front of you—then my people will turn their attention to you. We do not believe in quick death, Adrian."

"You have no soul," he said.

She smiled. "So they say. But I suspect that it is the other way around, for we are guided by our ghosts, and you must rely on stories told to you by old men. Perhaps that is why your 'holy' water kills us—because we have something inside that can be touched by the supernatural."

"I will work for you," he said, "but I will not like it."

"You don't have to like it," she said. "You simply have to do it well."

SIXTY-TWO

COULTER was talking. His baby voice rose and fell as if he were having a conversation. Eleanora heard excitement in his tone and a kind of joy, as if he found this conversation special. She sat up in bed and wiped a hand over her face. The room was dark, but a thin sliver of moonlight came in the window. The blanket had fallen to one side. She had been asleep for quite a while, but not long enough. She felt groggy.

The baby conversation continued. He laughed, a wonderful soprano trill, followed by the pat-pat of baby hands applauding. How odd. He always slept through the night. He had ever since they'd come there, when fear and exhaustion had overwhelmed him. Sometimes she thought he went through deep grief for his parents, but the others told her he was too young for that. Still, she remembered the feelings: the anger, betrayal, and sadness all mixed together. For the first few months of his life with Eleanora, Coulter had been a difficult child. She had soothed that away by making him the center of her world.

He cooed, and then she woke up enough to remember the cat. She let out an exasperated sigh. She had kept the door to Coulter's room closed, and her door open, thinking the cat would come to her. But there was no cat in sight. And Coulter sounded awfully loud for a baby talking behind a closed door.

She pushed the wisps of gray hair off her face, careful not to pull any. She hated the way her hair had got thin in the last few years, the way she could feel her scalp through the strands. Sometimes she wondered if she would live long enough to bring Coulter into adulthood, and she prayed that she would. He needed someone who loved him, needed to be cared about. And she needed to be valuable in the last years of her life.

Coulter laughed again. Not a dream, for sure, then. That baby was probably playing with the cat.

Eleanora swung her feet off the cot Helter had made for her and adjusted her nightdress. The cabin was cold in the middle of the night because she let the fire go out. She always wrapped the baby well and made sure he was comfortable before putting him down. She didn't plan on his playing in the moonlight.

Still, the thought made her smile. It pleased her that Coulter had become such a happy child. It meant she was doing something right.

The wooden floorboards were cold. She stood, feeling the ache in her bones that had become more and more common. She was eating well now, but somehow that only made her ache more, as if the additional weight in her body put too much pressure on her legs.

The darkness in the room did seem odd. It took a moment for her to realize what was different. Her door was closed. She never closed her door.

She crossed the rag rug and pulled the door open. The door to Coulter's room stood open, and she heard him clap again, little giggles making him hiccup.

He had not done this before.

She felt chill, trying to tell herself it had to do only with the cold night air. But something was wrong here.

The cabin was too small to have a real hallway. Her door opened into her room, as did Coulter's, and the doors faced each other at the edge of the living area. There was no way the cat could have accidentally closed one door and opened the other. And Coulter's bed had bars around it, thanks to Helter. The boy couldn't have got free.

She almost called out Coulter's name, then stopped. No sense alarming the boy, especially when he sounded so happy. She stepped into his room, and froze.

The moonlight streamed through his window, making the room almost as bright as day. Coulter stood up in his bed, his little hands reaching through the protective bars. He turned to Eleanora and smiled, joy radiating from his face.

A woman stood next to his bed. She wore a shift that was too short for her. Her feet were bare, and her hair hung down to the middle of her back. She was tall and slender, and had an unusual grace.

Eleanora didn't have to see her eyes to know the woman was Fey.

"Get away from my child," Eleanora said.

Coulter's baby face puckered in confusion. He obviously hadn't expected the anger in Eleanora's tone.

"Oh?" The woman's voice was light, airy, and musical. "He's your child? I didn't think Islanders could have children so late in life."

"He's my child," Eleanora said. She took a step into the room, her fists clenched. The death of Coulter's parents still haunted her nightmares. "Your people killed his family, and I saved his life. I've raised him. He's mine."

Coulter hiccuped again, and his lower lip jutted out. He was going to cry.

"I think he's something quite special," the woman said.

"Yes, he is," Eleanora said. She took another step into the room. She wasn't quite sure what she was going to do. The woman was young and supple and, being Fey, could probably kill with a single touch. "Stay away from him."

The woman laughed, a throaty, almost purring, sound. "You think I would hurt him? I'm not a Foot Soldier. My magick is nothing so crude as that. No, this child is valuable alive."

Eleanora's heart was pounding hard. "This child is valuable because he's an individual. And he is mine."

A big tear ran down Coulter's cheek. He sniffled and clung to the bars. Eleanora had never seen him cry this way. It was as if her anger raised something in him—a memory, perhaps? It couldn't be the woman. He had been laughing with her.

"I know he's yours," the woman said, keeping her tone level. "But I want you to give him to me."

"What?" Eleanora gasped the word.

"Give him to me," the woman said. "I will raise him with the same love and care that you would give. I will teach him things that he can do, things he could never learn from you. You're an old woman. You will probably die before he can live on his own. And then what will happen to him? Do you think that neighbor of yours is enough of a Rocaanist that she will take in a stray child?"

This woman had been watching her. She had been watching them all.

"He's my child," Eleanora said again. "He loves me. He's had enough disruption in his life. He can't afford more."

Another tear ran down Coulter's cheek. He gripped the bars as if they held him in place.

"The child needs more than love," the woman said. "He needs knowledge of his abilities and power."

"What abilities?" Eleanora asked. Maybe if she kept the woman talking, she could figure out a solution to this. Maybe someone would notice voices coming from her cabin and bring help. Maybe she could catch the woman off guard and get her away from Coulter.

"He has a magick all his own that brought me to him, and that I can feel even now. Most of you lack that magick and have no idea how to train it."

"He's a baby," Eleanora said. "Babies always have magic."

"Not like this," the woman said.

Coulter gave a shuddering sigh and hiccuped in the way that precluded a major yell. *Go, baby, yell all you want,* Eleanora thought to him, wishing he could hear her. *Yell so loud that we'll get help.*

"I want you to give him to me," the woman said.

"I can't," Eleanora said. "I watched you kill his parents. How do I know you won't kill him?"

"You have my word," the woman said. "I would not harm a hair on his beautiful head."

"Word? Word?" Eleanora's voice rose. "How can I believe that? You people have invaded us, murdered my friends, ruined our homes. How can I believe you won't hurt my child?"

Coulter screamed and both women jumped. He started to sob, deep, yelping sobs that seemed to come from the depth of him.

Eleanora ran to him and scooped him up, holding him against her chest as she had done when he was a baby and she was hiding him from the Fey. He grabbed her with all of his strength, wrapped his tiny legs around her body, and clung to her neck. His tears soaked through her nightdress.

She put her hand on his small head, protecting it, and ran from the room. She couldn't hear the woman following her, only her own footsteps in the front room. As she opened the main door, the cat shot out of the house and ran down the steps. Eleanora followed, her balance precarious as she cradled Coulter.

The cat blocked her way. She nearly tripped over it and extended a hand to keep her balance. Coulter gripped her tightly, not screaming anymore, his little body shuddering. The moonlight caught the cat at an odd angle, making it seem bigger than it was. Eleanora regained her footing. No. The cat *was* bigger. It was changing, quickly, like a rain cloud turning into a storm.

Then the woman stood in front of her, in place of the cat. She was naked. Eleanora screamed, and Coulter clung even tighter. The woman reached for Coulter, grabbing him around the waist and tugging. Eleanora kicked her, and the woman wrapped her leg around the one Eleanora had used to brace herself, then pulled Eleanora to the ground.

She wrapped her arms around Coulter as she fell, hoping she could protect him. She felt the woman's hands beneath her upper arms, warm against her skin. As Eleanora hit, the air left her body, and she heard something snap. Her arms loosened, and the woman pulled on Coulter. He cried out and grabbed harder.

Eleanora screamed "No!" as she scrambled for a good grip on her baby, but the woman unhooked his hands and pulled him away. He kicked at her and started to wail. "Maaaaaaaa!" he cried, his baby voice high and fine. "Maaaaaaaaa!"

Doors opened around them. She heard Helter's voice over her son's screams. She tried to stand, but couldn't. There was a deep pain in her chest, and another in her right leg. She screamed for help.

The woman cradled Coulter much as Eleanora had done. She pressed his face against her bare shoulder, muffling his cries. He did not hold her. His little arms reached around her neck, his hands open and grasping.

"She's stealing Coulter!" Eleanora cried. "Please, help!"

Helter ran down his stairs, and she heard others follow. The woman glanced over her shoulder once, at Eleanora, a look full of pity, and then loped across the clearing.

Coulter screamed, his high, angry, frightened scream. She pushed herself on her elbows, ignoring the pain in her chest. "No!" she cried. "He's mine!"

But the woman didn't seem to hear, or if she did, she didn't notice. She crossed the moonlight field with the speed of a cat. The men were far behind her.

"Stop her!" Eleanora shouted, but no one seemed able to catch the woman. As she reached the edge of the clearing, Coulter wriggled his head free. He screamed for Eleanora, his gaze on her, his face pleading, and his tiny hands reaching for her.

Then the woman bounded into the woods, and Eleanora could see Coulter no more.

The men hurried after her, feet crackling in the underbrush. She could hear them from this distance. The woman could probably hear them even better. They would never catch her.

Eleanora lay back on the ground, her throat raw from screaming, the feel of Coulter's frightened grip still imprinted around her neck. *Don't let him die*, she prayed to whoever was listening. *Not after all he's been through. Please. Don't let him die.*

SIXTY-THREE

RUGAR had to admit the scene was affecting. He stood at the opening to Shadowlands, near the Meeting Block, Jewel and Burden beside him, two Domestics on the other side, and four Infantry near the door itself. The young male prisoner stood in front of the door, his father at his side. Rugar still wasn't sure if he approved of Jewel's bargain—he believed they could have got the information another way—but her point was that they hadn't yet. It was better to have a source inside the Shadowlands, especially one who had a stake in being honest.

Jewel looked haggard. She had been looking tired for weeks now, complaining of the grayness in Shadowlands, but the last few days had taken their toll. The fight with Caseo, and then the work with the prisoners, had exhausted her. And the night before, staying up all night with the Domestics and Spell Warders to make certain that the boy had the proper links to Shadowlands, had tired her even further.

The spells sounded good. They had enchanted him just enough and wove a linking spell into his hair, so that they could find him at all times. The Warders had done the linking spell over Caseo's objections and had made it general enough that no one Warder owned it. That way, if they all died before the prisoner did, a new generation of Warders could still track the boy.

The boy had no idea he had been spelled. He ate and slept the night in the Domicile while the Fey cleaned him up. Jewel negotiated with the Dream Riders to weave dreams for him, dreams that he would confuse with memories, so that his experiences as a prisoner would be more pleasant. She let them add her into the dreams in a more important role, since the boy was of an age with her. Rugar had initially opposed that, but she told her father that she wanted the boy's link with Shadowlands to have several layers.

Until these last few weeks in Shadowlands, Rugar hadn't realized that his daughter was so devious. In her fight with Caseo, in her approach to him, and in her treatment of the prisoners, she reminded him of her grandfather. No wonder the Black King had been so angry when Rugar had wanted to bring her to Blue Isle. None of Rugar's other children had ever shown the kind of manipulative thinking and powerful sense of self that Jewel had.

The two Islanders were talking softly in their own language. Jewel had found a Fey who understood Islander to translate. Rugar could understand none of it. Jewel was listening intently to the translation, her mouth curving downward as she did. Rugar put his hand on Jewel's arm. "Enough of this mawkishness," he said.

Jewel nodded once; then she glanced at him. "It would work better," she said, "if you stopped the proceedings instead of me."

It would look as if he had the power, as if she were trying to stop him. He understood the game, but he never quite knew how to think up twists for himself. Perhaps that was why his father was relieved to see him go. With Rugar out of the way, someone with a more devious mind could rule the Fey.

He stepped forward and clapped his hands.

"In Nye," she reminded him softly, so softly that no one else could hear her.

"Enough!" he said, his Nye harsh and accented. He never could lose the accent, which always annoyed him. He had a mind for warfare, not for the delicacies of speech. "Any more of this talk and the boy stays."

The boy actually shot Jewel a mooncalf look, which his father, fortunately, did not see. The father had turned toward Jewel almost in supplication, but Rugar spread his feet and crossed his arms, staring down at them so that no one would argue with him. The father nodded once, although the movement seemed to be against his better judgment, and drew his son in close.

The boy's expression was equally sad. It wasn't as if they would never see each other again. Islanders—their sentimentality would be their weakness.

"Burden," Rugar said in Nye. "Escort the boy to the edge of Jahn."

Burden left Rugar's side and took the boy by the shoulders, easing him away from his father. The father grabbed the boy's arms as if he would not let go.

"Adrian," Jewel said softly in Nye. "We had an agreement."

The man caressed his son's arms as he let go. Then he bit his lower lip and watched as Burden took the boy to the Circle Door. Burden chanted the opening spell for those without the ability to open the Door on their own. The Circle appeared wide and beckoning. Through it Rugar could see the black bark of the trees, the green of the forest floor, and a bit of blue sky. The scent of evergreen flowed in on the wind.

Burden stepped through the Circle Door, pulling the boy alongside him. The Door shimmered as the boy stepped through. The father took a step forward as the boy went through the Door. One of the Domestics grabbed his arm and held him in place. The Circle Door closed, and the man turned to Jewel.

"I'll keep my part of the bargain," he said in Nye, "but you'd better keep yours."

"I keep my word," Jewel said.

"I hope so," the father said. A Domestic took his arm, and he followed her to the Domicile. Jewel and Rugar remained beside the Meeting Block.

"I hope you haven't made a mistake," Rugar said in Fey.

"I expected something from him," Jewel said. "This was

rather mild. I thought he might leap through the Door with his son."

"And then what would you have done?" Rugar asked.

"Kill them both," Jewel said without any emotion at all. Rugar glanced at her. She wasn't just the Black King's granddaughter. She was also his daughter. That ruthlessness was his.

Rugar smiled and put his hand on her shoulder, wishing for a moment for the closeness he had seen between the Islander father and son. Such affection had never been his way. "You've done well," Rugar said.

"Thanks," Jewel said. She put her hand on top of his. As she did, the Circle Door opened. Rugar turned. He could feel the sudden stiffness in Jewel's shoulder. They both expected Burden to come back in to report a problem with the boy.

Instead Frill and Ipper stepped through. Frill was a boy who was so slender as to be almost frail. Ipper had been spying for Rugar since Rugar had taken his first command. He had the thickness of age, but a grace that the younger boy did not have. They were both frowning as they came through.

Rugar took his hand off Jewel's shoulder. "Have you messages for me?" he asked.

Ipper nodded. "Is there somewhere we can talk?"

So the messages were not simple ones. Rugar sighed. He had been hoping for simple. Just an acknowledgment that the Doppelgängers were in the religious center would have been enough.

"My cabin," he said. "Jewel, you'll come with us."

He led the way. The muscles in his shoulder were tight. They had been tight all year, and his stomach was growing more and more upset. He was tired of all this concern, all this lack of control. It was time that things turned in the direction of the Fey.

When Jewel reached their cabin, she bounded up the steps and opened the door. A faint odor of woodsmoke met them, even though the fire was out and the cabin dark. Jewel awoke the Fey Lamps as Rugar pulled out chairs. Ipper shut the door.

"All right," Rugar said. "What is it?"

"Tel disappeared," Frill said. He straddled the chair nearest the door, his long, sticklike legs extended before him.

"Disappeared?" Jewel asked.

Frill nodded. "He was supposed to meet me at midnight. I waited until dawn, when Ipper came and got me. Tel never showed."

"Any possibility that you were in the wrong place or had the wrong time for the meeting?"

"We set up the meetings with Solanda before she left on her jaunt," Ipper said. "Unless you believe she could get her information wrong."

Rugar smiled. Solanda had a memory that was long and detailed. He knew that from personal experience. "She never gets her information wrong."

"Quest showed for our meeting," Ipper said. "And he had news."

"Does he know the secret?" Rugar couldn't keep the excitement from his voice.

"No." Ipper pulled out his chair and sat down. "And his news wasn't promising."

"Oh, dear." Jewel sat as well.

Rugar continued to stand. He would hear this all out.

"Quest managed to get into the Tabernacle, but he wasn't able to become a Black Robe with a high rank. He figured he could get into position to do that better from the inside. The problem is that only two of the Black Robes know what's in the poison—and they're the ones who create it. They must touch it at all times. He isn't even sure he can become one of them. He's afraid he will die right away."

"He's checked this information?" Rugar asked. "He's sure that his person doesn't have the information wrong?"

"Oh, he's sure. All the religious types know that learning the secret to the poison is one of the perks of that job. It is as if a Fey can switch his magickal talents as he becomes more experienced. It would be as if I learned Visions or how to be Solanda." Ipper sighed. "I think, since Tel didn't appear, that he tried to become one of the Black Robes and died."

"Otherwise he would have been able to come see us," said Frill. "He knows better than to miss a meeting. He hasn't since we've come to Blue Isle and I've worked with him."

Rugar swore under his breath. Of the six Doppelgängers he had brought along, three had died in that Tabernacle. Two had died in the palace. One remained at risk in that Tabernacle and might be dead even as this discussion took place.

"Papa?" Jewel said. Someone had been speaking to him.

"Sorry," he said. "Thinking."

"Forgive me, sir," Ipper said, "but I'm thinking we should get Quest out of there. If he can't learn anything without dying, then he's not going to be of value to us."

"I can't think of a better place to have him at the moment," Rugar said.

"But he's the only Doppelgänger we have left," Jewel said.

Rugar frowned. The anger had come back, thick and strong. He hated being trapped there. He hated being at the mercy of the Islanders' poison. He needed to think his way out of this, but in a year of trying, he had come up with very little.

"When are you meeting him again?" Rugar said to Ipper.

"Tomorrow," Ipper said. "He hoped he would have better news for us then."

"Did he have a plan?" Rugar said.

Ipper shook his head. "Only that he would observe the two Black Robes who make the poison and see if it was a part of them. If it wasn't, he would meet me in his new form."

Rugar let out his breath slowly. It seemed nothing on this island was easy. "If he is in his new form, he will know the answer to the poison, am I right?"

Ipper nodded.

"If he's not, he will have trouble or die getting the information." Rugar glanced at Jewel. She was watching him intently. "When you meet him tomorrow, have him come back to Shadowlands."

"No matter what?" Ipper asked.

"No matter what." Rugar templed his fingers together. "If we can't discover the secret to the poison this way, at least we'll know who to torture to get it."

SIXTY-FOUR

IT had been weeks since Alexander had been out of the palace. The wind ruffled his hair, and a strand fell in his eyes. He had borrowed one of Nicholas's leather thongs to tie it back, but his hair was shorter than his son's, and it didn't stay as well.

He wore the breeches and tunic of his guards in an effort to be inconspicuous. Lord Stowe worried that the Fey might try to assassinate Alexander to weaken the morale of the Isle. While that might have been a serious crisis a year before, it wasn't now. Nicholas had grown into his role as Prince, and he was ready to become King. If anything, Alexander's death would rally his people to fight the Fey even harder.

Still, he went everywhere with a contingent of guards. Since he was going outside the palace this afternoon, the guards were all around him. Some had even been planted along the route. Just once he wished he had the freedom to go where he chose when he chose. But he did not. He was valuable, not just to himself, but to Blue Isle.

The keep was located at the back of the guards' quarters, on the other side of the palace gate. The keep itself was isolated from the rest of the town by a row of trees, planted in a square around the building. Guards stood inside that grove of trees, watching the entrances anytime there was a prisoner. The punishments were very harsh, since the guards used this building to discipline their own.

When Monte had come to him saying that they had a Fey prisoner whom Monte did not want to bring to the dungeons, Alexander's senses went on alert. Any captured Fey disappeared in captivity—or, if they lacked the ability to do that, they found a way to kill themselves. No Fey prisoners taken in any of the battles and skirmishes had come back to Jahn alive.

Nicholas had wanted to interrogate the prisoner himself, but Alexander wouldn't allow it. He had heard that the Fey could charm and enchant, and he suspected that such a thing had already happened to Nicholas when he'd met the female Fey the day of the invasion. Nicholas, because of his youth and inexperience, might be too susceptible to this kind of magick. Alexander shouldn't be interrogating the prisoner himself, but he wanted to judge whether the prisoner was bluffing or not. Alexander planned to maintain as much distance between himself and the prisoner as possible.

When he reached the keep, he found Monte waiting for him at the door. Alexander handed one of his guards a vial of holy water and kept his distance while the guard tested Monte. Then Monte nodded, and Alexander followed him, stepping inside.

The building smelled of sweat, fear, and urine. Torches hung from the wall more than an arm's length between each door. That meant that the big oak doors were cast into darkness. Sometimes, through the small slit carved eye level in the door, he could hear rustling as prisoners moved in the straw or cried for help. The keep had five prisoners now, not counting the one Alexander was coming to see. Two of the five had been imprisoned for theft in the palace itself, one was in for dereliction of duty, and two for attempting to desert their position in the guards when the Fey invaded. Privately, Alexander had understood that desertion: they had both claimed that they wanted to make certain their families were all right. But the King's guards all took an oath which put their God and King above their family, and so abandoning their posts was a serious crime.

The other fifteen who had done the same thing had

already been executed. These two Alexander could not quite finish punishment on: both were so young and innocent, they reminded him of Nicholas.

Monte took him down a corridor he had never been in before. It twisted past the first row of cells, toward the back of the keep, where the ancient torture equipment was kept. Finally Monte stopped in front of a door. He took a torch from its peg, handed it to one of Alexander's guards, and bade the guard stay away from the prisoner. Then, using the ring of keys attached to his belt, he unlocked the heavy oak door and went inside. After a moment Alexander and two of his guards followed.

Alexander took a deep breath. He had not been close to a Fey since that girl over a year before. She had frightened him with her fierceness and certainty. Even though she had been his prisoner, he had had the feeling that she was stronger than he was.

This cell was shaped differently from the others. The floor was made of stone. There were pegs on the walls beside the door. Monte used his torch to light the other torches.

The additional light revealed another structure inside the room. A square area had been blocked off with bars, and there was another door with a lock in that square. Also inside were a pile of straw and food and water. The room smelled faintly of urine, but due to the room's size, the odor wasn't as bad as it had been in the corridor.

A small man stood just inside the bars, with his hands wrapped around them. He watched the contingent as they came toward him. Alexander was stunned at the man's size. He had always thought that Fey were tall and thin. He had not expected someone shorter than he was, and much heavier, although he noted that the heaviness was due to the little man's stocky build, and not to fat.

"I don't remember this room," Alexander said.

"It is, I believe, the first room built in the keep." Monte smiled and set his torch on a peg. All of the pegs were way out of the prisoner's reach.

Alexander turned to the little man and asked in Islander, "What's your name?"

The little man answered with a guttural word that Alexander didn't quite catch. That was a good sign. The little man wasn't trying to hide his knowledge of the language.

Then the little man smiled. "The translation in Nye means 'Scavenger.' "

Alexander told him how to pronounce "scavenger" in Islander, and the little man practiced for a few minutes, delighted at the sound. Alexander stood in front of the bars, out of arm's reach, and watched the little man.

He had that same upswept look that the woman had had, only on his square face it looked as if someone had sketched in his features too quickly. His eyebrows were dark and rode like wings onto his forehead, a Fey trait. His black eyes snapped with intelligence, and his cheekbones were so high that they made his cheeks concave. His skin was paler than any Fey's Alexander had seen before, and his clothing was covered with brown stains. He had an odor to him that was faintly suggestive of death.

Alexander clasped his hands behind his back. "Monte tells me that your own people tried to kill you. He says you want protection from us in exchange for information. It sounds to me like the perfect setup on the part of your people: to get us to trust one of you and to have you betray us all."

The little man, Scavenger, stopped laughing. He pushed as close to the bars as he could get and peered back at Alexander. "Who are you?" he said. "Clearly someone important. Those men beside you act as if you're worth all the land in the world."

Alexander wasn't going to identify himself. "I'm the last person you're going to talk with. And then we'll decide what to do with you."

Scavenger sighed. "Once powerless always powerless," he muttered. He leaned his forehead against the bars. "Look, I'm going to be honest with you. Things can't get much worse than they are now. I can't go back to my own people, and your hospitality leaves a bit to be desired." He looked up, his dark eyes glittering in the light. "My people don't need someone as inept as I am to spy for them. We have Doppelgängers."

He said the word as if Alexander should know what it meant. This was going to be a long afternoon. "Doppelgängers?"

"Fey who can mold themselves into one of you folks. There were three in the palace area that I knew of."

Alexander's mouth went dry. He remembered the look of terror on Stephen's face, and Nicholas's voice: *He's not Stephen. If he was Stephen, he would not need to be frightened of the holy water.*

The little man smiled at Alexander's silence. "Ah, I see you've met one of them." His smile grew. "They are able to kill, of course, but only in the process of changing bodies. Which makes them great spies and terrible assassins. In case you were wondering how you managed to stay alive with vipers in your lair."

Alexander *had* been wondering, but he wasn't about to let the little man know that. "Who are the three?"

"I know them as"—he said three words Alexander did not recognize—"which means Quest, Tel, and Silence. I have no idea who you would know them as. That could change from day to day. Have you found any odd bones lying around or perhaps a few puddles of blood? Those are the traces a Doppelgänger leaves, especially one forced, due to circumstances, to clear the area of change quickly."

A shiver ran down Alexander's back, and he straightened his own posture to make certain his unease did not show. At least one Fey in the Tabernacle, and three in the palace. The idea terrified him. "How many Doppelgängers live on Blue Isle?"

"About six," the little man said, "unless some of the youngsters came into their magick, and had Doppelgänging ability."

Six. Six could have done a great deal of damage in a year's time.

The little man gripped the bars tighter. The smile left his face. "See how valuable my information can be?" he said. "I suppose you haven't seen a stray cat around here, have you? She is one of our most gifted Shape-Shifters. They claim to be the most perfect Fey, although I have my doubts about that."

Alexander cleared his throat. "I haven't asked for this information. Why are you telling it to me?"

"Because I want you to believe I am sincere," the little man said. "I want you to know that we are on the same side. I have no home with my former comrades. I thought I might get a home with you."

"A home?" Monte's voice held surprise. Alexander held up one hand for silence.

"What do we get if we allow you to live in our midst?"

"My knowledge of Fey magick and hierarchy," the little man said. "I know everything you need to know about how to fight them."

"We seem to be doing quite well on our own," Alexander said.

The little man shrugged. "Until they discover the secret to your poison. Then they will use all the information they have gathered and destroy you."

"Threats don't scare me," Alexander said.

"It's not a threat," said the little man. "It's the truth. I have lived through the Nye campaign. I know the history of my people. We do not lose."

"Then what happened here?" Monte asked.

The little man's smile was back. It touched his lips but made his eyes seem empty. The look sent more chills through Alexander. "You have won the battles, but the war continues. We are Fey. We do not quit until we have won—at all cost."

"That's not what I'm asking," Monte said. "You say your people do not lose, and yet you have been trapped here for a year, with no reinforcements, and no way of defeating our holy water. That seems like a loss to me."

The little man sighed. For the first time he seemed rattled. "It is unusual, I will admit. And that is why they are taking desperate measures. They begin with lowlifes like me and will progress upward. They are trying to determine what makes your poison work. They were going to pour some on me to see if I survived. They figured I would, because I have no magick."

"Do you believe that would happen?" Alexander asked.

The little man shook his head. "Would you take that risk? Would any sensible person? I know of two Red Caps who did not return from the First Battle of Jahn. This tells me that they died, and Red Caps are never in the middle of the fighting. We do all our work after it is over."

"What work is that?" Alexander asked.

"We strip the bodies of useful parts," the little man said.

Bile rose in Alexander's throat. "You decapitate people?"

"Nothing so crude as that. We strip the skin, muscle, and

blood tissue from the bone. But the victims are already dead. The bodies would rot anyway. And our Spell Warders use the parts in spell development. Children use some parts as they gain their magicks. It would be a waste to allow such good material to rot."

Alexander couldn't speak through his shock. The little man seemed so calm about all of this, as if it were normal. Apparently it was for him. Alexander couldn't even imagine what it was like doing that kind of job, let alone believing it was necessary.

"That shocks you," the little man said.

Alexander glanced at Monte. Monte looked away. Neither of them liked how perceptive the little man was. "What do you gain from coming to us?" Alexander asked. "If we win against your people, you will have no way to return home. And if we lose, you will be killed for betraying them. We have a different culture, different beliefs, and we could just as easily slaughter you here. Now."

The little man smiled. "I gamble on your lack of aggressiveness. I also know, from your actions, that your lack of knowledge about the Fey will eventually lead to your death, if not the death of your people."

"You seem confident of that."

"It takes little to be confident of that," the little man said. "You didn't know you had spies in your midst. How close did one get to your person, Your Highness? For you are the King, aren't you? No one else I have seen in this city has such a protective retinue."

Alexander started, although he struggled to suppress the response. If this perceptive man was one of the lesser Fey, how clear-sighted were the real Fey?

The little man's smile grew. "I am adept at seeing power, Your Highness, because I lack it. Not all of my colleagues are as gifted. Most of them rely too much on their magicks. Since I have none, I rely on myself. It hasn't gotten me anywhere, except to this place, but at least it works."

Alexander had to act quickly to regain control of the conversation. "The only kind of knowledge I care about is knowledge that will help me defeat the Fey quickly."

"Then you are a fool," the little man said. "Because you might have all of your plans in place to defeat them, only to learn that your most trusted advisers are Fey themselves. It has happened to more than one King in more than one difficult battle."

"None of those other leaders had the advantage of poison, which all of my advisers touch before they are even allowed in the room with me."

"Such advantages can disappear overnight," the little man said. "And if they do, they leave you with nothing."

"If I choose to let you work with me," Alexander said, "what happens to you when we are done?"

"Depends on what you want me to do," the little man said. "But what I ask for is this: that you set me up with a home among your people and that you then allow me to live a normal life. No more corpses, no more intrigue. Just a simple home with a bit of sustenance and a future."

It sounded reasonable. Alexander was about to open his mouth to agree when Monte said, "You are our enemy. You have the look of the enemy. Many of our people have lost family and friends to your people. You will not gain a peaceful life in Blue Isle no matter what you do."

"Then you place me among those who would understand what I have done, and you guarantee my personal safety."

"It would not be comfortable," Monte said.

"You think I'm comfortable now?" the little man snapped. "I shred corpses so that I stay out of the way of those more 'gifted' than I am. No one speaks to me except other Red Caps, unless they have an order for me. They house us in a different part of camp. They do not let us near their children for fear we would pollute them. If we talk back, as I have done, they encourage the Spell Warders—not obviously, mind you, but encourage nonetheless—to use us in their experiments. More Red Caps die in times of peace than in times of war. We have no value to them at all. At least here I would have a bit of value. I might enable you to save Blue Isle."

"But you would still live apart," Monte said. "You will still threaten the children."

Alexander put a hand on his arm. "We have never had an outsider move into Blue Isle and attempt to be one of us. We have had Nyeians here, and they are treated with courtesy. We have the example of our Roca, who did not kill his enemies, and we have a religion that preaches compassion.

Perhaps, in these circumstances, Scavenger will do better on Blue Isle than he will with his own people."

Monte started to respond, but Alexander squeezed Monte's arm. He didn't care if his assessment was right. He merely wanted to convince the little man that it was.

"If you help me," the little man said, "I will tell you what you need to know."

"You know how to defeat your own people?" Alexander asked.

"It is not as simple as one single blow," the little man said. "But with knowledge of all the tricks, you would have a much better chance."

Monte started to speak, but Alexander touched his arm. "All right," Alexander said to the little man. "We will work with you. But for now, we shall keep you under guard, and you shall work on my terms. Is that clear?"

The little man pressed closer to the bars, as if the information pleased him. "It is very clear," he said.

"Good," Alexander said. "Monte, I want you to find this man quarters with a real bed. I want you to make certain he is fed and comfortable. I also want him far away from any curiosity seekers or any other unsuspecting souls. Keep a large contingent of guards around the building, so that he will know that he is still a prisoner and under our control."

He turned to the little man. "We shall move you to a better place, and you and I will talk again. You are not to share any information about the Fey with anyone but me. Do you understand?"

"Yes, Sire," the little man said.

"I did not give you my title," Alexander said. "Do not presume."

"Sorry," the little man said. "I do want you to know, however, that I appreciate your efforts."

Alexander turned away from the little man, his guards closing in around him. "Come, Monte. We have other matters to discuss."

He left the room and stepped into the hallway. The air was fresher there, and not as close. He did not wait to see if Monte was behind him. Instead, he went down the hallway and to the front door of the building. He let himself out and took a deep breath, glad to be away from the stench.

The little man had frightened him, not so much in looks,

although the fierceness hidden in those whimsical features seemed a part of the Fey aggression, but in perception. The little man saw too much. If he was, indeed, to help the Islanders, that perception would be valuable. But if he was lying so that he could spy, such perception would help the other side.

Working with the little man would be a risk. But Alexander would take a risk if he had to. This was the opportunity they needed.

SIXTY-FIVE

THE baby was crying and struggling. Twice his little feet had caught Solanda in the ribs. She was glad she had taken him at night, because he was not wearing shoes. Shoes would have done damage.

She was on the path outside Shadowlands. The day was dawning pink on the horizon, the sky barely visible through the gaps in the leaves. She had lost somewhere in the woods the men who were chasing her—she was able to move more silently than they were, even though she couldn't change into her feline form. But the baby had nearly alerted them several times. He had cried out only once, and she had jammed his face into her collarbone. The pain must have stunned him—it stunned her—because he did not cry again. Indeed, he did not move again for such a long time that she feared she had hurt him.

If only the old woman had given Solanda a few more moments. Moments in which to wrap the child in some clothing, to grab a blanket, and to get some clothing for herself. Instead, she escaped the cabin in her feline form, and when she became a woman again, she found she had left the shift somewhere in that meager house.

Her own nakedness bothered her less than that wail. It

would haunt her dreams. She should have killed the old woman instead of letting her live to see the boy taken from her. But Solanda hadn't had time. The cries had drawn the others, and they had nearly caught her.

Solanda's breath was coming in small gasps, and near the fork in the path she had gained a stitch in her side. The boy had gone through one of his periodic struggles—he seemed to believe that he would be better off on his own toddling feet than in her arms—and she had had to grip him more tightly than she wanted. She hoped she hadn't bruised him: the Domestics would yell at her. But she was never cut out for motherhood or carrying children, and the fact that the Powers had entrusted this infant to her annoyed her.

Yet she had to follow the magick.

She stopped to catch her breath. The breeze was cold, and she was frozen except where the warm child pressed against her. The boy shuddered too, but she kept her arms wrapped around him. She had tried, for a while, to capture his tiny feet with one of her hands, but he had braced himself on her and tried to push off, so she'd had to let go.

The boy shoved her hard with his fists until his upper torso pulled away from hers. He peered into her face, the light of dawn illuminating his small features. She hadn't believed anything that young could feel anger, but she couldn't read his expression any other way. His brow was furrowed, his lips pursed, and his eyes blazed. If he had had more than a smattering of baby talk, he would have ordered her to take him back to the old woman.

Solanda was of half a mind to do so. Her job had never before called her to witness someone else in pain. She usually did a quick spy job, or let the others know the leaders' plans. She always went into areas where no other Fey could go, and sometimes she seduced families, rulers, or soldiers. They always took her for a pet and confided in her. Then she left them, with no blood involved.

"Mama!" the little boy said, the Islander word clear. The tone was a command, not an inquiry. He knew that the old woman was his mother, and he wanted to go back.

"No," Solanda replied in the same language. "You're coming with me."

"No!" the little boy shouted, and pounded on her with his fists. They connected with her breastbone and sent a lot of pain through her. She hadn't realized that toddlers were so strong.

She grabbed his fists with her free hand and held them against his own chest. "No," she repeated, then pulled him against her body, a bit more gently this time than the last.

Then she took a deep breath and stepped off the path. The sooner she got rid of this little bother, the better.

The grass was wet against her feet, and she flinched at its chill. She wanted nothing more than to be warm again. She pranced across it, using cat skills, touching as lightly as she could. The oddness of her movements seemed to catch the boy's attention; he stopped wriggling in her arms and held on as if he was afraid she would drop him.

As she got closer to Shadowlands, the stench of rotting flesh floated on the cool air. The child sneezed and pressed his face against her skin. She wrinkled her nose. She had hoped the Red Caps would be finished by now.

The Ground Circle was as she expected it. No one stood outside it. The Red Caps were probably working closer to the river. Tiny lights indicated the circular opening; they seemed faded in the growing daylight.

She held her breath as she stepped into the clearing. A deer was feeding on a nearby tree. When it saw her, it startled and ran off into the woods, its hooves crunching the underbrush. The child clung to her even more tightly. Something about the clearing seemed to spook him.

Her arms were getting tired. She pried him off her shoulder and balanced him on her left hip—as much for his protection as for relief for her muscles. It was said, although she thought it a superstition, that anyone who went into Shadowlands with his eyes closed would never see real daylight again. Somehow she wanted more for this child.

The boy saw the lights revolving in a circle, whimpered, and buried his head in the soft flesh of her breast. She pushed him away, holding him so that he could not cover his eyes again. Immediately they filled with tears. She looked away.

Her footprints left a shiny path in the dew. She stepped over the Ground Circle, put out her hand, and felt the warmth of the Circle Door. A tear plopped on her left thumb, followed by another, and another. The tears rolled into her palm before falling onto the dirt. She glanced at the boy. He had put one finger in his mouth, the tears streaming down his face. He was not snuffling or even sobbing. The tears seemed to be as natural as breathing.

But much more unnerving. It was as if he knew where she was taking him, and knew he would lose something precious if he went. She glanced at her footprints in the dewy grass, to the sunlight hitting the trees, and the path beyond. She could take him back and leave him in the clearing near the old woman's house. They would think it merely an odd incident.

Or they would think him enchanted and kill him as the Nyeians had done with any children taken by the Fey during that war.

This magick child could not die.

She held him carefully so that he couldn't lean against her; then she stepped through the circle. The lights warmed, then burned her skin, as they always did. The boy screamed as they passed through, a high, wailing scream, not of pain, but of fear.

And then she was inside, in the mist and the grayness that was Shadowlands. No one stirred. The air was warmer there, and stuffy, with a touch of woodsmoke that would probably vanish if a wind came up. The mist was thick around her feet, but it warmed them instead of chilled them. The Meeting Rock was empty, and the cabins had that closed look that buildings gain when their inhabitants are sleeping within.

The boy's scream ended as suddenly as it had begun. He buried his face in her arm and began sobbing, hard, steady sobs as if she had broken his heart. She didn't need this any longer. Whatever tie she had felt with the child had been broken once she went through the Circle Door. She was supposed to bring him there; she had done that. Now she needed to return to her usual routine.

With a sigh she headed for the Domicile. They would know what to do with him. He grabbed her nipple with one hand, making her bite her lower lip to hold back the pain. With the other he grabbed a handful of hair and tugged. The little brat was punishing her for bringing him inside.

When she reached the Domicile, she knocked loudly. The baby's grip tightened on her breast, and twisted. She bit back a cry of pain. No one answered her knock, so she pushed the door open.

She had forgotten that this door opened into the infirmary. She was surprised at the moaning Fey in the beds. Fey who got injured in battle usually died. But they were used to fighting experienced warriors. Perhaps more Fey lived through these battles because the Islanders were so inexperienced. The room smelled of pus, sweat, and urine. Two of the men on the beds looked up at her; the rest continued to moan as if she hadn't arrived. She closed the door and let the building's heat warm her.

Dello came out of the back room. Her clothing was rumpled, and her long black hair was slipping out of its braid. She had lost weight since the arrival on Blue Isle. Her cheeks were gaunt and hollow. She stopped when she saw Solanda.

"You stole a baby?" she asked, her voice flat and soft. Baby theft was the bane of adult Shape-Shifters. Their bodies never stayed constant enough to nurture a child within, so they stole children. But often they stole babies from other Fey, not from the people they were fighting. Beast Riders, Foot Soldiers, and Weather Sprites were the ones who stole from the enemy.

"Get this boy off me, would you?" Solanda asked.

Dello came over and delicately removed the boy's tight fist without touching Solanda's breast. "He's Islander," she said in wonder.

"I'm not so sure," Solanda said. She unhooked the boy's other hand and passed him to Dello. The boy immediately started to sob. "He hasn't slept all night, and I haven't had a chance to feed him. He also misses the woman who raised him."

"His mother?"

"His mother is dead."

Dello frowned at her. "We have no facilities for children here."

"I know," Solanda said, "but we have people who know how to raise them. Let's put him in good temporary care, some Sprites, maybe, or someone else who won't die in a battle."

One of the men had propped himself up. He wasn't

wounded that badly, because he was staring at Solanda's naked form with appreciation.

Dello's lips tightened. She patted the baby gently, soothing him.

Solanda glanced at her breast. It was red and marked with welts from the boy's fingers. Served her right, she guessed. If she could get away with a kidnapping so easily, then she was as lucky as she thought she was.

"Is there anywhere I can get some food—and some clothes? It's cold out there."

"You shouldn't be talking to me," Dello said. "You should be talking to Rugar."

Solanda crossed her arms. She hated it when someone quoted the rules to her. She wanted to make it through this short stint in Shadowlands without seeing Rugar at all.

"He'll have to know about the child," Dello said, anticipating Solanda's response. "You might as well tell him now. It's better than having him ambush you about it when you least expect it."

She had a point, and Rugar's temper could be fierce with someone who did not follow the rules. The man was still watching her. She could stand it no longer. She sighed and then slipped into her cat form. The warmth of the fur enveloped her even as the body changed. The boy watched her from Dello's arms, his tears forgotten. This trick, at least, fascinated him.

Solanda didn't say anything as she hurried out the door. Once outside, she paused. She probably should have said something to the child. But he was too young. It didn't matter to him if she followed the niceties of life.

Unlike Rugar. He would hate this.

A few more people stirred in Shadowlands. She saw a couple more Domestics going about their morning tasks, although how they could tell it was morning was beyond her. The mist was almost to the level of her chin. She scrambled as quickly as she could, then climbed the steps up to Rugar's cabin.

The wood was wet and slick. How had they created the mist? Or was Shadowlands deteriorating again? It had scared her when it had deteriorated the first time. She thought about changing into her woman form to knock on the door, then changed her mind. She butted her entire body against the frame, as a real cat would.

A sleepy Jewel pulled the door open. Her hair fell straight down her back, and she wore a woven wrap that had a faint scent of cinnamon.

"I need to see your father," Solanda said. "I also need clothes, and some breakfast."

Jewel stared at her for a moment. "Yes, it's nice to see you too," she said. "I was wondering where you had got to. Of course I'll get my father for you. And here, a wrap."

She took hers off and dropped it. Solanda wasn't able to move quickly enough, and the wrap landed on her head. The smell of cinnamon was overpowering. She poked her face out in time to see Jewel striding naked into the corridor.

Solanda made a small huff of disgust. Then she crawled from underneath the wrap and closed her eyes, putting on her woman skin. The air grew colder as she felt her limbs stretching. Finally the change ended. She opened her eyes, grabbed the wrap, and wound it around her.

The cinnamon indicated a spell for extra warmth, something she was profoundly grateful for. She stepped inside to see Jewel, dressed in another wrap, cross the hall and knock on a different door.

The cabin was plain. A fireplace graced one wall, and a table with food and stools for chairs nearly filled the room. Quite a comedown from Rugar's place in Nye. He had taken over a bank building there, slightly smaller than his father's, and had used the vault for a bedroom.

Solanda picked a slice of bread off the table and took a bite. It tasted a bit stale. She didn't care. She hadn't eaten since the day before.

Rugar came out of the back room, Jewel at his heels. He was rubbing his hand through his hair in an attempt to comb it. He had pulled on a pair of breeches, but his chest was bare. She was surprised at the flatness of his belly, and the muscles lining his chest and sides. She had always thought Rugar a bit soft: a man who talked about fighting but who had never done any himself.

"What's so important that you had to wake me up?"

"I woke *you* up," Solanda said, taking another slice of

bread and breaking it into small pieces. "Not your daughter."

Rugar gave Jewel a pointed glance. She shook her head as if she could not believe what Solanda had said, then disappeared down the hallway.

"I wanted to tell you what I've done before the Domestics did," Solanda said.

"The Domestics?" Rugar sat down. He still looked half-asleep. With his left hand he picked up a pitcher and poured himself and Solanda water.

She nodded, then took a sip of water. It tasted good. "I brought a baby to them this morning. Actually, not a baby, really, more like an infant or a toddler. He has some language and he can walk on his own."

Rugar set his cup down. She had his full attention now. "Where did you get this child?"

"Near Daisy Stream. Apparently some of our soldiers killed his parents a year ago, and an old woman took him to safety. I brought him here."

"Whatever were you thinking?" Rugar asked. "What are you doing with an Islander's child? If you had wanted a child of your own, you should have told me. I think we could have resolved the problem without resorting to theft of an Islander."

"I don't think so—" Solanda said.

"I do. Do you know what this will do? They will come after us even stronger now. We're not just trying to kill their soldiers. We're going after their babies."

Solanda straddled a stool, unshaken by his anger. "Rugar, you should trust me."

"Trust you? You may have escalated the war without consulting me, and you ask me to trust you?"

"Yes," she said. She leaned forward until her face was inches from his. "That's precisely what I'm asking you. I have never brought you a child before, and when I have done something without consulting you, it has usually been right."

He moved away from her. "Usually."

"I'm right in this case," Solanda said. "That child called to me. I found his home, the one where his parents were killed, and then I tracked him."

"I thought you said his parents died a year ago."

She nodded.

"Then how—?" He stopped himself. She could tell from the look in his eyes that he had the answer. "It's not possible."

"It happened," she said. "He *called* to me. Not a conscious thing. I think he left a trail for his parents to follow if they had lived. Only I'm the one who followed it."

He crossed his arms. "The Islanders don't have magic."

"This little one does," Solanda said. "Which is probably why their holy water works as it does. They just don't acknowledge their powers as magick. They couch it in religion."

Rugar shook his head. "We would know."

"We do know," Solanda said. "We know very well. Our people have died for that knowledge. I think it is time we realize that we may not be the only magick people in the world."

"If they were magick, they would live differently."

"They live no differently from some of the Fey settlements. They have just incorporated magick into their life in an unusual way."

Rugar's frown grew deeper. "It doesn't seem like magick to me."

"It would if you look at this child," Solanda said. "He has a second voice, one I can hear in my head. I would never have found him if it weren't for that voice. And it developed young. He must have been in swaddling when he left that trail I followed."

"I don't like the implications of this," Rugar said.

"Just because you don't like it doesn't mean that it's not true," Solanda said. "I think you need to let the Spell Warders know they're working with a new kind of magick, and they need to figure out what to do with it. To neutralize it, perhaps, as they would a bad Fey."

"I'll see the child first," Rugar said.

Solanda shrugged. "Do as you want. I'm going to finish some of your bread, and then I'm going to get some sleep. If you haven't found any work for me by the time I wake up, I'm going back on the prowl to see what oddities I can find."

"I thought you wanted this child."

She shook her head. "I brought the child for you. I do

think he should be raised here. I don't think the Islanders should be allowed to have anything so powerful."

"What do you suggest that we do with him?" Rugar asked. "We can't use the powers of a baby to fight a war."

"Not yet," she said. "But we can use him in the future. And that's what you need to be looking toward, Rugar. You keep thinking this is an ordinary campaign, and it's not. The Fey will be on Blue Isle for a long time, and I, for one, will not spend that time in this gray and dismal place."

"We're safer in Shadowlands," Rugar said.

"Probably." Solanda took a sip of water. "But safety is never a consideration in war, particularly if you want to win."

SIXTY-SIX

HE felt like a thief in his own home. The Rocaan crept down the corridor, carrying a small lamp in one hand, a vial of holy water in the other. The lamp's light was faint, barely illuminating the floor and the wall beside him. He was shaking, not with exhaustion, which he felt in every ache of his body, but with fear.

The Rocaan should not be frightened of anything.

But he was no better than the people he decried. He was going to one of his Elders to see if the man had been tainted by enemies of his people. He was not acting like a Rocaan. He was acting like a soldier.

Only he couldn't help himself. He had to know.

The doors in the Elders' wing had locks, but the Rocaan had a ring of keys to open all of them. He was the only person with access to all of the rooms in the Tabernacle.

He stopped at the door to Matthias's chambers and rested his head against the door frame. He could change his mind now. He could ask Matthias what was going on.

And risk hearing lies.

All the talk of bodies and blood and bones had spooked him. Reece's comments about the tainted holy water had spooked him even more.

The Rocaan stood up and stuck the vial into his pocket. Then he took the key ring from his sash and quietly unlocked Matthias's door.

The Rocaan's heart was pounding twice as fast as usual. Sharp pains shot from the bottom of his feet to his knees. He needed rest, and soon. But he couldn't rest until this was all settled.

Matthias's chambers were dark. Light from the moon floated in an uncovered window, making all the furniture look like gray lumps. The Rocaan slipped in and eased the door shut so that it made no noise as it closed. The latch clicked, sounding like thunder in the quiet rooms.

Even breathing came from the secondary chamber. Coals in the fireplace there burned red, giving everything an orange glow. The Rocaan set his lamp on a table by the door, so that the minuscule light wouldn't awaken Matthias. Then he crept toward Matthias's sleeping room.

The Rocaan took the vial from his pocket and held it in his fist. His shaking had grown, as had his feeling that what he was doing was very wrong. It was against all his beliefs, against all that he had been taught. A man believed his friends and colleagues. He did not test them without their knowledge, especially with a test that might kill them in a horrible manner. A man did not even do a thing like that to his enemies.

The red glow in Matthias's bedchamber grew as the Rocaan stalked closer to it. As his eyes adjusted, he saw the bed, piled with blankets. Books and scrolls covered the floor beside the bed. Matthias was asleep on his back, one hand resting on top of the covers, his shoulder bare.

The Rocaan stared at him for a moment. He had sponsored this man. He had chosen him to become an Elder despite his youth and strange looks. The break between them since the invasion had been hard. It was difficult to remember that, on the day of the invasion, Matthias had been the Elder that the Rocaan had trusted the most.

His hand hurt because he clutched his fist so tightly. He was half-afraid the vial would shatter. He stood over Matthias, watching his chest rise and fall with each even breath.

It would be so easy. A single drop would tell him everything he needed to know.

But he would never be able to live with himself again,

and God might turn his Ear even further from the Rocaan than he already had.

The Rocaan reached out with his empty hand and touched Matthias's arm. Matthias started but didn't awaken. The Rocaan grabbed Matthias's wrist and shook it, whispering Matthias's name. Finally Matthias's eyes opened.

"Holy Sir, what—?"

The Rocaan put a finger to his lips, although he wasn't sure why he insisted on silence. "Get dressed, then come to the other room and talk with me."

Matthias nodded. He ran his hand through his hair—the curls were in complete disarray—and sat up.

The Rocaan hurried back into the main room. He used his small lamp to light a candle and then went from lamp to lamp, so that the entire room was ablaze in light. It was cold there. The fire had gone out in this chamber long ago.

He would tell Matthias what he had been thinking. If Matthias acted badly—although what "badly" meant the Rocaan didn't know—then the Rocaan would toss holy water on him. If Matthias acted well, the Rocaan would still insist on a test. Matthias would just have to understand.

When Matthias emerged from his sleep chamber, he wore a simple black robe and nothing on his long, slender feet. His hair was still mussed, and shadows under his eyes made them appear sunken.

"Is there an emergency, Holy Sir?" he asked. His voice was roughened from exhaustion. Matthias was probably as tired as the Rocaan. Only Matthias was younger. He could take the strain on the body better than the Rocaan could.

"Sit down," the Rocaan said.

Matthias chose a chair near the cold fireplace. The Rocaan sat in a chair opposite him. His legs protested, and he knew he would have trouble getting up.

"Forgive me," the Rocaan said, "but I would like to ask you to allow me to sprinkle some of my holy water on you."

"Certainly." Matthias extended his left hand. It was clean and well manicured. He did not shake as he held his hand in the air.

But the Rocaan did. He unstopped the vial and poured four drops of holy water onto Matthias's hand. The drops pooled in Matthias's palm.

"Do you want to say a Blessing?" Matthias asked.

"Do you need one?" the Rocaan said.

"Everyone needs one these days," Matthias said.

So the Rocaan murmured a short version of the Blessing over Matthias. The Rocaan's voice shook as much as his hands had. *He had been wrong. He had been wrong. He had not believed, and he had been wrong.*

When the Blessing was over, Matthias looked at him. "Am I to find out what this is about, or should I go back to bed?"

The Rocaan shook his head, although he knew Matthias wasn't certain which question he was answering. "I am sorry," the Rocaan said. "I needed to know."

Matthias picked up a small sword from the table, a sword that should have been on a chain or sash, and dipped it into the water in his palm. Then he rubbed the water over the sword, murmuring part of the Midnight Sacrament. When he was done, he put the sword in a small ceramic bowl and rubbed his hands together.

"Forgive me, Holy Sir," Matthias said, "but I would have thought that my work with the holy water would be enough to prove that I have not been touched by the Fey."

The Rocaan nodded. "So would I. But tonight I discovered that the holy water used in the Midnight Sacrament was not real holy water."

Matthias leaned back just a little. "And you knew you hadn't done that, so you suspected me. Are you sure of your source?"

"Very," the Rocaan said. He couldn't tell Matthias who or how he knew. No one else among the Elders knew of the peculiarity in the Cliffs of Blood. Another of the Secrets.

Matthias rubbed the sleep from his eyes. The movement was boyish. The Rocaan had forgotten how young Matthias really was. "Then we need to know if there is more than one vial," Matthias said. "I trust the one you Blessed me with is one you made yourself?"

The Rocaan nodded.

Matthias sighed. He ran his fingers through his hair like a comb, and this time the curls fell into place. "All right. Are you up to checking this out tonight? I think we need to know before Morning Sacrament."

The Rocaan's body felt as if it were about to collapse underneath him, but he wasn't going to admit that to Matthias. Matthias was right; they had to check this immediately, and the Rocaan wouldn't be satisfied unless he did the work himself.

He extended an arm. "Help me up."

Matthias stood and braced the Rocaan's elbow with his hand. The Rocaan stood slowly. The ache that he usually had in his feet and joints in the morning had arrived this evening. The stress that he suffered was affecting his body. He wasn't certain how much longer he could continue at this pace.

"We have no idea who could have done this," Matthias said. "We must trust no one else."

The Rocaan smiled to himself. At least he and Matthias were thinking along the same lines. And at least Matthias understood what had prompted the Rocaan's actions a few moments earlier.

"I brought a small lamp," the Rocaan said, pointing to the one on the table.

Matthias picked up the lamp. "Perfect."

He opened the door and helped the Rocaan out of it. They walked down the corridor in silence, the only sound the Rocaan's shoes whispering on the carpet.

They took a side staircase to the sanctuary. Matthias led them through the back chamber and into the sanctuary itself.

The sanctuary looked different in the dark. The sword hanging from the ceiling had the look of a wild thing swooping at them. The Sacrificial Table looked larger, and the pews seemed to extend forever into the blackness.

Matthias set the lamp on the Sacrificial Table. The scars in the wood became prominent. On the shelves beneath it, the glass vials gleamed.

"There are only a few," the Rocaan said. "They must be left over from the Midnight Sacrament."

He grabbed the table to keep his balance and reached for the vials beneath.

"Wait!" Matthias said. "You don't know if the liquid inside is something that might harm us. Let me do the dangerous work. There are ten Elders. You are unique."

The Rocaan hated the argument, but he agreed. He straightened, ignoring the protest of his back.

Matthias took a vial from beneath and unstopped the

cork. Then he sniffed loudly. The light flowed upward onto his face and reflected through the glass, distorting his features. His frown seemed ominous.

"It smells wrong," he said.

He tilted the vial and poured some of the liquid onto the same hand that had held the Rocaan's holy water earlier. "It feels right, though."

He leaned closer to the light, and the Rocaan leaned with him. The water was brownish and had bits of sediment. The first act of creating holy water was to strain any sediment from the water used.

"Well, we know what it's not," the Rocaan said.

Matthias nodded. "I don't want you to touch it," he said. "In fact, I don't want anyone to touch it except me. Then I'll wash my hands in holy water and see if something happens. I think I can take care of things from now, Holy Sir."

"No," the Rocaan said. "I will stay here. We need to get rid of this liquid, and we need to put some new holy water here for Morning Sacrament."

"It could be an all-night task," Matthias warned.

"Then we won't get any sleep," the Rocaan said. "I will make a new batch of holy water tonight and have an Aud bring it down. You can get rid of these vials however you please. I don't believe they should be reused. Then come to me when we're through."

"You have a suspicion," Matthias said.

The Rocaan nodded. "I think there are Fey here, and I think they're substituting something for holy water. I think that's why you discovered those bones and that blood. I think one of the creatures made a mistake and died."

Matthias shook his head. "If that was the case, then the Fey that I doused with holy water that day would have been reduced to a pile of bones and a pool of blood. I covered them with the stuff. They died, but still had skin. No. Those bones and blood mean something else. But I do agree with you. I do think Fey were here."

"It seems the only explanation, doesn't it?" the Rocaan said.

Matthias set a bottle next to the lamp. "I'm afraid it does. What are we going to do about that?"

"We have to do something." The Rocaan pushed away from the table. "And we have to do it soon."

SIXTY-SEVEN

DELLO stood over the baby, her stout frame guarding his cradle as if she were afraid Jewel would harm him. Jewel waited behind her, off to the side so that she could see the child for herself. Her father had seen him and had come back to the cabin angry. He had refused to talk with her, so Jewel had come herself.

The Domestics were keeping the baby in the Domicile until Rugar decided what to do with him. They had placed him in a room no bigger than a closet, with a cradle that was handmade. The cradle surprised Jewel. Someone had to have needed it. She was sure her father hadn't asked who, if anyone, was pregnant.

The boy was sound asleep, his eyes puckered and his nose red from too many tears. He was wrapped in a blue woven blanket decorated with comfort symbols. The magick in that blanket would keep him warm and calm—or calmer, if his distress was too great.

"It's all right, Dello," Jewel said. "I'm not going to wake him."

Dello didn't move from her stance over the cradle. "It's just that it took so long to get him to sleep. He cried as if his heart was broken. If I didn't think Solanda was right, I would say that we should take him back to the people who raised him."

"Right about his magick?" Jewel felt cold. She had somehow thought that Solanda was justifying her outrageous action. That would explain Rugar's reaction.

Dello put a finger to her lips. "Let's talk outside," she said. She led Jewel from the room. Jewel took one more glance at the little boy. He was pretty in a round sort of way. She had always thought of baby faces in terms of angles and slashes, but this human child had round eyes, a bow-shaped mouth, a tiny nose, and no cheekbones to speak of. Even though he slept, there seemed to be an energy radiating from his body.

She stepped into the hallway. Dello closed the door after her. "The child has magick," Dello said. "And it's odd magick, too."

"I thought children didn't have magick," Jewel said. "It doesn't develop for ten years."

"Shape-Shifters do," Dello said, "and others have potential. We just never discuss it—we don't want parental expectations to get too high. Sometimes all that a child will ever show is potential. The adult will have only glimmerings of magick. I don't believe that's what's going on for this child."

"Islanders don't have magick," Jewel said.

"Well, this child is not Fey, and he has magick. It's strong. And it's mostly confined to mental survival tricks at the moment. He can charm, and he can lay paths. I'm sure he laid one right to Shadowlands so that his people could find him."

"But they can't get in," Jewel said.

"If they have magick, they can," Dello said. "It's any magick, Jewel, or the knowledge of the chant. We have just not had to worry about other magicks before."

Jewel glanced at the door and bit her lower lip. Dello was right about that. There had been threats of other magick, but no real magick before. And if that was true, then Caseo would have a hard time discovering the secret to the poison. It might not be a poison, but something enchanted.

For all her egotistical ways, Solanda had seen this child clearly, and she had understood his importance to the Fey.

"Does Solanda want to keep the boy?" Jewel asked.

"I think she was happy to be rid of it," Dello said. "He certainly was glad to see her gone."

"Had she hurt him?"

"Not physically. But this child is extremely perceptive. He knew she had taken him away from home."

Jewel nodded. The idea of magick on Blue Isle had her reeling. She touched Dello's arm and thanked her, then went out the back door.

No wonder her father had been angry. He understood the implications as well as Jewel did, perhaps better. If there was another magick system here, one they didn't understand, then the Fey might not be the most powerful people in the Isle. The defeat that had been clouding their work since their arrival might be more than a fluke; it might be their future.

She detoured to Adrian's lean-to. When she allowed Caseo to take Ort, she had a Domestic clean the place. The Domestic cast a spell of cleanliness to get rid of its odor and found a bed, extra clothes, and blankets. Now the place was at least livable. Besides, all the bedding had been spelled as well, so that Adrian's desire to leave Shadowlands was tempered.

Jewel knocked, then pushed the door open. Adrian had a real lamp lit on the ceiling, and he was standing beneath it, putting on a shirt. He was already wearing pants, but his feet were bare.

"Where'd you get the lamp?" Jewel asked in Fey.

"I'm sure you didn't barge in here to ask me that," Adrian said in Nye. His Fey was improving, but not quickly enough. "But since you want to know, I asked for it. I found out how you make your lamps, and I figured I didn't want to live around the dying light of my countrymen's souls."

"How noble." Jewel switched to Nye also. She leaned against the door. "I have a question to ask you."

"And here I was hoping this was a social call."

"The sarcasm doesn't help you."

He smiled. "Ah, but it does. There is nothing in our agreement that says I can't express myself. I must only be truthful with you all."

Jewel hooked her thumbs on the waistline of her pants. In truth, she liked Adrian's sarcasm. It was an example of his spirit that she didn't want to see broken. "I want to know about Islander magick."

"Magick?" Adrian deftly tied the wrist thongs on his right sleeve with his left hand. "We have none."

"You know what will happen if you lie," Jewel said.

He stopped tying. "I'm not. I have been truthful every waking moment of my life in this dreary place."

"Then what do you call your extraphysical abilities?"

"We have none," Adrian said.

"None?"

"Of course not," Adrian said. "We don't turn into cats, and we don't conjure rooms clean, and we don't practice warfare with another culture's blood. We have no magick."

"We have twice discovered evidence of magick here," Jewel said, "and that makes it no coincidence."

Adrian sighed and slowly tied his left sleeve. "Look," he said in a measured tone. "If we have 'magick,' we don't know it, and we certainly don't use it. If some of our people practice magick, I have never been around them. It isn't part of us."

"What of your religion?"

"It always comes back to that, doesn't it? If you wanted an expert on Rocaanism, you should have kidnapped an Aud."

"We have you," Jewel said.

"And I know nothing about holy water, or magick, or any of that. I barely know who the advisers to the King are —and I have already shared that information with your father. Pretty soon you're going to have me teaching classes in Islander because I don't have any more information to share." He crossed his arms over his chest. "When you made a bargain like this, you should have thought about who you were pumping for information."

"It's not solely for information that we kept you here," Jewel said. "It's also for interpretation. Now, I've asked questions about magick, and you've dodged them. I want a straight answer."

"I have given you a straight answer," he snapped. "I don't know."

"Then interpret."

He uncrossed his arms and sat on the bed. "I don't have enough facts to interpret."

"You know what the poison does to us. That's magick. Now one of our people has found an Islander who leaves a mental trail. That, too, is magick. What do you make of it?"

" 'Beyond what we see, an entire world exists, a world beyond our understanding.' " He spoke in a half chant and smiled when he was finished. "The Words Written and Unwritten, the foundation of our religion."

She took a deep breath, about to curse him for being obtuse, when she realized that for all his sarcasm, he wouldn't risk lying to her. Not this early. Not with the memory of his son still fresh. "So you just accept things you don't understand as part of that unseen world?"

He nodded. "Unless we are taught that it should matter to us, we figure that we do not understand it. We leave it to God and our betters to make sense of such things."

"God and our betters." She frowned. "You have no curiosity at all?"

"Curiosity is a different matter altogether," he said. "We all have curiosity. We just never satisfy it."

"You have seen things like this before? Magick things?"

"I have seen things I don't understand," he said. "I don't understand why a people who have conquered half the world would want our small island. I don't understand why the sky is blue, or why storms rage strongest near the Stone Guardians. But I have accepted those things. They are all beyond my capability to change."

"Such a philosopher," she said.

He shook his head. "A realist. I will never learn the answer to all my questions. So I accept the fact that there are things I will never, ever know."

"And you said you weren't a philosopher," she said. "I have business to attend to. Are you sure you have nothing more to say on Island magick?"

"If I think of anything, Princess, you'll be the first to know."

"Thanks a lot." She closed the door and headed back to her cabin. The sensation she had had since she'd seen the child was building. A bit of terror mixed in with everything else. She hurried up the stairs to the cabin and opened the door.

Her father was inside, standing in his favorite spot beside the fireplace. He was holding Jewel's wrap, the one Solanda had worn earlier. Jewel knew that he wasn't thinking of her, but of the child and the knowledge Solanda had brought them.

"I tried to talk with Adrian," she said without greeting him.

"And what does he say about their magick?" Rugar crumpled the wrap in his hand.

"He says there is none. And so I challenged him on it, and he quoted some religious text to me about not understanding the world around them."

"Is he lying?"

She could sense the blood-thirst beneath Rugar's words. He wanted someone to pay for this new twist.

So did she.

"I don't think so," she said. "It seems as if they shrug off magick and grant the abilities to powers beyond them."

Rugar turned. He tossed the wrap onto a chair. "If they don't understand what they have, then they can't use it."

She shook her head. "They may have already found a way to use it without recognizing it for what it truly is. As they did with their poison. If they don't know what they're capable of, Papa, then neither do we."

He sighed, sat down in the chair next to him, and rubbed his eyes. "I've gotten us into quite a mess, haven't I?"

"Yes," she said. "And it frightens me."

He studied her for a moment. "Frightens you?"

Normally he would have ignored that sentence, but this time he focused on it. She felt a flush build in her cheeks.

She nodded. "If they do have magick, then the slaughter we suffered on the First Battle for Jahn was not a fluke. We could lose the entire force, and Grandfather would not be the wiser. He might not send anyone to Blue Isle for some years, but eventually someone would come. And more Fey would die."

"What should we do? We can't fight them one on one until we learn the secret of their poison."

She took a deep breath. He was going to hate this idea, so she braced herself for his anger. "If we discover the secret to the poison, we attack. If not, we negotiate."

"Negotiate?" His voice rose higher than she had ever heard it. "Fey don't bargain with their enemies, girl. Especially not when we were the ones initiating the battle."

She swallowed, hard. "I know. But sometimes we make agreements with a government after they have lost, and then break those agreements. We did it in Nye when we said they would have complete control over their local governments. And from what Grandfather said, we've used that tactic a number of times before."

Rugar brought his head up. His interest was obvious. "You're saying we should make an agreement and then break it?"

"Negotiate a peace," Jewel said. "We should do it in a convincing manner, so they think we might coexist here. If they don't want us to do that, they can give us the way out of the Stone Guardians, and we can go back to Nye. Then we can talk to Grandfather and attack when he's ready, after we have learned the secret to the poison."

"They would be fools to give us the way out of the Stone Guardians," Rugar said. "They would know that we would get reinforcements. The Black King would never suffer a defeat under his rule. It's a nice idea, Jewel, but not workable."

"I'm not done." The phrase came out harsher than she wanted it to, almost imperial. Rugar raised his eyebrows at her tone. Despite the urge to apologize, she didn't. "If they refuse to let us have the route, then we play the defeated people. We give them a show of faith—return the prisoners, turn in our weapons, something—and once we learn their secrets, once they're complacent, we attack again. This time we know their weak points, we'll probably have access to their King, and we'll win the Isle."

"You make it sound simple, Jewel."

"It is," she said.

He shook his head just a little. "Treachery is never simple. We have to keep this secret from most of our forces. Some might rebel. Then we have to watch for the right moment, the right time to attack. It might take years. Do you want to stay in Shadowlands for years?"

"Why won't you consider this?" she asked.

"I've already considered it," he said. "It's a nice idea, but not necessary. We will find the secret to the poison. Once we do, we attack. They'll surrender more quickly than any other people we've ever encountered. They're used to winning and haven't really experienced the pain of losing. They'll do whatever we want."

Jewel stared at him for a moment. She didn't remember him being this blind in the past. He had always been able to see a situation clearly, whether it looked like the Fey had an advantage or not.

"I hope you're right, Papa," she said. "I hope you're right."

SIXTY-EIGHT

ELEANORA'S ribs hurt so badly, she could barely stand. The fact that Helter made her lean on a pair of handmade crutches didn't help. Pier had made a splint and tied it to Eleanora's right leg, keeping her foot bent and off the ground. Her good leg was tired, and her armpits ached.

She had been waiting now most of the afternoon. Helter had wanted to take her to the palace, but he was told she wasn't important enough. Somehow he got her a meeting with one of the King's advisers, a Lord Stowe, in his home.

Lord Stowe's home was the size of a palace. Eleanora had never seen a house so big. It took up most of a block. Helter had wanted to come in with her, but she had asked him to wait outside. She had wanted to tell this story herself.

Helter had accompanied her to Jahn. He'd borrowed a friend's horse-drawn cart, which had bumped so hard against the ruts in the road, it had made tears run down her face. Helter had found lodgings for the two of them with a friend, and in the morning Eleanora had been so stiff, she couldn't move. Helter had offered to go in her stead, but she had come so far, and endured so much pain, she'd figured she could stand a little more.

She hadn't expected to be waiting in a room with furniture so ornate she was afraid to sit down.

Helter had taken her to the back door, and a servant had led her through the kitchen into a room that was the size of the cottage she had shared with Drew. The room smelled faintly of woodsmoke even though the fireplace wasn't in use. A pipe sat in a tray near an overstuffed chair. Someone liked spending time there.

The servant had bade Eleanora sit, but even after the servant had left, she remained standing. Furniture crowded the room, chairs against walls, tables and seating arrangements in the middle of the thick carpet. Her makeshift crutches caught on the nap, and she had to place one forward to keep from falling.

She leaned on the crutches and stared at the shelves, and the tiny things everywhere. Small carvings on the tables, a tiny silver sword built into one of the lamps, a painting of an elderly man over the fireplace. She had never seen so many possessions in all her life—and these were in one room of a huge house.

Finally the door opened. The man who entered was wearing breeches tied at the knees and a white shirt, and he had his brown curls pulled back behind his head. He was balding, and he had deep circles beneath his eyes.

"Good day, miss," he said. "I'm Lord Stowe. Your man said this was urgent."

She nodded. "I'm afraid I'm unable to courtesy, sir."

He looked her over, his tired gaze taking in her crutches and splint. His smile was sympathetic. "I completely understand," he said. "I hope you haven't been standing this entire time. I would beg you to sit."

"No, sir," she said. "I couldn't. I've been traveling in these skirts."

"I'd rather you muddy a chair than pass out on my rug," he said.

She flushed and sat on the red stuffed sofa. The sofa was hard, even though it looked as if it should have been soft. Aches grew in her body. She hadn't realized how very tired she was. "Forgive me for taking your time, sir," she said. "But I would hope you can help me."

"I will try." He sat in the overstuffed chair and turned it to face her, his hands folded in his lap.

"My child was kidnapped. The woman who took him was Fey."

Lord Stowe gaped, then recovered and closed his mouth. "Did someone see the woman? Are you sure the child didn't —forgive me—wander off?"

Eleanora bit her lip, then ran her tongue over the spot her teeth had touched. She decided to ignore his unintentional assumptions about her child-rearing skills. She took a deep breath, then looked away from him, studying her hands. They were gnarled and covered with spots. The hands of an old woman.

"This will sound crazy, sir," she said, "but I brought a cat in the day before. She looked hungry, and my boy liked her, and I gave her some leftover food and some water. It seemed all right. I've always shared with God's creatures and never had any trouble before. But in the middle of the night, sir, my baby woke me up. He was laughing. When I went into his room, a Fey woman stood in the moonlight wearing one of my shifts. She was playing with him. She said she would take him away from me, so I grabbed him and ran. He is just a little thing—he didn't weigh much, but I can't move very fast. The cat ran out ahead of me—and here's where it sounds crazy, sir—it changed into the woman, only this time she wore nothing. She was younger than I am, and stronger. She broke my ribs and my leg, and took my boy. Some of the men chased her, but they lost her on the trail. At dawn they followed her path as best they could. They think it led to the Fey place."

"Shadowlands?" Lord Stowe asked.

She nodded. The retelling had brought tears to her eyes.

"And you're convinced this was not a dream."

She brought her head up. He was holding the unlit pipe, turning it over and over in one hand. He appeared interested in her answer, again seeing nothing wrong with the question.

"Oh, no, sir," she said, keeping her voice calm. She had come to him for help. She had to remember that. "Others saw the woman, too, although I'm the only one who saw her change."

He nodded, brow furrowing. "How old was your boy?"

"A year and a half, sir."

"So he was not a Fey child." He muttered the last, as if he had been thinking it all along.

Her cheeks grew hot. "No, sir. The Fey killed his parents. I got him out before they could find him."

Lord Stowe set his pipe down. He pushed himself out of his chair and walked over to the fireplace, his back to her. "Do you think they wanted him for a reason?"

The memory came unbidden. The slender woman looking natural in the moonlight, her voice so confident, so sure she could treat Coulter better than Eleanora could. "She said he had magick. That if he grew up with her, he would learn how to use that magick, but if he stayed with me, he would not understand his power at all."

"Magick." Lord Stowe turned around so that he could see her face. He grabbed the back of the chair nearest him and leaned on it. "Are you sure he was born on Blue Isle?"

Eleanora nodded. "I helped with the birthing, sir. I knew his parents since their marriage, long before the Fey came."

"And his parents were Islanders?"

"His mother was born near Daisy Stream. I watched her grow up."

"And his father?"

"Was from the Snow Mountains, sir. He was a good man, very handy at wood carving. The Fey killed them on the day of the invasion, and I sneaked the baby away, or they would have killed him too."

Lord Stowe rubbed his chin. "They have an Islander whom they claim has magick."

He shook his head, then studied her for the second time. Somewhere in the last few moments he had come to regard her differently. She could see it in his face. She was no longer a poor woman, little better than a servant. She was someone who had lost a child.

"What do you want me to do?" he asked.

Tears filled her eyes. She thought her need obvious. "I want you to find him and bring him home."

He let out his breath slowly. In the silence she heard Helter's voice. *You're crazy, woman, to think the King will help you. You don't even know the boy is alive. For all you know, that creature killed him like his parents. Maybe they need to kill a whole family to make their own magick work.*

"It would take another attack on their homeland to find

the boy," Lord Stowe said. His voice was gentle. "I will have to speak to the King about this. I doubt we can risk the men."

"He's only a baby!" Her voice rose into a wail. She took a deep breath and calmed herself. "He's all I've got. He needs me."

A touch of red dotted both of his cheeks. Lord Stowe stood and came over to her, patting her shoulder. "We'll do what we can, ma'am," he said. She had been wrong. Her pain meant nothing to him. He saw Coulter's loss as a technical problem, unexplained behavior by the Fey.

"Please," she said. "Please help me."

He took his hand off her and stepped away. She felt his absence more than she saw it.

"I will," he said softly. Then he stared at her for a moment before speaking again. "I will send in one of my servants to help you up. We'll also find you an easier way home."

"Thank you," she whispered. She didn't look up. He wasn't going to help her. No one could.

His footsteps made the floor creak. She heard the other door open, but it didn't close. Finally she looked in that direction. He was still studying her.

"Have you heard of the Fey taking other children like this?" he asked.

"No," she said.

"Neither have I. It's peculiar, isn't it?" And with that he left the room.

Peculiar? Perhaps it was, from a lord's point of view. But from hers, the loss of Coulter meant the loss of everything. And she had no idea how to get him back.

SIXTY-NINE

VOICES woke him.

Tel had been sleeping lightly—it had taken him hours to settle down after the Midnight Sacrament. But the cot was comfortable when he put enough blankets on it, and after he'd built a fire in the bedchamber's fireplace, he had relaxed enough to sleep.

He strained to hear, and his Andre memories recognized the tones of Matthias and the Rocaan. Tel's mouth immediately went dry. The only way he would learn the secret of holy water was through those two, and he hadn't thought he would have a chance to be near them both so soon.

Tel threw back the covers and got off the cot, slipping on the black robe that Andre had always worn when he was going somewhere in the middle of the night. Only unlike Andre, Tel put on sandals as well. He didn't want to risk walking on anything dangerous.

He combed his hair with his fingers, then grabbed the small stiletto he had brought with him and slipped it into the pocket of his robe. The voices grew even closer. They must have been in the hall outside. He opened the door.

The corridor was wide and long, with no furnishings in that section, only paintings of previous Rocaans and Elders.

Matthias and the Rocaan stopped only a few feet away from Tel, and both looked guilty. The Rocaan carried a small lamp, which illuminated their faces. Matthias was carrying a tray of vials. Tel froze. He couldn't attack them. Not when they had the very thing that would kill him.

"I—ah—I heard voices," he said.

"Sorry, Andre," the Rocaan said. His voice was as warm as his gaze. "We didn't mean to wake you."

Matthias held himself at a distance. He didn't smile as he looked at Tel. Instead his expression was wary. "We didn't expect anyone to be up."

They spoke softly. The other Elders slept in that wing.

Tel felt the knife heavy in his pocket. He glanced at the tray of holy water, wondering if he could maneuver around it. "Is there a problem?"

The Rocaan started to speak, but Matthias shot him a warning glance. The Rocaan seemed to ignore it. "We discovered that the holy water in the sanctuary had been tampered with. We're replacing it."

Tel's entire body went cold. He slipped one hand into his pocket. If they accused him, he would attack them—holy water be damned. They would throw it at him anyway. He couldn't protect himself from them if they wanted to go after him.

"How did you discover it had been tampered with?" he asked. "Did something happen?"

The Rocaan shook his head. "Something didn't happen."

His remark made no sense in the light of anything Andre remembered. There was no physical reaction to holy water, except among the Fey.

"What do you mean?" This time he glanced at Matthias, who was watching him closely. "Was there Fey? I don't understand."

"You're not meant to," Matthias said. His tone was cold.

"Nonsense, Matthias," the Rocaan said. "He's an Elder."

"And we haven't touched him with real holy water all day. I'm not telling him any secrets. Would you mind a Blessing, Andre?" Matthias asked.

Tel clung to the stiletto. He didn't understand the level of menace in Matthias's voice. Did Matthias have a suspicion about who he was? "A Blessing would be fine," Tel said, hoping his voice wasn't shaking too badly. It would bring the other two men closer to him and would give him a chance to catch them off guard. Perhaps.

"You are not wearing your sword," Matthias said with a touch of rebuke. "You will need to get it if we're going to Bless."

With his free hand Tel touched his chest, pretending surprise that the sword wasn't there. Andre never took his off, but Tel hadn't wanted anything around his neck while he slept.

"I had taken it off because part of it snagged on a nail," he said. "I thought it had broken. I must have forgotten to put it back on. It's in the room. I'll go get it. Would you like to come in?" His entire body was shaking, as much with anticipation as fear. If he could get them into his chambers, he could get Matthias to set the tray down and move away from the water. He would slit Matthias's throat and use the blood to become the Rocaan. The old man wouldn't be able to move quickly enough to get away.

The Rocaan swayed a little, as if he could feel the dilemma that Tel was going through. The Rocaan touched Matthias's arm, careful not to upset the tray. "Forgive me, Andre," the Rocaan said. "But I think Matthias and I should finish this task first. We still need to check the Servants' Chapel, Matthias."

Matthias glanced at him. "You could stay with Andre and Bless him while I finish."

The Rocaan shook his head. He looked exhausted. The old man usually never allowed himself to go without sleep. It was a secret of his endurance. "I would like to finish the task myself."

Matthias sighed as if he didn't approve. He turned back to Tel. "Until later, then."

"Later," Tel said.

The two men came toward him. Tel opened his door. He loosened his grip on the stiletto and pulled his hand out of his pocket just as Matthias tripped and tilted the tray toward him.

Tel didn't have time to jump out of the way. Only one vial fell off, and he caught it in his left hand, the stopper still on. The glass felt cool against his hand. No burning. No sudden change. Nothing had spilled.

He could feel the panic bubbling through him, but he refused to let it overtake him until the others were out of sight. Keeping his hand steady, he replaced the vial on the tray. As he did so, he noted Matthias watching him carefully. Matthias had spilled the tray on purpose.

"Would you like some help, Matthias?" Tel asked. There were other ways to learn the secret of holy water.

"Sorry," Matthias said. "We've been at this all night."

"I appreciate the offer of help," the Rocaan said, "but it would take longer to teach you than it would to get the task done. We will see you at Morning Sacrament, Andre, and I will do the Blessing afterward."

"If he comes to Morning Sacrament, there's no need for a Blessing, is there, Holy Sir?" Matthias asked.

Tel's heart was pounding so hard, he was surprised it hadn't smashed a hole through his chest. Did they know? It seemed as if they did.

The Rocaan sighed. "Thank you, Matthias. You are always looking after me."

"I try, Holy Sir," Matthias said. He looked over his shoulder at Tel. "I'll see you after dawn."

"Until the Sacrament," Tel said. "Good night, Holy Sir."

"Andre."

And with that they walked off down the corridor. Tel slipped into his chamber. He closed the door and leaned against it, near collapse. He hadn't been that frightened in all his life. He had nearly died out there.

Maybe he would die. Maybe they had changed the formula somehow. He picked up a flint. His hands were shaking so badly, he could barely get a spark. But he managed, and he lit the lamp near the door. Then he stared at the palm of his left hand.

It looked no different. From what he had seen in the battles, the victim died almost immediately. The change was sudden and devastating. His palm looked normal. Nothing had changed.

He closed the hand into a fist and took a deep breath. They didn't know, but Matthias suspected something. After all, Tel had been the one conducting the service. Maybe he should have noticed something unusual with the holy water. If the Aud reported that Tel had ordered it brought down, they all would know.

He made himself take a deep breath and think. Auds didn't talk to Elders unless asked a direct question or unless they were performing a service. In all of Andre's years in the Tabernacle, an Aud had never approached him with tales of another Elder. He was probably safe on that one.

But the difference in holy water. He had thought no one could tell. So had Andre. Obviously there was a secret he didn't know. The switch wouldn't work again. He would have to figure out a new way to protect himself.

Especially since he had only an hour or so until Morning Sacrament.

Tel pushed away from the door and wandered to one of the couches. There he perched on the edge, rested his elbows on his knees, and reviewed what Andre remembered of the Morning Sacrament.

In many ways it was the same as the Midnight Sacrament. Only the message was different, and he didn't need to concern himself with that. He had to concern himself with the holy water. And since he wasn't conducting the ceremony, he wouldn't have to touch the vials—only one, the one passed down the pew in which he sat. The Danite would remove the stopper and then each worshiper would dip their cloth into the water and use it to wipe the sword. With the stopper already removed, he couldn't fake the movement.

Or could he?

No one cared about the color or type of cloth used. That kind of strict regulation had been banned by the Fifth Rocaan when he'd realized that his parishioners all had differing economic circumstance. Rather than ban them from worshiping, he loosened the regulations on the symbols carried by those parishioners.

Any color cloth. And black would not show a water stain.

Tel took a deep breath. It would be risky—his entire position there was risky—but he could chance it twice a day. Andre had access to black cloth because he made certain that the Auds and Danites were properly robed. The lesser Rocaanists didn't wear velvet robes. They wore a good sturdy linen weave: thick and heavy enough to minimize the damage. If he threw away the cloth after the ceremony, it wouldn't matter if the water got onto it, as long as he never touched that water.

He leaned his head back, feeling some of the adrenaline ease out of him. He would have to make it through another day. But not many more than that—because he had to find a way to get to the Rocaan alone. Then Tel would know the secret all the Fey were looking for.

SEVENTY

ALEXANDER stood outside Scavenger's quarters. This would probably be his last meeting with the little man. He had gained all the knowledge he believed he could, and it seemed as if the little man was telling the truth. Now Alexander would have to decide what to do with the prisoner.

Monte and the guards watched him, probably wondering at his hesitation.

At the end of the last meeting Scavenger had said he had completed the litany of all the things the Fey could do. Alexander had seen some of the things: the desecrated bodies, and that terrifying Doppelgänger trick. Lord Stowe had told him more about the cat, and there had been reports in the outer regions of creatures that were half-human and half-beast. Alexander had confirmation for all of it if he only looked.

The problem was that all of this information terrified him. The things they could do left him chilled. He had had nightmares the past two nights running. He didn't understand how his own people had managed to survive. But Scavenger had assured him that the holy water was a potent weapon, more potent than anything the Fey had encountered since swords.

Still, it was not enough, and Alexander knew that. If the Fey found a way around holy water—and they were trying—they had the capability to defeat soundly and quickly any army Alexander tried to put together. The fact that the Isle had survived this long was sheer dumb luck.

Protection from God, the Rocaan would probably say.

Alexander opened the door.

They had moved Scavenger to what had once been a guard's quarters. The room was small, square, and cramped, little more than a cell in Alexander's opinion. But he had wardrobes bigger than this, and he knew to expect more was unrealistic.

Still, he didn't like to be this close to the little man.

The guard's quarters had rare glass windows. Alexander didn't ask, but he suspected that Monte had had the windows installed before he'd moved Scavenger in there, so that the guards could watch the conversations between Alexander and Scavenger in case the little man tried to do anything to harm the King.

In two days of talks Scavenger hadn't made a move.

That hadn't stopped Alexander from covering his body in holy water before he went into the room and bringing vials in with him. The guards were armed with the same, and Monte always accompanied Alexander inside, carrying a pitcher of holy water. Then Monte would leave, and Scavenger would explain the horrors of the Fey to Alexander. Alexander didn't want anyone else to hear. He didn't want the rumors to start.

On this day Scavenger sat on one of two wooden chairs, his head bowed and his legs spread. His elbows rested on his thighs, with his hands hanging between his knees. The picture of dejection. Alexander still wasn't quite certain what Scavenger wanted, but being locked in this tiny room clearly wasn't it.

Alexander took the other chair and moved it away from the wall. Each night, apparently, Scavenger moved some of the furniture to give himself space. Once Alexander had asked a guard what Scavenger needed room for. The guard had said that the little man paced until the wee hours.

Monte gave Alexander a nervous glance—the same one he had used for days now, and Alexander ignored it. He knew the risks. He hated it when Monte reminded him. Besides, if nothing had happened by now, nothing would.

At Alexander's signal Monte left the room. Alexander leaned on the back of his own chair, refusing to sit down. Scavenger looked up at him.

The little man's face had a small web of lines running across it, accenting the already fluid nature of his features.

"Tell me, Scavenger," Alexander said, speaking Nye, "what would have happened to you if you had stayed in Nye?"

Scavenger started at the question. Obviously it hadn't been one he expected. "I had no choice but to leave," he said.

"Did you do something?"

He shook his head. "I was part of Rugar's team. Most of Rugar's team had a choice, but the Red Caps didn't. We have no choices at all. We're supposed to do what we're told."

"And what would have happened if you had stayed?"

He shrugged. "I suppose the Black King would have had me killed as an example to the others."

"No farm, no normal life, no dream?" Alexander asked, remembering what Scavenger had told him that first day.

Scavenger laughed. "Farm? Cottage? And who would live beside me? Another Fey? No, sir. My choice was made as a young man when it became clear I wasn't going to grow any more, and I didn't have any magick. I could help some of the Domestics with the things they couldn't do by magick, and maybe, if I was good, I could marry—but probably not, since most Fey would fear that my children would be as deformed as I am."

"Deformed?"

Scavenger stood and turned around, arms held over his head. "I'm not even as tall as you are, and among my people, you're short. I have no magick. I am not slender. Do you know that Red Caps don't live to a ripe old age? When they are no longer strong enough to do their work, they are killed, or they wander off never to be seen again. I talked back to Caseo, which in some circles is a death warrant for Red Caps."

"Is it to Rugar?"

"Probably," Scavenger said, "if it gets in Caseo's way.

Rugar sees Caseo as our only hope to get out of here, to defeat that poison of yours." As he mentioned the holy water, he glanced at the pitcher on the end table. In one of their earlier meetings, he had asked that it be removed, and Alexander had refused. Scavenger knew he was a prisoner, and part of him didn't like it at all.

"I've been thinking about this for days." Alexander walked around his chair and sat down. The room was hot and stuffy. "Right now our people have yours held back, but we can't seem to gain any advantage. You tell me that Fey do not negotiate or strike bargains, so that leaves me no choice but to insist they leave Blue Isle. If I let them go, they will return home and get reinforcements, maybe figure out the solution to holy water, and maybe not—but it probably won't matter, because they will come back with such force we would have to fill the Cardidas with holy water in order to fight them off."

"You're beginning to understand," Scavenger said.

"But I don't want them here," Alexander said. "I want you to tell me a way that I can gain an advantage."

"You would have to slaughter us all to get rid of the Fey now," Scavenger said. "Even if you did win a battle, even if you did soundly defeat us, you can't prevent a ship or two from going back to Nye. Such a defeat would send the Black King, eventually. The Fey cannot afford that kind of loss. People would know we are defeatable."

Alexander stood. "I don't want Fey on Blue Isle for the rest of my life."

"You have no choice," Scavenger said. "From the moment the ships came through the Stone Guardians, your people had no choice but to coexist with the Fey. The question is, how will you do it?"

Alexander sighed. He had been afraid of that answer. He had hoped Scavenger would say something else, that the Fey would move on, leave Blue Isle alone once they saw they had no hope. But Alexander knew better. The Fey were here, and he had to find a way to get rid of them without bringing more Fey to the Isle.

He leaned on the small table, his hand near the pitcher, not because he distrusted Scavenger, but because he wanted a measure of safety for the next series of questions. "If we defeat the Fey, soundly defeat the Fey, will the Black King come for us?"

Scavenger shrugged. "He should have come already. No one knows why he's not here. There's talk that he can't get ships through those Stone Guardians."

Alexander had heard no report of ships outside the Guardians, but he had sent the Guardian Watchers to the Snow Mountains. "Do you think he will come?"

Scavenger shook his head. "He didn't even see the ships off, and that's his custom. I think he's trying to get rid of his son."

Scavenger's response so startled Alexander that he nearly knocked over the pitcher. Scavenger backed away from him. "His son? He would kill his son?"

"He has four grandchildren. He doesn't need Rugar."

Alexander looked up. "Would a man be that ruthless with his own family?"

"The Black Kings are. Black Queens even more so. One of them had five of her oldest children killed so no one would contest the succession of the youngest."

A shiver ran down Alexander's back. He couldn't imagine killing Nicholas for any reason. These Fey were beyond him. Perhaps the Rocaan was right. Perhaps they had not a shred of decency in them.

Still, Alexander would have to trust Scavenger's opinions. Alexander would have to base his plans on the theory that the Black King would not arrive. It was the Isle's only chance.

Alexander watched Scavenger closely, hoping the man would answer the next question truthfully. "So what would happen if Rugar died?"

Scavenger started. The question had surprised him. Apparently Red Caps thought of killing Spell Warders, but not leaders of any kind. "I don't know," he said slowly. His face had gone white. "I don't know."

He stood, too, and Alexander inched his own hand closer to the pitcher. But Scavenger turned his back and pushed the chair aside. He put his hands behind him and walked to and fro, muttering and shaking his head.

This was the pacing the guard had been talking about, and it bothered Alexander. He slid his fingers around the base of the pitcher. The ceramic was cool to his touch.

"No one likes the Shadowlands," Scavenger said, almost to himself. "And some don't believe in Rugar's Visions anymore. Jewel is too young for Visions." He looked up at Alexander, eyes wide. "They would fight for leadership, and some would run. They would find a safe place among your people, or try to go up the river."

"No new leader would take their place? Doesn't Rugar have a succession plan in case he dies in battle?"

"Visionaries don't die in battle," Scavenger said. "They're too well protected." And then he smiled. "Except here, where he could get splashed."

Alexander didn't smile. He watched Scavenger's face. Even though he tried to control his reaction, the very idea disturbed him. It disturbed Alexander as well. The second murder. Only this one would not be by his own hand.

"Rugar's death would destroy us," Scavenger said.

"I thought that was what you wanted," Alexander said.

Scavenger shook his head, just a little. "I want Caseo dead."

"What would happen to Caseo?"

"He would try to take over and"—this time a beatific smile crossed Scavenger's face—"someone would kill him. No one likes him. They would all want to be rid of him. No matter who leads, if anyone does, they won't put up with Caseo. He has too much power. He's too dangerous. And he made a mistake bringing that young, talented Spell Warder with him."

"A mistake?" Alexander asked.

Scavenger nodded. "He's replaceable. He doesn't think he is, but he is."

"So if Rugar dies, you would be free to live as you want, and you would get your revenge."

Scavenger stared at him as if he were speaking great heresy. And he probably was. But the man was in Alexander's custody. Alexander could say what he wanted. The little man wouldn't get out unless Alexander wanted him to.

"If Rugar died," Scavenger said slowly, "things would change here. On Blue Isle."

"As long as the Black King didn't arrive."

"Maybe not even then," Scavenger said. "It depends on how long it would take him to get here."

He sounded convinced. Or at least he sounded as if he was thinking it over. Alexander couldn't rush this. If he did, he might lose Scavenger forever.

"But Rugar is a young man," Scavenger said. "Fey sometimes live to be twice his age. And he's well protected."

"How well?" Alexander asked.

"Whenever he's out of Shadowlands, he has two bodyguards at all times. And they can protect him against anything."

"What about in Shadowlands?" Alexander asked.

"You can't get into Shadowlands." Then his eyes widened. He sat down abruptly, like a child losing its balance. "Oh," he said. "You mean me."

Alexander nodded, unable—afraid—to say anything.

"I can't kill Rugar. I—no one would forgive me."

"But you aren't going to live with those people anymore."

Scavenger shook his head. "You don't understand. They would send someone after me."

"Only if two things happened," Alexander said. His eagerness made him want to rush the words. He forced himself to speak calmly. "First, you would have to be seen. And second, they would have to have some kind of organization in order to come after you. You said the society would disintegrate. Were you wrong about that?"

"No." He rubbed his knees. "No. I'm right about that."

"Then you're safe."

"No." He spoke the word softly, as if he couldn't say anything else. "Someone will see me. Shadowlands is close quarters. Like this place."

"But you said no one notices Red Caps. Would they notice you? And if they did, would they know it was you that they saw and not someone else?"

He looked up. His mouth was open, and the tips of his fingers traced his lips as if he couldn't remember their shape. "No one would notice me."

"Then you could do it."

Scavenger's eyes were wide. He took his hand away from his mouth and frowned just a little, as if he were imagining the death. Alexander's throat was dry. He had never tried anything like this before. And Scavenger's silence disturbed him. "If you help me, you'll be a hero to my people," Alexander said. He had no idea if he was speaking the truth.

Scavenger slowly turned his face toward Alexander. "With a place of my own? And no more bodies?"

"Yes," Alexander said.

"And no more Caseo," Scavenger whispered. "I would get rid of him, too, and I wouldn't even have to kill him myself."

"That's right," Alexander said. He pushed off the table and stood upright. This was his cue to go. He walked to the door.

"Wait!" Scavenger said. "I need a guarantee. I mean, what if I kill him, and then you kill me?"

Alexander frowned. What an alien thought. "I wouldn't do that."

"Right," Scavenger said. "And I'm not sitting in your makeshift jail talking about killing the leader of my people."

He believed it. He truly believed that Alexander would betray him. "I give you my word."

"Your word?" Scavenger said. "As what? I don't even know who you are. Not really. I've only guessed so far."

"My word as King," Alexander said. The words made him feel light-headed. Fear rising, fear at revealing himself.

"And that's supposed to make me feel better?"

"I've never broken my word," Alexander said.

"Not ever, in all the years of being King?"

"Not ever," Alexander said.

But Scavenger didn't look convinced.

Alexander let go of the knob. "Is it common for Fey to go back on their word?"

"It is an art form."

"Then how can I trust you?"

"I'm not true Fey, remember?" Scavenger said.

"It doesn't matter. If it is customary to make a promise and then break it among your people, then you will follow custom."

Scavenger stared at him. "I will do as you ask."

"And so will I," Alexander said. "The problem is that now neither of us will trust the other to do as he says."

"Have you anything of value that you can entrust to me?" Scavenger asked.

"I already have," Alexander said. "My life."

"I can't take your life," Scavenger said. "There are guards outside."

Alexander shrugged. "How am I to know that you can't? Your people have magick. You could have lied to me or failed to discuss the one thing that you possess."

"I have no magick."

"And I have only your word on that." Alexander smiled. "I can trust you. Can you trust me in return?"

Scavenger stared at him for a long time. "My choices seem fairly obvious," hè said. "I guess I will have to trust you."

SEVENTY-ONE

THE infant frightened him. Rugar sat on the Meeting Block, the grayness swirling around him. He spent too much time there, staring at the Circle Door, wishing he were anywhere but in Shadowlands. In the distance, voices echoed as the Domestics installed the last water tank. No one was hammering today. Most of the building was done—at least until another group went for wood. None of the inhabitants of Shadowlands wanted to leave until the last of the bodies had been cleaned up near the circle. Only Solanda had left through the Circle Door since morning.

Leaving the baby. As if it frightened her too.

An Islander should not have any magick, and yet it was there, in the baby's eyes. If he hadn't had that glint that so few Fey children had at his age, Rugar would have discounted Solanda's action as the first in a Shape-Shifter deterioration. But she had been right. This child was important to all of them.

The boy doomed them to life on Blue Isle.

Unless Caseo and the others could figure out the spells. Rugar would give Caseo only another week to find a way around the poison, and then Rugar would start making other plans. He wasn't sure what those plans would be yet. He wanted some time to factor in this problem with magick.

None of the other Islanders evidenced any magick. No other Fey had reported any encounters with Islander magick. He refused to believe that the poison was magick. It was probably something as simple as a sword. The Islanders probably got it from some stream somewhere, and once the Fey found it, they would be able to win any battle they initiated.

But the idea that they had magick they didn't understand bothered him more than he wanted to admit. The prisoner that Jewel kept, the man Adrian, had told both Jewel and Rugar there was no magick. Yet the baby refuted that claim by his very existence.

When Rugar had been a little boy, he had learned in school of the Co. The Co had inhabited a small region in the Northeastern tip of Galinas, and they had had powers that enabled them to command all the wild beasts to kill Fey. Fey were slaughtered for years before a Spell Warder discovered that the Co's magic was not a conscious one. If they did not feel threatened or powerless, they couldn't summon help. So the Fey planned a midnight raid, knowing that the Co would be asleep in their beds. The stealthiest Fey went on the raid—those that could move silently, including the Wisps and Dream Riders, who helped only on special occasions. The Dream Riders kept the Co from waking by giving them good dreams. The Wisps kidnapped all the babies under one year of age—children that could be molded to the Fey way—and the rest of the Fey slaughtered the Co in their sleep. Co magic failed them. Except for a bit of Co blood in the Fey bloodlines, the Co no longer existed at all.

But to hear the stories, it seemed that the Fey suffered some losses of their own before they figured out a way to defeat the Co.

Rugar's breath caught in his throat. He was always one step behind his father. Rugar had forgotten about the Co until this moment. And he had forgotten about the pattern.

The Black Queen had sent a small contingent of Fey to attack the Co, but she had done so warning them that they would have no assistance. She was testing a new warrior-leader. If he did not find a way to defeat the Co, he would not lead her troops. He had found a way, but it had taken him years. By the time he returned, she was dead, and another led in her place. Another who cared nothing for a warrior who had been trapped in a war that he had nearly lost.

He had learned the story of the Co as a coda to Fey history: one of the few battles that the Fey had nearly lost, led by a renegade warrior who should never have disobeyed his Queen. The warrior's disgrace was twofold: that he had gone off on his own, and that it had taken him years to win a war that should have ended in months. But the new Black King had taken over the Co's land and had taken credit for the defeat, even as he discredited the warrior who had finally achieved that defeat.

Rugar rubbed a hand over his mouth. His father was an expert on Fey history. He had more than once told Rugar that a Fey who did not understand history was ignorant not just in the ways of the past but in the ways of the future.

The ways of the future.

Rugar felt cold. His father had heard something about Blue Isle, and then he had goaded Rugar into going, as a sort of rebellion, much like the fight against the Co. If Rugar failed, it would be his fault for disobeying his father. If he succeeded, then he would be his father's tool, finding the way around the Islanders, and solving what could have been a very serious defeat for a large Fey force.

Rugad the Black King had not lost his urge to fight. He had merely used his excellent talent at treachery against his own son, a son who was worthless to him because he had grandchildren who could carry on the tradition of leadership. Rugar would be old when he became King, and a Black King should be young at first, young enough to shoulder the burdens of command.

"Bastard," Rugar muttered.

The lights around the Circle Door suddenly began rotating. He leaned forward on the block. The lights weren't supposed to do that. They either lit outside when it was dark, or they lit inside when someone without magick or the password tried to get in. They never lit inside and *rotated*.

Another Fey stopped beside him. A husbander, who usually worked outside the Circle. "What is that?" he whispered.

"Something different," Rugar said. "Go get Jewel as well as some of the Infantry. We need to be prepared for this. Oh, and that prisoner. Let's bring him too."

"Which one, sir?" the man asked.

"The younger one. The one who is supposed to help us. Him." Rugar stayed next to the block. As far as he could tell, he was too far away to be splashed if Islanders somehow got inside the dirt circle, managed to open the door, and throw poison inside.

The lights flashed brighter, and spun faster, until they became a blur. Heat emanated from the door, melting the mist around it, making the base of Shadowlands look like glass. Rugar thought he could see grass below, but he wasn't willing to get closer to look.

Voices grew louder behind him. He recognized Jewel's and Burden's. He suppressed a flash of irritation, wishing that young, magickless Infantryman would leave her alone. As they got closer, Rugar saw the husbander with them, and the prisoner Adrian, looking confused.

Then the Circle Door opened, and a Black Robe stumbled inside. Rugar gasped. The Black Robe looked around wildly. The approaching Fey stopped. Only Adrian, the prisoner, came forward.

He held out his hands, as if he were to protect them all from the poison. "Religious Sir," he said, "you are in a dangerous place."

"I am in a safe place," the Black Robe snapped. "You are the one who is in danger. Rugar, I need to talk with you."

Rugar stood very still. The accent and emphasis made the phrasing sound like Quest, but he couldn't tell—not for sure. Still, he had ordered the Doppelgänger to return if he couldn't find anything. But that didn't explain the door.

"The Circle Door had trouble with you," Rugar said, careful not to use any names. "Is there a reason for that?"

"I don't know," the Black Robe said as he grabbed Adrian by the throat and held him aloft without any effort at all. Adrian coughed and kicked, but couldn't reach the Black Robe. The Black Robe took a knife from his pocket. "Should I decapitate this one and get a real body back?"

"Let him go!" Jewel said.

The Black Robe looked from her to Rugar.

"Let him go! He's mine, and I promised him protection."

Adrian's kicks were getting weaker. His face was turning blue. The Black Robe looked at Rugar. Rugar shrugged. "Let him go. He's supposed to help us."

The Black Robe dropped Adrian. He landed with a thud, both hands going to his throat as he coughed and gasped for air.

"Get a Healer," Jewel said.

"You're awfully suspicious of a Doppelgänger who has returned home on your orders," the Black Robe said.

"I have never seen the Circle Door behave that way before," Rugar said, "and I should have. I'm the one who designed it."

"I got in, didn't I? Without the passwords. I couldn't have those, I've been gone for too long."

Rugar nodded. If it was Quest, then that was true. Quest would not have known the password. But something had disturbed the door. "Take off the robe," Rugar said, "and all the religious trappings and pass through the door again."

The Black Robe sighed, then slipped the robe over his head. He took off the tiny sword around his neck. His feet were already bare. His body was thin, with ribs showing, and legs as thin as sticks.

He stepped over the robe, turned, and went through the Circle Door. This time the lights did not show. The Door merely opened, giving Rugar a glimpse of the twilight meadow beyond. A breeze wafted through, carrying the scent of pine. Jewel tilted her head toward the breeze and took deep breaths, her eyes closed.

Then the door closed and she stopped, a flush building in her cheeks. Apparently her longing for the outdoors was overcoming her pride. Rugar said nothing, but stared at the empty grayness where the door was.

After a moment the door opened as it would for any Fey. No lights, no rotation. Quest stepped in. His penis had shriveled with the cold, and goose bumps had risen on his flesh.

"I really don't understand what the problem was," he said.

Rugar was not going to respond. Not yet. "Now," he said, "pick up that robe and hold it near the door."

"I wouldn't mind putting it back on," Quest said, but he bent and picked up the robe anyway. He held it near the door, and the lights came on, just as they had before. And then they began rotating.

Rugar sat down. The lights came on only when someone who was not Fey tried to get in, or when someone didn't know the password. And they never rotated.

"Try it again with the sword this time," he said.

Quest dropped the robe and picked up the sword like a small weapon. He held it near the Circle Door. This time the lights were even brighter, and they rotated even faster.

"Put it down," Rugar said tiredly.

Quest turned. "What does that mean?"

Rugar didn't answer him. The fear that had haunted Rugar all morning felt like a block of ice in his belly.

"I want you to take those things to Caseo, then put on some real clothes and come to my cabin to see me," Rugar said. "I don't want anyone else to touch that piece of jewelry or the robe. Is that clear? Even if Caseo wants to work on them, I want you there, Quest."

Quest glanced at the others. They were displaying no emotion. So he shrugged and picked up the material. "Mind if I get Caseo's help finding my old form?"

"Yes," Rugar said. "Right now I do. I want to see you as soon as possible."

Quest sighed but said nothing else. He headed down the path between buildings. Rugar sat for a moment. His heart was pounding as if he had run for miles, and he was having difficulty catching his breath. Everything was spiraling out of control. He couldn't even control the reaction of the Circle Door he had created from a recipe designed by a Visionary centuries before. The last Shadowlands had slowly disintegrated around them, and this one had gained a mind of its own. He was simply not equipped to cope with this.

His books and references were back on Nye. He had no other Visionaries to ask whether this feature of the Circle Door was normal. Because he had never seen it before, he suspected it was not—and he had seen some strange things come into Shadowlands in his time.

"Papa?" Jewel was crouched in front of him. He hadn't seen her approach. "I'm sure Quest will be waiting for you."

Rugar nodded. He had her still, but what would she think if she knew he had holes in his Vision, holes that could cause something like this?

"Do you know what caused the Door to react that way?" she asked.

"I wish I did," he said. Then he stood. His body was cramped, not from sitting too long, but from tension. He shook some of it loose and headed for the cabin.

He didn't want to think about what Quest's return there alone meant. If Tel truly was dead, then Quest was the only remaining Doppelgänger. The Black King had once said that Rugar relied too much on his Doppelgängers. But in this place they hadn't done him much good.

The problem was that Solanda became his only eyes and ears in the world of the Islanders. And she wasn't always reliable. Her insights were accurate, but she was never around when he needed her.

Quest was waiting outside the cabin, wearing a loose pair of breeches and a shirt that was too big for him. His Islander body looked tiny this close; the shortness made his thinness look unhealthy.

"Let's go in," Rugar said. "It's better to have this talk alone."

Quest followed him inside. Once in, Rugar lit a fire in the fireplace. He had to get rid of the chill in his body. He suspected that the chill had less to do with the air than with his own tension; but, still, a fire might help.

He stood, placing his hand on his knee to brace himself. "All right," Rugar said. "Tell me how to make the poison."

Quest looked at his hands. "I don't know."

"You came in here dressed as a Black Robe. How could you not know?"

"I thought Ipper told you that Danites weren't privy to the information."

"And I thought you were smart enough to find out anyway."

Quest sat down. Rugar bit back irritation. He hadn't told Quest to sit. But he would let it go for now.

"It's dangerous there," Quest said. "Anything can kill you. Anything at all. They put their poison on a lot of things, and as a Danite, I was expected to hold vials of it, and pour it on things. I had to touch it all the time."

"Did you?" Rugar asked.

Quest shook his head. "I only had to hold a vial during one of the Midnight Sacraments, and then it didn't hurt me.

I think I managed to keep it off myself. The other times I made sure I didn't come close to the stuff. People were watching me. I think they were getting suspicious. Even if you hadn't ordered me out of there, I would have had to leave."

"Risking your life was worthless if you didn't learn the secret to that stuff."

Quest kept his head down. "I did learn some things about it."

"Such as?"

"That it doesn't come from some stream or pond like we thought. That the Rocaan makes it. The secret is passed from one Rocaan to the next. No one else knows it."

"I thought you told Ipper that two people knew it."

Quest nodded, raising his head. His cheeks were flushed. "I guess the day we invaded, the Rocaan taught one of the Elders the secret because he was afraid he would die. So now two of them know. But I couldn't get near either of them. They're too well guarded."

Rugar clenched his fist. "What about one of the higher-ups? Why didn't you see if you could become one of the guards?"

Quest shook his head. "It wasn't that easy. No one is alone in that place. I had to ask for a special audience just to get my Danite alone. And even then he was wary. Good thing I moved fast."

Rugar's nails dug into the flesh of his palms. They were getting nowhere on this. Quest did not have the information, and short of sending him back in, Rugar couldn't get it from him.

"Did you see evidence of any other Doppelgängers in the Tabernacle?" Rugar asked.

"Others?" Quest frowned. "I saw no others, or if I did, they were well hidden."

"What about talk? Any suspicious folk? Any blood or bones?"

"My change was very messy," Quest said. "Someone walked in almost as soon as it was over, and I had to leave before being seen. It took me a while to integrate into this one. This Danite was a true believer, and taking on his person was tough. At first his soul thought I was God."

Rugar smiled, although he didn't want to. He didn't like

the details of Doppelgänger existence. Nothing. No others. The others had to be dead. Which meant that Quest was the only remaining Doppelgänger. Everything was getting too hard.

Quest frowned. "But shortly after I got there, they did have a big meeting, looking for something. And from what I could tell, that was unusual. So I don't think we should send anyone else back in there. The Islanders are getting too suspicious."

"There's no one to send in," Rugar said.

"What?" Quest's voice had a shocked edge to it.

"You're the only one left. I need to keep you here for now." Rugar's voice was soft. He hated that—hated the necessity behind keeping Quest in Shadowlands. He was becoming too protective. They lived like besieged people, guarding every resource and making do with nothing.

All that effort, all those lost Doppelgängers, and nothing to show for it.

Rugar sighed. He wouldn't be able to get any more out of this conversation. "All right," he said. "We'll debrief about the religion later. Go to Caseo and see if you can help him."

"Yes, sir." Quest didn't sound happy. He stood and with a bow let himself out of the cabin.

Rugar stared at the closed door for a long time. He was suffocating there, worse than any of them. Suffocating on his own sense of failure.

SEVENTY-TWO

MATTHIAS had had no sleep. His eyes felt dry and gritty. He had gone to both Morning Sacraments to make certain everything was all right, and by the time he'd got back to his own chambers, he'd been too keyed up to rest. He ate a large breakfast and paced before being summoned by the Rocaan.

The Rocaan's rooms were too warm, as usual. He sat in his favorite chair, wrapped in a blanket, a glass of milk beside him. Deep shadows made his eyes look sunken, even though he assured Matthias that he had slept. The incident with the holy water had frightened them both, and if such disruptions continued, Matthias was afraid the Rocaan's precarious health would fail.

Matthias couldn't allow that to happen, not without knowing where or if the Fey were in the Tabernacle. He couldn't very well present himself to the Council of Elders as the only choice to be the next Rocaan because he was the only person he was certain had not been touched by the Fey.

"All right," Matthias said, sitting on the overstuffed chair beside the Rocaan, wishing he could open a window and let cool air in. "Tell me this idea."

The Rocaan shook his head. "It's not an idea, Matthias. It's what we're going to do."

Matthias hated it when the Rocaan got like this. This attitude had created his exhaustion in the first place, with his presiding over burials like a simple Danite, and keeping track of each piece of news about the Fey. "What are we going to do?" Matthias asked.

"We're going to meet with the Fey."

Matthias sat up. He hadn't heard this. Had this been the point of Nicholas's second visit the night before? "The King set this up?"

The Rocaan shook his head. "You will set this up. I have given it great thought. We will meet their leaders at the kirk near Daisy Stream."

"We? Who is 'we'?" Matthias asked. His heart was pounding.

"A few of us from the Tabernacle. Not many."

"No one from the palace?" Matthias asked. "Aren't we presuming to run the affairs of state when we should be concerned with affairs of the soul?"

The Rocaan lifted his head. His round eyes had a shine to them that Matthias had seen only a few times. "Sometimes affairs of the state are affairs of the soul. I think our problem has been that we have failed to recognize this in the past."

"Forgive me, Holy Sir," Matthias said, "but what can you hope to accomplish?"

The Rocaan drew his blanket tighter around his body. "I hope to drive the Fey from this Isle."

"By meeting with them?" Matthias shook his head. "They don't listen to reason. Everything we know about them tells us that."

"I don't think it would be reason. I think God will help us." The Rocaan slipped a hand out from under the blanket. "Hear me out."

Matthias's mouth was dry. A bead of sweat ran down the side of his face and dripped onto his robe. The chamber had become stifling. "All right," he said.

"We already know that God is with us, or He would not have provided us with the holy water and its unique properties. It has taken me a year to be reconciled to these properties, to see the Fey as inhuman creatures from the netherworld who are trying to take over this one. But in all of this time, I have seen no goodness in them. The longer that we wait to fight them, the more vicious they become. Defiling the Tabernacle is merely one step. Soon they will get rid of the holy water altogether."

"But if God is with us, He wouldn't allow that," Matthias said.

"God has given us tools, Matthias, but we must use them. You were right about that. And forgive me for my arrogance. I was wrong."

Matthias brushed more sweat off his forehead. The fire crackled beside him, sending a wave of sparks into the chimney. "You were wrong about holy water?"

The Rocaan nodded. "Your instincts were right, but you acted for the wrong reason. You acted out of fear and justified it using the Words. Somehow, though, the Holy One guided you and gave you the correct solution. I have been studying this for the last year and have come to a similar conclusion, but for many different reasons."

The heat was making Matthias light-headed. He was having trouble concentrating. "Mind if I open a window?" he asked.

The Rocaan smile was rueful. "I get cold when I do not get enough sleep," he said, and it sounded like an apology. "Go ahead, but please get me another blanket."

Matthias stood and pulled the tapestry from the nearest window. Then he took a throw off the nearest chair and brought it to the Rocaan. A cool breeze blew in from the window, freshening the air and taking the staleness from the room.

The Rocaan wrapped the throw around his legs. "The Words Written make mention of the Enemy, but never explain who it is. The Words Unwritten tell early stories of the Enemy stealing hardy souls from God and the Roca. Then the Roca fights the Soldiers of the Enemy. I have spoken to Elder Eirman, and he says that several old stories of various regions say the Enemy created a netherworld and kept the souls inside it. Other stories say that the Enemy killed those souls, while still others say that the Enemy took the life from the souls so that they could not return to Blue Isle in the form of children. None of these are mentioned in the Words."

"You think the Fey are that Enemy?" Matthias asked.

The Rocaan shook his head. "I am not as simple as all that. But I think they are Soldiers of the Enemy, just as there have been Soldiers of the Enemy in the past."

"The ones mentioned in the Words," Matthias said. The temperature in the room was easing. He was finally getting comfortable.

"I believe there have been others, some we can recognize and some we can't. During the Peasant Uprising," the Rocaan said, "there had to be Soldiers of the Enemy, only the Church did not recognize them, and the Rocaan did not act properly."

"We've had this discussion before," Matthias said. "I thought it had come to nothing."

"No," the Rocaan said. "For once I did the study, not you. And the conclusion I have come to is this: the Roca gave us the way to defeat the Soldiers of the Enemy time and time again. The ritual we perform each day once saved the lives of his people."

"We don't know that," Matthias said. "There is no evidence for that."

"Ah, but there is," the Rocaan said. "And it is the most obvious evidence of all."

Matthias suppressed a sigh. He hated these kinds of games.

The Rocaan didn't wait for Matthias to ask. "We're here. The religion is here, and Blue Isle is in our domination. If the Soldiers of the Enemy had won, we would not worship the way we do."

A thread of excitement wound through Matthias's stomach. The Rocaan was right. It was so obvious that everyone had missed it. Of course they had won. That was why they revered the Roca.

But Matthias didn't like where the conversation was heading. "So you want to meet the Fey leaders in a little kirk near Daisy Stream to reenact the ceremony?"

The Rocaan nodded. "It will defeat them."

"And if it doesn't?"

"Have faith, Matthias."

Matthias shook his head. "It is not my function to have faith. It is my duty to question. And I question this. What if we lose?"

"Then we die," the Rocaan said.

"And the secret to holy water dies with us. That is not smart, Holy Sir. We can at least defend our people with holy water."

The Rocaan shot him a sideways look. "I did not say we would both be going. I am bringing only men of faith, Matthias."

Matthias sat back as if he had been slapped. He clasped his hands in his lap. "If you die, I would have to become Rocaan. I am the only one who knows the secret."

"To holy water. There are other secrets as well, Matthias. I would prepare my successor carefully."

Matthias felt a surge of disappointment, then flushed. He didn't want to covet the job of Rocaan, but apparently he did on some deep level. "Whoever you choose would have to stay behind."

"I know," the Rocaan said. "Which is why I am choosing you. You have no faith, but the Holy One guides you, and such a thing is of equal value."

Matthias froze. "How do you know that's of equal value?"

"The Holy One pointed to you, by giving you the knowledge of the hidden powers of holy water. And then you forced me to use those powers. Sometimes faith is not enough. Sometimes faith dies. But guidance from the Holy One is rare, and I'm sure it will never forsake you."

Matthias shook his head. This made no sense. "I threw the holy water at the Fey because I was frightened of them and had no other weapon, not because I heard a still, small voice. Forgive me, Holy Sir. I would love to be Rocaan—for probably all the wrong reasons—but I think I would be a poor choice. Pick someone else and let me advise him. It would be safer all around."

The Rocaan slid a hand out from under his wad of blankets and patted Matthias's knee. "You are my choice, Matthias."

"You expect to die on this trip, don't you?"

The Rocaan snaked his hand back under the blankets. He frowned. "I don't know. We have only the very old stories. I may not come back. I may not be successful. If I fail, though, I expect I will return. Not even the Fey would murder a very old man."

Matthias rubbed his clasped hands together. All of this

made a perverse kind of sense, and if he let it happen, there was a good chance he would be Rocaan. But he couldn't let it happen this way. "If you leave me here, I will have to inform the King."

The Rocaan frowned at him. "Matthias, haven't you always wanted to be Rocaan?"

"Of course," Matthias said. "I think any Elder who tells you otherwise is lying, no matter how pure his faith. But I will not have it happen by letting you commit suicide in a particularly noble fashion, just because you feel guilty about this entire war."

The Rocaan leaned back in his chair. He seemed to have shrunk. "Is that what you think I'm doing?"

"There is no other explanation," Matthias said. "You are not the Roca. He did not face those soldiers expecting to be a martyr. You are. And that's wrong. That's as arrogant as my letting you go so that I can be Rocaan."

The Rocaan closed his eyes. For a moment Matthias thought he had passed out. Then the Rocaan said, "You know, I have held this position so long I no longer think of myself as anything other than Rocaan. If you asked me my given name, I would tell you I'm the Rocaan before I would tell you who I am." His voice sounded thin, reedy.

Matthias sat very still. Perhaps the Rocaan was going to back down now.

"I have thought about this many times. What is better than being Rocaan? Being the second Roca of course. Saving my people. Perhaps I am being arrogant. Perhaps I am." He opened his eyes and focused on Matthias.

Matthias didn't move. If he could talk the Rocaan out of this idea, then they would all be better off.

"But what happens if I am so afraid of being arrogant that I fail to do the right thing? What happens if, in my quest to be completely humble, I fail to do the very thing that I am supposed to do?"

Matthias had no answer to that. The dilemma of the faithful. He cleared his throat. "The still, small voice is supposed—"

"The still, small voice. The still, small voice hasn't spoken in generations!" The Rocaan sat forward. Now he looked fierce. The blanket fell away from his shoulders. They were small and bony, certainly not shoulders that could hold up an entire people. "And perhaps it hasn't spoken because the Rocaans have failed to do as they should. Perhaps we are all supposed to be martyrs in our own way and in our own time."

"You twist the logic," Matthias said. "We don't know what happened to the Soldiers of the Enemy after the Roca died. We don't know. Maybe his own people got so angry that they drove the soldiers from the Isle. Maybe there was nothing in this from God at all."

The Rocaan turned white. "That's blasphemy," he whispered.

"Well, if it is, you need to hear it now," Matthias said. "And you need to keep me from succeeding you. Because I will wonder about that until we find the answer. Yes, you're right. The Soldiers of the Enemy probably left Blue Isle somehow. The Roca's people were successful somehow. But we don't know if in their stories they glorified a man who gave them courage and little more. We don't know, Holy Sir."

The Rocaan stared at Matthias for a moment, his eyes small and beady. "If we knew," the Rocaan said softly. "If we knew, Matthias, there would be no reason for faith. We wouldn't have to believe. We would know. God asks more of us. And I think He is asking more of me. I know He will ask a lot of you if you become Rocaan. But I think you are the best choice we have."

Matthias wasn't certain if he should be grateful or not. The idea of becoming Rocaan had its benefits, but he wasn't certain he was the best one to lead the others. "I have never had faith," he said softly. "I came into this profession like a man goes into the guard, because my family wanted it."

"I know," the Rocaan said. "We can't help how we are chosen. The fact is that you are here now."

Matthias licked his lips. "Am I to be your permanent successor? Or will I just hold that position while you are in Daisy Stream?"

"You are my choice, Matthias. I toyed with Andre for a while—he certainly has the most faith of any of the Elders —but he lacks the strength you have. And a Rocaan needs strength and a certain love of knowledge. You have both of those."

"I would want the Church to be led by someone who believes," Matthias said.

"Why?" the Rocaan asked. "You don't believe yourself. What should it matter to you?"

Matthias couldn't express the disquiet he was feeling. He stood and smoothed his robe, then walked over to the window. The breeze had become chill. Twilight had fallen, putting the courtyard below in shadows.

"I have always thought that my failure to believe was *my* failure," Matthias said. "Having a Rocaan who believes, being surrounded by those who believe, reinforces that feeling. But if the Rocaan doesn't believe either, that makes Rocaanism a hollow shell. An institution with no heart, a hypocritical place that pretends to provide comfort and answers and in truth can provide nothing."

"There have been disbelieving Rocaans in the past."

Matthias nodded. "Yes, and one was assassinated, and another nearly brought the Church down with him. I don't want to be that kind of man, Holy Sir. I can't be."

"You won't be," the Rocaan said.

"But I will. If you make me Rocaan, you won't be able to make me believe. And I will make this a hollow, empty place like those other men did."

"They did not destroy the Church."

Matthias unhooked the edge of the tapestry and covered the window. The scene was a familiar one: the building of the courtyard and the Blessing of the workers. "You just told me they might have," he said. "You said they failed to act when needed. No Rocaan has followed the path set by the Roca. No Rocaan. How could an unbeliever do it?"

"You won't have to," the Rocaan said. "I will."

"And if you fail—" Matthias thumbed the edge of the tapestry, unwilling to look at the Rocaan. "If you fail, I will not even have the hope of belief. There will be nothing left in this place."

"I will not fail," the Rocaan said.

SEVENTY-THREE

SCAVENGER shoved his hands into his pockets as he walked, feeling lighter than he should have been feeling. No pouches, no equipment, no blood. He had been clean for almost a week—longer than he had ever been in his adult life.

The road was quiet. The trees draped over it like a canopy, and the shadows carried a chill. Sunlight didn't make it through that canopy, except in small dappled specks. Birds chirped overhead, and occasionally something crashed in the underbrush. He concentrated, though, on each and every sound. He didn't want to be caught, a lone Fey, walking calmly down a road outside the city of Jahn. But he couldn't hurry back as the Islander King had wanted him to. He needed to think.

For a week he had not felt like himself. He had been someone important, someone a King spent time listening to. At nights, when the King was gone and only the guards remained, Scavenger dreamed of his own people: Caseo threatening to kill him, Rugar looking through him, Solanda calling him a troll. They had no concept of how important he could be. Just because he lacked magick didn't mean that he lacked intelligence.

And now he needed that intelligence more than ever, because he wasn't quite sure how he would explain his absence, especially if some of the other Red Caps had seen him fighting with the Islanders. If he claimed he had been captured, he would die. Returned prisoners were not celebrated; they were murdered as potential spies. It didn't matter that the Islanders were not sophisticated enough to think of that themselves. The Fey were, and that would be enough.

He needed a story, and it had to be a good one. It also had to be as close to the truth as he could make it, because he was a terrible liar.

The edge of his foot caught a rock, and he nearly stumbled. He stuck out one arm for balance and then continued. He had only one thing he could say. He would say that he ran away because he was frightened of Caseo. Then he found two Islanders in the woods—no, he couldn't say that. Because if he killed them, then where was the skin? And if he didn't, he was back to the first problem. Everyone would think he had been captured and polluted. It would take so little for them to turn on him. He had no value there.

The big tree that led into the clearing was just ahead. He would say he ran away from Caseo, but he wouldn't say anything more. If someone had seen him with the Islanders, then he would make up a story, but the less he said, the better off he would be. Besides, it wouldn't matter for long. When he killed Rugar, no one would care where he had been. They would worry only about themselves.

He stopped by the tree to catch his breath. Of course, he had yet to figure out how to kill Rugar. That thought had haunted him since the King had brought it up. Rugar was a leader, a Visionary. He had guards around him at all times.

Except in the Shadowlands.

Even then, though, his daughter was around, and more than Rugar, Scavenger was afraid of Jewel. He had seen her in battle. She was fierce. He didn't want her to catch him.

And that was the crux of it, really—being caught. He could kill Rugar. Killing any Fey was not difficult. They bled just like everyone else. The problem was not to let the powerful ones understand they were under attack, so that they could attack first.

Scavenger stepped into the clearing, bracing himself for

the stench of bodies. But the air was fresh there, and except for some bloodstains and scuff marks on the ground, there was no sign that any battle had taken place. They had managed to get everything cleaned up since he had gone.

A path had been worn to the Ground Circle marking the Circle Door. A lot of traffic lately. He was about to cross into the Ground Circle when he heard voices.

". . . don't know why he wants bones."

"And all broken up. I wish we could just toss 'em like we usually do."

"I think he's going crazy."

"No sleep they say since he started working on the poison."

They were talking about Caseo. And he recognized the voices. Vulture and Uences, two of the Red Caps. Vulture worked often. Uences was older and preferred to work only during battle. It must have taken a lot of effort to get her out of the Shadowlands.

He braced himself for the recriminations about his absence. He still didn't have a complete story, but he had enough. He rounded the Ground Circle and followed the sound of voices.

"No sleep can destroy anyone's mind."

"Wonder what happens to a Warder when he goes crazy?"

"Becomes Caseo."

"He's just ambitious. Thinks he's the Black King."

"He's scary."

"No scarier than the rest of them."

Vulture and Uences were standing near a pile of skeletons just inside the woods. The flesh was gone, and so were the organs. If Scavenger hadn't known better, he would have thought the bodies had been there a long time.

He cleared his throat.

Both Vulture and Uences looked up guiltily. Vulture was covered with brown stains, his clothing filthy, his hair standing on end. Uences looked cleaner—she had obviously not been pulling the flesh off bodies—but patches of sweat stained her shirt under her arms and down her back.

"About time," Uences said. "Do you know how long we've been waiting for someone to relieve us?"

"They promised somebody at dawn. We haven't seen

anyone except that Domestic they have doing the running."
Vulture held a tibia. He used his knife and sliced the edge of
the bone away as he would whittle on a piece of wood,
putting the shavings into his pouch.

Scavenger opened his mouth, about to give the answer
he had planned, when what they said reached his brain.
They thought he had come from outside. No one had noticed he was missing. A little shiver of anger went through
him. He could have been killed by the Islanders and no one
would have cared. No one at all.

"Didn't they tell you I was coming?"

Uences shook her head. A strand of hair fell alongside
her face. "They don't tell us anything. I don't even think
they care what happens to us as long as we get the work
done."

"And Caseo has this thing about Islander bones today.
Yesterday it was Fey bones. The day before it was kidneys. I
don't think he knows what he's doing," Vulture said.

Caseo certainly seemed to know when Scavenger had
gone to see him, but Scavenger said nothing. The less he
said, the better off he would be.

"He just likes to keep us busy," Uences said. "We've
never had to strip bones before, not even in L'Nacin."

"How do you remember L'Nacin?" Vulture asked. "You
were a baby."

"I was a girl. My parents served there. They came home
covered in blood. I would have remembered if they had to
do bones."

The two of them must have been arguing throughout the
entire job. Scavenger was glad he hadn't been there.
"Which of you do I replace?" he asked.

"Me." Uences stuck her knife into its small hilt, let the
bone she was holding drop, and handed him her half-filled
pouch. "I don't do this kind of work."

"Now, wait one damn minute," Vulture said. "I haven't
slept in two days. You can wait until the next relief comes."

"As if there's going to be a next relief," Uences said.
"They promised me I could leave at dawn. Does it look like
dawn to you?"

"No," Vulture said. "I can barely see. Next thing you
know, I'll cut off my own finger."

Scavenger looked back and forth between them. He

really didn't want to work with Uences, but he knew what it was like to slave for days with no recognition. He also knew that whoever went inside now would probably be back in a few hours when Tazy sent for replacements.

"How long have you worked, Uences?" Scavenger asked.

"Since twilight," she snapped at him. "And they only provided one Fey Lamp—and the souls in that one were withering. How do they expect you to do good work when you can't see? Talk about almost losing a finger. I almost lost *two* of mine in the dark."

"I'm sorry," Scavenger said, knowing he would be even more sorry in a few hours. "But I'm going to relieve Vulture."

Vulture clapped him on the back so hard, the sound rang through the forest. "My man!" He grinned. "I finally get to sleep. And I don't have to listen to her chatter anymore." He put his knife in its scabbard, handed the scabbard to Scavenger, and threw the finished pouch on the pile of pouches to wait for the Domestic. Then he took the half-filled pouch from Scavenger's hand and made a show of giving it back to Uences. "Have a good time, all," he said, and scampered for the Circle Door.

"What did you do that for?" Uences picked up a bone and began shaving it, her cheeks red. "I have seniority."

"And he needs to sleep sometimes."

She brought her face up. "Let me tell you something, little man," she said, using the tip of her knife to emphasize her words. He took a cautious step backward, and she followed. "I have seniority. That ain't much, but it's something. Red Caps don't get respect, or love, or even like, but we do get seniority, which gives us the permission to do whatever we want whenever we want. I *earned* that, and that's about all I will have ever earned. When you get to my place, you'll understand that seniority is more important than sleep. It's more important than food. It's more important than anything."

"Yes, ma'am." Scavenger took out Vulture's knife and grabbed a femur.

"Don't 'yes ma'am' me," Uences said. "You'll understand when you're my age and have nothing to show for years of work. Years of filthy, stinking work and the taunts and the lack of respect. You'll understand."

"I'm sure I will," Scavenger said.

She pushed the tip of her knife against his breastbone. "Are you making fun of me?"

He grabbed her wrist with his free hand. The knife could shred him in a matter of moments. "No," he said as evenly as he could. "I wouldn't dream of it."

She apparently took him seriously, for she removed the knife.

"I'm sorry," he said softly, "about letting Vulture go."

She grinned for the first time since he arrived. "Don't worry about it, kid," she said. "If I had really thought I should go, I would have. Seniority, you know. You got even less power than I do."

He knew that. He knew that very well. He sighed and settled in to work. Soon someone would replace him. When they did, he would go inside and kill Rugar, just as he promised. And the hell of it was, he could kill Rugar in front of a thousand Fey, and most would never notice him. They would notice only that Rugar had died. The Red Caps might see Scavenger, and those who did wouldn't be angry at him for the deed.

They would cheer.

SEVENTY-FOUR

NICHOLAS had built a fire in the west-wing library. He welcomed the warmth on his right side, even as he sat in his favorite window seat overlooking the servants' quarters. He had finally decorated the room a bit, adding cushions and a few chairs since he spent so much time alone there. He was hoping for a glimpse of Charissa. He had been dreaming of her every night, passionate dreams in which he held her in his arms. But midway through she always turned into the Fey woman he had captured, and his passion increased. The desire he felt for that woman, the fact that he hadn't been able to get her out of his mind for over a year, disturbed him more than he cared to admit to anyone.

A knock on the door startled him. He thought he had complete privacy. He got out of the window seat. "Who is it?"

"Lord Stowe."

Nicholas grabbed the vial of holy water he now kept beside him at all times, unstopped it, and hid it in his right hand. "Come."

Lord Stowe opened the door and closed it very carefully. Nicholas kept his distance. He no longer trusted anyone, not until they proved themselves. He tossed the open bottle at Lord Stowe. When Stowe caught it, water splashed all over him. He smiled.

"Nice test, Highness." He crossed the room, clutching the vial, and handed it back to Nicholas. Half the liquid was gone. Nicholas replaced the stopper and put the vial in his pocket. He did not apologize. He didn't have to.

"I have a young man outside," Lord Stowe said, "and he has quite a story. I think you should talk with him."

"Me?" Nicholas asked. "What can I do? Why aren't you taking him to my father?"

"I'm not sure he should get near your father, and someone needs to hear this besides me."

"Anyone can go near my father if you test with holy water."

Lord Stowe smiled. "Wait until you see what happens when you try that."

The hair on the back of Nicholas's head prickled. The idea of danger intrigued him. "Where is this man now?"

"Outside the door," Lord Stowe said. "With several guards. I would like to bring him in without the guards, if that's all right by you."

"What am I seeing him for?"

"His story," Lord Stowe said. "It's quite fantastic."

"Do you believe it?"

"I won't prejudice you, Highness, one way or another."

Nicholas walked back to his window seat and perched on it as if it were a chair. A few days before he had hidden another bottle of holy water beneath the cushion. He moved the cushion aside slightly to see if the vial was still there. It was, with the same strand of hair wrapped around its cork that Nicholas had placed there.

"All right," Nicholas said. "Show him in."

Lord Stowe bowed and backed to the door, then stood and pulled the door open. He spoke for a moment to someone in the hallway; then a man came in—a boy, actually, a few years younger than Nicholas. He was squarely built with a hint of future power. His face was gaunt and acne-scarred, and his eyes were dark blue and wide with fear.

"Highness, if you please, your holy water," Lord Stowe said as he held out his hand. With his other hand he pushed the door closed. Nicholas left the stopper on the vial this time and tossed it at Lord Stowe. He caught it, took the stopper off, and sprinkled some on the boy.

Where the water touched the boy, it turned green and glowed for a moment before fading away. If they had poured a bucket of holy water on him, the entire boy would have glowed.

"What are you?" Nicholas asked.

The boy bowed and remained bent until Lord Stowe spoke softly to him. Then the boy stood. Lord Stowe put his hand on the boy's back and propelled him forward until they were only a few feet from Nicholas.

"My name is Luke," the boy said. "I live with my family near Killeny's Bridge, or I did until I volunteered to help fight the Fey."

"You were born here on the Isle?" Nicholas asked.

Lord Stowe was watching the boy with concern on his face. He hadn't taken his hand off the boy's back.

"Yes, sir. I didn't glow green till they sent me back, sir. I don't know what it is!" The boy's voice rose with each word, wobbling in panic. The panic, Nicholas realized, was not from the boy's proximity to the Prince, but from the green glow itself.

"Yet nothing happens to you, except the glow?"

The boy nodded.

"He was one of the Fey prisoners," Lord Stowe said. "They set him free."

Now Nicholas's attention was fully caught. "They set you free?"

"Yes, sir. My father, he bought my freedom, sir, by promising to stay with them forever and telling them all they needed to know about Islanders."

Nicholas glanced at Lord Stowe, whose gaze met his. The concern on Lord Stowe's face mirrored the concern Nicholas felt. "What does your father know?" Nicholas asked.

"Not much," the boy said. "I doubt they got much from the bargain. He don't even go to Sacraments, beg pardon, sir."

"Who is the boy's father?" Nicholas asked Lord Stowe.

"He's a farmer near Killeny's Bridge. Apparently he joined up early on, and then when his son joined, he stayed with him, to protect him. He's never been near the King, and he's never met anyone more important than a Danite, so far as we can tell." Lord Stowe had done his homework before bringing the boy in. But Nicholas did understand why they didn't want him anywhere near the King. His father was taking enough risks talking with the Fey prisoner. He didn't need another.

"I come to Lord Stowe, sir, to ask him to rescue my father. But then his people poured holy water on me—and it glowed. But I feel fine. I do." The boy shook. His terror was almost palpable.

Nicholas stood. "What happens when you touch him?" Nicholas asked Lord Stowe.

"Nothing. I can pour holy water onto my hand when I'm touching him. He glows and I don't."

Nicholas nodded. He touched the damp spots on the boy's tunic. The area felt warm from the boy's skin. But there was no glow, nor any transfer of great power, so far as Nicholas could tell.

"What did they do to you, boy?"

"He was there for a number of days," Lord Stowe said. "I will brief you later."

So too much to recite in a short visit. "Did they give you anything before you left?"

The boy shook his head. "Just the clothes. I wore them to Jahn, but when we found the green glow, I took them off. The glow stays."

"The clothes glow, too," Lord Stowe said.

Nicholas touched the boy's skin. It was soft, not the skin of a laborer, and tanned. But again he found nothing unusual. "Did you come to Lord Stowe of your own free will?" he asked.

Lord Stowe started. Apparently he had not thought to ask that question. But, then, he hadn't heard most of the stories from the Fey prisoner.

The boy nodded. "I come to ask him if he would rescue my father."

Nicholas let go of the boy. He was afraid to ask the next question, afraid he might not want to hear the answer. "Where are they keeping your father?"

"In their place, the Shadowlands," the boy said. "It's horrible there, all gray with nothing growing. It's like they put a box in the sky. Please. I could hardly stand it. My dad loves the green. He'll go crazy in there."

All gray with nothing growing. Nicholas couldn't even picture it. "I'll do what I can," he said, uncertain even what that was. His father said he had a plan for bringing down the Fey, but they had had plans before.

Lord Stowe patted the boy's shoulder. "I'll rejoin you outside in a few moments."

The boy nodded, turned, and stopped. Then he turned again, bowed, and backed out of the room in proper fashion. When he had shut the door behind him, Nicholas took a deep breath and leaned against the window seat.

"They did something to him, didn't they?"

Lord Stowe nodded. "But we can't tell what it is. As far as we know, his story is accurate, and I had Theron—the man who led the attack—check him over. He recognized the boy, said there was nothing different. Although Theron did say there was a third man taken prisoner. When I asked the boy, he got tears in his eyes and refused to talk about it."

"Dead?"

"I don't know," Lord Stowe said. "I think we have to assume this boy is dangerous in some way, a way we can't comprehend yet. I recommend placing him in protective custody until we can figure out what to do with him."

Nicholas tugged on his ponytail. "He seems very, concerned for his father."

"I believe that's genuine," Lord Stowe said. "But the Fey might be using that as a way to lure us into Shadowlands. I think we tell the boy we're doing what we can, but stay away from their Shadowlands for the time being."

Nicholas sighed. "Choices. I dislike these choices. You were going to tell me what happened to him inside."

Lord Stowe smiled. "Apparently, he and his father got lenient treatment because one of the Fey women took a liking to the boy."

"Seems odd that she would let him go in that case, doesn't it?"

"No. He shows a curious loyalty to her."

Nicholas frowned and stared at the door. It was sturdy oak, but with the boy just outside, Nicholas didn't feel safe. Actually, that was wrong of him. He hadn't felt safe since he'd learned of the various Fey magicks, and how close they had come to doing away with him.

"I was thinking, Highness, of keeping him under guard at my place," Lord Stowe said.

"Why would you do that?"

"So that I can watch over him."

"No," Nicholas said. "The quarters are safer."

"Beg pardon, Highness, but I disagree. If we have the same guards watching over him in my place with strict procedure, we're better off with him there. You can check me each time I come into the palace and do the same with the regular guards. In the quarters too many people have access to him."

"What about the man who led the attack? Can the boy stay with him?"

Lord Stowe shook his head. "Too risky. That man is the one who brought the Fey prisoner to us. We have no idea if he has been infected by a different kind of magic."

"And you brought the boy to me. The same kind of problem could exist." Nicholas smiled. "I see your point, Lord Stowe. Have a contingent of twelve guards rotating every few hours watch him. Set up an elaborate check and double check with holy water. I'll inform my father of him and see what we can come up with between the two of us."

Lord Stowe bowed. As he stood, he said, "One other thing, Highness. A woman saw me just before the boy came. She swears that a cat stole her baby."

"What?" Nicholas said. "A cat?"

Lord Stowe nodded. "A golden cat who changed into a woman in the moonlight. The woman sounded a bit deranged to me, but since things have been quite odd around here this last year, I thought you would want to know."

"I do want to know," Nicholas said. He braced his hands on the window seat, letting the sharp stone edge bite into his palm. "What did the cat do with the child?"

"Took it to the Shadowlands," Lord Stowe said.

"And you're sure it was an Islander child?" The stone was turning Nicholas's hands cold.

"Positive. It was too old to be Fey, for one thing, and the woman could name its parents."

"I thought she was its mother."

Lord Stowe shook his head. "The Fey murdered the parents. She rescued the baby and hid it until the Fey left."

"So they may have been after this child before." Nicholas's mouth was dry. That cat was connected to the Doppelgängers. Maybe the child was one too.

"So it would seem."

Nicholas nodded. "Thanks for letting me know. When you take care of the boy, let me know what you've done with him."

Lord Stowe bowed again, apparently understanding the dismissal. He backed away and let himself out, closing the door behind him.

Nicholas closed his eyes and fell against the window seat cushions. All of this was too much. That cat—if it was only one cat—had a lot to do with the problems happening near the palace. And the boy, touched by the Fey in a way that was not comprehensible yet.

Or maybe he was Fey. Maybe they had discovered a way around holy water. But if that was true, why hadn't he attacked Nicholas? Tried to take a place in the palace?

The Fey never did things logically. After a year of battling them, Nicholas knew that much. He sighed and sat up. Time to talk with his father. The only thing he could hope was that his father's plan was a good one.

SEVENTY-FIVE

CASEO'S hands were shaking. He had to stop working or he would spill. He sat in one of the chairs, and it squeaked under his weight. The cabin was cold. He had been inside for days. He couldn't remember the last time he had eaten.

Touched was sitting in the other chair, staring at the ceiling as if it had secrets to reveal. Two Warders were asleep in the back room, and the others had gone to their own places for sleep, being too afraid to spend much time in this place, near the poison.

Caseo wished he could sleep, but his mind was too busy. After the discussion with Touched and Rotin a few days ago, he had dreamed a solution: an elegant spell with twists and turns that benefited a Master Warder. But when he awoke, he couldn't remember the details of the spell, only the sense of it. He had sent for Touched and explained what he could remember before he forgot it, and since then the two of them had worked almost nonstop. They were no closer to a solution, but it seemed to them as if they were.

Sometimes that sense of confidence made all the difference.

At least Caseo knew what direction he was going in. Touched had been right. They needed to create a spell of their own. But Caseo had come up with the aspects of the spell that would make it work for the Fey.

The spell would have to make the poison deadly to Islanders, and Islanders only. It would have to be cast from a distance, and in a situation of extreme stress. Only a handful of Fey could throw spells, and even fewer could do so under stress. His best choices were Warders themselves, or Weather Sprites. But there were too few Warders to waste, and the problem with Sprites was that they usually worked in private. The same, for that matter, could be said about Warders. Domestics might be able to do the work, but they would have to be right over the poison, and that was too dangerous. Still, as Rotin had pointed out, better to lose a few Domestics than not to solve the problem at all.

Caseo shifted his feet. They brushed against something on the floor, and a tingle ran up his leg. A bit of magick. He glanced down. The robe that Quest had brought in. Robe and sword. Religious icons, Quest had said before he ran off to a meeting with Rugar. Quest had promised to come back, but never had. Caseo had forgotten about the robe until now.

"Touched," he said.

Touched was still staring at the ceiling. He didn't appear to hear Caseo.

"Touched!"

Slowly Touched leaned forward. His eyes focused on Caseo. "What if—" Touched's voice rasped. "What if we forget about Sprites and Domestics? What if we use an Enchanter?"

Caseo resisted the urge to roll his eyes. "A great idea," he said, "except that we don't have an Enchanter with us on this trip."

Touched blinked and frowned. "But we do. We have one in camp. Can't you feel it?"

Caseo couldn't feel it. He had never been able to feel Enchanters. It was one of his only failings as a Warder. But he was not about to admit that to Touched. "I will check with Rugar. If we have an Enchanter in camp, it is not something he wants others to know."

Touched bit his lower lip, then let go. He had bite marks in the flesh. "It would work as an Enchanter spell. An Enchanter has the distance and the power, and he wouldn't have to work a bottle at a time. He could do it all at once."

The idea was brilliant, but worthless without an Enchanter. If the boy was feeling one, then something odd had happened. Perhaps one of the children had come into puberty with full Enchantment powers. But Caseo would have had hints. Enchanters, like Shape-Shifters and Warders, showed their powers from childhood. Only in glimpses and promises, but the powers existed. He would have known if Rugar had brought an Enchanter.

Besides, Enchanters were so rare that the Black King probably couldn't spare one. It was quite normal for long-distance campaigns to operate without one.

"It's a good idea," Caseo said, "but I think we have to stick with the Domestics and the Sprites for now. Better to work with the powers we have."

"Shame," Touched said. "It was a good idea."

Caseo almost contradicted him. A good idea was one they could use. But he had been harsh enough with the boy lately. And at least he was visualizing spells. That was better than the other Warders were doing.

"Did you get any others?" Caseo asked.

"I was working on that one." Touched bit his lip again. He would have to change that habit, or one day he would bite through.

"All right, then," Caseo said. "Do you remember what Quest said when he brought the robes in this morning?"

"He said that it had caused lights to rotate inside the Circle Door when he arrived. Rugar made him take off the robe and sword, and then the lights stopped."

"Odd," Caseo said. He kicked the robe again. The tingle ran through his leg. "Pick this up, would you?"

Touched got up with a sigh. He wasn't shaking like Caseo, but he had been working as hard and had gone pale with exhaustion. He crouched and put a hand on the black cloth, then drew back with a cry, as if it had burned him.

"It's alive," he said.

"It certainly has power, doesn't it?"

Touched looked at his hand. "It doesn't seem to have hurt me. Quest wore this all the time?"

"For a few days. He seems fine. Yet we have the small matter of the inside lights."

"Do they ever rotate?"

"No, never," Caseo said. "Shadowlands is a purely functional spell. Whatever is built into it serves a small purpose. The lights have always given us the information we have needed, but they have never acted on their own accord before."

Touched frowned and leaned back. "Are they Fey Lamps?"

Caseo shook his head. "They are part of the Shadowlands itself. Just a construct from Rugar's Vision. I almost dismissed the boy's story this morning. Rugar's Vision has been spotty, and that can sometimes create anomalies. But now I'm not so certain. You and I have both felt power from this robe, and I wager if I wake up the others in the back, they would feel it too."

"What does it mean?" Touched said.

"I don't know," Caseo said. "Quest said these are religious garments, and the sword is a religious symbol, as is the poison. Perhaps their religion has a power they don't understand or know how to use."

"What makes you think they don't know how to use it?" Touched said.

"Because if they knew, we would be dead. They would have defeated us," Caseo said.

"You can't know that," Touched said.

Caseo smiled at him. "I can, and so can you if you learn to observe. This robe has enough power to jolt us, who happen to be guarded against other beings' magick. It also has enough power to cause the Circle Door to behave strangely. Whatever you may think of these things, Touched, these are not small matters. It suggests a great power."

Touched ran a finger over the robe, wincing as he did so. "Then we need to study it as well. Maybe it holds the secret to the poison."

"Maybe," Caseo said. He didn't want to rule anything out. "But I think we can solve the riddle of the poison without it. If you say you have developed a spell for an Enchanter, then we are not far from developing one for others."

Touched dropped the robe. He wiped his hands on his own robe as if he were cleaning them off. "I think we should check with Rugar first and find out about the Enchanter we have here."

"No," Caseo said. "That's taking the easy way. He's keeping the Enchanter from the rest of us for a reason. We're better off with a wide-ranging spell; one that can be done by a variety of people." He looked at Touched. "If you can devise a spell for an Enchanter, you can devise one for a Sprite."

Touched seemed to grow even paler, his eyes dark circles in his narrow face. "I work best with Enchanters," he said.

"We all do, boy," Caseo said. "They fill in the gaps for us, make spells that are awkward seem elegant. But we don't have a choice here. We will work with the Domestics and the Sprites."

"I can't," Touched whispered.

Caseo froze. "You . . . can't?"

Touched shook his head. He wasn't looking at Caseo. "My Domestic spells never work. And I don't understand Sprites."

"Your Domestic spells seem to work fine," Caseo said. He felt odd—lighter than usual, as if part of him was elated that Touched couldn't work and the other part was very, very angry.

"Rotin helped. She's always finished them."

The anger took over. Caseo had to struggle to keep the emotion off his face. "She has?"

Touched nodded. "She said I wasn't to tell you, but I don't know how I could avoid it here. I can't translate the spell over to the Domestics or the Sprites. My talent seems to lie in the large spells, like an Enchanter's, or the bloody spells like the ones the Foot Soldiers use."

And here Caseo had always believed that Touched would be the next great genius of Spell Warding. Rotin had been playing with him, just as she had been playing with Touched a few evenings ago. Her manipulation was going to stop. Caseo would see to that. Touched was no more talented than the rest of them. In fact, he had the normal weaknesses that any new Warder had.

Which didn't help them now.

"Tell me your Enchanter spell," Caseo said. "I'll translate it."

Touched frowned at him. "Will you be able to? I thought only the spell's creator could translate."

Caseo shook his head. "It's easier for the spell's originator to translate. But anyone can do it. It will just take me more time."

Touched ran a hand along the table. "Even if you do figure it out," he said, "how will you test it? We can't use Jewel's pet. She'll hurt us somehow."

"Rugar and I came to an agreement," Caseo said. "Jewel gets to keep her pet and to set the boy free. In exchange for my willingness to go along, I get the old prisoner. The disagreeable one. And I've been saving him for a moment like this."

"We'll have only one chance, then," Touched said.

Caseo smiled at him. "We need only one. If he dies, our spell will have worked exactly as we planned." He leaned forward, his tiredness forgotten. "Tell me your spell, boy. Let's defeat these Islanders once and for all."

SEVENTY-SIX

TITUS cried as the road wound into the trees outside of Jahn. He knew he shouldn't cry, just as he knew he shouldn't have cried when his parents had sent him to the city two years before. The Holy One was supposed to watch over him, carrying his prayers to God's Ear. But he had never seen the Holy One, and he had seen a Fey, and, God forgive him, he believed in the Fey. He knew what they could do.

The tears came in bursts. He had been crying for most of the day now, although at the moment he was merely sniffling. His eyes felt swollen, and his throat was raw. If people saw him, they would think him daft.

But he had never been this far to the west of Jahn. He could hear the river burbling far below. The trees overhead provided a cool shade against the hot sun. He had forgotten how much he liked trees—and how much he missed them. When he had agreed to become an Aud ("Second son," his father reminded him. "Second sons always get religion"), he hadn't realized he would be sent to the city, where everything was hot, smelly, and dust covered.

His father was proud of him. ("They're sending you up, son, because you're smart. Only the smart ones get to go to that Tabernacle.") His father would be even prouder if he knew the honor the Rocaan had bestowed on Titus. Titus had never met the Rocaan before dawn that morning, had seen him only in official ceremonies. Once he had shaken the Rocaan's hand, when he had come to Aud's Day in the Servants' Chapel, and once, a few weeks before, he had received the Rocaan's Blessing along with all the other Auds.

This morning he had received the Rocaan's Blessing again. Only Titus had been alone in the room. Up close, the Rocaan was an old man who smelled. The base of his robe had stains on it, something the Danites would have chastised Titus for. He hadn't liked seeing that. It almost made him believe the Rocaan was human. When the Blessing was over, the Rocaan had touched Titus's shoulder and asked him if he was courageous.

He had said yes. What else could a boy say when faced with the link to his God?

The Rocaan had smiled and then given him his first Charge. The other second-year Auds were jealous. What Aud got his first Charge from the Rocaan himself? But if they knew what the Charge was, they would be glad the Charge had come to Titus.

Titus stopped and wiped his eyes with the back of his hand. He wouldn't cry anymore. He wouldn't. The Rocaan had told him it was holy to die in God's service.

But he was only fourteen years old. Why would God want him now?

Ahead, he saw the huge oak he had been warned about. Soon he would see the clearing that led to the Fey place.

He sniffled, then headed for a large stump off the side of the road. When he sat, he bent over and pressed his face against his knees. The vial of holy water burned like a torch in the pocket of his robe. The Rocaan had told him not to bring any, but Elder Matthias had argued that he should.

He is not going as an enemy, the Rocaan had said.

He is certainly not going as a friend, the Elder had replied.

The problem was Titus didn't understand why he was facing the Fey at all. Alone.

His feet were cold, and he wished for the millionth time since he had become an Aud that he was allowed to wear shoes. Even more than his shaved head, he resented the bare feet. He hated being cold, and coldness always started with his feet.

The Rocaan had insisted he travel without any protection except God's. But wasn't holy water God's protection? Apparently the Rocaan did not think so. But the Rocaan hadn't stipulated where the Charge began. So Titus planned to carry the holy water all the way up to the Fey place.

The threat of tears subsided a bit. He stood. He wanted to get to the Fey place before nightfall. He couldn't imagine anything scarier than being there in the dark.

The bottoms of his feet were hardened by years of being barefoot, so he scarcely felt the rocks. But when he turned at the oak, the chill of the damp grass made him wince. He heard voices echo in the clearing. They used a language he did not understand.

He swallowed. The Rocaan had assured him that the Fey would speak Nye, maybe even Islander. If they all spoke this odd, guttural language, his Charge would be for nothing.

He couldn't see the speakers. They had to be farther away from him than they sounded. Their voices were raised; it almost sounded as if they were fighting. He sniffled again, but not from any threat of tears. The possibility of tears was gone. He was too frightened for that.

Slowly he crossed the clearing. He saw the dirt circle the Rocaan had told him about. He was supposed to go there and wait, see if someone found him. His entire body was trembling. He tried to tell himself it was from the cold. And he was cold. His toenails had turned blue, and his fingers were little blocks of ice.

Clutched in those blocks of ice was the vial. He had forgotten to put it down before he reached the clearing.

"Forgive me, Holy Sir," he whispered, as if the Rocaan were sitting on his shoulder, watching him.

He glanced around for a place to leave the vial, but didn't see any. Finally he set it just outside the dirt circle, letting the vial fall away from the circle onto the grass.

As the sky grew darker, he realized that the clearing had too much light. He glanced up and saw small lights hovering over the dirt circle. The lights were in the shapes of human beings. When they saw him, they all reached toward him, their tiny lips moving.

He couldn't move. So this was what happened to the

people the Fey captured. He wanted to turn and run, but he couldn't. If he did that, he would fail his Charge. Any Aud who failed his Charge would lose his place in the Church. His father would never accept him back home then.

He closed his eyes and stepped across the dirt circle. When he opened his eyes, the little beings were all crouched, their heads buried in their hands as if his movement had frightened them. A bit of warmth radiated from the lights, and the grass beneath his feet was hot.

This was the place the Rocaan had told him to come to. Titus recognized it from the description of the trees and the circles. The clearing had an otherworldly sense, the same kind of sense he had felt when he'd stepped into the Tabernacle for the first time, as if this were a holy place, and he was trespassing.

But that couldn't be. The Fey were heathens, godless, and unclean. Some of the Auds even believed the Fey were little demons sent by a jealous rival to destroy the followers of Roca. Titus knew of nothing in the Words to support that theory, but for the first time since he'd heard it, he did not dispute it. There was a power there, a power so great that it made him shudder.

Then the lights went dark, and a shadow moved across the sky. He felt a change in the wind, as if someone had closed all the doors and windows around the dirt circle. The air was still. With a shaking hand he reached behind him, and his fingers hit an invisible barrier like glass over the dirt.

He couldn't get out. He was in a Fey prison, his holy water outside it. He was trapped. He swallowed down the panic—panic did not suit a man of God—and made himself stand in a place where he was warm for the first time in days.

A door opened in front of him. The door was suspended a few feet off the ground, and it was round. It took him a moment to realize the door's outlines traced the lights that had been there a moment before. Inside, he saw a gray swirling mass, and beyond it, buildings. A Fey stood just beside the door, with others gathering behind him. This Fey was slender, and just a few years older than Titus, but his face had a fierceness that was both beautiful and terrifying.

"Tel?" the Fey asked in his guttural voice.

Titus didn't move for what seemed like forever. Tell? Was that a command? Or did it mean something in their language? He opened his mouth, then closed it again. His breath was coming in small gasps. Finally he managed, in Nye, "I am from the Rocaan. I have a message."

The Fey at the door looked stunned. Then he glanced at someone beside the door whom Titus couldn't see. They spoke for a moment in the other language; then the door closed.

After all that light, the darkness was absolute. Titus backed up, but the invisible barrier was still there. He couldn't get out, he couldn't see, and the Fey knew he was there.

His lower lip trembled, and he bit it. Then his eyes burned. He couldn't cry in front of them. He had done nothing but cry since he had become an Aud two years before. Every night, in his bed, he would sob silently and wish he could go home.

He wanted to go home now more than ever, but he couldn't. He might never again.

At least it was warm, and his feet were warm. Something positive. Concentrate on something positive. But that didn't help him. He was more frightened than he had ever been in his life. More frightened than he had been when the Danites had come and taken him away. More frightened than the day he'd first seen Jahn.

He crossed his arms over his chest, gripping his thin robe, and stifling the urge to pray. The Danites said that praying for one's self only angered God, and that all prayers should be for others. He could pretend that he was praying for his father, that his father wouldn't want him to die in disgrace, but the truth was that his father would never know. He would know only that Titus had died on his Charge, and to die in the Lord's service was an honorable thing.

The door opened again and flooded him with light. More Fey stood near the door, and he thought he saw a Danite he recognized, although that wasn't possible. He backed up all the way to the barrier, his feet brushing the dirt circle. An older Fey stood in the door now, his face craggy but still upswept, as if age had given his features wings.

"You're one of the holy ones, aren't you, boy?" he asked in Nye.

Titus swallowed. "I-I'm an Aud. I have a message—for you, one of you, from the Rocaan. Please. It is my Charge."

The Fey who looked like the Danite spoke in the other language, a quick, rapid sentence, which the man waved off. "Is the message for anyone in particular?" the man asked.

"It's for whoever is in charge. The Rocaan asks forgiveness that he doesn't know your names." The sentences were coming easier. Things were progressing as the Rocaan had said they would.

"How do I know this isn't a trick? That you aren't covered with poison and won't try to destroy our homeland?"

Titus glanced at the vial on the outside of the barrier. "I—I, ah, was told to leave my holy water outside and to come to you naked if I had to." He held out his arms, as the Rocaan had told him to do. "You can search me. I won't do anything. On the Roca's Ascension, I won't."

The Fey who resembled a Danite spoke again. The older man nodded. He snapped his fingers at the boy who had opened the door. The boy shot a glance of pure hatred at the older man, then stepped out the door.

"You try to kill me," the boy whispered to Titus, "and I will see to it that your entire family dies."

Titus shook his head. What if the boy accidentally died? The Charge couldn't include Titus's whole family, could it? Still, he didn't move. The boy searched Titus, then stopped, his hand hovering over the sword.

"Take that off," the boy said.

"I—I can't," Titus stammered. "I made an oath. Auds aren't supposed to forsake the sword."

"You said naked if you had to. Well, you don't have to take off that robe, but you have to take off that sword," the boy said.

The Rocaan had said naked, and he had said to cooperate. Titus bit his lower lip. Did his oath to the Rocaan take precedence, or the vow he had made as an Aud? Or was this part of the test? He didn't know. He wasn't smart enough to make these kinds of choices.

And what did it matter? They would probably kill him. He had to prepare himself to meet his God.

"I can't," he said. "I'm sworn."

"Oh, for God's sake." The Danite in the back came forward. He had a familiar face. He spoke in Islander. "The sword is just a symbol, son. What matters is in your heart."

True enough. But the symbol became real when the faith

was true. They had learned that too. But Titus didn't say that. Instead, he said in Islander, "Did the Rocaan send you too?"

The Danite looked behind him, at the others, as if he were asking for confirmation. His mouth was a thin line when he turned back to Titus. "No," the Danite said. "I'm here on other business."

Titus nodded, even though he didn't really understand. "I need to speak to the head of the Fey," he said.

The Danite smiled at him a bit sadly. "No Fey is going to talk with you while you wear that sword."

"I can't take it off." Titus clung to the sword. He felt as if it were his only piece of security in this place.

The Danite sighed and spoke in Nye. "You're not going to get him to change his mind. You'll have to find another way."

A woman in the back said something in the Fey language; then another agreed with her. They spoke at once, and finally one of them ran out of Titus's field of vision.

The boy stood calmly beside Titus. While the others seemed to wait for something, the boy looked at Titus and grinned. "You know," he said in Nye, "we could as easily kill you as we could listen to you."

"I know," Titus said. If he had thought he was safe, he would risk removing the sword. How stupid did they think he was?

Finally the woman came back with a bowl of water. She handed it down to the boy. He held it out to Titus.

"Wash the sword off, and wash off anything else that might have been touched by the poison."

Titus stared at the water. They could as easily be trying to harm him. But that was part of a Charge, to take risks. He would have to take a large risk here, and he would have to give in, even a little, in order to complete his mission.

With a trembling hand he picked up the sword and dipped it into the water, washing the blade with his fingers. Then he reached into his pocket and removed his cleaning cloth, dropping it onto the ground. He couldn't think of anything else that had touched the holy water, but he washed his hands for good measure.

The older man spoke to the boy in Fey. The boy pursed his lips—obviously not liking the comment. He set the water bowl down. Quickly, almost defiantly, he reached out and wrapped his hand around the sword.

All of the Fey gasped. Titus could feel the boy's fear. But the boy stared him in the face as if memorizing his features in case they met on the other side.

After a moment the boy let go of the sword, stared at his hand, then held it up for the others to see. "I'll live another day, Rugar," he said in Nye.

The older man—Rugar—seemed unconcerned. "Bring the boy up," he said.

Titus swallowed hard. He took one glance over his shoulder at the real world, which he might never see again. Then he allowed them to pull him into the opaque gray mass.

SEVENTY-SEVEN

SCAVENGER climbed into the Shadowlands, bent double
with the weight of the pouches. Caseo never thought things
through. Pouches filled with bone—even bone shavings—
were heavy, and tired people should not carry them. The
Domestic had collapsed a few hours before—at least, that's
what Scavenger assumed happened, since she had not returned.

He had worked longer than he'd planned, following
Uences to the river. They had carved up dozens, maybe
hundreds, of skeletons. Scavenger's right hand was sore from
clutching a knife. His palm was covered with tiny burst
blisters, and a large blood blister still threatened on his
thumb.

He regretted leaving Uences out there. Once Vulture
had left, she had been quite civil. But he had no choice. He
could keep working until he was so exhausted he was of no
use to anyone, or he could take the pouches himself, go
inside, and find Rugar.

As he walked up the hill, he swayed, and then steadied as
he crossed the clearing. But that final step into Shadowlands was one of the most difficult he had ever made.

Shadowlands itself looked nearly empty. A single man

pounded nails into a board he had braced on the ground, but Scavenger couldn't tell what the man was building. A few Domestics worked around the Domicile. A group of Infantry were leaving Rugar's cabin, but other than that, he saw no one. Smoke rose out of the chimney of the Warders' cabin, and outside sat several dozen pouches filled with bone. Vulture slept next to them, his clothes and face still filthy from the work he had done earlier.

Scavenger crouched beside him and shook his shoulder. Vulture opened his eyes slowly and rolled them when he saw who was trying to wake him.

"Go replace Uences. She's been working since you left."

"I deserve more sleep," Vulture said.

"Go on." Scavenger gave him a push.

Vulture sat up and rubbed his eyes. "Why aren't you going back? You've been there the shortest."

"I have some things to deliver to the Domicile, then I'll be back out there. But they said it might take a few hours. Better to relieve her now."

Vulture sighed. "And I get to do it. Lucky, lucky me. How much more is left out there?"

"Enough for another afternoon's work." Scavenger lowered his voice. "Know what they need the bone for?"

Vulture shook his head. "Caseo said something about a wonderful new spell, but you know how he is."

Caseo. Scavenger shuddered. Yes, Scavenger knew how Caseo was. He ran a hand through his hair. "Go help her. I'll be back in an hour or two."

Vulture heaved himself off the pouches. "If I come back and find you asleep, I'll cut off your fingers."

"Then I really won't be able to help you."

They grinned at each other. Behind them the Warders' door swung open, and Caseo stood there, hands on his hips.

"Just put the pouches down, boy, and leave us," he said. "We're trying to do legitimate work in here." Then he slammed the door shut.

"Touchy, touchy," Vulture said.

Scavenger said nothing. His heart was pounding so hard against his chest, he thought his ribs might burst. He was staring at the door. Caseo didn't even seem to recognize him. Just as he'd thought. No one saw the Red Caps. No one would know when he killed Rugar.

But that knowledge no longer held any consolation for him. How can a man threaten to kill someone one day and a week later not even recognize him? Was Caseo that cold?

Or was Scavenger that small?

Vulture punched him on the shoulder. "Hey, buddy, you all right?"

Scavenger nodded, forcing his gaze away from the door. "Yeah," he said. "I got things to do. I'll meet you outside."

Vulture watched him, and Scavenger headed for the Domicile. Vulture would notice anything Scavenger did, and Scavenger didn't want to do anything out of the ordinary until Vulture was gone.

Vulture took his time getting from the Warders' cabin to the Circle Door. When he finally left, he moved slowly out the door as if being banished to the outside was worse than death. Scavenger let out a huge sigh, then walked back to Rugar's cabin.

Smoke came from that chimney as well, thin gray plumes of it, puffing up and brushing against the apparent roof of Shadowlands, then disappearing altogether. Scavenger didn't understand why the smoke didn't collect in Shadowlands—someone had tried to explain it to him once, but the explanation made no sense. This was the second Shadowlands of his life. The first was in the Nye campaign, and it was not nearly as elaborate as this. The Fey slept on the gray, cloud-covered ground in thick blankets made especially for the campaign by the Domestics. They had sewn something into those blankets; he'd never slept so well in his life, before or since.

He gripped the hilt of the knife that he had got from Vulture and wondered when Vulture would notice that he didn't have it. Would he work at all, or would he wait for Scavenger to come back? Probably Uences would force her blade on him and then leave, and Vulture would have to work by himself until the news of Rugar's death reached him.

Scavenger didn't even feel sorry for that.

He stopped in front of Rugar's cabin. The Infantry were huddled a few cabins away, watching him. The skin on the back of his neck crawled. If he concentrated, he could hear voices from inside the cabin. Something was going on. This was not the time to knock on the door and confront Rugar.

The Spell Warders' cabin wasn't that far away. Maybe Scavenger should just grab a few empty pouches and go back outside to relieve Uences. The King had not given Scavenger a deadline. Scavenger could take all the time he needed.

He stopped outside the Warders' cabin. The smoke coming from the chimney was a dark-gray, almost charcoal, color, and it smelled of roasting meat. He had been fooled by Warder smells before, and even though his stomach growled, he knew that what they were cooking inside was probably not anything he wanted.

No one had left the empty pouches where they were supposed to be. He needed an armload to go back outside. No sense working without them.

Still, knocking on the door was quite a risk for him all alone. It gave Caseo another chance to experiment on him. Scavenger put his hand on the hilt of his knife. He would be prepared, and then Caseo wouldn't be able to grab him.

He went to the door, knocked, and backed away from it. The door opened almost immediately. Caseo blocked the light from inside.

"What now, boy?"

"I need some pouches so that I can finish the job outside."

Caseo grinned. "You're afraid of me, aren't you, boy?"

Scavenger shook his head quickly.

"Afraid I'm going to take you inside and turn you into a mass of jelly?"

His grip on the hilt tightened. Again he shook his head.

A female voice cried from inside, "Leave him alone, Caseo. We have to finish this."

"You can't finish without me," he said. "And I'll be just a moment." Then he stepped out and closed the door behind him. "They think your life might have value. They think I'm cruel for taunting you. You think that, too, don't you?"

There was a huge lump in Scavenger's throat. He had to swallow twice before he could speak. "I—ah—I need those pouches if I'm going to do the work you need."

"We really don't need you. That's the whole truth. If Rugar was smart, he would stop transporting creatures like you to each battle site and just kill you when it becomes clear that you're not real Fey."

"I'm as much Fey as you are," Scavenger said.

"Really?" Caseo's grin was wide. "Then prove it. Come with me. Let me test the poison on you."

"That's a stupid test!" Scavenger's voice rose as he spoke. "If I prove I'm Fey, I die. I'm not that stupid. And if I don't die, you'll say I'm not Fey. Think about this. Three Red Caps never came back from the First Battle for Jahn. Maybe the poison got them. They had to have died. *Had to.* So, therefore, we're Fey. *We're Fey.* We're just not as mean as you are."

Caseo laughed. "You are an amazing little man. As if I were to trust your perceptions on something as important as saving the lives of our people. Listen, little man, we're experimenting on a new type of poison. I promise not to use the Islander poison on you. I'll use the new poison on you when it's finished. Then we'll know if it works."

"No!" Scavenger was shaking. There was no one around to help him. The other Warders were inside working, and they would side with Caseo. Even though Scavenger was shouting, no one came out of the other cabins. They probably peeked through the door, saw Scavenger fighting with Caseo, and thought it not worth interrupting.

Caseo took a step toward him. "You'd be remembered as helping all Fey."

Scavenger backed up. "I don't want to be remembered."

"Come, now," Caseo said. "Being remembered is better than being ignored while you live."

"Maybe for you," Scavenger said. He pulled the knife out of its sheath.

"Ah, threats, little man?" Caseo didn't seem frightened. He came closer.

Scavenger took another step back and nearly fell down the stairs. "Just stay away from me. I don't know why you pick on me. Just stay away from me."

"I 'pick' on you, boy, because you offend me. I don't want people like you passing yourselves off as Fey. You're an abomination, and it's an absolute shame that some people consider you my equal."

"I can be your equal," Scavenger said. Energy flowed through his body, making him bounce. His breathing was coming in shallow gasps.

"Can you, little man? I doubt it. I very much doubt it."

"We're all equal at two points in our lives," Scavenger

said, his grip on the hilt so tight that the metal dug into his palm. "When we're born and when we die."

Caseo's smile was broad. "Not even then, boy," he said. "Some of us have talent when we're born—it's just latent—and some have talent when we die."

"But you die just the same." Scavenger waved the knife at him. "I came for pouches. I came here to help you. Now, leave me alone, and I won't ever bother you again."

Caseo shook his head. "Can't do that, boy. Until Rugar changes things, you are my assistant, like it or not. And I need your assistance. Now, be a good boy and come inside with me. It won't take very long, and it will help all of us."

Scavenger swiped at Caseo with the knife. "Stay away from me."

"You won't hurt me, boy. The penalty for attacking a Warder is death by mutilation. Another difference, since there is no penalty when a Red Cap dies." Caseo grabbed Scavenger's arm—the one without the knife. His flesh was hot. He had no fear in his face. "Now, we're going inside."

"No!" Scavenger said, and plunged the knife into Caseo's chest. Caseo took a surprised step backward, but did not let go of Scavenger's arm. Scavenger pulled the knife from Caseo's chest—blood spurted, as it had when Silence had used his knife—and he hacked at Caseo's fingers, in a panic to get them off him. Caseo let go, and the knife gouged into Scavenger's arm. He bit back a scream of pain.

Caseo dropped to his knees, his other hand over his chest. The blood was coming in spurts. His eyes were wide with shock, his mouth open, but no sound was coming out. There was no one else outside, and no one seemed to be moving in the Warders' cabin.

"I'm sorry," Scavenger said. He hadn't meant to become as bad as Caseo. He hadn't meant anything bad at all. Now they would know who did it. The other Warders would know that a Red Cap had hurt Caseo. He had to get away.

His feet slipped in the blood on the porch. The blood was flowing down the steps and disappearing into the gray mist that was the ground. He jumped over the steps and ran for the Circle Door, repeating the chant over and over until he arrived. The Door opened for him, and he dived out, tossing the knife away as he did so.

He had planned to do this, but not after killing Caseo.

He had planned to kill Rugar, and he didn't even know where Rugar was. Now he had no way to find out.

Scavenger slipped into the woods and ran away from the skeleton pile, down the embankment to the side of the river. There he stopped to catch his breath. He was covered in blood, and the blood smelled no different from any other kind. No different at all.

SEVENTY-EIGHT

THEY took Titus to one of their buildings, but only the older man went inside with him. Titus was unprepared for the darkness inside the building. The older man knocked on a lamp, and a small creature stood up, extending light in all directions. He knocked on another, and another, until the room glowed.

A table and several chairs furnished the front. A fireplace stood off to the left, the fire only embers now. A woman peeked in the door and asked a question. The older man shook his head. She nodded, slipped back out, closing the door behind her.

"What's your message, child?" the man asked in Nye.

Titus didn't know how to speak to this man, if there was a protocol or not. He merely bowed his head, then said, "The Rocaan wishes a meeting with you. He wants to end this war, and he believes that you two can do so together."

"I thought the Rocaan was your religious leader."

"Yes, sir."

"But I should have that discussion with your King."

Titus shook his head. "The Rocaan says the King has handled this long enough, and this is a spiritual matter."

"Ah," the older man said. "So we go in to see your Rocaan, and he kills us all."

"No. He would not do that," Titus said. "He would like to speak with you about power, spiritual power, yours and his."

"I see." The older man slid a chair near Titus. "Sit, boy, and be comfortable. I won't hurt you."

Titus sat as he was bade. He entwined his fingers together and kept his head bowed.

"This Rocaan of yours, he is the one who leads all of you in religion, doesn't he?"

Titus nodded.

"And he makes the poison that kills us."

"He never meant it to kill you. He didn't know." Titus spoke with strong emphasis, just as the Rocaan had. His emphasis would have been strong, even if the Rocaan's hadn't. "Holy water has been part of our religion since the beginning. We didn't know its properties, until an Elder discovered it by accident."

"By accident?" The older man's smile was cold. "How do you kill by accident?"

"He threw a bottle at your people to keep them away from him. It shattered, and they died."

The older man's eyes opened a little, then returned to their hooded gaze. "I see. Then he told your people, and the killing started."

Titus swallowed. The Rocaan said he wasn't supposed to talk back to the Fey, but he would have loved to point out that they had started the killing, not the Islanders.

"Must I see your Rocaan alone, or may I bring guards?"

"He would like you to come as you would, as long as you promise not to attack him. He says he will come with friends as well." Titus licked his lips. "He wants to perform a Blessing to cleanse us all of hatred, but to do that, he will need to use some holy water. He promises not to turn it on you. Likewise, he says you may bring weapons if you promise not to use them against him."

"He's a trusting sort, is he?"

Titus nodded. "He is a good man, sir. He would not kill anyone."

"What of all the Fey he has killed?"

Titus was so relieved that the Rocaan had thought of all

the answers to these questions. Titus never would have been able to think of them himself. "He has killed none personally, sir, and he wishes the others were still with us. But he begs you to consider the circumstances, and to ask yourself whether or not you would have done the same as he did in handing out holy water."

The Fey smiled. "What I would have done is immaterial. What he has done is the issue, and what he plans to do is even more important."

Titus peeked through his eyelashes at the Fey. "What he plans to do is to make you acceptable to God so that this fighting might end, and we might all find a peaceable solution."

"And what if I don't want a peaceable solution?" the Fey asked.

Titus shrugged. "Then, sir, I guess things will remain the same."

The Fey put his finger beneath Titus's chin and raised the boy's head. The older man smelled of pine trees and leather. His skin was covered with faint lines and was darker than that of a man who had worked all his life in the sun. "Can you guarantee that your Rocaan will be at this meeting?"

"Yes, sir," Titus said. "It is his idea, and he has given his word. He never goes back on his word."

The Fey smiled. "Then tell your leader that I will meet him. I will bring a full contingent of warriors who will have magick as well as swords. Tell him that if he does not show, I will slaughter any Islander I see. Tell him also that if he betrays me in any way, I will do the same to him."

"Yes, sir," Titus whispered. A shiver ran through him that he could not control. This man, this Fey, meant what he said.

"Tell him the next time he wishes to send a message to me, he will send a man, not a child. I have no more sympathy for children than I do for men. I will kill one as easily as I will kill the other."

Titus swallowed hard. "Yes, sir."

Then the Fey chucked Titus's chin and smiled at him. "Now, tell me where this meeting will take place."

"Two days hence in the kirk near Daisy Stream."

"A kirk?" The Fey raised one eyebrow. "Isn't that a religious spot?"

"Yes, sir, but he begged me to remind you that you may come armed."

"I would prefer to meet in a place that does not hold religious significance to your people."

"He says he understands that, sir, but he begs your forgiveness. He says if he meets you in a kirk, no one will question him, and the King will not send troops."

The Fey's smile faded. "Your Rocaan is a wily man."

"No, sir," Titus said. "He is a good man who wishes for peace before he dies."

The Fey crossed his arms, leaned against the table, and sighed. "All right. Tell your Rocaan that I agree to his terms, and warn him that if anything is different from what you have told me, I will take revenge. Warn him that Fey adore taking revenge." Then the Fey smiled, a cold, forbidding smile. Titus shuddered in spite of himself.

"You're dismissed, boy. You'll find Burden outside where you left him. He will let you out of Shadowlands."

Titus stood. His legs wobbled beneath him.

"And, boy, be sure to tell your Rocaan everything that I have told you, because I will hold you responsible for that meeting as well as him."

"Yes, sir." Titus bowed his head, uncertain what the Fey meant by that comment, but it frightened him nonetheless.

"You're dismissed, boy."

"Thank you, sir." Titus made himself walk to the door. He couldn't run, couldn't show weakness in front of these people. he pulled the door open and stepped into the grayness. The boy who had brought him was waiting with a group of other Fey by a nearby building. When the boy saw Titus, he came over.

"So," the boy said. "He decided to spare you."

Titus put his chin up. "I have a message to take back to Jahn."

The boy shrugged. "I won't stop you, not when our illustrious Rugar thinks you should go free."

Titus didn't answer. He hurried down the steps and walked through the ground mist back to the place where he had come in. Only there was no door.

"You shouldn't hurry, little mouse," the boy said. "You can't leave without my help."

Suddenly Titus's throat went dry. What was to stop the

boy from killing him and not telling his leader? Then they would have an excuse to rain terror on the Rocaan. But if they could do that, they already would have. "Your leader said I could go."

The boy smiled. "And so he did. This time. But when he decides that you will do as we want, you'll be mine. I'll make sure of that."

He waved his hands, and the door opened. Titus jumped out, rolled on the grass, and landed outside the dirt circle. The barrier was gone. He grabbed his bottle of holy water and looked up in time to see the door close. Darkness surrounded him, but for the first time since he had left Jahn, he felt safe.

SEVENTY-NINE

THE cabin had an odd smell to it. Jewel pushed aside with her foot the chair the Islander boy had sat on. She would have a Domestic clean it. She refused to sit on it herself. Her father was watching her closely.

"All right," he said. "Tell me what you're thinking."

"That you're a fool." The words hurried out of her, almost unbidden. She hadn't realized how angry she was until she said them. "You shouldn't have agreed to their meeting. You should have set up your own. And with their religious leader? What can he do except kill you? You should be seeing their King."

"Their King can't help me." Rugar leaned against the fireplace. The morning's fire had burned to ash.

"And this religious leader can?" Jewel threw her braid over her shoulder and faced her father. He was smiling at her. That irritated her even more.

"He is the keeper of the secrets. We will learn about their magick."

"If they don't do away with us first. Papa, this is a trap. Go after that little boy and make him change the meeting."

Rugar shook his head. His eyes crinkled with an amusement he couldn't hide. "Jewel," he said quietly, "once we learn their secrets, we can win this war."

"I refuse to believe he would set up a meeting with you in order to teach *you* the secrets that give them an advantage." She stood, too, so that she faced him. She was as tall as he was, and it gave her a feeling of power. "He is probably planning to kill you, and if any Islander can, he can."

"He won't kill me. He's letting me go in there with weapons."

Jewel bit back anger. She had never seen this stubborn side to him before, although she had heard her grandfather speak of it. This was the side that had brought them all to Blue Isle in the first place. "If you go in with weapons, he'll go in with weapons. He'll kill you one on one, and then where will we be?"

"You'll be in charge."

"And our people will want to return to Nye. They won't listen to me. I'm still a young girl to many of them. They don't even know that I have my Vision."

He raised an eyebrow in that measuring look she hated. "And whose fault is that?"

"One Vision does not a Visionary make," she said. Then she put her palms on the back of her chair and leaned toward him. "What does your Vision say about this meeting?"

Color rose in his cheeks, but he didn't pull his gaze from hers. "I have had no Vision about this."

"Well, then," she snapped before she could help herself, "at least we know you won't die."

"That's a folktale," he said. "If Visionaries see their own death, they don't talk about it."

"I know it's a folktale." She said each word with such force she spit as she spoke. She resisted the urge to cover her mouth. "I was being sarcastic, and underneath it, I'm frightened. Caseo says you have lost your Vision. Is that true?"

Rugar stared at her for a long time without saying a word. The color in his cheeks grew deeper.

"Is that true?" she asked again.

"Not all events require a Vision."

"No," she said. "Only the important ones. I think a meeting between the Fey and their local enemy leader is an important event, particularly since one or both of you could die. And you have no Vision about it? Has anyone? Have you checked with the Shaman?"

"She would tell me if she saw something bad."

"Would she? Does she know that she is supposed to do that, or will she assume that you have Seen as well?"

"Why are you being so forceful, Jewel?"

"Because you're being stupid. And I don't want you to die." Her voice shook a little on the last word. His death would devastate her, and she would have to be the one to carry on, not just for herself but for the force on Blue Isle. "I'm going to talk to the Shaman."

"No, Jewel." Rugar used the commanding voice he had used when she and her brothers had misbehaved as children. The voice stopped her, even now. "The Shaman is not supposed to be disturbed on mundane matters. If she has a problem, she will come to me. Now, let this go. I will take care of this. You aren't thinking it through."

Jewel crossed her arms. "I am thinking very clearly. Why don't you tell me what you believe I'm missing?"

"Quest."

Jewel frowned. "Quest?"

Rugar nodded. "He goes, takes over the Rocaan, and we know the secret to their holy water. It is the opportunity that Quest missed in the Tabernacle. And we have guards around him so that nothing will happen to him."

"He'll have Islanders around. They won't let that happen to their religious leader."

"Who is going to stop us? How fast can we kill a handful of Islanders?"

"And what happens if one of them manages to spray poison on you or on Quest?"

"We'll protect him."

"What happens if that Rocaan has some kind of force in his body, some magickal force that will kill Quest on contact? What happens if there are powers in his robe, like the one that Quest brought back?"

"It didn't hurt him before. It won't hurt him now. And if it does, we'll designate a runner. We'll bring one Warder, so that Quest can blurt the secret immediately, and we'll send them both back to Shadowlands."

Jewel rubbed her temples with her thumb and forefinger. "This seems like quite a risk to me."

"Funny," Rugar said quietly. "It seems like our last chance to me."

EIGHTY

ALEXANDER sat in the sun on the courtyard bench, not far from the door to the kitchen. It was just after sunrise, and he had been awake all night, the stories he had heard from Scavenger whirling in his head. He had been thinking of the little Fey since the man had left, wondering how he was doing—and how he would know if Scavenger succeeded. Scavenger would come back if he could, but Alexander held that as faint hope. Alexander knew if anyone murdered him, that person would die instantly. The guards would see to that. He suspected the Fey would have the same methods.

The air still had the dampness of early-morning dew, and the cold that came with the night hadn't yet burned off. The stone bench was cold beneath his legs. Four guards stood as unobtrusively as possible near him: one beside the palace, one near the stable, and two behind him. Still, anyone looking for them would see them.

He was staring at the kitchen door, and just as his chamberlain had predicted, the chef came out with scraps of food and bowls of milk. Dogs and cats came running from all parts of the courtyard.

Alexander watched the cats. Five black cats, some with

white markings, several gray cats, and three orange tabbies. The chef clucked at them as he knelt, petting the few who would let him get close. Some of the cats sat behind the bowls, waiting for the others to finish. The dogs didn't have that politeness. They wrestled over bones and growled over scraps of meat. The chef ignored them, watching the cats instead.

Even more cats came from the stables: some pure white, others with brown markings, as varied and diverse as horses. Alexander had had a cat as a boy, a young female who neglected him only when she had kittens, and who had died, trampled under the hooves of his father's favorite stallion.

Alexander hadn't allowed a cat near his rooms since. The heartbreak had been the greatest he had felt up to that point, and he hadn't wanted to feel it again. Banishing cats, of course, hadn't protected him from sorrow—he still felt the death of his second wife as if it had happened that morning—but it gave him the illusion of control.

Just as this new measure would.

Everything that he had been able to check about Scavenger's stories had been true. The little Fey hadn't been lying to him—or if he had, he had done it in a way that was extremely subtle. Then the stories that confirmed what he said, stories that the little Fey couldn't know, like the one Nicholas had told him the night before, about the woman whose infant had been stolen by a cat. An orange tabby, like the ones seen in the palace and the stable before the two servants had disappeared.

Shape-Shifter, Scavenger had said. *She's considered the purest Fey, the best of all of us. I've never understood it, since Shape-Shifters are prone to odd lapses. In their old age they steal children because they can't have any of their own. They raise those children as if they were Fey.*

The Shape-Shifter also carried messages back and forth, according to Scavenger, and often learned much about enemies by living in their houses. Scavenger had apparently hated her, for reasons he would not explain, but even that didn't prevent Alexander from seeing what a threat she was to his own people.

All the Fey were a threat. They had destroyed much of his faith in himself. He no longer trusted his perception. He wasn't as quick as Nicholas, who tossed an open vial of holy water at anyone who came near him, but he had the same suspicions. He was afraid that no one was the person he had once known. Sometimes he even doubted himself.

The cats had finished eating and had scattered about the yard, cleaning themselves, wiping scraps off their whiskers, and enjoying the meal all over again. Any one of the orange tabbies could be the Shape-Shifter. Any one of the cats could be her. Scavenger had not said that her form was limited in color, only in shape. She had a feline counterpart. Some of the Shape-Shifters took on other shapes, but once the secondary shape was chosen, it was theirs forever.

But there was only one Shape-Shifter on Blue Isle. And Alexander had a good chance of getting rid of her if he took one action.

He stood and stretched. The guards all came to attention, watching him closely to see what he would do. The cats scattered at his movement, some going into the shadows and the crooks of the palace walls to finish their baths.

Until last year his reign had been easy. He had had to make political decisions regarding various matters. He had had to find ways to move crops across the Isle to help with a bad harvest or two near the Snow Mountains. He had had to resolve disputes and decide matters of property. But until the Fey had arrived, he had never had to make a difficult decision. In the last year he had sent men and boys to their deaths, and he had fought, as best he could, against a foe that threatened to take over his whole world. He felt lost with each decision he made.

The decree was simple, and it was the right decision: no cats inside. No cats near the palace. No cats. Any cat found should be sprinkled with holy water or killed outright. No cats allowed in the city limits, no cats anywhere in Blue Isle.

And maybe, just maybe, the Isle would get rid of one of the biggest threats the Fey had yet presented.

He wanted this war to end—the sooner the better, for all concerned.

EIGHTY-ONE

THE Rocaan's rooms were a flurry of activity. Auds racing back and forth, Danites rolling bits of the Words Written in tiny scrolls and placing them next to the filigree swords on the Rocaan's special sash. Porciluna, Reece, Vaughn, and Fedo were sprawled on couches, looking comfortable. Eirman stood near one of the windows, holding up a tapestry with his right hand and staring out. Matthias leaned against the fireplace, arms crossed, watching the Rocaan, who was supervising all the activity with a liveliness neither Tel nor Andre had ever seen before. The other three Elders had not arrived yet.

Tel didn't like all the movement. He found a corner and stood in it, a careful distance away from everyone else so no one could spill anything on him. He held his hands behind his back and watched closely, wondering what was going on. He knew it was futile to ask. Porciluna had asked once, and Matthias had snapped at him to wait until the Danites were done.

Linus, one of the Elders, came through the door. His blond hair was cut in a bowl shape, making his face round, his eyes even rounder. He was squat and older than most of the Elders. He often used that as an excuse to get out of some of the duties, an ability that Tel wished he had, but one that Andre used to hate. Linus didn't even bother to ask what was going on. He just sank into a chair beside Porciluna and watched the activity.

The Rocaan smiled at Linus and continued directing the Auds. They were packing another bag, this one with a silver ceremonial sword the size of a real sword. This kind of behavior was extremely abnormal: Andre had no memory of it at all. Tel's skin crawled. He was terrified and he didn't know why.

The door opened again, and this time Ilim entered. Tel had never seen this Elder up close. Ilim always managed to keep to himself, taking on the spiritual leadership of the lowliest servants as his main task. Unlike Linus, Ilim worked all the time. But they looked like brothers, except Ilim's hair was long and worn in a ponytail that ran down the middle of his back.

Behind him came Timothy, the last Elder. Andre had considered him a boy, even though there were Elders younger. Perhaps it was because Timothy wasn't very bright and his naïveté gave him a youthful quality no measure of years could take away. His hair had touches of gray in it, but he moved with the quickness of youth. He came over and stood by Tel, trapping him in the corner.

"Ah, finally," the Rocaan said. All the Elders had arrived, which was apparently the moment he had been waiting for. He took the sash from one of the Danites, saying that they had put enough on it, and then fastened it around his robe. "We'll finish later," he said to the others.

The Auds and Danites bowed their heads and left through the main chamber door, a few of them casting curious glances over their shoulders. Tel could feel their desire to be included, and most of them never would be. There were countless Auds (although he was sure someone —probably Linus—knew the exact number) and exactly half that number of Danites, an even thirty Officiates, ten Elders, and one Rocaan. Yet each Aud believed he would someday become Rocaan, only to find himself old and stuck somewhere in the Church system without power, and without a future.

The last Aud closed the door. The Rocaan stood in the center of the room, beaming like a child on his naming day.

His sash was weighted with tiny swords and scrolls. More had been stuck in his biretta, which sat on the table beside him. He clasped his hands in front of himself and turned so that he could see all of the Elders.

"I am probably going to offend some of you," he said, "and if that's so, please forgive me. Please understand that I think all of you have value, and that you all serve, in some way, God's purpose. The evaluation I will give this afternoon reflects my opinion and not that of the Church itself."

Tel's mouth was dry. Did that mean the Rocaan knew about him? Was he going to reveal Tel for who he was and then test the other Elders to make certain that they were not Fey? He rubbed his thumbs together, glad the nervous movement was hidden behind his back.

"I am leaving when we are through here and heading to the kirk on Daisy Stream for an important spiritual meeting. I am taking with me three of you whom I know to be strongest in their belief. This does not mean that the rest of you do not have faith, but merely that yours is not as pure as I need on this mission." He smiled, and the smile was sad. "Mine is not as pure as I need, either, but there is nothing I can do about that because I am needed on this trip."

"Can you tell us what this is about?" Porciluna asked. His posture hadn't changed, but the tension in his body had grown. Despite his outward appearance of calm, Porciluna was extremely competitive. Andre had fallen victim to that competitiveness more than once. For that reason Tel had stayed as far away from Porciluna as possible.

"Matthias and I have discussed whether or not to tell you the details of this spiritual matter," the Rocaan said, "and we have decided not to. The matter is not open to debate. If we succeed, you shall know it, and if we fail, you shall know it. Until then it is better that you are as ignorant as possible."

Tel stopped twisting his thumbs together. A spiritual matter was not about him. This was something different, something he didn't need to care about. The others did, though. They leaned forward, watching the Rocaan closely, as if everything depended on his next few words.

"I am taking with me Timothy, Reece, and Andre."

Tel started. Andre was one of the great believers? Andre seemed to have pure faith, but couldn't the Rocaan sense that something was different? Wasn't faith something that could be felt?

The other Elders stirred at this news. Some set their mouths tightly, their anger apparent. Others looked down as if they were ashamed of their lack of belief. The Rocaan didn't seem to notice.

"The Auds are packing your belongings even as we speak. When this meeting is through, we shall finish a few things here and leave."

Tel was numb. The Auds were going through his things. They might pack poison instead of his fake holy water. He would have to be extremely careful.

"The rest of you will go about your daily business and say nothing of this trip to anyone. You will have to juggle the Sacrament schedule, but that should not be a problem."

The Rocaan paused and looked at all of them, as if seeing for the first time their reactions. "I find you all to be very good men, and worthy of being this country's spiritual leader. But I can choose only one of you to succeed me."

Everyone in the room stirred except Tel and Matthias. Tel held himself rigidly. If the Rocaan picked Andre, Tel's problems would be solved, quickly and easily.

"I should have done this years ago, many years ago, given my age. I did not, probably out of pride and a bit of arrogance, the belief that I would live forever. I should have done this formally a year ago, when the Fey arrived and any of us could have died in an instant."

He paused, then glanced at all of them one at a time. When he was finished, he said, "Matthias will be our next Rocaan."

Porciluna looked at Matthias. Vaughn did as well. Tel went cold. Of course the Rocaan would choose Matthias to follow him. It made perfect sense. He had already given Matthias the secret to holy water. He would teach him the other secrets as well.

A rumble went through the room as it dawned on the other Elders that what they feared had finally come true. For the first time in their religious careers, they had been passed over. Linus made an odd groan and pushed his chair back.

The Rocaan raised his hand, and all sound stopped. "I will not justify my choice to you except to say that Matthias seems to have God's Ear. He will remain my choice throughout the rest of my days. I don't want any of you to think I made this decision hastily because I am worried about this trip."

"Well, I'm worried," Porciluna said. Vaughn and Ilim looked at him as if he were crazy. Matthias watched it all with an amused expression on his face. "If you four die on this trip, you're saying we'll be led by a nonbeliever and none of us will keep the faith."

"You misunderstand me, Porciluna," the Rocaan said, keeping his hand up as if to stop other protests. "A person cannot become Elder without faith. But I need pure faith to come with me. I'm afraid that I believe the people who remain have faith tainted by other things."

"Other things?" Eirman asked. His question sounded particularly sharp. Tel remembered hearing that he and the Rocaan had had words just a few days before.

"Ambition," Matthias said, stepping in before the Rocaan could answer the question. "Greed, or in my case, a belief in the power of knowledge versus the sanctity of faith."

The Rocaan shot Matthias a grateful smile. "I do not consider myself pure of faith. I was not, even when I became Rocaan. Pureness of faith has its own drawbacks, one of which is a startling naïveté in worldly matters. A Rocaan needs to understand the world as well as God."

There was enough greed, ambition, and anger in the room to light a dozen Dream Riders' imaginations. Tel didn't care about the petty politics of the Church. He wanted out of the room. He wanted to be able to check his possessions before the group left.

"I thought you weren't going to defend your decision," Tel said.

The Rocaan glanced his way, and a slight frown creased his forehead. With some surprise Tel realized that the Rocaan was wondering what had prompted the outburst. Tel made himself smile.

"The choice of a Rocaan is, after all, a matter of faith," he added.

"Good point," Timothy said.

The silence in the room was as thick as the sound had been. Tel could feel the stress in his back. The Rocaan glanced around, only the nervous twitch of his right hand showing his discomfort over the whole proceeding.

"We have duties," the Rocaan said. "If any of you have questions about your own future, I will answer them when I return. Until then do your best, and remember that we will all be rewarded in the Absorption."

The others stood. Matthias didn't move from his post near the fireplace, and neither did Tel, preferring to wait until the others had gone before he left. He didn't want to risk bumping against any of them.

Despite the odd packing problems, he was relieved to be leaving this place. He wouldn't have to worry about each move knocking something over and killing him. He would be outdoors again, walking, and feeling the air on his face. It had been over a year since he'd left Jahn.

He was halfway across the room himself before he realized that this could be more than a temporary respite. For the first time since he had become Andre, he would have a moment alone with the Rocaan. At night, near Daisy Stream, he would be able to attack the Rocaan and take over his form long enough to learn the secret to the poison. Then he would return to Shadowlands a hero, and the Fey would conquer this Isle easily, as they had been meant to do. An elation he hadn't felt in a long time filled him.

The long, dark night of defeat was almost over. He was nearly home.

EIGHTY-TWO

NICHOLAS felt as if he were running to his father over each small thing. He and his father had talked about the Fey prisoner, the cats, and the mysterious bones. Now Nicholas was climbing to the War Room again. He hated that room, even though his father seemed to be spending more and more time in it, pacing, thinking, and staring at maps. Nicholas still saw the spot in the corner where Stephen—or the thing that had passed for Stephen—had melted into a hideous, unrecognizable mass.

Two guards stood at the door to the War Room, arms crossed. More guards had been at the entrances to the tower below. Nicholas had refused the guards his father had assigned to him. He wasn't certain if having guards was such a good idea. He was afraid it made the Fey's access to him that much easier. Yet not having guards was also difficult. No one protected him from the surprise attack.

He nodded to them as he grabbed the doorknob. The guards nodded back. Then Nicholas pushed the door open.

New maps covered the walls, and the room shone with polish. Someone had cleaned the stains off the floor long ago, but Nicholas still saw them. This was the place where he had grown up, where he had learned that even if he loved someone, love did not mean he could trust. He missed that easy faith in the people around him. Its loss made him feel lonely.

His father was sitting at the head of the table, staring at a scrolled list that seemed to extend forever. When he saw Nicholas, he smiled and waved a hand, indicating that Nicholas should close the door. Nicholas did.

"Do you realize," his father said, "that we have lost over a thousand lives in the skirmishes since the invasion? And those are just the official lives. They don't count women or children or men who stayed home to defend their families. Only the men who worked as guards or volunteered to defend an area. And it doesn't count the people in the invasion."

"I don't know why you're torturing yourself with that," Nicholas asked with a touch of impatience. "We're at war."

Something in Nicholas's tone must have alerted his father. He let go of the scroll, and it rolled on its own. "What's happening?"

"I don't know," Nicholas said. He stopped at the edge of the table. The room smelled faintly of ink and parchment. "I was hoping you could tell me. Has the Rocaan told you of any plans to leave Jahn?"

"No," his father said. "I haven't spoken to him in a day or so, but I'm sure he would have told me."

"Well, he hasn't," Nicholas said. "I was riding near the bridge tonight when I saw his entourage cross. I spoke to an Aud. The Rocaan and three Elders are headed to Daisy Stream."

"Some kind of ceremony?"

"In the past maybe. But not now. The road to Daisy Stream leads them past the Fey encampment."

His father rolled up the scroll and tied a ribbon around it, placing it on the table behind him. "Why didn't you speak to the Rocaan?"

"I tried. The Rocaan and the Elders won't speak to anyone until they return."

"And they knew it was you?"

"Yes." And that was the strangest thing. The Rocaan's entourage had not stopped for him.

His father let out a breath and leaned back in his chair. It squeaked under his weight.

"Their determination and secrecy bother me," Nicholas said. His father's silence was not the reaction he had expected. "Combine that with the problems in the Tabernacle with the bones and the blood, and we have a serious problem. The Rocaan makes our holy water. If he dies or it gets contaminated—"

"I understand the problems, Nicholas," his father snapped. He ran a hand through his long blond hair. "I take it you came straight to me."

"Yes," Nicholas said.

"We could send someone to the Tabernacle, but it would take too long." His father frowned. "We'll send a contingent of guards to follow them and see if anything's wrong."

"I already sent the guards," Nicholas said. He was trembling, although he didn't want to show it. This was the first time he had taken action without his father's permission.

"You what?"

Nicholas swallowed. "There wasn't time to contact anyone and get permission. So I found Monte, explained that I needed guards, and sent them after the Rocaan."

"To do what, if I might ask?"

Nicholas ignored the sarcasm. "To keep an eye on him, in case something happens."

His father leaned back and rubbed his jaw reflectively. He took a deep breath. "It is what I would have ordered."

"I know," Nicholas said.

"What I don't understand is why you were in such a hurry to see me, if you had already taken action."

"I want to go with them as well."

His father stared at him for a long moment, his expression unreadable. "Why?"

"Because I think something is going to happen, and I want to be there."

"What would you do there?"

Nicholas shrugged. He couldn't tell his father he was tired of indecision. It was his father's indecision that bothered Nicholas. He wanted to go with the Rocaan because he felt that the Rocaan had a purpose. "I would be able to report back here, probably much more clearly than any of the guards could."

His father shook his head. "Your first instinct was right. This is not a place for you. The Rocaan is a smart man. If this is his doing, then it might be a simple ceremony. He has said in the past he does not like being held hostage to the Fey. If it is not, the guards will inform us. I don't want you in the middle of this."

"Like it or not, Father," Nicholas said, "I am in the middle of this. I fought during the invasion beside kitchen staff, I sat next to a Fey in this very room, and I suspect I've seen even more. Trying to protect me won't accomplish the job. Either I die or I don't."

His father's cheeks flushed. "It's not that simple. You're the heir. If something happens to me, this country needs you."

Nicholas sighed and sat down. He knew his father would say that, and he really had no argument against it. Fey leaders fought beside their men, but Islanders were not Fey. "Father," he said, "I would like to know what the Rocaan is doing because he is doing something. And it's time. We can't let these Fey stay on our lands. They have too many tricks, and someday they'll outsmart us. We have only one advantage. They have several."

"I've thought of this," his father said. "But I have no ideas. We can't let them through the Stone Guardians. They'll just get reinforcements. The Fey prisoner told me a lot, and I have him attempting something that might help us, but I don't know if I can trust him to work for us. And now the Rocaan, the source of holy water, has left the city. Each change leaves me more and more unnerved. More and more confused. I take an action, and I wonder if I've gone far enough. Then I take another action, and I think I may have gone too far. I am not prepared for this kind of leadership, Nicholas. Nothing in our history teaches the kind of thinking a man needs to fight an invasion. Internal dissent, yes, but an invasion—" he shook his head.

Nicholas stared at him. He knew his father was having trouble with all of the changes, but he had never thought of him as weak. The evidence was becoming clearer and clearer, though. Alexander was failing to act, to press any advantage that the Islanders had. And someday the Islanders would no longer have an advantage.

"We have two choices," Nicholas said. "Either we fight them and defeat them completely—kill them all—or we somehow learn to live with them. This halfway stuff where occasional skirmishes break out, and people die, is not going to work for much longer. We've already had one Fey come over to our side. How many Islanders will they convince to go over to theirs?"

His father looked stricken. He had obviously not thought of that. He glanced at the scroll, tied in red ribbon, then back at Nicholas. "What would you suggest?"

"We go into their Shadowlands with the strongest force we can gather, get them to open up, and throw all the holy water we can inside. It might not kill them, but it might."

His father shook his head. He had argued against this once before in front of all the advisers, worrying that the supply of holy water would disappear and the Islanders would have gained nothing. Nicholas had thought then that his father's argument was faulty.

"We even have a way in," Nicholas said. "Lord Stowe introduced me to a boy yesterday who was one of the prisoners the Fey held. His father is still inside. He might be able to get us into the Shadowlands, just enough that we could make this plan work."

His father stroked his chin. His eyes held a sadness that had been growing all year. "Even if we can talk the Rocaan into making enough holy water," Alexander said, "we still would not be certain we have all the Fey. They don't all look like us. Some are tiny wisps, and others shape-change, and still others duplicate themselves into us."

"We could get them over time," Nicholas said. Why was his father waiting? If his father's actions hadn't been consistent since the Fey arrived, Nicholas would have thought the King on their side. "What would they do without their friends? They would be stuck here and would probably live as quietly as they could."

His father looked away. Nicholas followed his gaze. His father was staring at the scroll. A thousand dead. No King had ever presided over so many deaths. Nicholas sat down. It was finally becoming clear. "And what if we decide not to annihilate them?" his father asked. "What if we decide to make peace?"

Nicholas started. Peace? Peace with the Fey would change Blue Isle forever. But war with the Fey had changed it too. And Nicholas had also seen the dead. He just hadn't ordered their deaths. He thought for a moment, then said,

"We would need a guarantee, something to show that they would never double-cross us, that we could learn to coexist peacefully on this small stretch of ground. And we would have to continue our self-imposed exile here. We couldn't have any contact with the outside world, because if any Fey left, they might bring reinforcements."

"Reinforcements might come anyway," his father said. "We don't know if they were scheduled to arrive after so much time has passed. What if we slaughter them all and the Black King's entire army arrives? What then?"

"We fight again."

"We don't have those kinds of resources, Nicholas," his father said. "The more men we lose, the fewer we have to fight with."

"But holy water—"

"Is a weapon. We always will need someone to wield it."

His father actually had a point. Perhaps what Nicholas had seen as weakness was consideration for life. "And if we make peace?" Nicholas asked.

"Then we do so in a way that they can't break that peace. No matter who arrives." His father picked up the scroll and hit it against his palm. "Let's see what the Rocaan is about. He's a wise man. When he returns, we'll ask his advice. We'll let him settle this once and for all."

"I sure wish you would let me go with him," Nicholas said.

His father smiled. "I know, Nicky," he said. "But part of learning to rule is realizing that you will never be able to do what you want."

EIGHTY-THREE

THE kirk at Daisy Stream was a small building the size of a cottage in Shadowlands. The building was made of wood and stone. The wood was so old that it had been bleached white by the elements. The stone was crumbling. Rugar had no idea how long the kirk had stood there, but he knew it had probably stood for centuries. The wood, even though it was white, looked as if it had been replaced more than once.

He did not touch anything. He waited until his lieutenants had touched each part of the exterior before he even went near it. They also pushed down the weeds that surrounded the building on three sides. Only the front, with the dirt path leading to the open door, had no weeds.

The kirk appeared to be well used, for all its age.

It stood at the edge of the stream. The water burbled beside it, down a bank so steep that the water had no chance of rising over it. Rugar had made Burden dip a finger into the water itself, half hoping that Daisy Stream was the source of the poison, but no such luck. Burden had removed his hand with an exclamation about the chill, and nothing more.

Rugar had brought Burden with him because he didn't want to leave the Infantryman alone with Jewel. Over the course of the year, Burden had got too bold. A childhood friendship was not enough for Burden to base his confidence on—he seemed to think he would be the next addition into Rugar's family. Jewel didn't appear to give him that idea, but Rugar wanted to take no chances. Better to have Burden with him.

Rugar also brought Quest, two Beast Riders who remained in the woods some distance from the kirk, and the remaining Infantry leaders, as well as his own personal guards. He also brought three Domestics and one Healer on the off chance that something might go wrong. He had considered bringing the Islander Adrian, but thought that might be tempting fate.

This meeting had Rugar both excited and frightened. He wasn't sure what the Rocaan was up to, but Quest assured him that the purpose had to be benevolent. Quest believed that the Rocaan had been opposed to the fighting, and even opposed to the use of holy water as a poison. But Quest hadn't been sure what the old man would offer Rugar.

Rugar would accept nothing. He wouldn't have to.

The air smelled faintly of moss and damp grass. The stream had its own rich, musty odor. Rugar had had his people survey the entire area, to see if any Islanders were setting up traps or encampments. He found neither, and he found that strange.

Finally he sent one of the Infantrymen inside the kirk with a Fey Lamp. Rugar stood at the door and watched the man's progress, expecting the lamp to go out. It did not. It illuminated a single room, the size of his own meeting room. A sword had been tacked to the far wall, and a small structure had been built in the middle of the floor. The structure had a cushion on its pedestal, and a small table about chest high, with an empty candleholder on it. The rest of the room was empty.

After the soldier had touched everything, Rugar went in. The musty smell was stronger there. The floor was made of stone, and even with the light of the Fey Lamp, the place had a dark, ominous look to it. He couldn't imagine worshiping in a place like this: he almost expected cobwebs and ghosts instead of religious ecstasy. But, then, he was never raised in any kind of religious tradition, and barely understood it.

He left the kirk and stepped into the sunlight, blinking at the brightness. With a snap of his fingers, he ordered two more men inside, and then Quest, who would know better than any of them what should be there and what shouldn't. It bothered Rugar that he couldn't find any poison, or any preparations for the meeting at all. Perhaps it was as Quest had said: perhaps the Rocaan had a nonmilitary reason for the visit.

Still, if there was anything in and around the kirk that would harm Fey, Rugar would find it before the Rocaan arrived. Then the Fey would set up their own defensive systems. The Rocaan would never know how many people Rugar had brought with him. And he wouldn't know about Quest.

Rugar waited on the path out front, glancing inside occasionally, and watching as his lieutenants combed the area around the kirk. From all evidence, it looked as if no one had been near the place in weeks. But he knew better than to trust his eyes.

Finally Quest came out and stood beside Rugar. The other men were still inside, shining the Fey light in corners and gingerly touching the large sword.

"Nothing is out of place," Quest said. "The sword is symbolic of the religion, but the blade is tarnished. It hasn't been used in even as much as a ceremony in a long time. The altar in the center shows more sign of recent use. The pillow is worn, and there are no cobwebs on it, and no dirt, for that matter. But there's also no holy water, which means whoever is using it is not a member of the clergy."

"What's the purpose of this building?" Rugar asked. He had been expecting something much bigger and more accommodating for the kind of meeting the boy had asked them to.

"Some areas have only a limited number of residents, and it's not worth the time for a Danite or an Aud to stay there permanently. So they travel through and hold a Sacrament or a Blessing here when they arrive. Otherwise the faithful in the area tend to their own religious needs. Whoever has been using this place has been praying, and little more. There hasn't been a big service here in a long, long time."

"Do you know that from your last host, or does evidence in the building tell you that?"

"Both, actually," Quest said. "The Danite assigned to this region should be farther west right now. And if there had been a ceremony, the weeds would be trampled, and there would be less dust in the building itself. Maybe even some holy water. Frankly, that Danite might get into trouble for letting the sword tarnish. The symbolism there is probably not one the Rocaan wants."

"So no one has been here except a few worshipers." Rugar turned and stared at the building. It held his future, and he wasn't certain he liked that. "No preparation for this meeting, or do you think we merely got here ahead of them?"

"No preparation would be my guess, at least here," Quest said. "If they prepared at all, they probably did so in the Tabernacle."

"But they could have sent the boy here before he saw us. It's not that far away."

Quest nodded. "They could have. But I'll wager they didn't. Auds are servants and message bearers, as far as Tabernacle staff are concerned. If they wanted someone to do something of more complexity, they would have sent a Danite."

"This meeting makes no sense," Rugar said. He put his hands on his hips and surveyed the area. "Perhaps if I understood why they wanted it, I would be able to plan better myself. It's not an ambush, because we got here first and they're clearly not here. They also allowed us to bring weapons."

"The Rocaan is not an easy man to understand," Quest said. "At least from all I've heard about him. He does things for religious reasons, not for the sake of logic."

"Clearly," Rugar said. He peered inside the kirk again. The Infantryman had located a small mouse nest in the back corner. The mouse had used some of the stuffing from the pillow to line its little home. If anyone else had asked for this meeting, Rugar would not be there. But the opportunity to use Quest to get the information from the Rocaan was too great. It would finally allow the Fey to take Blue Isle.

Rugar glanced at Quest. "Are you ready?"

Quest nodded. He glanced nervously at the door. "I am most afraid that the old man will be so holy in his own right that he will poison me."

"We have yet to encounter anything like that," Rugar said.

"Until we came here, we had yet to encounter anything like their holy water."

Rugar ignored the point. Now that he knew the kirk was secure, he had his own preparations to make. He wasn't going to let that Rocaan get away, nor was he going to lose his entire squad to these Islanders. If they were too stupid to prepare, that was not his problem. That benefited him.

But this might be his only chance at winning the Isle. He wasn't going to allow any mistakes.

EIGHTY-FOUR

THE Fey were already waiting at Daisy Stream. They were all tall, thin, and dark, their features upswept and narrow. They stood in a group lining the entrance to the kirk. The kirk's door was open, and it was clear the Fey had already been inside.

The Rocaan gripped Andre's hand, and Andre jumped. The Fey made Andre nervous. Reece was sitting at the edge of his seat in the carriage, his hands folded in his lap, his body rigid. He was staring out the small window as if his gaze could control the Fey. Only Timothy had his eyes closed. His lips were moving, and the Rocaan didn't want to interrupt him.

They could use all the prayers these believers could muster.

The Rocaan's heart was pounding. His body ached worse than usual. In the last few days he had got no sleep, and he had lost the support of some of his Elders. Time had slowed. He felt as if he had lived years instead of hours. Matthias had wanted him to delay the meeting a day, but the Rocaan wasn't sure his health would hold.

He gripped the seat of the carriage. He had imagined himself performing the ceremony a hundred times in this small kirk, but he had never imagined the greeting. He had also imagined the Fey's presence, but not what he would say to them to get them to stand through the ceremony. He should have listened to Matthias. They should have run through the whole event just one time.

The riders in front of the carriage stopped; then the horses leading the carriage stopped as well. The Rocaan let go of Andre's hand. Andre gave him a weak smile and moved his arm away. Andre had not been himself on this trip. Nervous, unwilling to brush against anyone, he had sat as close to the carriage wall as he could, and kept his eyes shut most of the time. The Rocaan almost regretted bringing Andre along. If there had been one other true believer among the Elders, the Rocaan would have left Andre behind. But there hadn't been. And the Words Unwritten said the Roca performed his ceremony with three of his most faithful companions at his side.

The Rocaan's body kept swaying even though the carriage had stopped. Apparently he was frightened too—and too numb to feel it. He mouthed a quick prayer, then pushed open the side door. An Aud was already waiting for him at the bottom of the stairs. The Aud took his hand and smiled timidly at the Rocaan. Then the Rocaan recognized him as the boy to whom he had given the Charge: young Titus, who had returned against all predictions, his black robe grass stained, his feet cold and filthy, and his eyes wild. Titus had been inside the Fey enclave and lived. He was a good talisman to have on this mission.

The Rocaan squeezed the boy's hand, then stepped down. His swaying had ceased, although his legs felt shaky. He waited until the others had got out of the carriage before facing the Fey.

The Fey surrounded one man. This man was older; his skin had a leathery look that the Rocaan had often seen in laborers who spent their days in the sun. The man's black eyes snapped with intelligence. Age had worn his features to a point—his chin was sharp, his cheekbones high. Everything about him gave the impression of upward movement.

The Rocaan nodded his head. "Welcome to the kirk at Daisy Stream," he said in Nye. "I am very pleased that you could come. I am the Rocaan, and these are my Elders, Andre, Reece, and Timothy."

The Fey's smile seemed sincere. "I am Rugar, the Black King's son. My assistants do not need to be named, since this negotiation is between you and me."

Negotiation. Without apparently planning to, the Fey had given the Rocaan a way to begin. "I am honored," the Rocaan said, "to be in the presence of the Fey leader on Blue Isle."

"And I am honored," Rugar said, "to be in the company of a great religious leader. Your people are the first in a long time to stop a Fey drive across a country. I must say, for that reason, this meeting has piqued my curiosity."

"My people are not by nature warlike," the Rocaan said, hoping his words wouldn't sound like a judgment. "Our religion forbids using anything—including death—for personal gain. I had thought, perhaps, we might discuss what you want on Blue Isle to see if we can come to some kind of terms."

"Terms?" Rugar raised an eyebrow. His voice remained level, but he clasped his hands behind his back and spread his legs slightly. He appeared braced for trouble. "You are winning this war. You should not be asking for terms."

"In my religion," the Rocaan said, uncomfortable with the war terminology, "it is our custom to have a brief Blessing before we have any serious discussions. I said in my message that it would be all right if you brought your weapons, because our ceremony uses some of the things you would consider to be weapons—the sword and the holy water."

Rugar let his arms fall to his sides. Although none of his features changed, the tension in his body did. The Rocaan could feel his fear.

"I won't touch you or your men with any of these. Before God, you have my word," the Rocaan said. He glanced at the door of the kirk. A few of the Fey had let the horror seep into their expressions. The man standing next to Rugar, a shorter Fey with rounder features and startling blue eyes, nodded once. Then Rugar smiled.

"We won't interfere with your ceremony," Rugar said. "But we won't participate, either."

"You do not even have to come into the kirk," the Rocaan said, "although it would be better if some of your people did so. It would feel, then, as if the Blessing affected all of us."

One of the Fey near the door burst out into a torrent of guttural words, words that the Rocaan did not understand. Rugar did not look at him, but raised one hand to silence him.

"My associate cautions me that if your holy water works on us in such a strong fashion, your Blessings might be even stronger," Rugar said. "I will send in four of my people, but I'll remain out here and will watch the ceremony from the door."

The Rocaan nodded. That was more than he could hope for. He hadn't even expected the Fey to be there, much less be willing to cooperate with him. The Holy One was watching over them. The Rocaan knew this was the right path. No one else had had the courage to do this before, that was all. He hoped that he would be able to see the changes this meeting would bring. Maybe, maybe it would even make Matthias believe.

The Rocaan turned to his own people. "I need the Elders, two Danites, and an Aud," he said in Islander. He waited until the Danites and the Aud came to him before asking them to go down the path before him. He was a bit disappointed that the young Aud, Titus, had stayed near the carriage. It seemed appropriate that the boy be at the Rocaan's side. But the Rocaan always believed in allowing things to take their natural course. If the boy chose to stay behind, he did so for a reason that was between him and God.

The Danites and the Aud walked down the path, holding their hands at their sides, and keeping their heads down as if they were in an Absorption Day processional. Andre and the Rocaan followed, with Timothy and Reece behind. The distance down the path was short, but it felt long, with all those Fey lined up along the sides. The Fey watched silently, and it seemed to the Rocaan that they felt as much fear as the Rocaanists did. He sent up a silent prayer through the Holy One:

I hope this is what you meant.

The Danites crossed the threshold into the tiny kirk and then lined up in front of the blade, as they had been told to do. The Aud stood behind the altar. As the Rocaan stepped inside, he noted that Andre flinched. The Rocaan glanced to his right. Nothing out of the ordinary, except that the cobwebs one normally found in a rarely used kirk were gone.

The Rocaan took his place in front of the altar. Timothy and Reece stood half a step behind him. He could no longer see Andre. Timothy held out the sword. The Rocaan took it and extended it in front of him, as the Words instructed.

Then he waited for the Fey to join them.

EIGHTY-FIVE

QUEST stepped inside the kirk, and all the fear he had felt in his short days as a Danite nearly overwhelmed him again. Rugar, the coward, remained outside. The Rocaan already held his sword, which was odd, since the Rocaanists never used a real sword for a Blessing. Something was going on here, on their side as well. Somehow that made him feel better.

Despite all the people in such a small space, the kirk still had an empty feel. The dampness was so thick, it seemed as if water dripped off the ceiling. But Quest already knew that the ceiling was safe. He had checked the building himself for any hidden religious tricks. There appeared to be none, but he hadn't really known what he was looking for. Until the Rocaan pulled that sword, Quest had thought that the Islander religion was fairly straightforward.

The four other Fey who came in with Quest were Infantry leaders, minor Visionaries whose death would be of little importance. Even that thought made the hair on the back of Quest's neck rise. Rugar was willing to sacrifice them all to learn the secret of the poison. He was even willing to put himself at risk.

The Rocaan was watching closely, waiting until they

were all inside. Quest sidled up next to Elder Reece, who took one small step away. Then Quest put his left hand behind his back and rested the other on the hilt of his knife. Only the Fey could see the position of his right hand.

Rugar stood just outside the door, along with some of the other Fey. A few Auds also stood close, but not mingling, just close enough to see. The Auds were young and unthinking. The older Rocaanists came nowhere near the Fey.

"We're ready, then," the Rocaan said in Nye. "Part of this service requires holy water. I will keep it away from you all and place it only on my sword. You will be safe. You have my word on that."

It sounded as if the Rocaan was performing Midnight Sacrament, not a Blessing. Quest frowned at Rugar. Rugar shrugged one shoulder, then glanced from the Rocaan to Quest. Act now, he appeared to be saying. But if the Rocaan was performing Midnight Sacrament, he had poison on his person. Quest wanted to wait until the poison was visible before acting. It would do them no good for him to take over the Rocaan and die instantly.

"There will be sword movement," the Rocaan said. "None of it is meant to be threatening."

The Fey glanced at each other, and two moved closer to the door than they had been.

"Nye does not have some of the words for this ceremony," the Rocaan said. "So I will perform it in Islander. Andre will translate for you."

Elder Andre started and shot a frightened glance at the Rocaan. Quest tilted his head. How odd the small subtleties in the Islander group. No one but the Rocaan seemed to know what was going on. Quest moved another step closer. He would take advantage of any opening he found.

The Rocaan looked meaningfully at Andre and said in Islander, "Quote the Blessing to them."

Andre nodded. His jaw worked, and he glanced at the Fey as if looking for help. Quest did not like this development, but he would let it run as long as he could. If it threatened any of the Fey in any manner, he would take immediate action.

The Rocaan swung the sword over his head and caught its tip with his left hand. "There are enemies without," he said in Islander.

"Th-the Blessing begins," Andre said in Nye.

Quest shot a quick glance at Rugar and shook his head slightly. The Rocaanists were performing the wrong ceremony. Quest clamped his jaw hard so that he wouldn't have to say anything. If he moved quickly, the type of service they performed didn't matter. But he would have to move quickly.

"'And within,'" the Danites, Aud, and Elders responded.

"'We are surrounded by hatred—'" the Rocaan said.

"'—greed,'" the Danites, Aud, and Elders said—

"'—lust,'"

"'—cruelty,'"

"'—and loss.'"

"Th-this is a quote from the Words Written and Unwritten that is a metaphor," Andre said in Nye. "It has no meaning in literal translation."

Quest had gone cold. He inched around Elder Reece, who was watching the Rocaan and not paying attention. Maybe Quest could see the poison. If he could see it, he could act now.

The Rocaan brought the sword down with both hands so that the flat of the blade faced the Fey. "'We choose to fight, not with weapons—'"

"'—or cunning,'" the Danites, Aud, and Elders said—

"'—but with faith.'" Slowly he brought the sword down and laid it flat on the altar.

Quest expected him to say the part of the ceremony mentioning taking the troubles to the Ear of God, but the Rocaan didn't. He was quoting only the Words. They were up to something.

The poison would come out next.

Andre glanced at the Fey. "Loosely translated," he said in Nye, "what went before means, 'Blessed be these strangers before us.'"

Quest tightened his grip on the hilt of his knife. With all the poison in the kirk, he would not have time to slit Elder Reece's throat, then go for the Rocaan. He would have to use the more difficult trick of using the host as victim.

The Rocaan raised his hands again, this time without the sword. The sleeves of his robe fell away, revealing his bare arms. "'When the Roca asked for God's Ear,'" he said, "'he begged for safety for his people. Yet they were besieged by enemies, and it appeared that God did not listen. . . .' "

Quest shot a panicked glance to Rugar. They were trying to get rid of the Fey using the old ceremony, the thing the Roca had done generations before. A chill ran down Quest's back. He understood this ceremony, and their gamble. The chance might work. No one understood Islander magic. Not even the Islanders.

Quest's palms were damp. He would have to act quickly. He couldn't wait for the safety of knowing where the poison was.

" '. . . the Roca thought to strike them down himself, but he thought, 'Would that mean that I believe I am better than God? For if God is not willing to do this thing, He in his wisdom must have a reason. . . .' "

With a quick, practiced movement, Quest grabbed the Rocaan's head with one hand and slashed his throat with the other. The Fey moved beside him, pinning the hands of the Elders as the blood spurted on Quest. Other Fey came in and grabbed a Danite just as he pulled the stopper off his poison vial.

Don't watch, don't watch, Quest admonished himself. Instead he stared at the Rocaan, whose mouth was still moving, trying to speak the words of the ceremony as his blood gushed all over Quest. He leaped on the Rocaan, wrapping his legs around the old man's torso to hold his position, his elbows in the old man's neck to brace his arms. The blood hit him full in the chest, and the skin was growing pale. He was almost too late.

Quest stuck his fingers into the Rocaan's eyes, and his thumbs into his mouth. Around him people were screaming. Elder Andre had taken a step back, shock on his face, his hand to his mouth. The Danites were screaming in Islander, something about enemies.

Quest pried the old man's teeth open, and pushed hard against the back of the throat. Then Quest pulled and pulled. Something seemed to pull back. For a moment he felt himself loosen from his own being, but the old man was dying. He couldn't fight. Quest was glad he hadn't tried this with someone else's blood. He yanked with all his strength. The old man's essence broke free and fluttered between them for a moment.

"Absorption!" Elder Timothy screamed and grabbed Quest's back. He felt a momentary struggle; then someone must have pulled him away.

Quest bit into the mist that was the old man and sucked it inside. Then Quest's body molded and twisted and expanded until it was squat and old and terrified. He combed the Rocaan's mind. The secret was there, but tantalizingly out of reach. *Meld, meld, meld.* He willed it to happen.

Rugar was gesturing to him to come outside. Then Quest looked around himself and saw the chaos. Several of the Rocaanists held poison. The Rocaan's bottle was on the ground by his feet. Terror filled him, deep and abiding, and in it, he knew the secret of the water. It had a recipe, like wine, filled with herbs and potions that came only from the Isle.

Quest pushed his way toward the door. He had to get out. He couldn't shout the recipe at Rugar; verbally, the spell made no sense. Quest had to explain it carefully, and then write it down for the Spell Warders to see.

The Fey would win now. Blue Isle was theirs.

EIGHTY-SIX

THE thing that looked like the Rocaan lurched toward the door. It wore no clothes, its ancient body pale and wrinkled. Titus grabbed his bottle of holy water and clutched it in his left hand as he struggled to get the stopper off with his right. The other Auds had run, but he wouldn't. The Fey had made a mockery of the whole ceremony. The Rocaan had vowed not to hurt them, and the Fey had killed him, mimicking the Absorption as they did so.

His hands were shaking, and some of the water spilled onto the Fey next to him, who immediately started screaming. The old man Fey, the one whom Titus had spoken to, saw that and ran to the side. He was screaming at the Rocaan-thing in that guttural language, but the Rocaan-thing did not respond. It just kept hurrying forward as if it could escape the kirk.

Another Fey grabbed for Titus's hand. Titus splashed him, then waited until he had a clear shot. He tossed the bottle toward the Rocaan-thing as Matthias had done the day of the invasion. Water splashed on all sides. The Rocaan-thing screamed and raised its arms to its face to ward the water off.

A stench like burning flesh rose around Titus, bringing

with it a mist. He could barely see. He stepped forward, toward the kirk, as the living Fey around him ran.

Water splashed on the Rocaan-thing. For a moment nothing happened. The thing looked up at Titus with both relief and anger. Then the water started to work, for the thing grabbed its arms and screamed. Another Fey came close, talking to it, begging it in their language, but the Rocaan-thing didn't seem to hear. Its face was twisting as it had done moments before. As the face changed, Titus recognized the Danite he had seen in the Fey place, then a man he had seen around the palace. Then he saw a Nye face, and another, and another, followed by a series of Fey faces before all the features washed away and the Rocaan-thing fell to the ground in a large heap of cloth and twitching limbs.

Some of the Fey from inside the kirk pushed past Titus. Others were twisting as the Rocaan-thing had done. There was blood on the altar and foul-smelling mist in the air. Fey screams trailed away along the stream.

Titus stood in the door, clutching his second vial. Elder Reece was pouring water onto a lump that had been the Fey holding him. Elder Timothy was crouched on the floor, hands in the blood, praying, as if that would bring the Rocaan back to life. One of the Danites was shaking an empty bottle in the air as the other Danite struggled with his Fey captor. The Aud hid behind the altar, pulling the bloodstained wood over him like a cover.

Elder Andre was pressed against the wall, his hand over his mouth in horror. He was staring at Titus as if he had never seen him before. Tears were running down Andre's face. As Titus moved closer, Elder Andre seemed to be trying to disappear into the wall itself.

But Titus stopped when he reached the Rocaan-thing. It was dead now. Its body had stopped twitching. It no longer looked like the Rocaan. It no longer looked like any living thing Titus had seen, just a lump of flesh and bone on the wet floor.

Titus bent over it. During the Sacrament, as the Rocaan had been quoting the Words, Titus had finally understood what the Rocaan was doing. He was trying to get the Ear of God. Maybe if God was paying attention, he would free them all from the Fey invasion. Maybe, maybe from the beginning the Roca had meant this Sacrament to help fight beings like the Fey.

But the Rocaan had done it wrong. The Fey were too close and too cunning. Maybe the Words had caused that Fey to go crazy and try to become the Rocaan. Whatever happened, the Rocaan was dead. And so was his attacker.

Titus looked up. Only Andre watched him, with great terror. There were no Fey behind him, and the Fey in the kirk were dead. The Auds who had run to the carriage had fought their own Fey and were standing over them like victors at a palace ceremony. A lot of the Fey had got away.

Titus touched the face of the Rocaan-thing. It felt soft and mushy. A few feet away from him, on the floor, was the sword the Rocaan had been using, and an unused vial of holy water. Titus got up, picked up the sword, and laid it flat over the Rocaan-thing. Then he took the stopper off the holy water.

He took his Sacrament cloth from the pocket of his robe and held it over the mouth of the bottle. Then he poured the holy water onto the cloth and picked up the sword. " 'Without water,' " he quoted, " 'a man dies.' " He cleaned the sword methodically, as he had been taught, only this time his movements took the blood off the sword's blade. " 'A man's body makes water. His blood is water. A child is born in a rush of water. Water keeps us clean. It keeps us healthy. It keeps us alive. It is when we are in water that we are closest to God.' "

The Danites stood and bowed their heads. The Aud picked up the altar and moved it so that he could stand. Timothy remained bowed, but Reece stood behind Titus. Only Andre didn't move.

" 'A man dies only when he is not pure enough to sit at the feet of God,' " Titus said. He finished cleaning the sword and handed it to Reece, wishing in his deepest heart that the Sacrament would have brought the Rocaan back. But it did not. It was an object lesson to the dead and dying Fey.

Titus looked down at them, huddled lumps around his feet, some of them still moving. " 'When you touch water,' " he said to them all, " 'you touch the Essence of God.' "

THE MEETING
(THREE WEEKS LATER)

EIGHTY-SEVEN

HER father left her no choice. During the three weeks it took to set up the negotiation sessions, Jewel barely spoke to him. Instead, she worked through her own people, sending Burden and others from her decimated Infantry unit into Jahn to speak to the King's representatives. Her father spent most of his time in front of the fireplace, staring at the flames. Twice he tried to talk with her—once to apologize—and she didn't even let him finish. What had he been thinking, to allow their people inside a holy place? She had thought he would have had enough sense to have the meeting outside. Or to act quickly. From all reports, he waited and let the old man lead the proceedings. Things were too far gone when Quest made his move.

Five Infantry leaders dead. Two Beast Riders missing. Their only remaining Doppelgänger dead. All for nothing. Quest, even though he took over the religious leader, never gave Rugar the secret of the poison. And that didn't even count the loss of Caseo, whom, if the Warders were to be believed, was the only Fey who knew the entire formula for the breakthrough experiment on the poison.

If she allowed her father to continue command, they would have no one left. No one left at all.

So she stood on the hilltop with Burden at her side, staring down the rock-littered sides to the flat stone where the meeting tables had been set up. Wind whipped her hair, pulling it from its braid. Her father was in the party, but shunted aside. She didn't want him anywhere close. The negotiations just to choose the site had been difficult. They finally had to settle near the channel where the Fey had first invaded the Cardidas River. The rocks had risen up, forming a bowl, protected all around. The base was a flat piece of ground that created a natural—and open—negotiations site. Both sides had seen it before, and both sides knew that neither one could dominate there.

The Stone Guardians ringed the mouth of the channel like sentries blocking a palace. Through them lay freedom, and her grandfather, whom she would probably never see again. The black water around the Guardians churned, covered with a thin layer of foam. Waves broke against the stone, sending spray across the rocks. The mist was in the air, fresh and bracing after the stale, smoky smell of Shadowlands. If she weren't so terrified, she would have been happy to be outside.

She had given this meeting a lot of thought, ever since her father had returned with news of his defeat. They had killed the religious leader, and they still had the Black King as a threat on the horizon. They weren't entirely powerless.

It only felt that way.

The key, her grandfather would have told her, was to act as if they still had all of the power. But she knew that the Islanders could keep whittling away at the Fey on the Isle until none were left. She had to count on the fact that the Islanders didn't know that. She had to buy time. She had to make an offer that would someday work in the Fey's favor.

Her father came up beside her. She half turned her back on him. He would sit at her side, and if he said anything, she would stop him. She would undercut him in front of the Islanders. She should have had a Warder on her other side, but she needed someone she trusted.

She needed Burden.

She should have listened to him since the First Battle for Jahn. He had said her father was Blind. She should have listened.

On the hill on the other side of the bowl stood Nicholas,

the King, and an adviser. As previously agreed, the Fey guards made their way down the rocky slope to the flat surface at the same time the Islander guards did on the other side. They brought some Black Robes, probably knowing that the religious representatives would strike more terror into the Fey than anything.

They were right.

When the guards were in place, Jewel, her father, and Burden made their way down the hill. Jewel watched as Nicholas, the King, and the other adviser kept pace with them. They all arrived on the flat stone surface at the same time. So many details, so much delicate negotiation, even before this meeting could start. They crossed the stone together, reached the table, pulled back the chairs, and sat with the unison of people used to ritual.

The wind wasn't as harsh in the bowl, although the spray had turned into a fine mist that coated everything with water. Jewel pushed the stray strands of hair off her face. Nicholas was staring at her with the fascination that she remembered. In the year since she had seen him, his face had acquired an almost Fey-like leanness, and lines had formed around his mouth. She longed to touch him, to see if his skin was rough. He no longer looked like an untried boy, more like the man who held her with such tenderness in her Vision.

She hoped today's meeting would change that Vision.

Nicholas sat to his father's right, across from Jewel's father. Burden and the Islander adviser sat on Jewel's right. Jewel and the Islander King sat in the middle.

Jewel swallowed. She nodded at all of them, then started the proceedings since she was the one who had called them.

"My name is Jewel," she said in the language of the three Islanders who faced her. Her words sounded stilted, even to herself. Adrian had coached her long and hard on the next few sentences. "I am the Black King's granddaughter. My father, Rugar, is the one who met your Rocaan at Daisy Stream. My adviser, Burden, will listen in as well. I will be speaking for the Fey. I would hope, once the formalities are passed, that we can speak in Nye, since my Islander is still limited."

"It is nice," the King said in Nye, already acquiescing to her needs, "to learn who you are. My son Nicholas sits with me, and my adviser, Lord Stowe. I will negotiate for Blue Isle."

Jewel nodded at his kindness. "I called this meeting because I believe it to be in all of our interests to call a truce."

"I thought the Fey don't negotiate," the King said.

Rugar began to speak, and Jewel grabbed his thigh. She dug her fingers in so tightly that he had to pry them loose. "The Fey have never lost before," she said, amazed at her ability to say the words. When she had rehearsed this, alone, they had stuck in her throat. "We would like to return to Nye."

Her father's hand froze on hers. He had not expected her to say that. She even knew what he was thinking: they couldn't return to Nye in defeat. He would never be able to stand before his father again.

Nicholas's eyes were wide. He was watching her closely. She did not allow herself to look at him, although she felt his presence, as strong as her own.

The King's smile was gentle. "You know we can't allow that. You will return with more ships and more Fey, and finally overrun us."

"You would have our oath that no such thing would happen," Jewel said, trying to conduct this negotiation as skillfully as she could. If they did return to Nye, they would do exactly as the King said. But if she could convince him otherwise, they might have a chance to leave this Isle of defeat.

The King rested his hands on the damp wooden table, fingers clasped. "And if you broke your oath, what then? We simply fight in a war we did not want in the first place."

She pushed her father's hand away from hers. His emotions were distracting her. He hadn't wanted this meeting either, and he had insisted on going along only so that he would knew what she was doing.

"Well, then." Jewel pushed her chair out and leaned back. Panic flared in Nicholas's face, then disappeared. She wasn't sure what he thought. Was he afraid she would attack them? "We have a problem. You could slaughter all of us, if you could find us all, but that's only a temporary solution."

Her father was stiff beside her. Burden hadn't moved. He was the good listener she had thought he would be.

"Temporary?" the King said. "We could go back to our lives."

She nodded. "Until the Black King comes to Blue Isle, looking for his son and granddaughter."

"Why hasn't he come yet?" Nicholas asked. The question wasn't impertinent: he sounded curious, as if he had been wondering this for a long, long time.

"He has the details of his own rule to deal with on Galinas. He expects us to report back to him. There is quite a window of time for that—wars are never quick and easy things—and if we haven't reported back after what he considers to be too long, then he will send ships for us."

"Too long?" Lord Stowe asked. His face betrayed no nervousness, but his voice shook a little. "What's that?"

Jewel shrugged. "Three years, five, ten. I don't know. If my grandfather has died, it will take a bit longer because my brother will have to get used to the reins of power. Once he is used to being Black King, he will come here."

"Eventually," Rugar said in his command voice even though he didn't know what Jewel was trying to do, "the Fey will come to Blue Isle in such numbers that we will rule this place."

The King took his hands off the table. A little pool of dryness outlined the place where they had been. "Such threats do nothing for your position," he said. "We can still wipe you all out."

Jewel leaned forward. "If you were able to wipe us out," she said softly, "you would have done so already. You have had several chances, and you have never managed to destroy us."

"Given time—" Lord Stowe started.

"Given time," Jewel agreed, "we would probably die. But you don't know how much time you have. If the Black King does arrive while you're still killing us, you are in even more trouble. And so are we."

Rugar stiffened beside her. Burden shifted slightly in his seat. Neither of them knew what she was going to do or what she was going to offer. She had discussed this with no one, even though she had been thinking about it for weeks.

Go with the magick, her grandfather would say. And she was.

The King started to speak, but she put up her hand.

"Give me just a moment to explain," she said. "You can kill us, small group by small group, but some of our people will survive. It is just our way. You can't reach all of the magicks at once. We, on the other hand, would live in constant fear, making small raids on your people and holding skirmishes in order to survive. We would probably find a place like Daisy Stream, which is easy to defend, and take it over, and then there would be battles for that spot. More of your young people would die, and so would our people—one at a time, slowly and painfully, and with no gain."

"It seems we would gain if you go away," Lord Stowe said.

Jewel gave him a gentle smile. She saw how they were playing this. The King was the reasonable one, while he had given Stowe the opportunity to argue the extreme position. She didn't quite know Nicholas's role yet. She was sure she would find out.

"But that's my point, Lord Stowe," she said. "We won't go away. You might have a year or five or maybe even a decade without us. But then the Black King will arrive, and he will have no mercy for you. You will have killed his troop and his family. In those circumstances the Black King *cannot* show mercy, or someone might try such a thing again."

"You obviously have a plan, something to propose that will benefit all of us?" the King said.

The mist still fell, thin and cold, leaving little drops on her skin and her hair. It felt as if the sky were crying. She licked her lips, felt the cool water on her tongue. She did not look at her father as she spoke. "I propose an alliance," she said.

"Between us?" the King said, his voice rising with surprise.

Jewel nodded. "It must be an alliance that the Black King recognizes. One that he cannot break."

"There is no such alliance," Lord Stowe said. "The Fey are known for betraying agreements when the agreements no longer suit them. We would be fools to negotiate such a thing."

"You would be, yes," Jewel said, "unless we can offer you something that would make the alliance impossible to betray. Something the Fey would have to agree to. Something your people would have to honor as well."

"What do you have in mind?" the King asked.

Jewel raised her chin. Her heart was pounding and her mouth was suddenly dry. "I would like to marry your son."

Burden gasped beside her. The King's pale face turned even whiter. Lord Stowe opened his mouth in surprise. Rugar grabbed Jewel's arm and she shook his hand off. But Nicholas stared at her, his blue eyes warm. He appeared thoughtful, as if the idea had not occurred to him before.

"Marriage is sacred among the Fey," Jewel said before anyone else could speak. "We mingle bloodlines, we mingle magick. We do not do such a thing lightly, and marriage vows cannot be broken. From what I understand, anyone married within your religion cannot break those vows either, and members of the royal family, once pledged, are wedded to that person for eternity, even into death."

The King's smile was a shaky attempt to cover his discomfort. "Eternity, yes, but we are allowed to remarry after death. The family grows bigger then."

"So," Jewel said, "I take that to mean you agree with my proposal?"

The King's smile grew wider but did not reach his eyes. "No. It's out of the question."

Nicholas put his hand on his father's, then leaned forward so that his face was closest to Jewel's. She could feel the warmth of his skin. Her gaze met his. His eyes were a deep blue.

"It would have to be a true marriage," Nicholas said.

"Nicky!" his father said.

Nicholas ignored him. He was staring at Jewel with an intensity Jewel had seen only once—when they had met in battle. She felt the spark between them. They were equals, whether he had magick or not.

"I mean for it to be a true marriage," she said. "I do not suggest such things lightly."

"Jewel, a nonmagick bloodline—"

"Hush, Papa," she said.

"A true marriage," Nicholas said, as if her father hadn't spoken, "means, for Islanders, children."

Jewel nodded. It wouldn't be hard to make children with this man. She had thought of it often enough. "Children would be the only security," she said. Then she looked at the King. "If I am with child when the Black King arrives, or if we have a child already—if the bloodlines are mingled —the Islanders become honorary Fey."

"So we lose after all," the King said bitterly.

"No," Jewel said. "It is the only way you can win. The Black King will not attack the Isle. There will be no more war, and your family remains in power. You will continue to rule, and then Nicholas, as it is done here, and then our child. Nothing changes except that one day Blue Isle will have an important position in the Fey Empire, not as a conquered place, but as a place where Fey rule."

"Jewel," Burden whispered. "You can't do this. You have no authority—"

She whirled on him. "I am the Black King's granddaughter. I have all the authority I need."

He leaned back, away from her. She had never turned on him before, not in all their years of friendship. She had never had to.

The King was watching her. When she turned her attention back to him, he said with a seriousness she hadn't expected, "I need to talk with my son."

"Please do," she said. It would give her a moment to calm her own people.

The Islanders withdrew to the edge of the bowl. They huddled together so that the Fey couldn't see their faces.

"You have no right to do this," Rugar said in Fey. "You pollute the Black King's bloodline."

Jewel sighed. "I have every right. We have married into nonmagickal families before. It always makes the magick stronger. You know that. It is the best way."

"But the Black King will have to acknowledge these people."

"Only the ones I designate as family," Jewel said. "I may choose to designate no one but my own children."

"Jewel," Burden said, "you can't copulate with that thing, not even for the sake of the Fey. You can't—"

"I can do as I choose," Jewel said. His self-interest at this time angered her more than her father's blundering. "What, did you think that you and I would become mates? If I am going to chose a nonmagickal being, Burden, I will choose someone whose blood will enhance my line."

A flush built in his cheeks, and he stared at her, his eyes wide.

"You need to think of someone other than yourself, Burden," Jewel said. "If this works, and the Black King never comes, we have a chance to rebuild our own force. The children will grow. We will have new fighters, new Doppelgängers, new Shape-Shifters. We can develop a new strategy and, with my help, know where the weaknesses are in the Islander defenses."

"It seems wrong to me," Burden said.

Rugar was watching the Islanders speak. Finally he turned to her, a frown bringing the tips of his eyebrows down. "Jewel," he said so softly only she could hear, "all of those people were at that ceremony in your Vision."

"Except Lord Stowe," she said.

"A wedding is a ceremony, Jewel. You will make your Vision come true."

She shook her head. "No, Papa. If I do this right, I make that Vision a false one. We control the ceremony. In that Vision I was caught by surprise. It will not happen. We will allow none of their poison near us during the service. It has to be a condition of this agreement."

Rugar took her hand, thereby giving her his permission. "You take a large risk, daughter."

"Without some risk," she said, "we will not survive."

EIGHTY-EIGHT

THE mist tasted of salt. Nicholas's ponytail was heavy and wet against the back of his neck. He wished he had clothes like the Fey, clothes that kept the water off everything but his skin. This bowl near the Stone Guardians was a dismal place, even though the sky was blue and the air smelled fresher than anything near Jahn.

His father glanced over his shoulder. The Fey were sitting at the table, Jewel in the center, arguing with her father and with the young man beside her. She seemed thinner than she had been before, but her thinness only accented her cheekbones. Her exotic eyes flashed with intelligence and humor each time she looked at Nicholas, as if remembering their first meeting. And when he had said he would marry her, he felt a flush of warmth that she seemed to feel as well.

"You had no right to speak," his father said in Islander. "I was conducting this negotiation."

"Marry a Fey, boy, what were you thinking of?" Lord Stowe asked.

Nicholas took a small step backward, his calves hitting the rock incline. The mist fell around him like a soft rain. "I was thinking of several things," he said. "While it seemed to me you were reacting and not thinking at all."

His father's eyes narrowed. Water beaded on his face, making him look older. "You have no right, Nicky—"

"I have every right," Nicholas said. "They need this alliance more than we do at the moment. But when they killed the Rocaan, they almost destroyed the Tabernacle. Matthias doesn't have the strength to lead the Rocaanists. He can't give them the moral direction that the Rocaan did, and he can't make enough holy water for a war on his own. I've talked with him. Have you?"

His father crossed his arms. "A bit."

"Then you understand his dilemma. If he gives someone else the secret to holy water, they can overthrow him as Rocaan. The last thing we need in the middle of this crisis is a political crisis in the Tabernacle."

"It's not as bad as all that," Lord Stowe said. His cheeks were ruddy with the cold, his blue eyes pale as the sky. He actually seemed to believe what he said.

Couldn't he see that the loss of the Rocaan was the loss of the spiritual heart of Blue Isle? For all of his father's complaining about Nicholas's lack of religious training, it seemed Nicholas was the only one who understood that the death of the Rocaan was the beginning of a crisis, unless someone acted. His father had got even more indecisive since the Rocaan's death. The news of it had paralyzed him for days.

Nicholas brushed his forehead with the back of his hand. On the other side of the rocks, the sea boomed. "It's worse than you both think. Forgive me, Father, for speaking plainly, but you missed another opportunity when the Rocaan died. Instead of letting everything in the Tabernacle fall into disarray, you should have gathered an army and attacked the Shadowlands. Everyone would have backed you. We might have been able to get rid of the Fey."

"We can still do that," his father said.

Nicholas shook his head. Cool water dripped down his cheeks and onto his shoulder. "No, Father. You had a window of maybe a day where the Fey were in as bad a condition as we were. After that, they expected it."

"I thought Scavenger—"

"You put faith in one of their people," Nicholas said, still unable to believe in his father's trust.

"You would do the same," Lord Stowe said.

Nicholas ignored him. "Have we heard from Scavenger? Do we know that he actually left Jahn? No. We are not skilled at intrigue. Someday we will make a bigger mistake than the Rocaan made. Someday we might lose Blue Isle for good."

His father glanced over his shoulder. Nicholas had been speaking too loudly. The Fey didn't seem to notice. They, too, were arguing. Jewel—the name suited her—was speaking with force, using her hands to punctuate her thoughts.

"And," Nicholas said, "Jewel brought another point we rarely talk about. The Black King."

"I thought about the Black King," his father said. "That's why I haven't allowed the Fey to leave, why we no longer have any trade at all."

"But you did not think beyond that," Nicholas said. "She's right. If we destroy them, we are asking for a greater retaliation somewhere in the future. It may not happen on your watch, Father, but it will happen on mine."

"So we prepare for it," Lord Stowe said. "Holy water, and lots of it. Guards here at the mouth of the Cardidas."

"And what if they find a way around holy water? What if they bring other kinds of Fey with them, kinds the young Fey did not describe to you? How do you know that your friend Scavenger told the truth about any of the others? You don't. We have nothing now. We were better off before the Rocaan died." Nicholas was almost shouting again. He took a deep breath.

"You want to do this," Lord Stowe said. "You want to bed the girl. Your Highness, tell the boy such lusts pass."

Nicholas flushed. He couldn't deny his lust for her. They probably saw it in each of his glances. Since the negotiations started, his dreams had been intense, and she had been in all of them, naked and beguiling.

His father was studying him. "You believe in this, don't you, Nicky?"

Nicholas nodded. "I think this will work."

"The Fey, Scavenger, told me that the Fey won't keep their agreements."

"Obviously, since he didn't," Nicholas said. "But how

can they go back on this one, without sacrificing the Black King's granddaughter?"

"They're ruthless, Nicky," his father said softly. "They might be willing to sacrifice her for their own good."

Nicholas swallowed. That made no sense to him. "But it's her idea."

"It *appears* to be her idea," his father said.

Nicholas hadn't considered that. He glanced over to the table. Jewel was pounding on the table. She looked strong enough to defend herself. She couldn't be anyone's pawn. No one would dare treat her that way.

"What if we don't take her up on this, and she's right?" Nicholas asked. "How many other creatures do they have? Can they kill Matthias too? Or you?"

"And what if this is a ploy to get closer to us?" Lord Stowe asked.

"Then they could have done something here, like they did with that meeting with the Rocaan." Nicholas shook his head. "This offer is on the level. It will help all of us."

"It won't return things to the way they were," Lord Stowe said. He leaned against the rock, his face half-shrouded in mist.

"Our lives changed forever the moment the Fey passed through the Stone Guardians," Nicholas said. "No matter what we do, we can never go back. We have to figure out a way to live with the changes. A way that will benefit all of us."

"If you wed this woman," his father said, "it will be something else that we can't turn away from."

"I understand that," Nicholas said. "I think it's time we take a risk. I am willing to."

"She might kill you the moment she's alone with you," Lord Stowe said.

Nicholas didn't want to think about the magicks that she might have in store for him. He hoped she wouldn't trick him that way, but he would have to come up with a way to protect himself. Asking for children, as he had done, might be enough. "I think she'll work with us," Nicholas said.

"Perhaps we can wed her to someone else," his father said.

Nicholas shook his head. He didn't want anyone else to touch her. "She's the Black King's granddaughter. Someday she could rule the Fey. To offer her anyone less than you or me would insult her, Father. Do you want to marry her?"

His father started. He apparently hadn't considered it. The look of revulsion on his face was answer enough.

"We insist that she stay in the palace," Nicholas said. "Then she is taking an equal risk. I could just as easily kill her the moment we are alone as she could kill me."

His father sighed. The sound was shaky. "If this doesn't work, we will lose Blue Isle."

"If we don't try something, we will lose Blue Isle anyway," Nicholas said. "The question is whether we will take a chance to save her."

His father took Nicholas's hand. His father's fingers were cold. "You're my only child, Nicky. If something happens to you—"

"If something happens to me, you appoint a regent in case of your death, and have another child. You're still a young enough man. It's possible, maybe even advisable, given the fact that at the moment we're at war."

The coldness of Nicholas's tone surprised even himself. Someone had to make a decision, and this seemed to be the best one. No country had stood against the Fey. Even the ones that had fought for decades eventually fell to Fey ingenuity, Fey magick. If Nicholas played this right, he would capture a bit of Fey magick for himself. He wouldn't be able to fight the Fey on equal terms, but his children would if they had to. And being half-Fey, they might not need to.

His father was staring at his hands. Lord Stowe was waiting for someone to speak.

"I will marry her," Nicholas said. "And you will have another child, father. And we will make certain that we negotiate everything we can before the ceremony, and we will cover our backs."

"Nicky—" his father started.

Nicholas shook his head. "Do you have a better idea?" he asked. "Something that will make the Fey leave us alone forever?"

Lord Stowe was staring at him as if he had never seen Nicholas before.

"Look at a map, gentlemen," Nicholas said. "To get from Galinas to Leut, you must pass Blue Isle. The Fey, in their attempt to conquer the world, will not sail past Blue Isle. At one point they will try to conquer us again. And at some point they will win. We've been lucky, but luck doesn't hold forever."

"I don't like this kind of risk," his father said.

Which was precisely why they were in this position. Nicholas took a deep breath. Maybe if his father had prepared even as the Fey were attacking the Nye, then Blue Isle would have been safe from Fey aggression. But he hadn't, and he hadn't fought well against the Fey, and because of all that, the Fey had a toehold on the Isle, and they killed the Isle's heart.

"We still have negotiations to do before we can hold any kind of ceremony," Nicholas said. "Let's see how much of the risk we can minimize."

He broke out of the huddle and headed back to the table. The Fey stopped talking among themselves as the Islanders approached. Jewel watched Nicholas, her lips parted. She was as tall as he was, and perhaps even more powerful. But he was just as smart.

Nicholas smiled at her. "What does a Black King's granddaughter bring to a marriage besides herself?"

Jewel's answering smile was warm and playful, as flirtatious as a maid in the hall. "Those terms we need to discuss." She held out her hand and he took it, desire for her suddenly so strong, it was as if he had never felt desire before.

Nicholas would not lose himself over a woman. He would not lose Blue Isle to his own drives. He took his hand from hers and sat between his father and Lord Stowe, directly across from her.

"We have a lot to negotiate before we reach any sort of agreement," Nicholas said, "including where to hold the ceremony."

Jewel's glance was measuring. "I'm sure," she said softly, "we'll have no trouble reaching a compromise."

THE SACRIFICE
(Two Months Later)

EIGHTY-NINE

JEWEL wore green, the color of joy, which Rugar found to be an abomination. The gown had wide skirts in the L'Nacin tradition, a narrow bodice that revealed a lot of breast. For the first time Jewel looked not like his soldier daughter, but like a woman.

Rugar braced himself at Jewel's side, his sea legs not with him yet. The Islander's new Rocaan—a man as tall as the Fey but with the face of a child—had insisted on holding the wedding ceremony over water since he could not use their holy poison in the joining. Jewel's hair was down, a flowing black mass that draped to her knees.

Rugar wore his war clothes: his black leather and tunic. He had thought of ordering the Weather Sprites to make certain that it rained, but he decided it would gain nothing, only make him seem more petty than he was. Still, the war clothes kept him alert. He had to pay attention to every detail. He had tried to convince Jewel that some Visions couldn't be controlled, but she wouldn't listen to him. She believed if she was in charge of this ceremony, her Vision would not come true.

The barge was flat and undecorated. It floated in the center of Jahn Harbor, too far away from any shoreline for a successful attack by Islander or Fey. King Alexander had forbidden his people to watch from the streets, and Rugar had advised against his even coming to Jahn for fear of fights breaking out between the two groups. Still, he knew that Islanders watched from windows, and some Fey had taken over the abandoned warehouses from which Rugar had fought the initial attack. Everyone wanted to see the strange joining of a Fey and a nonmagickal being.

Only a handful of guests were allowed on this barge. Jewel had even insisted that the barge be jointly constructed —the first project completed by Fey and Islanders. Of course, the Fey had done most of the work, with the Islanders looking on to make certain there were no magickal traps (as if they could spot them), but the plan appeared to ease everyone's mind. For now. Jewel's truce with the Islanders seemed like a good idea, but Rugar didn't think it practical. The Fey might trust this arrangement for a while, but then they would get impatient, especially the seasoned soldiers. Jewel had told Rugar that it was his duty to keep the Fey in line.

He would do his best.

King Alexander stood to the left of his son, Lord Stowe behind him. Both were wearing formal black robes, but the Prince wore a coat with long tails, and pants tucked into his boots. His hair hung freely too—he had decided to do that after Jewel had told him that for Fey, unbound hair meant a gift happily given. Rugar stood beside Jewel. She permitted no one else to attend her.

She also permitted no symbols of the religion to be hung on the barge. She had seen a worship sword as well as a bottle of poison in her Vision. She didn't want them near her. If she could have prevented the Rocaanists from wearing their robes, she would have. There had been a moment of diplomatic crisis when the new Rocaan had refused to perform the ceremony, but somehow King Alexander had convinced him to do so anyway. Jewel had had to compromise on the clothes.

The Shaman stood beside the new Rocaan. She looked even older next to his blond youth. Her hair was white and it sprung off her head like weeds. Her face was wizened, her mouth a small oval amid wrinkles. Only her eyes were bright—sparkling black circles of light in a dying face. She had said nothing about this union. She offered no suggestions for the ceremony; indeed, she had not even seemed surprised by the whole thing.

Jewel had used that as another example of the correctness of her position, but Rugar wasn't so certain. He had spent all of his life thinking about Visions. The Shaman was less inclined than he was to interfere in a Vision's course. She might have seen the moment. She might even know where it was heading. But she might not be willing to do anything to change the future. Her job was to provide sanctuary in the present.

Rugar had been on alert for nearly two hours waiting for the ceremony to start. It would be in two parts. The Fey part would go first. The Shaman and the new Rocaan had been talking for several minutes. Finally the Shaman clapped her hands.

"We are ready," she said in Nye. "These children shall be watched by our Powers and your Roca. We shall appeal to the Powers first."

The guests became silent. The new Rocaan stood to the side. Rugar took one step back so that he could watch the man.

The Shaman smiled at Jewel and the Prince. "Please join hands," she said in Nye. They glanced at each other—shyly, it seemed—and then their hands entwined. Rugar let out the breath he had been holding. He remembered that moment of uncertainty from his first marriage.

Then the Shaman waved her wand over the couple's heads. "The Powers will watch over you," she said in Fey. "And your children shall be a credit to you. May you add to the Magick." Then she smiled at them. "You may join your other hands."

They had to face each other to do so. Rugar saw the Prince's face clearly. His eyes were sparkling as he looked at Jewel. She had said the boy had been tender in her Vision. Maybe that part was right. Their other hands met.

"You have completed the circle," the Shaman said. "You shall be One, always."

Then she turned to the new Rocaan. He shook his head. King Alexander and Lord Stowe frowned. Apparently they didn't understand that the Fey ceremony was done. But the

Prince did. He kissed the backs of Jewel's hands before turning to face the new Rocaan.

"It's yours now," the Shaman said in Nye to the new Rocaan. He glanced at the King, who shrugged. Rugar would have smiled if he hadn't been so intent on this part of the ceremony. The religious Islanders were tricky, and this new Rocaan had a motive for revenge. If he brought out any water at all, Rugar would run to him and knock the water away from Jewel.

The new Rocaan was speaking in Islander. Rugar did not understand a word of it. He watched the new Rocaan's hands move with the words. The man had thin fingers, magickal fingers. Perhaps the magick for the poison came from within the soul of the Rocaan and not from without. A few Fey had such abilities—Shape-Shifters, Shamans, Visionaries.

Then Jewel and the boy bowed their heads. The new Rocaan looked at Rugar. Rugar frowned, then remembered. He pulled the cloth Jewel had instructed him to bring from his breast pocket and placed it on her head. She had explained that it would protect her from the touch of the Rocaan, in case he had any poison residue on his fingers. Rugar was shaking. He stood so close to Jewel that he could feel the warmth of her skin.

Then the Rocaan put his hand on the cloth and on the Prince's bare head and spoke again. This speech seemed to go on forever. Rugar stood at attention, his gaze focused on the new Rocaan's hands.

But nothing happened. The new Rocaan took his hands away. Jewel removed the cloth and smiled at the Prince. He smiled back. He seemed to be feeling the same odd joy that Jewel was.

In Nye the new Rocaan said, "It is done."

His tone made Rugar look at him. The new Rocaan was no happier about this than the rest of them. But Jewel didn't seem to notice. She hugged her father. "We made it," she whispered.

"Yes," he said. They had made it through the treacheries of her first Vision. The Shaman stood beside him—he could smell her faintly cinnamon scent. Jewel put her arm through the Prince's—Nicholas. Rugar would have to remember that since they had just become relations—and she spoke to the Islander King.

"We will have peace now," the Shaman said in Fey.

Rugar gave her a startled look. She was watching Jewel laugh.

"This will work?" Rugar asked.

"Parts of it," the Shaman said, her voice soft and raspy at the same time. "You always forget, Rugar, that children hold the key to the future. It is a place we travel ever so briefly, a place they will know intimately."

A cool breeze had come up from the water. It ruffled his hair. "You're telling me that Jewel made the right choice," Rugar said.

The Shaman continued to follow Jewel's movement through the barge. "Jewel made the only choice for peace. Would that you always do the same, Rugar."

He straightened. "You forget yourself," he said. "I am a warrior."

"I forget nothing," she said, and walked away from him, her white robes trailing on the wood. He bit back a curse. He always had such elliptical discussions with her, and he hated them.

The barge started moving back toward the harbor. Jewel and her new husband stood at the rail, watching the shore come up to meet them. She had decided to live in the Islander palace, the symbol of power on Blue Isle, she had reminded him. He had said nothing. He knew how much she wanted to be out of the Shadowlands.

She waved him over. Rugar took a deep breath and crossed the deck. He hated moments like this, moments after the wars ended, when the Fey and their former enemies had to coexist as best they could.

When he stopped beside her, she took his hand with her free one. Her fingers were warm, her grip tight. "We beat the Visions, Papa," she said in Fey.

"Yes," he said again. He could say no more. He didn't want to spoil her obvious joy. They had defeated her Vision, but not his. He had always seen her walking through the halls of the Islander palace as if she owned it. Only he had thought they would come to that moment through a military victory, not through loss and treachery.

"We are sailing toward the future," Nicholas said softly in Nye. His words were meant for Jewel, but Rugar heard them.

The future. The Shaman said it had no place for warriors. Rugar wondered if she was right.

ABOUT THE
AUTHOR

Kristine Kathryn Rusch is an award-winning fiction writer. She has published six novels under her own name: *The White Mists of Power: Afterimage* (written with Kevin J. Anderson); *Façade, Heart Readers, Traitors,* and *Sins of the Blood.* Her short fiction has been nominated for the Nebula, Hugo, World Fantasy, and Stoker awards. Her novella, *The Gallery of His Dreams,* won the Locus Award for best short fiction. Her body of fiction work won her the John W. Campbell Award, given in 1991 in Europe.

In her spare time, Rusch edits the *Magazine of Fantasy and Science Fiction,* a prestigious fiction magazine founded in 1949. She won the Hugo award for her work as editor in 1994. She started Pulphouse Publishing with her husband, Dean Wesley Smith, and they won a World Fantasy Award for their work on that press. Rusch and Smith edited *The SFWA Handbook: A Professional Writers Guide to Writing Professionally,* which won the Locus Award for Best Non-Fiction. They have also written several novels under the pen name Sandy Schofield.

She lives and works in the coastal mountain range outside of Eugene, Oregon. Along with succeeding books of the Fey, among her forthcoming projects is a *STAR WARS* novel, *The New Rebellion.*

Turn the page for a special preview of

THE
CHANGELING

The Second Book of The Fey

by Kristine Kathryn Rusch

The uneasy truce between Blue Islanders and the Fey will soon explode in deceit and violence in Book Two of this exciting series, *The Changeling*. As Nicholas and Jewel carve out a precedent-shattering life together, sinister forces are at work on both sides of the battle. In this, the opening scene from *The Changeling*, a furtive event will change the course of history on Blue Isle. **Don't miss THE CHANGELING, on sale in May 1996 from Bantam Spectra Books.**

THE THEFT

ONE

He put words to the memory years later, when he tried to tell people of it. Some doubted he could remember, and others watched him as if stunned by his clarity. But the memory was clear, not as a series of impressions, but as an experience, one he could relive if he closed his eyes and cast his mind backward. An inverse Vision. None of his other memories were as sharp, but they were not as important. Nor were they the first:

Light filled the room. He opened his eyes and felt himself emerge like a man stepping out of the fog. One moment he had been absorbing, feeling, learning —the next he was thinking. The lights clustered near the window, a hundred single points revolving in a circle. The tapestry was up, as if someone were holding it.

He turned his head—it was his newest skill—but he saw only the curtained wall of the crib. Voices floated in from the other room—his mother's voice, sweet and familiar, almost a part of himself; and a man's voice—his father's?

His nurse sat near the fireplace, her head tilted back, her bonnet askew. She was snoring softly, a raspy sound that sometimes covered the voices. He could barely see her face over the edge of his crib. It was a friendly face, with gentle wrinkled features, a rounded nose, and a generous mouth. Her eyes were closed, her mouth open, her nostrils fluttering with each inhalation. He reached toward her, but his fingers gripped the soft blanket instead.

A cool breeze touched him tentatively, smelling of rain and the river. The lights parted to let a shadow in. The shadow had the shape of a man, but it was dark and flat and crept across the wall. He put his baby finger in his mouth and sucked, eyes wide, watching the shadow. It slid over the tapestries and across the fireplace until it landed on his nurse's face. Her snoring stopped.

He whimpered, but the shadow did not look at him. Instead, it molded itself against his nurse's features. Her hands moved ever so slightly as if to pull it off, then she began twitching as if she were dreaming. Her eyes remained closed, but her snoring stopped.

His mother's voice penetrated the sudden silence. "You will not give him a common name! He is a Prince in the Black King's line. He needs to be named as such!"

The nurse's breathing became regular. The twitching stopped. Except for the blackness covering her face, she appeared almost normal.

"I thought Fey named their children after the customs of the land they're in." His father's voice.

"Names have to have meaning, Nicholas. They are the secret to power."

"I do not see how your name gives you power, Jewel."

The breeze blew over him again. He peered over his blanket at the window. The lights were no longer revolving. They had formed a straight line from the window to his curtained crib. The lights were beautiful and tiny, the size of his fingertips. They gathered around his crib, twinkling and sparkling. Suddenly he was warm. The air smelled of sunlight.

"I'll agree to the name if you tell me what it means." The voices moved back and forth, near and away, as if his parents were circling each other in the next room.

"I don't know what it means, Jewel. But it has been in my family for generations."

"I swear"—his mother sounded angry—"it was easier to make the child than it is to name him."

"It was certainly more fun."

He turned to the curtained wall, wishing he could see through it, wishing they would come to him. The lights hovered above him. They were so beautiful. Blue and red and yellow. He pulled his finger out of his mouth and raised it toward the lights.

By accident, he touched a blue light and pulled his hand away with a startled cry. With the smell of sulfur and a bit of smoke, the blue light became a tiny naked woman with thin wings shimmering on her back. Her skin was darker than his, her eyebrows swept up like her wings, and her eyes were as alive as the lights.

"Got him," she said.

His fingers hurt. He sniffled, then looked at his nurse. The shadow still covered her face, and she was still breathing softly. He wanted her to see him. But she slept.

The tiny woman landed on his chest, put her hands on his chin, and looked into his eyes. "Ah," she said. "He's ours, all right."

Her hands tickled his skin. The other lights gathered around her. With a series of pops, they became more winged people, all dark, all graceful and small. The men had thick beards, the women, hair that cascaded over their shoulders.

They landed around him, their bare feet making tiny indentations on the thick blanket. He was too startled to cry. They examined his features, poking at his skin, tugging on his ears, tracing the tiny points.

"He's one of ours," the woman said.

"Skin's light," one of the men said.

"Lighter," another man corrected. Their voices were tiny too, almost like little bells.

In the other room, his mother giggled. He moved at the sound, knocking some of the little people over. He stretched out a hand, reaching for her. She giggled again, deep in her throat.

"Nicholas, it's been just days since the babe."

His father laughed too.

The little people got up. One of the men came very close. He squinted, making his small eyes almost invisible. "Nose is upturned."

"So?" the woman asked, her wings fluttering.

"Our noses are straight."

"He has to have some Islander."

"Rugar said leave him if there is no magic."

The woman put her hands on her hips. "Look at those eyes. Look at how bright they are. Then tell me there's no magic."

"The magic is always stronger when the blood is mixed," said another woman.

In the other room, his mother's laugh grew closer. "Nicholas, let's just see the babe. Maybe we can decide what to call him then."

The little people froze. His hands were still grasping. Outside the protection of the crib, the air was cold. The little people had brought deep warmth with them.

"Stay for a moment," his father said.

"The Healer said—"

"Healers be damned."

The little people waited another moment, then the woman snapped her fingers. "Quickly," she said.

Their wings fluttered, and the group floated above him, as pretty as the lights. He wasn't sure of them. Touching them had hurt, but they were so lovely. So lovely.

They fanned out around him, holding strands as thin as spiderwebs. They flew back and forth, weaving the strands. The woman stood near his head, outside of the strands, clutching a tiny stone to her chest.

"Hurry," she said.

"Nicholas, really." His mother laughed again. "Stop. We can't."

"I know," his father said. "But it's so much nicer than fighting. Maybe we shouldn't call him anything."

"Can you imagine?" she said. "He's a grandfather and his friends all call him 'baby.' "

The strands had formed a piece of white gauze between him and the world. The shadow moved on his nurse's face, lifting away a tiny bit and glancing over its flat shoulder at the flying people.

"Not yet," the woman said.

The shadow flattened out over the nurse once more.

The gauze enveloped him and his blankets. He felt warm and secure. The little people held the edges of the gauze and lifted him from the crib.

He could see the whole room. It was big. His nurse sat in one corner, the shadow over her face, her eyelids moving back and forth. A bed with filmy red curtains sat in the far side of the room, and chairs lined the walls. All the windows were covered with tapestries, and the tapestries were pictures of babies—being born, being held, being crowned. Only one window was open—the window the people had come through.

Floating was fun. It felt like being held. He snuggled into his blankets and watched the little woman put the stone on his pillow.

Then the door handle turned. The little woman floated above the crib, shooing the others away with her hands. "Hurry!" she whispered. "Hurry!"

"We might wake him up, Jewel," his father said.

"Babies sleep sound."

"Wait," he said. "Let me find out what the name means. Then we can have a real talk. If it has no meaning, then—"

"Find out who had the name before," she said. "That's important."

They were almost to the window. He had forgotten his mother. He wanted her to float with him. He rolled over, making the little people curse. The net swung precariously. He cried out, a long plaintive wail.

"Shush!" the little man nearest him said.

The shadow lifted off the nurse's face. She snorted, sighed, and sank deeper in sleep. The shadow crawled over the fireplace toward the window.

He cried out again. The nurse stirred and ran a hand over her face. His feet were outside. It was raining, but the drops didn't touch him. They veered away from his feet as if he wore a protective cover.

The nurse's eyes flickered open. "What a dream I had, baby," she said. "What a dream."

He howled. The little people hurried him outside even faster. She went to the crib and looked down. His gaze followed hers. In his bed, another baby lay. Its eyes were open but empty. The nurse brushed her hand on its cheek.

"You're cold, lambkins," she said.

The little woman huddled in the curtain around the crib. She moved her fingers and the baby cooed. The nurse smiled.

He was staring at the baby that had replaced him. It looked like him, but it was not him. It had been a stone a moment before.

"Changeling," he thought, marking not just his first word but the arrival of his conscious being, born a full adult, thanks to the Fey's magic touch.

He screamed. The little people pulled him outside, over the courtyard and into the street. The nurse looked up and went to the window, a frown marring her soft features. He cried again, but he was already as high as the clouds and well down the street. The nurse shook her head, grabbed the tapestry, and pulled it closed.

"Hush, child," the little man floating above him said. "You're going home."

JOIN

STAR WARS®

on the INTERNET

Bantam Spectra invites you to visit the Official STAR WARS® Web Site.

You'll find:

< Sneak previews of upcoming STAR WARS® novels.

< Samples from audio editions of the novels.

< Bulletin boards that put you in touch with other fans, with the authors behind the novels, and with the Bantam editors who bring them to you.

< The latest word from behind the scenes of the STAR WARS® universe.

< Quizzes, games, and contests available only on-line.

< Links to other STAR WARS® licensees' sites on the Internet.

< Look for STAR WARS® on the World Wide Web at: http://www.bdd.com

SF 28 1/96

REALOOS OF FANTASY

The biggest, brightest stars from Bantam Spectra

Maggie Furey

A fiery-haired Mage with an equally incendiary temper must save her world and her friends from a pernicious evil, with the aid of four forgotten magical Artefacts:

AURIAN ___56525-7 $5.99

HARP OF WINDS ___56526-5 $5.99

Robin Hobb

One of our newest and most exciting talents presents a tale of honor and subterfuge, loyalty and betrayal:

ASSASSIN'S APPRENTICE: Book One of the Farseer

___37445-1 $12.95/$17.95 Canada

Katharine Kerr

The mistress of Celtic Fantasy presents her ever-popular Deverry series (most recent titles):

DAYS OF BLOOD AND FIRE ___29012-6 $5.99/$7.50

DAYS OF AIR AND DARKNESS ___57262-8 $5.99/$7.99

Ask for these books at your local bookstore or use this page to order.

Please send me the books I have checked above. I am enclosing $_____ (add $2.50 to cover postage and handling). Send check or money order, no cash or C.O.D.'s, please.

Name _____

Address _____

City/State/Zip _____

Send order to: Bantam Books, Dept. SF 29, 2451 S. Wolf Rd., Des Plaines, IL 60018
Allow four to six weeks for delivery.
Prices and availability subject to change without notice.   SF 29 1/96

REALMS OF FANTASY

The biggest, brightest stars from Bantam Spectra

Michael A. Stackpole

An antique warrior, from 500 years in the past, is resurrected to save his kingdom from an evil he unwittingly propagated:

ONCE A HERO ___56112-X $5.99/$7.99

Paula Volsky

Rich tapestries of magic and revolution, romance and forbidden desires:

ILLUSION ___56022-0 $5.99/$6.99
THE WOLF OF WINTER ___56879-5 $5.99/$7.99

Angus Wells

Epic fantasy in the grandest tradition, of magic, dragons, and heroic quests (most recent titles):

LORDS OF THE SKY ___57266-0 $5.99/$7.99
EXILE'S CHILDREN: Book One of the Exiles Saga
___37486-9 $12.95/$17.95

Ask for these books at your local bookstore or use this page to order.

Please send me the books I have checked above. I am enclosing $___ (add $2.50 to cover postage and handling). Send check or money order, no cash or C.O.D.'s, please.

Name _____

Address _____

City/State/Zip _____

Send order to: Bantam Books, Dept. SF 29, 2451 S. Wolf Rd., Des Plaines, IL 60018
Allow four to six weeks for delivery.
Prices and availability subject to change without notice.   SF 29 1/96